Jilly Cooper is a novelist and journalist who has
also worked in the public relations and publishing fields.
She wrote her first book, *How to Stay Married,* in 1969 and
since then has written or helped to compile twenty-seven
others, including seven romantic novels and four children's
books about a small dog named Mabel whose social
insecurities cause her endless problems.

The Common Years, Jilly's delightful chronicle of life with
her family, dogs, and neighbors in London, was a bestseller.
RIDERS, the marvelous novel you're about to fall in love with,
was #1 on British bestseller lists for many weeks.

For over thirteen years, Jilly Cooper entertained readers of
the *London Sunday Times* with her outrageous and funny columns.
These have been collected and published in five volumes.
She also wrote a television series, *It's Awfully Bad for Your
Eyes, Darling,* and has often appeared on television herself.

Jilly has been married to publisher Leo Cooper for
twenty-three years. They have two children, Felix and Emily,
five cats, and three dogs. They live in an old house in the
Cotswold area of Gloucestershire.

RIDERS

By JILLY COOPER

BALLANTINE BOOKS
NEW YORK

Library of Congress Catalog Card Number: 85-91185
ISBN 0-345-33332-2

Cover painting by James Griffin
Text design by Ann Gold

Manufactured in the United States of America

First American Edition: June 1986

10 9 8 7 6 5 4 3 2

To Beryl Hill,
the Artur Rubinstein of the typewriter,
with love and gratitude

ACKNOWLEDGMENTS

Since I started *Riders* fifteen years ago, an enormous number of people have helped me with the book. They are all experts in their fields. But this being a work of fiction, I took their advice only as far as it suited my plot, and the accuracy of the book in no way reflects on their expertise!

They include Ronnie Massarella, Caroline Silver, Alan Smith, Brian Giles, Douglas Bunn, Michael Clayton, Alan Oliver, Bridget Le Good, John Burbidge, Diana Downie, Raymond Brooks-Ward, Harvey Smith, Dr. Hubert and Mrs. Bessie Crouch, Dr. Timothy Evans, Heather Ross, Caroline Akrill, Dick Stilwell, Sue Clarke, Sue Gibson, Andrew Parker-Bowles, John and Tory Oaksey, Marion Ivey, Rosemary Nunneley, Elizabeth Richardson, Elizabeth Hopkins, Julia Longland, Susan Blair, Ann Martin, Kate O'Sullivan, Marcy Drummond, John and Michael Whitaker, David Broome and Malcolm Pyrah.

I owe a special debt of gratitude to dear Sighle Gogan, who spent so many hours talking to me about show jumping, and arranged for me to meet so many of the people who helped me, but who tragically died in January last year.

I should also like to thank my bank manager, James Atkinson, for being so patient and Paul Scherer and Alan Earney of Corgi Books for being so continually encouraging, and Tom Hartman for being one of those rare people who actually makes authors enjoy having their books edited.

An award for gallantry must go to the nine ladies who all worked fantastically long hours over Christmas, deciphering my appalling handwriting and typing the 340,000 word manuscript. They include Beryl Hill, Anna Gibbs-Kennet, Sue Moore, Margaret McKellican, Corinne Monhaghan, Julie Payne, Nicky Greenshield, Patricia Quatermass and my own wonderful secretary, Diane Peter.

The lion's share of my gratitude must go to Desmond Elliott for masterminding the whole operation so engagingly, and all his staff at Arlington, who worked so hard to produce such a huge book in under five months.

Finally there are really no words adequate to thank my husband Leo and my children Felix and Emily, except to say that without their support, good cheer and continued unselfishness the book would never have been finished.

1

*B*ecause he had to get up unusually early on Saturday, Jake Lovell kept waking up throughout the night, wracked by terrifying dreams about being late. In his first dream he couldn't find his breeches when the steward called his number, in the second he couldn't catch any of the riding ponies to take them to the show, in the third Africa slipped her halter and escaped, and in the fourth, most terrifying dream he was back in the orphanage screaming and clawing at locked iron gates, while Rupert Campbell-Black rode Africa down the High Street, until turning with that hateful, sneering smile, he'd shouted:

"You'll never get out of that place now, Gyppo, it's where you belong."

Jake woke sobbing, heart bursting, drenched in sweat, paralyzed with fear. It was half a minute before he could reach out and switch on the bedside lamp. He lit a cigarette with a trembling hand. Gradually the familiar objects in the room reasserted themselves; the Lionel Edwards prints on the walls, the tattered piles of *Horse and Hound*, the books on show jumping hopelessly overcrowding the bookshelves, the wash basin, the faded photographs of his mother and father. Hanging in the wardrobe was the riding coat Mrs. Wilton had rather grudgingly given him for his twenty-first birthday. Beneath it stood the scratched but gleaming pair of brown-topped boots he'd picked up second-hand last week.

In the stall below he could hear a horse snorting and a crash as another horse kicked over its water bucket.

Far too slowly his panic subsided. Prep school and Rupert Campbell-Black were things of the past. He had been out of the orphanage for four years now. He mostly forgot them during the day; it was only in dreams that they came back to torment him. He shivered; the sheets were damp with sweat. Four-thirty said his alarm clock; there were already fingers of light under the thin yellow curtains. He didn't have

1

to get up for half an hour, but he was too scared to go back to sleep. He could hear the rain pattering on the roof outside and dripping from the gutter, muting the chatter of the sparrows.

He tried to concentrate on the day ahead, which didn't make him feel much more cheerful. One of the worst things about working in a riding school was having to take pupils to horseshows. Few of them could control the bored, broken-down ponies. Many were spoiled, others, terrified, were only riding at all because their frightful mothers were using horses to grapple their way up the social ladder, giving them an excuse to put a hard hat in the back seat of the Jaguar and slap gymkhana stickers on the windshield.

What made Jake nervous, however, was that, unknown to his boss, Mrs. Wilton, he intended to take Africa to the show and enter her for the open jumping. Mrs. Wilton didn't allow Jake to compete in shows. He might get too big for his boots. His job was to act as a constant nursemaid to the pupils, not to jump valuable horses behind her back.

Usually Mrs. Wilton turned up at shows in the afternoon and strutted about, chatting with the mothers. But today, because she was driving down to Brighton to see some rich uncle who had no children, she wouldn't be putting in an appearance. If Jake didn't try out Africa today, he wouldn't have another chance for weeks.

Africa was a boarder at the riding school, owned by an actor named Bobby Cotterel who'd bought her in a fit of enthusiasm. A few weeks later he had bought a Ferrari and, apart from still paying her board, had forgotten about Africa, which had given Jake the perfect opportunity to teach her to jump secretly.

She was only six, but every day Jake became more convinced that she had the makings of a great show jumper. It was not just her spirit and courage, her fantastic turn of speed and huge jump. She also had an ability to get herself out of trouble which counterbalanced her impetuosity.

Jake adored her—more than any person or animal he had known in his life. If Mrs. Wilton discovered he'd taken her to a show, she'd probably fire him. He dreaded losing a job which had brought him his first security in years, but the prospect of losing Africa was infinitely worse.

The alarm made him jump. It was still raining; the horror of the dream gripped him again. What happened if Africa slipped when she was taking off or landing? He dressed and, lifting up the trap door at the foot of his bed, climbed down the stairs into the tackroom, inhaling the smell of warm horse leather, saddle soap, and dung which never failed to excite him. Hearing him mixing the feeds, horses' heads came out over the half-doors, calling, nickering, stamping their hooves.

It was seven-thirty before he had mucked out and fed all the horses. Africa, feed finished, blinking her big dark blue eyes in the low-angled sun, hung out of her box, catching his sleeve between her lips each time he went past, shaking gently, never nipping the skin. Mrs. Wilton had been out to dinner the night before; it was unlikely she'd surface before half past eight; that gave him an hour to groom Africa.

Rolling up his sleeves, chattering nonsense to her all the time, Jake got to work. She was a beautiful horse, very dark brown, her coat looking almost indigo in the shadows. She had two white socks, a blaze of white down her forehead, huge shoulders and quarters above lean strong legs. Her ears twitched and turned all the time, as sensitive as radar.

He jumped when the stable cat, a fat tabby with huge whiskers, appeared on top of the stable door and, after glancing at a couple of pigeons scratching for corn, dropped down into the straw and curled up in the discarded warmth of Africa's blanket.

Suddenly Africa jerked up her head and listened. Jake stepped outside nervously; the curtains were still drawn in Mrs. Wilton's house. He'd wanted to braid Africa's mane, but he didn't dare. It would unbraid all curly and he might be caught. He went back to work.

"Surely you're not taking Africa to the show?" said a shrill voice. Jake jumped out of his skin and Africa tossed up her head, banging him on the nose.

Just able to look over the half-door was one of his pupils, Fenella Maxwell, her face as freckled as a robin's egg, her flaxen hair already escaping from its elastic bands.

"What the hell are you doing here?" asked Jake furiously, his eyes watering. "I said no one was allowed here till ten and it can't be eight yet. Push off home."

"I've come to help," said Fenella, gazing at him with huge blue eyes fringed with thick blond lashes. Totally unabashed, she moved a hard candy to the other side of her face.

"I know you're by yourself till Alison comes. I'll get Dandelion ready . . . please," she added, "I want him to look as beautiful as Africa."

"Shut up," hissed Jake. "Now shove off."

"Please let me stay. There's nothing to do at home. I couldn't sleep. I will help. Are you really taking Africa?"

"Mind your own business," said Jake.

Fen took the candy out of her mouth and gave it to Dandelion, who was slavering over the next half-door, then kissed him on the nose. Her shirt was already escaping from the jeans she wore over her jodhpurs to keep them clean.

"Does Mrs. Wilton know?" she asked.

"No," said Jake.

"I won't tell her," said Fen, swinging on Africa's door. "Shall I make you a cup of tea? Four spoonfuls of sugar, isn't it?"

Jake relented. She was a good kid, cheerful and full of guts, with an instinct for horses and a knowledge way beyond her nine years.

"You can stay if you keep your trap shut," he said. "I don't want Mrs. Wilton waking up yet."

After she had spilled most of the tea in the saucer, Fen tied Dandelion up outside Africa's stall and settled down to washing his white patches, managing to get more water over herself than the pony.

Jake half-listened as she chattered on incessantly about her sister Tory coming out this season but not enjoying the deb parties at all, and who often had red eyes from crying in the morning.

"She's coming to the show later."

"Does your mother know you're here?" asked Jake.

"She wouldn't notice if I wasn't. She's got a new boyfriend called Colonel Carter. Colonel Cart-ah, he calls himself. He laughs all the time when he's talking to Mummy and he's got big yellow teeth like Dandelion, but somehow they look better on a horse.

"They're coming to the show too. Colonel Carter is bringing a lot of soldiers and guns to do a display after the opening jumping. He and Mummy and Tory are going to lunch up at the Hall. Mummy bought a new blue dress specially; it's lovely, but Tory said it was jolly expensive, so I don't expect she'll be able to afford to buy me a pony yet; anyway she says Tory being a deb is costing a fortune."

"Shampoo and set, darling," she said to Dandelion twenty minutes later as she stuck the pony's tail in a bucket of hot soapy water. "Oh, look, Africa's making faces; isn't she sweet?" The next moment Dandelion had whisked his tail at a fly, sending soapy water all over Fen, Africa's blanket and the stable cat, who retreated in high dudgeon.

"For God's sake concentrate," snapped Jake.

"Mummy's picture's in *The Tatler* again this week," said Fen. "She gets in much more often than poor Tory. She says Tory's got to go on a diet next week, so she'll be thin for her cocktail party next month. Oh no, Mrs. Wilton's drawing back the kitchen curtains."

Hastily Jake replaced Africa's blanket and came out of her stall.

Inside the kitchen, beneath the ramparts of honeysuckle, he could see Mrs. Wilton, her brick red face flushed from the previous night's drinking, dropping Alka Seltzer into a glass of water. Christ, he hoped she'd get a move on to Brighton and wouldn't hang around. Picking up the brush and the curry comb he started on one of the ponies.

Mrs. Wilton came out of the house followed by her arthritic

yellow labrador, who lifted his leg stiffly on the mounting block, then as a formality bounded after the stable cat.

Mrs. Wilton was never known to have been on a horse in her life. Stocky, with a face squashed in like a bulldog, she had short pepper and salt hair, a blotchy complexion like salami, and a deep bass voice. All the same, she had had more success with the opposite sex than her masculine appearance would suggest.

"Jake," she bellowed.

He came out, curry comb in one hand, brush in the other.

"Yes, Mrs. Wilton," and she'd repeatedly asked him to call her Joyce.

They gazed at each other with the dislike of the unwillingly but mutually dependant. Mrs. Wilton knew that having lost both his parents and spent much of his life in an orphanage Jake clung to the security of a live-in job. As her husband was away so much on business, Mrs. Wilton had often suggested Jake might be more comfortable living in the house with her. But, aware that he would have to share a bathroom (and if Mrs. W. had her way, a bedroom) Jake had repeatedly refused. Mrs. Wilton was old enough to be his mother.

But, despite finding him sullen and withdrawn to the point of insolence, she had to admit that the horses had never been better looked after. As a result of his encyclopedic knowledge of plants and wild flowers, and his incredible gypsy remedies, she hadn't had a vet's bill since he'd arrived, and because he was frightened of losing this substitute home, she could get away with paying him a pittance. She found herself doing less and less. She didn't want to revert to getting up at six and mucking out a dozen horses, and it was good to be able to go away, like today, and not worry.

On the other hand, if he was a miracle with animals, he was hell with parents, refusing to suck up to them, positively rude to the sillier ones. A number had defected and gone to Mrs. Haley across the valley, who charged twice as much.

"How many ponies are you taking?" she demanded.

"Six," said Jake, walking towards the tackroom, praying she'd follow him.

"And you'll get Mrs. Thompson to bring the halters and the water buckets in her car? Do try to be polite for once, although I know how hard you find it."

Jake stared at her unsmiling. He had a curiously immobile face, everything in the right place, but without animation. The swarthy features were pale today, the full lips set in an uncompromising line. Slanting secretive dark eyes looked out from beneath a frowning line of brow, practically concealed by the thick thatch of almost black hair. He was small, not more than five foot seven, and very thin, a good jockey's weight. The only note of frivolity was the gold rings in his ears. There was something watchful and controlled about him that didn't go with youth. Despite the heat of the day, his collar was turned up as if against some imagined storm.

"I'll be back tomorrow," she said looking down the row of box stalls.

Suddenly her eyes lit on Africa.

"What's she doing inside?"

"I brought her in this morning," he lied easily. "She yells her head off if she's separated from Dandelion and I thought you'd like to sleep in."

"Well, put her out again when you go. I'm not having her eating her head off."

Despite the fat fee paid by Bobby Cotterel, thought Jake.

She peered into the stall. For an appalling moment he thought she was going to peel back the blanket.

"Hello Mrs. Wilton," shrieked Fen. "Come and look at Dandelion. Doesn't he look smart?"

Distracted, Mrs. Wilton turned away from Africa.

"Hello, Fen dear, you're an early bird. He does look nice; you've even oiled his hooves. Perhaps you'll bring home a ribbon."

"Shouldn't think so," said Fen gloomily. "Last time he ate all the potatoes in the potato race."

"Phew, that was a near one," said Fen, as Mrs. Wilton's car, with the labrador's head sticking out of the window, disappeared down the road.

"Come on," said Jake. "I'll make you some breakfast."

Dressing later before he set out for the show, Jake transferred the crushed and faded yellow tansy flower from the bottom of his left rubber boot to his left riding boot. Tansy warded off evil. Jake was full of superstitions. The royal gypsy blood of the Lovells didn't flow through his veins for nothing.

*B*y midday a blazing sun shone relentlessly out of a clear blue sky, warming the russet stone of Bilborough Hall as it dreamed above its dark green moat. To the right on the terrace, great yews cut in the shape of peacocks seemed about to strut across the shaven lawns down into the valley where blue-green wheat fields merged into meadows of pale silver-green hay. In the park the trees in the angelic softness of their new spring growth looked as though the rain had not only washed them but polished them as well. Dark purple copper beeches and cochineal-red may added a touch of color.

To the left the show ring was already circled two deep with cars, and more cars in a long gleaming serpentine were still inching slowly through the main gate, on either side of which two stone lions reared up clenching red and white bunting between their teeth.

The horse show mothers were out in full force, caught on this first hot day of the year, their arms pale in sleeveless dresses, silk-lined bottoms spilling over camp chairs, shouting to one another as they unpacked picnics from the trunks of cars. Hunt terriers yapped, labradors panted. Food in dog bowls, remaining untouched because of the heat, gathered flies.

Beyond the cars, crowds milled around the booths selling horse equipment, moving aside to avoid the occasional competitors riding through with numbers on their backs. Children mindlessly consumed junk food, clamored for ice cream, balloons, and pony rides. Fathers hung with cameras, wearing creased lightweight suits smelling of mothballs, wished they could escape back to the office, and for consolation, eyed the inevitable hordes of nubile fourteen-year-old-girls with long wavy hair and very tight breeches who seem to parade permanently up and down at horse shows.

Bilborough Hall was owned by Sir William Blake, no relation to the poet but nicknamed "Tiger" at school. Mingling with the crowds, he gossiped to friends, raised his hat to people he didn't know and told everyone that in twenty years there had only been one wet Bilborough show. His wife, in drooping tweeds and a felt hat, whose passion was gardening, sighed inwardly at the ground already grey and pitted with hoof marks. She had already instructed the under-gardener, to his intense embarrassment, to go around with a spade and gather up all the manure before it was trodden into the ground.

"Oh there you are, William," she said to her husband, who was genially trying to guess the weight of a piglet. "People are already arriving for luncheon; we'd better go and do our stuff."

Down by the horse lines Jake Lovell, tying up a weedy grey pony more securely, was slowly reaching screaming point. The family of the unspeakably hopeless Pattie Beasley (none of whom had ever been on a horse) had all turned up in jodhpurs. Sally-Ann Thomson's frightful mother hung around the whole time, talking at the top of her voice, so all the other competitors turned around and laughed at her.

"It doesn't matter about winning, dear," she was now telling Sally-Ann, "Competing and having fun is all that matters."

"Bloody rubbish," thought Jake, "they all sulk if they don't place."

After Sally-Ann's pony had bolted with her and Pattie Beasley's cob had had a kicking match with the priceless winner of the under

13.2 showing class, causing loss of temper on all sides, Jake had refused to let any of the children ride their ponies until the jumping in
the afternoon. He had nearly had a mutiny on his hands.

Jake's head throbbed. He might as well get a job as a nanny. No
wonder sheepdogs had nervous breakdowns. No wonder mothers battered babies and babies battered mothers. He wanted to turn off the
din and lie down in the long lush grass by the river and go to sleep.

His eye ran over the row of bored, depressed-looking ponies
standing on three legs, tails swishing ineffectually against the flies,
occasionally flattening their ears at one another. They're trapped like
me, he thought.

His face became less frosty as he came to little Fenella Maxwell,
standing on a bucket, rebraiding the long-suffering Dandelion's mane
for the third time. She was a a good kid. Surprisingly she wasn't
spoiled by her bitch of a mother, who would be guzzling champagne
up at the main house by now.

His eyes softened even more when they came to rest on Africa.
Not dozing like the ponies, she looked around with her huge eyes
taking everything in, reassuring herself constantly that Jake was still
there.

The prospect of the open jumping and the risk he was running
made him steadily more sick with nerves. He lit another cigarette.

Next minute a huge horse van drew up, a groom got out, unfastened the ramp and led out a beautifully braided grey, sweating in a
crimson rug with dark blue binding. A girl wearing a white shirt, a
black coat, skin-tight breeches and long black boots walked over and
looked the horse over critically. She had a haughty pink and white face.
Jake thought how attractive some women looked in riding clothes, the
austerity and severity of the uniform contrasting with the wild wan-
tonness beneath. He imagined her long thighs thrashing in ecstasy,
while the hat, tie and haughty pink and white face remained primly in
place. He imagined laying her on a bed of straw, as tempting as a
newly made bed.

As if aware of Jake's scrutiny, she turned around. Jake looked away
quickly, determined not to give her the satisfaction of knowing she was
being admired.

"Lavinia!" A handsome dark boy, white teeth gleaming in his
suntanned face, pulled up his chestnut horse beside her.

"Christopher. Hello. I thought you were in Marbella."

"Just got back."

"Come and have a dwink." She couldn't say her Rs. "Mummy's
parked the car by the collecting wing."

"Love to." He rode on.

Bloody upper classes, thought Jake, all making so much bloody
noise. He was fed up with wearing a cheap riding coat and second-hand

boots that were killing him. He wanted a shiny van, and a groom whisking out different horses like a conjurer producing colored handkerchiefs, and a tackroom wall papered with blue ribbons, and a beautiful pink and white girl asking him respectfully how many strides there were between the gate and the rustic poles.

A shrill piping voice brought him back to earth.

"I've bought you an ice cream," said Fenella Maxwell. "You ought to keep up your strength. Oh look, they're bringing out the jumps for the junior jumping. I know I'm going to let Dandelion down. Mummy and Tory'll miss it if they don't stop stuffing themselves."

Inside Bilborough Hall Tory Maxwell, Fenella's elder sister, looked up at a large Rubens in which a huge pink fleshy Venus was being pursued by half the satyr population of Ancient Greece, while adoring cherubs arranged her rippling pearl-strewn hair. "She's much fatter than me," thought Tory wistfully. "Why wasn't I born in the seventeenth century?"

Tory had huge grey eyes and long straight light brown hair, which her mother insisted she wear drawn back off her forehead and temples and tied in a bow on the crown of her head. A style which made her round pleading peony red face look bigger than ever. She was tallish and big boned, with a huge bust that bounced up and down as she walked. No matter how she stood on the scales, she weighed one hundred sixty pounds.

She'd just got the curse, which made her feel even fatter, and, however many layers of makeup she put on, a large red spot on her chin glowed through like a lighthouse. She was getting hotter and hotter, but she couldn't take off the jacket of her red suit because the skirt was fastened precariously with a safety pin. Her ankles had swelled and, having kicked off her tight shoes, she wondered if she'd ever be able to get back into them again. She wondered if she'd ever been more miserable in her life. Then with a stab of pain she remembered last night's dance and decided she was comparatively blessed.

During the weekdays she was at a finishing school in London, learning to cook, to type and to arrange flowers by ramming bits of rhubarb into chicken mesh. By night she practiced the art of wallflower arrangement, going to cocktail parties and dances and trying to appear as though she belonged to one of those chattering laughing groups of debs and their admirers. Occasionally hostesses took pity on her and brought up wilting, reluctant young men who talked politely or danced one dance, then drifted away.

The more miserable she got, the more she ate. But never at dances, never in front of her mother. She would wait for everyone to go out or to bed, then wolf three bowls of cornflakes swimming in heavy cream. Yesterday she'd eaten a whole box of chocolates, which had

been given to her mother by an admirer, and then had to rush out to
the store and buy another box to replace it before her mother got back.

Why couldn't she be like Fen, and have something like horses to
be passionately interested in and keep her nose out of the trough? Why
did she have to stay inside on this lovely day when she wanted to be
outside picnicking with Fen and Jake? At the thought of Jake, dark-
faced and unpredictable, whom she had never spoken to, her stomach
felt weak, her mouth dry. Oh Jake!—at night she wrote him long
passionate letters which she always tore up. Small men were supposed
to like big girls; look at D.H. Lawrence and Stanley Spencer. Perhaps
having no parents, and being brought up in an orphanage, he might
be looking for a mother figure, but he didn't seem to be showing
much sign so far.

Tory's mother, Molly Maxwell, had enjoyed her lunch *enormously*.
She was delighted to be asked. Colonel Carter, who had accompanied
her, had enjoyed himself too. It had been fun being able to introduce
him to Sir William, and they'd got on well talking about the war. She
combed her hair surreptitiously; Gerald had done it beautifully this
week. Why was Tory hanging around like a wet blanket? Sir William's
sons were there. All of them Old Etonians, nice looking and so suitable, and Tory hadn't addressed a word to any of them all through
lunch, just sat like a pig, taking a second helping of pudding when she
thought her mother wasn't looking.

"Poor Molly," she could imagine people saying, "poor Molly to be
saddled with such a lump."

She was really enjoying Tory's season. The society page had described her as "the chic and most attractive mother of Tory Maxwell."
At least one escort and several fathers had declared themselves madly
in love with her. And now Colonel Carter was getting really keen and
sending roses twice a week.

Molly was a bit short of cash at the moment. Her rather stolid
husband had paid her a great deal of alimony, but when he inconven-
iently died he had left all his money, unaccountably, in trust for Tory.
That was another grudge; what did Tory want with an income of
£5,000 a year?

Tory looked across at her mother. "I'm the fruit of her womb, and
I hate her, hate her, hate her," she thought, "for her ankles slender as a
gazelle's, and her flexible high insteps, and thin legs, and her painted
malicious face, and her shrill clipped voice."

And that dreadful Colonel Carter, Colonel Bogus more likely,
handsome as an aging movie star, matinee-idling about, a cliché of
chauvinism, his large yellow teeth gleaming beneath his greying
moustache, as he blamed even the weather on the socialists.

Tory spotted Sir William hurrying across the room to welcome
the two judges, Malise Gordon and Miss Squires, who, on a tight

schedule, had only time for a quick bite. Malise Gordon, having accepted a weak whisky and soda, refused to follow it with any wine. He took a small helping of salmon but no potatoes, not because he was worried aout getting fat but because he liked to practice asceticism. An ex-Cavalry officer, much decorated after a good war, Colonel Gordon not only farmed but also judged at shows all around the country during the summer, and was kept busy in the winter as a local M.F.H. In addition to these activities, he played the flute, restored pictures in his spare time, and wrote poetry and books on military history. He was tall and lean with a handsome hawklike face, high cheekbones and dark hair hardly touched with grey.

That is easily the most attractive man in the room, thought Molly Maxwell, eyeing him speculatively as she accepted Colonel Carter's heavy pleasantries, and let her laugh tinkle again and again round the room. Malise Gordon was now talking to Sir William's wife, Lady Dorothy. What an old frump, thought Molly Maxwell, that dreadful brown cardigan with spots on it and lace-up shoes and the sort of baggy tweed skirt you'd feed the chickens in.

As an excuse to be introduced to Malise, Molly got up and, wandering over to Lady Dorothy, thanked her for a delicious lunch.

"Absolutely first rate," agreed Colonel Carter who'd followed her.

"Would you like to see the garden?" said Lady Dorothy.

Malise Gordon looked at his watch.

"We'd better go and supervise the junior jumping," he said to Miss Squires.

"Oh, my daughter's in that," said Molly Maxwell, giving Malise Gordon a dazzling smile. "I hope you'll turn a blind eye if she knocks anything down. It would be such a thrill if she got a ribbon."

Malise Gordon didn't smile back. He had heard Molly's laugh once too often and thought her very silly.

"Fortunately, jumping is the one event in which one can't possibly display any favoritism."

Colonel Carter, aware that his beloved had been snubbed, decided Malise Gordon needed taking down a peg.

"What's the order for this afternoon?" he asked.

"Junior jumping, open jumping, then gymkhana events in ring three, then your show in ring two, Carter."

A keen part-time soldier, Colonel Carter was organizing a recruiting display which included firing twenty-five pounders.

"We're scheduled for 1700 hours," snapped Colonel Carter. "Hope you'll have wound your jumping up by then, Gordon. My chaps like to kick off on time."

"I hope you won't do anything silly like firing off blanks while there are horses in the ring," said Malise brusquely. "It could be extremely dangerous.

"Thanks, Dorothy, for a splendid lunch," he added, kissing Lady Dorothy on the cheek. "The garden's looking marvellous."

Colonel Carter turned purple. What an arrogant bastard, he thought, glaring after Malise's broad, very straight back as he followed Miss Squires briskly out of the drawing room. But then the cavalry always gave themselves airs. Earlier, at the briefing, Malise had had the ill manners to point out that he thought a horse show was hardly the place to introduce a lot of people who had nothing better to do with their afternoons than play soldiers. "I'll show him," fumed Colonel Carter.

Outside, hackney carriages were bouncing around the ring, drawn by high-stepping horses, ribbons streaming from their striped browbands, while junior riders crashed their ponies over the practice fence. By some monumental inefficiency, the organizers of the show had also ended up with three celebrities who'd all arrived to present the prizes and needed looking after. The first was the Lady Mayor who'd opened the show and toured the exhibits and who had now been borne off to inspect the guides. The second was this year's Miss Bilborough whose all-day-long makeup had not stood up to the heat. The third was a radio celebrity, with uniformly grey hair and a black treacle voice called Dudley Diplock. Having played a doctor in a long-running soap opera, he talked at the top of his voice all the time in the hope that the public might recognize him. He had now commandeered the microphone for the junior jumping.

Fen felt her stomach getting hollower and hollower. The jumps looked huge.

"Please God, let me not have three refusals, let me not let Dandelion down."

"Oh here comes Tory," she said as Jake helped her saddle up Dandelion. "She went to a dance last night but I don't think she enjoyed it; her eyes were awfully red this morning."

Jake watched the plump anxious-faced Tory wincing over the churned-up ground in her tight shoes. She didn't look like a girl who enjoyed anything very much.

"Did you have a nice lunch? I bet you had strawberries," shrieked Fen, climbing onto Dandelion and gathering up the reins. "I'm just going to put Dandelion over a practice fence.

"This is my sister, Tory," she added.

Jake looked at Tory with that measure of disapproval he always bestowed on strangers.

"It's very hot," stammered Tory.

"Very," said Jake.

There didn't seem much else to say.

Fen came back from jumping the practice fence. Immediately Dandelion's head went down snatching at the grass.

"You pig," squealed Fen, jumping off and pulling bits out of his mouth. "I just cleaned that bit. Where's Mummy?" she added to Tory.

"Going over the garden with Lady Dorothy," said Tory.

"She must be bored," said Fen. "No, there she is on the other side of the ring. Colonel Carter stayed last night. I couldn't sleep and I looked out the window at about five o'clock and saw him go. He looked up at Mummy's bedroom and blew her a great soppy kiss. Think of kissing a man with an awful droopy mustache like that."

"Fen," said Tory blushing scarlet. She looked at Jake out of the corner of her eyes to see if he was registering shock or amusement, but his face was quite expressionless.

"Number fifty-eight," called out the collecting ring steward.

A girl in a dark blue riding coat on a very shiny bay mare went in and jumped clear. Some nearby drunks in a Bentley tooted loudly on their horn.

"How was her ladyship's garden." asked Colonel Carter.

"I think I was given a tour of every petal," said Molly Maxwell.

"You must have been the fairest flower," said the Colonel, putting his deck chair as close to hers as possible. "My people used to have a lovely garden in Hampshar."

The radio personality, Dudley Diplock, having mastered the microphone, was now thoroughly enjoying himself.

"Here comes the junior champion for Surrey," he said. "Miss Sarah Cock, I mean Cook, on Topsy."

A girl on a heavily bandaged dappled grey came in and jumped a brisk clear round.

Next came Sally-Ann Thomson.

"Here's my little girl," said Mrs. Thomson, pausing for a moment in her discussion of hats with Mrs. Maxwell. "I wonder if Stardust will go better in a running martingale."

Stardust decided not and refused three times at the first fence.

"We really ought to buy her a pony of her own," said Mrs. Thomson. "Even the best riders can't do much on riding-school hacks."

Mrs. Maxwell winked at Colonel Carter.

"Another competitor from Brook Farm Riding School eliminated," said Dudley Diplock.

"Teach them to fall off there, don't they?" said a wag.

The crowd guffawed. Jake gritted his teeth. He was aware of Tory standing beside him and, sensing her sympathy, was grateful.

"It's your turn next," said Jake, going up to Fen and checking Dandelion's girth. "Take the double slowly. Everyone else has come around the corner too fast and not given themselves enough time. Off you go," he added, gently pulling Dandelion's ears.

"Please God, I'll never be bad again," prayed Fen. "I won't be foul to Sally-Ann or call Patty a drip, or be rude to Mummy. Just let me get around."

Ignoring the cries of good luck, desperately trying to remember everything Jake had told her, Fen rode into the ring with a set expression on her face.

"Miss Fenella Maxwell, from Brook Farm Riding School," said the radio personality. "Let's have a round of applause for our youngest competitor."

The crowd, scenting carnage, clapped lethargically. Dandelion, his brown and white patches gleaming, gave a good-natured buck.

"Isn't that your little girl?" said Mrs. Thomson.

"So it is," said Molly Maxwell, "Oh look, her pony's going to the bathroom. Don't horses have an awful sense of timing."

The first fence loomed high as Beecher's Brook and Fen used her legs so fiercely Dandelion rose into the air clearing it by a foot.

Fen was slightly unseated and unable to get straight in the saddle to ride Dandelion properly at the gate. He slowed down and refused; when Fen whacked him he rolled his eyes, swished his tail and started to graze. The crowd laughed; Fen went crimson.

"Oh poor thing," murmured Tory in anguish.

Fen pulled his head up and let him examine the gate. Dandelion sniffed, decided it was harmless and, with a whisk of his fat rump, flew over and went bucketing on to clear the stile, at which Fen lost her stirrup, then cleared the parallel bars where she lost her other stirrup. Rounding the corner for home, Dandelion stepped up the pace. Fen checked him, her hat falling over her nose, as he bounded towards the road-closed sign. Dandelion, fighting for his head, rapped the fence, but it stayed put.

"I can't bear to look," thought Tory, shutting her eyes.

Fen had lost her hat now and, braids flying, raced towards the triple. Jake watched her strain every nerve to get the take-off right. Dandelion cleared it by inches and galloped out of the ring to loud applause.

"Miss Fenella Maxwell on Dandelion, only three faults for a refusal, jolly good round," coughed the microphone.

"I had no idea she'd improved so much," said Tory, turning a pink ecstatic face towards Jake.

Fen cantered up grinning from ear to ear.

"Wasn't Dandelion wonderful?" she said, jumping off, flinging her arms around his neck, covering him with kisses and stuffing him with sugar lumps.

She looked up at Jake enquiringly: "Well?"

"We could see half the show ground between your knees and the saddle, and you took him too fast at the gate, but not bad," he said.

For the first time that day he looked cheerful, and Tory thought how nice he was.

"I must go and congratulate Fen," said Mrs. Maxwell, delicately picking her way through the dung the gardener had not yet gathered.

"Well done, darling," she shrieked in a loud voice, which made all the nearby horses jump. "What a good boy," she added, gingerly patting Dandelion's nose with a gloved hand. "He is a boy isn't he?" She tilted her head sideways to look.

"Awfully good show," said Colonel Carter. "My sister used to jump on horseback in Hampshar."

Mrs. Maxwell turned to Jake, enveloping him in a sickening waft of Arpège.

"Fen really has improved. I do hope she isn't much of a nuisance down at the stables all day, but she is utterly pony mad. Every sentence begins, 'Jake said this, Jake says that'; you've become quite an ogre in our home."

"Oh Mummy," groaned Fen.

Jake, thinking how silly she was and unable to think of anything to say in reply, remained silent.

"How gauche he is," thought Molly Maxwell.

The junior class, having finished jumping off, were riding into the ring to collect their ribbons.

"Number eight-six," howled the collecting ring steward, "Number eight-six."

"That's you, Fen," said Tory in excitement.

"It couldn't be. I had a refusal."

"You're fourth," said Jake, "go on."

"I couldn't be."

"Number eighty-six for the last time," bellowed the steward.

"It is me," said Fen, and, scrambling onto Dandelion, plonking her hat on her head and, not wearing a riding coat, she cantered into the ring where she thanked Miss Bilborough three times for her ribbon. Success went to Dandelion's head and his feet. Thinking the lap of honor was a race, he barged ahead of the other three winners, carting Fen out of the ring and galloping halfway around the show ground before she could pull him to a halt in front of Jake. He shook his head disapprovingly.

Fen giggled. "Wouldn't it be lovely if Africa got one too?"

The afternoon wore on, getting hotter. The Lady Mayor, sweating in her scarlet robes, had a bright yellow nose from sniffing Lady Dorothy's lilies. The band was playing "Land of Hope and Glory" in the main ring as the fences for the open jumping were put up, the sun glinting on their brass instruments. Mrs. Thomson and Mrs. Maxwell moved their deck chairs to the right, following the sun.

"Wasn't Dandelion wonderful?" said Fen for the one-hundredth time.

Tory could feel the sweat dripping between her breasts and down her ribs. She'd taken off her red jacket and hung her white shirt outside over the straining safety pin.

Competitors in the open jumping were pulling on long black boots, the women tucking long hair into hairnets and warming up their horses over the practice fence. With £100 first prize there was a lot of competition from neighboring counties. Two well-known show jumpers, Lavinia Greenslade and Christopher Crossley, who'd both jumped at Wembley and for the British junior team, had entered, but local hopes were pinned on Sir William's son Michael, who was riding a grey six-year-old called Prescott.

Armored cars and tanks had started driving up the hill for the dry shoot and the recruiting display. Soldiers, sweating in battledresses, were assembling twenty-five pounders in ring two.

"Christ, here comes Carter's circus," said Malise Gordon to Miss Squires.

"Hope he can keep them under control."

"My chaps have arrived," said Colonel Carter to Mrs. Maxwell. "I'm just going to wander over and see that everything's all right."

Jake gave Africa a last polish. Tory, noticing his white face, shaking hands and chattering teeth, realized how terrified he was and felt sorry for him. He put a foot in the stirrup and was up.

"If only I weren't so frightened of horses I might not be frightened of life," thought Tory, cringing against the rope to avoid these great snorting beasts with their huge iron feet and so much power in their gleaming, barging quarters.

The band went out to much applause and, to everyone's dismay, came back again. Jake rode up to Tory and jumped off.

"Can you hold her for a minute?" he said, hurling the reins at her.

He only just made the men's room in time.

Looking into the deep, dark well of the portable toilet and catching a whiff of the contents, he was violently sick again. He must pull himself together or Africa would sense his nerves. Mrs. Wilton wouldn't find out; the kids could cope in the gymkhana events for half an hour by themselves. He'd be all right once he got into the ring. He'd walked the course; there was nothing Africa couldn't jump if he put her right. He leaned against the canvas and wondered if he dared risk another cigarette.

Tory was not happy. Excited by the microphone and the armored cars and the crowds, Africa pulled and fretted as she jogged up and down.

"Thanks very much," said Jake, taking the horse from her.

Tory, noticing his pallor and shaking hands, felt so sorry for him. "I get just the same before dances," she blurted out.

Jake smiled slightly.

"Take your partners for the torture chamber," he said, mounting Africa again.

He rode very short, almost jockey length, crouching over the mare like a cat settling down into the creaking leather. Africa, a netted cord of veins rippling under her shining coat, tugged at the reins, now this way, now that. Trying to shake Jake off, she danced over the grass, shying at the tea tent, the ladies lavatory, the flags. Jake didn't move in the saddle.

Even Tory's uncritical eye could see that he rode wonderfully lightly; his hands hardly touched Africa's mouth. Taking her away from the crowd he popped her over a couple of practice fences.

Colonel Carter sat down beside Molly Maxwell announcing that his chaps were itching to get started. At that moment a competitor on a huge grey paused in front of them to chat to some friends. The grey promptly stuck out its penis. Mrs. Maxwell caught the Colonel's eye and giggled.

The Colonel looked at his watch.

"Half an hour to blast off," he said. "I hope Malise Gordon gets his finger out."

There were nine jumps in all, a brush fence, a stile, a gate, parallel bars, the road-closed sign put up to a nasty five feet, another brush with a pole on top, a water jump which had been drained by various dogs, a wall, and a triple.

The two stars, Lavinia Greenslade and Christopher Crossley, sat on their horses side by side slightly apart from the other competitors.

"The jumps are much too low and flimsy," said Lavinia. "Bound to be loads of clear wounds. We won't get away for at least an hour and I did want to look in at Henwietta's cocktail party."

"Not much competition anyway," said Christopher.

The first competitor trotted out, an enormously fat girl with a huge bosom.

"Give herself a couple of black eyes every time she jumps with those boobs," said Christopher.

The girl went clear.

"I told you there were going to be loads of clear wounds," said Lavinia petulantly.

"I can't see, I can't see," said Fen in a shrill voice.

"You come through here then," said a man on a camp chair, making a gap in the crowd through which Fen dragged a desperately embarrassed Tory to the ropes.

A chestnut came in ridden by a boy with a big nose who jabbed his horse in the mouth over every fence.

"Jumps well," said Tory.

"Horse does," said Fen. "Rider should be shot. Bloody hell," she added as he went clear. The man on the camp chair who'd let Fen through looked at her with less indulgence.

Lavinia Greenslade was next, the grey peering seductively through the long forelock of its mane, Arab ears curling upwards like eyelashes.

"Her father spends a fortune on her horses," said Fen. "That one was third at the Horse of the Year Show last year."

Sure enough, the grey bounced serenely around the course like a ping pong ball, followed by Sir William's son who also went clear.

To the course builders' relief, a man came in on a horse wearing so much leather it looked like a bondage victim and proceeded to demolish the course completely. Fear traveled through the collecting ring and for a dozen rounds no one went clear. The wall, the principal bogey, had to be laboriously rebuilt each time.

Colonel Carter looked at his watch. Five minutes to go. Time and the Colonel waited for no Malise Gordon.

Lavinia's boyfriend Christopher then went in and killed the jinx by jumping a very fast, clear round. Jake envied the casual way he threw his whip to his groom, slid off the horse and went back to the ringside to join Lavinia watching the rest of the rounds.

The next competitor was an old woman in a hair net with a raddled face, scarlet lipstick and withered cheeks embedded with rouge.

The old lady rode as though she was steering a Rolls Royce. Her cob went clear without any visible effort.

"Jake's after this," said Fen, as a girl with a bun escaping from her hairnet came in on a mangy brown mare and proceeded to scatter every fence. As she came to the wall the mare dug in her toes and skidded four feet into the wall; then, as the bricks collapsed around her, she bolted on to totally demolish the triple.

"Oh poor Jake," said Fen, as they waited and waited for the course to be repaired.

At last they called number 195. Out came Jake from the gap in the crowds, his face a grey mask. By contrast, Africa, who danced and plunged, merry eyes gleaming at the crowd, coat rippling like a furniture polish advertisement, looked the picture of joy.

"Jack Lovette," said Dudley Diplock, the radio personality. "From Brook Farm Riding School."

"Not another one," Malise Gordon groaned inwardly.

Tory could see Jake's lips constantly moving, as he reassured Africa.

"Only time he talks is to horses," grumbled Fen.

Once in the ring Jake found his nervousness had gone. He shortened his reins and stood up in the stirrups. Africa bounded towards the first fence.

"Too quick," muttered Fen.

But Africa was over safely and Jake's eyes were already trained on the post and rails ahead, which she cleared easily. At the gate, catching sight of a balloon in the crowd, she stopped concentrating and rapped her hocks hard. The gate swung, but miraculously didn't come down.

"That'll teach her," said Fen, as Africa dragged her leg for a couple of paces.

"Rides well," said a voice in the crowd.

"Horse carrying a lot of condition."

"Isn't that Jake Lovell?" said Molly Maxwell.

Africa slowed down at the wall, then changed her mind and cleared it with a violent jerky cat jump, which would have unseated most riders. Haven't seen that boy before, thought Malise, handles that horse very well. She's not at all an easy ride. With increasing pleasure he watched Africa clear the post and rails and the parallel bars and sail over the water jump and the wall.

But, as Jake turned her towards the triple, Malise realized it was unnaturally high. One of the arena stewards who'd been crossed in love, and been in the beer tent all afternoon, had just seen his beloved saunter past on the arm of a rival and had put the top bar up to six feet.

Malise Gordon stepped forward to protest, but it was too late. Africa had turned and was approaching the triple at a steeplechaser's pace, her feet drumming on the ground, fighting for her head.

"Steady darling," crooned Jake.

The top bar, white against pitted grey-green turf, was higher than Africa's ears. For a second she hesitated, caught on a short stride, then, like a helicopter, rising off her hocks, she made a colossal jump. It seemed to the gaping crowd that she had taken off like a bird into the sky and bore no relation to the white poles below her.

"Christ," said Malise.

The crowd gave a long sigh of rapture and sent up a great cheer.

Colonel Carter looked at his watch.

"Bloody good round," said Christopher Crossley.

Jake jumped off Africa, patting her, determined not to betray the surge of exultation that was sweeping over him.

"That's it," Malise Gordon told the arena party. "Restrict it to six jumps, raise the pole over the first jump and the gate, put another row of bricks on the wall and set the triple at five feet. Buck up, or Carter will start letting off his guns.

"That's seven clear rounds," said Fen, counting on her fingers.

Colonel Carter heaved himself out of his deck chair.

"Are you off?" said Molly.

"Enemy wouldn't wait, would they? The men will start the display in ten minutes," he said, striding past Malise.

"Don't be bloody silly," snapped Malise. "If you fire a single shot before the last horse has jumped, you'll cause chaos—and accidents."

"Quarter of an hour; should give you ample time."

"I'll send someone to give you the O.K."

Colonel Carter ground his big yellow teeth. He was tired. Last night with Molly had been wonderful but rather exhausting. He hadn't had much sleep; the effects of Sir William's hospitality at lunchtime had worn off and, worst of all, he resented Malise's complete refusal to take his display seriously.

In ring three, near the chestnut trees, the gymkhana events were already starting, with a burst of music for musical chairs.

"Can you help me saddle up Swindle, Mr. Lovell?" said Pattie Beasley.

"Give me a quarter of an hour," said Jake.

The horses waited in the collecting ring, maddened by flies, the heat and the rumble of approaching thunder.

"If you win, will you tell Mrs. Wilton?" asked Fen.

"God, no. If she knew how good Africa was, she'd persuade Bobby to sell. Wish I could buy her myself, but I'd have to win the lottery or marry an heiress."

"Marry Tory," said Fen with a giggle. "She's going to be frightfully rich one day, and you could keep lots of horses, and I could come and live with you."

"Fen," said Tory, going crimson.

She really was a champion blusher, thought Jake.

Fen watched Sally-Ann Thomson bumping off to take part in the musical chairs.

"Good thing Mrs. Wilton's in Brighton," she said. "She'd be jolly cross if she knew you weren't keeping your eyes on her darling pupils."

Mrs. Wilton eased her car through the traffic. It had been a most unsatisfactory day. Her rich homosexual uncle, irritated by the heat and the refractoriness of his male hairdresser friend, had been so quarrelsome at lunchtime that she had walked out in a huff. One look at Brighton beach, packed with tourists avid for a day in the sun, and she had decided to drive back home to avoid the rush hour traffic. The trip, in fact, had been so easy that she decided to look in at the Bilborough Show. It never hurt to turn up unexpectedly; it kept Jake up to the mark. She rummaged in her bag for lipstick and applied it without even looking in the mirror.

Colonel Carter's blood pressure rose with the temperature. Bugger Malise Gordon, he would not only lose the respect of his soldiers, dying of the heat in their battledress, but also of the sizeable crowd who'd turned up at five to witness some bangs and were now drifting away.

"People are getting bored with waiting, Sir," said his adjutant.

"Take this to Colonel Gordon," said Colonel Carter, handing him a note: "The guns will be fired at 17.20 hours. Carter."

It was just like the Charge of the Light Brigade, thought the young soldier, as he returned two minutes later with the same bit of paper, on the back of which Malise Gordon had scrawled:

"Imperative to wait end of last round, Gordon."

Colonel Carter tore up the note in a fury.

The girl with the big boobs had seven faults, Sir William's son had eight. The horse whose rider jabbed him in the mouth had had enough and refused the brush fence twice, the stile once, and was eliminated. The old lady covered in makeup went next; she took a brick off the wall and knocked the top bar of the triple.

Mrs. Wilton parked her car. It looked as though the open jumping was still going. Colonel Carter examined his watch.

Christopher Crossley was about to start his round.

"Shall we divide, Lavinia," he said, "if we both go clear?"

"Fire!" The word of command rang out of the midgy, steaming air. Crash went the twenty-five pounders, causing immediate pandemonium in the collecting ring, horses rearing, bucking, plunging and scattering the crowd.

Lavinia Greenslade's grey was barging around like a bumper car. Jake jumped straight off Africa and was clinging on to her bridle trying to calm her.

White with anger, Malise Gordon left Miss Squires and the green baize table and sprinted across to ring two, where he was joined by Sir William asking, "What the hell is going on?"

"That megalomaniac Carter," said Malise, striding up to Colonel Carter.

"What the bloody hell are you playing at? Stop those guns at *once!*"

Colonel Carter's reply was drowned in another crash.

A horse that dumped its rider bolted past them reins and stirrups flying, followed by the girl with the big boobs who was also being carted.

"Look at that," said Malise. "There'll be a serious accident in a minute."

"Your people should be able to control their mounts," said Colonel Carter. "If you're incapable of keeping to a time schedule, you should accept the consequences."

Another gun exploded.

"Think you might hang on five minutes, Carter," said Sir William, "Only three horses left to jump."

"Hold your fire, Colonel," said the Lady Mayor, who had put her hands over her ears.

Carter decided he was outnumbered.

"All right, if you want to make a mockery of the whole display we'll wait another ten minutes."

"Maniac," said Christopher Crossley, whose horse was leaping around as though someone was burning the grass under its feet, its nostrils as red as a peony. Jake, who was trying to sooth a trembling, sweating Africa, admired the way Christopher went into the ring, and jumped a beautiful round, only taking a brick out of the wall.

Lavinia Greenslade's grey, however, who'd been completely unhinged by the guns, crashed round the course, leaving it as though an earthquake had hit it.

Once again Jake had to wait until it was repaired, the strain telling on both his and Africa's nerves.

"Bad luck," said Christopher Crossley as Lavinia rode out, looking furious.

"I'm going to object," she said.

Molly Maxwell joined Colonel Carter.

"Are you having a cease-fire?" she said with a giggle.

"Bloody Gordon, insisted on finishing his jumping."

"You should have started half an hour ago," said Molly. "I wouldn't stand for that. Wellington would never have taken Waterloo that way."

"Oh my God," gasped Fen, seeing Mrs. Wilton pushing briskly through the crowd. "Look who's over there, Tory. She'll go potty if she sees Jake. We'd better distract her. Hello, Mrs. Wilton, we thought you were in Brighton."

"Decided to come back. Had a good day?"

"I was fourth in the Junior Jumping."

"Your first ribbon. Well done. Has anyone else done anything?"

Fen shook her head.

"Where's Jake?"

"Supervising the gymkhana events, I think," said Tory desperately.

"Yes, he is. Come and find him, and you can see how sweet Dandelion looks in his ribbon on the way," said Fen, seizing Mrs. Wilton's red hand. "And then come and see Mummy. I know she wants to buy you a drink. You must be hot after your journey." She looked a picture of guilt as the words came tumbling out.

"What happened in the open jumping?"

"It's finished," said Fen.

The course had been set to rights.

"In you go," said the collecting ring steward.

Jake rode quietly into the ring.

"That's a nice horse," thought Malise.

"Oh there's one more competitor," said Mrs. Wilton.

"Come and see Dandelion," said Fen desperately.

"Why it's Jake," said Mrs. Wilton in tones of outrage, "and he's riding Africa."

Africa bounded up to the first fence, as tense as a catapult at full stretch.

The ten minutes were up. "Fire" said Colonel Carter for the second time.

The gun went off like clap of thunder.

A dog bolted into the ring, barking hysterically, a child dropped its ice cream and let out a wail of rage. Africa went straight up on her hind legs, eyes rolling in terror, and dropping again, with a bound bolted towards the first fence clearing it by inches.

Jake sat down in the saddle and tried to hold her. Another gun went off. Africa crashed into the gate and sent the stile flying.

The crowds looked on, helpless. Tory and Fen watched, frozen with horror, as the maddened mare swung round the corner, with Jake hauling futilely on the bit, aware only of Africa's hooves thundering on the dry earth and the white terrified faces flashing past.

As she raced to the triple, ten yards off, another gun went off. Jake tried to check her, but she'd missed her stride and took it completely wrong, jumping sideways and catching her foreleg in the wing of the jump. It was all flying colored poles as horse and rider came crashing down into the middle of the jump. The crowd gave a moan of terror.

Africa lay under three poles, legs flailing like a centipede, making desperate attempts to get up. Jake staggered groggily to his feet, stars in his head. Praying against hope that Africa hadn't broken a leg, he lurched towards her still holding onto the reins.

Another gun went off; Africa threw off the poles and struggled to her feet, standing trembling all over, holding up her off hind hoof.

Malise ran up.

"You all right?" he said.

Jake nodded: "Not so sure about the horse; can't put her foot down."

Malise took Africa's bridle, stroking her gently, then he led her forward a step, Africa hobbled, then stopped. Malise ran his hand down the foot; she winced but let him touch it.

"Nothing broken, I wouldn't think. Might have pulled a tendon. Better get the vet."

Another gun went off. Africa trembled violently but was finished.

"Sorry about that," said Malise. "She jumped very well in the first round. Look, sit down on the grass," he added as Jake started to sway.

But the next moment Mrs. Wilton rolled up, marching with a far more military stride than Colonel Carter.

"So this is what you get up to when I'm away," she shouted. "How dare you jump that horse, how *dare* you!"

Jake looked at her. Through a haze of pain he saw her red angry face like a baron of beef receding and coming towards him.

"Leave him alone," snapped Malise. "Can't you see he's in a state of shock."

Mrs. Wilton turned on Malise furiously.

Jake said nothing and, after another look at Africa's foot, led her habbling out of the ring. Mrs. Wilton followed him, shouting abuse. She wanted to fire him on the spot, but she couldn't afford to, as there'd be no one except that half-wit Alison, who only worked part-time, to look after the horses. Grooms were so hard to get.

As he came out of the ring, Fen rushed forward.

"Oh poor Jake; are you all right? Do you have a concussion? Can you remember what day of the week it is and what you had for lunch?"

Christopher Crossley passed them going into the ring to collect first prize. He pulled up his chestnut horse for a minute.

"That was bloody bad luck," he said, "and that's a very nice mare. If you ever want to sell her I'm in the North Hampshire telephone dirctory under Crossley. Those bloody soldiers should turn the guns on themselves."

Jake nodded.

As they approached the horse lines, Fen gave a scream.

"Dandelion, he's not there.

Rushing forward, she found his halter still tied to the fence.

"He's a valuable horse now that he's a prize winner," she wailed. "He's probably been kidnapped."

After a nasty quarter of an hour, in which Mrs. Wilton trailed after Jake calling him every name under the sun, Dandelion was discovered in the brave new world of Lady Dorothy's vegetable garden. Having laid waste to the herbaceous border, dug holes in the newly sprinkled lawn, cut a swathe through the rose beds and de-formalized the formal garden, Dandelion was now imitating an untamed bronco, galloping about snorting, showing the whites of his eyes, with a large carrot sticking out of his mouth like a cigar.

Every time Jake or Fen got close he whisked out of range, snatching bites to eat.

When at last Jake caught him, abuse from Lady Dorothy, Mrs. Wilton, and Mrs. Thomson, was cascading over his head like Niagara.

Finally it was time to go home. Africa had been checked by the vet, who said she was suffering a bad sprain, no more, and should be rested. Malise Gordon then hurried home himself because he was going to the theater. Fen had come in second in the potato race and was in a state of ecstasy. Miss Bilborough had a date with one of Colonel

Carter's men. Dudley Diplock had been asked for his autograph three times, but had not been thanked for doing the commentary.

Back at Brook Farm Riding School a still dizzy Jake was putting the ponies to bed.

"Hear you're in the dog house," said Alison, the Irish girl who helped out on weekends. "Old Ma Wilton's hopping. I knew she'd catch you out sooner or later."

Jake didn't answer; he was putting a poultice on Africa. He'd already rubbed one of his gypsy medicines (ointment made from marshmallow flowers) gently into her leg. He was finally sweeping up about nine-thirty when Mrs. Wilton turned up. Her face looked unappetizingly magenta in the naked light bulb of the tack room and he could smell whiskey on her breath.

"I want to talk to you, Jake," she said, speaking slowly to show she was quite sober. "Do you realize you've ruined the reputation of Brook Farm Riding School?"

"What reputation?" said Jake. "You can't descend from the basement."

"Don't be cheeky. No need to answer back."

Jake swept up the straw on the floor. Phrases like "absolute shambles," "endangering best horse in the yard" and "duty to our young pupils" flowed over his head. His face had taken on an almost Asiatic aloofness.

"Why can't he ever show any contrition?" thought Mrs. Wilton. "If he apologized just once it would make a difference."

The diatribe continued. "I'm very disappointed in you, Jake," she went on. "I really trusted you, gave you some responsibility and you just kick me in the teeth. yet I still feel *deep down* that you really like me." For a second her voice was almost obscenely conciliatory.

"No, I don't," Jake said flatly. "Deep down it's much worse."

Mrs. Wilton caught her breath. The next minute vindictiveness was warming her blood. She played her trump card. "You'd better get Africa's leg better; she won't be with us much longer."

Jake looked up, eyes narrowed.

That jolted him, she thought.

"Sir William's just rung. I thought he was going to raise hell about Lady Dorothy's garden, but he only wanted to know how Africa was and if we'd be interested in selling. He wants her for his youngest son to hunt next season. She might do very well with a decent rider on her back."

Turning, she walked unsteadily out of the tackroom. Jake felt suddenly exhausted, near to tears, overwhelmed with black despair.

Going out of the tackroom, he walked down the box stalls until he came to Africa. Even though she was eating she left her manger and hobbled over to him, nickering with joy, nuzzling at his pockets. He put his arms around her neck and she laid her head against his cheek. Soppy old thing, she'd stay like that for hours, breathing softly while he scratched her behind the ears.

In his mind, he jumped that beautiful first round again, reliving that wonderful amazing last jump. What a star she was; he couldn't give her up, and he knew more than ever that the only thing he could ever be in this world was a show jumper. Working for Mrs. Wilton for over a year, he was constantly aware of time running past, time wasted. He had left the orphanage at eighteen and spent two years in a racing stable. It was there that he made the discovery that difficult horses became easy when he rode them, and that he could communicate with them as he never could with people. Even having his first girl, and subsequently others, wasn't nearly as exciting as that sudden breakthrough when a horse that had been written off as hopeless became responsive under his touch. Finally there was the joy over the past months of discovering Africa and slowly realizing how good she was. It was worth putting up with the horrible little girls and their frightful mothers. No mother had ever protected and fussed over him the way they did, he thought bitterly.

And now he'd blown it; it was only a matter of time before Mrs. Wilton would fire him. He supposed he could get another job as a groom, but not as a rider. Africa nuzzled him gently.

"I'm still here," she seemed to say.

"But not for much longer," sighed Jake, "although I'll fight like a bugger to keep you."

Tory Maxwell lay on her bed, bitterly ashamed of herself for eating three helpings of strawberries and cream. She looked around her extremely tidy bedroom and wished she had a photograph of Jake. The scent of lilac and lilies of the valley kept drifting in from outside, as insistently as he kept drifting into her thoughts. Not that he had noticed her. His eyes had flickered over her as a man flips past the woman's fashion page in his daily paper, knowing it had nothing to interest him.

Her mother had gone out with that monstrous murderer, Colonel Carter. After what he'd done to Jake, Tory couldn't even bring herself to talk to him. How *could* her mother sleep with him? She imagined him climbing on top of her like an ancient dinosaur.

Looking in the mirror, she tried on a different color lipstick and put her hands over the sides of her round face. If she were thinner, she might just be pretty. Out of the window, against a brilliant drained sapphire sky, she could see the sliver of a pale new moon, followed by a little star. "Just like me following Jake," she thought.

"Oh please," she prayed, "give me Jake Lovell, and then I could buy him all the horses he wants."

Colonel Carter and Mrs. Maxwell were on their third gin and tonic in the bar of the Grand Hotel, Guildford. They had pulled Malise and Jake to shreds, had a good bitch about Sir William and Lady Dorothy and were in a mood of great mutual self-congratulation about having found one another.

"You're looking particularly lovely tonight," said Colonel Carter.

He always says that, thought Molly, but then perhaps it's true. She caught sight of her glossy reflection in the rose-tinted bar mirror. What should she wear to get married in? Perhaps oyster silk with a matching hat; it couldn't be the same thing she wore to Tory's party.

In future the Colonel could cope with all her bills.

In the corner the pianist, who had unnaturally vermilion hair, was playing "Someone to watch over me."

"Just a little lamb that's lost in the wood," sang the Colonel.

It was nice to take an attractive woman out again. He had always been unfaithful to Jennifer, his wife, but it had been a shock when she died. She'd done everything for him.

"I was very lonely when Jennifer died," he said.

"I was very lonely when Alastair died," said Molly. No reason to add that she and Alastair had been divorced for six years before he was killed in that car crash. It was so much more romantic to be a widow than a divorcée.

The waiter presented them with a huge menu, which they studied with too much attention (Colonel Carter in particular noting the prices) for people in love.

"I'm glad I stood up to that bastard, Gordon," he said.

"I wish I knew where I'd gone wrong with Tory," said Molly Maxwell.

Fen was in her bedroom, down the hall from Tory's. She'd been sent to bed in disgrace for cussing Colonel Carter about frightening Africa with his twenty-five pounders. Her bed was full of cookie crumbs and she was reading *The Maltese Cat* for the hundredth time with a flashlight. Then she turned the flashlight on her ribbons, white and red, then looking out of the window, caught sight of the new moon.

"Make me the greatest show jumper in the world," she wished.

Sunday started badly for Tory Maxwell. Unable to sleep, she had heard the floorboards outside her room creaking as the Colonel crept out at dawn. But he was back by 12:30, spruced up in clean clothes, moustache brushed and bearing a bottle of gin, and he and Molly Maxwell sat on the terrace drinking dry martinis while Tory cooked the lunch.

"As I have to fork out so much for this cooking and typing course," said Molly, "I might as well make use of her."

"What a charming garden," said the Colonel.

"The lawn needs mowing," hinted Molly Maxwell. "But I seem to have so little time this summer."

The white sauce for the cauliflower went lumpy because Tory was trying, at the same time, to read an article in one of the color supplements on deb's escorts. The piece included a profile of Rupert Campbell-Black. After three years in the Blues, he was now too busy making a name for himself as a show jumper to go to many deb parties, but whenever he did he caused a rumpus.

"You can say that again," sighed Tory, adding more milk to the sauce. She had been a victim of Rupert's bitchy asides on numerous occasions. He had got that cold blank stare of complete indifference to perfection. The sight of his cruel, arrogant face looking out at her made her feel quite sick. Particularly as her mother thought he was absolutely charming and kept nagging Tory to ring him up and make sure he'd got the invitation and was coming to Tory's party.

Tory was dreading the party. She didn't think anyone would come and she was sensitive enough to realize that, although some of the fathers and the young men flirted with her mother, the mothers thought her pushy and pretentious.

At 1:30, although Fen still wasn't back from the stables, they started lunch. Colonel Carter carved. Conditioned by wartime austerity, he cut very thin slices. Tory noticed he touched her mother's hand when he passed her a plate. She knew they found her presence a strain. Her mother found fault with everything. The white sauce was too lumpy and thin, the meat overdone, and the roast potatoes soggy. Molly, who wanted the Colonel to think she had an appetite like a sparrow, pushed hers to the side of her plate.

"I don't mean to nag," she said, "but one day you'll get married and have to cook for some chap, and he'll expect decent grub."

Some hope, thought Tory. As she cleared away in an excess of misery, she ate the two roast potatoes her mother had rejected and two

more left in the dish. When her mother came in, weighed down by the
gravy boat, as an excuse to powder her nose in the kitchen mirror, Tory
had to swallow frantically.

Halfway through dessert, when Molly was grumbling that the
meringue was just like toffee, Fen walked in with a filthy face and
hands and the same shirt she'd been wearing yesterday, which triggered off a storm of reproof which Fen accepted with equanimity. The
Colonel droned on about bridge.

"Jolly good roast potatoes," said Fen, "Are there any more?"

"There were two in the dish," said Molly.

Tory blushed: "I threw them away."

"I bet you ate them," snapped Molly. "Really Tory. D'you want to
look like a house for your dance?"

"Did you have a good ride, Fenella?" asked Colonel Carter.

"Not very," said Fen. "Jake was in a foul temper."

"Nothing new," said Molly. "Would you like some Stilton, Bernard?"

"Hardly surprising," said Fen, glaring at Colonel Carter. "Africa
might have been ruined for life."

"Shut up," snapped her mother.

"Malise Gordon dropped in to see if Africa was all right, but Jake
says both he and Sir William are after her. It's a rotten shame. Jake's
worked so hard on her; no one gets her going better than he does. And
he's got the most awful bunch to take out this afternoon—fat grown-
ups who can't ride, and in this heat they've booked a whole two hours.
I'm going back to help him after lunch."

"You are *not*," said Molly Maxwell firmly. "You spend too much
time hanging around that place. You're coming out to tea with the
Braithwaites."

"Whatever for?" wailed Fen.

"Because they asked us."

"Tory as well?"

"No. Tory's got to do her homework and write her thank you
letters."

"It's not fair. I loathe Melanie Braithwaite. She's a drip and she's
not my age."

Molly Maxwell insisted on taking Fen with them as otherwise she
would have to go back to the Colonel's house on the way home and
spend an hour in bed with him. That was the tiresome thing about
men, she thought, they always wanted sex all the time and she so
much preferred the flirting and the wining and dining.

Tory watched Fen, scrubbed and mutinous in a new dress, being
dragged off to the Braithwaites. She then wrote five thank you letters
in her round careful hand, and then accepted four more invitations.

Being fat and plain and no threat to prettier girls, and because many of
the deb's mothers had known and liked her father, she was asked to
quite a lot of parties. Each one spelled disaster.

"I'm like a terrible first night, but first night's are lucky enough
to fold, while I have to flop on forever," she said to herself.

Letters finished, she started on her homework, gazing at a page of
shorthand until the heavy and light lines swam before her eyes.

"We are in receipt of your letter, yours faithfully, yours truly," she
wrote.

Oh, she'd be faithful and true to Jake. Then she wrote "Jake" in
shorthand, the dark backward sloping J and light horizontal K on the
line, with two little commas underneath to show it was a proper name.
Then she wrote "Lovell"; it was the same sign as Lovely. He was lovely
too. She tried to visualize his face, but she could only picture his body
and a blur. She felt impossibly restless. The telephone interrupted her
daydreams; perhaps by a miracle it might be him, but it was only her
mother saying that the Braithwaites wanted to play bridge and had
pressed them to stay on for an early supper, so they'd be home at about
ten and could Tory pack Fen's lunch and see that she had a clean uniform and leotard for tommorrow? Poor trapped Fen, thought Tory.

The evening stretched ahead of her. Jake would be back from his
ride now and settling the horses. The longing became too much for
her. She'd go down to the stables on the excuse that Fen might have
left her whip behind.

Quickly she washed her hair. Her mother liked it drawn back
from her forehead but today she was jolly well going to let it flop loose.
If only she had a slimming black dress, but her mother said she was too
young and anyway she couldn't go down to the stables dressed for a
funeral. Ponchos were fashionable, they covered all the spare tyres, but
when they slid down on the shoulders they showed her bra straps, and
if she didn't wear a bra she flopped all over the place. If only she had a
waist she could wear a long skirt to cover her fat legs, but it made her
look like a barrel. In the end she gave up and wore a navy blue T-shirt
outside her jeans. Her hand was shaking so much she couldn't do the
clasp of her pearls, so she left them off. In a fit of loathing, she drenched herself in her mother's scent and as it was drizzling slightly, borrowed her mother's white trench coat, with the belt trendily done up at
the back. It didn't matter if it didn't meet over her bust.

As she passed the church people were coming out of Evensong,
putting up umbrellas. On the village green cricketers huddled disconsolately into the pavilion, hoping the apricot glow on the horizon
meant that the rain was about to stop and they could finish their
game.

The Brook Farm Riding School tackroom was overcrowded but
very tidy—saddles and bridles occupying one wall, food bins another,

and medicines, principally Jake's gypsy remedies, yet another. Room had also been found for a few faded ribbons and old calendars. The schedule book was open. Sunday, full of bookings, had been crossed off. Tomorrow was comparatively empty, except for a group of children who wanted to ride after school. Jake sat on a rickety chair, cleaning a bridle and reading the same article on Rupert Campbell-Black. The bastard was obviously going to make it in show jumping, just when Jake's world seemed to be falling apart, throwing him straight down to the bottom of the ladder, without even being within clutching distance of the first rung. The two-hour ride had really taken it out of him; his head was pounding and every bone in his body had been bruised by the fall yesterday.

After a night's rest and Jake's marshmallow ointment Africa's limp was barely perceptible. Mrs. Wilton had gloatingly told him of Malise's interest that morning and Sir William had just called again. No one could do anything about it, as Bobby Cotterel was in France till the end of the week, but it was only a matter of time.

He heard a step and, looking up through the dusty cobwebbed window, saw Fen's fat sister approaching. That was all he needed. Now she was stopping to comb her hair. Then her great blushing face, like a Dutch cheese, appeared round the door.

"Yes," he said bleakly.

"Did, I mean, I was wondering," she stammered, "if Fen left her whip here?" The feebleness of the excuse made her blush even more. "It was—er—one our grandmother—gave her for Christmas, so she was worried."

"I haven't seen it. She's so spacy she probably dropped it on the way home."

How pinched and dark under the eyes he looked, thought Tory. Sympathy overcame her shyness. "I'm so sorry about people wanting to buy Africa. Fen told me."

Jake nodded. She shifted from one foot to another and Jake was enveloped in a waft of Molly's scent, which did not evoke happy memories.

"Is her leg better?"

"She's all right."

Why was she hanging around? Getting up, he ran the sponge under the tap and plunged it into the saddle soap, adding:

"The whip—it isn't here."

Tory gazed at her feet, twisting a button on Mrs. Maxwell's coat. Then she noticed what he was reading.

"Oh there's Rupert Campbell-Black. Horrible man."

Jake looked up, slightly more accommodating. Tory blushed again.

"I'm sorry. Is he a friend of yours?"

There was a pause.

"I hate his guts," said Jake.

"Oh, so do I," said Tory. "He's so vicious and contemptuous and, well, bloody-minded. How did *you* come across him?"

"We were at school together."

Tory looked amazed.

"Prep school," added Jake. "I was a day boy. Mum was the cook, so the headmaster let me in free."

"Oh goodness, he must have been an absolutely poisonous small boy."

Taking a nail, Jake pushed out the saddle soap that had got stuck in the cheek-strap holes.

"Poisonous," he agreed. "He made Eichmann look like a fairy godmother."

"He's so rich," said Tory, "that lots of mothers are after him, but he's only after one thing."

"What's that?" said Jake to embarrass her.

Tory swallowed. "Well sex and things. He's awfully promiscuous."

She pronounced it promise-kew-us. "And he never answers invitations; just rolls up with his current girlfriend and leaves after half an hour if he's bored. He set off firecrackers at Queen Charlotte's. Lady Surrey was livid."

"He obviously hasn't changed," said Jake. "I should have thought Harrow or the army might've knocked it out of him."

"I think it made him worse," sighed Tory, "He gets a little gang of cronies round him and manages to be even nastier."

Nothing unites people like a good bitching session, Jake let her rattle on as he put the bridle together again and hung it up. Then he went to reapply Africa's poultice. Troy followed him, longingly watching the tender way his hands ran over the mare, caressing her polished shoulder and her sleek veined legs. Africa nuzzled him, breathing through her velvet nostrils with love and trust.

"She's so beautiful," said Troy wistfully.

The swelling had practically disappeared. Jake redid the bandages and readjusted her summer blanket. He wished Tory would buzz off and leave him alone to nurse his misery. As he came out of the stable, shutting the door behind him, the rain stopped. He looked at her round anxious face, her clean flopping hair and enormous monobosom straining against the dark blue T-shirt. There was kindness in her eyes. He looked at his watch.

"Let's go and have a drink."

Tory looked at him stupidly.

"A drink," he repeated mockingly, "The pubs are open. You're eighteen, aren't you?"

"Yes, of course I am. Gosh, thanks awfully."

As they walked to the pub, Jake noticed the hawthorns were rusting slightly but still smelled like fresh soap, and the wet hot nettles gave off a heady, blackcurrent scent. The cricketers were running out onto the pitch, anxious to get all the game they could into the last half hour.

It was the first time Tory had been taken by a man into a pub, in fact the first time a man had voluntarily asked her out at all. My first date, she thought excitedly. An old woman was buying Guinness and putting it in a black canvas bag. In the corner two men with sun-reddened faces, their wives wearing white orlon cardigans and lots of cheap jewelry, had decided to break their journey on the way back to London and were drinking Pimm's. What on earth was she going to drink? She hated beer, her mother said gin and orange was common and she knew Buck's Fizz involved champagne which was expensive. Her mind was a complete blank, She looked desperately around.

"I'd like a Pimm's," she said.

Jake sighed. He' d hoped she'd drink something cheap like beer, or better still orange juice. That meant he'd have to have beer instead of the double whisky he so badly needed.

The pub was cool and dark and restful inside; the side door had been fastened back, and outside was a little garden full of wallflowers and irises and pale pink clematis scrambling over some rustic poles.

At first the conversation was very stilted, but after a couple of Pimm's Tory's tongue was loosened and suddenly, like a washing machine that's been tugged open half-way through its cycle, everything came gushing out. What a disaster she was at dances, how she hated her finishing school, how ghastly Colonel Carter was and how she couldn't get on with her mother.

"Mummy likes Fen, because she's pretty and funny, and because she's so young, but I'm an embarrassment to her and living proof that she's over forty-five."

"She made you go to all these dances because she's looking for a husband," said Jake. "D'you think she's found one?"

"Oh, I hope not," said Tory. "He's so phoney. He was hanging a picture for Mummy the other day and hit his thumb with the hammer and," she went even redder, "he said booger instead of bugger."

Jake hadn't even brushed his hair before he came out, but it fell into place automatically, Tory ached to touch it. She felt as though someone had bewitched her, as though she was drowning and there was no coming up for the third time. In a panic, she noticed he'd finished his drink. She'd been reading about Women's Lib; it was all right for women to buy drinks these days. She got a fiver out of the bag and handed it to Jake.

"Go on," she said with a giggle, "we're all equal."

Jake shrugged and went to the bar. The cricketers had finished
their game and flocked into the pub, and the barmaid was serving
them with huge jugs of beer to pass round, so it was a few minutes
before Jake got served. Tory sat in a haze of happiness; the longer he
took, the longer they'd have. She looked at him slumped against the
bar. He was so thin beside the beefy cricketers; she wished she could
feed him; she was sure he wouldn't grumble about overdone beef and
soggy potatoes. On the door near the Ladies Room a group of men
were playing darts. Oh dear, Cupid had scored a double top, straight
into her heart.

Jake returned with the drinks and a bag of potato chips. "I don't
know why I've been telling you all these things," said Tory. "You're the
one who needs cheering up. But you're such good listener."

"I get plenty of practice. When you've got to take stupid women
on long rides you develop a listener's face. It doesn't necessarily mean
you're listening."

Tory's face fell. "I'm sorry," she said humbly, starting to eat the
potato chips. "I didn't mean to bore you."

"You haven't," he said irritably.

"Who taught you to ride?" she asked.

"My father. He put me on a pony almost before I could walk."

"How long ago did he die?" said Tory.

"I don't know that he's dead."

Tory looked startled.

"He was a gypsy. He met my mother when he was hop-picking
on part-time work. Her father was the keeper at the big house. He
tried to settle down with my mother and get a steady job, but it was
like caging a lark. One day, the wanderlust became too strong and he
walked out when I was about eight."

"You must have missed him."

"I did." The third pint of beer had loosened his tongue and the
world seemed a more hospitable place.

"So did my mother. She cried a lot behind locked doors, and my
grandfather went through all the photograph albums cutting my
father's picture out of the family groups."

"So you might suddenly bump into him one day?"

"I doubt it," said Jake, although he never passed a gypsy encampment or fairground without having a look.

"Was he very good looking?"

"My mother thought so. Two years after he left she waved me off
to school and said she'd be in to cook the school dinner later. Then she
put some cushions in front of the gas oven and that was that. All I
remember was that all the masters and boys were particularly put out
because we were supposed to be having treacle pudding that day."

He suddenly glared at Tory, whose eyes had filled with tears.

What the hell was he telling the soppy cow all this for? He hadn't talked about his mother in years.

Tory couldn't bear it. He'd lost his mother and his father and now he was going to lose Africa.

"Do you think Bobby Cotterel will really sell her?" she asked.

"Course he will; doesn't give a damn about her. He was grumbling the other day because Mrs. Wilton was threatening to raise the boarding fees."

"What will you do if Africa goes?"

"Get another job."

"Around here?"

"No, up north probably, I doubt Mrs. Wilton will give me a reference."

"Oh you mustn't," said Tory aghast, "I mean—it's so cold up north. I must go the john."

She had difficulty negotiating the way the Ladies Room, cannoning off tables and chairs like a baby elephant.

"Oh hell," thought Jake, as she narrowly missed a flying dart, "she's drunk."

Tory collapsed on to the toilet and realized with the shock from the slab under her bottom that the seat was still down. She lifted it up. "If I can manage to go on peeing for over twenty seconds, Jake will take me out again," she said to herself. By wriggling she made it last for twenty-two. When she found she had put her bag in the basin and washed her hands over it, she realized she was very tight. She couldn't bear Jake to go away. She pressed her hot forehead against the mirror. "Gypsy Jake," she murmured to herself.

Then it became plain that she must buy Africa. She had the money. Jake could pay her back, or she could be the owner and he the jockey. She had visions of herself in a big primrose yellow hat, leading Africa into the winner's enclosure with two mounted policemen on either side. She was a bit hazy about what went on in show jumping. She found a phone booth and looked in the telephone book, but there was no Bobby Cotterel. He must be unlisted, but the Mayhews had had the house before Bobby Cotterel. She spent ages finding the M's. Oh god, the page was missing. No, it ws the first number on the next page. Sir Edward Mayhew, Bandit's Court. Her hand was shaking so much she could hardly dial the number.

"Hullo," said a brusque voice.

She was so surprised she couldn't speak.

"If that's burglars, " said the voice, "I'm here plus fifteen guard dogs and you can fuck off."

Tory gasped. "No it isn't," she said, "Is that Mr. Cotterel?" She must speak very slowly and try and sound businesslike.

Jake finished his glass of beer and ordered a large whisky.

"Come here often?" said the barmaid, who worked in the pub on Sunday to boost her wages and in the hope of finding a new boyfriend.

"No," said Jake.

He glanced at his watch. Tory had been away for nearly a quarter of an hour now. He hoped the stupid cow hadn't passed out. He'd need a fork lift truck to carry her home. He went out to look for her. She was standing by the telephone with her shoes off.

"That's fine," she was saying in a careful voice.

If Bobby Cotterel had not come back a week early from the South of France because it was so expensive, and been promptly faced with a large income-tax bill, he might not have been in such a receptive mood. Africa troubled his conscience, like his daughter's guinea pig, whose cage, now she'd gone back to boarding school, needed cleaning out. He was not an unkind man. This girl was anxious to buy Africa for four times the price he'd paid for her and he wouldn't have to pay any commission to Mrs. Wilton.

"The board's paid up for another three weeks," he said.

"I'll take that over," said Tory. "Can we come round and give you the check now?"

"Of course. Come and have a drink, but for Christ's sake don't tell anyone I'm back."

Tory turned towards Jake with shining eyes.

If she lost twenty or thirty pounds, she'd be quite pretty, he thought sourly, What the hell had she got to look so cheerful about?

"You O.K.?"

"Wonderful. I've just bought Africa."

"Whatever for? You don't like horses."

"For you, of course. You can pay me back slowly, a pound a week, or we can go into partnership. I'll own her, you can jump her."

A dull red flush had spread across Jake's face.

"You're crazy. How much did you pay?"

"I offered eight hundred and he accepted. He's just had a bill for his income tax. I said we'd take the check round now, before Mrs. Wilton starts blabbing about Sir William and Malise Gordon."

"Have you got that amount in the bank?"

"Oh yes, I got £5000 on my birthday."

"Your mother'll bust a gut."

"Hooray," said Tory.

"She'll say I got you plastered."

"No, you did not, I did it all on my own."

She bumped into a hat stand as she went out of the door.

Jake was finding it impossible to clamber out of the pit of despair so quickly. He might at least say thank you, thought Tory.

They walked to Bobby Cotterel's house and handed over the check. Armed with a receipt, he walked her home, both of them fol-

lowing the white lines in the middle of the road. Half-shafts of moonlight found their way through the beech trees on either side of the
road, shimmering on their dark grey-green trunks, Fortunately the
house was still dark.

"Oh good," said Tory, "I can put back Mummy's coat before she
finds out it's missing. I'm going to London tomorrow. I've got two
awful parties, then a dance on Wednesday, but I'll be home on Thursday. Mummy and Colonel Carter are going out to dinner. I've got to
babysit. Perhaps you could come round, after they've gone out, and we
can decide what to do."

"I think it may be a bit more problematical than that," said Jake.

He took the key, opened the door for her and turned on the hall
light. Oh God, thought Tory miserably, there was Fen's whip lying on
the hall table. Jake turned to her, a slight smile touching his lips. Was
it contempt, or pity, or mockery?

"Thank you very much," he said and was gone.

Fighting back her disappointment that he hadn't attempted to
kiss her, Tory then reflected that she would probably have tasted of
onion-flavored potato chips.

*T*he parties on Monday and Tuesday were bad enough for Tory,
but the dance on Wednesday was a nightmare. At the dinner party
beforehand some sadist had put her next to Rupert Campbell-Black.
On his right was a ravishing girl called Melanie Potter, whom all the
girls were absolutely furious about. Melanie had upstaged everyone by
turning up several weeks after the season began with a gorgeous tan
acquired from a month in the Bahamas.

Rupert had arrived late, parking his filthy Rolls Royce with the
blacked-out windows across the pavement. He then demanded tomato
ketchup in the middle of dinner, and proceeded to drench his sea trout
with it, which everyone except his hostess and Tory thought wildly
funny. Naturally he'd ignored Tory all the way through dinner. but
there was something menacing about that broad black back and beautifully shaped blond head, a totally deceptive languor concealing the
rampant sexuality. She wondered what he would have done if she'd
tapped him on the shoulder and told him she was the owner of an £800
horse.

Then they went on to the dance and she somehow found herself
piled into Rupert's Rolls Royce, driving through the laburnum-and-
lilac-lined streets of Chelsea. She had to sit on some young boy's knee,

trying to put her feet on the ground and all her weight on them. But she still heard him complaining to Rupert afterwards that his legs were completely numb and about to drop off.

The hostess was kind, but too distraught about gate crashers to introduce Tory to more than two young men, who both, as usual, danced one dance, then led her back and propped her against a pillar like an old umbrella, pretending they were just off to get her a drink or had to dance with their hostess. Thinking about Jake non-stop didn't insulate her from the misery of it all. It made it almost worse. Obviously it was impossible that he should ever care for her. If no one else wanted her, why should he? Feeling about as desirable as a Christmas tree on Twelfth Night, she was sitting by herself at the edge of the ballroom when a handsome boy sauntered towards her. Reprieve at last.

"Excuse me," he said.

"Oh, yes please," said Tory.

"If no one's using this," he said, "could I possibly borrow it?" and, picking up the chair beside her, he carried it back across the room and sat down on the edge of the noisy yelling group around Rupert Campbell-Black. As soon as they got to the dance Rupert had abandoned his dinner group and, taking Melanie, had gone off to get drunk with his inseparable chum Billy Lloyd-Foxe, who was in another party. Now he was sitting, cigar drooping out of his handsome curling mouth, wearing Melanie's feather boa, while she sat on his knee, shrieking with laughter, with the pink carnation from his buttonhole behind her ear.

Later Billy Lloyd-Foxe passed Tory on the way to the bathroom and on the way back, struck by conscience, asked her to dance. She liked Billy; everyone did; she liked his turned-down eyes and his broken nose and his air of life being a little bit too much for him. But everything was ruined when Rupert and Melanie got on the floor, Rupert, his blue eyes glittering, swinging Melanie's boa round like the pantomime cat's tail, had danced around behind Tory's back, making faces and puffing out his cheeks to look fat like Tory and make Billy laugh.

Tory escaped to the bathroom, shaking. She found her dinner party hostess's daughter repairing her makeup and gossiping with a couple of friends over the effrontery of Melanie Potter.

"Her mother did it on purpose. What chance have any of us got against a tan like that? She turned up at the Pately's party wearing jeans. Lady Surrey was absolutely livid."

At that moment Melanie Potter walked in and went over to the mirror, examining a huge love bite on her shoulder and trying to cover it with powder.

"You haven't got anything stronger, have you?" she asked Tory.

Humbly Tory passed her stick of cover-up.

"Oh how marvellous, that's amazingly kind. You were on Rupert's other side at dinner weren't you?" she added, wincing as she blotted out the red oval of tooth marks. "Isn't he a sod? I've just emptied a bucket of ice over him for biting me."

She handed the makeup back to Tory and combed her platinum blond hair more seductively over one eye. "He and Billy are taking me to Tramps now; why don't you come too? David Bailey's going to be there. Rupe wants him to photograph me."

And when Tory refused, insisting she was going home now because she had a headache, she only just persuaded Melanie not to make Rupert give her a lift home.

Unfortunately Tory found a taxi all too easily. When she got back to the flat, which Molly Maxwell had borrowed from a friend for the summer, it was only 11:30. She found her mother and the Colonel on the sofa. The Colonel was wearing a lot more lipstick than her mother.

Tory went to her room and as quietly as possible cried herself to sleep. She woke as she had on the last four mornings with a terrible sense of unease—that her mother would find out about Africa.

She came home in the evening to babysit and went up to her room to change and have a bath. It was still ludicrously hot.

"Don't use all the water," called out her mother. Through the crack in the door Tory could see her lying on her peach chintz bedspread rigid under a face pack.

Tory was undressed down to her bra and pants, and hoping, since she'd hardly eaten since her evening with Jake, that she might have lost a bit of weight, when she heard the telephone ring and her mother answering it in a self-consciously seductive voice:

"Hello." Then, more matter of fact, "Oh hello, Mrs. Wilton, how are you?"

There was a long pause, then Molly said:

"No, it couldn't possibly be her. Tory's terrified of horses. Maxwell's quite a common name, you know. Well, just wait while I shut the door."

Tory felt as though icy water was being dripped slowly down her spine. She was tempted to climb out the window down the clematis; instead she got into bed, pulled the duvet over her head and started to shake.

Five minutes later her mother barged in, ripping the bedclothes off the bed. She was still wearing her face pack like some malignant mime of catastrophe. As first she was so angry she couldn't get the words out.

"Did you or did you not ring up Bobby Cotterel on Sunday and buy Africa?" she spluttered.

"I don't know what you mean," mumbled Tory.

"Don't lie to me; who put you up to it?"

"No one. It's my money, why shouldn't I buy a horse if I want to?"

"And I can't afford to buy little Fen a little pony." Molly spat out the littles. "Get up, you fat lump." She reached forward and tugged Tory to her feet by her hair.

"It was that little swine, Jake Lovell, wasn't it?"

"No it wasn't."

"Course it was." Molly Maxwell was shaking Tory by the shoulders until she thought her head would snap off. "He's obsessed with that horse, spends all his time on it. But he won't much longer," she added, her eyes suddenly lighting up with venom. "Mrs. Wilton's just given him the sack."

"Oh no," said Tory, aghast. "It was nothing to do with him. I rang Bobby Cotterel. I did everything myself."

"Why?" hissed Molly, powder from her drying, cracking facepack drifting down to the floor. "You've got a crush on that boy. I saw you mooning over him on Saturday at the show. That's why you've been such a colossal flop at all those dances, not trying with all those suitable young men, because you've got hot pants for some common stable boy. Well you won't get him by buying him expensive presents."

Tory couldn't bear to look at her mother any more. She gazed down at her mother's feet, noticing the newly painted scarlet nails, cotton wool keeping each toe apart.

"He's a friend," she sobbed. "Nothing more."

"Well he's not having Africa. He's going back."

"He's a she and she's not."

"Sir William and Colonel Gordon are both prepared to top your offer. I'm going round to see Bobby Cotterel to make him tear up that check."

Molly pictured herself, in a new dress, rather low cut, driving up to Bobby Cotterel's house, and pleading with him:

"My daughter's not responsible for her actions."

And Bobby Cotterel, who she suspected was between marriages, would pour her a stiff drink and comfortingly say, "Tell me all about it, preferably over dinner."

She was brought back from her reverie by Tory sobbing,

"It's my money and I can do what I like with it."

"And how are you going to look after a horse?" hissed Molly. "It can't live in the potting shed, and now Jake Lovell's lost his job he'll be moving on."

Tory was in such despair she hardly heard her mother's tirade about all the expense and trouble she'd gone to to give Tory a season until, catching sight of her face like a dried-up river bed in the mirror, Molly realized she had better get her pack off. Tugging open the door, she found Fen, who'd been listening avidly at the keyhole and nearly fell into the room on top of her. Fen gave a giggle and, waving in time with a half-eaten popsicle, started singing:

"My mother said that I never should play with the gypsies in the wood."

"Shut up," screeched Molly. "It's your fault too for always hanging round the stables. You're not going down there tonight. Go to your room, do your homework and don't talk to Tory. I must ring Bernard. I can't possibly go out and play bridge after all this."

"Want to bet?" said Fen, as her mother went into the bedroom, slamming the door behind her. Immediately they heard the ping of the telephone, followed at intervals by other pings.

Molly couldn't get through to Bobby Cotterel but, if she couldn't get him to tear up the check, there was always the possibility of reselling Africa to Sir William or Malise.

That had possibilities too, she reflected. She'd like to meet Sir William again and she still had the hankering of the summarily rejected for Malise Gordon. She saw herself with less make-up and a higher neckline than for Bobby Cotterel, and Malise's hawklike face softening, as he took her hand, saying:

"When I first met you at Bilborough, I thought you were just a lovely face."

After all, Colonel Carter hadn't popped the question; it would be good to make him jealous.

As Tory predicted, the Colonel talked her mother into going out for dinner.

"Bernard's friends have gone to a lot of trouble cooking and they'd be so disappointed if we begged off at the last moment," she told Tory coldly, as if she was making a supreme effort to go out. Not that she'd enjoy a second of it, with all this worry (as well as Bernard's friends' cooking) on her plate.

Tory was still sitting on her bed in her bra and pants as though turned to stone.

"Do you hear me, Tory? I'm putting you on your honor not to talk to Fen and not to telephone anyone or put a foot outside the house while I'm away."

She said it three times, but wasn't sure Tory had understood.

Jake sat in the tackroom chain-smoking and watching the nearly full moon peering in through the window. Round and pink, with turned down eyes in an anxious chubby face, it reminded him of Tory. Poor kid, he hoped that cow of a mother wasn't giving her too bad a time. He'd like to have got in touch with her to find out the score, but he didn't dare ring the house. Africa was much better; he'd turned her out for a few hours and just laid down thick clean straw in her stall next to the tack room. He was just going to get her when he heard a step outside, and Tory come timidly through the door. Christ, she looked all blotchy like a parship that's been beaten up by the frost. The next minute, she was sobbing in his arms.

"I'm so sorry to get you sacked."

"Doesn't matter, I was going to leave anyway. Plenty more fish-wives in the sea."

"But you haven't anywhere to go."

"Mrs. Wilton can't chuck me out till she's found someone else, so I've got a bit of time. Did your mother give you a hard time?"

Tory nodded. "She's determined to give Africa back or sell her."

She was shaking so violently, Jake sat her down on the rickety chair and made her a strong cup of coffee with four tablespoons of sugar. She didn't normally take sugar, but she found the sweetness comforting.

Jake lounged against the feed bin, watching her.

"Look," he said, dropping his half-smoked cigarette down the sink, "why did you buy me that horse."

Tory lowered her eyes, "Because I like you," she whispered.

Jake took her hands, which felt damp and chilled.

"How much?" he said gently.

Tory glanced up. He was so beautiful with his thin watchful face and his glinting earrings.

"Oh, so very much," she said.

And suddenly, like a horse that's been locked up in a stable for a long time and sees the door opening onto a huge field of clover, the idea that he'd been battling all week overwhelmed him. A rich wife, that's what he needed. Not very rich, but enough to buy him a few horses and give him a start, so he could get to the top and wipe that self-satisfied smile off Rupert Campbell-Black's face.

His arms were suddenly full of Tory. She was kissing him, suck-ing at him like a great vacuum cleaner—Christ she'd pull his teeth out soon and her arms had him in a vice and the huge friendly breasts were pressing against him.

"Oh Jake, oh Jake."

Without fumbling, he undid the buttons of her dress and switched off the light, and they were on the bed of deep clean straw, with the light of the moon now filtering in through the skylight. He unfastened her bra and the splendid breasts overflowed, soft and sweet-swelling, like a river bursting its ddam.

For a small, slight man, Jake was sexually well endowed, but he spent enough time fingering a spot which Tory afterwards discovered was her clitoris, and she was so slippery with longing that she hardly felt any pain after that first sharp thrust inside her. She'd always heard it was awful the first time, but despite the scratching of the straw on her bare back she felt only ecstasy.

"Any minute Africa'll wander in and say who's been sleeping in my bed," said Tory with a giggle.

"Not much sleeping," said Jake.

He rested his head on her breasts. Actually she was much less fat without her clothes on, rather marvellous in fact.

"I didn't hurt you too much?"

"No, no. It was lovely."

"And you do like me?" he said.

Tory nodded in the dark, then kissed him passionately, adoringly uncritical, like a dog greeting a returning master.

"Enough to marry me?"

Tory gasped, and stopped kissing him.

"I know I can make big money out of horses, once I get started," Jake said. "I just need a break."

"I'll help you," said Tory in excitement. "I've got £5,000 a year." Admittedly a lot of that had gone on Africa and been given to her mother for new clothes and the cocktail party. But if she married Jake, she wouldn't have to go to any more dances.

Five thousand a year, thought Jake. That must mean at least £100,000 in the bank. If only he could get his hands on that, they could buy a place and a dozen horses.

"We've got to find somewhere to live," he said. "There's no point in getting anywhere too small. We need stables and at least fourteen acres; the house needn't be big."

"I could paint it," said Tory.

"And I could build the jumps," said Jake.

She could feel him hot with excitement beside her.

"The only trouble is that I've only got about £1500 in the bank at the moment. That won't buy us a house, and everything else is tied up in trust till I'm twenty-one."

Back came the black gloom, the pit, the despair; the stable door was locked and bolted on him again. It wasn't going to be any good after all. Jake slumped back on the straw.

Then he realized that Tory was full of plans to break the trust.

"The capital's mine. After all Daddy left it to me. It's just sitting there, and there's a whole lot more to come when Granny dies."

It was as though she was talking about having a good crop of string beans in the garden and another crop coming up in a few months.

"I can't just take your money," he said.

"Of course you can," she said. "I'm only crying because I'm so happy. We'll go and talk to Granny Maxwell. She'll help us."

They tried to keep their visit to Granny Maxwell secret. Tory arranged to go and see her the following Saturday. Alison the stable girl would lend them her car to drive up to Warwickshire. Molly, however, distrusting Tory's almost too passive acquiescence, guessed something was up and intercepted a letter from Tory to Jake which fell out of Fen's pocket on the way to the stables.

The letter spoke of them marrying as well as the visit to Granny Maxwell, and the scenes that followed were terrible. Molly's hysteria knew no bounds. How could Tory be ungrateful and stupid enough to throw herself away on this penniless, illegitimate nobody? In fact, Molly suddenly realized that she would no longer have her daughter as an unpaid babysitter, cook, cleaner, shopper and errand runner. She would have no one on whom to vent her rage, to grumble to and about, no one so easy to cadge money off. She was in danger of losing her whipping boy and she didn't like it one bit.

She despatched a reluctant Colonel Carter to have a man-to-man talk with Jake, the meeting wasn't a success. "Dumb insolence," were the Colonel's words for it. "Fellow just gazed out of the window and read the paper upside down. Anyway how can you expect a chap who wears earrings and hair down over his collar to see reason?"

In the face of Tory's intransigence, Molly buried her pride and rang Granny Maxwell, her ex-mother-in-law, whom she'd always hated and suspected of plotting against her.

"Yes, I can see he doesn't sound very suitable," said Granny Maxwell, "but I prefer to judge for myself. Tory is bringing him down to meet me on Saturday."

Molly felt silenced and snubbed.

Fen, although horrified at dropping the letter, was thoroughly overexcited by the whole thing.

"I wish I was old enough to marry him. You are lucky, Tory. Have you mated with him yet? I can't think why Mummy minds so much about his being intermediate."

The heatwave continued, making the long drive up to Warwickshire sweaty and unpleasant. The sun blazed down on the top of the car, until Tory longed to escape down some woodland glade or picnic in a field by a winding river. The white chestnut candles lit up the valley, the bluebells made an exquisite contrast to the saffron of the young oaks, cow parsley rampaged along every verge, but Jake was not interested in scenery. He seemed to find Alison's car difficult to drive and kept grinding the gears and stopping in fits and starts. Probably hasn't had much practice, thought Tory, watching his bitten nailed hands clenching the wheel. He answered all her questions in monosyllables, so she fell silent. She was dreading the meeting with her grandmother, who could be very rude and difficult. She couldn't see Jake getting on with her if he was in this mood. And if she won't help us, thought Tory in panic, perhaps he won't marry me after all. Then again, what did she know about this strange taciturn young man with

whom she was hoping to spend the rest of her life? At least she'd shed
nine pounds since she met him, and now could get easily into a size 16
skirt.

Dozing, then waking up, she realized they'd just gone through
Cirencester. She looked at the map. "Aren't we a little off course?"

"No," said Jake curtly, putting his foot on the accelerator.

Climbing to the top of a very steep hill, he pulled into the side of
the road saying: "Get out for a minute."

They had a magical view across the valley to where a golden-grey
manor house lay dreaming against its pillow of beech woods. In front
was lush, stream-laced parkland dotted with big bell-shaped trees,
under which horses sought the shade swishing their tails against the
flies. To the left a good deal of building and excavations were going on.
But here one large flat field had been left unploughed; on it every kind
of colored jump was set up. Jake studied the place at length through
binoculars.

"Where are we?" asked Tory. The last signpost had been buried in
cow parsley.

"Penscombe." Jake suddenly looked drawn, a muscle was flickering in his cheek. "Rupert Campbell-Black's place."

Going back to the car, he scooped all the rubbish off the floor and
from the ashtrays, which brimmed with cigarette butts, and tipped it
over the wall into Rupert's land. One of the workmen, looking across,
shook his fist at their departing car. "Serve him right," said Tory with
a giggle. But when she looked at Jake she saw he was not smiling.

Tory's grandmother lived sixty-five miles further on in an equally
beautiful but more sheltered position. Gabled and russet, the house
peered out from its unkempt mane of Virginia creeper like a Yorkshire
terrier.

A troupe of pekes and pugs came yapping around the side to
welcome them. Despite the beauty of the day, they found Granny
Maxwell sitting in the drawing room, watching racing on the television. She was also trying to read _Horse and Hound_ and a gardening book
at the same time, with three pair of spectacles hanging around her
neck like trapezes. She had a strong face, broad-browed, hook-nosed,
the peaty-brown eyes glittering imperiously beneath their black brows,
the wrinkles deeply etched around the wide mouth. On her head she wore
a grey-green curly wig, slightly askew and held on with scotch tape.

"You're wearing your nightgown, child," she said looking at
Tory's floating white dress. "I like your blue pants."

Then she held out a wrinkled black-nailed hand to Jake.

"I assume this is Mr. Wrong," she added with a cackle of laughter.

"Granny," said Tory blushing.

Jake grinned.

"Sit down, sit down; no, not in that chair," she said, as Jake was almost bitten by an ancient rheumy-eyed Jack Russell already parked on it.

The pekes and pugs lay at her feet snuffling and panting. She wore an ancient cardigan, a lace shirt, obviously for the second or third day running, and a tweed skirt with a droopy descending hem.

She and Lady Dorothy must go to the same tailor, thought Jake. But aquamarines and diamonds flashed on the grimy hands as she talked, and the pearls round her neck were each as big as a mistletoe berry.

"I suppose you want a drink; young people drink at the most extraodinary hours these days. There are some tins of iced beer in the fridge, Mr. Lovell, unless you'd like something stronger? Then, go and get them, Tory."

The room had the glorious overcrowded look resulting from the exodus from a larger country house. Jake's hands rested on the rough carved mane of a lion. The carpet was the blurred pink and green of an impressionist painting.

As Tory went out, Granny Maxwell studied Jake, who was surreptitiously looking at the horses circling at the start. At least he didn't fidget.

"Epsom," she said handing him the paper, "I've had a bet in this race. Any tips for the 3:30?"

Jake glanced at the runners.

"I'd have a fiver on Malmaison."

"I'm surprised you haven't chosen Marriage of Convenience. Or how about Fortune Hunter?" she added maliciously. "He's 100-1."

Jake looked at her steadily.

"I'll stick to Malmaison," he said flatly. "And if I wanted to pick an outsider, I'd choose Whirlwind Courtship."

"No, you haven't known Tory long, have you?"

"Not very, but I like outsiders."

At least he's not frightened of me, thought Granny Maxwell; that in itself was a novelty. Old and bored and waiting for death, she was aware that her family only came to see her when they were in financial trouble. She sometimes felt she was only kept alive by feuds and tyranny.

Tory came back with the cans of beer and a glass, and was immediately sent up to talk to Mrs. Maggs who was sorting out the laundry.

"She's made you cake and gingerbread men for tea. She thinks you're still eight. You look very tired, child," she added in a gentler voice, "and you've lost a lot of weight."

She turned to Jake. "Bring your glass of beer and walk round the garden," she said, struggling to her feet. She walked very stiffly and had to be helped over the French windows. One hip was obviously very painful.

"Rheumatism," she explained. "It's difficult to be a very nice old woman when everything hurts."

Having picked several heads off a coral pink geranium, she set off along the herbaceous border. It was the most glorious overpacked garden; peonies jostled with huge oriental poppies, lupins and irises. Catmint, not yet out, stroked their legs as they passed.

The pack of dogs, some on three legs, panted after them grumbling and yapping.

"This is what I call a beautiful garden," said Jake.

"As opposed to what?"

"To Tory's mother's. All the flowers seem to stand in their own patch of earth there, in serried ranks. Thou shalt not touch."

"Like a park," said Granny Maxwell.

A bird flashed by, yellow as laburnum.

"Yellowhammer," said Granny Maxwell.

"Golden oriole, I think," said Jake. "Very rare for these parts; it must be the heat."

Suddenly a jaunty mongrel with a tight brindle coat came bounding across the lawn and was greeted by much yapping and every sign of delight by the pack, particularly a little blond peke, who wagged her tail and kissed him. Granny Maxwell turned to Jake.

"We used to call them 'butcher dogs' in my day, because they followed the butcher's van. Owners get very fussed when mongrels try to mate with their pedigree dogs. I imagine that's why my daughter-in-law is making such a fuss about you. I made a fuss when my son threw himself away on Molly. Her father was a hairdresser. Remember that if you ever think about her."

"I try not to," said Jake.

"She never got over being the toast of Hong Kong."

"Now she's the sliced bread of Bilborough."

Mrs. Maxwell gave a cackle of laughter.

"Tell me about yourself. You had polio as a child?"

He nodded: "When I was six I was in hospital for 18 months learning to walk again. It left me with a wasted leg."

"And a raging desire to prove yourself presumably," said Granny Maxwell dryly. "And your father was a gypsy?"

Jake nodded.

"My mother's family tried to re-settle him, but he missed the wandering life and the horses. He was a genius with horses. So he pushed off soon after I came out of the hospital.

"And your mother committed suicide. You blamed yourself for that, I suppose?"

"I think she was let down by some chap who she took up with after my father left, but I didn't know that at the time."

"What happened after she died?"

"The school where I went free as a day boy made me board. I hated it, so I ran away and joined a group of gypsies. They taught me all I know, to poach and to look after horses and train dogs. There was an old grandmother there; she taught me all the medicines she'd learnt from her great grandmother."

He took Granny Maxwell's arm and guided her down some stone steps to a pond filled with irises and marsh marigolds. She caught her breath at the pain.

"An infusion of the leaves of Traveller's Joy works wonders for rheumatism," he said. "I'll make you some up to try, or if you prefer it you can carry the skin of a dead frog against your skin."

Granny Maxwell watched the dogs lapping out of the pond. The mongrel got into the water, drinking, paddling and making a lot of splashing.

"I always feel very badly about the gypsies," she sighed. "It's one of the great unnecessary tragedies of progress. They should never have been forced into compounds to settle and sell scrap metal. Before the war they always used to park in our fields for the seasonal piece work. My father often kept them employed from March till Christmas.

"I miss the sight of their fires at twilight, with that marvellous smell of rabbit stew, and the gaudy washing on the line, and the shaggy horses and silent lean dogs. They knew a thing or two, those dogs."

Jake didn't say anything, but felt an emotion nearer love than he had ever felt for a human being.

"How long were you with the gypsies?"

"Three years. Then I was picked up by the police and put in an orphanage."

"Can't have been much fun."

"It was better than prep school. The kids were less vicious. They even accused me of having a posh accent."

They walked back across the burnt lawn.

"We need rain badly. And what about this horse Tory appears to have bought?"

When he spoke about Africa his face took on a tinge of color.

"She's just the best horse I've ever ridden; she's got so much potential and such a lovely nature."

"Are you sure you don't love her more than Tory?"

Jake thought for a minute, frowning then said:

"I'm not sure, but if I take care of Tory as well as I look after Africa she won't do too badly. Anyway she couldn't be worse off than she is at the moment with that bitch of a mother. She'll have a nervous breakdown if she has to go to many more of those smart parties. It's like putting a carthorse in a hack class, then beating it if it doesn't win."

"And I gather Molly has a new boyfriend, some Colonel?"

"He's a jerk; they don't want Tory."

"Why are they so reluctant to let her go, then?"

"Molly likes something to sharpen her claws on. Tory's her cat-scratching board."

She bent down to pull a bit of groundsel, then asked Jake to uproot a thread of bindweed that was toppling a lupin.

"It's hell getting old. I can only prune sitting down now. And what's in it for you?" she asked.

"I couldn't marry her if she weren't rich. I've got to get started somehow. And I think Tory and I could make each other happy. Neither of us has ever really had a home before."

That was the nearest he was going to get to placating her.

"Aren't you banking too much on that horse being a winner? she might break a leg tomorrow."

"I'll get more horses. This is only the beginning. To make it work as a show jumper you've got to have at least half a dozen top horses and novices coming on all the time. The gypsies taught me how to recognize a good horse, and I can ride them, and I've got patience."

"Let's go and watch the 3:30." said Granny Maxwell.

Malmaison was second, Whirlwind Courtship nowhere. That's torn it, thought Jake. At that moment Tory came in with a tray.

"Are you ready for tea yet Granny?"

"Put the tray down on this table in front of me, thank you, and sit down. I have something to say to you both."

For a minute she looked at them both with speculative eyes.

"I'm not going to give you any money. Young people should get along by themselves. Tory has a considerable income and you'll soon save enough to buy and sell a few horses."

Jake's face was expressionless. That was that. His hopes crashed.

"I've no intention of breaking the trust," Granny Maxwell went on, picking up the blond peke and rolling it onto its back, "until I see if you're capable of making Tory happy. In three years time she'll get the money anyway. However . . ."

Jake stiffened, fighting back hope, as with maddening deliberation Granny Maxwell poured tea into three cups, and went into a long would anyone like milk, sugar or lemon routine, and then handed out plates, and asked whether anyone would like a sandwich.

"However," she repeated, "Mr. Binlock is retiring to a cottage in the middle of June, which means the Mill House at Withrington—that's about twenty miles north of here—will be empty. You can have that."

Tory turned pale. "But Granny, it's got stables and fields," she stammered.

"Exactly, but it's tumbledown and very damp. I hope you haven't got a weak chest," she added to Jake, "but it's yours if you want it."

"Oh Granny darling," said Tory, crossing the room and flinging her arms around her grandmother.

"Don't smother me child, there's no need to cry. And as you don't appear to have any wheels, I'll buy you a decent horse van for a wedding present."

Jake shook his head. "I can't believe it," he said.

"There is one condition," Granny Maxwell went on with a cackle of laughter. "That the first time you appear at Wembley, you buy me a seat in the front row. I'm a bored old woman. In time, if you do well, I might buy a couple of horses and let you ride them for me."

"If you really are going to buy us a van," said Jake, "I'd better learn to drive properly and take a test."

*S*ix long months after she arrived in London Helen Macaulay met Rupert Campbell-Black. Born in Florida, the eldest daughter of a successful dentist, Helen was considered the brilliant child of the family. Her mother, a passionate Anglophile and the daughter of a Presbyterian minister, was constantly reminding people of her English ancestry. In fact, a distant connection had come over, if not on the Mayflower, perhaps by the next boat. Mrs. Macaulay glossed over this fact and from an early age encouraged the young Helen to read English novels and poetry and admire all things English. Helen majored in English Literature in college, where she was confidently expected to get a brilliant degree.

Deeply romantic on the one hand, Helen was also repressed by the rigid respectability of her family. The only proof that her parents had ever copulated at all were the four Macaulay daughters. Helen had never heard her mother and father argue, or seen either of them naked. Her mother, who always insisted on women doctors, never mentioned sex except to imply that it was degrading and wicked. Neither of her parents ever told her she was beautiful.

Until she was nineteen Helen never gave her parents a moment's trouble. She worked at school, helped her mother in the house, never had acne or gained weight, and never answered back. In college at the beginning of the seventies, however, she came under the influence of the women's movement—anathema to her mother who believed a woman's place was in the home. Her mother did, however, support the feminists' view that a woman should never allow herself to be treated as a sex object, nor admired for her body rather than her mind.

To her parents' horror Helen started getting caught up in student protest movements, demonstrating against the Vietnam war and joining marches. Even worse, she came home for vacation and said disparaging things about Richard Nixon. But far worse was to come. During her third year Helen flunked out with a nervous breakdown, pregnant by her English professor, Harold Mountjoy.

Heavily married, but accustomed to the easy conquest of female students, Harold Mountjoy was quite unprepared for the torrent of emotion he unleashed in Helen Macaulay. It was Jane Eyre and Mr. Rochester all over again, except that Helen was a beauty. On campus she was known as the fair Miss Frigidaire; Harold Mountjoy set about defrosting her. Seeing her huge hazel eyes fixed on him during lectures like amber traffic lights, he should have read caution. Instead, one day after class he kept her back to answer a complicated question on Browning's "Paracelsus."

Discussing ambition in life, Harold had lightly quoted: "I am he that aspired to *know,* and thou?" To which Helen had instantly almost despairingly, quoted back: "I would *love* infinitely, and be loved!"

Harold Mountjoy realized he was on to a good thing and asked her out for a drink. Secret meetings followed; self-conscious letters weighed down by literary allusions were exchanged, and finally Helen's virginity was lost in a motel twenty-five miles from the campus, followed by fearful guilt, followed by more motels and more guilt. Under Harold's radical guidance Helen embraced radical causes and shocked her parents even more.

Finally, towards the end of the spring term, Helen fainted in class. Her roommate, who had regularly been reading her diary, went to the dean. He, in turn, was highly delighted because for years he had been looking for an excuse to dump Harold Mountjoy, whom he regarded as not only immoral but, far worse, intellectually suspect. Helen's parents were summoned. Appalled, they removed her from college. Her father, being a dentist, had the medical contacts to organize a discreet abortion. Helen and Harold were forbidden to see one another again. Harold, clinging to his job, terrified his wife would find out, complied with the request. This was the last straw for Helen. Losing her virginity had meant total commitment. She had expected Harold to tell her to keep the baby and to divorce his wife.

Desperately worried about her, her parents, who were kindly if rigid people, packed her off to England in the hope that this other great imagined love of her life would distract her. She was to stay for at least a year. Helen rang Harold Mountjoy in despair. He urged her to go. They would both write. In time they would meet again. There was a possibility he'd get over to Europe in August. At last Helen agreed.

The dean wrote to his London publishers giving Helen an excellent reference and praising her diligence, and they agreed to give her a job, reading manuscripts, writing blurbs and copy editing. He also found her a room with a female author in Hampstead.

So Helen pieced her broken heart together and came to England in October, unable to suppress a feeling of excitement that she would soon be able to visit St. Paul's where John Donne had preached, and Wimpole Street where Robert Browning had courted Elizabeth Barrett. She might even get up to the Lakes to see Wordsworth's cottage, or Haworth, home of the Brontës.

Sadly, England proved a disappointment. Accustomed to year-round Florida sunshine, Helen arrived at the beginning of the worst winter for years. She couldn't believe the cold.

By day she froze in her publishing house, by night she froze in her room which was awful. The female author was an ancient lesbian who watched her every move. Upstairs was a lecherous boarder who made eyes at her at meal times and kept coming into her room on trumped-up excuses. The place was filthy and reeked of a tom cat which her landlady refused to castrate. The landlady also used the same dishcloth to wash up the cat's dish and the human's plates. The food was awful; they seemed to eat carbohydrates with carbohydrates in England. She found herself eating cookies and candy to keep out the cold, put on ten pounds and panicked.

On weekends she froze on sight-seeing tours, shivering at Stratford, at the Tower and on the train down to Hampton Court and in numerous art galleries.

The English men were a bitter disappointment too. None of them looked like Rochester, or Heathcliff, or Sebastian Flyte. None of them washed their hair enough. They also seemed de-sexed by the cold weather. Anyway, Helen was not the sort of girl who would have picked up men. As the days passed she grew more and more lonely.

Harold Mountjoy was another disappointment. After one letter: he didn't even write at Christmas or remember her birthday.

Finally, at the beginning of March, Helen decided she could bear her room no longer. On the same day that her landlady used a cat-food-encrusted spoon to stir the beef stew with, and the tom cat invaded her room for the hundredth time and sprayed on her typewriter cover, she moved into Regina House, an all-female hostel in Hammersmith exclusively catering to visiting academics, which was at least clean and warm.

Nor was her job in publishing very exciting. The initial bliss of being paid to read all day soon palled because of the almost universal awfulness of the manuscripts submitted. At first Helen wrote the authors polite letters of rejection, whereupon they all wrote back, sending her other unpublished works and pestering her to publish them; so finally she resorted, like everyone else, to rejection slips.

Her two bosses took very extended lunch hours and spent long weekends at their houses in the country. One of the director's sons, having ignored her in the office, asked her out to dinner one evening and lunged so ferociously in the car going home that Helen was forced to slap his face. From then on he went back to ignoring her.

The only other unmarried man in the office was a science graduate in his late twenties named Nigel, a vegetarian with brushed-forward fawn hair, a straggly beard, a thin neck like a goose and spectacles. They had long political arguments and grumbled about their capitalist bosses. Nigel introduced her to Orwell and bombarded her with leftist literature.

He was also heavily involved with the anti-fox hunting movement and seemed to spend his weekends rescuing foxes and hares from ravening packs of hounds, harassing hunt balls with tear gas and descending by helicopter into the middle of coursing meetings. Often he came in on Monday with a black eye or a bandaged wrist after scuffles with hunt supporters.

One Friday, towards the end of March, he asked Helen out to lunch. He was wearing a yellow corduroy coat, a black shirt, had clean hair and looked less unattractive than usual. Inevitably the conversation got around to blood sports.

"Why don't you come out with us tomorrow? We're driving down to Gloucestershire; It's the last meet of the season. We've got hold of a lot of firecrackers, it should be a good day."

Helen, unable to face another weekend on her own, wandering through galleries or visiting the house of some long-dead writer said she'd love to.

"And afterwards we might have dinner in Oxford," said Nigel. "They've opened a good vegetarian restaurant."

And now she was rattling down the M4 to Gloucestershire and wondering why the hell she'd agreed to come. The dilapidated car was driven by a bearded young zoology graduate named Paul, who had cotton wool in his ears and was already losing his hair. Beside him sat Nigel. Both men were wearing gumboots and khaki combat suits.

Even worse, she had to sit in the back with Paul's girlfriend, Maureen, who was large, and aggressively unglamorous. Between her heavy lace-up boots and the bottom of her khaki trousers were two inches of hairy unshaven leg.

Taking one look at Helen's rust corduroy trousers tucked into brown shiny boots, dark green cashmere turtleneck sweater and brown herringbone jacket, she said, "I don't expect you've ever demonstrated against anything in your life, Ellen."

Helen replied, somewhat frostily, that she'd been on several anti-Vietnam war marches, which launched Maureen, Nigel and Paul into an unprovoked attack on America and Nixon and Watergate, and how corrupt the Americans were, which irritated Helen to death.

They were off the highway now, driving past hedgerows starry with primroses. Buds were beginning to soften and blur the trees against a clear blue sky. Flocks of pigeons rose like smoke from the newly ploughed fields. Helen felt tears stinging her eyes.

"Spring returns, but not my friend," she murmured, thinking sadly of Harold Mountjoy.

Now Maureen, Paul and Nigel were bitching about someone they referred to as R.C.B.

"Who's R.C.B.?" asked Helen, and was told it was Rupert Campbell-Black, the one the saboteurs hated most.

"Male chauvinist pig of the worst kind," said Maureen

"Upper class shit," said Paul.

"Always rides his horse straight at us," said Nigel. "Broke Paul's wrist with his whip last autumn."

"What does he do?" asked Helen.

"Show jumps internationally," said Paul, "and allegedly beats up his horses. But he's so loaded he doesn't need to do anything very much."

Helen noticed the curling copies of the *New Statesman* and *Tribune* on the back seat and a tattered copy of Bertolt Brecht in the pocket of Maureen's coat. These are people who care about things, she reproved herself, I must try to like them better.

What do we do when we get there?" she asked.

"The basic idea, Ellen," said Maureen, "is to copy everything the huntsmen do. We bring our own horns—Paul here actually plays the horn in an orchestra—and use them to split the pack. We've perfected our view halloos, and we also spray the meet with a special mixture called Anti-mate which confuses the hounds."

Nigel looked at his watch, which he wore ten minutes fast on the inside of his wrist. "Nearly there," he said.

Helen got out her mirror, added some blusher to her pale, freckled cheeks, ran a comb through her gleaming dark red page-boy, and rearranged her tortoiseshell headband.

"You're not going to a party," reproved Maureen.

Defiantly, Helen sprayed on some scent.

They were beginning to overtake riders and horses going to the meet. A pretty blonde on an overexcited chestnut waved them past.

"You've no idea how we're going to cook your goose later, my beauty," Nigel gloated.

Soon the road was lined with vans and trailers, and Paul drove faster through the deep brown puddles in order to splash all those riders in clean white breeches standing on the grass verge. Now he was fuming at being stuck at 10 m.p.h. behind a huge horse box which kept crashing against the overhanging ash trees.

The meet was held in one of those sleepy Cotswold villages with a village green flanked by golden grey cottages, a lichened church knee-deep in daffodils, and a pub called the Goat in Boots. A large crowd had gathered to watch the riders in their black and scarlet coats saddling up, supervising the unloading of their horses and grumbling about their hangovers.

Paul parked his car on the edge of the green and, getting out, they surged forward to exchange firm handshakes and straight glances with other saboteurs. Both sexes were wearing khaki parkas or combat suits as camoflage, but with their grey faces and long straggly hair and beards, they couldn't have stood out more beside the fresh-faced, clean-cut locals.

"Here's your own supply of Anti-mate," said Nigel, dropping two aerosol cans into the pockets of Helen's coat, "Spray it on hounds or riders whenever you get the chance."

Helen thought irritably that the cans would spoil the fit of her coat.

Two sinister-looking men walked by with a quartet of small, brighteyed yapping dogs.

"Those are the terriers they use to dig out the fox," whispered Maureen.

Helen noticed several magenta-faced colonels and braying ladies on camp chairs giving her dirty looks. She was beginning to feel distinctly uneasy. She edged slightly away from the group of saboteurs, then said to herself firmly, "I am a writer. Here is a golden opportunity to study the British in one of their most primitive rituals."

Listening to the anxious whinnying from the trailers, she breathed in the heady smell of sweating horse, dung and damp earth. The landlord of the pub was dispensing free drinks on a silver tray. His wife followed with a tray of sandwiches and sausage rolls. Helen, who had had no breakfast, was dying to tuck in, but felt, being part of the enemy, that she shouldn't.

Nigel and Maureen had no such scruples.

"Good crowd," said Nigel, greedily helping himself to three sandwiches, "Oh dear, they're ham," he added disapprovingly, and removing the fillings, he dropped them disdainfully on the ground where they were devoured by a passing labrador.

Suddenly, as the gold hand of the church clock edged towards eleven o'clock, there was a murmur of excitement as a dark blue Porsche drew up.

"There he is," hissed Maureen as two men got out. Helen caught a glimpse of gleaming blond hair and haughty, suntanned features as

the taller of the two men vanished in a screaming tidal wave of teenagers brandishing autograph books. Others stood on the hoods of their
parents' cars, or clambered onto each others' shoulders trying to take
photographs or get a better look.

"Worse than that Dick Jagger," snorted an old lady, who'd been
nearly knocked off her camp chair by the rush.

A girl stumbled out of the melée, her face as bright pink as the
page of the autograph book she was kissing. Half a minute later she
was followed by her friend.

"He used this pen," she sighed ecstatically. "I'm never going to
use it again."

Gradually the crowd dispersed and through a gap Helen was able
to get a better look. The man had thick blond hair, brushed straight
back and in two wings above the ears, emphasizing the clear, smooth
forehead and the beautiful shape of the head. His face, with its Greek
nose, high cheekbones and long, denim-blue eyes was saved from
effeminacy by a square jaw and a very determined mouth.

Totally oblivious to the mayhem he had caused, he was lounging
against the Porsche, talking continuously but hardly moving his lips,
to a stocky young man with light brown curly hair, a broken nose,
sleepy eyes, and a noticeably green complexion. The blond man was
signing autograph books automatically and handing them on to his
companion.

"What a beautiful, beautiful guy," gasped Helen.

"Yes, and knows it," snapped Maureen, "That's R.C.B. and his
shadow, Billy Lloyd-Foxe."

The landlord pressed forward with the tray.

"Morning Rupe, morning Billy, want a hair of the dog?"

"Christ, yes." Reaching out, the stocky light-brown-haired boy
grabbed two glasses, one of which he handed to Rupert. Then, getting
out a tenner and two flasks from his pocket, he handed them to the
landlord adding:

"Could you bear to fill them up with brandy, Les? I'll never fight
my way through Rupe's admirers."

"Bit under the weather, are you, Billy?" said the landlord.

"Terrible. If I open my eyes, I'll bleed to death."

A groom was lowering the ramp of a nearby trailer and unloading
a magnificent mare, sweating in a dark blue rug edged with emerald
green with the initials R.C.B. in the corner, and looking back into the
box whinnying imperiously for her stable companions. Rupert turned
around.

"How is she, Frenchie?"

"Bit over the top, Sir," said the groom. "She could use the exercise."

He swept the rug off the sweating, shuddering mare and slapped on a saddle. Suddenly she started to hump her back with excitement, dancing on the spot as the hunt arrived in a flood of scarlet coats, burnished horses and jolly, grinning hounds, tail wagging frenziedly, circling merrily, looking curiously naked without any collars.

Helen felt her heart lift; how beautiful and glamorous they all looked.

"Little people get on big horses and think they're gods," said Nigel thickly in her ear. "Those hounds haven't been fed for three days."

But Helen was gazing at Rupert Campbell-Black who was taking off his navy blue sweater and shrugging himself into a red coat. Goodness, he was well built. Usually men with such long legs had short bodies, but Rupert, from the broad flat shoulders to the lean muscular hips and powerful thighs, seemed perfectly in proportion.

Just as he and Billy mounted their horses the local photographer arrived, pushing his way through the ring of admirers.

"Hello, Rupert, can I have a photograph of you and Billy?"

"O.K.," said Rupert, gazing unsmiling into the camera.

"I'm not looking my best," grumbled Billy. "I haven't washed my hair."

"Good chance for publicity," said Maureen sententiously, and barging her way through, she handed Rupert an anti-hunting leaflet.

"Thank you very much," he said politely. "Can I have one for Billy?"

Maureen turned round to face the camera between them.

"Can I borrow your lighter, Billy?" said Rupert. Next minute he had set fire to the two leaflets and dropped them flaming at Maureen's feet.

"You're not even man enough to read them," she said furiously.

Rupert looked her up and down. "It's rather hard to tell what sex you are," he drawled, "but you're certainly not good looking enough to hold such extreme views. Go away, you're frightening my horse."

The crowd screamed with laughter. Maureen flounced back to Helen.

"The bastard, did you hear what he said?"

Over Maureen's head for a second, Rupert's eyes met Helen's. Then he looked away without interest. They're right, he's poisonous, she thought.

The next moment the hunt clattered off. Helen was amazed to see Nigel suddenly leap out of a hawthorn bush and squirt the hounds with Anti-mate. Next minute a little girl had rushed up and kicked him so hard on the ankles that he dropped the aerosol can with a yell.

"Stop it you horrid man," she screamed.

Rupert Campbell-Black, who was passing, grinned down at her: "Well done, angel. I'll marry you when you grow up."

The saboteurs leapt into their cars.

"Keep your eyes peeled for foxes," hissed Paul. Nigel was still grumbling about his ankle.

The saboteurs moved off in search of fresh sport, but they got stuck in the mud. Two footfollowers, not realizing who they were, pushed them out.

The next two hours were like being at a race meeting permanently under starter's orders. Every time the hunt picked up a scent the saboteurs managed to foil them.

Later Maureen and Helen hung over a gate watching a sluggish stream choking its way through overhanging osiers and pussy willows. Fat celandines were pushing their way through the dead leaves. Helen gloried in the spring sunshine beating through her dark green sweater.

"Are the saboteurs anti-fishing as well?" she asked.

"Oh yes," said Maureen earnestly. "Our more extreme members feel it's cruel to the worm."

Helen's stomach gave an ominous rumble.

"I'm starving," said Maureen. "Thank God I had a cooked breakfast. We're all rendezvousing at the Spotted Cow at one o'clock."

Helen, who had had no breakfast and only scrambled eggs last night, had visions of gin and tonics and steak and kidney pie. But in the end they only stopped at the village shop to buy oranges and some Perrier.

"Can't squander the saboteurs' funds on food and drink," said Nigel, offering her his bottle of Perrier.

Helen suddenly thought how much she'd prefer to share a flask of brandy with Rupert Campbell-Black. If she'd been out with him, she figured, he'd have made sure she was properly fed.

The saboteurs were parked outside the Spotted Cow as the hunt came past.

"Pull the choke out," whispered Paul. "It'll muddle the hounds."

In the back Nigel was noisily sucking an orange. Getting out of the car, Helen caught her breath, for there, slowly riding up the hill, came Rupert Campbell-Black, his gleaming bay mare and his red coat the only splashes of color against the greens and browns. Gaining the top of the hill he paused, trying to work out which way the hounds might run. The sun, which had been hovering in the wings like an actor waiting to make an entrance, broke away from the clouds, warming the brown fields. Nigel got out of the car, wiping his hands on his trousers.

"I think they're going to draw this covert," he said, vanishing into the beech copse, followed by Paul.

A hound spoke. Then the triumphant chorus rang out and there was the wild cry of the true horn, Suddenly, with the master cheering them on the line, hounds streamed down the valley in a dappled cloud. Then came the field, galloping, jumping, barging through gates with a clash of stirrups. There was Rupert, looking in a completely different class from the others, riding easily and fluidly, almost nibbling his horse's ears as he seemed to lift her over a huge hedge.

"Wire on the other side," he yelled back to Billy, who gathered his black cob together and cleared it just as easily. There was a clattering of hooves as they jumped into the road and out again, and set off towards the beech wood which had been liberally sprayed with pepper and Anti-mate. Nigel and Paul stood on a nearby fence and started to blow a horn concerto, utterly muddling the hounds who, distracted by the pepper and the Anti-mate, charged around, frenziedly zigzagging back and forth, whimpering with frustration as they tried to pick up the scent.

Helen suddenly felt furious with Nigel and Paul. What right had they to spoil everyone's day? The next minute Rupert Campbell-Black galloped around the corner, riding straight at them, his eyes blazing.

"He won't touch the girls," screamed Nigel, promptly plunging his horn down Helen's new cashmere sweater and stretching the neckband, before disappearing over the hedge. "Chivalry will prevent him," he called over his shoulder.

Chivalry prevented Rupert doing no such thing. He rode straight up to Helen, reined in the plunging mare and, before Helen could stop him, leaned over, put a warm hand down the front of her sweater and retrieved the horn.

"A good-looking Anti," he said in mock-wonder. "I never expected to see one. What's a pretty girl like you getting mixed up with a desiccated creep like Nigel?"

"How dare you?" gasped Helen, hand to her breast as though she'd been violated.

"How dare *you*?" said Rupert. "This is private property. You're trespassing. I'd go back to London and not get involved with a lot of rent-a-crowd lefties."

"All right, Helen?" asked Nigel, emerging from the undergrowth.

"Not getting much help from you," said Rupert. "She's got a good body though."

Blushing crimson, hopelessly aware how unbecoming it was with her red hair, Helen gazed fixedly at Rupert's highly polished boot as he nodded in Maureen's direction. "What d'you use that one for, breaking down elevator doors?"

For a second he made the mare plunge towards Nigel, who retreated into the hedge, then, wheeling around, he was off.

Rupert was simply the most wrong but romantic thing Helen had ever seen. She was appalled how violently she felt attracted to him.

She could still feel the warmth of his leisurely hand and remember the way the brilliant blue eyes had moved over her, assessing, clocking up data like a computer.

"My only love sprung from my only hate," she whispered.

As Rupert cantered back to join the despondent remains of the hunt, he had a sudden yearning for the whippet-slim Anti, with hair the color of the bracken still strewing the rides.

"What a bloody useless day," he thought.

He was relieved to see Billy emerging from the wood, his head buried in his horse's neck to avoid the branches.

"I feel better, " said Billy. "I've been sick behind a holly bush. Have you got any brandy left, Rupe?"

"Not much," said Rupert, handing him the flask. "Better finish it."

It had started to spit with rain, Old ladies hurried home, putting on head scarves. Women rushed out into the cottage gardens, taking in washing.

Rupert and Billy trudged back to their van through the pouring rain, discussing which horses they should take to the Crittleden Easter Meeting which started on Friday. Billy, who'd put his collar up and turned his hat back to front to stop the rain running down his neck, was trying to light a cigarette.

"Did you see the girl with the Antis?" asked Rupert in that deceptively casual way that meant he was interested.

"Bit thin," said Billy.

"Marvellous face, though. Doesn't sound English. How the hell did Nigel get hold of her?"

"Perhaps she likes his mind."

"Hardly likely to like him for anything else."

Rounding the corner, fifty yards away, they saw Nigel busily letting the air out of the tires of Rupert's van. He hadn't heard them coming.

"Leave this to me," said Rupert softly.

Sliding off the mare, throwing the reins to Billy, he sprinted down the road and, taking a flying leap, landed on Nigel with a crash, knocking the breath out of his body. Next minute he had dragged him up to a grassy side lane and was systematically beating him to a pulp. It was Billy who dragged Rupert off.

"For God's sake, that's enough. You don't want to be done for murder."

At that moment Frenchie, the groom, woke up from sleeping off his lunch and appeared out of the front of the van, rubbing his eyes.

"Where the hell have you been?" snarled Rupert. "Getting drunk as usual, I suppose. Here take the horses and get me some rope."

Pulling off his stock he stuffed it into Nigel's mouth, then systematically stripped off Nigel's clothes, looking down with distaste at the white skinny body. As Rupert tied his hands and feet with spare halter ropes, Nigel gave a groan and started to wriggle.

"Think he'll be all right," said Billy.

"Sadly, yes, the little shit," said Rupert, giving him a kick in the ribs. "It'll take him half an hour to wriggle down the road. It'll still be light; someone'll pick him up. Pity it's such a warm night."

He picked up Nigel's combat jacket and removed his address book from the inside pocket. As he flipped through it they hitched a ride in the van back to the blue Porsche.

"How riveting," said Rupert, "he's got Fiona's telephone number and mine, the little bastard, and yours too. What did he call that girl? Helen, I think. Here's one. Helen Macaulay, Regina House, W. 14. Where the hell's that?"

"Shepherd's Bush or Hammersmith."

"Frightfully unsmart," said Rupert. "I wonder if that's her."

Helen got in around midnight. Nigel had never turned up and Pual had dropped her off at Regina House after dropping off Maureen at her apartment.

Now she sat in her room looking at Harold Mountjoy's photograph, which seemed to have lost all its appeal. She noticed the slightly weak expression, the hair carefully combed forward to cover the lined forehead and the crows' feet round the eyes.

"My only love sprung from my only hate," she whispered. She'd never see Rupert again. He obviously had millions of girls after him. She looked at the primroses she'd picked with their ochre centres and pastel petals. She'd have to put him in her novel, then she could dream about him. Slowly she undressed, gazing at her body in the mirror. She'd never really studied it before, and yet he'd said it was beautiful. She found she'd put her nightgown on inside out; that was supposed to be lucky. She could do with some luck. She jumped at a sudden pounding of the door. It was the Principal of the hostel in a camel hair dressing gown, hair in net.

"Telephone," she snapped. "Person says it's an emergency. Can't see how it can be."

Helen sighed; it must be Nigel. Perhaps he'd been arrested and needed bailing out, or was grumbling because Paul had driven off without him.

In the telephone booth someone had left a copy of Lorca. Helen picked up the receiver: "Hello."

"May I speak to Helen Macaulay," said a voice. She'd recognize that clipped, light drawl anywhere. Her palms went damp, her knees turned to jelly.

"This is she."

"Well this is the enemy speaking—Rupert Campbell-Black."

"How did you get my number?"

"It's a long story."

"Is Nigel all right?"

"As right as he ever could be. What are you doing tomorrow?"

"Going to church in the morning."

In the background she could hear the sounds of music and revelry.

"Shut up, you maniacs," yelled Rupert. "Look, I'll take you to church, and then I'll give you lunch. I'll pick you up at half past ten."

She liked the way he pronounced it: "H'pp'st'n".

*H*elen flew upstairs to her room and rushed to the mirror, just to reassure herself that she was still there and that such a thing could have happened.

"He called," she whispered, before collapsing onto the bed. "He really called."

She must pull herself together. Rupert was probably a womanizer who attracted far too effortlessly, no doubt leaving a trail of destruction in his wake, like Macheath. Perhaps she shouldn't go; her heart hadn't mended after Harold Mountjoy; a second break would be far more difficult to repair. But the thought of not seeing him made her faint with horror. She felt quite out of control, swept along like a branch chucked into a raging torrent.

Besides, there was no way she could get in touch with him to say she had changed her mind. And how would she ever be any good as a writer if she didn't experience life?

It had been a very long day. If she didn't want dark circles under her eyes the next morning she ought to get some sleep, but instead she sat down at her typewriter and covered six pages describing the day. These she slotted into a folder marked "England". Then she brushed her teeth for two minutes, using dental floss between each tooth, and sank to her knees to say her prayers.

She woke in wild excitement, but elation soon gave way to panic as clothes littered the normally tidy room; what should she wear?

On and off, on and off, went the grey angora dress that went best with her hair, but might be too hot if they went to a crowded restaurant. On and off went the yellow silk shirt which brought out the color of her eyes, but, worn with a grey suit, made her look too much like an efficient secretary. The rust suit was too autumnal, the steel blue wool dress was lovely, but she was perspiring so much with nerves she might have great embarrassing dark circles under the arms. Finally she settled for a kilt and matching beret and green velvet coat she had bought from the Scotch House, worn with a frilly white shirt.

Then, what about makeup? She knew you shouldn't wear much for church, but too much for God would be too little for Rupert. It was very hard dressing for both. Perfume was wrong for church, too Delilah-ish, so she settled for pouring half a bottle of cologne over herself instead. Much against her principles, she'd taken one of the tranquillizers she'd been given when she split up with Harold Mountjoy. It was having no effect at all.

She was ready by 10:15, waiting in the dark polished hall. Various dowdy lady academics were milling around, getting ready for outings to museums or galleries. If only one of them would tell her she looked nice; but lady academics don't notice such trivialities.

She took a surreptitious glance in the full-length mirror and suddenly decided that she looked ludicrous in the matching beret and kilt, just like an airline stewardess. Racing upstairs, she changed back into the grey angora dress. Oh God, there was lipstick on it. She covered the mark with a pearl brooch. Her newly-washed hair was all over the place from so much dressing and undressing. She rammed it down with a grey velvet hairband.

She couldn't stop shaking. It was now twenty-five to eleven. At first the minutes crawled by, and then they started to gallop. He couldn't be coming; it was 10:50. Perhaps she'd heard him wrong, but she was sure he'd said half past ten. She tried to read a long analysis of the Watergate crisis in the _Sunday Times_ but the words kept blurring, so she gave up and gazed at some horrible shocking pink hyacinths that were twitching outside in the cold wind.

Perhaps in her state of cardiac arrest she'd given him the wrong directions to Regina House, saying left when she meant right. It was two minutes to eleven; she mustn't cry, it would make her mascara run, but what did it matter when he obviously wasn't coming anyway? It was just some diabolical plot to raise her hopes and then dump her from a great height because she was part of the saboteurs.

In utter despair, fighting back the tears, Helen turned to stumble upstairs, but just as the hall grandfather clock struck eleven the front door pushed open and Rupert walked in, coming towards her with that lovely loping stride. Unlike most people, he didn't automatically lower his voice when he entered an institution:

"Darling, darling, I'm desperately sorry. I had to look at a horse in Newbury on the way up; the traffic was frightful," he lied. "Are you all right? Did you think I wasn't coming?"

He walked up to her and, taking her hand, kissed her on the cheek.

Helen gazed up at him, unable to get a word out. Overnight she'd turned him, in his red coat, into some kind of devil, and here he was looking like just the kind of preppy man of whom her parents would approve. The severity of the impeccably-cut dark suit, striped shirt and blue tie only served to set off his dazzling good looks. A shaft of pale sunlight coming through the window gilded the smooth blond hair. It was as though a light had been turned on in the dark hall.

"You want to go to church, don't you?"

Helen nodded, still speechless.

"Well, it's not too late. We'll probably miss the B film and the ads, but get in for the big picture," he said, putting his arm through hers.

"I've never been to Hammersmith before," he said opening the car door for her.

"It's a fascinating ethnic cross-section," said Helen earnestly.

In the back of the Porsche, sitting muddily on a huge pile of unopened letters, newspapers and old copies of *Horse and Hound*, sat a grinning black labrador.

"This is Badger," said Rupert. "He's the only being in the world who thinks I can do no wrong."

Badger thumped his thick black tail joyfully, scattering the letters, and, leaning forward, gave Helen a great slobbery kiss.

"Don't pre-empt me, Badger," said Rupert, driving off so fast that the dog nearly fell off the back seat.

"Badger insisted on coming today," Rupert went on, "to see if you were as pretty as I said you were."

Embarrassed, Helen said, "Don't you ever open your mail?"

"Not if I can help it. It's always people wanting my money or my life."

He drove her at great speed to the Guards' Chapel. As soon as they'd crept into a back pew Helen sank to her knees. Rupert, sitting sideways to accommodate his long legs, noticed she really prayed, eyes shut, lips moving. Confessing in advance the sins she's going to commit later this afternoon, he thought dryly. While she was kneeling he examined the freckled hands with their slender wrists and colourless nail polish, the small beaky nose, the very clean ears, the lipstick drawn not quite to the edges to disguise a large mouth, the frightful head band holding back the gorgeous dark red hair—it was the color of drenched fox rather than bracken. Wondering if she had a ginger bush, he felt the stirrings of lust. He'd tank her up at lunchtime and take her back to his mother's house. As she sat up he noticed the perfect ankles, slightly freckled beneath the pale pantyhose.

"Nice scent," he whispered.

For a second she looked at him, her huge, wide-apart yellow eyes, flecked like a Conference pear, then smiled shyly.

Christ, she's adorable, he said to himself.

He had deliberately not picked up a hymnbook on the way in so he could share hers. As their hands touched she jumped as though burned; then, realizing she was overreacting, tried to relax.

"Forty days and forty nights, tempted and yet undefiled," sang Rupert loudly and quite out of tune.

During the sermon Helen found her thoughts straying as she glanced at the crimson and gold banners topped with little gold lions with crowns on their heads, and breathed in the scent of a nearby arrangement of white lilac and narcissi. Among the congregation were several lean men in dark suits with strong carved features and very straight backs, accompanied by conservatively dressed women with good enough cheekbones to get away with turbans or hats with no hair showing. The altar was draped with purple for Lent. Helen was horrified to find herself wondering whether a dress in that color would suit her.

She must concentrate.

Rupert had no such intentions, after staring at the priest for a few minutes with half-closed eyes, he extracted a paint chart out of his pocket and studied the colors, finally marking a Prussian blue square with a cross. Then he produced yesterday's evening paper and, folding it up into a small square, started to read the racing results.

"Hooray," he whispered, "I've won £50—pay for a lunch."

Helen tried to ignore him and stared stonily in front of her. But as the sermon droned on a loud snore suddenly rent the air. Rupert had fallen asleep and the next moment his head had flopped on to her shoulder.

A woman in a red turban glanced around in disapproval. Helen nudged Rupert sharply in the ribs. He woke up with a start, glanced round in bewilderment and then grinned at her totally without contrition. The smile suddenly softening the arrogant dead-pan features and, creasing up the long blue eyes, reduced her to complete panic. Harold Mountjoy had never affected her like this.

She was relieved when the organ galloped through the last hymn and they surged out into the sunshine. Rupert nodded to several of the congregation but didn't stop to talk until one of the men called out to him.

Rupert stopped, said, "Hello, Tommy," and introduced Helen.

After the inevitable swapping of mutual acquaintances, Tommy said, "You've been doing very well; meant to come and buy you a drink at Olympia. Look," he added, lowering his voice, "there's a horse that might interest you at the barracks. Bought him in Ireland just before Christmas—make a top-class Puissance horse."

"Can I come and look at him after lunch?"

"About four."

Helen wondered if she were included in the invitation and was shocked by her relief when Rupert said, "We'll be there."

Before lunch he insisted on taking Badger for a walk in the park. It was a perfect spring day. Thickening crimson buds fretted a love-in-the-mist blue sky. The banks were draped with crocuses of the same lenten purple as the altar cloth. A host of golden daffodils, retarded by the bitter winter, had just reached their prime and nodded their pale heads in approval. Helen longed to dawdle, but there was no chance of wandering lonely as a cloud. Rupert, with his brisk military walk, set off at a rapid pace. Helen, her high heels sinking into the soft grass, was soon panting to keep up.

"I'm starving," he finally said. "Let's go and have some lunch."

"Will it be very smart?" asked Helen.

"Not until we get there," said Rupert.

The restaurant, despite being sandbagged up to the gutters against IRA bomb attacks, was extremely smart inside with cane chairs and tables, a black and white checked floor and a forest of glossy tropical plants, emphasizing the jungle atmosphere. From the kitchen came a heady waft of garlic and herbs.

The head waiter rushed forward:

"Meester Campbell-Black," he said reproachfully, "You deedn't reserve."

"I never reserve," said Rupert.

"But I 'ave no tables."

"I'm sure you can find us one, nice and private. We don't want people bothering us."

"And you cannot bring dogs in 'ere. The health inspectors, they will shoot me."

"Badger's different," said Rupert, "He's a guide dog for the blind drunk. Now buck up, Luigi, don't keep us waiting."

Sure enough within half a minute, Luigi beckoned. It was quite an experience walking through a restaurant with Rupert and Badger. Every head turned, necks craned, nudges were exchanged as people looked first at him, then at Helen, trying to work out who she was, if anyone. The restaurant seemed to be packed with beautiful people, the girls all wearing fashionable flared trousers down to the ground with never a boot showing, their red nails tapping on their slim thighs, smoothing back their streaked hair and calling "Hi Rupe" as he passed.

Luigi installed them at a table divided from the rest of the restaurant by a dark green wall of tropical plants. Immediately Helen fled to the Ladies Room. She felt so drab in her grey dress with her pale church face gazing back from the mirror. Savagely, she ringed her eyes with pencil, added a coral dot of blusher to each cheekbone, painted her mouth to match and emptied so much Miss Dior over herself that it made her sneeze.

Back at the table, Rupert had ordered a bottle of Dom Perignon and removed his tie. Badger, lying at his feet, thumped his tail. Breathing in the newly applied Miss Dior, Rupert noticed the additional make-up. All good signs.

"I haven't been in London on a Sunday for ages," he said, "It's nice, and it's the first time I've had a chance to look at you properly—that's even nicer. You'r really an astonishingly beautiful girl. What the hell were you doing with Nige?"

"We work together."

"In publishing?"

"I read manuscripts and write blurbs. Actually," she blushed, "I'm also working on a novel."

"Can I read it?"

"It's only a first draft."

"Well, you must put me in it then. I'll be Prince Charming. Nigel can be the toad. You're not his girlfriend?"

"No, I am not," said Helen with some asperity. "He just asked me out with the Antis yesterday. How did you get my phone number?"

"Well, Billy and I found Nigel letting down the tires of our van, so I shook him till his lentils rattled, then left him trussed up like a Christmas turkey and appropriated his address book. What did you think of your day out?"

"Very cruel. All those people tearing after a poor defenseless fox, ripping it apart for fun. Why d'you do it?" asked Helen primly.

"Because I enjoy it. I enjoy riding hell for leather across country. It's one of the best ways of teaching young horses to jump anything, or keeping an older horse from getting stale. Horses love it, so do hounds, so do the people doing it. You just don't like to see people enjoying themselves."

Luigi arrived with the menu. Helen noticed there were no prices.

"What are you going to eat? Why not be really decadent and have a large rare steak?" asked Rupert.

Luigi particularly recommended the scampi made with a cream pernod sauce or the filets of wild duck with juniper berry sauce.

"No, I don't want any of your mucked about rubbish, Luigi. My guest would like. . . ." Rupert turned to Helen.

"Oh, paté, and a small steak and a green salad."

"And I'll have smoked salmon, and grilled lamb chops, very rare, with some fried potatoes, and can you bring an extra steak for Badger? He likes it well done, and we'll have a bottle of No. 6, and another bottle of this while we're waiting."

While he was ordering, she admired the beautifully lean curve of his jaw. Unlike most Englishmen, and particularly one who spent so much time out of doors, there was no red tinge to his complexion which, even without the tan, would have been pale olive. Glancing around, he caught her gazing at him. "Well," he said.

"You're very tanned."

"Skiing last month,"

"I hear you're an expert rider."

Rupert grinned. "You could call it that. The show jumping season's about to start in earnest. It's Crittleden next weekend. Why don't you come down on Saturday?"

He was touched to see how thrilled she was.

"I'd just love to. I'd love to see you ride."

"With any luck you might be seeing me ride before that," he said, smiling at her with those wicked, dangerously direct eyes. Helen chose to ignore the innuendo. Was it Badger or Rupert under the table, pressing against her leg?

Under the influence of drink Helen found herself more and more at ease. As their first course arrived she found herself telling him about her first room and the unfixed tom and the lecherous lodger.

"I gained ten pounds."

"Well it seems to have gone on in the right places," said Rupert, gazing at her breasts. He ate very fast, finishing his smoked salmon before she was a quarter way through her paté.

"This is excellent paté," She pronounced it 'part-*ay,*'. He wondered idly if her accent would get on his nerves. "I'm afraid I can't finish it, I'm awfully sorry."

Off her feed, thought Rupert, another good sign.

"Now is the time for all good dogs to come to the aid of the part-*ay*," he said, spearing it with his knife and handing it under the table to Badger, who gobbled it up with more thumping.

As their second course arrived she tried to steer the conversation on to safer topics. Did he enjoy reading?

"Not a lot. The best book I've read in years is *The Moon's a Balloon.*"

"Do you go to the theater a lot?"

"Well, I went once," said Rupert.

He was picking his chop bones now, tearing the meat off with very strong white teeth.

"Have you any brothers and sisters?" she asked.

"Only one. A brother, Adrian. Very bright. My mother's favorite. He runs an art gallery."

"Oh, which one?" asked Helen eagerly.

"The Bellingham, specializes in modern stuff."

Helen said she'd been there often.

"Awful tripe, don't you think?" said Rupert. "Adrian gets frightfully miffed when I tell him Badger could do better with his tail dipped in a paint pot."

All these remarks were drawled out with a completely deadpan face.

She couldn't tell if he was putting her on.

"At least you must go to the movies."

"No," said Rupert. "Quite honestly, if you've got nearly thirty horses, as Billy and I have, many of them novices that need bringing on or top-class horses that need keeping up to the mark, you don't get much time for anything else. We've got a man and three girl grooms, but we still get up at 6:30 and seldom leave the barn before nine or ten at night. Horses still need looking after on weekends. And you've got to keep looking at other horses all the time in case you miss something. Nearly all the year round we're traveling non-stop from show to show all over the world. You don't get to the top by going to French films or hanging around art galleries."

"I'm sorry," said Helen, feeling corrected. "Do you do the same sort of thing as Mark Phillips?"

"He events, I show jump. Ours is the serious stuff; eventing's for gifted amateurs."

"D'you know Mark Phillips?" Helen felt ashamed for asking.

"Yes, he's a very nice bloke."

"Will he marry Princess Anne?"

"So he tells me," said Rupert, filling up her glass. Helen tried not to betray how impressed she felt.

She couldn't eat any more of her second course than her first. Rupert gave her steak to Badger.

"It's so expensive it's awful," said Helen in distress.

"It isn't offal, it's steak," said Rupert, again imitating her accent.

Luigi brought brandy for Rupert and coffee and chocolate peppermint creams for Helen.

"No thank you," she said. "I've given up candy for Lent."

"I've given up women," said Rupert, taking her hand, "except you."

Almost on cue an exquisitely beautiful girl with long blue black hair barged into their jungle glade.

"Rupert Bear," she screamed, "what are you doing skulking away like a babe in the wood? Aren't you frightened of all the wild animals?" she added to Helen.

But before Helen could answer the girl had rattled on.

"Nicky Cripps is absolutely livid with you, Rupe. He booked this table weeks ago and you just pinch it from under his nose. Aren't you going to offer me a drink, Rupert Bear, just for old times' sake?"

"Beat it," said Rupert icily.

"Oh well, I'll have to help myself," and, picking up Rupert's glass of brandy with a shaking hand, she drained it. Suddenly there was a tremendous thumping from under the table and Badger emerged grinning, pressing his black face into the girl's crotch.

"Hullo Badger," she said in a choked voice. "You've always been keener on me than Rupert Bear."

Glancing at Rupert's face, Helen tried to lighten the atmosphere. "Why do you call him Rupert Bear?" she asked.

The girl looked at her pityingly, "Don't you know? Rupert B-A-R-E, because he spends so much time with his clothes off." Reaching over, she picked up the cross that hung round Helen's neck. "And don't think that'll keep you safe. You won't be able to ward him off anymore than anyone else. Afterwards he'll just spit you out like a grape pip."

Rupert got to his feet. "Get out," he said in a voice that made Helen shiver. "You're drunk and you're boring us."

The girl fled. Helen escaped to the bathroom. She felt quite sick. Her face was flushed, her eyes inflamed.

As she slapped on some makeup, two girls came in, shouting to each other over the partition,

"Bianca's just had a showdown with Rupert Bear," said the first.

"And all in front of his new girlfriend."

"She won't be new by next week," said the second, "She'll be an ex like the rest of us."

As Helen emerged from the john, Rupert, having paid the bill, was waiting for her.

"What's the matter? You're shaking."

"I want to go home."

"Don't.be silly." Taking her hand, he led her back to the car. "Now, what happened?"

"Two girls were talking in the john."

"What did they say?"

Helen told him.

Rupert grabbed her hands again, holding them tightly.

"Look, I'm sure it upset you, and what Bianca said too. But if you and I are going to have anything going together, and I feel we can, you must shut your eyes and ears to gossip. If you're any kind of celebrity, which I suppose Billy and I are, people will always bitch about you. If they don't know you, they make it up; if they catch you snapping at a parking meter attendant they'll assume you're always bloody-minded. I had a brief fling with Bianca. I broke it off. I've even had girls accusing Billy and me of being queer because I haven't made a pass at them. You listen to me, not anyone else. Is that clear?"

Helen nodded, speechless.

"You're terribly sweet." Leaning forward, he kissed her very gently.

At first she resisted, then, as her lips parted, he drew away.

"Come on, we've got to see that horse."

"Jesus, Tommy," he said a quarter of an hour later, as a huge black horse with a white face clattered out of the stable, tugging a helpless, terrified trooper on the end of a rope, "are you trying to sell me an elephant?"

"He's a good horse," said Tommy. "Jump the Harrods building with all four feet tied together."

Rupert approached the plunging animal, ignoring its rolling eyes and snapping teeth, and caught the other side of the halter.

Together he and the trooper managed to steady him.

"Come and have a look," he said.

From a safe distance, Helen watched Rupert's practiced hands moving over the horse, running down a leg here, picking up a hoof there, examining his teeth, looking at him from front and back.

"Lovely courageous head," said Tommy, dodging hastily sideways to avoid a diving nip.

"What's his background?"

"Dam was an Irish draught mare, father was clean bred, won a few races in Ireland. We got him from Jock O'Hara."

"Doesn't usually miss a good horse," said Rupert, walking round him again.

"His wife was having a baby at the time. He was a bit more abstracted than usual."

"And he's being discharged? What's wrong with him?"

"Well, quite honestly, he's a bit of a problem; run away with nearly every trooper in the regiment, fidgets on parade, breaks ranks, naps on duty and won't obey orders."

Rupert laughed. "And you're suggesting I buy him?"

"You could always sort out difficult horses and I promise you he can jump. He dumped a trooper in the King's Road last week. A milk truck was crossing the road; old Satan stood back on his hocks and cleared it by inches. Several witnesses saw him. That has to be some horse."

"O.K.," said Rupert, taking off his coat, "tack him up."

A trooper stood nervously in the center of the indoor ring, wait-

ing for Rupert's orders. Tommy and Helen, to her relief, watched from
the gallery. At first Satan walked round as though butter wouldn't
melt in his mouth; only his eyes rolled and his tail twitched. His white
face and the one white sock that came above knee and hock gave him a
comic appearance. Rupert pushed him into a canter; with his huge
stride he circled the ring in seconds. Then, suddenly, the horse seemed
to gather itself together and, as they rounded the corner, he humped
his back in a series of devastating bucks that would have unseated a
rodeo rider.

Helen gave a gasp, putting her hands over her eyes.

"It's all right," said Tommy, "He's still there."

"O.K.," said Rupert to the trooper. "put all the fences up to four
foot, six."

Tommy got out a silver cigarette case and handed it to Helen,
who shook her head. "Watch this," he said.

As Satan bucked toward the upright, Rupert put him at exactly
the right spot and cleared it by a foot. It was the same with the parallels.

"Put them up to five foot, six," said Rupert.

"Known Rupert long?"

"No," said Helen, "and it won't be much longer at this rate," she
added nervously as Satan thundered toward the upright, then put in a
terrific stop. The next moment Rupert was beating the hell out of the
horse.

"Poor Satan," murmured Helen.

Rupert turned him again. Satan cleared the upright, then, careless, stargazing at some pigeons in the roof, he rapped the parallel so
hard that only Rupert's immaculate riding held him together and
saved them both from crashing to the ground.

"Put it up to six feet," said Rupert to the white-faced trooper.

"He's mad," moaned Helen.

"Crazy," agreed Tommy, "but he always liked riding something
over the top."

This time Rupert cantered down quietly and Satan cleared the
upright with several inches to spare. Rupert pulled him up. Coming
out of the ring the horse appeared positively docile. Sliding off, Rupert
reached for his coat which was hanging on the door and, taking a
packet of Polos from the pocket, gave a couple to Satan who looked at
him suspiciously, then ate them curling his upper lip in the air.

"I think we'll get along," he said, "I'll buy him, Tommy. You'll
discharge him as uncontrollable, will you? And I'll have a word with
Colonel Cory up at Melton Mowbray."

Helen was astonished at how much the sight of Rupert mastering
that huge, half-wild horse had excited her. He might not have heard of
Francois Truffaut or Kandinsky, but when it came to horses he was

obviously a genius. Suddenly, she felt a spark of pure envy; however much she slaved at her novel, she could never display such joyful, spontaneous talent as Rupert.

The sun was going down now, firing the barracks windows. Dog walkers were hurrying home from the park. As Rupert sorted out the details of the sale with Tommy, Helen did her face yet again. She turned on the radio and found the middle movement of Schumann's Piano Concerto. Listening to the rippling romantic music she looked uneasily at the pile of mail on the back seat. Many of the envelopes were mauve, or peppermint green, or shocking pink. Someone had addressed a letter:

"To Rupert Campbell-Black, the handsomest man in England."

And so he was, thought Helen, as he walked back to the car, Badger at his heels. He looked very happy.

"That is one hell of a good horse. I reckon I could take him to the Olympics if he doesn't kill me first. Let's go and have a drink at my mother's house."

"That'd be nice," said Helen. Privately, she didn't feel quite up to meeting Rupert's mother.

Rupert listened to the Piano Concerto for a minute. "I suppose this is the sort of music you like?"

"Yes," said Helen. "Are your parents happily married?"

"Yes," said Rupert.

"How lovely," said Helen.

"But not to each other. My mother's on her third marriage. My father on his fourth."

"Were you very traumatized when your parents split up?" she asked.

Rupert looked surprised: "Not at all. I stayed with Mummy and Nanny."

"But you must have had endless step-parents?"

"Oh, legions."

"Weren't they sort of awful?"

"I was very unkind to them. I was a little sod when I was young. They got their own back by never visiting me at school. Nanny came down by train occasionally and brought me fruit cakes. I spent most of the holidays with Billy's family."

"What about Adrian?"

"Oh, he was my mother's darling—far too delicate and sensitive to go away to school."

Rupert spoke without bitterness or self-pity. He was not given to introspection and never considered that anything his parents had done could have affected his behavior.

Helen, who'd studied psychology, felt differently. Still hazy and emotional from an excess of champagne, she was flooded with compassion for poor Rupert. Parents who'd never loved him, step-parents who neglected him, a mother who preferred his younger brother. No wonder he felt the need to beat other riders all the time and to seduce women to bolster his self-confidence. I could change him, she thought expansively, I could arrest the rake's progress and show him what real love is like.

Rupert's mother lived in one of those large white Georgian houses looking over an emerald green fenced-in square. The garden was filled with grape hyacinths, scillas and white daffodils. An almond tree was already scattering pink petals on the sleekly shaven lawn. Every window was barred. Rupert opened the door with several keys and sprinted in to switch off the alarm.

"Well, your mother certainly won't get robbed," said Helen.

"No, but you're just about to, my treasure," said Rupert under his breath.

They went into the drawing room. As Rupert switched on the lights, Helen gave a cry of pleasure.

"What a gorgeous room."

There were pale primrose walls and carpets, old gold watered silk curtains, and sofas and armchairs covered in faded pale blue and rose chintzes. Two tables with long pale rose tablecloths were covered in snuff boxes. The walls held portraits of handsome arrogant men and beautiful women, their faces lit up by fat strings of pearls. Orchids in pots added to the exotic atmosphere. On the grand piano were photographs—one of Rupert's mother as a deb and several men in uniform who were presumably step-fathers. There was also a picture of Rupert on a horse being handed a cup by Princess Margaret. What caught the eye was a photograph of an extraordinarily beautiful youth, very like Rupert, but more fragile of feature.

"That's my kid brother," said Rupert. "What d'you want to drink?"

Helen shook her head. As Rupert poured himself a large glass of brandy, Helen caught sight of a study next door, the walls lined with books, all behind grilles.

"May I look?"

"Of course. Most of the ones on the left are first editions."

Helen gave a cry of excitement: "Why, here's John Keats' *Endymion,* and Shelley's *Prometheus Unbound,* and *Mansfield Park*. Your mother must be a very cultured woman."

This seemed to amuse Rupert. "She's never read any of them."

On the study desk was a huge pile of letters.

"Doesn't your mother open her mail either?"

"It's a family failing."

"Will she be home soon?"

"She's not here," said Rupert, draining his glass of brandy. "She's in the Bahamas escaping from the taxman."

Helen looked at him appalled.

"I must go. If I'd known she wasn't going to be here, I'd never have come."

"You haven't come yet, sweetheart," said Rupert softly, taking her in his arms, "but you soon will, I promise."

She was almost overwhelmed by the warmth and sheer power of him, so different from Harold Mountjoy, who'd been a bit of a wimp.

"No," she yelped.

"Yes," said Rupert into her hair. "You need some material for your 'narvel'."

"You shouldn't have pretended your mother was here." She struggled to get away from him.

"I didn't. Anyway, all's fair in love and war and I don't imagine it's going to be war between us," and he bent his head and kissed her. For a few seconds she kept her lips rigid, then, powerless, she found herself kissing him back, her hands moving up to the sleek, surprisingly silky hair.

Rupert pulled her down on the faded rose pink sofa.

"I haven't stopped thinking about you for a moment since I first saw you," he said. He was running his hands over her back now, assessing the amount of underwear, planning where the next assault should come from. There was no zipper on the grey dress; it would have to come off over her head, which might frighten her if removed too soon. Over her shoulder he met the jovial eyes of one of his forebears. "Atta boy," he seemed to say.

"No," said Helen, trying to pry off his hand which was barnacled over her left breast.

"You're repeating yourself, angel. You must realize I'm unfixed like your landlady's cat."

Through her dress he expertly undid her bra with his left hand. The thumb of his right hand began to strafe her nipple.

"No, I'm not like that."

"Like what?" whispered Rupert. "D'you want to spend the rest of your life unopened, like those first editions?"

Helen burst into tears. At first Rupert couldn't understand what she was saying. Then the first storm of weeping gave way to shuddering sobs and gradually the whole story came pouring out. How respectable her family was, what a terrible shock it had been when she got pregnant by a married man and flunked her exams. How her parents had sent her to Europe to get over it all.

"This afternoon you appeared to be getting over it very well," said Rupert. "Perhaps I should send your father a bill. What did you say this married man was called?"

"Harold Mountjoy."

"Should have been called MountHelen."

"I loved him," said Helen. "I thought he loved me. But he only wrote once. He forgot Christmas, my birthday, Valentine's Day."

"Mother's Day?" asked Rupert grinning.

"The pregnancy was terminated," said Helen with dignity.

"I promise I won't let you get pregnant," said Rupert gravely.

He got out a blue silk handkerchief and wiped away the mascara that was running down her cheeks. He had enough experience of women to realize that if you backed off and were kind and considerate on a first occasion, they dropped into the palm of your hand on the next.

More important, he suddenly felt terribly tired. Phenomenally strong, he could go for long periods without sleep, but he realized that he hadn't been to bed for three days. He had to drive home to Gloucestershire tonight, a dealer was coming to see him first thing in the morning and he wanted to buy Satan quickly before the Army started producing all kinds of red tape. He also had a string of novices to take to an indoor show tomorrow evening.

"All right," he said getting to his feet, "go home to your narvel. Let me put on a sweater and I'll drive you back to your coven."

Helen felt absolutely miserable, convinced that she'd lost him. The sun had set and the trees and the houses, losing their distinctive features, were darkening against a glowing turquoise sky. Rupert didn't speak on the way to Regina House, nor did he say anything about taking her to Crittleden. Let her work up a good lather of anxiety, he thought. Helen felt worse and worse.

All the lights were on in Regina House as they drew up. A blackbird was singing in a nearby plane tree. Helen sat for a second, overwhelmed with tiredness and despair, tears about to spill over again.

"I'm sorry," she said in a choked voice, "I didn't mean to give you a hard time."

Rupert yawned.

"On the contrary, sweetheart, it was me intending to give *you* a *hard* time."

He got out of the car, but before he could open the door for her she had scrambled out, standing up so they faced each other a foot apart.

"Good night," he said brusquely, intending to get back into the car and drive straight off.

"I w-will see you again won't I?" Helen stammered.

Her face with its huge, brimming, mascara-smudged eyes, had lost all its color in the dusk. He took it in his hands.

"Of course you will, my little red fox. I've let you escape this time, but I'll get you in the end. Try and go to ground, you'll find the earth blocked; disappear down another hole, I'll get the terrier men to dig you out."

His white teeth gleamed. As he bent and kissed her, Helen trembled with fear and longing.

"Don't listen to Nige," he said, getting back into the car. "He's not my greatest fan. I'll ring you later in the week about Crittleden," and he was gone.

Helen stood in the twilight, listening to the church bells, thinking about weddings and the attraction of opposites.

Rupert drove down the M4 thinking about Satan. He toyed with the idea of stopping off at the Newbury turn to see a married girlfriend whose husband was away, but he was too tired. At Exit 15 sleep overcame him and the moment he was off the highway he pulled off the road, climbed into the backseat and, hugging Badger for warmth, fell asleep.

The Frogsmore Valley is considered by many to be the most beautiful in the Cotswolds. On either side fields checkered by pale stone walls and dotted by lush woodland and the occasional farm fall steeply down to jade green water meadows, divided by the briskly bustling Frogsmore stream.

At the top of the valley, curling round like a horseshoe, lies the ancient village of Penscombe. Here for the past hundred and twenty years the Campbell-Blacks had made their home, alternately scandalizing and captivating the local community by their outrageous behavior. On Rupert's twenty-first birthday, a month before he came out of the Army, his father, Edward Campbell-Black, had deeded him the house, Penscombe Court, and its surrounding 200 acres. The motive for this altruistic gesture was that Edward had just further scandalized the community by leaving his third wife and running off with the beautiful Italian wife of one of his Gloucestershire shooting cronies. On reflection too, Eddie decided he was bored with running the estate at a loss, and his beautiful Italian prospective bride decided that neither of them could stand the bitter west winds which sweep straight off the Bristol Channel up the Frogsmore Valley to howl round Penscombe Court throughout the winter. So they decamped permanently to the South of France.

Young Rupert further scandalized the community by moving back into the house with his friend Billy Lloyd-Foxe and a floating population of dogs and shapely girl grooms. Even worse, hell-bent on making the place profitable, Rupert promptly dug up the famous rose garden and the orchard, built stables for thirty horses, turned the cricket pitch, where the village used to play regularly, into a show-jumping ring and put up an indoor ring beyond the stables to buttress them from the bitter winds.

Gradually over the next four years the gossip subsided as Rupert and Billy started winning and were frequently seen on television clearing high fences and being awarded silver cups by members of the Royal family. Journalists and television crews came down and raved about the charms of the village and the valley. Suddenly Penscombe had two local heroes and found itself on the map.

Penscombe Court was, fortunately, situated on the north side of the valley, half a mile from the end of the village, so any late-night revelry was deadened by surrounding woodland and didn't keep the village or the neighboring farmers awake too often. Rupert was generaly considered capricious and arrogant, but Billy, who loved gossip and spent a lot of time in the village chattering to the locals, was universally adored. Any inseparable friend of Billy, it was felt, couldn't be all bad; besides, the locals had known Rupert since he was a child and had seen step-parents come and go with alarming regularity; and, being a tolerant and generous community, felt allowances should be made. They also realized that Rupert, like the rest of his family, was indifferent to public opinion, so that their disapproval would not make any difference, anyway.

Just before midnight Rupert woke up from his nap and set off for home. He never saw the signposts to Penscombe without a leap of joy and recognition. As he drove along the top of the south side of the valley, Badger woke up and started snuffling excitedly at the crack of an open window. Ahead in the moonlight gleamed Penscombe church spire. Although it was after midnight, Rupert looked across the north side and cursed in irritation to see half the lights in the house blazing. Billy must have gone to bed plastered without switching them off.

As he stormed up the drive through the chestnut avenue planted by his great-grandfather, he could see the pale green leaves opening like parachutes. Behind white railings, three dozing horses in New Zealand rugs blinked as he passed. The car crunched on the gravel in front of the house. There was a great baying and yapping. As Rupert opened the front door, two Jack Russells, a Springer spaniel, a yellow labrador and a blond mongrel with a tightly curled tail threw themselves on him in delight, growling and fighting each other. Finally they all started pestering Badger, jealous because he'd been the one to go on a jaunt. Rupert kicked them gently out of the way. His suitcase was still lying in the hall where he'd left it that morning. In the drawing room the fire was going out, Sunday papers half-read and a pile of entry forms lay scattered over the sofa. One of the dogs had shredded his hunting tie on the rug in front of the fire.

"Jesus," said Rupert, slamming the door shut.

In the kitchen he found Billy trying to read *Horse and Hound,* clean the brown tops of a pair of black boots, drink whisky and fork oysters out of a can all at the same time.

"Hi," he said looking up. "How did it go? Have you joined the Antis?"

Billy was not a handsome young man, his nose was broken and his sleepy dark brown eyes were seldom visible because they were always creased with laughter, but he had a smile that could melt the Arctic Circle. Rupert, however, was not in a mood to be melted.

"This place is a pigsty," he snapped, pointing to the sink which was piled high with plates, glasses and dog bowls. "Can't you even put things in the dishwasher?"

"It's full," said Billy calmly.

"Or in the garbage can," went on Rupert, pointing to the empty cans of dog food and milk cartons littering the shelf.

"That's full too," said Billy.

"And one of your dogs has crapped in the hall."

"It was one of your dogs," said Billy without rancor. "Anyway, I've been bloody busy."

"Drinking my whisky and reading the Sunday papers."

"The hell I have. By the way, there's a nice piece about you in *The Observer*."

"What did it say?"

"Oh, some sycophantic rubbish about you being the best rider in England."

"Don't try to placate me, and why's the telephone off the hook?"

"To stop Bianca, and Gabriella, and goodness knows who else ringing up."

Rupert replaced the receiver. Five seconds later the telephone rang.

"See what I mean?"

Rupert picked it up. Both of them could hear squawking. Putting the receiver in a nearby cupboard, Rupert shut the door.

Billy grinned: "Anyway, I repeat, I've been bloody busy."

"Doing what?"

"Taking care of the entire stable single-handed. I've even sold a couple of horse for you."

"How much d'you get?"

"Ten grand for Padua and eight for the grey with the ewe neck."

"Not enough," said Rupert, looking slightly mollified.

"Never is for you, and I worked out everything we're going to need tomorrow. Admittedly I was so hungover first thing I saw four ears every time I looked down a horse's neck."

He speared up another oyster. "And I think I've sorted out why The Bull keeps stopping. He's terrified of water."

"So am I," said Rupert, "unless it's got whisky in it."

He picked up the bottle and, not finding any clean glasses in the cupboard, poured it into a tea cup.

"Where the hell was Diane today?"

"Said she's got the curse; worked for a couple for hours, then collapsed into bed."

"Rubbish," said Rupert. "She had it a fortnight ago. She'd have stayed working if I'd been here. And Tracey?"

"It's her day off."

"And Marion?"

"Quit, and flatly refused to work. She was pissed off because you forgot to take her to some party on Saturday night. She's been reading the want ads in *Horse and Hound* all day and left them deliberately lying on the table for us to find."

He handed the magazine to Rupert.

"Oh hell, let her go, I'm fed up with her tantrums."

"You cause most of them," said Billy reasonably. "You know perfectly well that Mayfair and Belgravia, not to mention The Bull and Kitchener, will all go into a decline if she leaves. And we can't afford that at the beginning of the season."

He held out his glass for Rupert to fill up.

"And just remember how tremendous she is with customs men. They're so transfixed by her boobs they never bother to even glance at our papers."

"Are you after her or something?" said Rupert.

"No, my heart belongs entirely to Mavis," said Billy, looking down at the blond mongrel who was now curled up on his knee, slanting eyes closed, head resting on his collarbone.

"Oh, all right," said Rupert, "I'll go and see her in a minute."

"She'll be asleep by now."

"Not her, she'll be tossing and turning with desire and frustration."

From the pantry next door the washing machine was thundering to a halt. Wiping the boot polish off his hands on to Mavis's blond coat, Billy set her gently down on the floor. Opening the machine, he removed a tangle of white ties, shirts, breeches, socks and underpants and threw them into the dryer.

Rupert looked disapprovingly around the kitchen which was low beamed with a flagstone floor and a window looking over a valley. A bridle hung from a meat hook and every shelf seemed to be covered with spilling ashtrays and unopened bills.

"We must get a housekeeper. I'm fed up with chaos."

"It's pointless," said Billy. "You'd only employ pretty ones, then you can't resist screwing them. Mrs. Burroughs is coming in the morning. She'll tidy the place up."

"I want it neat on weekends. Perhaps we ought to get Nanny back."

"She'd have a heart attack at the goings on. Perhaps you ought to get married. Wives are supposed to do this sort of thing. How was your red-headed Anti?"

"Interesting. Very uptight."

"Not the easy lay you expected?"

"You've put your finger on the spot," said Rupert, draining his whisky, "which is certainly more than I did. She's rather sweet, but frightfully intense, kept wanting to talk about books and the theater."

"Must have taxed your brain. Are you going to see her again?"

"I might. I don't like unfinished business. By the way, I bought a bloody good horse today from the barracks. No one was around so Tommy let me try him on the Q.T. Never seen a big horse so good in front. Despite his size he jumps like a pony. Needs some sorting out though."

"Don't make me tired. I've done enough sorting out for one day," said Billy, picking up the yellow mongrel. "Mavis and I are off to bed. See you in the morning."

"I'll go and placate Marion," said Rupert.

He went upstairs, brushed his teeth and his hair, then took the dogs out.

At the end of the lawn two black yew trees crouched like great gelded tomcats. Behind the house rose the wood, stretching for half a mile. Four vast Lawson cypresses rose in front of the bare beech trees like spires of a cathedral. Moonlight flooded the valley, silvering the lake and blanching the first daffodils. On the opposite side a car driving along the top towards Penscombe lit up the trees lining the road. Rupert felt his heart expand with pride and love. This was his home and his land to do what he wanted with. He must keep on winning to keep it going, to make it better and better.

The dogs weaved about lifting their legs on rose bushes and young trees. From the stables he could hear the occasional snort and stamp, and resisted the temptation to go and wake the horses up. As he expected, the light was still on in Marion's apartment over the tack-room. He shut the dogs in the house. Marion took a long time to answer the door. She was pale and puffy-eyed, but nothing could disguise the voluptuousness of her body, nor the length of leg revealed by the clinging nightshirt with the baleful figure of Snoopy on the front.

"What d'you want?" she said in a choked voice.

"You," said Rupert.

"Bastard." Snoopy rose and fell as her breast heaved.

"That's no way to address one's boss."

"You're not my boss anymore. I've given my notice. Didn't Billy tell you?"

"Yes," said Rupert moving toward her and putting a hand between her legs. "And I haven't accepted it."

"Don't touch me," she sobbed.

But as he splayed out his fingers and increased the pressure she collapsed into his arms.

*H*elen found the next week extraordinarily trying. She could think of nothing but Rupert, which made sleep, work and her very existence impossible.

In the evenings at Regina House she read love poetry endlessly and played Schumann's Piano Concerto over and over again, very quietly with her door an inch open, in case she missed the telephone ringing downstairs.

By day she had to put up with Nigel. He limped in after lunch on Monday with a black eye and two cracked ribs. She was appalled by his detailed account of the brutality of the beating. But when he started describing how he'd been tied up and left naked behind a hedge she suddenly remembered Rupert's remark about trussing a Christmas turkey and had to gaze out the window so Nigel wouldn't see her laughing.

"Even worse, Helen," Nigel added, his unblacked eye gleaming behind his thick glasses, "R.C.B. appropriated my address book."

"Oh dear," said Helen. "Will he find any important numbers?"

"Crucial," said Nigel sententiously. "With that book in his hands, R.C.B. can smash our entire network. I'm sure that's why he beat me up because he was so anxious to get his hands on it."

"Sort of like Watergate," said Helen, fighting a terrible desire to giggle.

As the week crawled by, she was filled with an increasing restlessness and sat at her typewriter playing he loves me, he loves me not with the raindrops cascading down the window from the incessant April showers, quite incapable even of typing "Dear Sir," because the only sir who was dear to her hadn't called.

She'd learned from the paper that the Crittleden meeting started on Good Friday and lasted over the Easter weekend.

On Thursday at lunchtime, in anticipation of seeing Rupert, she went out and spent nearly three weeks' salary on the softest beige suede dress.

She spent a miserable Good Friday going to the three-hour service, praying for resignation and trying not to ask God to remind Rupert to call her.

On Saturday afternoon she went downstairs and, sitting on a straight-backed chair in the television room, tried to watch Crittleden, but had to wait until a Charlie Chaplin film had finished on the other channel before she could switch over. By this time the B.B.C. had left Crittleden and gone over to an extremely noisy stock car race. Seeing the pained expressions on the lady academics' face, Helen explained that a friend of hers was jumping at Crittleden, which should be on at any minute.

At last the camera switched back to the show ground. It was pouring rain and it was not until the five riders, none of them Rupert, had demolished the course, the the announcer told them that the winner was a German rider who had produced the only clear. An Irishman was second with four faults, and Rupert Campbell-Black for Great Britain was third with eight faults. Billy Lloyd-Foxe and three other riders had tied for fourth place with twelve faults apiece.

After the incessant rain, said the announcer, the Crittleden Arena was like a quagmire and any rider who got around was to be congratulated. Through the downpour the German rider came into the ring, followed by the Irish rider in his holly green coat. Helen's heart started pounding and her mouth went dry, as Rupert followed them on a huge chestnut. The black collar of his red coat was turned up, his white breeches splattered with mud.

As they lined up, a man in a tweed suit and a bowler hat came out holding an umbrella over an attractive, middle-aged blonde in a dark grey suit, who delicately picked her way through the mud. Another bowler-hatted man in a tweed suit followed them carrying a huge silver cup and shielding a tray of ribbons from the rain under his coat.

"Here comes Lady Pringle, a fine horsewoman in her own right, to present the prizes," said the announcer. Helen could see Rupert chatting and laughing with Billy and, as Lady Pringle reached him, he took off his hat and, bending down, kissed her on both cheeks.

"Lady Pringle and Rupert Campbell-Black are obviously old friends," said the announcer as she handed him a lemon yellow ribbon, "and she's obviously delighted to have a British rider in the first three."

"Isn't that the young man who picked you up last Saturday?" said one of the female anthropologists, changing her spectacles to have a better look. But Helen had fled upstairs to sob her heart out on her bed. How could Rupert look so cheerful and carefree when she'd been going through such hell waiting for him to call?

"Lady Pringle, indeed," she sobbed and, taking the photograph of Rupert which she'd surreptitiously cut from one of Nigel's *Horse and Hounds* out of her diary, she tore it into tiny pieces. He was nothing but a stud.

She was crying so hard, at first she didn't hear the knock on the door.

"Telephone," said a voice.

When she got downstairs it was Rupert.

"Angel, I'm sorry I haven't rung before. I left your number at home and I've only just remembered the name of your coven. We've been up at the South Lancashire Show and the van blew out on the way down, so we only arrived in time for the big class."

"How did you do?" asked Helen. She was damned if she was going to let him know she'd been watching.

"Not bad. I was third, Billy fourth. The going was terrible, bogs in front of every jump. Are you coming down?"

"I d-don't know," said Helen, thinking of her swollen eyes and lack of sleep. "I can't tonight."

"Come down tomorrow. I'd come to collect you, but I've got classes in the morning. Get a taxi."

"But it's miles," said Helen, appalled, thinking of all the money she'd squandered on the midi dress.

"It's only an hour from London. I'll pay," said Rupert. "Come to the main entrance. I'll leave the cash and a ticket with the man at the gate."

Rupert's estimate of the time it would take to drive down to Crittleden was very different from the taxi driver's. She nervously watched the fare jerk up and and up. £25—£35! She was sure the driver wouldn't take an American check and she couldn't call up her bank as it was a Sunday. Scrabbling around in her purse she only found £1.30. Perhaps he'd accept her gold watch until she could find Rupert. Even worse, two miles from Crittleden they ran into a huge traffic jam. A glorious mild day had followed yesterday's downpour. Every young green leaf and blade of new grass sparkled with raindrops and all the people who'd given the Show a miss yesterday seemed to have decided to go today. For the thousandth time Helen checked her face in the mirror. Her hair looked okay, the suede dress brought out the amber of her eyes, but she still looked tired.

"Got him bad, 'ave you?" said the taxi driver as the third application of Miss Dior in ten minutes fought with the diesel fumes. She'd looked rich enough when she'd got into the car, the dress must have cost a packet and Americans were rarely short of a few bob.

"Been to Crittleden before?"

Helen shook her head. "One of the show jumpers has invited me. You may have heard of him, Rupert Campbell-Black."

"Rupert Campbell-Black," said the driver. "I know Rupert, 'ad him in the cab, and his mate, Billy Lloyd-Foxe. 'E's a lad is Rupert. Did you see him at the 'orse of the Year Show in one of the novelty classes on the last day? Dressed up as Miss World, wiv coconuts in his dress. They fell out as he rode over the jumps, brought the 'ouse down. 'E's a lad is Rupert. I got 'is autograph for my missis, she's mad about Rupert, she is."

At last they reached the main gates.

"Help," thought Helen in panic. There seemed to be half a dozen men in yellow coats on the gate.

The taxi driver had no such reserve. Winding down the window he shouted: "I've got a lidy here for Rupert."

Immediately one of the yellow-coated men leapt forward and peered into the cab.

"Might 'ave guessed it," he said with a gap-toothed grin. "Rupert certainly goes for lookers," and getting a sheaf of tenners out of his pocket he handed them to Helen. "I think he's given me most of his winnings yesterday. If you hang on quarter of an hour, mate, I'll get you a fare back to London."

After Helen had paid the taximan sixty pounds, which seemed an appalling amount of money, the man in the yellow coat took her off to find Rupert. It was so muddy she was thankful she'd worn boots.

"I'm a bit late," she said.

"Not surprised in that traffic. Got a good crowd here today, although it looks like rain later." He pointed to indigo clouds which were beginning to mass on the horizon above the pale acid-green elm wood.

They found Rupert in the schooling ring, cantering very slowly around on a magnificent bay gelding, totally oblivious of the crowd of nubile teenagers gazing at him.

The man in the yellow coat was about to call out when Helen stopped him. "I want to watch for a second," she said. "Thank you so much."

Rupert was wearing green cords tucked into rubber boots, a dark blue quilted vest over a dark blue sweater, and no hat.

"I told you he was lovely," said a teenage girl eating an ice cream.

"I never thought he'd be that lovely," said her friend.

"That's his groom, Marion," said the first girl, pointing to a sulky looking blonde who was standing by the practice fence. "She was interviewed in _Honey_ about what it's like working for Rupert. She said he doesn't get enough sleep."

At a word from Rupert the sulky blonde, who was wearing a red T-shirt with "I only sleep with the best people" printed across her bosom, put up the pole to five feet. Rupert cleared it effortlessly.

"Wish I was the horse," said the girl.

Helen had had enough.

"Rupert," she called as he came past.

It was some comfort that he seemed pleased to see her. Instantly sliding off the bay gelding and handing him to Marion, he ducked under the fence to join her. Immediately the autograph hunters surged forward.

"Bugger off," snapped Rupert. "Can't you see I'm busy?" and, putting his arm around Helen's shoulders, he pushed impatiently through the crowd.

"How are you?" he said.

"Wonderful," said Helen, suddenly realizing she was.

"You certainly look it," he said, running his hand down her suede arm. "I adore that dress. It's the same texture as Belgravia when he's just been clipped, but I don't like that bloody headband," and removing it from her hair, he tossed it into a nearby trash can.

"That was my favorite headband," she said outraged.

"And your last one," said Rupert.

And he turned her to face him, running his hands through her red mane so it fell tousled and shining over her forehead and around her face.

For a second she gazed at him mutinously, then she laughed.

"Christ," said Rupert. "I'd forgotten how beautiful you were," and drawing her towards him, he kissed her full on the mouth, in front of the crowds.

"We can't here," she said pulling away, blushing furiously.

"We can absolutely anywhere," said Rupert. "Come on, let's go back to the trailer and have a drink." He looked at his watch. "I've got a class in an hour and a half."

On their way they passed the stables. Horses lolled their heads over the half-doors, gnawing at the wood, flattening their ears at each other and at passers-by.

A crowd of people were hanging around one box stall. "That's Belgravia," said Rupert.

As he went towards the half-door the crowd dispersed to a respectful distance, but the horse rolled its eyes and took a threatening nip at Rupert's sleeve.

"Ungrateful sod," said Rupert, punching him gently on the neck. "He doesn't like me; I mean hard work to him. You'd better be in top form this afternoon."

Leaving the horses, they walked through the mud up the hill to the trailer park where the riders lived during the show. Rupert's was easily the biggest vehicle and the only one painted dark blue piped with emerald. In the window hung a string of ribbons.

"We had a good morning," said Rupert.

Inside the trailer Badger thumped his tail joyfully and wriggling up to Helen, goosed her briskly. On the table sat Billy Lloyd-Foxe. Mavis, the yellow mongrel, sat perched on his knee. On the bench seats sat a mousy-haired man with big ears and his mouth open, a fat man with short legs, and a pretty brunette with a note-pad. They were all watching yesterday's competition on the videotape. Billy's horse was coming up to a big oxer and scattering poles.

"Freeze it," said the fat man. "You went in too close, Billy."

"Not enought impulsion," said Rupert. "Got to jump an extra

foot in mud like that. I wish you'd all stop cluttering up my trailer. This is Helen Macaulay."

They all stared at her.

"This," continued Rupert, "is my unstable companion Billy Lloyd-Foxe."

Billy grinned. "Hi. I saw you across a crowded meet, but sadly Rupe got in first."

"This is Joanna Battie from the *Chronicle,* who's interviewing Billy," said Rupert introducing the dark girl, "and Humpty Hamilton." The fat man nodded. "And this is Ivor Braine, singularly misnamed because he's so thick." The man with big ears opened his mouth even wider.

Rupert got down two glasses and another bottle.

Once Helen had been given a drink they all ignored her and went back to watching the video, tearing everyone's round to shreds, which gave her a chance to look at the trailer. It was extremely luxurious, with an oven, a fridge, a washing machine, bench seats, a double bed that folded up completely and a great deal of cupboard space.

At the end of the tape Rupert switched over to racing, picking up the paper in order to look at his horoscope.

"Good day for shopping," he read. "Perhaps I'd better buy that grey gelding. 'Evening starred for romance.'" He grinned at Helen. "I should bloody well hope so."

At that moment Marion walked in, still looking sulky. She was chewing gum which gave her a particularly insolent air.

"You haven't met Helen Macaulay, Marion," said Rupert, a slight note of malice creeping into his voice.

"I've met her namesake," said Marion sourly. "Arrived Friday morning; bitten me three times already."

"My namesake?" asked Helen bewildered.

"The black horse I bought at the barracks. He's been showing Marion who's boss. I decided to call him Macaulay."

Helen blushed crimson. "Oh, how sweet of you."

"Are you going to make us something to eat?" said Rupert.

"Haven't got time," said Marion. "Class starts in three-quarters of an hour. I've got to help Tracey tack up Belgravia and The Bull. There's smoked salmon and brown bread." She flounced out of the trailer, slamming the door behind her.

"What a lovely nature that girl's got," Humpty said, getting up. "We'd better go, Ivor. Thanks for the drink."

"I'll come with you," said Joanna. "You'll want to get changed. I presume you're all going to Grania Pringle's party tonight. O.K. then, I'll have half an hour there with you, Billy. Good luck both of you."

"Do you want me to go out while you change?" asked Helen.

"As long as you don't mind underpants," said Rupert.

"I'll make you some sandwiches." She went to the fridge which was packed with an upscale medley of paté, smoked salmon, smoked turkey and several bottles of champagne. She also noticed a great many empties already in the trash can.

"Bread's in the bin on the right," said Rupert. Lifting her hair, he planted a kiss on the back of her neck, then when she swung around, he kissed her on the mouth, his hands feeling for her breasts. Helen tried to leap away but she was rammed against the oven.

Rupert laughed and let her go. "Mustn't raise my blood pressure too much before a class."

As Helen spread unsalted butter on slices of bread and placed smoked salmon, red pepper and a squirt of lemon on top, she allowed herself the brief fantasy of living with Rupert in the trailer like a couple of gypsies, cooking him ingenious dinners on the stove every night, shutting out the rest of the horsey world except for Billy. Billy, she decided, was terrific.

"How's Nige?" asked Rupert.

"Very overadrenalized," said Helen, cutting the crusts off the sandwiches, "and overly concerned that you've appropriated his address book and now have access to all the names and addresses of the saboteur underground."

"The only name and *add*-ress I was after," said Rupert mimicking her accent again, "was yours. After that I threw the book into the Thames so no doubt a lot of fishes are about to reveal the Antis' darkest secrets in the *Angling Times*."

Helen turned around with the plate of sandwiches to find Billy already dressed in breeches and a shirt, tying his white tie, and Rupert wearing nothing at all. She nearly dropped the sandwiches on the floor.

"Very good sandwiches," said Rupert. "D'you want some, Billy?"

"No thanks," said Billy, lighting a cigarette. "It never fails to amaze me how you can eat before a big class. I'm about to throw up last night's dinner."

There was a bang on the door. It was Humpty Hamilton.

"We can walk the course in five minutes," he said. "It looks a sod."

"I'm definitely going to ask Lavinia Greenslade out tonight," said Billy, shrugging into his red coat.

"You'll have to take her parents along as well," said Rupert, grabbing his coat and a couple more sandwiches as they went out of the trailer.

10

*H*elen, as a result of three glasses of wine and no sandwiches, was feeling very unsteady. She was glad Rupert took a firm hold on her arm.

"Can you remember where I'm jumping?" he asked Billy.

"Fifteen," said Billy. "I've got to wait until thirty. I'm last. Christ, look at that upright."

They left Helen in the riders' stand while they walked the course. She saw Joanna, the deadpan girl from the *Chronicle*, pointing her out to some of the other journalists who laughed and shrugged their shoulders. She wished she'd brought a coat; the suede dress wasn't very warm.

She watched the riders splaying out over the emerald green arena. There were a few girls in black or very dark navy blue coats, several Irish riders in Army uniform or holly green, but the majority wore coats as red as a poppy. Some of them were pacing out the number of strides between jumps, like seconds in a duel, others put their hands up to rattle a pole to check how firm it was in the cup, others stood eyeing a turn or an angle, seeing how safe it was to cut a corner or come in sharply.

Several riders climbed up the famous Crittleden bank to examine the fence halfway across on the top. The jumps were absolutely colossal. Humpty Hamilton, looking stouter than ever in a quilted vest, couldn't even see over half of them.

And there was Billy, puffing on yet another cigarette, gloomily examining the water jump, while Mavis drank from it.

The indigo clouds had rolled away leaving the softest pale blue sky above the acid green wood which had only a few sad grey streaks where the odd tree had died of Dutch elm disease. On the hill Helen could see the gleaming armadillo of parked cars and the trailers.

Mostly her eyes were drawn to Rupert, who seemed to be spending more time ribbing his fellow competitors than studying the course and, unlike the others, he didn't look bandy-legged or stout, or diminished by not being on a horse. All around the ring crowds were gathering with binoculars. Helen reluctantly imagined every eye was on Rupert.

Two men in checked suits and bowler hats, flushed from lunch, were going up into the judges' box.

As the riders came out joking and laughing on the nervous high before a big class, the cameramen went in, most of them in jeans, gathering round the water jump. A large lady with a huge bust strode round the course with a tape measure, checking the height of each fence.

Tracey and Marion rode down to the collecting ring, one on the dark bay, Allenby, nicknamed The Bull, the other on the chestnut, Belgravia.

"God, I hate Rupe before big classes," said Marion. "He's so picky, checking and re-checking everything. Stop it, you monster," she snapped, as Belgravia, oated up to the eyeballs, fidgeted and spooked at everything he passed, scattering the crowd with his huge hind quarters.

"Seems on top of the world," said Tracey.

"Wish I was," said Marion gloomily. "You haven't seen Rupe's new girl friend."

"What's she like?"

"Not really his type: red-headed, breedy-looking, quivering with nerves rather like Belgravia."

"Sounds like all the rest," said Tracey.

"Even worse, she's called Macaulay."

"Blimey," said Tracey. "He's never done that before."

Helen was joined by Rupert, Billy and Mavis in the riders' stand. "I wish you'd leave that dog behind, Billy," said a steward fussily.

"She brings me luck."

"Can't see why she can't bring you luck in your trailer."

The first riders were crashing their horses over fences in the practice ring under the oak trees. Members of the public leaned forward to pat their equine heroes as they passed in their colored rugs.

"What was the course like?" asked Helen.

"Bloody. You can park a double-decker bus between the parallel bars," said Rupert. "There are only two and a half strides between the double, and the wall isn't as solid as it looks. If you catch it on the way up, you're in dead trouble."

"Zee vater must be at least six metres," said a German rider gloomily. Billy looked green and lit another cigarette.

A man in a felt hat with long sideburns and a raffish face stopped on the way to the commentary box. "Hello boys," he said in a carefully modulated put-on voice. "We're on the air in two minutes. How did the course walk?"

"Not very good, but it may ride better than it walks," said Rupert.

Surely ride and walk aren't transitive verbs, thought Helen. "Who's that?" she asked as he moved on.

"Dudley Diplock—does all the commentaries. He's a jerk, knows nothing about show jumping."

Everything went quiet as the first rider came in—yesterday's winner, Ludwig von Schellenberg on Brahms, a splendid horse, impeccably schooled.

"He's the one to watch," Billy told Helen. "He's the best rider in the world, and was virtually unbeaten last season."

British spirits were not raised, however, when the mighty Ludwig had a most uncharacteristic twelve faults.

"Shows how bloody difficult the course must be," said Rupert. "And here comes the despair of the Pony Club." Ludwig was followed by Humpty Hamilton on Porky Boy.

Humpty certainly rode in a very unorthodox fashion, pouter pigeon chest stuck out, hands held high, feet pointing down like a dancing master, showing a great patch of blue sky as he rose nearly a foot and a half out of the saddle over every fence. Nevertheless he acquitted himself well over the punishing course, and only had two fences down and a foot in the water for the same number of faults as Ludwig.

After that everyone went to pieces. Disastrous round followed disastrous round, slowing the proceedings up because the course had to be rebuilt every time.

Rupert got to his feet:

"I'd better go and show them how to do it," he said.

He kissed Helen on the cheek. "I won't be long, darling."

Without his red-hot warmth beside her, Helen suddenly felt cold. A brisk wind was unfurling the flags and spreading out the horses' tails. On television it had looked like a game for children with toy horses and toy fences. The camera had caught nothing of the colossal height of the jumps, the pounding hooves, the heroic splendor and sheer size of the horses. Suddenly Helen felt scared for Rupert.

"Aren't you terrified?"

"Terrified," said Billy, clutching Mavis for comfort and lighting another cigarette, "particularly as Malise Gordon has just arrived and parked himself below us."

"Who's he?"

"One of the selectors and the new chef d'equipe. He manages the British team and goes abroad with them to keep them in order."

"What's he like?" said Helen, admiring the taut aquiline features, the high complexion and the dark hair greying at the temples. "He looks kind of attractive."

"Bit of a tartar, stickler for discipline, always has spats with Rupe—well, you can never tell what Rupe's going to do next. Going to bed sober, early and alone has never been his strong point. Although I'm sure," Billy added hastily, worried that he might have hurt Helen, "now he's met you, he'll mend his ways. Mind you, it's getting to the stage when Rupe's so good Malise can't afford to leave him out."

Helen watched Rupert saunter across the concrete below them, then vault over the fence into the collecting ring. Goodness, he must be fit. He went up to Marion and Belgravia, bending down to adjust the bandages on the horse's front legs.

"Is he that good?" Helen longed to talk about him.

"Christ, yes. Doesn't have any nerves, cool as an icicle before every class, and he's so fast and he meets the fence just right. Knows what risks he can take too. And he's got the killer instinct. Even in novice classes he's always out to win."

Ivor Braine was in the middle of a good round. The television man ran nimbly after him with the boom, recording the grunts and snorts of his horse.

"Sounds like a live sex show," said Billy.

Ivor was followed by a handsome Frenchman in a blue coat with a crimson collar who proceeded to demolish the course. As he came thundering down to the water the horse jammed on its brakes and the Frenchman took a leisurely somersault through the air, landing with a huge splash.

"*Il est tombé dans l'eau*," said Billy. "I know that's going to happen to me and The Bull. Now they'll have to rebuild the course and Belgravia won't like the wait.

A colossal cheer went up as Rupert erupted into the ring through the red brick arch. In the private boxes people came out on to the balconies to watch, clutching their gin and tonics. Belgravia stood still just long enough for Rupert to take his hat off.

Humpty Hamilton sat down beside Helen as Belgravia gave three colossal bucks. Rupert laughed and didn't move in the saddle. As the klaxon went off the horse bounded forward.

"Complete tearaway," muttered Humpty disapprovingly. "Steerable, but not stoppable."

"That horse would benefit from some dressage," thought Malise Gordon disapprovingly. "If it weren't for Rupert's colossal strength, he'd be quite out of control."

Over the brush sailed Belgravia, over the post and rails, over the rustic poles, driven on by Rupert's erotic pelvic thrusts. When he came to the massive upright he flew over it as though it was a tiny log.

At the gate with Crittleden written across it in large red letters he came in too fast, slipped, just righted himself, and rapped the fence hard as he went over. For a second it swung back and forth giving Rupert's fans heart attacks. Rupert didn't even bother to glance around. With his long stride, Belgravia managed the double in three strides. Now he was rounding the corner. Next moment Helen saw Belgravia's pricked ginger ears appearing over the top of the bank, then his lovely head with the white star, and then Rupert. They were on top, popping over the little fence, then tobogganing down the other side, Belgravia on his haunches. Only Rupert's superhuman strength again stopped the horse from running into the fence at the bottom. He was over; the crowd gave a cheer. Over the wall and the combination, which caused him no trouble. Then he kicked Belgravia into a gallop and sailed over the water, yanking him back to get him in line for the final triple.

"Too fast," said Billy in anguish. "He's going to hit it."

Helen shut her eyes, listening to the thundering hooves, waiting for the sickening thud of falling poles and the groans of the crowd. Instead there was a mighty roar of applause. Helen opened her eyes.

"Ouch," said Billy.

Looking down, Helen realized she'd been gripping his arm.

"I'm sorry."

"Be my guest. Brilliant round, wasn't it?"

"Wonderful." Helen watched a delighted Rupert letting his rein slack and walking Belgravia out of the ring, slapping his lathered neck, pulling the ginger ears with joy. Belgravia's coat, dark, bronzed and shiny with sweat, looked like uncooked liver.

"That puts me in joint second, which means £500, but there are still fifteen to go," said Humpty.

Helen noticed the arrogant way Rupert ignored the cheers. Sliding to the ground, he patted the horse once more and turned towards the riders' stand. Stopped by admirers on the way, in an exultant mood, he was prepared to sign autographs.

"Once you get a clear people realize it can be jumped and you'll probably get a lot more," said Billy. "If I watch any more rounds I'll start getting the heeby-jeebies."

He lit another cigarette. Mavis closed her slanting eyes to avoid the smoke.

"How long has your mount suffered from hydrophobia?" asked Helen."

"What?" Billy looked alarmed.

"Been frightened of water."

"Oh, ever since I had him. I think he might have nearly drowned in some tiny river when he was a foal because it really scares him. Last week I managed to get him over a six-foot stream at home, but he trembled for ages afterwards. I just don't know how he'll go today. He's such a good horse," he went on, his face lighting up. "So kind, and such a trier, he'll get himself into all sorts of trouble rather than duck out, and he's so bright. Over and over I put him wrong and he just brakes at the last moment and sails over, and he's so cheerful, never moody, and so gentle, a child could lead him up to London on a piece of string like a little dog."

Helen smiled. "I think Mavis is getting jealous," she said.

"Oh Mavis knows she's my favorite dog, and there goes my favorite girl," said Billy, as a blonde with a pink and white complexion on a grey horse waited to go into the ring.

"Look at her bloody father telling her to give it a whack at the water, and her mother telling her not to. Poor girl's in such a muddle. I could sort her out," he said longingly. "Good luck darling," he called down. Lavinia looked up, waved her whip and smiled. Her parents looked simply furious.

How nice he is, thought Helen, and he's Rupert's best friend. There couldn't be much wrong with Rupert if he inspired friendship like this. In anguish, Billy watched poor Lavinia, after a nervous, tentative round, meet the same fate as the poor Frenchman, flying through the air into the water.

"At least she won't have to wash her hair before she goes out with you this evening," said an amused voice. It was Rupert. He was eating an ice cream.

"Congratulations," said Helen.

"Bloody well done," said Billy.

"That should wrap the whole thing up," said Rupert, shooting a sideways glance at Billy. "Don't imagine there'll be any more clears."

"Thanks a lot," said Billy. "I've still got to jump. Oh, look at poor darling Lavinia coming out in tears."

"She looks like a seal," said Rupert. "She may just be dwipping water, not cwying. Lavinia," he added to Helen, "can't say her 'R's."

"It was a good round until she came to the water," protested Billy. He got up. "Can you hold Mavis for me?" he asked Helen.

"Good luck," said Rupert.

As he went downstairs the dog whined and strained after him.

"Shut up," snapped Rupert. Mavis gave him a cold stare, then climbed on to Helen's knees and settled down with a sigh of deep martyrdom.

Helen was grateful for the warmth. Seeing she was shivering, Rupert put his red coat round her shoulders. The heat left from his body was like a caress. Riders kept returning to the stand, many of them on twelve faults. Everyone congratulated Rupert. He was in tearing spirits until Malise Gordon came over and sat down on his other side. Rupert was about to introduce Helen when Malise said, "Not a bad round, but a big hit and miss."

Rupert's lips tightened, his face suddenly expressionless.

"Belgravia could do with a lot more work on the flat," went on Malise, "and a lot less corn."

"He never felt in any danger to me," said Rupert coldly.

"You were very lucky at the gate, and at the rail after the bank, and you came in much too fast at the triple. That's a good horse, but you won't get him out of trouble every time."

Rupert stared stonily ahead.

"We ought to be thinking of him in terms of the Olympics or the World Championships," said Malise in a slightly more conciliatory tone.

"Belgravia'd be the ideal horse," said Rupert, relenting slightly too. "In the World Championship," he explained to Helen, "the four finalists have to jump each other's horses. Belgravia's such a sod, no one would have a hope on him."

"Hardly cricket," said Malise.

"Course it isn't," said Rupert insolently. "I thought we were talking about show jumping."

"By the way," asked Malise, "have you come across a rider called Jake Lovell? He's been jumping on the northern circuit. I think he's very good."

Rupert paused for a second. "No. Is he good enough to make the British team?"

"He will be in a year or two."

"You'd do much better with Billy," said Rupert quickly.

"Billy has yet to convince me he has the killer instinct," said Malise, standing up. "I'll probably see you at Grania's."

Helen could see exactly why he and Rupert struck sparks off each other.

Down in the collecting ring Billy went up to Lavinia Greenslade and commiserated with her.

"Same thing's bound to happen to me," he said. He walked over to The Bull who nickered with joy and stuck his nose inside Billy's coat. Built like an oak tree with vast girth, short, wide-apart well-shaped legs and surprisingly small feet, it was the wide forehead and rather small eyes that made him look like a bull. The wide blaze down his forehead gave him an added appearance of placid contentment.

"How is he?" he asked Tracey.

"Gorgeous," said Tracey. "Always is. Didn't Rupert jump champion?"

Billy rode off, trying to control his nerves. Rupert had been so cocky, he felt needled into producing something better. Other riders, having finished jumping, were all too ready to offer him advice. But it was no good listening to other people at this stage, he'd only get muddled. Over the years he'd schooled himself to tackle the problem by himself. In the ring you were on your own.

The collecting ring steward called his number. Good lucks came from all round. Billy was very popular.

As he waited for the last rider—the German, Hans Schmidt—to come out of the ring, a little girl bent over and stroked The Bull's nose.

"Good luck Bull," she said shyly.

Billy smiled and thanked her, wishing the butterflies in his stomach would go away. He couldn't even remember which fence to jump first. The Bull, however, showed no such fears, striding out briskly, ears pricked, tail up, merry eyes sparkling, taking everything in.

"Take your hat off, Billy," whispered a ring steward.

The crowd roared with laughter as Billy started and hastily whipped off his hat, damp curls sticking to his forehead. Malise stopped talking to Grania Pringle in the President's box.

"I want to watch this round," he said. "Must say The Bull looks marvellous."

"More than can be said for Billy," said Grania. "He's pea green."

"Take it slowly," Billy told himself over and over again. If you can go clear, even with time faults, you'll be second. "You're the best, you're the best," he whispered to The Bull as he leaned forward and started cantering as the klaxon went.

The Bull bucketed over the first three fences, giving huge scary leaps with inches to spare, then he settled down, trundling merrily along, little legs going like pistons, meeting everything just right.

"God, that horse has improved," said Malise, as he flew over the double. "Billy's really been working on him."

Helen held her breath as The Bull scrambled up the bank which, after much use, was extremely slippery. On top Billy steadied him. Just for a second The Bull looked dubious. The crowd crossed their fingers in case he stepped back which would have constituted a stop, costing Billy three faults, but he popped over, tobogganed down the other side and took a huge jump over the tiny rail, snorting with disapproval, ears flat, tail swishing.

"Didn't enjoy that," laughed Humpty. "Look at his tail going. Who did you say his dam was, Rupert?"

"Probably a cow," said Rupert.

Helen giggled.

The combination, three good solid fences, held no fears for The Bull.

"He's faster than you," said Humpty with some satisfaction.

"I know," said Rupert coldly.

Now it was only the water, and the final triple. Turning The Bull, Billy thundered down, his red coat like a spot of blood against the dappled crowd.

"Come on Billy," howled Rupert.

Ahead Billy saw the water glinting as wide and as blue as the Serpentine. On each side huddled the photographers, waiting for the third ducking.

"Go on, go on," Billy whispered, "you're a star, you can do it, we can do it."

He felt The Bull tense. He's probably thinking it's twenty feet deep, thought Billy, Just for a second the horse hesitated. Then suddenly he seemed to relax and put his trust in Billy.

People who were close swear to this day that The Bull closed his eyes. Standing back, he took a mighty leap off his hocks, soaring about six feet in the air, and landed three feet beyond the tape on the other side. People claim it was the longest jump they had ever seen. As he landed the ring erupted in a bellow of cheers: "Go on Billy, you can do it, go on."

He had only the triple to jump and that had caused no problems to anyone. But to the crowd's amazement, Billy suddenly pulled The Bull up, hugging him, patting him, running his hand up and down his mane, and telling him what a king he was.

"You've got one more fence to jump," yelled the photographers.

"You've missed the last fence. Go back. You've still got time," shouted the ring steward who'd reminded him to take his hat off.

"I know," said Billy, and, raising his whip to the judges to show he was retiring, he cantered slowly out of the ring in front of the stunned crowd.

Rupert met him in the collecting ring, absolutely white with rage.

"Bloody maniac, what the fuck are you playing at? You've just chucked away £1,000 or £750. It was only you and me in the jump off."

"I know," said Billy, "but he was so frightened, and he jumped the water so bravely, I thought I'd call it a day, so he could remember how good he'd been."

Rupert looked at him incredulously, "You must be crazy."

Billy slid off The Bull, burying his face in the brown shiny shoulder, hugging him, patting his chest.

"Good boy, clever boy."

Rupert suddenly realized Billy's eyes were filled with tears. Tracey rushed up and, removing the rug which she'd been wearing round her shoulders for warmth, put it over The Bull.

"What happened?" she said in concern. "Did he hurt himself?"

Billy shook his head.

"No," he said in a choked voice, undoing a packet of Polos, all of which he gave to The Bull. "I was so pleased with him, winning didn't seem to matter any more."

Rupert sighed. "I'm afraid Malise Gordon will feel differently," he said. "I hope you realize you've blown you chances of going to Rome."

He put an arm round Billy's shoulders. "All the same, it was a bloody good round. You were up on the clock on me."

Marion came up with Belgravia. "They want you in the ring, Rupert."

As Rupert rode off to collect his first prize, Billy turned to Tracey.

"I'm sorry," he said humbly. "Perhaps I shouldn't have done it."

"Course you should. He's got years ahead. Look how pleased he is."

The next minute they ran slap into Malise who took Billy and The Bull aside.

"That was a bloody silly thing to do," he said.

Billy hung his head.

"I'm sorry, but it's the first time he's ever jumped water and it was such a tremendous jump."

"Well, don't do it again." Malise patted The Bull. "I must say he looks terrific. So don't get carried away and over-jump him in the next three weeks. I'll certainly be needing him for Rome, if not for Madrid."

Billy looked up incredulously.

"What did you say?"

"Don't go blathering it around to everyone, but I'd like you to bring him to Rome." He gave The Bull another pat and stalked off.

"What ever did he say to you?" said Tracey. Then, seeing there were tears in Billy's eyes again, "Did he bawl you out?"

"No, yes, no, I don't know," said Billy in a dazed voice. "I think I'll ride The Bull back to the stable myself."

After winning a major competition, Rupert was usually in a manic mood. But today he felt that Billy had somehow stolen his thunder. Malise Gordon's remarks had niggled him. He resented the implication that Belgravia's win had been a matter of luck. If Billy hadn't pulled The Bull up in that stupid fashion, Rupert would have been able to prove Malise wrong by routing Billy in the jump-off against the clock. Anyway, he'd like to see Malise or anyone else controlling Belgravia. He was further irritated that Billy, despite having chucked away £750 prize money without a thought, was behaving as though Malise had kissed him under the mistletoe.

After the competiition, the heavens opened and journalists and other riders crowded into Rupert's trailer to get out of the rain. But after drinking to Rupert's health in Rupert's champagne out of the huge silver cup he had just won, they were far more interested in talking about The Bull's amazing jump and Billy's retirement. Rupert loved Billy, but he did not like playing second fiddle. He might have been indifferent to public adulation, but he liked it to be there, so he could be indifferent to it.

Leaving them all gossiping together, he took half a bottle of champagne into the shower. As the drumming of raindrops on the trailer roof drowned the noise of the hot water, he was gripped by the lust that always overwhelmed him after a big class. Normally he would have screwed Marion in the back of the van, but he doubted if she would oblige with a quickie with Helen around. Anyway, he didn't want Marion; he was amazed by his violent craving for Helen. He must get her into bed tonight. Only that could restore his *amour propre* and remove the ache from his loins. He'd already told Billy to find somewhere else to shack up for the night as he needed the trailer for Helen and himself. But, although he knew she was hooked on him, he was by no means sure she was going to be a pushover. He'd have to make her jealous.

Helen, in fact, was feeling absolutely miserable. Since he'd won the cup, Rupert had been competely withdrawn. And now all these people were guzzling his drink, talking shop and ignoring her.

Billy (who was still being interviewed by Joanna Battie from the *Chronicle*) could do little more than smile apologetically and shove the bottle in Helen's direction from time to time.

She longed to be able to shower and change before Lady Pringle's party. She'd never met a member of the British aristocracy before and wondered if she ought to curtsey. To hell with it, she thought, helping herself to another drink.

One of the journalists was calling up his newspaper on Rupert's telephone. "I want the news desk," he said.

At this moment Rupert came out of the shower, a dark blue towel around his hips, blond hair dark and otter sleek. Helen felt her stomach give way.

"I want to change, so would you all fuck off," he said coldly. "And get off my telephone, Malcolm."

He ripped the telephone wire out of its socket.

"I was on to the news desk, singing your praises," said Malcolm indignantly.

"I don't care. Beat it."

Grumbling, they all dispersed into the driving rain, running with their coats over their heads, until only Billy and Helen were left. Rupert re-plugged the telephone. It rang immediately. At a nod from Rupert, Billy picked it up. Rupert came over and kissed Helen. He tasted of toothpaste and smelt faintly of eau de cologne. In the safety of Billy's chaperonage, she allowed herself to melt against him, kissing him back until she could hardly stand. Rupert put his hand on her breast.

"I can feel your heart," he said softly, "and it sure is racing."

"Ahem," said Billy. "Sorry to interrupt, but it's Dick Brandon. He wants to drop in for a drink to talk about that horse."

"Hell, oh all right, tell him to come over. Go and have a shower, darling, the water's baking."

"Will it be very fancy tonight?"

"Not particularly."

"Shall I wear pants?"

Rupert's eyes gleamed. That *was* getting somewhere. "Certainly not," he said.

Helen was relieved to find that the shower, unlike the showers at Regina House, gushed out constant hot water. But there was no lock on the door and Helen imagined Rupert barging in, so she showered with frantic haste. She put on a black silk jersey dress with a discreetly low back and pale grey pantyhose that stuck to her legs because they were still wet.

Outside, she found that the double bed had been let down from the wall. Joining the two bench seats, it formed a huge area. On top of the dark blue duvet lounged Rupert wearing a striped shirt and grey trousers.

"Christ, Rupe is a lucky sod," thought Billy. "She gets more stunning by the minute."

11

*A*nother bottle of champagne was consumed and the rain had stopped before they set out for Grania Pringle's party. The setting sun was firing the puddles and bathing the dripping trees with soft pink light.

Rupert and Billy, both already slightly tight and in raging spirits, walked on either side of Helen, putting their inside arms through hers and lifting her over the muddier ground.

"Where my caravan has rested, flowers I leave you on the grass," carolled Billy in a quavering baritione. Mavis ran on ahead, picking up her blond feet like a hackney pony, delicately tiptoeing along the runnels of the puddles.

On the way they stopped to check the horses who were dozing in nine inches of wood shavings. The Bull was looking out of his stall and Mavis scampered up and licked him on the nose. Helen couldn't help noticing how both The Bull and Kitchener snickered with pleasure to see Billy, nudging at his pockets for Polos, but both Belgravia and Mayfair and the younger novice horses flattened their ears and backed off as Rupert approached.

"Got to show them who's boss," said Rupert lightly, but adding that it was getting chilly, he put an extra rug on Belgravia.

"Don't forget the anti-freeze," said Billy, and promptly burst into song again. Then he said, "I'm going to make the most enormous play for Lavinia Greenslade tonight."

"Wavish her in the whododendrons." said Rupert. "Like hell you will. I'll give you a tenner if you get to first base."

The Pringles lived in a large Georgian house behind the Crittleden elm wood, looking over a lake and a cherry orchard whose white blossom was now tinged almond pink by the last rays of the sun.

Helen gave a gasp of pleasure.

"Loveliest of trees, the cherry now," she quoted expansively, "Is hung with bloom along the bough."

"Hung with bloomers," said Rupert, deliberately mishearing her. "Sounds just like Nanny. What were those bloody great things she insisted on wearing winter and summer?"

"Directoire knickers," said Billy.

"That's right. When she hung them on the line on washday we always thought they'd carry the house away like an air balloon."

They both collapsed with laughter.

In order not to be spoilsport, Helen tried to join in.

From the noise issuing from the front door the party was obviously well under way. As Helen changed out of mud-spattered boots into black high-heeled shoes, a handsome blonde, scent rising like incense from the cleavage of her splendid bosom, came out to welcome them.

"Rupert, darling, how lovely to see you."

She gathered him into a braceleted embrace. Over his shoulder her sootily mascaraed eyes appraised the rest of them, affording Helen and Mavis about the same amount of enthusiasm.

That's Grania Pringle, thought Helen. Close up she didn't look very ladylike.

"Must you bring that creature in here?" she said to Billy.

"Love me, love my dog," said Billy unrepentantly. "Sorry, Grania, but she howls if I leave her behind."

"Well, I don't have any difficulty loving you, but I do draw the line at Mavis."

"You haven't met Helen Macaulay," said Rupert, extracting himself from her clutches. "She comes from Florida where tomatoes, she informs me, are the tertiary industry."

"Tomatoes," said Lady Pringle. "How extraordinary. Your mother gave me a marvellous recipe for tomato provençale last time I saw her, Rupe. We all stank of garlic for weeks afterwards, but it was simply delicious." She turned back to Helen, "Are you a horsey girl?"

"No, thank God," said Rupert, "she works in publishing. Have you invited any intellectuals for her to talk to?"

"Only Malise Gordon," said Grania. "He writes books, frightfully clever chap, you must meet him. But he's rather hemmed in by Lavinia Greenslade's parents twying to persuade him to take Lavinia to Wome."

"Must be mad," said Rupert. "She couldn't even stay on the wocking horse at Hawwods."

"Shut up," said Billy, grinning.

"Billy's rather a fan of Lavinia's," explained Rupert. "He's longing to wape her."

"And Lavinia's Daddy will be so cwoss he'll come and wun me over in his Wolls Woyce," said Billy.

Grania screamed with laughter. She was beginning to get on Helen's nerves.

"You boys are awful. Come and have a drink."

"If Greenslade *mère* and *père* are bending Malise's ear, that means Lavinia must be unchaperoned for a second and I'm off," said Billy, and vanished into the crowd in the next room.

"I'm afraid I've hidden the whisky, Rupert," said Grania. "You know what pigs this lot are, but you'll find some in the decanter in the library and there's another bottle in the kitchen cupboard."

Whisky, however, was only for Rupert. Helen had to make do with a glass of very indifferent sparkling wine. The next moment Grania had swept her away from Rupert and thrust her into a loudly arguing group consisting of several show jumpers and Joanna Battie.

"Now then, Joanna," said Grania briskly, "you can't monopolize all these delicious chaps. This is Helen Macaulay, boys; she's frightfully clever and works for a publisher in London. Now I know all of you show-jumpers are writing your autobiographies, so why don't you get her to publish yours? Come along Rupert, my sister's dying to meet you."

And off she swept, leaving Helen scarlet with embarrassment. "Hi again," she mumbled to Joanna. "Are you all writing books?" she asked the ring of men.

"Too busy keeping them," said a man with brushed forward hair and a pale, pinched, disapproving face who was drinking tomato juice. "Joanna's the writer round here, aren't you Jo? Except she gets it all wrong." The man then introduced himself as Brian Driffield.

Helen gritted her teeth. Across the room she could see Rupert hemmed in by women, all braying like Grania. Every few minutes, she noticed, Grania fed in another one and saw to it that Rupert's glass of whisky was constantly topped off. Every so often he looked across and mouthed "All right" to Helen and pride made her nod back.

She was certain Grania had deliberately thrust her into a group of small men. She topped all of them in her high heels. Separated from Rupert, she wanted him to be able to see her as the center of attention, being madly courted, but in this bunch she felt as attractive as a Great Dane among a lot of Jack Russells. She bent her legs slightly.

Now they were discussing who'd bought what horses during the winter and which looked as though they were going to be the most promising novices. One of the German riders, Hans Schmidt, wearing slightly too fitted and too bright blue a blazer, came up, clicked his heels, and kissed Helen's hand.

"Ha, Mees Helen of Troy," he said. "I have heard of you."

Helen turned to him gratefully, but next minute he was caught up with others, discussing some potentially unbeatable Hanoverian mare.

Over in the corner Billy was hanging over the back of an armchair shared by Mavis and Lavinia Greenslade. After her dunking in the water she'd washed and curled her hair. A belted peacock-blue dress showed off her tiny waist. Her small hand rested on Mavis's head. Billy and she'll have very curly-haired children, thought Helen. She wished Rupert would look after her like that. She must pull herself together and try and be more outgoing.

The group had moved on to discussing the best roads to take the next show which was in the West country.

"The A40's much quicker," said Humpty Hamilton.

Suddenly they were joined by an amazing woman of about sixty. Squat, with a discernible black moustache on her upper lip, she was wearing a hairnet, a red flannel nightgown, and bedroom slippers. She looked, thought Helen, not unlike President Nixon in drag.

"Hullo, boys," she said in her deep voice. "If we don't get something to eat soon, you'll have to carry me home." She was just about to move on when she caught sight of Helen, gave her the most enthusiastic glance she'd received all evening and joined the group.

"Who's that?" whispered Helen, holding out her glass to a passing waitress.

"Monica Carlton," whispered Humpty. "Law unto herself, breeds Welsh cobs, always comes to parties in her nightgown, then can get absolutely plastered and doesn't have the hassle of undressing when she gets back to her trailer."

"While that waitress is here, she might as well fill me up too," said Miss Carlton, thrusting her glass at Humpty. "You look familiar," she added to Joanne Battie.

"We met at Olympia last Christmas," said Joanna. "I write for the *Chronicle*."

"Dreadful rag," boomed Miss Carlton, retrieving her full glass. "Still, it comes in useful for wiping up puppies' piddle."

Helen giggled. Scenting enthusiasm, Miss Carlton turned towards her. "You're a lovely little thing," she went on. "We certainly haven't met. I'd have to remembered you." She looked Helen up and down approvingly. "Don't belong to any of these boring little farts, do you? Might have guessed it; too good for any of them."

"I resent that," said Humpty. "The amount of times I've given you a fireman's lift home from parties, Monica."

"Well, perhaps you're better than some. Now, where are you from, my beauty?" she said, turning her full attention on Helen. "Are you going to be here tomorrow?"

"I don't know," stammered Helen.

"Well, if you are, I'll take you for a spin round the countryside in my trap. You'd enjoy that. My two chaps travel at a spanking pace."

And she was off, describing the merits of her two cobs who, it seemed, had won prizes at every show in England. As she talked, her eyes wondered over Helen's body and the hand not clutching a glass squeezed Helen's waist on every possible opportunity. Around them, Helen was vaguely aware of all the show-jumpers' amusement. None of them made a move to rescue her.

"Everyone all right?" It was Grania flitting past.

"Just admiring your antiques," called out Helen desperately. "I'm a real Chippendale freak."

"Oh, you Americans are always mad about old things; you *must* meet my husband. I see you've already met naughty Monica. She patted Miss Carlton's bristly cheek. "Grub's up downstairs, by the way."

"Thank God for that," said Humpty. "I'm starving. Come on everyone."

Rupert caught up with her just as she was entering the dining room. "All right, darling? Sorry to neglect you; I'm in the process of selling a horse."

"I'm fine," said Helen, hardly able to trust herself to speak. "Just fine."

"You must be starving. I'll get you a plate."

But the next moment he'd been lassooed by a large woman in red, asking him what had happened to some horse she'd sold him last year. Next minute the crowds had closed around him. Turning around, Helen saw Miss Carlton bearing down on her with two huge plates of chicken and rice. "Coo-ee," she shouted.

Desperately, Helen fled in the other direction where she could see Billy and Mavis and Lavinia sharing another armchair. She'd just have to play fifth wheel.

"Please," she rushed up to them, "can I talk with you? Rupert's with some woman, and Miss Carlton's on the warpath."

"Of course," Billy got to his feet. "You haven't met Lavinia, have you? Are you having an awful time?"

"I haven't seen much of Rupert," she said, trying to keep the bitterness out of her voice.

"I know. I'm sorry. He's still haggling with Dick Brandon and it's the first real show of the season. No one's seen each other all together for ages, if you know what I mean. They've got a lot to catch up on."

"Oh Billy, darling," said Lavinia, "I've forgotten to put any

Fwench dwessing on my lettuce. Can you get me some, and do see if there's any more of that delicious garlic bwead."

For a second Helen's eyes met Billy's, but both of them managed not to giggle.

"Well, if Monica comes up, you must protect Helen."

"He's weally nice, isn't he?" said Lavinia dreamily. "Mummy doesn't appwove because he's such a fwiend of Wupert's. Mummy thinks Wupert leads Billy astway. Is this your first date with him?"

"No," said Helen, finding herself chewing and chewing on the same piece of chicken, "my second."

"Goodness," said Lavinia, her china blue eyes widening, "that must be a wecord."

Billy came back and they were joined by Humpty and Ivor Braine with a bottle of red wine.

"I say, Helen," said Humpty, "you certainly made a hit with Monica."

"Oh dear," said Helen, blushing.

"Thinks you're the prettiest filly she's seen in years," said Ivor and roared with laughter. "Going to take you in her trap tomorrow, she says."

"Better watch out. She breeds her own welsh cobs; they say she doesn't even need a stallion," said Billy.

"Well at least she's better than Driffield," grumbled Ivor. "Since he's given up booze he's gotten so bad-tempered."

"The big fairy," said Humpty. "Let's chuck him in the lake after dinner."

Next moment Hans Schmidt joined them carrying a plate of trifle.

"Mind my dog," said Billy, as the German prepared to sit heavily on the sleeping Mavis.

Hans rolled his eyes in the air. "Always zee same, zee English, zee dog sleep in zee chair or zee bed, zee husband sleep on the floor. You are American, Fraulein Helen. Are zey not crazy people? Why not come back to Germany wiz me?"

"I say, Hans off," said Humpty. "You'll have to fight a duel with Monica."

"You might also have Rupert to contend with," said Billy, giving Mavis the rest of his chicken.

"No, Rupert is no problem. I can beat him any day of zee week, how do you say it, against zee cock? But Monica, she is different proposition, she is Superman. If Monica stake a claim, I can only love you from afar."

Helen felt suddenly happy. In their clumsy way they were paying attention, accepting her, teasing her as they teased each other.

"Oh blast," said Lavinia, "here come Mummy and Daddy.

They've been talking to Malise an awfully long time. Talk to me like mad, Helen, then perhaps they won't suspect anything. Where did you get that lovely dwess?"

Once again, Helen felt overwhelmed with pleasure, particularly when Driffield suddenly brought her a plate of fruit salad.

"This moment must go down in history," said Humpty. "It is the first time Driffield has even done anything for anyone else in his life. Where's Joanna? She must put it in the *Chronicle*."

"Are you feeling all right, Driffield?" said Billy.

Driffield went scarlet and looked irritated and pleased at the same time. They were all laughing. Then Helen looked across the room and her happiness evaporated. There was Rupert standing by the sofa signing autographs for some girl and talking to a man named Dick Brandon who was sitting down. Beside Brandon sat Grania talking to another woman. Helen watched frozen as she saw Grania slide her hand up and down the inside of Rupert's thigh, those beautiful brown muscular thighs she'd seen earlier. Rupert did not move. Grania carried on. Leaping to her feet and spilling the fruit salad mostly over the carpet and Mavis, Helen fled from the room.

"Darling," yelled Rupert as she passed. He caught up with her in the hall.

"Where are you off to?" Then, seeing her stricken face, "What's the matter," and, taking her hand, he pulled her into a nearby room which turned out to be an office with desks and ledgers and a calendar of spiky-legged race horses on the wall.

Rupert leaned against the door.

"Now, what's the matter? I thought you were having a good time."

Helen backed away until she found herself sitting in a wire basket.

"I'm fed up with all these people treating you like public property," she said.

Rupert shrugged. "Come back to the trailer now and I promise you my undivided attention until morning."

"Like hell! In five minutes someone'll be banging on the door trying to sell you a horse, or asking for your autograph for their great aunt."

Rupert laughed. "Temper, temper. I'm sorry about all these people."

"It was positively obscene, all those women hanging around you like bears around a honey pot."

Rupert felt a surge of triumph. It had worked. She really was jealous.

"I'm fed up with them all, and worst of all Grania; if she's a lady, I'm the Queen of Sheba."

"Don't be silly. No one ever suggested she was. She married a peer and father made his fortune selling laxatives. Do you honestly think I fancy her? She's like some geriatric canary."

"You didn't think so two minutes ago when she was running her hand up and down your thigh."

"I was hemmed in. Autograph hunter to the right, prospective buyer to the left, I couldn't just pry her off. It might have distracted Dick Brandon. Do you realize I've just made twenty grand?"

"Bully for you; you've also just lost a good woman."

He put his head on one side and grinned at her.

"Have I just?" he said mockingly. Then his voice softened. "Don't be such a crosspatch," and he came towards her, pinning her against the table so she couldn't escape.

"Now *you're* hemmed in, and don't you like it?" he said, drawing her towards him until he was holding her tight against his body, which was so smooth and hard it seemed to curve into hers like expensive soap.

For a second she melted; her longing for him was so strong, her relief to be in his arms. Gently he pulled down the shoulder of her dress and began to kiss her along her collar bone.

The other hand glided over her bottom: "Chicken, you *are* wearing pants."

"I am not, I'm wearing a dress."

"What's this then?" he snapped the elastic.

"Panties," said Helen quickly.

Rupert sighed. "There is a language barrier," he said.

"You thought I'd go to a party without underwear?" she said in a shocked voice.

"I hoped you might, seeing as how you're going to take off all your clothes for me later this evening."

"No," said Helen, struggling away. "I'm not going to be another of your passing fancies, just to be spat out like chewing gum when the flavor's gone."

Rupert started to laugh. "Tasty morsel, what an extraordinary phrase. And I don't like chewing gum. Nanny always said it was common."

"Why do you trivialize everything?" wailed Helen. "I just don't want to be rushed."

"Oh really," drawled Rupert. "Would you rather we made a date for the year 2000? Would January 5th be O.K., or would the 6th suit you better? I'm afraid I can't make it the 7th. Perhaps you could check your diary."

"Oh stop it. I just don't believe in jumping into bed with people who don't give a damn about me."

"You haven't given me much chance. You can hardly expect me to swear eternal devotion on the second date."

"I don't," sobbed Helen, "I truly don't. I just don't want to get hurt again. Harold Mountjoy. . ."

"Oh dear, now we're going to be subjected to another sermon on the Mountjoy. Is that it? You only go to bed with married men? If I get married to someone else, then can I fuck you?"

"Please don't use that kind of language."

"What's wrong with the word fuck? That's what we're discussing, aren't we? Stop being so bloody middle class."

"I am middle class."

"Personally I think prick-teaser is a much worse word than fuck. Why the hell did you come down here then?"

"I wanted to see you."

"You can, all of me, come back to the trailer."

"No," screamed Helen. "I'm going back to London."

"How?" asked Rupert.

"Where's the nearest train station?"

"About ten miles away. And, frankly, I'm not going to drive you. Nor am I going to lend you one of my horses, although I suppose you could borrow a bike from one of Grania's children. Or perhaps Monica could whizz you home in her trap."

Helen burst into tears. Running to the door, she ran straight into Grania Pringle.

"Oh there you are, darling. I've been looking for you everywhere, Rupert. Can I borrow you for a sec?"

Helen gave a sob and fled down the hall. She locked herself in the bathroom. Twice someone came and rattled the door, then went away again. The party was still roaring away downstairs and, from the shouts and catcalls, seemed to be spilling out into the garden. She washed her face and combed her hair.

Creeping out into the hall she saw the huge red nightgowned back of Monica Carlton. She was talking to Mrs. Greenslade. Terrified, Helen shot into reverse, taking the nearest door on her left.

*H*elen pushed open the door and found herself in a library where the only gaps in the walls not covered with books were filled with vast family portraits. In one corner on a revolving stand stood a globe of the world with the map of America turned towards her, the states all blurred together and sepia with age. A fire leaping in the grate gave off a sweet, tart smell of apple logs, reminding her of her grandmother's house in the mountains, and filling her with such homesickness that she had to choke back her sobs and blow her nose several times on an overworked tissue.

She was halfway across the room before she realized a man was sitting in an armchair in front of the fire reading.

"I am sorry," she said with a gulp. "I didn't mean to disturb you."

"You're not. I'm hiding."

"From Mrs. Greenslade?"

"Et alia. We weren't introduced this afternoon. Malise Gordon." He put out his hand.

"Helen Macaulay," she mumbled.

"Sit down. I'll get you a glass of Algie's brandy."

"Please don't bother."

He didn't answer and went over to the cocktail tray. He was wearing a pinstripe suit, threadbare but well cut across the shoulders. She noticed the upright, military bearing, the thin mouth, the steely eyes. He was the kind of Englishman you used to see in old war movies, Trevor Howard or Michael Redgrave, who hid any emotion behind a clipped voice, a stiff upper lip and *sang froid*.

"What were you reading?" she asked.

"Rupert Brooke."

"Oh," said Helen in surprise, "how lovely. There's one Rupert Brooke poem I really love. How does it go? 'These laid the world away,'" she began in her soft voice,

"'poured out the red
  Sweet wine of youth; gave up the years to be
  Of work and joy, and that unhoped serene,
  That men call age; and those who would have been
  Their sons, they gave, their immorality.'"

Her voice broke as she was suddenly stabbed with grief at the thought of Harold Mountjoy's child that she had lost.

"It's so beautiful, and so sad," she went on.

For a second the color seemed to drain out of Malise Gordon's face. Then he handed Helen the glass of brandy.

"How extraordinary," he said. "I was just reading that poem. My father was at Rugby with Rupert Brooke."

"What was he like?"

"Oh, awfully nice, according to my mother."

"Your father must have some marvellous stories about him."

"Probably did. Unfortunately he was killed in 1918 in the last advance of the war."

"That's just terrible. You never knew your father. Did you go to Rugby too?"

He nodded.

"I so enjoy the Rugby poets." said Helen. "Walter Savage Landor, Clough, Arnold, they have a deep melancholy about them which I find very appealing. I did the Victorian poets for my Major. I think Matthew Arnold is by far the most interesting."

Seeing her curled up on the sofa having kicked off her shoes, the firelight flickering on her pale face, Malise thought she was the most beautiful girl he had ever seen. Her ankles were so slender, he wondered how they could bear the weight of her body, or her long slender neck the weight of that glorious Titian hair. Quivering with misery, she was like a beech leaf suddenly blown by the gale against a wall; he had the feeling that, at any moment, the gale might whisk her away again. He would like to have painted her, just like that, against the faded gold sofa.

"Where is Rupert?" he asked.

"Being enjoyed by his adoring public. Actually, he's just been 'borrowed' by Lady Pringle."

"She's never been very scrupulous about giving people back."

"She's glamorous, but rather old," said Helen. Then, realizing that Grania must be younger than Malise Gordon, added hastily, "for a woman, I mean—or rather a Lady."

"Hardly," said Malise, echoing Rupert.

"Oh, I know about the laxatives," said Helen, "but all these ancestors?" She waved her hand round the walls.

"All fakes," said Malise, cutting the end off a cigar. "I restore pictures as a sideline. Grania's great-grandmother over there," he pointed to a bosomy Victorian lady, "was actually painted in 1963."

Helen giggled, feeling more cheerful.

"You and Rupert just had a row?"

Helen nodded.

"What about?"

"He wants to go all the way."

Malise raised his eyebrows.

"In England I think you call it the whole hog."

"Ah, yes."

"He's so arrogant. He ignores me all evening, selling some horse, then expects me to go meekly back and spend the night with him. I said I was going back to London, so he told me to find my own way. I just don't know what to do."

"I'll take you. I'm going back to London tonight."

"But I live in Shepherd's Bush; it's way out. Rupert claims he's never heard of it."

"Rupert on occasions can be very affected. It's about a mile from my flat. It couldn't be easier to drop you off."

Cutting through her stammerings of gratitude, he started to ask her about herself, about America, her family, her ambition to be a writer and her job. He even knew her boss:

"Nice chap. Never read a book in his life."

"But no one seems interested in books over here," sighed Helen, picking up the Rupert Brooke. "This is a first edition and they haven't even bothered to cut the pages. I don't understand the British. I mean they have all this marvellous culture on their doorstep and they're quite indifferent to it. They don't even know who's painted their ancestors."

"Unless it's a Gainsborough they're going to sell at Christies for half a million," said Malise. "Then they're fairly sharp."

"That bunch out there can't talk about anything but horses," said Helen bitterly.

"You musn't blame them," said Malise. "For most of the season, which goes on sadly for most of the year now, they're spending twenty-four hours a day with their horses, studying them, schooling, worrying about their health, chauffeuring them from one show to another. That lot you met next door have battled their way to the top against the fiercest competition. And it hasn't been easy. We're in the middle of a recession; prices are rocketing; overheads are colossal. Show-jumping's a very tough competition sport and only a few make it, and unless they keep on winning, they don't survive."

He got up and walked over to the globe and spun it around, pointing to the tiny faded pink shrimp that was England.

"Most of them would never have left the villages they were born in if they hadn't been brilliant horsemen. Now, as a result of this brilliance, they are kings to the public, household names, ambassadors to Great Britian all over the world. Rome today, Madrid tomorrow, New York the day after, constantly on television; yet most of them haven't a college degree between them.

"Often you'll hear the winner of a competition gabbling to his horses all the way around, coaxing him over those huge jumps. Yet, ask him to describe that round in a television interview afterwards and he'll be completely tongue-tied. They're physical people, and they think in physical terms, and they're far more at home with horses than they are with humans, and they're suspicious of any kind of learning, because it makes them feel inadequate. But don't understimate them. Because they lack the gift of tongues, it doesn't mean they don't feel things deeply."

He paused, frowning at her, then smiled:

"I'm sorry, I didn't mean to lecture you. I know what you've been going through today. Ever since I was appointed Chef d'Equipe last year I've been trying to break down these barriers of suspicion. You simply can't apply army discipline and expect them to jump into line. They are all deeply individualistic, chippy, very highly strung. Despite their deadpan exteriors, they get terribly het up before a big class. But once they accept you, you're in for keeps unless you do something very silly."

He thought it was time to change the subject. "Is your firm publishing any decent books this summer?"

And they went back to talking about literature which Malise

enjoyed because she was so adorably pompous and earnest, and because
he could see how she was relaxing and gaining confidence, and just
watching that exquisite face gave him pleasure. He was tempted to ask
her to sit for him.

"I wish I could meet someone like Rupert Brooke," she was saying, "I guess he can be regarded as the most charismatic personality of
his generation."

Malise Gordon winced and put another log on the fire. "I wish
your generation wouldn't so wilfully misuse words."

Helen laughed. "I guess then that Rupert was the most glamorous character of his generation."

"Taking my name in vain," said a voice. Rupert was standing in
the doorway, his face quite expressionless.

"No," said Malise Gordon. "We were discussing another
Rupert—a poet."

"Quite unlike me," said Rupert lightly, "Helen knows I'm an
intellectual dolt, don't you darling?" He turned to Helen, still smiling, but she knew beneath that bland exterior he was angry. "I wondered where you'd got to."

"Talking to me, since Grania—er—borrowed you."

"How nice," said Rupert. "So no doubt you've discussed every
exhibition and play and foreign film on in London. Perhaps you've
even graduated to Henry James."

"We hadn't got around to him yet," said Malise.

"That'll have to wait till next time," said Rupert. "Come and
dance," he added to Helen. It was definitely an order. But before she
could move, a sound of screams, whoops and catcalls rent the air,
drowning the deafening pounding of music. The noise was coming
from outside. Malise drew back the heavy dark green velvet curtains. A
group of men was running through the moonlit cherry orchard carrying something that was wriggling frantically, like a sheep about to be
dipped.

"They're throwing Driffield in the lake," said Rupert.

"Isn't that lake polluted?" asked Helen in worried tones.

Rupert laughed. "It soon will be, if they throw Driffield in," He
took Helen's wrist. "Come on, darling."

Malise took his watch out of his waistcoat pocket.

"We ought to head for home," he said.

"*We?*" asked Rupert, his fingers tightening on Helen's wrist.
Then she said, all in a rush,

"Colonel Gordon's going back to London tonight. He's very
kindly offered me a lift."

"That's ridiculous."

"There isn't anywhere for me to sleep."

"Grania'll give you a bed. Party's hardly got going yet."

"Events would bely that," said Malise, as bellows, guffaws and sounds of splashing issued from the lake. "I hope Driffield doesn't catch cold. It's hardly the weather for midnight bathing. As for Grania putting Helen up, I'm sure every bed and sofa in the house is already heaving with occupants. Shall we go?" he turned to Helen.

She nodded, unable to speak. Part of her longed to stay with Rupert.

She'd never seen anyone so angry. His blue eyes narrowed to slits, his face pale as marble. He picked a white narcissus out of the flower vase, examining the crinkly orange centre.

"I'll drive you back to Vagina House," he said.

"Don't be silly," said Malise crushingly, "you've got classes early tomorrow and you've had far too much to drink. Police always patrol the Worthing-London road at this hour of night. Not worth risking your license. You can't afford to be off the road for a year."

"I am quite capable of driving," said Rupert through gritted teeth.

"And then you'd have to turn around and drive all the way back. Be reasonable."

Rupert turned to Helen. "You really want to go?"

"I guess so."

Looking down, Rupert found he had shredded the narcissus. One petal was left. "She loves me not," he said.

"I'll get my coat," said Helen.

Fleeing from the room, she nearly fell over Monica Carlton, fast asleep in her red nightgown, propped against the gong. On her lap lay a plate of chocolate mousse which Mavis was busy finishing up.

In the room where she'd left her coat and boots a couple were heaving on the bed. It was Billy and Lavinia.

Billy was going to win his tenner, thought Helen. As she grabbed her belongings and let herself out of the room Mavis shot through her feet to join in the fun.

Outside she found Hans Schmidt swaying in front of her.

"Fraulein Helen," he said triumphantly, "come and dance wiz me."

He was just about to drag her off in the direction of the music when Malise and Rupert came out of the library, both looking wintry. To make matters worse, Hans insisted on coming out to the car with them and roaring with laughter when he discovered what was going on.

"You are losing zee touch, Rupert," he kept saying.

"Fuck off," snarled Rupert. Then as Helen got into the car, "Your things are still in the trailer."

"Only my dress," said Helen.

"I'll get Marion to mail it to you," said Rupert and, without even saying goodbye, turned on his heel and stalked back into the house.

"There's absolutely no need to cry," said Malise, as the headlights lit up the grass and the pale green undersides of the spring trees.

"That's definitely thirty-love to you."

"D'you think he'll ever call me again?" said Helen with a sniff.

"Course he will. It's a completely new experience for Rupert not getting his own way. Very good for him."

Malise slipped a Beethoven quintet into the tapedeck. Helen lay back, revelling in the music and thinking how much Rupert would hate it.

"All right?" said Malise.

"Sure. But is it worth it? Me going out with him again, that is if he does call me?"

"Depends if you've reached the stage when you can't not. In which case any advice I give you will be meaningless."

"Explain him to me," pleaded Helen. "All I hear is people gossiping who hardly know him."

"I've known his family for years. Rupert's mother was exquisitely beautiful but deeply silly. She couldn't cope with Rupert at all and abandoned him to a series of nannies, who all spoiled him because they were frightened of him, or felt sorry for him. He learned far too early in life that, by making himself unpleasant, he could get his own way. The only decent relationship he had was with old Nanny Heald, and she was his father's old nanny, so she didn't look after Rupert very long. Rupert's mother, of course, was besotted with Adrian, Rupert's younger brother, who was sweet, curly-haired, plump, easy going, and who, of course, has turned into a roaring pansy.

"As a result I don't think Rupert really likes women. He certainly doesn't trust them. Subconsciously, I think he enjoys kicking them in the teeth, just to pay them back as a sex for letting him down when he was a child. He's bright, though, and enormously talented. Funnily enough, the one thing that might save him could be a good marriage. But she'd have to be a very remarkable girl to take the flak."

As they reached the highway, he put his foot on the accelerator.

"Wouldn't it be easier," he said, "to find a respectable young lawyer or a bright young publisher?"

Helen shrugged. "I guess so, but he is kind of addictive. You take a lot of trouble with all these guys. Have you got kids of your own?"

"We've got a daughter. She events."

"Oh," said Helen, "That's what Mark Phillips does, as opposed to Rupert."

"That's right."

"Any sons?"

"No." There was a pause. Then he said in a measured, deliberately matter-of-fact voice, "We had a boy. He was killed in Northern Ireland last year."

"Oh," said Helen, aghast, "I'm terribly sorry."

"He drove into a booby trap, killed outright, which I suppose was a mercy."

"But not for you," said Helen. "You weren't able to say goodbye."

Oh hell, she said to herself, that's why he was reading that Rupert Brooke poem. And I came barging in with all my problems.

"Were you very close?" she asked.

"Yes, I think so. The awful thing was that I'm not sure he really wanted to go into the army at all. He was really rather a rebel. We had an awful row before he died. He'd gotten some waitress pregnant, felt he ought to marry her. He didn't love her, he just had principles. We tried to dissuade him. His last leave was all rows, my wife in hysterics."

"What happened to the baby?"

"It was a false alarm, which made the whole thing more ironic. Now I wish it hadn't been. At least we'd have something of him left."

They had reached London now. When they got to Regina House he got out as well. A few stars had managed to pierce the russet haze hanging over London. Lit from behind by the street light, there were no lines on Malise's face.

Helen swallowed, took a deep breath to conquer her shyness and stammered, "I always dreamed English men would be just like you, and it's taken me six months in this country to find one," and, putting her hand on his shoulder, she kissed him quickly on the cheek. "Thank you so much for the ride. I do hope we meet again."

"Absolutely no doubt about that," said Malise. "Young Rupert'll be on the war path in no time. But listen to an old campaigner, play it cool, don't let him have it all his own way."

Malise let himself into his Lowndes Street flat and switched off the burglar alarm. It was a cheerless place. His wife had conventional tastes, tending to eau de nil wallpaper, overhead lights, and Sloane Square chintz. She was away in the country, eventing with their daughter. The marriage had not been a success. They had stayed together because of the children, but now there was only Henrietta left. In the drawing room, on an easel standing on a dust sheet, was an oil painting of a hunting scene Malise was restoring. He could finish it in two hours. He didn't feel tired. Instead, he poured himself a glass of brandy and set to work, thinking about that exquisite redhead. She was wasted on Rupert. He was not entirely sure of his motives in whisking her back to London. Was it a desire to put Rupert down, or because he couldn't bear the thought of Rupert sleeping with her tonight, forcing his drunken hamfisted attention on her? For a minute he imagined painting her in his studio, not bothering to turn on the lights as dusk fell, then taking her across to the narrow bed in the corner and making love to her so slowly and gently she wouldn't realize it had been miraculous until it was all over.

He cursed himself for being a fool. He was fifty-two, thirty years her senior, probably a disgusting old man in her eyes. Yet she had stirred him more than any woman he had met for years.

She'd have been perfect for Timmie. He picked up the photograph on the piano. The features that smiled back at him were very like his own, but less grim and austere, more clear-eyed and trusting.

Were Rupert and Billy and Humpty merely Timmie substitutes? Was that why he'd taken the job of Chef d'Equipe? After six months he was surprised, almost indignant, at the pain. Putting the photograph down, he slumped on the sofa, his face in his hands.

As Helen let herself into Regina House the telephone was ringing.

"Shush, shush," she pleaded, and, rushing forward, reached the receiver just before the principal of the hostel, furious and bristling in her hair net.

"It's one o'clock in the morning," she hissed, "I won't have people ringing so late."

But Helen ignored her, hunching herself over the telephone to ward off the outside world. Praying as she'd never prayed before, she put it to her ear.

"Hello," said a slightly slurred voice, "can I speak to Helen Macaulay?"

"Oh yes, you can, this is she."

"Bloody bitch," said Rupert, "waltzing off with the one man in the room I can't afford to punch on the nose."

Helen leaned joyously against the wall, oblivious of the gesticulating crone in the hair net.

"Are you O.K.?" Rupert went on.

"Fine. Where are you?"

"Back in my horrible little trailer—alone. I've got your dress here, like a shed snake-skin. It reeks of your scent. I wish you were here to fill it."

"Oh, so do I," said Helen. Again at a distance, she felt free to come on more strongly.

"Look, I'm on the road this week and most of next. I haven't really got myself together, but I'll ring you towards the end of the week, and I'll try and get up to London a week from Monday or Tuesday."

"Rupert," she pleaded, "I didn't want to go off with Malise. It was just that you seemed so otherwise engaged all evening."

"Trying to make you jealous didn't work, did it? Won't try that again in a hurry."

*F*or the next few weeks Rupert laid siege to Helen, throwing her into total confusion. On the one hand he epitomized everything she disapproved of. He was flip—except about winning—spoiled, a philistine, hedonistic, immoral, and very right-wing—eating South African oranges just to irritate her. The few dates they were able to cram in between Rupert's punishing show jumping schedule and Helen's job always ended in arguments because she wouldn't sleep with him.

On the other hand she had very much taken to heart Malise's remarks about Rupert's disturbed childhood and the possibility that he might be redeemed by a good marriage. Could she be the one to transform this wild boy into the greatest show jumper of his age? There was a strong element of reforming zeal in Helen's character; she had a great urge to do good.

Princess Anne had also just announced her engagement to Mark Phillips and every girl in England was in love with the handsome captain, who looked so macho in his uniform and who, despite being pretty taciturn when interviewed on television, was obviously a genius with horses. Princess Anne looked blissfully happy. And when you considered that Rupert was just as handsome as Captain Phillips, and extremely articulate when interviewed about anything, did it matter, pondered Helen as she tossed and turned in her narrow bed in Regina House, reading A. E. Housman and Matthew Arnold, that she and Rupert couldn't talk about Sartre and Henry James? He was young. He could learn. Malise said he was bright.

Anyway, all this fretting was academic because Rupert hadn't mentioned marriage or said that he loved her. But he called her from all over Europe and managed to snatch an evening with her, however embattled, every couple of weeks. He had invited her to fly out to Lucerne for a big show at the beginning of June, so she had plenty of hope to sustain her.

Meanwhile the IRA were very active in London exploding bombs; everyone was very jumpy, and her mother wrote her endless letters, saying that London sounded very dangerous and why didn't she come home. Helen wrote back saying she was fine and she had a new beau.

Rupert sat with his feet up on the balcony of his hotel bedroom overlooking the Bois de Boulogne. After a class at the Paris show that ended at midnight last night, he was having a late breakfast. Wearing nothing but a bath towel, his bare shoulders already turning dark

brown, he was eating a croissant with apricot jam and trying to read *War and Peace*.

"I can't understand this bloody book," he yelled back into the room. "All the characters have three names."

"So do you," said Billy, coming out on to the balcony, dripping from the bath and also wrapped in a towel. He looked at the spine of the book. "It might help if you started with Volume I, not Volume II."

"Fucking hell," said Rupert, throwing the book into the wooded depths of the Bois and endangering the life of two squirrels, "that's what comes of asking Marion to get books from the library."

"Why are you reading that junk anyway?"

Rupert poured himself another cup of coffee. "Helen says I'm a philistine."

"She thinks you're Jewish?" said Billy. "You don't look it."

"I thought it meant something to do with Sodom and Gomorrah until I looked it up," said Rupert, "but it just means you're pig ignorant, deficient in culture and don't read enough."

"You read *Horse and Hound*," said Billy indignantly, "and your horoscope and the racing results, and Dick Francis."

He bent down to pick up his hairbrush which had dropped on the floor, and winced. "I don't know what they put in those drinks last night but I feel like hell."

"I feel like Helen," said Rupert. "I lost her number and spent all night trying to ring her up. I got hold of the London directory, but I couldn't find Vagina House anywhere."

"Probably looking it up under cunt," said Billy.

Rupert laughed. Then a look of determination came over his face. "I'll show her. I'll write her a really intellectual letter." He got Helen's last letter, all ten pages of it, out of his wallet. "I can hardly understand her—it's so full of long words." He smoothed out the first page. "She hopes we take in the Comedie Francaise and Louvre, and then says that just looking at me elevates her temperature. Christ, what have I landed myself with?"

"Don't forget to put Ms. on the envelope," said Billy.

"Marion even got me a book of quotations," said Rupert, extracting a couple of sheets of hotel writing paper from the leather folder in the chest of drawers. "Now, ought I to address her as Dear or Dearest?"

"You 'Darling' her all the time when you're with her."

"Don't want to compromise myself on paper." Rupert picked up the quote book. "I'll bloody outquote her. Let's look up Helen." He ran his fingers down the index. "Helen, here we are. 'I wish I knew where Helen lies,' Not with me, unfortunately. 'Sweet Helen make me immortal with a kiss.' That's not going nearly far enough."

"Are you going to buy Con O'Hara's chestnut?" asked Billy, who was trying to cut the nails on his right hand.

"Not for the price he's asking. It's got a terrible stop. 'Helen thy beauty is to me.' That sounds more promising." he flipped over the pages to find the reference. "'Helen thy beauty is to me . . . Hyacinth hair.' Hyacinths are pink and blue, not hair-colored. Christ, these poets get away with murder."

"Why don't you just say you're missing her?" asked Billy reasonably.

"That's what she wants to hear. If I could only bed her, I could forget about her."

"Sensible girl," said Billy, "Knows if she gives in she'll lose you. Hardly blame her. You haven't exactly got a reputation for fidelity."

"I have," said Rupert, outraged. "I was faithful to Bianca for at least two months."

"While having Marion on the side."

"Grooms don't count. They simply exist for the recreation of the rider. Helen's not even my type if you analyze her feature by feature. Her clothes are terrible. Like all American women, she always wears trousers, or pants, as she so delightfully calls them, two sizes to big."

"Methinks the laddy does protest too much. Why don't you pack her in?"

"I'm buggered if I'll give up so easily. I've never not got anyone I really wanted."

"What about the nun in Rome?" said Billy, who was lighting a cigarette.

"Nuns don't count."

"Like grooms, I suppose."

"'Sweet Helen, make me immortal with a kiss,'" read Rupert. "'Her lips suck forth my soul. Come, Helen, come, give me my soul again.'"

"That's a bit strong," said Billy. "Who wrote that?"

"Chap called Marlowe. Anyway it's not my soul I want her to suck."

Billy started to laugh and choked on his cigarette.

Rupert looked at him beadily. "Honestly, William, I don't know why you don't empty the entire pack of cigarettes onto a plate and eat them with a knife and fork. You ought to cut down." He returned to the quote book. "This bit's better: 'Thou art fairer than the evening air, clad in the beauty of a thousand stars.' That's very pretty. Reminds me of Penscombe on a clear night." He wrote it down in his flamboyant royal blue scrawl, practically taking up half the page.

"That'll wow her. Anyway, I should be able to pull her in Lucerne. She's coming out for a whole week."

"D'you know what I think?" said Billy.

"Not until you tell me."

"Unlike most of the girls you've run around with, Helen's

serious. She's absolutely crazy about you, genuinely in love, and she won't sleep with you not because she wants to trap you, but because she believes it's wrong. She's a middle-class American girl and they're very very respectable."

"You reckon she's crazy about me?"

"I reckon. Christ, Rupe, you're actually blushing."

Rupert soon recovered.

"What are we going to do this evening?" he asked.

"Go to bed early and no booze, according to Malise. We've got a Nations' Cup tomorrow."

"Sod that," said Rupert, putting his letter into an envelope. "There's a stunning girl who's come out from *The Tatler* to cover the—er—social side of show-jumping. I would *not* mind covering her. I thought we could show her Paris."

"Sure," sighed Billy, "and she's brought a dog of a female photographer with her, and guess who'll end up with her? I wish to Christ Malise would pick Lavinia for Lucerne."

"Not while he's imposing all this Kraut discipline and trying to keep his squad pure, he won't," said Rupert. He looked at his watch. "We've got three hours."

"I'm going to give The Bull a workout."

"Tracey can do that. Let's go and spend an hour at the Louvre."

After a couple of good classes in which they both placed, Rupert and Billy felt like celebrating. Pretending to go to bed dutifully at eleven o'clock, they waited half an hour, then crept down the back stairs, aided by a chambermaid. It was unfortunate that Malise, getting up very early to explore Paris, caught Rupert coming out of the *Tatler* girl's bedroom.

In the Nations' Cup later in the day Rupert jumped appallingly and had over twenty faults in each round. In the evening Malise called him to his room and gave him the worst dressing-down of his life. Rupert was irresponsible, insubordinate, undisciplined, a disruptive influence on the team and a disgrace to his country.

"And what's more," thundered Malise, "I'm not having you back on the team until you've learned to behave yourself."

Helen sat in the London Library checking the quotations in a manuscript on Disraeli before sending it to press. Goodness, authors are inaccurate! This one got everything wrong: changing words, leaving out huge chunks, paraphrasing long paragraphs to suit his argument. All the same, she was glad to be out of the office. Nigel, having recently discovered she was going out with Rupert, was making her life a misery, saying awful things about him all the time. In the middle of a heat wave, the London Library was one of the coolest places in the West End. Helen was always inspired, too, by the air of cloistered quiet and erudition. Those rows and rows of wonderful books, and the photographs of famous writers on the stairs: T. S. Eliot, Harold Nicolson, Rudyard Kipling. One day, if she persevered with her novel, she might join them.

Being a great writer, however, didn't seem nearly as important at the moment as seeing Rupert again. She hadn't heard from him for two weeks, not a telephone call nor a letter. Next Monday she was supposed to be flying out to Lucerne to spend a week with him, and it was already Wednesday. She'd asked for the week off and she knew how Nigel would sneer if she suddenly announced she wouldn't be going after all. And if he did call and she did go, wasn't she compromising herself? Would she be able to hold him off in all that heady Swiss air? God, life was difficult. A bluebottle was bashing abortively against the window pane. At a nearby desk a horrible old man, sweating in a tweed suit, with eyebrows as big as moustaches, was leering at her. Suddenly she hated academics, beastly goaty things with inflated ideas of their own sex appeal, like Nigel and Paul, and even Harold Mount-joy.

She wanted to get out and live her life; she was trapped like that bluebottle.

"Have you any books on copulation?" said a voice.

"I'm afraid I don't work here," said Helen. The she started violently, for there, tanned and gloriously unacademic, stood Rupert.

Her next thought was how unfair it was that he should have caught her with unwashed hair, shiny face and no makeup. The next moment she was in his arms.

"Angel," he said, kissing her, "did you get my letter?"

"No, I left before the mail arrived this morning."

"Sssh," said the man with moustache eyebrows. "People are trying to work."

"Are you coming out for a drink?" said Rupert, only slightly lowering his voice.

"I'd just love it. I've got one more quote to check. I'll be with you in ten minutes."

"I'll wander around," said Rupert.

Helen found the quotation, and was surreptitiously combing her hair and powdering her nose behind a pillar when she heard a loud and unmistakeable voice saying: "Hullo, is that Ladbrokes'? My account number's 8KY85982. I want a tenner each way on Brass Monkey in the two o'clock at Kempton, and twenty each way on Bob Martin in the two-thirty. He's been scratched has he? Change it to Sam the Spy then, but only a tenner each way."

Crimson with embarrassment, Helen longed to disappear into one of the card index drawers. How dared Rupert use the private phone and disturb such a hallowed seat of learning?

"Funny places you work in, he said as they went out into the sunshine. "I bet Nige feels at home in there. Come on let's go to the Ritz."

They sat in the downstairs bar, Helen drinking Buck's Fizz, Rupert drinking whisky.

"Don't go and get tarted up," he said, as she was about to rush off to the powder room. "I like you without makeup sometimes, reminds me of what you might look like in the mornings." He ran the back of his fingers down her cheek. "I've missed you."

"And I've missed *you*. How was Paris?"

"Not brilliant."

"I read the papers. Belgravia was off his form."

"Something like that. I bought you a present. They're all the rage in Paris."

It was an ivory silk shirt that tied under the bust, leaving a bare midriff.

"Oh, it's just gorgeous," said Helen, "I'll never take it off."

"Hm, we'll see about that."

"Such beautiful workmanship," said Helen, examining it in ecstasy. "It'll be marvellous for Lucerne. I've bought lots of clothes. I hope the weather's nice."

Rupert's fingers drummed on the bar. He beckoned for the barman to fill up his glass.

"There isn't going to be any Lucerne."

"Why not?" Helen was unable to hide her disappointment.

"I've been dropped," said Rupert bleakly.

"For a couple of bad rounds in a Nations' Cup? That's insane. It wasn't your fault."

"Well, it was actually. Malise told us to go to bed early. I never sleep before a Nations' Cup, so I took Billy out on the town. We got more smashed than we meant to. Next day, every double was a quadruple."

"Oh Rupert," wailed Helen, "how could you when you were jumping for Great Britain? Surely you could have gone to bed early one night? And to involve Billy. Malise must have been so disappointed."

Rupert had expected sympathy, not reproach bordering on disapproval.

"Poor Malise, who's he going to put in your place?"

"I don't know, and I don't want to talk about it."

Helen could see he was mad, but could not stop herself saying, "I'm so disappointed. I really wanted to go to Lucerne."

"We'll go some other time. Look, I'm off to the Royal Plymouth tomorrow morning. It's an agricultural and flower show with only a couple of big show-jumping classes a day, so I shan't be over-occupied. Why don't you take the rest of the week off and come too?"

Helen was sorely tempted.

"When are you leaving?"

"Now. I want to avoid the rush-hour and I've got a lot to catch up on tonight after three weeks away."

"I can't."

"Why not?"

"I've got an editorial meeting at three o'clock, and I've got to get this manuscript off to production by Friday. I was planning to have everything clear before Lucerne."

"And I screwed up your little jaunt. Well, I'm sorry." He certainly didn't sound it. Helen warmed to her subject.

"And I do have some sort of responsibility towards my colleagues, unlike you. To go and get drunk before a Nations' Cup is just infantile. And Malise said you could be the finest rider in Britain if you took it a bit more seriously."

"Did he indeed?" said Rupert, dangerously quietly. Draining his glass and getting a tenner out of his wallet, he handed it to the barman. "Well, it's no bloody business of yours or his to discuss me."

He got to his feet. Helen realized she'd gone too far.

"Malise and I only want what's best for you," she stammered.

"Sweet of you both," said Rupert. "Have a nice meeting. It's high time you took up with Nige again. You two really suit each other."

And he was gone.

Rupert returned to Penscombe at eight o'clock the following morning, just as Marion and Tracey were loading up the van for the four-hour drive down to Plymouth. He looked terrible and proceeded to complain bitterly about everything in the yard; then went inside to have a bath and emerged twenty minutes later looking very pale but under control.

"What's up with him?" said Tracey.

"Had a tiff with the flame-haired virgin, I should think." said Marion.

Her suspicions were confirmed when Rupert started to quibble about the order in which the horses were being loaded.

"Who are you putting next to The Bull?"

"Macaulay. I thought it would settle him."

"Don't call him that. I'm not having him named after that bitch any more. He can go back to being Satan. Suits him much better."

With Billy driving, Rupert slept most of the way down to Plymouth. The showground was half a mile outside the town. It was a glorious day. Dazzling white clouds scampered across a butcher-blue sky. The horses, clattering down the ramp, sniffed the salty air appreciatively. Once in the trailer which Marion had driven down, Rupert poured himself a large glass of whisky.

"Tears before sunset," said Marion to Tracey.

On their way to the Secretary's tent to declare, Billy was telling Rupert about Ivor Braine's latest ineptitude.

"He was popping out to the shops, and I asked him to get me a packet of Rothman's. I said 'If you can't get Rothman's, get me anything,' and he comes back with a bloody pork pie."

Billy suddenly realized he had lost his audience. Glancing around, he noticed that very still, watchful, predatory expression on Rupert's face, like a leopard who's just sighted a plump impala. Following Rupert's gaze, he saw a suntanned blonde in a pale pink sleeveless dress. Probably in her mid-thirties, she was laying out green baize on a table.

"Gorgeous," murmured Rupert.

"Married," said Billy.

"Good," said Rupert. "I'm fed up with born-again virgins."

The blonde looked up. She was really very pretty, Billy decided.

Rupert smiled at her. She smiled back, half-puzzled, assuming, because his face was so familiar, that they'd met before. On the way back from declaring they found her lugging a huge challenge cup out from the car. Other cups were already lined up on the table.

"Let me," said Rupert, sprinting forward and seizing the cup.

"Oh," she jumped, "how very kind. Oh, it's you." Suddenly, as she realized who Rupert was, she blushed crimson. "I expect you'll win it later."

"Hope so," said Rupert, setting it on the green baize. Then he looked at the inscription. "This one's actually for lightweight hunters. I'm certainly a hunter," he shot her an appraising glance, "when the prey's attractive enough. But not that lightweight."

She seemed to think this was very funny. It was nice to have someone who laughed at his jokes.

"Shouldn't your husband be helping you unload this stuff?" He handed her another cup.

"He's away in Madrid. Some trouble over an order. He had to fly out this morning."

Better and better, thought Rupert, running his eye over the outline of her round, tight buttocks, as she peered into the back of the car.

"Blast," she said. "I picked a big bunch of sweet peas for the table. I must have left them behind."

"They might have slipped under the front seat," said Rupert, affording himself another good view.

"No." She emerged, flushed and ruffled. "Oh dear, and I was

going to tie them up with ribbon, as a bouquet for the Lady Mayor."

"I'll drive back and pick them up for you."

"You can't. It's awfully sweet of you, but it's twenty miles."

Rupert patted her arm. "Leave it with me. I'll find you a bouquet."

He went back to the trailer and had another couple of stiff whiskies and then went on the prowl. He peered into the horticultural tent; it was dark and cool, and smelled like a greenhouse, the huge flower arrangements making a rainbow blaze of color. Up at the far end he could see a group of judges poring over some zucchini, handling them like vast Indian clubs.

It didn't take long to find what he was looking for, a deeply scented bunch of huge, dark crimson roses, with a red first-prize card, and a championship card beside them. Without anyone noticing, he seized the roses and slid out of the tent.

Back at the trailer he put the roses in a pint mug.

"Where did you get those?" demanded Billy, who was pulling on his breeches.

"Never you mind."

"Inconstant Spry," said Billy, as Rupert arranged them, then poured himself another whisky.

"You better lay off that stuff," warned Billy. "And don't get carried away. We've got a class in three-quarters of an hour.

"Here you are," Rupert said to the pretty blonde.

"Oh, they're lovely," she said. "Ena Harkness, I think, and they smell out of this world. You didn't go and buy them?"

Rupert smirked non-committally.

"You did, and you've even beaten the stems so they won't wilt. I've got some ribbon in the glove compartment. I'll hide them in the shade for the moment. I must repay you. Come and have a drink after you've finished your class. My name's Laura Bridges, by the way."

Rumor raced round the collecting rings as the riders warmed up their horses.

"I hear Rupert's been dropped," Driffield said to Billy with some satisfaction.

"Is it twue Malise caught him in bed with a weporter from *The Tatler*?" giggled Lavinia. "He is awful."

"For Christ sake, don't say anything to Rupe," said Billy. "He's not in the sunniest of moods."

"What about that gorgeous redhead?" said Humpty. "I wouldn't mind having a crack at her myself but I gather she doesn't put out."

"Shut up," said Billy. "Here he comes."

As Rupert cantered up on Macaulay, scattering onlookers, Humpty said, "That horse is new."

"Where d'you get him?" sneered Driffield. "At a pig fair?"

Everyone laughed, but the smiles were wiped off their faces half-way through the class when Rupert came in and jumped clear. He had reached that pitch of drunkenness when he rode brilliantly, total lack of inhibition giving an edge to his timing. He also made the discovery that his new horse loved crowds. Used to the adulation of being a troop horse through the streets of London, he really caught fire and became a different animal once he got into the ring and heard applause.

"If you're going to be that good, perhaps it's unfair to call you Satan again," Rupert said as he rode out, patting the horse delightedly.

Over the crowd he could see that the Mayor had arrived, and, surrounded by officials, was progressing towards Laura Bridges' green baize table, no doubt to receive her bouquet. Vaulting off the horse, he handed him to Marion and ran off to have a look.

Harold Maynard, horticultural king of Plymouth, had won the rose championship at the Royal Show for the last six years. Going into the tent, confident he had swept the board for the sixth year, he was thunderstruck to find his prize exhibition missing. He was about to report the loss to the show secretary and get it paged over the loud-speaker, when he suddenly saw his lovingly-tended Ena Harkness roses, now done up with a scarlet bow, being handed over to the Mayor by a curtseying Brownie.

"What very choice blooms," said the Mayor, who prided herself on being good with kiddies. "I've never seen roses so lovely."

With a bellow of rage, Mr. Maynard pushed through the crowd and seized the roses.

"How dare you steal my Ena Harkness?" he shouted.

The Mayor swelled. "They've just been presented to me by this young lady."

"And where did you get them from?" Mr. Maynard turned furiously to the quailing Brownie.

"Mrs. Bridges gave them to me," she whispered.

"And who may she be?" roared Mr. Maynard, brandishing the roses like a policeman's club.

"I'm me," said Laura Bridges, "and don't shout at that poor child."

Rupert arrived to find Laura Bridges, Harold Maynard, a number of Harold's horticultural chums, several show officials and the Lady Mayor in the middle of a full-dress row. The Brownie was bawling her head off.

"What's up?" he said.

"This lady's stolen my Ena Harkness," screamed Mr. Maynard, glaring furiously at Laura Bridges.

Next minute, Rupert had grabbed him by his coat collar. "Don't you speak to her like that, you revolting little shit. She did *not* steal them, and you bloody well apologize."

"Those are my roses, and don't use foul language. I'm calling the police," screamed Mr. Maynard.

"You are bloody not," said Rupert, and picking Mr. Maynard up, he hurled him backwards into the nearby horticultural and produce tent. A second later four of Mr. Maynard's chums had landed on Rupert. Shaking them off, he dived into the tent after Mr. Maynard, picking up a lemon meringue pie and smashing it in Maynard's red roaring face. Turning, Rupert started pelting Mr. Maynard's cronies, who were trying to storm the tent in pursuit, with iced cakes. Next minute a Bakewell tart flew over their heads and hit the Mayor slap in the face. Just as Maynard's buddies were advancing on Rupert, brandishing huge zucchinis, reinforcements arrived in the form of Billy, Humpty, Ivor Braine, and Driffield, who, picking up every vegetable they could find, hurled them at Mr. Maynard's chums. Carrots, turnips, cabbages, rhubarb pies and layer cakes flew through the air.

"What the hell's going on?" Humpty asked Billy. "We've got to jump off in a few minutes."

The next minute a vast Black Forest cake, hurled by Mr. Maynard and meant for Rupert, hit Humpty in the middle of his forehead. Roaring like a little bull, rubbing cream out of his eyes, Humpty jumped on Mr. Maynard, hammering him with his fists. Driffield, behind the safety of a long white table, was lobbing sponge cakes into the mêlée, stopping to take a bite from time to time. Three of the chums had Billy on the ground now and were belaboring him with vast parsnips.

"Stop it you wotten cowards," screamed Lavinia Greenslade. "Thwee against one isn't fair."

Suddenly there was the wail of police cars.

"We better beat it," said Humpty.

"Come on," said Driffield, stuffing pieces of shortcake into his pockets and running towards the tent opening. But they were too late, for the next minute the tent had filled with policemen. Slowly show jumpers and horticulturalists picked themselves off the floor.

"Now, who started this fight?" said the Sergeant, getting out a notebook. "Morning Mr. Lloyd-Foxe, morning Mr. Hamilton."

For a minute no one said anything. Then, from the corner, pulling himself up by the trestle table, Rupert staggered to his feet.

"I did officer," he said, weaving towards them. "But *he* provoked me," and picking up the last prize-winning fruit cake, he flung it at Mr. Maynard. Unfortunately it missed, knocking off a policeman's helmet.

"Book him," said the Sergeant.

"You can't," said Humpty in tones of outrage, wiping chocolate icing out of his hair. "He's got to jump off."

A noisy argument ensued, only ended by the police threatening to book all the show jumpers.

"You can't do that," said the show Secretary in horror. "The public have come specially to see them. They've got two more big classes after the jump off."

"Well, I'm booking him," said the Sergeant, slapping handcuffs on Rupert. "Never heard such abusive language in my life."

On the way out, Laura Bridges stopped him.

"I'm so sorry. It was all my fault."

Rupert grinned. "Don't give it a thought sweetheart."

"I'll get you out of there," promised Billy.

"Not now," said Humpty. "Bail him out after the classes."

In the early evening Billy and Laura Bridges, who'd pulled every string in the book, arrived at the police station. The police agreed to let Rupert go as long as he appeared in Court first thing tomorrow. They found him sobering up in the cells and playing poker with a couple of constables who happened to be show-jumping fans. The story had made the late editions of the evening papers and the show ground and the front of the prison were swarming with press. Rupert was smuggled out the back door.

Despite the heat, he was shivering like a rain-soaked puppy. He looked terrible.

"Better come home with me," said Laura. "Keep the press out of your hair and at least give you a decent night's sleep."

Billy, who wanted to see Lavinia, went back to the show ground.

In the car, Rupert lay back and shut his eyes.

"How d'you feel?"

"Bit of a headache. Don't know if it's hangover or flying zucchini."

"Presumably you did take those roses from the tent?"

"Yes."

She patted his knee. "It was very sweet of you."

"Can I go and have a bath?" he said when he got to her house. "Just to wash the frosting out of my hair."

Downstairs, changed into a sweater and jeans brought by Billy, he found her in the kitchen. She had changed too, into a long pale blue cotton dress with a halter neck, which showed off her beautiful brown shoulders.

"When did you last have something to eat?" she asked.

"I don't remember."

She gave him a glass of ice cold milk. "Do you good," and got a large piece of steak out of the fridge.

"You can put this on your eye if you like, or I can broil it for you."

Rupert decided he was very hungry.

"Two newspapers rang for you while you were in the bath," she said.

"I said you'd gone to stay with friends in Exter."

Rupert went up to her, dropping a kiss on her bare shoulder.

"What a very very nice lady you are."

They ate outside in the dusk, not talking much, but the silence was companionable. Afterwards Rupert wandered into the drawing room and examined the photograph of the man on the desk.

"Your husband?"

She nodded. "My Charlie."

"Good-looking man. You happy with him?"

"Very."

She also had three children. The last had just gone to prep school. "I love them, but you've no idea the bliss after thirteen years of marriage of having the house to ourselves."

She was swinging gently on the hammock seat. Every time she came forward her blonde hair gleamed in the light from the window. Rupert longed to sit down beside her, but thought the swaying back and forth might make him sick.

"Ever get bored with each other sexually?"

She shook her head.

Reaching down, he took her hands, pulling her to her feet. She felt so honey-soft and nicely fleshed. His hand crept round to the back of her neck where the halter was knotted.

"I'm not sure you should," she said. "After that fight you can't be feeling very well."

"I know the one thing that'd make me better."

Slowly he unknotted the halter; her dress slithered to the ground. Underneath she was quite naked. On her warm gold breasts there were delicate blue lines. She had full thighs, and round curving hips. In a few years her body would collapse like a peony. Now it was superb. And, knowing it she gazed back at him without embarrassment.

Rupert pulled her towards him.

"I want to give you the best time in the world," he murmured. "Tell me what turns you on."

At three o'clock in the morning the telephone rang.

Laura stretched out an arm.

"Charlie, darling, where are you?" she asked with simulated sleepiness. "Oh, that's lovely. You can get a flight to Plymouth. I'll come and meet you. What an hour! You must be exhausted. Yes, I've been fine. The show was a great success. Love you, darling, all news when I see you. Bye."

"Where is he?" asked Rupert.

"Madrid. He'll be back in three hours. He's got his own plane."

Rupert laughed. "Good thing he didn't parachute in unexpectedly."

"I'll drive you back to the show ground on the way."

Rupert snuggled up against her splendid breasts. "Come on, we don't want to waste any time."

It was another beautiful day. An innocent cerulean sky hung over the deep green fountain of the oak trees. As they left the house dawn was just breaking. Rupert breathed in a smell of dust, roses and approaching rain.

"Laura," he said, as they reached the outskirts of Plymouth, "I was at a pretty low ebb when I met you yesterday. You've been very good to me. Feel I ought to write Charlie a thank you letter."

"Have you got a steady girlfriend?" she asked. "Apart from the multitudes, I mean."

"We've just packed it in."

"Why?"

"She's too serious-minded, and she won't sleep with me."

Laura braked at the lights. "Must be crazy. You're the eighth wonder of the world."

"I am when I'm with you." He put his hand between her legs, pressing gently. "That must have been one of the most glorious fucks I've ever had. If I wasn't absolutely knackered, I'd drag you back to the trailer for another go. D'you ever get away to London, or Gloucestershire?" he asked, as he drew up at the show ground.

"Sometimes, usually with Charlie."

"There'll be next year's show."

"Charlie'll probably be here next time."

He took her face in his hands and kissed it.

"We'll get together again sometime. I won't forget you in a hurry."

Laura watched him walking across the dew-laden grass, with that lovely athlete's lope, red coat slung over his shoulder. As he turned and waved, she thought it was a very good thing Charlie was coming back. The boy was quite irresistible. Underneath the macho exterior, he was very vulnerable. I could straighten him out, she thought wistfully.

Rupert headed for the stables. He couldn't remember ever having been so tired in his life. Due in Court at nine, he must get a couple of hours of sleep beforehand. He might even get suspended for a year. Malise would be charmed.

No one was up yet. Belgravia and Mayfair were lying down, Macaulay, however, who missed life at the barracks, welcomed any interruption and stuck his head out, nudging Rupert for Polos.

"From what I can remember," Rupert told him, "you jumped

bloody well yesterday. Over the next few months you and I are going to raise two hooves to Malise Gordon, until he can't afford not to have us back in the team. We'd better think up a new name for you; perhaps we ought to call you Bridges."

But as he walked wearily towards the trailer, remembering the day he had bought Macaulay, he felt kneed in the groin with longing for Helen. It must be tiredness that made it hurt so much. His resistance was weakened. Bloody hell, there was a light on in the trailer. Billy might be shacked up with Lavinia.

For a minute he thought he was hallucinating, For there, lying in the double bed, apparently naked, dark blue quilt over her breasts, lay Helen. There were huge circles under her eyes, and she'd obviously been crying. She looked waif-like and terrified. Not a muscle flickered in Rupert's face. For a few seconds he gazed at her.

"How did you get in here?" he said coldly.

Then as the tears began to roll down her cheeks, he went to her and took her in his arms. After Laura's opulent curves she felt as frail as a child.

"Sweetheart, it's all right."

"I'm so sorry," she sobbed. "I know you g-got drunk, and into that dreadful fight, because I was so mean to you the day before yesterday."

"You weren't."

"I was. You were down because you'd been dropped, and all I did was come on sanctimonious and blame you. I should have been supportive and kind. You're right; I am a prude. I love you and it's stupid to pretend I don't."

She was crying really hard now. Rupert got out his handkerchief, then not able to remember whether he'd used it to clean up Laura Bridges, shoved it hastily away and grabbed a handful of Kleenex from the box on the side.

"You can make love to me whenever you want to," she said.

"Only if you want to," he said gently.

"I do," her lip trembled, "more than anything else in the world. I'm just so scared of losing you."

Rupert tightened his grip on her. "You're not going to."

"I want you so much *now*," she pleaded.

Christ, Rupert said to himself, I come home smelling like an old dog fox, and I'm so pooped I can't do a thing.

He took her hands. "I respect you far too much to force you," he said gravely.

"You don't have to be kind. I really want to."

"It wouldn't be right." Then he had a brainwave. "Why don't we get married?"

"Married?"

"Why not? It's different."

"Are you sure you're not still . . . ."

"Drunk? Not at all, I haven't had a drop since yesterday lunchtime."

He pulled off his boots, then collapsed into bed beside her.

Then, removing his signet ring, he slid it on to her wedding-ring finger. "That'll have to do, 'til I get you an engagement ring."

She gazed at it, speechless, turning it over and over.

"You really mean it?"

"Really." He lay back and laughed. "I was so mad at you yesterday morning, I even changed Macaulay's name. Now you'll be changing yours, perhaps I'd better call him Campbell-Black. Christ, you're beautiful. I can fall asleep for the rest of my life counting freckles."

Next minute he was fast asleep.

He was woken by Helen an hour before the Court case.

"My God," he said, startled. Then, seeing his signet ring on her finger, he gradually brought the last few days' events into focus.

"Rupert," she said, frantically twisting the ring round and round, "when you came in this morning you asked me to marry you. But honestly, I'll understand if you've decided against it."

"Darling." As he pulled her into his arms he could smell tooth-paste and clean scented flesh. She must have been up for hours. "Of course I meant it. There's only one obstacle."

"What's that?" she said, going pale.

"I don't remember you accepting."

Helen flung her arms round his neck, kissing him fiercely. "Oh yes please. I'll learn about horses and be a real help in your career."

Rupert looked alarmed. "You don't have to go that far. I must go and have a pee."

When he came back her arms closed round him like a vice. He pushed her away. "Wait. I want to look at you first."

She was so so shy, hanging her head, as he admired the slender arms, the tapering waist, the jutting hip bones. Very gently he stroked the little snow-white breasts.

"They're beautiful," he murmured.

"Too small," she muttered. "I wish I had a wonderful forty-inch bust, the kind like pillows you could fall asleep on."

"Nanny always claimed it was much better for one's back to sleep without pillows," said Rupert. Then, realizing it was not the time for jokes, he kissed each chestnut nipple, waiting for them to stiffen under his tongue.

With a colossal feeling of triumph he pushed her back on to the bed and began to move downwards, kissing her ribs, then her belly.

"No," she gasped, grabbing his head.

Firmly he removed her hands. "Shut up. You're mine now, to do exactly what I like with."

Feeling her quivering with desire, he progressed down to the ginger bush. Then, suddenly, he encountered a sticky, lacquered mass.

"What the bloody hell?" he yelled. "Are you trying to poison me?"

"It's only vaginal deodorant," stammered Helen.

"It is bloody not, sweetheart, you've used hair spray by mistake."

Picking her up screaming, he carried her into the shower and held her under until he washed it off., then threw her dripping onto the bed.

"Now, let's get one thing straight. I like the taste of you. And I don't want it diluted by any damned deodorants. I'm going to wipe out that New England puritanism if it kills me."

In court he got off with a hefty fine. His lawyer, used to Rupert's scrapes, had traveled down overnight. Mr. Campbell-Black, he said, had had a row with his girlfriend the day before, which had upset him so much he'd proceeded to get drunk. Now the row was made up and he and his girlfriend were planning to get married. His client was very sorry. It wouldn't happen again. The press was so captivated by the news that they concentrated on the engagement rather than on the fight.

Later, between classes, Rupert bumped into Laura who introduced her husband, Charlie. Conversation was very amicable. As Charlie moved on to talk to some friends, Laura said in a low voice: "I'm so glad you're getting married to her."

Rupert grinned. "Will you sleep with me again as a wedding present?"

Laura looked reproving. "Your new wife would not like that very much."

"Ah," said Rupert lightly, "she'll have to take me as she finds me, if she can find me."

14

Nearly two years later Helen stood in the middle of her bedroom at Penscombe, trying to decide what she should pack for Rome and then Madrid. She and Rupert would be away for nearly three weeks, so she would need at least three bags to carry all the different clothes for sightseeing, swimming, sunbathing, watching Rupert in the ring, and the string of parties and dinners that always coincided with international shows abroad. She had started a hundred lists, then torn them up.

But even clothes littering every available surface couldn't detract from the beauty of the room with its high ceilings, huge Jacobean four-poster, old rose walls, pale yellow and pink silk striped curtains and fluffy amber carpet. On the dressing table and beside the bed were great bunches of yellow irises. The general effect of a sunrise provided the perfect foil for Helen's coloring. Or so the woman from *House and Garden* had said when she came down to photograph the house and the dramatic changes Helen had made to it.

On the primrose-yellow chaise-longue lay a copy of this month's Vogue with a photographic feature on the new beauties. Most beautiful of them all was undoubtedly the one of Mrs. Rupert Campbell-Black, showing Helen, huge-eyed, swan-necked, her Titian hair spread by a wind machine, Rupert's diamonds gleaming at her ears and throat. Also on the chaise-longue were guide books for Rome and Madrid and Italian and Spanish phrase books. Helen took her trips abroad very seriously, sightseeing and trying to learn as much of the language as possible. Beside the books lay Helen's journal. It was the same dark green notebook she'd had in Regina House. She was ashamed that since she'd married Rupert she'd filled in less than half of it, only sketchily recording events in what had certainly been the most exciting years of her life. But she'd been so busy living, she didn't seem to have had much time to write about it.

She remembered the day Rupert had asked her to marry him. That afternoon she'd been sitting in the stands with Doreen, Humpty Hamilton's even fatter, bouncier wife, mother of two children, watching Rupert and Humpty jump in a class. Helen, delirious with happiness, couldn't resist telling Doreen she was engaged. Doreen Hamilton was delighted at the news and promptly bore Helen off to the bar for a celebration drink, then offered her a word of advice.

"If you marry a show-jumper," she said, "involve yourself in his career as much as possible and travel with him as much as you can, even if it means sleeping in vans or trailers, or frightful pokey foreign hotels. And if he suddenly rings up when you're at home and says come out to Rome, or drive down to Windsor, or to Crittleden, always go—at once, even if you've just washed your hair and put it in curlers, or you've just got the baby to sleep. Because if you don't there'll always be others queuing up to take your place."

Helen, cocooned in the miracle of her new and reciprocated love for Rupert, was unable to imagine him loving anyone else, or any girl standing in line for fat little Humpty, but she had heeded the advice and gone with Rupert to as many shows as possible. Not that this involved much hardship; his trailer was extremely luxurious and when they went abroad Rupert insisted on staying in decent hotels or with rich jet-set friends who seemed to surface, crying welcome, in every country they visited. But it meant she always had to look her best.

Going to the window, with its rampaging frame of scented palest pink clematis, she gazed out across the valley, emerald green from weeks of heavy rain, remembering the first time she'd seen the house. Rupert and Billy, having both won big classes on the final day of the Royal Plymouth, decided to stay on for the closing party that night. After intensive revelry, Rupert suddenly turned to Helen and said, "I think it's time you had a look at my bachelor pad," and they loaded up the van and set out for Gloucestershire, Rupert driving, Helen sitting warm between the two men. "An exquisite sliver of smoked salmon between two very old stale pieces of bread," said Billy.

Helen went to sleep and woke up as they drove up the valley towards Penscombe. The sun had just risen, firing a denim-blue sky with ripples of crimson and reddening the ramparts of cow parsley on either side of the road. Suddenly the horses started pawing the floor boards in the back and Mavis and Badger, who were sprawled across Billy and Helen's knees in the front, woke up and started sniffing excitedly.

"Ouch," said Billy as Badger stepped heavily across him. "Get off my crotch. Why the hell don't you get his claws cut, Rupe?"

Helen looked across the valley at the honey-gold house leaning back against its pale green pillow of beech trees.

"What a beautiful house," she gasped. "I wonder who lives there?"

"You do," said Rupert. "That's your new home," and he and Billy laughed to see how speechless she was.

"I can't believe it," she whispered. "It's a stately home."

"You may not find it quite so splendid when you get close to," said Rupert, slowing down as they entered the village.

He drove straight around to the stables, where Marion and Tracey, who'd driven home the night before with the trailer, were waiting to unload the horses. Leaving Billy to see that everything was all right, Rupert whipped into the house, collected a bottle of champagne and two glasses and took Helen out on the terrace.

Below them lay the valley, drenched white with dew, softened by the palest grey mist rising from the stream that ran along the bottom. On the opposite hillside, the sun was filtering thick biblical rays through the trees, which in turn cast long powder blue shadows down the fields. And, sauntering leisurely down one of these rays like horses of the dawn, came three of Rupert's sleek and beautiful thoroughbreds, two greys and a chestnut. Tossing their heads, they broke into a gallop and careened joyously down the white valley, vanishing into the mist like a dream.

Leaning on the stone balustrade on the edge of the terrace, Helen gazed and gazed. Behind her the wood was filled with bluebells; thrushes were singing out of a clump of white lilacs to the left. Badger, after the long journey, wandered round lifting his leg on bright yellow irises, before happily plunging into the lake.

"It's the most beautiful place I've ever seen," she breathed. "You're not a closet Earl or anything are you? I feel like King Cophetua and the Beggar Maid."

"King who?" asked Rupert, hitching a hip on to the lichened balustrade and edging open the champagne with his thumbs. The cork flew through the air, landing in a rosebush.

"Is it all yours?"

"As far as that village on the right." He filled a glass and handed it to her. "Anyway it's yours too now, darling, every inch of it."

Looking up, she saw he was smiling. Even an eighth of an inch of blonde stubble, and a slight puffiness around the wickedly sparkling eyes, couldn't diminish his beauty.

"Just as every single lovely inch of you belongs to me from now on," he added softly.

Then she realized it was not King Cophetua he reminded her of, but the Devil tempting Christ in the wilderness, saying, "All this will I give you."

Just for a second she had a premonition of unease. Then Rupert chinked his glass against hers and, draining it, said, "Let's go to bed."

"We can't," stammered Helen. "What will everyone think?"

"That we've gone to bed," said Rupert.

Upstairs he pulled the telephone out, but didn't bother to lock the door.

"Well at least I'm going to draw the curtains," said Helen.

"I wouldn't," said Rupert.

But the next minute she'd given the dark red velvet a vigourous tug and the whole thing descended, curtain rail and all, on her head in a huge cloud of dust. In fits of laughter, Rupert extracted her.

"I told you not to pull it!" Then, seeing her hair covered in dust, "My god you've gone white overnight. Must be the effect of saying you'll marry me."

He pulled her into the shade of the great ancient four-poster and began unbuttoning her shirt. Next minute she leaped out of her skin as the door opened. But it was only Badger, dripping from the lake, trying to join them in bed.

"Basket," snapped Rupert. "And you might bloody well shut the door," he added, kicking it shut.

After Rupert had come, with that splendid driving flourish of staccato thrusts which reminded Helen of the end of a Beethoven Symphony, he fell into a deep sleep. Helen, lying in his arms, had been far too tense and nervous of interruption to gain any satisfaction. Looking around the room, she took in the mothy fox masks leering down from the walls, the Munnings and the Lionel Edwards, and surely that was a Stubbs in the corner, very much in need of a cleaning. All the furniture in the room was old and handsome, but it too was desperately in need of a polish, and all the chairs and the sofa needed re-upholstering. There were angora rabbits of dust on top of every picture, and sailors could have climbed up the rigging of cobwebs in the corners. Judging by the color of the bed linen, it hadn't seen a washing machine for weeks. Helen began to itch and edged out of Rupert's embrace. She was touched to see a copy of *War and Peace* by the bedside table. At least he was trying to educate himself. Writing "I love you" in the dust, she wandered off to find a bathroom.

She found the john, and was less than touched to find a framed photograph on the wall of Rupert on a horse, being presented with a cup by Grania Pringle. Along the bottom Grania had written, "So happy to mount you—love Grania. " That's one for the tag sale, thought Helen, taking it off the wall.

The bathroom made her faint. A great white bath, standing six inches off the ground on legs shaped like lion's paws, was ringed with grime. Above it, a geyser on the wall spat out dust and then boiling water. The ceiling was black with dirt, the paint peeling like the surface of the moon. On another beautiful chest of drawers, which was warping from the damp, stood empty bottles, mugs and two ashtrays brimming over with cigarette butts.

Having found a moderately clean towel and spent nearly an hour cleaning the bath, she had one herself, then set out to explore the house, finding bedroom after bedroom filled with wonderful furniture, carpets and china, with many of the beds recently slept in but not made. At the end of the passage she discovered a room which was obviously Billy's. On the chest of drawers was a large photograph in a frame of Lavinia Greenslade, and an even larger one of Mavis. There were glasses by the bed and drink rings on everything.

A bridle hung from the four-poster. There were sporting prints on the wall and more framed photographs of horses jumping, galloping, standing still and being presented with ribbons. On the chest of drawers was a pile of unopened brown envelopes and more overflowing ashtrays.

Going down the splendid staircase with a fat crimson cord attached to the wall to cling on to, she admired a huge painting of Badger in the hall. Underneath it two Jack Russells were having a fight. She found a pair of Springer spaniels shut in the drawing-room.

Every beautiful faded chair and sofa seemed to be upholstered in dog hair. On the wall was a large lighter gap where a painting had been sold. The rest of the walls were covered by, among other things, a Romney, a Gainsborough, a Lely and a Thomas Lawrence. Next door, behind the inevitable wire cages, was the library. No wonder Rupert was indifferent to culture; it was all around him, to be taken for granted. For a minute, looking at more cobwebs and dust, she thought she'd strayed into Miss Havisham's house.

Then she stepped on something that squished.

"Oh my God," she screamed.

"What's the matter?" asked Billy, coming through the door, holding a pile of entry forms and a check book.

"One of those damned dogs has gone to the bathroom in the living room."

She couldn't understand why Billy laughed so much.

"It's not funny," she said. "I've never seen such a dump. Doesn't anyone ever clean it?"

"Suppose it is a bit of a mess," said Billy apologetically, "But we're not in the house much during the day and one never notices dust at night. We had a cleaning woman. She wasn't very good, but Rupert kept her on because she made him laugh. He said she had charisma. Then he came back and found her in one of the spare room beds drinking gin with the electric blanket on. After that even he had to sack her, so we haven't had anyone for about six weeks."

"Doesn't look as though you've had anyone for six years," said Helen, scraping her shoe on the gravel outside.

"Come and look at the stables; that should cheer you up . . . is Rupert asleep?"

Helen nodded.

"I know it's a mess," he said putting his arm through Helen's and leading her across the lawn, passing overgrown shrub roses that hadn't seen a prune in years and pink scented peonies collapsing on the grass. "But we're so frightfully busy, we haven't really got time to organize the house. That's why Rupert desperately needs a wife," he went on, squeezing her hand. "Not only are you the most adorably beautiful girl we've ever seen, but we really need you to look after us."

"Thanks," said Helen. "So in fact I'm really marrying two riders, four grooms, thirty horses, a million dogs and a stable cat. I feel like Milly in *Seven Brides for Seven Brothers*. But it's such a beautiful house, and it could be made so gorgeous."

"And I'm quite confident you'll be able to do it," said Billy happily.

The stables were built of the same honey-colored stones as the house, the doors painted the same dark blue Rupert had chosen on the color chart in church on their first date. Horses looked out in-

quisitively, eager for any diversion. Brick-red geraniums bloomed in
blue and white striped tubs. There was not a blade of straw or a speck
of dust anywhere. In the center was a circle of grass beautifully mown
around an ancient mulberry tree. It was like a toy stable.

Billy introduced her to the junior grooms, Susie and Janis, two
more pretty shapely blondes. Tracey and Marion, having the afternoon
off, had collapsed into bed, Marion, Helen suspected, to cry her eyes
out. She hadn't addressed a word to Rupert since she heard he was
getting married.

Billy led her into the tackroom, which was beautifully kept. The
tack was dark and gleaming, the bits shining, every inch of wall lined
with ribbons. Helen breathed in the smell of leather, linseed oil, saddle soap. "But I don't understand," she said. "It's as neat as a pin here.
Why is the house such a mess?"

Billy shrugged. "This is where the action is. If I were you I'd
move into Macaulay's stall. At least you'd get clean straw and regular
meals."

After a good night's sleep, Helen felt more able to cope. Next day
she went back to Regina House and the office. Despite Rupert's outraged protests, she felt she ought to get things straight and tidy up.
Nigel, when he heard she was going to marry Rupert, was outraged.

The next day the IRA blew up a shop and then a hamburger bar
in London, not far from Helen's office. Rupert was at a show in the
West Country, but he called Helen immediately.

"Are you all right darling? Christ, I've been worried. Look, I'm
not leaving you in London any more. You must move in at once. I can't
bear another night away from you."

"But what am I going to do with myself all day?"

"You can organize my life."

"Can I re-decorate your house?"

"If it makes you happy, as long as you let me burn your entire
wardrobe, and promise never to buy any more clothes without my
coming too. I haven't got a show next Monday," he went on. "I
thought we might get married."

And so they married at Gloucester Registry office. Helen wore a
grey silk suit chosen by Rupert. Billy and Humpty were witnesses.

They set off to Yorkshire on their honeymoon staying in an old
pub in the middle of the moors. On Tuesday Rupert went to look at a
horse which he decided not to buy. On Thursday he said he was fed up
with the pub and knew a better one over the Pennines.

As they were driving there Helen suddenly noticed signs and
advertising posters: "The Great Lancashire Show starts today." She said
idly to Rupert, "Is Billy going?"

"Yes," said Rupert, leaning across and kissing her, "and so are we".

When they reached the show, there were Billy and Tracey looking sheepish, and Marion looking bootfaced, and surprise surprise, Mayfair and Macaulay and Rupert's riding clothes. Helen looked down at the unusual ring of sapphires and emeralds Rupert had given her as an engagement ring and remembered what Doreen Hamilton had said about being a show-jumper's wife, and laughed instead of cried.

"Darling Mother," she wrote home that evening, "I got married on Monday. My husband is Rupert Campbell-Black. He is handsome and very famous in England, because he is a show jumping star. In England it is a big sport, rather like baseball. He has the most beautiful stately home near Shakespeare's birthplace, you will just go crazy about it. It is so old, and the village he lives in looks as though none of the houses have been touched since Elizabeth I's day. I enclose photographs of the house and of Rupert. I know you wanted me to get married in Florida and in white, Mother, but I promise you I am truly truly happy. I never believed being in love could be like this. Rupert had a very traumatic childhood, I'm surprised he hasn't been in analysis for years, but he is very normal. His mother lives in the Bahamas and is on her third husband, and his father is on his fourth wife.

"I haven't met them yet. But soon I'm going to meet Rupert's old Nanny, who is really the person who brought him up, and gave him security. He thinks the world of her. I'm going to make him happy, I love him so much I long to have you meet him, but summer is Rupert's busy time. At the moment he is at shows all week and weekends, but I promise the first weekend we're free, we'll fly over and see you. All my love, Helen."

Rupert's meeting with Helen's parents didn't take place until August and was not a success. The plan was that Helen should fly direct to Florida and Rupert, having looked at some horses in Kentucky, should join her a couple of days later. As it was in the middle of the show-jumping season, Helen explained, he would only be able to stay for the weekend before flying back to Europe for The Dublin Horse Show, where, having been forgiven by Malise, he had been picked to jump for Great Britain, but at least it would give her parents the chance to meet him.

Arriving home, Helen was appalled to find her mother had arranged a full-scale wedding party, with 300 guests to meet Helen's handsome English husband, with even a minister coming to the house to perform a service beforehand in which the happy couple would be blessed.

"I just don't feel you're married after a civil ceremony," said her mother.

"Rupert'll freak out," protested Helen.. "He didn't bring a cutaway, or even a dinner jacket."

"He can always rent one, or borrow one from Daddy," said her mother.

With a growing feeling of apprehension, Helen watched the preparations. In fact, her mother was so well organized that on Friday afternoon she and her four daughters were able to slip down to the beach below their house for a couple of hours' sun. Helen's three sisters, all lithe and beautiful, awaited Rupert's arrival that evening with intense excitement. They were amazed at the change in Helen. She looked beautiful and happy, and so much more self-assured.

"Look at that dreamy yacht," said Esme, the youngest sister, as a big boat with bright blue sails crowded with bronze half-naked people tacked close to the shore. The next moment one of them jumped ship. Wading through the shallows carrying a bag, he turned as he reached the sand and, brandishing it, shouted, "Thanks for the lift."

"Are you ready for that?" said Milly, the second sister, in wonder.

"It's Rupert," gasped Helen.

He was as blond and as brown as a beach boy, and he was wearing nothing except a rather small United States flag draped around his loins.

"Jesus," said Claudia, the third sister.

"Don't swear, Claudia," said Mrs. Macaulay.

Helen hurtled down the beach, flung her arms round Rupert's neck and only just stopped the American flag tumbling to half mast,

"Darling, we were expecting you tonight."

"I got a lift with some chums. I missed you."

On Palm Beach, home of the beautiful, he was still the most beautiful of all.

"Mother, this is Rupert," said Helen.

Mrs. Macaulay was vain enough not be very pleased at having to meet her new son-in-law when she was scarlet and sweating from the heat. She would have preferred to have parted the wisteria on the terrace, welcoming him in a pretty dress, hair newly set, makeup light but perfect. But she knew one must behave like a lady at all time, so she radiated graciousness.

"Hello, Rupert," she said holding out a hand slippery with suntan oil and trying not to look at the American flag. "I'm so pleased to welcome you as our son."

Rupert looked at her handsome, rigid, determined face with the greying red hair. He took in the well-controlled figure in its skirted bathing suit, he noticed the gold cross hanging between the crepey breasts, and he shuddered and vowed he would never let Helen get like that. Mrs. Macaulay averted her eyes and noted Rupert was not wearing a wedding ring. She must find him one before tomorrow.

"I'm not going to rent a morning coat," snapped Rupert, when at last he and Helen were alone in their bedroom, "nor am I going to be blessed by some Yankee poofter. We were married in England; that's enough for me."

"Hush darling, they'll hear you, and it's worth it for all the wedding gifts."

"Not if you look at them closely. Six magazine racks, two sets of monogrammed highball glasses, twelve egg coddlers, a dozen staghorn steak knifes. Jesus! two sets of glasses with polo players on. Polo, I ask you."

"Oh, that was great-aunt Grace. Doesn't know the difference between show jumping and polo. She was doing her best. There's a lovely dinner service, and some beautiful cachepots, and glass. The problem is how to get them all home."

"We'll have to hire a plane and hope it crashes on take-off."

Helen giggled, but she felt defensive about her parents and their friends. If only he would behave for the wedding, she knew everyone would love him. Rupert went moodily to the window.

"God, I miss Badger. Why don't your parents have a dog? I am not going through with this party. If I do I'll wear a suit."

"All right," said Helen soothingly. "But please, darling, be nice just this once. Mother's been arranging it for weeks and Milly's going to sing 'What is Life to Me Without You.' Mother's been coaching her, and Dad's even been out and bought himself an ascot and some striped pants. All you've got to do is show up and be polite."

Rupert behaved pretty well during the service. Later everyone crowded onto the lawn, and after champagne had been drunk for an hour or so, the most distinguished male relation rose to praise Helen, and to welcome Rupert to the family. Afterwards there was a pause.

"Speech, speech," shouted all the relations and friends and the large sprinkling of Dr. Macaulay's patients, flashing their beautifully capped teeth. Rupert, wearing a dark suit and not wearing the wedding ring his father-in-law had pressed on him rose to this feet.

"My heart is in my mouth at this wonderful party," he said charmingly, "but as my Nanny always told me not to talk with my mouth full, I'm not going to say anything, except to thank Dr. and Mrs. Macaulay. I could tell jokes about gay Irish dentists, but I don't think my father-in-law would like that. Thank you all for your wonderful presents," and with that he quietly slid under the table.

"But you weren't even drunk," said Helen, still furious, as their plane took off for England.

"I know, but I was bored. I'm sorry, darling, but the only relations I like are sexual relations."

"And you left Aunt Martha's paintings behind."

"I know," said Rupert. "I was terrified they might frighten the dogs."

Rupert's parents both wrote Helen delightfully vague letters. Rupert's mother sent her a diamond brooch with a broken clasp, Rupert's father a jar of caviar. Both promised they'd be over some-time—probably when they want to borrow money, said Rupert—and wished them every happiness.

Helen's meeting with Rupert's old Nanny was hardly more suc-cessful.

"What shall I wear?" she asked Billy beforehand.

"A skirt with horizontal stripes. All Nanny cares about is good childbearing hips."

Nanny's cottage in Wiltshire had been bought and furnished by the Campbell-Black family. They had filled it with pieces from their various houses which were far too large. It was an obstacle race to get across the sitting room. Nanny, almost the largest thing in the cot-tage, stood six feet tall, with big ears, a whiskery seamed face, a boxer's jaw and shrewd tough little brown eyes like Henry the Seventh. She was wearing a shiny high-necked navy blue dress with a white collar, which gave the impression of a uniform. Although it was a very hot day, she was watching fireworks on a black and white television with the central heating at full blast and none of the windows open. Perhaps years of Campbell-Black austerity and indifference to the cold had unhinged her, thought Helen. Every surface in the room was cov-ered in photographs of babies in long white dresses. The only others were of Rupert at every stage in his career, as a solemn blue-eyed baby, at St. Augustine's, Harrow, in the Blues and, mostly, of him show-jumping. Otherwise there was no evidence that she was remotely pleased to see him.

She hardly thanked him for the half-dozen bottles of her favorite disgustingly sweet sherry that he brought her. Pouring out three glasses, she gave the smallest to Helen.

"Isn't Helen beautiful?" said Rupert.

Nanny looked Helen up and down and sniffed. "Very beautiful face," she said.

"She's got a beautiful figure too," protested Rupert, laughing. "I know you'd have only been happy if I'd married some Flanders mare producing sons every eight months."

Nanny snorted and proceeding to berate Rupert for hell-raising in Paris and getting arrested in Plymouth and getting married without a proper wedding. Rupert accepted it with amazing mildness.

"I'm sorry we didn't ask you to the wedding; we didn't ask any-one. I couldn't face all my step-parents muscling in on the act. And my mother would have been bored to have been reminded of all her weddings."

"Who's your father married to at the moment?" said Nanny.

"Some Italian whore," said Rupert.

"I suppose you had to get married?" asked Nanny.

"No, we did not."

"Whatever happened to Bianca? And Melanie Potter? She was a bonny girl."

"She's married with two daughters. I told you last time."

Nanny knew everything about him, and every round he'd jumped in the last two years.

"Your mother remembered my birthday," she said accusingly. "More than you did, and so did your brother Adrian, I hear he's got a girlfriend."

"Are you sure?" said Rupert in amazement. "I don't think so."

"Never knew he was bi-spectacled," said Nanny.

Helen didn't dare to look at Rupert.

"Helen's American," said Rupert.

"So I read," said Nanny. "Never thought you'd end up with a foreigner. I've read about Watergate," she added, as though Helen were personally responsible.

Helen was so hot she took off her sweater, revealing her slender brown arms and waist.

"Not much of her, is there?" said Nanny. "Anorexic, I suppose."

Finally, when Helen thought she'd faint from the heat, she said, "I think we ought to go, Rupert."

Nanny was not at all upset; she didn't even come to the door. Desperate to get out into the fresh air, Helen made her goodbyes and fled, but not before she heard Nanny say. "Got money, I suppose? Only reason for marrying a foreigner really."

"Isn't she a gem?" said Rupert on the way home.

"She's a Machiavellian old monster," said Helen.

"Doesn't mean it; she's nearly eighty. All the same, I can't wait for you to have a baby so we can get her out of mothballs to look after it."

It became obvious as the months went by, that Rupert and Helen were very different. Rupert was spoiled, easily irritated and didn't flinch from showing it. His ambition in life was to get his own way and beat the hell out of the opposition. He had many moments of frustration and boredom, but very few of self-doubt.

Helen, on the other hand, was riddled with self-doubt. She believed that one should not only constantly strive to improve oneself and others, but that work would indeed keep the devil at bay.

To begin with, therefore, she made heroic efforts to interest herself in horses and learn to ride, but she was too tense and nervous and the horses sensed this, and the way she always caught her breath got on Rupert's nerves. Then Marion (Helen never knew if it were deliberate) put her up on one of the novices, who carted her through a wood with low-hanging branches and finally deposited her on the paved village street. Helen bruised herself very badly and gave up trying to ride.

She still took an interest in show-jumping, however, reading every book on the subject, scanning the papers for horsey news. She even started reading dressage books and discussing her theories with Rupert, trying to show him where he was going wrong. Rupert was not amused. He did not want gratuitous advice that Macaulay might go better in a running martingale, or Belgravia might profit from learning to execute half-passes.

"When all's said and done," he told her sharply, "I'm riding the fucking horse, not you, so belt up."

Helen, during the long, long hours that Rupert and Billy were occupied with the horses, turned her attention to the house and soon had the place swarming with builders, plumbers, electricians and painters.

"You'd think they were building the pyramids," grumbled Rupert.

But gradually the damp and the dry rot were eradicated, and a new heating and wiring system installed. Pastel colors replaced the crimson and dark green wallpapers and old brocades. Tattered silks and motheaten tapestries were replaced with new pale silks, glazed chintz and Laura Ashley flower prints.

Helen also hired a decent cleaning woman, Mrs. Bodkin, paid her well and managed to keep her. Mrs. Bodkin admired Helen. She found her formal and distant and not given to gossip, but she was kind and prepared to pitch in with the cleaning.

She certainly needed to. Rupert and Billy were appallingly untidy. Both dropped their clothes where they took them off, never brought a cup or glass downstairs, and, if they couldn't find a boot jack at the front or back door, trailed mud all over the hall and the new carpet, followed by a convoy of dogs with dirty paws.

The dogs drove Helen bananas, shedding hair, barking, fighting, claiming Rupert's attention. Also, the colder the winter got, and the last one was a killer (you could skate on the water in the john), the more the dogs tried to climb into bed with them. Rupert, who fell asleep the moment his head touched the pillow, didn't notice or mind Badger lying across his feet, or a Springer spaniel curled up in the warmth of his back. Helen, a nervous insomniac, was kept awake night after night, shoving dogs out of bed and listening to them licking themselves or scratching interminably in creaking baskets.

As the winter got colder, and the winds blew off the Bristol Channel, and the central heating was not yet installed, poor Florida-reared Helen developed a hacking cough.

Then there was the matter of the Augustus John drawing. Helen, having spent a long time deciding what would really please Rupert for a wedding present, blew her entire savings on a drawing of a horse by Augustus John.

Rupert was enchanted.

"I think that was the old roué who had an affair with my grand-mother."

He was studying the drawing in great detail when the doorbell rang. It was a man about the washing machine. When Helen returned a quarter of an hour later, Rupert had propped the drawing on the sofa and was looking at it with satisfaction.

"That's better."

"What?" said Helen. Then, noticing a pencil and eraser in Rupert's hand, gave a gasp of horror. "What *have* you done?"

"Re-drawn the near side hock. Chap simply hadn't got it right."

"But you can't tamper with the work of great artists," said Helen, appalled.

"I can, when they can't draw," said Rupert.

Although he insisted on buying her a completely new wardrobe, making her look, he'd told Billy, like the aristocrat she plainly isn't, on the whole he approved of the changes she made to the house. But he drew the line at coasters under glasses to stop the drink rings, and he tore down the net curtains in the first floor bedrooms and the down-stairs john, and he threw all the artificial flowers into the furnace.

Their worst row was triggered off, however, when Helen intro-duced discs into the lavatory tanks to disinfect the water and dye it blue. Rupert came roaring into the kitchen, one of the blue discs in his hand, dripping dye all over the floor.

"What the fuck is this?" he howled. "Have you gone mad?" Are you trying to poison my dogs?"

"They shouldn't drink out of the toilet," screamed Helen. "Then they go and lick everyone. It's disgusting. They've got water bowls in the kitchen, and a water trough, and a lake in the garden. Why do they bother with the toilet?"

"Because they always have. I'm not having you introducing any more of your dinky little American ideas. It'll be chiming doorbells and musical lavatory paper next. I want the water clear by the time I get home, and if any of the dogs get ill, I'll report you to the R.S.P.C.A." And he stormed out, slamming the door. Helen and Mrs. Bodkin removed the blue discs.

Poor Helen tried and failed to impose gracious living on Billy and Rupert. She yearned for candlelit dinners with the silver out, damask napkins, intelligent conversation and lingering over coffee and liqueurs. But, looking after horses, there was no guarantee what time Rupert and Billy would get in. After three attempts at boeuf en croute that turned out tougher than a tramp's boots, Helen found out that all they really wanted was sausages and potatoes, or Irish stew on their knees slumped in front of the television. Usually they argued about the day's events, or some horse they were thinking of buying. Rupert bolted his food, hardly noticing what he ate. Often they were so tired, they fell asleep in the middle.

But however much Rupert fell asleep over the television, he always woke up and wanted sex when they went to bed, and again in the morning, and often popping in, if he wasn't at a show, in the middle of the day, "I'm happy as long as I'm mounted," he used to say, "and you're so compulsively rideable, my darling."

If they ever had a row, Rupert had to make it up because he wanted to sleep with her. If she found his demands excessive, and she frequently didn't achieve orgasm herself, she never said so. But after nearly a year she still grabbed a towel when he walked into the bedroom and found her naked. She always locked the bathroom door, and she only really liked sex if she'd just had a bath. She was embarrassed by his unashamed delight in her body. She still couldn't convince herself that he really enjoyed doing those things he insisted he liked doing long enough to make her come, so she often wriggled away pretending she had, then felt desperately ashamed of faking. But she found him irresistible and she needed his constant assaults as evidence that he still doted on her.

For there was oodles of competition. Wherever they went girls ran after Rupert, clamoring for his autograph, mobbing him at parties, even pulling hairs out of his horses' tails as souvenirs. And although she got kudos, wherever she went, as Rupert's beautiful wife, and there was a great feeling of mutual congratulation in being such a handsome couple, it was Rupert people really wanted to see.

Marion troubled her too. She longed for Rupert to fire her (as he was always threatening to do) but was too tactful to say anything. But she remembered Marion's reddened eyes, particularly after their wedding. She tried to be particularly nice to the girl, giving her a beautiful black cashmere sweater for her birthday which Marion never wore, and was constantly urging Rupert to ask her to dinner and suggesting handsome young men to meet her. Marion politely refused and kept her distance, looking at Helen with the hostile sombre eyes of a prisoner of war.

Billy explained to Helen that Marion was so good with the horses that it was worth while putting up with her moods. Billy was such a comfort. He'd offered to move out when Helen and Rupert got married, but neither of them could bear to lose him. After all, he and Rupert had been inseparable since they were eight, and they were business partners, and Rupert needed someone to talk horses with. As the weeks passed Helen decided Billy was simply the nicest person she'd ever met. He was so kind, funny, easy-going and, she flattered herself, just a tiny bit in love with her. If she had a row with Rupert, Billy stuck up for her. If Rupert was irritable because the horses were going badly, she could dump on Billy, knowing she wasn't being disloyal, because Billy understood Rupert and loved him, at the same time knowing all his faults. It was a happy arrangement. Billy obviously wasn't serious about Lavinia Greenslade and wouldn't get married for years.

Rupert sometimes complained of being gentrified, but he and Billy soon found it a boon that the house was run like clockwork, that their suits and red coats were always back from the cleaners, that there were always enough clean white shirts, ties and breeches, that their boots were mended, that the house was ordered and tidy, that entry forms were filled in, that fan mail was answered, and endless requests to speak or open fêtes and supermarkets were politely refused by return mail.

This left Rupert and Billy to concentrate on the horses, which they certainly needed to do. The three-day week brought rocketing prices. Petrol in particular shot up. There were forecasts of economic doom for years to come and, with the Socialists coming to power, there was more chilling talk of a wealth tax, which would cripple Rupert's income. It became increasingly vital to win and win. And they did. There was no doubt that since Rupert married Helen he and Billy had calmed down, and were now both regular fixtures in the British team.

So now Helen, on the eve of leaving for Rome and Madrid, gazed out on the green valley. She was really looking forward to the trip. For the first time she felt she could leave the house without the workmen doing something frightful. She loved going abroad, picking up antiques and pieces for the house, visiting galleries and museums, learning new languages. Also it meant a vacation from all the dogs in the bed, and as Rupert was far less famous abroad they weren't constantly beseiged by groupies (or 'Rupies' as Billy called them). And Malise Gordon was there. She always enjoyed spending time with him. They often went to galleries and museums together when they were away, making Rupert slightly edgy. He was jealous of something that Malise and Helen shared, that he couldn't give her, so he continually mocked it.

Helen turned back to all the beautiful clothes Rupert had bought her. She realized above all that it was important to him that other men admired and fancied her, but like Meissen china in a glass case, the admiration had to be kept at a distance. Last year in Rotterdam, when a rather inebriated Dutchman asked her to dance in a nightclub, it had only been Billy's half nelson that had stooped Rupert from knocking him across the room. A slightly more persistent admirer at one of the Dublin Horse Show balls had been less lucky and ended up with a fractured jaw.

15

Jake Lovell rode across his fields at a leisurely pace. When he came to a hedge or wall he popped the grey gelding over it, but he was in no hurry. He'd already worked all the novice horses that morning, and the Grade A horses were having a rest after a three-day show. Besides it was a beautiful day and the cuckoo was yelling its head off in the hazel wood nearby. Wolf, Jake's shaggy adoring lurcher, was chasing rabbits but never letting his master out of his sight for very long, and Jake wanted to think.

It was nearly five years since he had married Tory and Granny Maxwell had given them the Old Mill at Withrington. And although they had been years of hard work and struggle, Jake knew they had been the happiest in his life. The Mill had been in a delapidated state when they moved in, but gradually he and Tory had painted the rooms, and gradually they had scraped together enough money to pull down the old stables and build new ones, so they now kept a dozen horses.

There had been terrible setbacks. Two Mays ago he'd been selected to ride for Great Britain for the first time, but the day he was due to leave Africa stepped on a rusty nail, which put her out of action for several months. One of the young novices, a really promising grey thoroughbred, had jumped out of its field, escaped on to the motorway, been hit by a truck and had to be destroyed. Then, as Tory had inherited the bulk of her capital by then and Africa was out of action, Jake spent rather too much money on a top-class horse to fill the gap, which had broken its leg and had to be put down at the first show he took it to.

Things had not gone according to plan in other directions either. At the start of their marriage, Tory had worked as a secretary to a local solicitor, her salary being the main thing that had saved her and Jake and the horses from starvation. For months they seemed to live on pork pies and baked beans bought with her luncheon vouchers. But within a year and a quarter she was pregnant, and in July of the following year she produced a son. They called him Isa, short for Isaac, after Jake's lost gypsy father, and Jake, who'd been very apprehensive, not particularly liking children and feeling most unready to be a father, found himself utterly besotted with the child. Perhaps it was because little Isa was his only blood relation, or because the boy was so beautiful, with his huge black eyes and white blonde hair, or because he was so sturdy and merry and placid and seemed to positively thrive in a cold damp house, and being permanently carted from show to show in a carrycot.

Jake was also pleasantly surprised to find how easy it was to be married to Tory, who was the ideal show-jumper's wife. She never made him feel guilty if he were late back from shows or up all night tending a sick horse. When he came in she always provided him with good food, a sympathetic ear, and sex if he wanted, but was never offended if he didn't. She understood his terrible nerves before big classes, and why often, if he were sorting out his relationship with a particular horse, he could be withdrawn and taciturn. She coped with all the paperwork, paying bills and sending off entry forms. When they married, she'd been terrified of horses, but Jake had helped her to overcome this, and although she'd never be much good as a rider, she soon picked up the rudiments of feeding and looking after a string, fussing over each animal as though she was its mother. So all the horses were happy and the stable ran like clockwork even when he was away.

She was also passionately proud of everything he did and nailed up every new ribbon with joy; a whole wall of the tackroom was now covered. Most important of all, she understood that his character was like a stray dog's rescued from Battersea Dog's Home. Constantly moving from one show to another satisfied some nomadic gypsy wanderlust in his blood, but he only felt safe doing this knowing he had a safe, loving home to come back to. Like many wanderers, only by going away could he test that home would still be there when he returned.

Two years ago he had had a special stroke of luck. He had gone to a horse sale in Warwick, not one of his favorite pastimes; sales always reminded him of the orphanage. All those horses, bewildered, frightened, displaced, often coming from wealthy homes or, after years of hard work, to be sold to the butcher, or to people who didn't know how to look after them, or who would abuse their willing natures.

The mare he'd been tipped off about went for more than he could afford, but suddenly he heard a horse squealing his head off. Get me out of this horrible place, he seemed to be saying. Wandering down the horse lines, Jake found a half-starved, dirty, flea-bitten grey gelding, standing about 16.3, with a wall eye, big feet, a coarse head, huge ears flapping like a mule, and ribs sticking out like a plate rack. He had to be the ugliest horse Jake had ever seen. He was obviously starving. But Jake looked at his teeth and was surprised to see the horse was only six or seven. He looked a hundred, but his legs were clean and strong, and when he was petted and scratched behind the ear, he stopped screaming and accepted Jake's attention with obvious pleasure.

"What's his history?" Jake asked the dealer who trotted him up and down.

"Some old nutter bought him as a pet for his wife, who had one foot in the grave anyway. They called him Sailor. One day the horse stopped suddenly in the yard and she fell off, catching her head on the mounting block, and croaked two days later. The old nutter was heartbroken, but too mean to have the horse put down, so he left him in a tiny paddock, virtually starving him to death.

"Finally the old nutter croaked himself. When they discovered his body they found the horse. The only thing he had to drink out of was a rusty bucket, with two inches of rainwater filled with dead wasps. As you can see, it's a case for R.S.P.C.A. but you can't prosecute a dead man."

For a second, Jake felt choked with rage.

"Poor old sod," he said stroking the ugly grey head, "had a bad time, have you?"

He had to pay £150 in order to outbid the horse-meat dealers, which he could ill afford at the time. Once home, he stuffed Sailor full of food and, during the day, turned him out with Africa. After three months he took him hunting and had one of the best days of his life. Sailor still looked like nothing on earth—it was always impossible to get any condition on him—but he could jump anything you put him at and keep going all day. And Jake experienced a surge of excitement he had not felt since he first jumped Africa.

Jake had had many arguments with Granny Maxwell because he refused to overface his horses and did not bring them on fast enough. But there was no need to bring Sailor on slowly. By the end of the next season he had placed in every class he entered and had upgraded himself to Grade A. The Northern show-jumping fraternity, who were a hard-boiled bunch, not easily impressed, laughed at Sailor when they first saw such an extraordinarily unprepossessing horse, but stayed to pray once they had seen him jump.

He was also the cleverest horse in the stable and, when he was bored, would unbolt his stable door and wander over to the house, putting his flea-bitten head in through the kitchen window, hoping for an apple or a piece of chocolate but just as happy with a petting. He never strayed beyond the yard. It was as though he couldn't believe his luck in having found a good home. He was also the gentlest horse, devoted to Africa, and Wolf the lurcher, and Tory's Jack Russell, Horace, who could lead him in from the fields tugging at his halter rope with his teeth. He was also a marvellous babysitter. Tory found she could leave baby Isa in Sailor's stall playing around the manger, clinging to Sailor's legs and often pulling himself up by the horse's rather skimpy tail. If he fell over and cried, Sailor would nudge him gently, breathing on him, until he laughed and got up again.

Today, on this ravishing day, Jake was riding Sailor around the fields just to check that all the fences were safe. He had a feeling things were at last coming good for him. Africa was fit again and jumping like a kangaroo. She had won two big classes in Birmingham last week, even beating the mighty Humpty Hamilton against the clock, and Sailor had placed three times. It had helped this year that he could at last afford to take on a full-time groom, a girl named Tanya, who was as good at riding as stable management. The idea was that Jake could now concentrate on schooling and competing, but he still found it hard to delegate, believing that no one understood or could look after his horses as he could.

Over the last four years he had traveled the Northern and Midland circuits, never venturing South because he hated staying away from home for the night, and because some niggling fear told him that he and his horses weren't yet quite ready to beat the hell out of Rupert Campbell-Black.

Rupert had never been far from his thoughts, however. He had watched him obsessively whenever shows were televised, and read every word about him in the papers, as one outrageous scrape followed another. In fact Jake suspected he had only been picked for the team the May before last (when he'd had to drop out because Africa was unfit) because Rupert and Billy had both been dropped for hell-raising in Paris, and then later getting into some frightful fight at the Royal Plymouth.

Soon afterwards, as though realizing he'd gone too far, Rupert had suddenly married a gorgeous American redhead who seemed to have had a dramatic effect on his behavior. Gone were the days of womanizing and wild drinking. Rupert appeared less and less often in the gossip pages and more and more on the sports pages, cleaning up at shows all over Europe, appearing as a regular fixture in the British team, and even being mentioned as a probable for the Olympic Games next year. Jake gnashed his teeth. He had a feeling that Rupert was pulling further and further away from him, that he would never catch up now.

Still, it was too nice a day to worry about Rupert. Ahead, flanked by pale green willows, he could see the Old Mill, its ancient red brick weathered to strawberry roan, tossing its shaggy mane of white roses, which no one had time to prune. It was a long low house. He, Tory, little Isa and Tanya the groom lived on the left-hand side. The right contained the old mill, with its store rooms and huge stone wheel which fifty years ago had been turned by a fast-rushing stream that still hurtled under the house, through the garden and eventually into the River Trent.

Behind the house, hidden from view, were the stables, and beyond that a ring of oak trees with huge acid-green lichened trunks, which protected them all from the vicious North winds.

Jake's ambition this year was to build an indoor ring. There were too many days in winter, with the dark mornings and long nights, or when it was frosty, wet or slippery underfoot, when it was impossible to work the horses outside. He'd eaten into Tory's capital so much, he'd have to get a loan from the bank. But ever since the three-day week and the socialists coming to power and the economic gloom, the banks had clamped down and were only lending money at colossal interest. He didn't want to sell more shares at the moment, as they'd have nothing to fall back on and nothing to secure any further borrowing they might need.

He was so deep in thought that it was a few seconds before he realized that Sailor had pricked up his lop ears, Wolf was bounding forward, and Tory was shouting from the house. Popping Sailor across the stream, he cantered up the lawn, which was more of a hayfield these days, as no one had time to mow it.

"Telephone," she yelled. "Hurry!"

She was standing by the willow tree, which permanently dangled its leaves in the stream. Eight months pregnant with their second child, she was about as fat now as she had been when he first met her. Her face was pink with excitement.

"Who is it?" he said, sliding off Sailor.

"Malise Gordon, ringing from London. I'll take Sailor."

Jake handed her the horse and ran into the house as fast as his limp would allow. He mustn't sound too eager. Probably Malise only wished to say he was coming North to watch Jake at some show. The telephone was in the hall, which Tory had painted duck-egg blue last February. Damp patches were already showing through. One day they might be able to afford a carpet.

"Hello," he said curtly.

"Hello, how are you?" said Malise in his brisk military tones, not stopping for an answer. "You had a good show at Birmingham, I hear. Glad Africa got her form back. Humpty was very irritated to be beaten, but very impressed how she was going."

"Thanks," said Jake, feeling Wolf curl up around his feet as he leafed through the neatly typed envelopes on the hall table. Tory had been busy sending off entry forms to the various show secretaries.

"You can't hide your light under a bushel forever," said Malise in a slighty hearty voice. "You ought to try some shows further South."

"I thought of having a crack at Crittleden in July, and perhaps Wembley in October."

Malise laughed. "I was thinking of *much* further South. How about coming to Madrid?"

It was a moment Jake had dreamed about for so long. His throat went dry and he had to clutch on to the rickety table for support.

"Madrid," he croaked.

"Yep, sorry it's such short notice. Ivor Braine's horses have all got the cough, and Driffield broke his arm over the weekend, so I thought you might like to go in his place."

Jake didn't answer, his mind careering from terror to elation.

"Hello, are you still there?"

"Just," said Jake. "I'd like to." Then, as an afterthought, "Thanks very much."

"The rest of the team'll be coming on from Rome," said Malise, "except for Humpty who's flying from Heathrow and sending his groom down by train with the horses. It's a bugger of a journey, takes three or four days, so I suggest you put your groom and your horses in Humpty's van. His groom, Bridie, can collect yours on the way and they can travel as far as Dunkirk together, then take the train the rest of the way. You can fly out to Madrid with Humpty," he went on, "and meet the horses there. No point both you and the horses arriving exhausted."

"No," said Jake sharply, "I want to travel with the horses."

"I really wouldn't recommend it."

"Anyway I can't spare my groom. Tory's about to have a baby and she can't look after the place on her own."

"Are you sure? You really won't enjoy that trip."

"I don't mind." Jake had never been abroad and the thought of letting his precious horses out of sight for a second on foreign soil filled him with horror.

"And you'll bring Valerian and Africa?" asked Malise.

"Valerian's been a bit pulled down by some virus. I've got a much better horse. He was placed in three classes at Birmingham."

"O.K.," said Malise, "you know your own horses. If we need you for the Nations' Cup you can jump Africa."

In the kitchen Jake found Tory talking to Wolf who was sitting on the kitchen table. She was also opening a bottle of champagne.

"Where did that come from?" he said, shocked at such extravagance.

"Granny Maxwell gave it to me just before she died. She said I wasn't to open it until you were selected. She had faith in you too. Oh Jake," she put down the bottle and flung her arms around his neck and he could feel the tears on her cheeks. "I'm so so proud of you."

In the week that followed Jake was almost too busy to be nervous. Although Tory repeatedly nagged him, he'd never bothered to get a passport, thinking it was tempting providence until he was actually picked. Now all sorts of strings had to be pulled by the B. S. J. A. and trips taken to the passport office. Africa and Sailor had to have passports too, which included a drawing of the horse. However many times Jake re-drew Sailor, he still looked like an old billy goat. They also had to have blood tests, and their health papers had to be stamped. Then shows had to be cancelled and Jake and the horses had to be packed for. With a four-day journey there and possibly back, he would be away for nearly three weeks. He would like to have rung Humpty and asked his advice about foreign customs and what to wear, but he was too proud. Meanwhile the village dressmaker sat up late every night making him a red coat.

He tried the coat on the night before he left, wishing he was taller and broader in the shoulders. At least he didn't have a turkey red face that clashed with it, like Humpty.

Tory was putting Isa to bed. Wolf, the lurcher, sat on his curved tail, shivering in Jake's suitcase, the picture of desolation. Normally he went with Jake to every show, but some sixth sense told him he was going to be left behind tomorrow.

Next minute Isa wandered in, in blue pajamas and a policeman's helmet on his head which he wore all day and in bed at night. His left wrist was handcuffed to a large teddy bear. He was at the age when he kept acquiring new words, and copied everything Jake and Tory said.

"Daddy going hunting," he announced, seeing the red coat.

"Not exactly," said Jake. "I'm going away for a few days, to Spain and you must take care of Mummy."

"Will you be back before Mummy gets her baby out? Will you bring me a present?"

Jake turned so he could look at the coat from the back. He wished he knew how hot it would be in Spain.

"What d'you want?"

"Nuvver truck."

"You've got about ten," said Jake. "For Christ's sake don't touch that briefcase."

"What's this?"

"Spanish money."

"Where is Pain?" said Isa, ignoring Jake and spreading out the notes.

"Over the channel. I said *leave* that case alone."

Normally he hated snapping at Isa, but last-minute nerves were getting to him.

"Daddy have a whicksey," said Isa, who regarded a stiff drink as the cure to all grown-up ills, "and get pissed up."

"I said *go* and find Mummy." Jake retrieved the notes and the health papers.

"Mummy's crying," said Isa.

Jake felt a burst of irritation. He felt guilty about leaving her, but what else could he do? She wanted him to get on; what the hell was she crying for? He found her in the bathroom bending her bulk down slowly to retrieve plastic ducks, boats and sodden towels. Her swollen ankles were spilling over her slip-on shoes. She had had those shoes since he married her.

"What's the matter?" he snapped.

"Nothing." She concentrated on squeezing out a washcloth.

"What the hell's the matter? I can't help going." His guilt at leaving her made him speak more harshly than he'd meant to. "It's not going to be much fun for me; fifteen hundred miles on the train in the blazing heat with two horses."

It was part of the bargain of their marriage that she never clung to him or betrayed her desperate dependency.

"I'm sorry," she mumbled. "I'm over the moon that you're going. I don't know what's the matter with me."

Her lip trembled. Jake put his arm round her, feeling the solid shape of the baby inside her, pressing against him. For a second she clung to him, lowering her guard.

"It's just that I'm going to miss you so much."

"It'll go very quickly," he said. "I'll ring you the moment I get to Madrid."

Next minute they heard a terrific banging, and Wolf barking. Looking out, they saw Tanya, obviously having to stand on a bucket, peering out of the tiny high tackroom window.

"Will someone come and rescue me? Your wretched son's just locked me in."

And yet next morning, getting up at first light, with the rising sun touching the willows and the milk-white fields, the Mill looked so beautiful that Jake wondered how he could bear to leave it. Tanya had already been up for two hours getting the horses ready. She had even borrowed two milk churns from a nearby dairy to carry water, in case Jake ran out on the train journey.

"I'm sorry you're not coming," he said.

"You can take me next time."

"If there is a next time," said Jake, lighting a cigarette.

"Nervous?"

Jake nodded.

Africa heard Humpty's van before Jake did. She had changed over the years, growing stronger, more muscular, and filling out behind the saddle. She was more demanding and less sociable, and could be moody and impatient, especially if she was in season. Now, aware that something was up, she darted to her half-door to look out, eyes bold, ears flattened, pawing at her straw, stamping with her forelegs. The other horses put their heads out of the stalls, ready to be jealous because they were not included in the trip. Only Sailor stayed in his stall, calmly finishing off his feed. Sailor calmed Africa down. But Jake was her big love.

Both Tory and Tanya felt a stab of relief that Bridie, Humpty's groom, wasn't all that pretty. Plump, with mouse brown curls, she had greasy skin and a large bottom.

"Just my luck to be stuck for four days with that," thought Jake. Inside the van they could see Humpty's three horses, with the resplendent Porky Boy on the outside, coat gleaming. By comparison, Sailor, shuffling up the ramp, looked as though he were going on his last journey. At least Africa, in her dark beauty, whinnying and prancing up the ramp, slightly redeemed the stable.

"Well I don't think you need have any worries about Jake getting off with that," said Tanya as the van heaved its way over the bridge, rattling against the willow branches.

"The forecast's awful," Bridie told Jake cheerfully. "I'm afraid it's going to be a terrible crossing."

In fact the whole journey was a nightmare. A storm blew up in mid-channel and the boat nearly turned back. Jake spent the entire journey trying to calm the horses. The crossing took so long they missed the train at Dunkirk and had to wait twelve hours before they caught another one, which took them to the Spanish border quite smoothly. There they got into trouble with both French and Spanish customs, who took exception to Jake's emergency passport. Jake, speaking no languages at all, and Bridie, who only had a few words of Spanish, found themselves shunted off to the side for a day and a half, fast running out of food. Bridie, who was quite used to such delays, whiled the time away reading novels and flirting with some handsome customs officials who didn't seem remotely put off by her size.

Jake nearly went crazy, pacing up and down, smoking pack after pack of cigarettes, trying to telephone England.

"If you're abroad, there are always hold-ups," said Bridie philosophically. "You'll just have to get used to them." He's as uptight as a tick that one, she thought. Any minute he'll snap.

At last Jake reached Tory, who managed to trace Malise in Rome, who pulled more strings, and eventually arranged for them to take the next Madrid-bound train. In the ensuing wait Jake started reading novels too, not realizing that only now was the real nightmare about to begin.

Their transport turned out to be cattle cars, with Humpty's three horses and Bridie in one, and Jake, Africa and Sailor in another. There were no windows, just air vents and a sliding door. "Porky Boy won't like this," said Bridie. "He's used to a light in his stall."

After lots of shunting and banging back and forth, until every bone in Jake's body was jarred, they were then hitched to a Spanish passenger express. Once the train started there was no communication with the outside world. No one to talk to, just total blackness and occasional flashes as stations flew past. The whiplash effect was appalling.

As they slowed down outside a big station, Jake heard crashing and banging and a scream from Bridie's cattle car next door.

"Porky Boy's gone off his head," she yelled. "I can't hold him still enough to dope him."

Risking his life and eternal abandonment in the middle of Spain, Jake leaped out of his car and ran along to Bridie's, only making it just in time, and narrowly avoiding being crashed to death by a maddened Porky Boy. Somehow, with the flashlight between his teeth, he managed to fill the syringe, jab it into the terrified animal and cling on, soothing and talking to him, until he calmed down.

Bridie was tearful in gratitude. Frantic about Africa and Sailor, Jake then had to wait until the milky white light of morning revealed rolling hills, dotted with olive trees, flattening out to the dusty leathery plains round Madrid, before the train slowed down enough for him to get back to them. Africa had a cut knee where she had fallen down, both were obviously saddened by his absence, but delighted to welcome him back. They swayed from side to side keeping their footing.

When they finally reached Madrid, the cattle cars were pulled into the passenger station. Jake and Bridie found the platform packed with chic Spanish commuters, soberly dressed for the office, and looking with astonishment at two such travel-worn wrecks and their dusty shabby horses.

After such a hellish journey, Jake was prepared for hen coops in which to stable the horses. But the Madrid show ground turned out to be the last word in luxury, with a sumptuous club house, swimming pools and squash courts, and a huge jumping arena next to an even bigger practice ring containing more than fifty different jumps.

"Humpty says its worth coming to Madrid just to practice over these fences," said Birdie as she unloaded a stiff weary chastened Porky Boy.

Even better, each foreign team had been given its own private stable with splendid box stalls. Next door, the victorious German team had just arrived from Rome and were unloading their huge horses and making a lot of noise. Jake recognized Ludwig von Schellenberg and Hans Schmidt, two riders he'd worshipped for years. Tomorrow, he thought with a thud of fear, he'd be competing against them.

He was distracted from his fears by another crisis. The stalls were all bedded with thick straw, which was no good for greedy Sailor, who always guzzled straw and blew himself up. Jake had run out of wood shavings on the journey down. How could he possibly explain to these charming, smiling but uncomprehending Spaniards what he wanted? Bridie's dictionary had "Wood" but not shavings. He felt a great weariness.

"Can I help?" said a voice.

It was Malise Gordon, who had just flown in from Rome; his high complexion tanned by the Italian sun, wearing a lightweight suit and looking handsome and authoritative. Jake had never been so pleased to see anyone.

Immediately Malise broke into fluent Spanish and sorted everything out.

"You look absolutely shattered," he said to Jake. "Sorry it was a bloody journey, but I warned you. Still, it was as well you were there to look after Porky Boy last night. Are your horses OK?"

While the Spanish grooms patted down the woodshavings for Sailor, Jake showed Malise Africa's knee, which mercifully hadn't swollen up.

"Where's your other horse?"

"Here. They've got his stall ready."

Sailor, a messy eater, had tipped out all his feed into the wood shavings and was busily picking it out. He gave Malise a baleful look out of his wall eye. After the four-day journey he loked perfectly dreadful.

"Christ," thought Malise, "we'll be a laughing stock entering something like that." But, he supposed, in the remote chance of Jake having to compete in the Nations' Cup, he could always ride Africa. Anyway the boy looked all in. No point in saying anything now.

"I'll take you back to the hotel. You'd better get some sleep." Malise looked at his watch. "It's only ten o'clock now. The rest of the team won't arrive till this afternoon. I suggest we meet in the bar around nine p.m. Then we can have dinner together and you can meet them all."

To Jake, who had never slept in a hotel, the bedroom seemed the height of luxury. There was a bathroom with a shower, and a tub as well and free soap and bubble bath, and a shower cap, and three white towels. In the bedroom there was a television, a radio, a telephone and a huge double bed. He was dying for some coffee but he didn't dare pick up the telephone in case they couldn't understand him. French windows led out on to a balcony that looked over a park. To the left, if he leaned out, he could see a street full of shops and cafes with tables outside. Already smells of olive oil, pimentos and saffron were drifting up from the kitchen. Drawing the thick purple curtains and only bothering to take off his shoes, Jake fell on to the suprisingly hard bed. The picture on the wall, of a matador in obscenely tight pink trousers shoving what looked like knitting needles into the neck of a bull, swam before his eyes and he was asleep.

Despite his exhaustion, however, he only slept fitfully. His dreams of disastrous rounds kept being interrupted by bursts of flamenco music or the screams of children playing in the park. By six the city had woken up and stretched itself after its siesta and Jake decided to abandon any hope of sleep. Outside, the streets were packed with cars rattling over the cobbles, hardly restrained at all by lights or frantically whistling policemen. Tables along the pavement were beginning to fill up, crowds to parade up and down. Looking across at the park, he saw a small child racing after a red ball, then tripping over a gambolling dog, falling flat on his face and bursting into noisy sobs. Next moment a pretty dark-haired mother had rushed forward, sworn at the dog and gathered up the child covering him with kisses. Jake was suddenly flattened with longing for Isa and Tory. He was desperate to call home, but he didn't know how to, he didn't even dare pick up the telephone and ask for some coffee.

Instead, raging with thirst, he drank a couple of mugs of water out of the tap, then unpacked, showered and, wrapped only in one of the white towels, wandered out on to the balcony. Instantly he stepped back, for there on the next balcony was a beautiful girl painting her toenails coral pink and soaking up the rays of the early evening sun.

She was impossibly slender, with long legs and arms, which, despite being covered with freckles, were already tanning becomingly to the color of weak tea. She wore a saffron yellow bikini and her hair was hidden by a big yellow towel. Beside her lay the catalogue of some art gallery, a Spanish dictionary, what looked like a book of poetry and a half-finished glass of orange juice. Obviously she could make reception understand her. The whole impression was of a marvellously pampered and over-bred race horse. As she stretched luxuriously, enjoying the sensation of being warm and alive, Jake felt a stab of lust. Why didn't one ever see girls like that in Warwickshire? He wished she would pick her nose or scratch her crotch; anything to make her more normal and less desirable.

Suddenly there was a commotion in the corridor. The girl jumped up. A man's voice could be heard shouting in the passage, "OK, we'll see you in the bar about nine."

The girl in the saffron bikini could be heard calling out in an American accent, "Darling, it's so good to see you."

There was a long pause. Then he heard the man's voice more clearly. It was a flat distinctive drawl which he would recognize anywhere and which made his knees disappear and the hairs prickle on the back of his neck.

"Bloody awful journey," said the voice. "Van kept overheating. We've been on the road for nearly thirty-six hours."

"Sweetheart," said the girl, "I'm so sorry. You must be exhausted-

Another pause followed, then the voice said sharply, "I don't care how fucking exhausted I am, get that bikini off."

The girl started protesting, but not very hard. Next moment there were sounds of lovemaking, with the bed banging against the wall so hard that Jake felt he was back in the cattle car. Mercifully it only lasted five minutes. Any more evidence of Rupert's superstud servicing would have finished Jake off altogether. Almost worse was the splashing and laughter as later they had a bath together. It was still desperately hot. Jake made his bed neatly and, wringing with sweat, had another shower and changed his shirt for something to do. He'd have liked to have washed some underpants and shirts and hung them out on the balcony, but he could imagine Rupert's derisive comments. Later he heard them having a drink on the balcony.

"Better get a few quick ones under my belt, so Malise doesn't think I'm alcoholic."

By nine o'clock Jake was so crucified by nerves and waiting that he couldn't bring himself to go downstairs until Malise rang up from reception saying they were all in the bar and had he overslept. Malise met him as he came out of the elevator. Noticing the set face, the black rings under the eyes, the obvious tension, he said, "Don't worry, they're all very unalarming."

There they were—all his heroes. Humpty Hamilton, puce from the heat, drinking lager. Lavinia Greenslade, whom he remembered from the first Bilborough Show. She was even prettier now that she'd lightened her hair, and wore it shorter and curlier. On either side, like two guarddogs, sat her mother, who wore too much cheap jewelry, and her father, who had ginger sideburns and a stomach spilling over his trousers. They didn't smile. Lavinia was too recent a cap herself for them to regard any new member of the team with enthusiasm. Billy Lloyd-Foxe had filled out and broken his nose since prep-school days, but looked more or less the same. He was laughing with a most beautiful red-headed girl, who was wearing black flared trousers and a white silk shirt tied under the breasts and showing off her smooth bare midriff. By her freckled arms and her coral pink toenails, Jake identified the girl on the balcony. Rupert had his back turned as he paid for a round of drinks and signed an autograph for the barman, but Jake immediately recognized the back of that smooth blond head and the broad blue striped shoulders. He felt a wave of horror and loathing.

"This is Jake Lovell," said Malise. "I'm sure he knows who all of you are."

Rupert swung round, smiling. In his brown face his eyes were as brilliantly blue as a jay's wing.

"Hi," he said. "Welcome to alcoholics not at all anonymous. I hear you had a worse journey than us, which seems impossible. What are you going to drink?"

Jake, who'd rehearsed this moment so often, and who was prepared to be icily aloof, found himself totally disarmed by such friendliness and muttered he'd like some Scotch. Billy got to his feet and shook Jake's hand.

"You've been cleaning up on the northern circuit. Don't venture up there often myself, too easy to get beaten."

"That was a good horse you were jumping at Birmingham," said Humpty, patting the empty seat beside him, "What's she called, Australia?"

"Africa," said Jake.

"Looks almost clean bred. Who was her sire?"

"Don't know."

"And her dam?"

"Don't know that either."

"Oh shut up, Humpty," said Rupert, handing Jake a very large glass of whisky which made Malise frown slightly.

Rupert lifted his glass to Jake. "Welcome to the British squad," he said. "Hope it's the first of many."

"Thanks," said Jake. He took a slug of his whisky, which was so strong it made his eyes water. He put his glass down at once, so they wouldn't see how much his hand was shaking.

"Lavinia's been capped for Great Britain six times," said her mother defensively.

"Oh please, Mummy."

"You should be proud of the fact," went on her mother. "The only girl on the team."

"What about Driffield?" said Rupert. "I've always thought his sex was slightly in question."

"No it isn't," said Humpty. "I've shared a room with him."

"That's enough," said Malise.

"Did you get to the Prado this afternoon?" Helen asked him.

Malise shook his head.

"I spent a couple of hours there," she said. "The Velasquez are out of this world, such power. I only managed to do two rooms, but I also looked at the cathedral. The nave is just wonderful."

Rupert stifled a yawn. "I prefer navels," he said, running his hand over his wife's midriff. Then, pushing down her black trousers, he fingered her belly button. "Particularly yours."

It was definitely a gesture of possession and he smiled across at Jake with that bullying, mocking, appraising look that Jake remembered so well.

Humpty turned back to Jake. "By the way, thanks for looking after Porky on the way down. Bridie said he might have damaged himself and her very badly if you hadn't stepped in."

"The train driver ought to be shot," said Jake.

"Spaniards don't like horses," said Humpty, "Porky's highly strung of course, but so was his dam."

And Humpty was off on a long involved dissertation on Porky Boy's breeding. Jake appeared to listen and studied the others. Mr. and

Mrs. Greenslade were discussing what horses Lavinia ought to jump tomorrow across Lavinia, who was gazing surreptiously at Billy. Billy was arguing fairly amicably with Rupert about whether a particular mare was worth selling and how much they'd get for her. Helen and Malise, having exhausted Velasquez, had moved on to Spanish poetry. She was an astonishingly beautiful girl, thought Jake, but too fragile for Rupert. Jake couldn't imagine him handling anyone with care for very long.

"I just adore Lorca," Helen was saying. "He's so passionate and basic; that poem that starts 'Green, Green, I want you Green.'"

"Sounds like Billy," said Rupert, "only in his case it's Gweenslade, Gweenslade, I want you Gweenslade."

"Shut up," hissed Billy, shooting a nervous glance in the direction of Lavinia's mother.

"Not unless you buy me a drink," said Rupert, handing Billy his empty glass.

"OK," said Billy, getting up. "Who needs a refill?"

"Jake does," said Rupert.

Jake had had plenty of time to finish his whisky. Having not had anything to eat for at least thirty-six hours, he was beginning to feel very tight. But before he could protest, Rupert had whipped his glass away and handed it to Billy.

"Not as strong as the last one, then," said Malise firmly. "that was a quadruple."

"He's not eighteen you know," said Rupert softly.

"How old are you?" asked Humpty.

"Twenty-six," said Jake.

"Same as me and Rupe," said Billy, hailing the waiter.

"It's funny we haven't heard of you before," said Lavinia. "Awfully womantic, to be suddenly picked out of the blue like that."

"I started late," said Jake.

"But I'm sure I've seen you before," said Billy, puzzled, as he handed double whiskies to Jake and Rupert.

"Probably in *Horse and Hound*," said Lavinia.

No it wasn't, thought Billy to himself. There was something about Jake that made him feel uneasy, layers of memory being slowly pulled back like an onion, not very happy memories, the kind you tucked into a corner of your mind and tried to forget.

They dined in a taverna a couple of streets away. The walls were covered in fans and castanets and pictures of ladies in mantillas. In a corner a fat tenor in a rather dirty white frilly shirt with greasy patent leather hair was dispiritedly strumming a guitar. The owner rushed out, shaking hands with Malise, Humpty, Rupert, and Billy and showing them their signed photographs on the wall, then going into a frenzy of ecstasy over Lavinia's blonde beauty. Redheads were less rare in Madrid than blondes, and Helen was a little too thin for Spanish tastes.

Jake was beginning to feel distinctly odd. He must get some food inside him. He found himself with Lavinia on his left and Mr. Greenslade on his right. Bottles were put on the table and Rupert immediately filled everyone's glasses. Completely incomprehensible menus came around.

"What's gazpacho?" he asked Lavinia.

"Tomato soup," said Rupert.

That sounded gentle and stomach-settling.

"And polpi?"

"Some sort of pasta," said Rupert.

"I'll have that," said Jake.

Suddenly he noticed Billy's hand caressing Lavinia's thigh under the table, where her mother and father couldn't see. The waiter arrived for their order. Firmly Jake said he'd like gazpacho and polpi.

"I'd like a large steak and french fries," said Humpty.

"So would I," said Billy, "but no potatoes, just a salad—my trousers are getting disgustingly tight—and Mediterranean prawns to start off with."

"You shouldn't drink so much," said Rupert, filling up his glass.

Helen turned to the waiter and started to address him in Spanish.

"Oh for Christ's sake," said Rupert irritably, "they all speak English."

"At least she can translate your horoscope in the Spanish papers," said Billy.

"And jolly useful at Customs," said Mrs. Greenslade, who admired Helen.

"We've got Marion for that," said Rupert. "She's got big boobs, which is more a language the Customs officers understand."

Apart from his hand stroking her thigh, Billy was studiously avoiding Lavinia for the benefit of her parents, so she turned to Jake.

"How did you get on in Rome?" he said. "I haven't seen any papers."

"I got a second and a third. Wupert did best. He won two classes and went clear in the Nations' Cup. But we were still beaten by the Germans and the Fwench. I don't think we'll ever beat them. Ludwig and Hans Schmidt are like computers, they just pwogwamme their horses and wound they go."

Jake was eating bread, desperate to mop up some alcohol. The fat flamenco singer, after a lot of stamping, launched into some mournful ditty.

"Sounds like Grand Hotel," said Rupert.

Now he'd had a lot to drink, Jake found his eyes continually drawn to Rupert, like a rabbit to a snake. He still felt the same sick churning inside. Rupert's whiplash tongue was still there. Soon he knew he'd be the recipient. He realized again what an evil man Rupert was behind his offhand jokey exterior.

It was very hot in the restaurant. Jake was drenched with sweat.

"OK?" asked Malise. "Grub should be up in a minute. That's one of the maddening things about Spain, no one dines before ten o'clock. At least we get a nice late start."

"I'm going to spend tomorrow morning sunbathing," said Lavinia.

"You are not," said her father, "You'll sort out that stop of Snowstorm's. We're not risking him ducking out again."

At last food began to arrive. A plate of soup was put in front of Jake. A great waft of garlic made him feel distinctly queasy, God knows what was in it. Little bits of fried bread, green peppers and cucumbers floated on top.

"This is a most interesting paella," Helen was saying as she speared a large mussel. Feeling slightly sick, Jake took a mouthful of soup and only just avoided spitting it out. He put his spoon down and took a huge gulp of wine, then a piece of bread to take the taste away.

What was he to do? Was it some diabolical plan of Rupert's, telling the waiter to bring him cold soup?

"What's the matter?" said Malise.

"Nothing," said Jake. He mustn't betray weakness. He took another mouthful and very nearly threw up. Glancing up, he saw Rupert eyeing him speculatively.

"Gazpacho good?" he asked.

"It's stone cold, if you want to know," said Jake. "They've forgotten to heat it up."

Rupert grinned. "It's meant to be," he said gently. "I should have warned you. It's a Spanish national dish."

Jake gripped the sides of the plate. For a second he felt such a wave of hatred he nearly hurled it in Rupert's face.

"I'll have the gazpacho," said Billy, leaning over, whipping away Jake's plate and handing him the Mediterranean prawns in return.

"Then you'll sleep alone," said Rupert.

"It seems I have no other choice," said Billy, smiling blandly at Mrs. Greenslade, and squeezing Lavinia's thigh a bit harder.

Rupert started discussing bullfights with Humpty Hamilton.

"We'll go to one later in the week."

"I'm not going," said Lavinia. "I thinks its vewy cwuel."

"Have you ever seen one?" asked Rupert.

"No."

"You're just like Helen. She was out with the Antis when I first met her."

She looks like a fox, thought Jake, beautiful, nervous, wistful, with those haunting yellow eyes, a tamed fox that might bolt at any minute.

"The El Grecos are wonderful," she was saying to Malise.

"I'm going back tomorrow morning. Why don't you come too?" she went on.

"Tomorrow, my angel," said Rupert with a distinct edge to his voice, "you are going to spend the morning in bed with me."

The second courses were arriving. Jake felt the mayonnaise and prawns mixing unhappily with the whisky and wine in his stomach. Pasta was just the thing to settle it. Next moment a plate was put down in front of him. He nearly heaved at the sight; it was full of octopus.

"I didn't order this!"

"Si, senor, polpi."

Jake turned dark red. "You said it was plain pasta," he hissed at Rupert.

"How silly of me," drawled Rupert. "Of course, polpi, octopus. I'd forgotten. What a pity you didn't ask Helen or Malise."

"You're a shit, Rupert," said Billy, "Look," he added to the waiter, "Take this back and get some risotto, or would you rather have a steak?"

Jake shook his head. He was feeling awful.

"I think I've had enough."

"Have some of my wice and chicken," said Lavinia, tipping it on to his side plate. "It's weally good, but I'll never finish it all. Did you know there were two men in the Spanish team called Angel and Maria?"

Dinner dragged on. Jake was dropping now. He picked at the rice Lavinia had given him but didn't manage to finish it. Once again he was overwhelmed with such homesickness he almost wept. If he were home now, he'd probably have just come in from a show. Tory would be waiting and together they'd go up and gloat over the sleeping Isa.

"Anyone want dessert?" asked Malise.

"I'd love some berries," said Helen, "Do they have any fresh berries?"

"In English you specify them," said Rupert through gritted teeth.

"Strawberries, raspberries, gooseberries."

"I'm sure there are some strawberries," said Malise, smiling at Helen.

"What about you, Jake?"

Jake shook his head and got to his feet. "Thank you for dinner. I'm off to bed," he said, "Can I settle up with you in the morning?"

"This is on the B.S.J.A.," said Malise.

"Well, thanks," said Jake.

"Sleep well," said Malise. "Order breakfast from Reception. They all speak English, and for Christ's sake don't drink the water in the taps."

"You going to bed?" said Rupert in surprise, "Sorry about the polpi and the gazpacho. New boy's tease you know."

"I know," said Jake bleakly, "only too well."

Looking at the set white face, in a flash Billy remembered. Lovell, J. Of course! He knew he'd seen him before. He was the gypsy boy at St. Augustine's, Gyppo Jake, whom he and Rupert had bullied unmercifully until he ran away. It was the one thing in his life he'd always been ashamed of. He wanted to say something to Jake, to apologize for the teasing at dinner, but it was too late. He'd gone.

Outside Jake took a taxi down to the show ground. Fortunately he'd remembered his pass and the guards let him in. He realized he was very drunk.

The Great Bear overhead kept disintergrating and re-forming, like a swarm of illuminated gnats. Crossing the exercise ring, he threw up behind a large Spanish chestnut. As he covered it with sand, he hoped one of Rupert's bloody horses would slip on it tomorrow.

Bastard, bastard, bastard, he hadn't changed at all. New boy's tease indeed. Nausea overwhelmed him again. He leaned against an oak feeling dizzy. Finally he made the stables. It was a comfort Africa and Sailor were so pleased to see him. Blinking sleepily, they smelled of hay and contentment. One arm around each of their necks, he clung to them, desperate for reassurance. They were *his* horses from *his* stable.

"Tomorrow," he said, "we'll go out and lynch him."

Jake never knew if it was a result of meeting Rupert again, or because he drank too much tap water, but in the early morning he was laid low with a vicious stomach ache. For the first few days of the show it was all he could do to stuggle up and crawl down to the stables to look after Africa and Sailor. Later in the day, he was either eliminated or racked up a number of faults in every class he entered. The jumps were huge and solid, with the poles fitting deeply into the cups, and the competition was fierce. Both Africa and Sailor were out of sorts after the long journey. Jake was so strung-up he transmitted his nerves to the horses, who jumped worse and worse as the week went on.

To make matters worse, none of the classes started before three o'clock in the afternoon, with an evening performance beginning at 11 p.m. By the time the final national anthem had been played it was three a. m. and often four o'clock before Jake fell into bed, to wake like a stone at six in the morning, his usual time for getting up, after which he couldn't get back to sleep again.

A doctor was summoned and gave him pills and advised forty-eight hours rest. But for a workaholic like Jake, this was impossible. He couldn't bear to be parted from his horses, his one link with home. He had no desire to sightsee with Malise or Helen, or lounge around the pool sunbathing with the others and be confronted with the contemptuous bronzed beauty of Rupert Campbell-Black.

So while the others relaxed and enjoyed themselves, Jake didn't miss a round jumped by another rider, or a work-out in the warm-up area. He was learning all the time, but not to his advantage. There were too many of his heroes around to influence him, and he got increasingly muddled as first he tried to ride like the Italians, then like the dashing Spaniards, then like the mighty Germans.

The rest of the team, except Rupert, tried to be friendly and helpful. They were all relieved he was not the white-hot savior predicted by Malise, but as one catastrophic round followed another and he became more monosyllabic and withdrawn, they gave up.

Rupert, on the other hand, was openly hostile. On the morning after they arrived in Madrid, he was riding round the practicing ring when Billy said, "You know that new chap?"

"The great gourmet and conversationalist?" said Rupert scornfully.

"Don't you recognize him? He's the same Gyppo Lovell who was at St. Augustine's with us."

"Can't be."

"Bloody is. Don't you remember his mother was the cook. Mrs. Lovell? She did herself in."

"Hardly surprising after producing an undersized little runt like that. Didn't he become a boarder?"

"Yes," said Billy bleakly: "he was in our dormitory. We gave him such hell he ran away."

"Perhaps we should repeat the experiment. With any luck he might do it again."

"You didn't help much last night," snapped Billy. "Making him order octopus. Poor sod, he's never been abroad before."

"Certainly doesn't know how to behave in a hotel," said Rupert. "I caught him making his bed this morning."

For a few minutes they rode on in silence, then Billy said, "I feel I ought to make it up to him somehow for being such a shit at St. Augustine's."

Rupert started to play on an imaginary violin. "Don't be so bloody soft. Little creeps like that deserve to be hammered. How the hell did he get started anyway?"

"Well that's the interesting part. D'you remember a hugely fat deb called Tory Maxwell?"

Rupert shuddered. "Only too vividly. Maxwell big as a House—unable to turn around without the use of tugs." He glanced sideways at Billy, relieved to see he had made him laugh. "And quite rich."

"That's the one. Well, Jake Lovell married her and evidently used all her cash to get started."

"No wonder he's undersized; squashed flat in the sack. Must be like going to bed with a steam roller. Who told you all this?"

"Malise. Last night. He thinks Lovell's brilliant."

"Well he's wrong. Lovell's just about as insipid as the food his mother used to cook. And, what's more, he kept Helen and me awake all night throwing up."

To rub salt into Jake's wounds, all the other members of the team were jumping well and in the money, particularly Rupert who won a Vespa on the third day and insisted on roaring around the show ground on it, to everyone's amusement and irritation. Jake's was the only part of the British tackroom without its share of ribbons.

Rupert never lost an opportunity to twist the knife. On the third day, just before the competition, he persuaded Marion to hid all Jake's breeches and his red coat and fill up his trunk with frilly underwear.

Marion was only too happy to oblige. Wandering around, heavily curvaceous in pink hot pants and a sleeveless pink T-shirt, she was the toast of the show ground, always followed by a swarm of admiring tongue-clicking Spaniards, and the recipient of endless bonhomie from the other male international riders.

Jake, resentful that Rupert not only had an exquisite wife but a spectacular groom, ignored Marion, a reaction she was unused to.

"He went bananas when he found his clothes missing," she told Rupert gleefully. "He's not as cool as he makes out."

Although Marion soon returned his clothes, what upset Jake more was that the yellow tansy flower he always wore in the heel of his left boot to bring him luck had somehow vanished. Without his talisman his luck was bound to plummet and as a result he lost even more confidence.

Most of all he was upset by Rupert's constant cracks about Sailor—that he must be a mule or a camel, and no wonder he'd frightened them at the customs; they must have thought they were letting a dinosaur into the country. Jake felt very protective towards Sailor, whom he loved very deeply, and his heart blackened against Rupert.

On the fifth day Malise announced the British team: Rupert, Billy, Humpty Hamilton and Lavinia, with Jake as reserve. In the evening he took Jake out for a drink and explained there was nothing else he could do given Jake's current performance.

"Don't worry," he said, spearing an olive out of his very dry martini. "This often happens to new caps."

"Not as badly as this," said Jake, gazing gloomily into a glass of soda water. He still felt too sick even to smoke. His eyes seemed three inches deep in his face. His face was grey and seamed with exhaustion; he must have lost ten pounds.

"It's a vicious circle," said Malise gently. "Everyone talks about the killer instinct and being hungry enough to go out and win, but you're so snarled up inside you're frightening the hell out of your horses. I know the fences seem huge and you're worried about overfacing them, but you *must* be more aggressive. The only way to tackle those fences is to attack. Be accurate, but ride on all the time. Those big heavy poles are so firm you can afford to clout them. Africa should be able to sail over them anyway."

Jake's face registered no emotion. A fly was buzzing around their heads. Malise flicked it away with yesterday's copy of *The Times*.

"Spanish fly," said Jake suddenly, with the ghost of a smile: "S'pposed to be good for sex, isn't it?"

Malise laughed. "Never tried it myself, more Rupert's province. Expect you're feeling homesick too, missing Tory and the baby, and you're pulled down looking after the horses by yourself. It's amazing how your first win will buck you up."

"If I ever do win."

"My dear boy, I've seen you at the top of your form. I know you're good. You've just got to calm down."

Jake suddenly felt an emotion close to adulation. He could imagine following Malise into battle without a qualm. If only he'd had a father like that, or even a father like Mr. Greenslade, who bossed you around all the time because he cared about you.

"I'm going to be very unorthodox," said Malise. He handed Jake a bottle with some red pills in. "Those'll make you sleep; put you out like a light. Don't tell the rest of the team I've given them to you. They'll play havoc with your reflexes, but you're not jumping tomorrow or in the Nations' Cup, and a couple of good nights' sleep'll put you right for the Grand Prix on Saturday. And don't tell me you don't approve of sleeping pills. Nor do I, except in an emergency. Tomorrow you're not going anywhere near the stables. Marion and Tracey will look after Africa and Sailor. You can go on the sightseeing jaunt with the rest of the team."

After fourteen hours sleep Jake woke feeling much better. He didn't know whether Malise had had a word with them but the team members were particularly nice to him as they set off out of Madrid in an old bus, across dusty plains, like the hide of a great slaughtered bull, then through rolling hills dotted with olive trees and orange groves. The road was full of potholes, sending sledgehammer blows up Jake's spine as the back wheels went over them. Rupert sat next to Helen with his arm along the back of the seat, but not touching her because it was too hot. Billy sat in front talking constantly to them, refereeing any squabbles, sticking up for Helen. Lavinia Greenslade sat with her father. Humpty sat with Jake and talked non-stop about Porky Boy.

Only Rupert didn't let up in his needling. Every donkey or mule or depressed looking horse they passed reminded him of Sailor or "Jake's Joke," as he now called him.

They lunched at a very good restaurant, sitting outside under the plane trees, eating cochinella or roast suckling pig. It was the first square meal Jake had been able to keep down since he arrived. While they were having coffee, a particulaly revolting old gypsy came up and tried to read their fortunes.

"Do tell your ghastly cousin to go away, Jake," said Rupert.

Helen, beautiful, radiant and clinging, was surprised Rupert was being so poisonous to this taciturn newcomer. She tried to talk to Jake and ask him about his horses, but he answered abruptly and left her in mid-sentence.

Afterwards they went to a bull farm and tried playing with the young bulls and heifers with padded horns and a cape. Rupert and Billy, who'd both had a fair amount to drink at lunchtime, were only too anxious to have a go. Humpty, who'd eaten too much suckling pig ("You might pop if a horn grazed you," said Rupert), refused to try, so did Jake.

Side by side, but each feeling very different emotions, Jake and Helen watched Rupert, tall and lean, a natural at any sport, swinging away as the little bull hurtled towards him. Determined to excel, he was already getting competitive. Billy, fooling around, couldn't stop laughing, and was finally sent flying and only pulled out of danger just in time by Rupert. In the end Rupert only allowed himself to be dragged away because they had to be in Madrid to watch a bullfight at six. Before the fight they were shown the chapel where the matadors pray before the fight.

"Do with a session in there before tomorrow afternoon," said Billy. "Dear God make us beat the Germans."

The bullfight nauseated Jake. Particularly when the picadors came on riding their pathetic, broken-down insufficiently padded horse. If they were gored, according to Humpty, they were patched up and sent down into the ring to face the ordeal again. They were so thin they were in no condition to run away.

The cochinella was already churning inside him.

"I say, Jake," Rupert's voice carried down the row, "doesn't that picador's horse remind you of Sailor? If you popped down to the Plaza de Toros later this evening, I'm sure they'd give you a few pesetas for him."

Jake gritted his teeth and said nothing.

After the bullfight the rest of the team went out to a party at the Embassy. Jake followed Malise's advice and went to bed early again.

On the morning of the Nations' Cup Jake woke feeling better in body but not in mind. The sight of fan mail and invitations so overcrowding Rupert's pigeon hole that they spilled over into Humpty's and Lavinia's pigeon holes on either side gave him a frightful stab of jealously.

Then in his own pigeon hole he found a letter from Tory, which filled him equally with remorse and homesickness. "Darling Jake," she wrote in her round childish hand, "Isa and Wolf and all the horses and Tanya and most of all me (or should it be I) are missing you dreadfully. But I keep telling myself that it's all in a good cause, and that by the time you get this letter, you'll have really made all the other riders sit up, particularly Rupert. Is he still as horrible or has marriage mellowed him? I know you're going to do really well."

Jake couldn't bear to read any more. He crumpled up the letter and put it in his hip pocket. Skipping breakfast, he went straight down to the stables. He wanted to work the horses before it got too punishingly hot.

Walking into the British tackroom, he steeled himself for whatever grisly practical joke was on the menu today, but he found everything in place. Because it was Nations' Cup Day everyone was far too preoccupied. The grooms were tense and abstracted, the horses edgy. They knew something was up. Jake worked both the horses and was pleased to find Sailor had recovered from his bout of colic earlier in the week, and Africa's leg was better.

Back in the yard he cooled down Sailor's legs with a hose, amused by the besotted expression on the horse's long speckled face. Nearby, Tracey was washing The Bull's tail. Beyond her, Rupert's groom, Marion, was standing on a hay bale to braid the mighty Macaulay's mane, showing off her long brown legs in the shortest pale blue shorts and grumbling about the amount of work she had to get through. Macaulay was so over the top that, rather than risk overtiring him, Rupert had decided to ride Belgravia in the parade beforehand and only bring out Macaulay for the actual class. This meant Marion had two horses to get ready.

Jake, who'd been carefully studying Rupert's horses, thought they were getting too many oats. No one could deny Rupert's genius as a rider, but his horses were not happy. He had surreptitiously watched Rupert take Mayfair, Belgravia and Macaulay off to a secluded corner of the huge practice ring and seen how he made Tracey and Marion each hold the end of the top pole of a fence, lifting it as the horses went over to give them a sharp rap on the shins, however high they jumped. This was meant to make them pick up their feet even higher the next time. The practice, known as rapping, was strictly illegal in England.

Jake, however, was most interested in Macaulay. He was a brilliant horse, but still young and inexperienced. Jake felt he was being brought on too fast.

In the stable the radio was blaring Spanish pop music.

The Italian team came past, their beautifully streaked hair as well cut as their jeans, and stopped to chat with Marion and Tracey.

As Jake started to dry Sailor's legs, the horse nudged at his pocket for Polos.

"How long have we got?" Tracey asked Marion.

"About an hour and a half before the parade."

"Christ," said Tracey, braiding faster. "I'm never going to be ready in time. Give over Bull, keep still." The Bull looked up with kind shining eyes.

"You want a hand?" asked Jake: "I've nearly finished Sailor."

"You haven't," said a voice behind him.

It was Malise Gordon, looking elegant, even in this heat, in a pale grey suit, but extremely grim.

"You're going to have to jump, after all," he said. "The stupid idiot Billy sneaked off this morning with Rupert to have another crack at bull-fighting and got himself knocked out cold."

Tracey gave a wail and dropped her comb. The Bull jerked up his head.

"It's all right. He'll live," said Malise irritably. "The doctor doesn't think it's serious, but Billy certainly doesn't know what day of the week it is and there's no chance of him riding."

Tracey burst into tears. Marion stopped braiding and put her arms around Tracey, glaring at Jake as though it was his fault.

"He's got a head like a bullet; don't worry," Marion said soothingly.

"Come on," said Malise, not unkindly. "Pull yourself together; put The Bull back in his stall and get moving on whoever Jake's going to ride. Africa, I presume."

Jake shook his head. "Her leg's not right. I'm not risking it. I'll ride Sailor."

For a second Malise hesitated. "You don't want to jump The Bull?"

Catching Tracey and Marion's look of horror, Jake shook his head. If by the remotest chance he didn't let the team down, he was bloody well not having it attributed to the fact that he wasn't riding his own horse.

"All right, you better get changed. You're meant to be walking the course in an hour, but with the General coming and Spanish dilatoriness it's impossible to be sure."

Luckily Jake didn't have time to panic. Tracey sewed the Union Jack on to his red coat. Normally he would have been fretting around, trying to find the socks, the breeches, the shirt and the white tie he'd worn the last time he'd won a class, but as it was so long since he had won anything, he'd forgotten which was the last set of clothes that worked. His face looked grey, his hands were trembling so much he could hardly tie his tie, and his red coat, which fitted him when he left England, was now too loose. Then suddenly, when he dropped a peseta and was searching for it under the feed bin, he found his tansy flower, slightly battered but intact. Overjoyed, he slipped it into his left boot. Aware of it, a tiny bump under his heel, he felt perhaps his luck might be turning at last.

Rupert arrived at the showground in a foul temper. He'd just had a dressing-down from Malise for going bull-fighting on the morning of a Nations' Cup. He was worried about Billy and he realized, with Billy gone, that their chances of placing were negligible. Helen's chatter about El Grecos and Goyas, and her trip to Toledo, "with the old houses silhouetted against the skyline," got on his nerves and he'd bitten her head off unnecessarily.

"God, it's hot," said Lavinia Greenslade as they sweated in the unrelenting sun, waiting for the go-ahead to walk the course. Her eyes were swollen and pink from crying over Billy's concussion. It had taken all Malise Gordon's steely persuasion, coupled with her parents' ranting, to make her agree to ride.

The rotund Humpty was sweating so profusely that great damp patches had seeped through his red coat under the arms and down the spine.

"Wish we could jump in our shirt sleeves," he grumbled.

"Not in front of the Genewal," said Lavinia. "He's weally hot on pwotocol."

Jake clenched his teeth together, so the others couldn't hear them chattering like castanets. Walking the course didn't improve his nerves. The fourteen jumps were enormous—most of them bigger than he was—with a huge combination in the middle and a double at the end with an awkward distance. You could either take three small strides between the two jumps or two long ones. He tried to concentrate on what Malise was saying as they paced out the distances.

In a Nations' Cup four riders jump for each country, jumping two rounds each over the same course. There is a draw for the order in which the nations jump. Today it was France, Italy, Spain, Germany then Great Britain last, which meant that a French rider would jump first, followed by an Italian, then a Spaniard, a German and finally a

British rider. Then the second French rider would jump followed by the second Italian, and so on until all the riders had jumped. Each nation would then total the scores of its three best riders, discarding the worst score. The nation with the lowest number of faults would then be in the lead at half time. The whole process is then repeated, each rider jumping in the same order. Once again the three lowest scores are added up and the nation with the lowest total over the two rounds wins the cup. If two countries tie there is a jump off. Nations' Cup matches are held all over Europe throughout the summer and autumn and the side that notches up the most points during the year is awarded the President's Cup. For the last two years this had been won by Germany.

Malise gave the order for the British team to jump: Humpty, Lavinia, Rupert, Jake.

"If you get a double clear," Humpty told Jake as they came out of the ring, "you get a free red coat."

"Can't see myself having much chance of wearing out this one," said Jake.

He thought so even more a few seconds later as Lavinia gave a shriek of relieved joy, bounded towards Billy, as he stood swaying slightly at the entrance to the arena, and flung her arms around him.

"Lavinia," thundered her mother and father simultaneously.

Lavinia ignored them. "Are you all wight? You shouldn't have come out in this heat. Does your poor head hurt?"

Billy was deathly pale, but he steadied himself against Lavinia and grinned sheepishly at Malise. "I'm terribly sorry."

"T'riffic," said Rupert. "You can ride after all."

"No he can't," said Malise firmly. "Go and sit in the shade, Billy, and take my hat." He removed his panama and handed it to Billy.

"For Christ sake," snarled Rupert, hardly bothering to lower his voice, "even concussed, Billy's more valuable than Lavinia or Jake. They simply haven't the nerve when the chips are down."

"I'm honestly not up to it," said Billy placatingly. "I can see at least six of all of you."

Fortunately an ugly scene was averted by a loose horse pounding through the collecting ring, its lead rein trailing and flysheet slipping. Nickering with delight, he shoved the rest of the British team summarily out of the way and rushed straight up to Jake, burying his nose inside his coat and nudging him with delight. It was Sailor; his feet were oiled, his coat polished, his thin mane coaxed into braids, his sparse tail fell jagged from the tube of royal blue tail bandage.

The next minute Tracey joined them, panting and laughing.

"The moment he saw you he broke away from me."

"Amazing that someone finds you attractive," said Rupert.

"That's enough, Rupert," said Malise icily. "You'd better warm up before the parade, Humpty."

The General, in true Spanish tradition, was late. So the parade started without him. The Germans came first. The famous four, Hans, Manfred, Wolfgang and Ludwig. Olympic gold medalists who had not lost a Nations' Cup competition for two years, they had reason to be proud. They rode with a swagger on their equally famous horses: four beautiful Hanovarian geldings, with satin coats, elegant booted legs, arched necks, and chins apparently soldered to their breast bones. As they passed, their grooms gripped the fence and cheered. They were followed by the French, beautifully turned out with the lighter and less obedient horses, and the Italians in their impeccably cut coats with the blue collars, riding with slapdash elegance, two of them smoking. Then there was a great ear-splitting cheer, sending a great communal waft of garlic up from the crowd, as the Spanish team came in. Beautiful riders on beautiful powerful horses, their manes flowing free, but somehow not coordinated like the Germans. The crowd, however, thought they were the greatest, and screams and shouts of "*magnifico*" and "*Olé*" followed them all around the ring.

The British team came last. Rupert rode on the magnificent Belgravia, chestnut coat gleaming in the sunshine. Not having been warmed up at all, (Marion hadn't even had time to walk him around), he was boisterous and uncontrollable, and the crowd, particularly the women, marvelled how this handsome Englishman hardly moved in the saddle, as the horse bucked and violently shied beneath him. On his left was Humpty on Porky Boy, then Lavinia on the grey Snowstorm, whose coat was already turning blue with sweat, and then Sailor, shuffling along, looking on his last legs, as though he could hardly stagger as far as the grandstand. The crowd laughed, jeered and pointed.

Jake gritted his teeth. He'd show them.

The wait that followed was interminable. The teams lined up in front of the grandstand and all, except Lavinia, removed their hats as each country's National Anthem was played. The band knew their own National Anthem and, confident the Germans would win, had been practicing "Deutschland, Deutschland" all week, but when they got to Great Britain, they launched into the Star Spangled Banner, which everyone thought very funny except the moustachioed bandmaster, who turned an even deeper shade of purple.

The horses meanwhile were going mad in the heat, except Sailor who stood half asleep, one back leg bent, hanging his head, twitching his flea-bitten coat against the flies, and occasionally flattening his ears at Belgravia, who was still barging around like a bee-stung bronco. Jake tried not to look at the jumps. All the women in the audience fanned themselves with their programs. Medallions nestling in a thousand black hairy chests glittered in the sunlight.

In the riders' stand, next to the collecting ring, Helen comforted a disconsolate Billy. "You'd be mad to jump," she said.

"Must say I've got the most awful headache. Jake's horse looks like I feel," said Billy.

As the teams came out of the ring, Sailor bringing up the rear, shuffling along head hanging, Helen looked at Jake's set face. She hadn't seen him smile once since he'd arrived. The knight of the sorrowful countenance, she thought.

"He's like Don Quixote," she said to Billy, "and that poor beaten-down old horse looks like Rosinante."

Billy wasn't interested in literary allusions.

"What a bloody stupid thing to do," he said. "Malise is livid."

"Doesn't look it," said Helen watching Malise, in dark glasses with a gardenia in the buttonhole of his pale grey suit, completely calm as he went from one member of the team to another, steadying their nerves, encouraging them.

"Lavinia's not wearing anything underneath that black coat," sighed Billy.

As the British team filed into the riders' stand, Malise gave Helen the jumping order on a clipboard so she could keep the score. The General still hadn't arrived, but it was decided to start. The arena went very quiet as the white doors opened and the first French rider came in and took off his hat to the judges. As he went past the start, the clock started ticking. It was soon obvious, as he demolished fence after fence, sending poles and bricks flying, that this was a far from easy course. The Italian who came second was also all over the place and notched up twenty-eight faults.

"*Viva España*," screamed the crowd as the first Spanish rider came in. Although they had applauded the earlier riders politely, they cheered their own hero unrestrainedly.

"Doesn't look very magnifico to me," said Rupert, as the horse went head over heels at the rustic poles, crashed through the wall and the final double, losing his rider again, and having to be led out impossibly lame.

"I've seen enough," said Humpty, running down the steps and out to the collecting ring to scramble on to Porky Boy as the first German rider rode leisurely into the ring. Hans Schmidt was the second best rider in the German team, but his dark brown horse didn't like the course any more than the others and came out with a most unusual twelve faults.

As he walked out ruefully shaking his blonde head and muttering *dummkopf,* he was practically knocked sideways by Humpty bouncing into the ring. The merry Porky Boy, ears pricked and fighting for his head, his black tail swishing back and forth across his plump cobby quarters, bucketed towards the first fence. The crowd was amused by him and his rider, who rose so high out of the saddle over the bigger jumps that it seemed the would never come down again. But he got around with a very creditable twelve faults.

Now it was time for the second Frenchman to jump.

No one went clear, as round followed round and disaster followed disaster. Several horses overturned and were eliminated. A Spanish horse burst a blood vessel and had to be destroyed later in the day. Despite Rupert's gloomy prognostications, Lavinia jumped well for only twelve faults, which meant the Germans and the English were level pegging on twenty-four faults at the end of the second round, with the other nations trailing well behind. The next German, Manfred, got eight faults, the best round so far. He was followed by Rupert, who did not jump well. Macaulay, like Belgravia, overoated and insufficiently warmed up, had been frightened in the collecting ring by three loudspeakers crackling fortissimo above his head. An enormously powerful horse, it took all Rupert's strength to stop him running away in the ring. By some miracle they went clear until they got to the upright, where Macaulay, put wrong, hit it sharply.

For a second the pole bounced agonizingly in the cup, then fell. Unbalanced, and taking off too early, Macaulay also had a foot in the water. Rupert came out of the ring looking bootfaced.

"He's dying to beat the hell out of that horse," said Jake to himself. He watched Helen, beautiful in her yellow hat, biting her lip with disappointment as she entered eight faults by Rupert's name. Jake didn't want to be around when Rupert came back. He'd seen enough rounds anyway.

Riding around the collecting ring, he felt sicker and sicker, trying to remember the turns and the distances between the jumps, but his mind had suddenly gone completely blank. He wished he could slip into the matadors' church to pray. He listened to the deafening cheer as the last Spanish rider went in and groan followed groan as he demolished the course.

Now it was time for the mighty Ludwig von Schellenberg, the greatest rider in the world, to go into the ring and show everyone how to do it, which he did, jumping clear. But so carried away was he by the poetry and stylishness of his round that he notched up one and a half time faults.

He came out grinning and cursing. Now, just as Jake was due to jump, the last rider in Round One, the General chose to arrive and everything ground to a halt while two lines of soldiers with machine guns formed a guard of honor and the band played the National Anthem several times. Dignitaries were introduced with a lot of bowing and shaking of hands, and the General was settled in his seat.

"This is a bugger," said Malise, after Jake had been kept waiting twenty minutes. "I'm sorry. They'll call you any minute. Just aim for a steady clear, take it easy and ride at the center of the fence."

Up in the riders' stand Helen was doing sums.

"If the Germans count Ludwig's, Manfred's and Hans' rounds, and drop Wolfgang's, that puts them on twenty-one and a half," she said. "We've got Rupert on eight, Humpty on twelve and Lavinia on twelve; that makes thirty-two."

"We won't get lower than that this half," said Rupert. "Jake's bound to be eliminated."

Ludwig von Schellenberg came into the riders' stand. "You look beautiful, Mees Helen, in that hat," he said, clicking his heels as he kissed her hand.

"She's a Mrs. not a Miss you smarmy Kraut, and keep your hands off her," said Rupert, but quite amiably. Ludwig was one of the few riders he liked and admired.

"Number 28," called the collecting ring steward.

Jake rode quietly into the ring. During the long wait he had counted Sailor's braids, found there were fifteen, his unlucky number, and had quickly undone them, so Sailor's sparse mane crinkled unbecomingly.

As the horse shuffled in, head hanging, Ludwig laughed and turned to Rupert: "Do you get your horses from zee butcher's yard now?"

"May I be Franco with you," said Rupert. "That is the ugliest horse anyone's ever seen."

Helen looked at Jake and repeated her remark about the knight of the sorrowful countenance to Malise, but Malise wasn't listening either; he was praying.

The audience was losing interest. There hadn't been enough clear rounds, the Germans were so far ahead it didn't look as though anyone, and definitely not the Spaniards, would catch up. The General was talking to his Energy Minister about oil prices. No one was paying much attention as Sailor cantered towards the first fence.

Tilting at windmills, thought Helen, filled with compassion.

"Never get over it," said Rupert.

But suddenly this extraordinarly ugly animal shook himself like an old music hall actor who realizes he's got a capacity crowd, gave a snort of pleasure and took hold of the bit.

"Christ, look at that," said Humpty Hamilton as Sailor cleared the first fence.

"And that," said Billy as he cleared the second.

"And that," said Malise, resisting a temptation to crow, as he cleared the third.

"And that," said Helen.

"Jesus, he can really jump," said Billy. "Look at the way he tucks up his feet."

The crowd, bored by Spain's poor performance, suddenly diverted by this extraordinary horse, laughed at first, then started to clap and cheer.

"He's going to get time faults if he's not careful," said Mrs. Greenslade, as Jake checked Sailor before the combination, but, pop, pop, pop, over he went.

"Christ," said Humpty. "That horse must have some good blood in him."

"Who is zees horse, Malise?" said Ludwig. "It is not permitted, I think, to jump mules. I shall lodge an objection."

Sailor was over the water. Now there was just the double left.

As he turned sharply to make up time, the sun shone straight into Jake's eyes, dazzling and blinding him. He had to leave it all to Sailor. The British team held its breath as the horse came trundling down, carefully positioned himself and cleared both parts beautifully. As he shambled out of the ring to deafening cheers, some people in the riders' stand could have sworn he winked his wall eye. Jake, his face blank, leaned forward, pulling Sailor's ears, running his hand repeatedly up and down the horse's curly mane.

"Beginner's luck," said Rupert.

"That horse isn't a beginner," said Billy. "He looks like an Old Age Pensioner."

"He's got half a time fault," said Helen, putting C for Clear by Jake's name. "That puts us in the lead."

In the collecting ring Sailor philosophically accepted the ecstatic embraces of Bridie and Tracey, but was more interested in getting his three Polos reward from Jake, who in his turn was trying to hide his elation. Having automatically checked Sailor's legs for any swelling or tenderness, he loosened his girth and put on his fly sheet.

"Well done," said Malise. "It's hard to believe that horse hadn't walked the course himself."

And as Humpty, Billy, Lavinia and both her parents surged around Jake to offer their congratulations, Malise added, "Delighted he's come good. Completely justified your faith in him. Get Tracey to walk him around in the shade and keep him quiet, and come and have a Coke or something."

But Jake couldn't bear to leave Sailor. Using a bucket of water brought by Tracey, he sponged the horse's head, throat and neck and between his back legs to cool him down. Putting a hand over Sailor's eyes he sprayed his head and ears with fly spray and as it wasn't wise for the horse to take in quantities of water he washed his mouth with a sponge to refresh him.

"Belgravia'd have your hand off if you did that," said Marion, who was walking a sweating Macaulay around the paddock. "He jumped well," she added, nodding at Sailor.

Was this the first round in peace talks? thought Jake. Marion, one of the Iron Curtain satellites, temporarily making diplomatic overtures towards the West.

"Thanks," he said.

The second half of the competition was much tougher. The delays had got to the horses and frayed the riders' nerves. The heat was stifling, the flies even worse. Sipping an ice-cold Pepsi in the competitors' stand, Jake tried to keep calm.

"It's the first time for ages the Germans haven't been in the lead after the first half," said Mrs. Greenslade. "But they're tremendously good at coming from behind."

"Sounds fun," said Rupert looking at Helen, who went pink.

The Germans, in fact, came back fighting, Humpty jumped well, but could only manage eight faults. Lavinia had four, to her parents' ecstasy.

But the first two Germans had only four faults each. Then Manfred came in and only got eight faults.

"Rupert's got to go clear," said Billy, looking at Helen's marks and counting on his fingers. "God, I wish I'd taken math."

Down in the collecting ring, Malise told Rupert the same thing: "Macaulay's a big brave horse. He can do it, if you keep calm and put him right."

But Rupert was still raging with Jake and Malise, and with Lavinia for being smug about getting four faults.

Macaulay was a big brave horse, but he'd suffered when Rupert was angry before, and he sensed Rupert was angry now and it unsettled him. Putting him over an unnecessarily high practice fence, Rupert had banged his fetlocks badly. Macaulay was a brave horse, but he didn't like being pushed around.

Rupert jumped clear until he came to the seventh fence, a huge oxer, then he turned Macaulay too sharply, put him at the fence wrong, pulling him up a stride too early. Despite a huge and heroic jump, Macaulay couldn't make it and had the pole down. This unsettled him for the combination. Fighting for his head, he almost ran away with Rupert and had all three elements down, then put a foot in the water, finishing up with twenty faults.

The British team groaned. This was the round they'd have to drop. It would be too much to expect Jake to repeat his brilliant first round. They been so near beating the Germans; now victory was slipping away. Rupert rode straight out of the ring ignoring the cries of bad luck spoken in five different languages, straight past Marion, out of the collecting ring and back to the stables.

Ludwig came in, stepped on it and, as expected, went clear without a time fault. It was all up to Jake. If he went clear, they would win by half a time fault. The volatile crowd was disappointed not to have a Spanish win, but they admired he courage of this gypsy boy and his hideous horse, and adopted him as their own. "Magnifico," they cried half in irony as he came into the ring.

"We're bloody well going to do it," whispered Jake into Sailor's ear as he leaned forward and shortened his reins. Sailor gave three bucks to show he hadn't fallen asleep and the crowd roared their appreciation.

Off Sailor went towards the first fence, and Billy, despite a blinding headache, felt that rare surge of pleasure that transcends any kind of jealousy when a new star is born.

"You're right," he said to Malise. "He's brilliant."

Malise, unable to speak because he felt so nervous and choked with emotion, merely nodded.

Suddenly Billy felt someone tugging his sleeve. It was Marion. One look at her horror-stricken face and he followed her down the steps.

"What's the matter?"

"It's Rupert. He's killing Macaulay."

"Where is he?"

"Back at the stables, in the stall. He's bolted the door."

As Billy sprinted the three hundred yards back to the stables, he was aware of a huge cheer that seemed to raise the sky. Jake must have gone clear.

Marion ran beside him, sobbing.

"The bastard, the bastard. It was his fault."

"Go and saddle up Belgravia quickly. Rupert'll have to ride him in the parade."

The white hot stone of the stables seemed to burn Billy's eyes. For a second he felt dizzy and thought he was going to faint. Then he heard the terrified screaming of a horse, and the sickening thud of a whip on flesh. He streaked across the yard. Both the half-doors of Macaulay's stall were shut.

"Rupert, let me in."

"Fuck off ."

"Bloody well let me in," shouted Billy, pushing his huge shoulders against the door.

"Mind your own fucking business."

Billy stepped back and ran at the bottom half-door. It began to give. Then he hurled his shoulders at it, nearly taking his head off as it caved in. For a second after the dazzling sunlight, he couldn't see a thing. Then he gave a flying leap and landed on Rupert, winding him and rolling him on the ground.

"Fucking horse," gasped Rupert. "Give me that whip or I'll use it on you."

"You bloody won't." Billy scrambled to his feet.

Macaulay was a pitiful sight. Cowering in the corner, the lather turned red with blood, he had weals all down his shoulder, and across his face just above the nostrils which were extended and as red as a poppy. His eyes were rolling in terror, his veins swollen, his sides heaving.

"You poor bastard," said Billy going up to him. The horse cringed away in terror: "It's all right," he said, catching his bridle: "It's all over." Rupert got to his feet, his face murderous: "Give me that whip, I haven't finished."

"You put him at it wrong," said Billy quietly. "You were a stride off; no horse could have jumped that fence. "It's all right, boy." He stroked Macaulay's trembling neck. "It's all right. You stupid bugger," he added over his shoulder, "you could be prosecuted for this."

"I'll deal with my horses as I choose," snarled Rupert. He was about to make a dive for the whip when they heard a clattering of hooves outside.

It was Marion with Belgravia.

"Go on," said Billy, "Don't you realize we've won? Jake went clear."

"So what?"

"You've got to go collect the cup. You won it too you know,. You only got eight faults in the first round. Go on, Belgravia's waiting."

"I'm not going."

"Stop behaving like a teenager," said Billy echoing Malise. "Do you want everyone saying you're a stinking loser?"

For a second he thought Rupert was going to take a slug at him. Instead he ducked out of the half-door and vaulted on to Belgravia's back.

"Here's your hat," called Billy after him.

Marion took it and handed it up to Rupert.

"You're a bastard," she hissed. "I'm quitting."

Mr. and Mrs. Greenslade, Malise and all the grooms were cheering like schoolboys as the British team rode into the ring. Even Helen, now over the disappointment of Rupert's twenty faults, was jumping up and down and waving her yellow hat in the air. Sailor, the hero of the afternoon, walked on the outside, wall eye looking suspiciously at the crowd but accepting with equanimity the deluge of cushions, flowers and handkerchiefs that descended around him. Jake managed to catch two pink carnations and threaded them into Sailor's browband.

As they lined up in front of the General's box a cushion flew through the air, and Rupert had to duck to avoid it. Jake turned to him. "Rather reminds me of pillow fights in the dormitory of St. Augustine's," he said softly.

Rupert gave him a look of pure loathing which would have withered most people, but Jake was beyond withering.

"They were also very keen at St. Augustine's on people being good losers," he said, and laughed in Rupert's face.

The British team stood in front, with the other teams fanned out behind them. Jake choked back the tears as the Union Jack rose in a series of jerks up the flag pole, and the National Anthem was played for the second time that afternoon, very badly and this time in a minor key.

Afterwards they had to walk rather apprehensively between an avenue of machine guns and meet the very distinguished General, who, despite his great age and the punishing heat, rose to his feet and congratulated them in perfect English. Rupert he appeared to know already, and inquired after his beautiful mother. But before Rupert could reply, a second commotion that afternoon was created by Sailor, who, dragging the unfortunate officer who was trying to hold him, refused to be separated from Jake and, undeterred by the armed guard, followed his master halfway up the stairs.

Fortunately the General had a sense of humor and allowed two of his minions to help him down the stairs to pat Sailor on the nose. Jake smiled. The General smiled, Sailor nudged the General in the pocket as though checking if he were armed too, and the photographers went wild.

"Sailor among soldiers," said the headlines next morning and the press went wild because it was the first time anyone had beaten the Germans in two years. The Germans, who were all very sporting, came up and shook Jake by the hand.

"I think we will have to pull the stocking up, no?" said Hans.

"Are you thinking of selling that horse?" said Ludwig.

As they galloped round the ring, ribbons streaming, sashes across their left shoulders, Jake clutched a solid silver bear, the symbol of Madrid, his prize as leading rider.

"I don't care what you say," said Humpty, swelling his chest at each cheer, "that horse must have some good blood somewhere."

"I must telephone Tory," said Jake as they rode out of the ring. "God I hate those telephones."

"Mummy'll do it for you," said Lavinia. "She speaks Spanish."

Billy was waiting for them.

"Well done," he said to Jake. "Good thing I got that concussion. I'd never have pulled off a double clear."

That night at dinner they went over every fence in every round and the Nations' Cup was filled and drunk out of again and again. And everyone, even Billy who'd deadened his headache with four aspirin,

was relieved that Rupert and Helen excused themselves from the celebration on the very genuine excuse that the General had asked them to
dinner.

Much later, not entirely sober, Jake went down to the stables to
check on his horses. Earlier he'd added salt and electrolytes to Sailor's
feed to make him drink because he'd been very dehydrated after sweating so much in the afternoon. Now he found his water bucket was
empty, and kicked over. Jake filled it up again. Rather laboriously he
repoulticed Sailor's legs to take away the aches brought on by such
strenuous jumping.

Then he went and looked at his darling Africa, walking her up
and down. Her leg was better; she'd be O.K. for the Grand Prix tomorrow. He couldn't resist going into the tackroom and shining his
flashlight on the ribbon he'd won earlier, rubbing it along his face,
kissing the hard cardboard centre.

"Maudlin idiot," he told himself, but he was still walking on air.

As he came out he saw a light in Rupert's stalls. Creeping towards
it, he looked over the half-door and found Marion redressing Macaulay's weals. Jake winced in distaste. It looked as though someone had
been playing tick-tack-toe with a knife on the horse's shoulder.

Macauley saw him first and cowered into the corner. Marion
swung around, instinctively pulling the rug over the damage.

"What the hell are you doing here?"

"Looking at my horses. I suppose that's Rupert's work?"

For a second Marion hesitated between discretion and outrage.
Outrage won. "Of course it was, the bastard." She peeled back the rug
and went on applying cream to the wounds.

"I've got some better stuff for that," said Jake. Returning to his
trunk in the tackroom, he got out a jar of ointment, which had turned
liquid in the heat.

"What's that?" said Marion suspiciously.

"An ancient Romany recipe," said Jake, opening the jar. "Steady
boy, I'm going to make you better." Gently he began to rub the ointment into the weals.

Macaulay trembled and flinched but did not move away; he
seemed to understand that Jake was trying to help him.

"He'd never let Rupert do that," said Marion.

"Who stopped him?"

"Billy did."

"Malise know?"

"No, and with Rupert's luck he won't find out. Macaulay'll be in
his stall tomorrow. Rupert's riding Belgravia in the Grand Prix, and
Mayfair in the class before. The day after we're flying back to England
first thing. He's a lovely horse, but Rupert's ruined him. He'll sell him
on now. Can't bear to be faced with anything that makes him feel

guilty. Helen'll go mad. Macaulay's the only horse she's interested in, because he named him after her."

Having treated the last cut, Jake patted the horse. Then, perhaps because he was more than a little drunk, he said, "Leave him to rest; come and have a drink."

Marion looked at Jake's expressionless face. He was like one of those birthday cards left blank so you could write your own message. "All right," she said. "I'm sorry I snitched your breeches."

"That's O.K. I knew Rupert put you up to it."

"He's really got it in for you."

"Makes two of us. I've really got it in for him."

They never made it to the bar.

"Rupert would really fire me if he could see me now," said Marion.

"Well he'll certainly hear you if you don't keep your voice down; they're in the next-door bedroom."

Marion laughed. "I quit today anyway."

"You going to leave?" asked Jake, unbuttoning her white shirt.

"I've quit so often he probably didn't believe me."

Accustomed exclusively over the last five years to Tory's bulk, Jake could hardly believe the slenderness of Marion's thighs or the springy breasts which didn't collapse under her armpits when she lay down. For a few minutes he stroked her body as wonderingly as if she were a £50,000 thoroughbred, and when he kissed her he was enchanted by the skill and enthusiasm of her response. They broke away. She smiled at him, touching a gold ear ring.

"Are you really a gypsy?"

"Half," said Jake.

She ran her tongue along the lifeline of his hand. "I'm crossing your palm with saliva."

It was a feeble joke but they both had to bury their faces in the pillow to muffle their laughter. Both got an extra buzz from knowing how angry Rupert would be if he could see them. Jake was small, thin and not very handsome compared to Rupert but his hands had a magical effect on Marion, soothing away all the tensions and frustrations she'd been bottling up since Rupert married Helen. Rupert's lovemaking was aggressive, like a power drill—her Campbell-Black and Decker, she used to call him. She enjoyed it only because Rupert was so wildly attractive and one melted at his slightest touch. Jake was gentle, considerate, yet seemed by comparison extraordinarily detached.

In fact Jake was extremely attracted to Marion and very glad he was able to prevent himself coming too soon by working out a plan of action.

Afterwards, when they lay sated in each other's arms, Marion

said, "That was wonderful. Who would have thought it? You're not looking for a groom are you?"

"I couldn't pay you as much as Rupert, and you'd distract me too much."

"You totally ignored me all week."

"That was deliberate. I hated you for being part of Rupert's entourage and you're so goodlooking you irritated the hell out of me."

"Prettier than Helen?"

"Much." He knew that was the judgment that would win her over.

"I wish Rupert thought so, the bastard."

"Is he faithful to her?"

"At the moment. I think he's rather captivated by the idea of his own fidelity. It's such a novelty. But they've hardly had a night apart since they've been married, and she sticks like a leech. Wait till she gets pregnant and can't go everywhere with him. That's when the trouble's going to start. He can't do without it."

"Nor can I, by all events. . . . Look," he said, pushing her hair back from her forehead: "You're fond of Macaulay aren't you?"

"Yes, I love him."

"All you have to do is let me know when Rupert's selling him."

"He'd never sell him on to you."

"Perhaps not, but someone else could buy him for me."

"He's too strong for you. Rupert can only just hold him and he's a sod in the stable."

"I don't control horses by brute strength," said Jake, "and my guess is that he won't jump for Rupert any more."

"Have you got a nice wife?" asked Marion, hoping he'd make love to her again.

"Very," said Jake.

"Rupe said you married her for money."

"Doesn't stop her being nice."

"Don't you feel guilty?"

"No," said Jake. "This is my reward for a double clear."

19

A month later Jake Lovell drove through the warm June evening doing sums. Late last night Marion had called him from a phone booth to tip him off about a horse named Revenge.

"He's a sod, but a brilliant one, and you'd better hurry. Rupert's after him too."

Wasting no time, Jake had driven all the way down to Surrey the next day to look at the horse, and he liked what he saw. Jake was seldom cheated when buying a horse. His stint with the gypsies had stood him in good stead. They taught him that dealers often disguise lameness by deliberately laming the opposite leg by shoeing it wrong, that they put black marks on a horse's teeth with hot wires so it'll pass for a six-year-old, or even shove mustard up its rectum so the animal prances along with its tail up in a travesty of high spirits. They had also taught him never to be carried away by a horse's looks.

He had to confess, however, that Revenge was the handsomest horse he'd ever seen, a showy red chestnut with zigzag blaze, a mane and tail that looked as though they'd been dipped in peroxide, and an air of intense self-importance. He had been bought by a doting millionaire father for his daughter, when she suddenly decided she wanted to take up show-jumping. Revenge had turned out far too strong for her. Allowed to get away with murder, he had learned to buck and spin at the same time, and tried to drag Jake off under some low hanging oaks at the top of the field. On the other hand, he had jumped a line of large fences without effort, landing like a cat, and showing not only an ability to get himself out of trouble, but incredible powers of acceleration.

Jake ached all over where the horse had thrown him three times, but he still wanted him. Unfortunately, George Masters, the dealer, wanted £5000, which Jake didn't have. He'd just sold two of his best novices in order to put down the deposit on the indoor ring. The balance on this would be owing by the end of the summer.

Darklis, the new baby, was adorable, but meant more work for Tory. Isa, jealous and demanding, needed extra attention, which meant Tory had less and less time for the horses. Tanya, the one groom, was hopelessly overworked. Jake desperately needed another groom, but to pay her he needed to go to more shows and win more money. To do that he needed another Grade A horse to fall back on when either Sailor or Africa was unfit. There's a hole in your bank balance, dear Jake, dear Jake, he told himself.

So deep was he in thought on the way home that he suddenly realized he'd taken the wrong turn and was driving through Bilborough. There was Bilborough Hall, russet and mellow in the evening sun, scene of his first show on Africa. If he competed there now, as a member of the British show-jumping team, would he be invited to lunch up at the house with the nobs? There was Brook Farm Riding School. He felt a sick churning relief that he no longer worked for Mrs. Wilton. There was the village green, and the church and Molly Maxwell's house.

Molly Carter she was now, the Colonel's Lady. Diplomatic relations had been resumed between Molly and Tory after Isa was born, but they were still uneasy. Jake had never forgiven the Colonel for firing his guns. Molly had never forgiven Jake for running off with her daughter, and even worse, making her happy.

Molly's marriage to Colonel Carter had not been happy. He was hardly back from his honeymoon at that hotel in Brittany that served English food before he realized what a bitch she was. Too old and too proud to split up, they were locked together in mutual enmity. The Colonel's retirement from the City had thrown them even more into one another's company. Molly took refuge in endless bridge. The Colonel tried to control Molly's spending and dickered with the stock market. Fen had been shunted off to boarding school when she was eleven, and was discouraged from visiting Jake and Tory during vacations because of Molly's quite unfounded suspicion that Jake would seduce her.

Driving slowly past the house, Jake could see his mother-in-law playing bridge with three other harpies in the drawing-room. The house had a burglar alarm now, and a yellow rose growing over the porch, and a swimming pool round the back, so the Colonel could do his ten laps every morning like an old walrus.

Jake suddenly felt hungry. He hadn't had any lunch and, with a hundred and fifty miles to drive home, he decided to drop into the next pub. Being early evening, he found it half-empty, but as he ordered a pint of beer and a pork pie, he heard a familiar bray of laughter. Not turning, he edged down the bar. There, in the mirror behind the bottles, he could see his step-father-in-law arched rather like a golden retriever over a brassy blonde who certainly wasn't his mother-in-law.

In amusement, Jake watched the Colonel putting his hand over the blonde's hand and lifting it with a clash of bracelets to his lips. Stupid old goat, he thought. Picking up his beer, he catfooted toward the table.

"Hello, Bernard," he said softly.

Colonel Carter dropped the blond like a wasp-filled pear and turned puce. Suddenly the ring on his paisley scarf seemed very tight.

"Hello, Jake," he said with a great show of heartiness. "Long time no see. What are you doing in this neck of the woods?"

"Looking at a horse."

"You've been doing very well this year. Getting your name in the papers. Even saw you on the tube the other night. Going to Crittleden are you? Sailor still going strong?"

"Of course he is," said the blonde. "He did well in Madrid didn't he? Double clear indeed, and Billy getting concussed, naughty boy. Macaulay was off form though. I think that Rupert Campbell-Black's dead cruel."

Jake found himself gazing into the heavily blue-mascaraed eyes of the true show-jumping groupie. She was showing a lot of crinkly bosom in a shiny blue and white dress, her shoe straps were biting into her fat ankles and she enveloped Jake in wafts of cheap scent, but her face was kinder than Molly's.

"Aren't you going to introduce us, Bernard?" she said.

"Well, as you obviously know, this is my son-in-law, Jake Lovell," said the Colonel even more heartily, "and this is Vivienne, a great friend of my late wife, Jennifer."

Vivienne didn't look as though she'd be the great friend of anybody's wife, thought Jake.

"Aren't you going to join us?" she said.

"All right, just for a minute, as long as Bernard doesn't mind," said Jake maliciously. "How's Fen?"

"Not too good really," said the Colonel. "Very moody, never brushes her hair, fights a lot with Molly, litters her clothes around the place. Moll sold her pony last week."

Then, seeing the expression on Jake's face, he added defensively,

"Wretched animal kept jumping out of the field. Had to go and collect it in the middle of the night."

"Probably lonely. Does Fen know?"

"Not yet."

"Break her heart," said Jake.

"Poor little soul," said Vivienne.

"How's she getting on at school?"

The Colonel shook his head. "Refuses to work. Just draws horses and gazes out the window. Wrong place for her, really. They don't have riding there. But Molly insisted."

"Don't know why people have kids, then send them away," said Vivienne, enjoying her disapproval of Molly. Then, turning to Jake: "Pity she can't live with you if she's so horse mad."

Jake, who'd been thinking the same thing, was biding his time. Fen was only thirteen, but was already showing distinct promise. If he could get her under his wing, he could mold her the way he wanted to, and she'd be very useful helping with the horses. They might even to be able to avoid getting a second groom.

"What d'you like to drink?" he asked.

"My round really," said the Colonel, not getting up.

"I'd like a gin and cinzano, Jake, with lots of ice, thanks," said Vivienne.

"If you twist my arm, I'll have a whisky and soda," said the Colonel, who'd been drinking beer before.

"Attractive, isn't he?" Jake heard Vivienne say as he went to the bar. "Shame about the little girl. Ought to go and live with them."

"Molly worries about what her friends think," mumbled the Colonel. "Likes to appear the devoted mother."

"On the other hand," said Vivienne slyly, "Fen'll soon be old enough to be competition. Won't be much fun when Molly's menopause clashes with Fen's adolescence."

The Colonel didn't think so either.

"Tell us about this horse," said Vivienne, when Jake returned with the drinks.

"He's called Revenge," said Jake, "And he's got acceleration like a Ferrari, and Christ he can jump, but he's got a very bad temper and has some bad habits."

"How much do they want?" asked the Colonel.

"Five thousand. I'm wondering how the hell to raise it."

He looked speculatively at the Colonel and then at Vivienne.

"That's awfully cheap," said Vivienne, "Three good wins and you'll get your money back."

The Colonel suddenly felt heady. His masculinity had been badly dented by Molly; she was always accusing him of being an old woman about money. He'd show her. It was time the lion roared.

"I'll buy it for you, Jake," he said. "Fun to have a flutter."

Vivienne clapped her fat hands together with more jangling.

"Oh, what a good idea. You can split the prize money."

Jake didn't react, determined not to betray his excitement. "Horse'll take a bit of sorting out; not going to hurry him; probably won't see any return for your money for a year or so."

"Go on, Bernard, it'll give you an interest. You've always wanted to own racehorses."

"What'll we tell Molly?" asked Jake flatly, "She wasn't ecstatic last time a member of her family bought me a horse in a pub."

"That I bumped into you," said the Colonel, "decided to help you out."

For a quarter of an hour they discussed technicalities. Rupert might well go higher, if so they'd scrap the whole idea.

Jake looked at his watch. It had Donald Duck on the face, and had been a birthday present to Isa that Tory had thought the child was too young for.

"Ought to get back; Tory's keeping supper."

"Bye bye Jake. Can I have your autograph?" said Vivienne.

"Nice lady," said Jake as the Colonel walked him out to the car.

"Old friend," mumbled the Colonel.

"Friend of Molly's too?" asked Jake.

"Needn't mention her to Molly, need we?"

"I never met her," said Jake. "You saw me going into the pub and you stopped to say hello and we had a drink together."

"Good man," said the Colonel, patting Jake rather gingerly on the shoulders. "Always felt sorry about that Tory business. Worried about Fen too. You'd be doing her a kindness."

Jake fingered the Colonel's check in his pocket.

"I'll think about it."

Jake waited until morning to ring up Masters. He didn't wish to appear too keen. He offered £4000.

"You must be joking," said Masters. "Anyway Rupert Campbell-Black's coming to look at him at eleven. He was the first one after the horse, so I ought to let him have first refusal."

"Four grand is my offer and I'm not topping it. If Rupert offers more, let him have it. I'm going to see another horse over Cheltenham way this afternoon and I want to know if I've got the spare cash to buy it, so I'd be grateful if you'd let me know what Rupert says one way or the other."

"I'll call you the moment I hear," said Masters. "Don't rush into that other deal too quickly."

Jake then had to spend the morning biting his nails. It was all nerve, allowing the elastic to go slack so the other person started pulling on it. When Masters called, he made Tory say he was out and would call back, which he didn't. Then Masters called again.

"That shit Campbell-Black never turned up, never bothered to call. The horse is yours if you want it."

"Four thou," said Jake.

"Four thousand five hundred."

"£4250."

"Done."

"I'll come and collect him now."

It was another hot wearying drive and it took three stable lads, George Masters and Jake, all their persuasive power, and a lot of bad language to get Revenge into the van, by which time the horse was drenched with sweat. As Jake drove away he could hear him stamping and kicking in rage, and wondered if he'd been mad to buy him.

Two miles on he was driving along a narrow country lane, brushing the buttercups and elder flowers, when suddenly a dark blue Porsche hurtled round the corner and only just avoided a head-on collision by skidding onto the shoulder and nearly removing a wild rose bush.

The driver, a blond man wearing dark glasses, swore and hurtled on. There was no mistaking Rupert, but Jake didn't recognize the brunette beside him.

"When you get there mate, you'll find the cupboard's bare," and he threw back his head and laughed. Revenge renewed his kicking and stamping.

"And you'd better be nice to me, boy," he called back to the horse. "You've no idea how lucky you are not to go to that bastard."

And all the way home, as the dead gnats peppered the windscreen, he kept laughing to himself, until at last, as the sun was setting, he saw the gleaming willows and red pink walls of the Mill and felt as always that wave of joy at coming home. Christ, he was tired. Darklis was still on four-hour feedings so they weren't getting much sleep. Tomorrow he had to get up early to drive up to a show in Yorkshire, and the next week on to the Royal at Stoneleigh.

Tory came out to meet him, with Wolf bounding ahead.

"You got him. You must be exhausted."

When they lowered the ramp, Revenge was cowering in the corner, shivering as though in a fever, despite the heat of the evening.

"Poor old boy, he must have had a bad time. But isn't he beautiful?" said Tory.

As Jake went towards him, Revenge bared his teeth and darted at Jake like a cobra.

"He's a bugger," said Jake, "No one's to go near him for the next day or so but me."

Having tied him up securely, Jake rubbed him down, put on a sweat rug, watered and fed him. But the horse didn't seem remotely interested in food and, once he was let loose, proceeded to pace round and round his stall.

"Leave him," said Jake. "He'll settle down."

"Thank God for Tory," he thought as he went into the house.

Everything was tidy. The toys that had been strewn around the hall when he left that morning were now all put away. The only evidence of babies was a pile of fluffy diapers folded in the hall. A smell of shepherd's pie drifted enticingly from the kitchen.

"How've things been?"

"Fine really, except for Isa posting all the entry forms down the toilet. Fortunately I'd typed them, rather than filling them in in ink, so they didn't run. They're drying off in the oven.

"By the way," she said, after she'd given him a glass of beer (they were still too poor to drink wine, except for special occasions), "Fen's here."

He looked up. "Run away from school?"

"Yes. She discovered Mummy'd sold the pony."

He found Fen, still dressed in her school uniform, slumped sobbing on the bed.

"How could she do it? She forgets my birthday, then next day, she sells Marigold. She won't even tell me where she's gone."

"Probably a good home. We'll find out," said Jake, "and she *was* too small for you."

"I know. I really tried not to put on weight so I wasn't too heavy, but she was the only thing I had. I loved her so much."

Jake patted her shoulder. For a second she was crying so hard she couldn't get the words out. Then she said, "I can't stand school any more. Its a horseless, dogless desert, going on and on." She reached out for Wolf who'd climbed on to the bed, and was trying to lick her tears away. "And I can't live with Mummy any more. I hate her and I loathe him. Please don't send me back."

Jake was shocked by her appearance. Last time he'd seen her, a year ago, she'd been a little girl. Now she was a teenager with lank greasy hair, pimples, and a pasty skin flecked with blackheads. Although she was terribly thin, he could see the first swell of breasts beneath the grassgreen school sweater.

"Please let me come live with you," she sobbed. "I won't be a nuisance. I'll babysit and I'll get up early, and work at night and weekends."

Jake stroked her hair. "I'll talk to Tory. Come downstairs and have something to eat."

"I can't, truly. I'd be sick. Oh, Jake, I'm so sorry. You must be exhausted, and to be faced with me after that drive. But I keep thinking of Marigold." Her face crumpled again. "How lonely and bewildered she'll be."

"I'll go and call your mother," said Jake.

"Fen's here," she heard him say on the downstairs telephone. "No don't talk to her tonight. She's fast asleep; must have walked most of the way."

Jake overslept next morning. Pulling on his clothes, he went downstairs to see how Revenge had survived the night. As he put on his shoes in the kitchen, he could hear Africa knocking her water bucket around and Sailor pawing the door and neighing, "Where's my bloody breakfast."

"All right, all right," grumbled Jake, "I'm coming."

Outside he froze with horror. Both halves of Revenge's door were open. Isa, fascinated by the horses, had developed a dreadful habit of standing on a bucket and letting himself into the stalls. Heart hammering, Jake ran across the yard as fast as his limp would allow. Inside he found Fen, her arms round Revenge's neck, feeding him carrots and kissing him on the nose.

"Good boy, good boy. You'll love it here and you're going to become a great and famous show-jumper. Jake'll see to that."

"Fen," said Jake, desperately trying to keep his voice steady, "come out of there."

She looked up at him with an angelic smile. "He's so sweet. Can I ride him later?"

Revenge glared at Jake, raised a threatening front hoof, and then darted his big white teeth in the direction of Jake's arm.

"Stop it," said Fen firmly, taking his halter and giving it a shake. "That's bad manners. You don't bite your master."

Revenge debated the matter for a minute, rolling his eyes and looking boot-faced.

"No," said Fen, even more firmly, "you're just showing off, you're an old softy really."

Revenge, deciding that perhaps he was, butted Fen in the pockets in search of more carrots.

"What's his name?" she asked.

"Revenge."

Fen grinned. "Revenge is sweet, he really is."

At that moment Jake decided to keep her.

"If you're so taken by him, you'd better feed him and skip him out."

"What's he been eating?" said Fen.

"Stable boys mostly," said Jake, "but I think we'll try and wean him off that habit."

Rupert drove home in a blazing temper. He'd tried everything to make Masters tear up the check, but when the man insisted he'd given the buyer a receipt, and refused to name him, Rupert lost his temper and an undignified shouting match ensued.

On the way home Rupert took it out on Sarah, the brunette he'd met at a show earlier in the week. He'd been furious with himself for bedding her that morning. He'd been on the way home from a dinner in London and had rung Helen to say he'd be home late, as he was making a detour to Surrey to look at a horse. The detour had also taken in Sarah's apartment. He hadn't enjoyed screwing her at all and he'd fallen asleep afterwards, which made him impossibly late for his appointment with Masters. He'd taken a stupid risk too. Masters might easily have called him at home and Helen smelled a rat and been hurt unnecessarily. He didn't feel particularly guilty about being unfaithful, but enraged that, through his stupid dalliance, he'd lost a really good horse. He'd have to get his spies out and track Revenge down. By the time he had chewed up a few more people, he might go even cheaper. Since Madrid, Macaulay had been a write-off, losing all his form and confidence. He'd have to go too, he thought as he dropped Sarah off.

"When'll I see you again?" she called after him anxiously.

But Rupert had driven off without a word. Even the sight of Penscombe in the height of its summer beauty didn't soothe him. Helen's clothes, her endless schemes for the garden—a lilac walk here,

a little heated swimming pool there, a 17th century stone nymph there
—cost a fortune. Billy worked hard, but he cost a fortune too, always
buying other people drinks and feeding Mavis chicken. The whole
shooting match is dependent on me, Rupert thought sulkily. I've got
to win and win to support it.

He drove straight around to the stables where he found Billy
working one of the novices in a nearby field. He admired Billy's patience, but why was he resting The Bull and Kitchener this week and
not at a show, winning money?

Billy pulled up and rode towards him, wiping the sweat from his
forehead.

"Did you get him?"

"Already sold on."

"Shit, that was bad luck. Who got him?"

"Wouldn't say."

"Might have been more trouble than he was worth. This is going
to be a very good horse by the way."

"Good. It's about time he started paying his way."

He found Marion in the tackroom, cleaning a saddle. She didn't
look up. Still sulking, thought Rupert. For a second he admired the
unsupported breasts in the tight blue T shirt, and the succulent thighs
in the denim skirt, which was only just buttoned up enough to hold it
up.

"Didn't get him," he said. "He was sold on."

"Who to?" Marion bent over the pommel, so Rupert couldn't see
how much she was blushing.

"Masters wouldn't say."

"Just as well. I quite like having two arms and legs."

"Particularly when they're such sexy legs."

She looked up: "Wasn't aware you'd noticed them recently."

"I always notice them."

"How was Sarah?" It was an inspired guess, but it hit home.

Rupert didn't flicker; then unable to resist a joke,added, "Rather
like Coventry Cathedral—ravishing from the outside, but very disap-
pointing once you got inside."

Marion started to giggle. "You are frightful."

He went up behind her, stroking the back of her neck. She lent
against him, furious with herself for feeling faint with longing.

"Rupert darling," called a voice.

"In here," said Rupert, moving away from Marion to examine the
diet charts.

It was Helen, also in navy blue, in a dress which must have cost
fifty times more than my skirt and T-shirt, thought Marion. Helen
was looking rather pale, her newly washed hair falling to her collar
bones, subtly smelling of Miss Dior, her blue high heels catching in
the ridges of the floor.

She's as out of place here as a tiger lily in a cabbage patch, thought Marion.

"Darling, how did you do?"

"I'm coming in," said Rupert. "I'm filthy. You can bring me a drink in the bath."

He was reading *Horse and Hound* in a foot of hot scented water when she walked in. Funny, he reflected, how even after two years she averted her eyes.

"Nice dress."

"It can go back if you don't like it."

"I do. You can take it off in a minute."

"Here's your drink," she said hastily, hoping to distract him.

Rupert took a deep gulp and went on reading Audax on the Derby.

"Why don't you come and soap my cock?"

Helen blushed. "Billy'll be in in a minute."

"So what? Not in here he won't. Come on."

Helen sat on the toilet seat and took a birdlike sip of her drink.

"Why are you drinking vodka?" demanded Rupert. (She usually had sherry.)

"It's Perrier actually,"

"What on earth for?"

"I went to see Dr. Benson today."

He looked up sharply. "You ill?"

"No," she took a deep breath, "I'm going to have a baby."

"You what?" The next moment he'd reared out of the bath like a great dripping whale and taken her in his arms, drenching her.

"Oh darling," he said in a choked voice, "are you sure?"

"Positive—Rupert, you're soaking me."

"Christ, that's fantastic. I can't believe it."

"It's wonderful isn't it?"

"You must rest. You mustn't carry anything heavy. Are you sure you're up to carrying that glass of Perrier? When did you think you were? Oh sweetheart, you should have told me."

"I wanted to be sure."

"I thought you were on the pill."

"I stopped taking it." Tears suddenly filled her eyes. "I was real scared after the abortion," she almost gagged on the word, "I wouldn't be able to conceive. Then I started feeling vile in Madrid."

"You never told me." Still dripping, he crouched beside her, kissing her again and again.

She was so pleased he was pleased, but she wished he'd get dressed. This rampant nakedness seemed incongruous somehow with the momentousness of the occasion.

Finally he stood up. "My father'll be knocked out. What shall we call him—Eddie?"

"He might be a girl."

Rupert started doing his sums. "He'll be able to ride in the 2000 A.D. Olympics."

He went to the bedroom window and opened it. "Billy, Billy."

"Put something on," urged Helen, wrapping a towel around him.

"Billee."

Next minute Billy appeared at the edge of the lawn still riding the grey.

"Yes."

"For Christ's sake, come here."

"Not across the lawn," wailed Helen. "Mr. Higgins'll go crazy."

"Helen's going to have a baby."

Billy threw his hat high up in the air and rode through some delphiniums.

"Fantastic."

"You can be fairy godfather," said Rupert, "and just think what a wonderful opportunity it'll be to get Nanny back to look after him."

Over my dead body, thought Helen.

At that moment one of the Jack Russells wandered into the bedroom and sicked up a few forthy blades of grass on the carpet. And the dogs are going to be kept outside once the baby comes, she said to herself. I'm not having them in the nursery.

20

*F*en never dreamed she'd have to work so hard. Jake's indoor ring was finished by the autumn, which meant, even as the days drew in, that she was able to get up at five in the morning and work the horses for two hours before school. Then she would come home, grab a quick bite to eat, dash off her homework, then back to the indoor ring until late in the evening. Often she fell asleep at her desk. Her teacher called Tory and complained. Fen was not stupid, just exhausted and totally unmotivated. It was the twentieth century; people didn't send children down the mines anymore. Her complaints fell on deaf ears. Tory remonstrated gently with Jake and tried to get Fen into bed by ten, but it was often midnight before they finished.

Jake was a very hard taskmaster. As Fen was tall for her age, it was pointless to waste time learning to ride ponies. She must go straight on to horses, and as she'd be competing initially against children who'd been riding in the circuit since they were seven, there was a lot of ground to catch up.

Fen found it hard to be patient. She only wanted to jump and jump, but Jake insisted she do the groundwork first, hardly letting her ride across the yard without coming to see if she were doing it properly. To straighten her back and deepen her seat, he gave her daily lessons on the lunge, without reins and stirrups, with her arms behind her back, and a stick through them to keep her shoulders straight. Cold weather didn't deter him. Sometimes they worked outside, with everything frozen, and the snow hardening to a sheet of ice. With the wind up their tails, the horses would give a series of bucks and, stirrupless and reinless, Fen would fly through the air and emerge from the shrubbery like a snowman.

Day after day she came in with raw bleeding knees and elbows, every bone in her body aching. Seldom did she complain, she was so frightened of being sent back.

On the whole she was happy, because she felt she was getting somewhere. Like Jake, she loved the cozy family atmosphere created by Tory. She adored the children, Wolf and the cats and the horses, and hero-worshipped Jake. Revenge, however, was her special pet. She spent any free moments in his stall, talking to him, calming him. In a way they were learning the ropes together. Like her, when he arrived, he was miserably displaced, suspicious of everyone. Gradually they got their confidence back.

Revenge was never worked in the same field twice. Horrendously highly strung, he was a picky eater, hated any stall but his own and was liable to kick any strange stable to pieces. He also fell madly in love with Africa, following her everywhere to Sailor's irritation, and yelling his head off if she went to shows without him. Jake brought him on with infinite slowness, never overfacing him, retiring him over and over again, going for slow clears to give him confidence, never exciting him by jumping him against the clock.

Revenge still put in the odd huge buck and had a piece out of Fen if he'd got out of bed on the wrong side. But she defended him to the death.

"He's really a kind horse," she would explain, "he always waits when he's bucked you off."

Tory and Fen got on well, but there were undeniable tensions. Although she helped in the stables, Fen made a lot of extra work at home. She was extremely untidy, dropping her clothes as she stepped out of them, forgetting to bring her washing down, spending hours in the bathroom washing her hair, gazing at her face in the steaming mirror and leaving the bath filthy and the drain blocked with hair. She was also terribly dreamy and, when she wasn't with the horses, her nose was always buried in some technical horse book or riding magazine, and if there were dishes to wash she always managed to find something to do in the stable. Tory tried not to resent Fen or to mind

her teenage moods, or to feel jealous that Jake and she spent so much
time together.

Fen adored Jake, but, unlike Tory, she saw his faults. Tory spent
hours making quiches and chicken pies for Jake when he was away at
shows, which he seldom touched because he got so nervous, and which
Tanya, the groom, usually finished up so Tory wouldn't be hurt. Jake
never laughed at Tory's jokes, seldom reacted, often didn't answer. She
noticed how Tory ended so many sentences with "Isn't it," to evoke
some sort of response, how she never answered Jake back. Jake and Fen
on the other hand had blazing rows.

One grey day towards the end of November Fen was particularly
tired. Her form mistress had sent her out of the class and the headmistress had come past and shouted at her. Her period was due any
minute, her pimples were worse than ever and she felt fat and edgy.
Jake was in a picky mood. Tomorrow he and Tanya were off to Vienna
and Amsterdam for two big shows. Everything had to be packed up
and ready. It was so mild that Tanya had tied Revenge up in the yard to
wash his tail. The dead dry leaves were swirling round his feet.

She had just finished, and Fen, who had fed all the other horses,
had Revenge's feed ready, when she suddenly remembered she hadn't
added any vitamins or chopped carrot to encourage him to eat. Putting
the bucket down beside Sailor's door, she rushed back to the tackroom
and here got sidetracked by the latest copy of *Riding* which had a piece
on her hero, Billy Lloyd-Foxe. Alas, Sailor who was on a diet and
incurably greedy, seeing the bucket, promptly unbolted his door. Having wolfed all Revenge's feed, he was discovered by Jake smugly licking
his lips.

Jake hit the roof. "Fen," he bellowed.

"Yes," she said nervously, coming out of the tackroom with a
carrot in one hand and the magazine in the other.

"Can't you fucking concentrate for one minute?" said Jake
furiously. "Filling your stupid head with dreams of Wembley, and lining up above Rupert Campbell-Black, with the Queen telling you
what a star you are. Well, you'll bloody well never get there unless you
pull your head out of the clouds."

"I'm sorry."

"What's the use of saying sorry? Sailor's just eaten Revenge's food.
You're bloody useless."

Fen lost her temper. "I hate you; you're a bloody slave driver."

Dropping *Riding* and the carrot, she raced across the yard, unty-
ing Revenge's halter. Leaping on to his back, she clattered across the
yard, clearing the gate out to the fields, thundering across them, clearing fence after fence, making for the hills.

"Come back," howled Jake. "That horse is valuable."

"I don't care," screamed Fen, picking up Revenge as he stumbled over a rocky piece of ground, galloping on and on until she'd put four or five miles between herself and the Mill.

As she passed a cairn of rocks, she realized how dark it had gotten. Then suddenly, like a blanket, the mist came down. Tugging Revenge around she retraced her steps. She came to a fork in the pathway. There was boggy ground to the right. She turned left, the path turned upwards and upwards. It must lead somewhere. Then she went rigid with horror as she realized they were on the edge of a ravine and had nearly tumbled over. She gave a sob of terror as she realized she was totally lost. Gradually the enormity of her crime hit her. Revenge didn't belong to Jake; he was Colonel Carter's and potentially the best horse in the stable, clipped and out in the cold in the middle of winter.

"I don't know what to do," she cried, flinging her arms around the horse's neck, shivering uncontrollably in her thin, mist-soaked sweater. "Oh God and Rev please help me."

For a few seconds Revenge snatched at the short grass. Then he sniffed the wind and set off purposefully. Fen tried to check him, terrified of more ravines, but he was quite determined. They came to marshy ground. Fen, petrified of getting bogged down, could feel his hoofs sinking in, and the sucking sound as he pulled them out. She jumped as tall rushes brushed against her legs. Now he was splashing through a little stream. On he plodded, avoiding rocks and boulders, checking carefully for holes. Fen tucked her frozen hands in his blond mane, clinging to him for warmth, letting him carry her. He couldn't know the way; he'd never been that far from home. They'd never find it.

The mist seemed to be clearing. She could see trees below, and oh, God, surely that was the same cairn of rocks? They were going round in a circle.

She gave a sob of despair as Revenge turned and started picking his way delicately down a steep hill. It seemed to go on for ever; any minute she'd fall off him and tumble crashing to the bottom. Then suddenly the mist seemed to slide away and dimly she could see lights ahead.

Jake, back at the Mill, was frantic. He'd been out on one of the novices, scouring the countryside for Fen, shouting, calling, finding nothing. No sound had come back through the thick blanket of fog. Every time he saw a car snaking along the road, he waited for a squeal of brakes and terrible screams.

He came home again. There was no news.

"Bloody stupid girl. Christ why did she do it?"

Tory took a deep breath. "You're too tough with her, Jakey. She's only thirteen."

"No time to be superstitious," snarled Jake, and rode off into the night.

Tory sighed and went back into the house. It was nearly nine o'clock. Darklis was crying, woken up no doubt by Isa, who was worried about Fen. She had just settled them when from the yard she heard Africa give her deep whinney. All the other horses immediately rushed to their half-doors, peering out at the clouds rolling back on a beautiful starlit night. The dry leaves circled and rustled, whipped by the wind. The horses turned to prowl around in the straw, then came back to the door and listened again, each nickering more excitedly.

Suddenly Tory heard hoof beats. Africa sent out a joyful neigh into the darkness. The other horses whinnied, snorting and pawing at their doors. Revenge didn't whinny back; his task wasn't over yet. Five minutes later he walked into the yard.

Tory ran out. "Oh thank God you're home."

Fen burst into tears. "Rev did it. He brought me back. I'm so sorry, so terribly terribly sorry."

Rushing out of the tackroom, Tanya caught her as she fell off the horse. "You're frozen, pet. There, don't cry. You're safe."

"Rev did it," mumbled Fen.

Revenge didn't want a hero's welcome. He stumped past the other horses without a glance, making disapproving noises about stupid teenagers who got lost and made him late for supper. He smelled of mist, sweat and exhaustion, and went straight to his stall and, with a long groan, folded up and began to roll, his feet shadow-boxing the air.

"Where's Jake?" muttered Fen, through frantically chattering teeth.

"Out looking for you. Go in and have a bath."

Even after a bath she was still cold. She put on her nightgown and three sweaters over it, looking around her little room. The green-sprigged Laura Ashley wallpaper, put up especially by Tory, was already covered in posters of Billy Lloyd-Foxe, and Ludwig von Schellenberg. The shelves brimmed over with every horse book imaginable. Every shelf was crowded with china horses which took Tory forever to dust. On her dressing table was the hedgehog which Jake had made her from teasels for her last birthday. They had been so good to her and she'd kicked them in the teeth.

Jake would be quite right to pack her back to her mother and the Colonel. She picked up Lester her battered teddy bear, named after Lester Piggott, cuddling him for comfort. Her heart sank even further at the sound of horse's hoofs on the bridge, muffled by the willows— Jake coming home.

He'd be insane with rage. He had a five o'clock start in the morning. His best horse had been sabotaged. Looking through a crack in the curtain she saw him slide off the big black gelding, hand him to

Tanya and go into Revenge's stall. Leading him out, he examined his legs, making Tory walk him up and down.

Fen trembled, terrified he'd find something wrong. But he merely nodded curtly and turned towards the house. Fen crept away from the curtain. Next moment she heard him coming up the stairs, and the boards creaking outside her room. I'm not going to cry, she thought desperately, he's bored by tears.

"I'm so sorry," she stammered.

"I should think so," he said bleakly. "Of all the bloody irresponsible things to do. You could have killed yourself and the horse."

"I didn't think." She hung her head.

"Time you started. Can't afford passengers."

"Please don't send me back." A tear splashed on to her hands. If she had looked up she would have seen his face soften.

It would make her swollen-headed if he told her that the only reason he was so harsh with her was because he knew how good she could be. He put a hand on her shoulder.

"It's all right, no harm done. Rev's O.K. Must like it here. After all, he came home."

Fen looked up, eyes streaming. "He did; he was so clever. I was completely lost. He brought me back home like Lassie." There was a pause.

"When is school out?"

"The eighteenth."

"Well you can leave two days early and come to Olympia with me."

She gazed at him unbelievingly.

For a minute she couldn't speak, then she flung her arms round Jake's neck. "Oh Jakey, thank you," she sobbed, "I love you so much."

Helen had honestly intended to go to the Olympia show. She still had some Christmas shopping to do. She'd catch up on a few matinées in the afternoons and spend the evenings watching Rupert. Friends who'd gone skiing had lent them a penthouse flat, looking over Holland Park, just a few minutes from Olympia. She was touched and a little ashamed by Rupert's delight that she would be with him. It was the first show she'd been to for ages. She'd been sick with the baby and felt so tired, and after a tidal wave of Rupert's female fans sent her flying and nearly trampled to death at the Royal International back in July, she'd decided not to attend any more shows.

Rupert had been competing abroad for much of the last five months, and during the separations she'd been very lonely and spent many restless nights worrying she might miscarry or the baby might be deformed. She took her pregnancy very seriously, eating the right food, resting, going religiously to prenatal classes and giving up drinking completely. So those jolly reunions after Billy and Rupert came back from successful shows, when even Helen got mildly tight, were things of the past.

She steeled herself not to mind when Rupert was away. She missed him, but subconsciously she built up other resources. She spent a fortune on baby clothes and another fortune on a new nursery, decorating the baby's room daffodil yellow and white and putting in a washing machine, a dryer and a small fridge next door, with a room for the nanny all done up in Laura Ashley beyond that.

She also liked being able to watch all the egghead programs she wanted on television, to listen to classical music all the time and not to have to cook huge meals when she was feeling sick.

Then Rupert would come home, bringing not tenderness but silver cups and suitcases of dirty washing. Invariably on his return he wanted a sexual marathon, and although her gynecologist reassured her that sex couldn't harm the baby, Rupert's lovemaking was so vigorous that she was terrified she'd miscarry and found herself tensing up and going dry inside.

She also had the feeling Rupert wasn't being supportive enough. He flatly refused to go to prenatal classes or be present at the birth.

"It's too Islington for words," he said by way of excuse. "I've pulled calves, I've pulled foals, but I'll be buggered if I'll pull my own baby. I've found you the best gynecologist in the country, booked you into a private room at Gloucester Hospital. Let them get on with it."

He also laughed his head off when he found her listening to Beethoven and Vivaldi in order to stimulate the baby in the womb.

"D'you want to give birth to a quartet?"

Throughout November and December he'd been away on a successful but punishing round trip to Geneva, Vienna and Amsterdam, which left only a hectic twenty-four hours at home before setting out for Olympia. Even so Rupert found time for sex. He'd won a polaroid camera as one of his extra prizes at Amsterdam and was determined to take photographs of Helen in the nude.

"Your boobs are so fantastic since you got pregnant."

Helen, conscious of her swelling stomach, couldn't get into the swing of things at all. Nor did she like being photographed first thing in the morning without any makeup on.

"It's not your face I'm interested in," said Rupert laying each photograph on the dressing table so they gradually took on color and shape, until he got so turned on he had to make love to her.

Afterwards she came out of the bathroom, wrapped in a towel, to find a naked Rupert joyfully poring over the photographs.

"For goodness sake put them away. Mrs. Bodkin might see them," she pleaded.

"This one's much the best. Come and look."

Helen approached cautiously; then embarrassment turned to rage as she realized he was admiring not her naked beauty but a photograph of Badger, lying grinning upside down in his basket, now banished to the landing.

"I must show Billy," said Rupert.

"Why not take one of Mavis too?" snapped Helen.

She was fed up with those wretched dogs and horses. It wasn't a question of playing second fiddle; she wasn't even in the orchestra.

Later Rupert and Billy had a session with their secretary, Miss Hawkins, catching up on the mail and checking that entry forms had been sent off for the next few months. When Helen came down with some washing she found the dark blue diary for next year on the kitchen table. They must have been working out the first six months show dates. Fondly she turned to March 7th, the most important entry of all, the expected date for the birth of the baby. But instead, to her fury, she found Antwerp, Dortmund, Milan scrawled across the first eighteen days in March, with red Pentel arrows stretching from page to page indicating they wouldn't be returning to England between shows. Helen couldn't believe it. Rupert intended to be away for the most momentous event of his life. She stormed into the drawing-room where Rupert was pouring himself and Billy pre-lunch drinks.

"Billy, will you please leave the room," she said in a dangerously quiet voice. "I want to speak to Rupert."

"Yes, sir, certainly sir," said Billy, grinning and making himself scarce.

"Earth's the matter?" asked Rupert. "Not still sulking about Badger's picture, are you? D'you want a drink?"

"You know I haven't touched liquor since I was pregnant. I'd like to know the meaning of this." She flung the diary at Rupert. "Look at March."

Rupert opened it. "Well? Oh, I'm sorry to be away three weeks on the trot, but they're all good shows and I'll be home a lot in January and February."

"Haven't you any idea what else is happening in March?"

Rupert looked blank. "Can't think."

"Our baby is to be born."

Rupert grinned in dismay. "Oh Christ, angel, I'm frightfully sorry. It completely slipped my mind. Don't worry, I can hop on a plane the minute you go into labor, or if you really think it'll arrive on the 7th," he glanced at the diary, "I could fly out late to Antwerp. They don't have the big prize money there till the third day."

Helen, for the first time since they were married, went beserk, screaming abuse at Rupert, her red hair flying like a maenad, her face scarlet.

Rupert looked at her in amazement. "Are you sure you haven't been drinking?"

The next minute she was hurling objects at him. The altered Augustus John went flying through the air and hit the wall with a splintering crash. Then she started on the bookshelf. *Burke's Landed Gentry* nearly landed on target, followed by *Ruff's Guide to the Turf*, followed by leather-bound volumes of *Paradise Lost*, and Dante's *Inferno*. Gibbon's *Decline and Fall* fell at Rupert's feet. Rupert, laughing and dodging out of the way like a boxer, annoyed her even more. As the top shelf was emptied, there was a knock on the door. It was Mrs. Bodkin in her hat and coat, quivering with curiosity.

"Was there anything else?"

"Yes," said Helen. "Bring me a jug of orange juice please."

Two minutes later Mrs. Bodkin puffed in with the jug and two glasses on a tray.

"Thank you, that'll be all Mrs. B. See you to-morrow," said Helen, firmly shutting the door on her. Then, picking up the jug of orange juice, she hurled it in Rupert's face and collapsed sobbing on the sofa.

Nothing Rupert could say would placate her. If he wasn't going to be with her when the baby was born, she wasn't coming to his bloody show. She still refused to speak to him when he and Billy set off to London that afternoon. Rupert, who'd always believed that a room full of roses and a gold bracelet could placate any woman, was slightly surprised when his gifts didn't sway her.

*O*lympia, the last show before Christmas, always has a holiday atmosphere. Most of the riders have a break afterwards until the middle of January. All the glamour of the sport is concentrated and enhanced by an indoor show. The collecting ring stewards and stable manager in charge of the 150 box stalls have increasing difficulty keeping high-spirited riders in order as the excitement mounts. Practical jokes and parties go on all week.

Neither Billy nor Rupert, however, was in a particularly festive mood as their van rolled into the trailer park on the eve of the first day. Billy was fretting because he suspected Lavinia Greenslade had transferred her affections to a handsome French count called Guy de la Tour. Rupert was still smarting over Helen's intransigence. Christmas shopping traffic jams were driving him wild.

"Fuck the masses, fuck the masses," he screamed, leaning on his horn.

Billy was further depressed to see a huge van carelessly parked like an acute accent with Guy de la Tour, Republique Francaise in huge letters across one side.

"Let's go and get drunk," said Billy.

Rupert's temper was not improved the following day when they walked past the exercise ring and saw Fen lunging Revenge.

"Nice horse," said Billy.

Although Revenge had been transformed into a picture of hard muscle, health and well-being over the past six months, he was still unmistakable with his strange zigzagging blaze and his two long white socks. For a second they paused to watch him.

"Don't recognize the groom," said Billy.

"I say, darling," shouted Rupert.

Fen swung around, turning crimson. She couldn't believe they were talking to her.

"What's the name of that horse?"

"Revenge."

"Who does he belong to?"

"Jake Lovell."

"Shit, that's where he's ended up," said Rupert. "The little bastard pulled a fast one on me. I wonder who tipped him off."

"Dear God," prayed Fen fervently, "make my zits go, give me some decent boobs and don't let me fancy Rupert Campbell-Black."

At the beginning of the week the collecting ring gossip was all of the two Italian horses who had escaped and had a lovely time galloping up and down the Westway. Now it had switched to Guy de la Tour's romance with Lavinia and to Jake Lovell's new horse. Every time Revenge came into the arena, afternoon or evening, people rushed to the ringside to have a look. At the beginning of the show the lights and the crowds had upset him, and he went around star-gazing and leaping two feet above the fences. After forty-eight hours he settled down.

There had been a bad moment, however, on the second day. Jake put his foot in the stirrup and Revenge put in a hell of a buck, landing Jake on top of a steaming pile of dung.

"Found your own level, Lovell," jeered Rupert as he rode past. Jake's reply was quite unprintable. It took all Fen's tact to calm him down.

"I'll soak your breeches," she said soothingly. "All the stains'll come out."

Nor were the fates being kind to Billy. Just when he was trying to woo Lavinia back, a local barber gave him a hideous, far too short haircut.

"I got so engrossed in *Playboy*, I forgot to watch him," moaned Billy afterwards.

Even worse, Billy turned The Bull too fast into the combination on the second night, forcing him to put in a refusal. Billy sailed over his head, landing on a pole and knocking out his two front teeth, which further damaged his beauty. There wasn't time to have them capped. He'd have to wait until after Christmas.

With no sign of Helen, Rupert's eye started to rove. Every day there were novelty events—the Army did a display of tent pegging, lady clowns did dressage. The Pony Club put on a demonstration of Snow White and the Seven Dwarfs. First amused by the fact that Snow White's horse had diarrhea, Rupert's eye fell on a ravishing girl playing Grumpy called Tiffany Bathgate. Gradually during the week he'd been buying her drinks and flirting with her. He even bought her a £150 gold watch from the Garrard's stand as a Christmas present, which she permanently showed off on her wrist like a dog holding out a sore paw.

By the last night Fen was absolutely exhausted. She hardly had the energy to wash her hair for the party that night. Living on junk food all week, her pimples were worse than ever. She longed and longed to be a rider or at least one of the elite bunch of grooms who all knew each other, swapped endless gossip and who had found time to go shopping and come back with pretty clothes. She admired from afar the handsome Guy de la Tour who had so captivated Lavinia. Love had made Lavinia prettier than ever. She had cut off her long curls and now with her hair as short as a boy's looked the epitome of French chic. Already half the show-jumping groupies, who hung around the place in breeches hoping someone might mistake them for a competitor, had followed suit and lopped off their long rippling manes as well. Fen also noticed Billy looking absolutely miserable. She felt so sorry for him, although he had cheered up a bit earlier that evening when he and Rupert won the fancy dress relay. Billy with a pipe in his mouth and a raincoat had dressed up as Harold Wilson, while Rupert cavorted around in high heels, a red dress and a blond wig. It had brought the house down.

Now all the grooms were getting their charges ready for the last event, the Radio Rentals Grand Prix. Fen, with both Sailor and Revenge to do, had her work cut out. Cries of "Give me the body brush," "Anyone seen my sponge?" "Christ they're calling us already" were coming from all sides.

"In the bleak mid-winter frosty wind made moan," sung the loudspeaker. Rupert and Billy sat side by side in the riders' stand, their long legs up on the back of the seats in front, watching Grumpy.

"Isn't she gorgeous?" said Rupert smugly. "She's coming out with me tonight."

"How old is she?" asked Billy.

"Sixteen, or so she claims."

"Shouldn't be playing Grumpy, she's grinning like a Cheshire cat," said Billy, as Tiffany Bathgate cantered by, pony tail swinging. "I'll report her to the District Commissioner."

"She's bringing Dopey with her," said Rupert. "Meeting me at the apartment. Just imagine having the two of them."

"You ought to be ashamed of youself," snapped Billy.

"Why don't you come too?"

"I'm going to the party afterwards, I must talk to Lavinia. She's been avoiding me all week. Her parents are wild about Guy because he's a count."

"A cunt," said Rupert.

"That too," said Billy.

"I wonder if Greenslade *père* realizes Guy hasn't a bean," said Rupert. "He needs the Greenslade cash to keep his place going in France. 'I cannot afford to 'eat the underrooms,' he told me last night. Do you think I should give Helen an English setter puppy for Christmas?"

"No," said Billy.

Snow White and her entourage cantered out of the ring, with Grumpy blatantly grinning at Rupert as the arena party were putting the finishing touches to the jumps for the Grand Prix. Now the rose red curtains which parted theatrically to admit each competitor were clashing with the scarlet coats of the riders as they walked the course to a jazzed-up version of "Oh Come All Ye Faithful."

The collecting ring was very hazardous. Belgians crashed their horses over the jumps crying "Numero Huit, Numero Sept" to their grooms and discussing where they were going for dinner. Rupert was having a row with an Irish rider (nicknamed Wishbone, because of his long bow legs) because they had both tried to jump the upright at the same time.

Fen walked her two horses around the outside, keeping out of trouble, Sailor calming Revenge who looked as beautiful as Sailor looked ugly. She was still shaking from her first encounter with her mother and Colonel Carter since leaving home. As owners, they'd come to the show to watch Revenge. Molly had been "absolutely livid" with Bernard when she discovered he'd blown £5000 on a horse for Jake behind her back. She'd denied him her bed for more than a month. But gradually she was beginning to appreciate the kudos of being a winning owner. Everyone was mentioning Revenge as an Olympic probable. Molly was already planning her wardrobe for the next Games, in Colombia next August. She enjoyed sitting in the riders' stand and talking about "My horse" in a loud voice. Molly was very relieved that Fen appeared to have totally lost her looks.

Certainly it had been Jake's show. Africa, Sailor and Revenge had all won big classes. You couldn't get into the van for silver cups. Sailor grew in popularity, the crowd was wild about the "Old Mule" with his mangy tail and his drooping head, who caught fire in the ring. Whenever he left the van Jake was mobbed by autograph hunters. And Fen told him someone had written "I love Jake Lovell" on the wall of the Ladies, and underneath lots of people had written "Me too." Joanna Battie had interviewed Jake for the *Chronicle,* gushing over his romantic gypsy looks. Jake pretended to disapprove, but secretly he was delighted and had re-read the piece several times. He had even been interviewed by Dudley Diplock as he came out of the ring. The fact that he hardly got a word out didn't seem to matter. He smiled, and when Jake smiled publicly, which was about once every five years, the world melted.

The bell rang, the riders left the arena. In the distance you could still hear the mournful cry of the men at the gate trying to sell programs to last-minute arrivals. The arena was flooded with light as the television cameras came on. As Rupert mounted Belgravia, he spat out his chewing gum.

"I want it," said a besotted teenager, rushing forward. A deafening cheer lifted the roof off as he rode into the ring.

"I can't help it," thought Fen. "He's vile, but he is attractive." Rupert jumped an untroubled clear and rode out as Ivor Braine rode in. The collecting ring steward, who had a headache from drinking too much at lunchtime, was shouting at late arrivals.

"I'm going to report Rupert Campbell-Black to the B. S. J. A. for calling me a fart," he grumbled. "And you're late too," he said to Humpty who was supposed to be jumping next.

"Get out of my way then, you little fart," said Humpty. "You're a worse nagger than my wife."

Humpty also went clear.

Billy, waiting to jump, felt near suicide. Lavinia was still avoiding him. Now Count Guy was in the collecting ring, crashing over the practice fence pretending not to understand the collecting ring steward who was now castigating *him* for being late.

"That man is a preek," he drawled to Lavinia, as he rode towards the rose-red curtains.

"Bonne chance, my angel," said Lavinia, blowing him a kiss.

Count Guy's dark brown stallion, however, took a dislike to the curtains and shied into a group of officials in pinstripe suits, dislodging for a moment the complacency of their smooth flushed faces as they scuttled for cover. Then with a flurry of Gallic expletives Guy rode into the arena and proceeded to lay waste to the course.

"Oh bad luck darling," said Lavinia as he came out, shrugging dramatically, reins dropped, palms of both hands turned to heaven.

"Fucking frog," muttered Billy as he passed him on the way in.

But he was so upset, he jumped badly and notched up twelve faults.

"I've got a splinter," grumbled Marion.

Ignoring her, Rupert went back to the riders' stand to watch the rest of the rounds. As he listened to a group of German riders chattering behind him, his thoughts contentedly drifted towards Tiffany Bathgate who, with her dumpy friend, would at this moment be washing themselves (as well as they could in the Olympia showers) for him. There were two bottles of champagne in the fridge. Perhaps he should offer them a proper bath when they arrived. Goodness knows where that might lead.

The next moment the two girls were forgotten as Jake and Revenge came in, jumping unevenly but very impressively. Revenge was fooling around between fences, but when he jumped he really tucked his legs up.

"I want that horse," thought Rupert grimly. "He's got everything I like, brains, temperament, good looks."

He was suddenly aware that the woman on his right was making a lot of noise.

"Do you remember me?" she said, turning to Rupert.

"I never forget a face like yours, but I'm terrible at names," said Rupert. It was his standard reply.

"I'm Molly Carter, Maxwell that was. Tory, my daughter, was doing the season in 1970. You were *such* a deb's delight. All the mums were in love with you, too."

"Tory. Of course I remember. Very shy, treated every man as though he was going to chuck snowballs with stones in at her."

"She married Jake Lovell, you know. It was a bit of a shock at the time, but he's done awfully well."

"Helped by Tory's money of course," said Rupert.

"Oh, of course. He'd never have made the grade without her." She gave a little laugh. "And my husband's been helping him out recently."

"Really," said Rupert, his brain beginning to tick.

"Revenge is our horse."

Not by a flicker of a muscle did Rupert betray how interested he was.

"Your horse?"

"Jake was short of cash last June and desperate to buy Revenge in a hurry. Some other buyer was after him, so Bernard put up the money. I was livid at the time, but he seems rather a good investment. Jake is rather maddening though."

"Yes?"

Under Rupert's blue gaze, Molly was becoming indiscreet. "He keeps retiring the horse because he doesn't want to push him. Feels he's not ready to jump against the clock."

"Rubbish," said Rupert. "When a horse is as good as that you've got to press on."

"Really," said Molly. "Oh do look, the Princess has arrived. I love her dress."

Everyone stood up with the usual clattering of seats. The band played the National Anthem. Round followed round, but only Ludwig and Jake on Sailor jumped clear.

"Helen's having a baby in March," said Rupert, getting to his feet. "So we're not going out much, but we must all have dinner sometime."

"That would be lovely," said Molly, giving him their telephone number. "Bernard usually goes to London on Wednesday morning to see his stockbrokers, but I'm always there."

"I'll remember that," said Rupert pointedly.

Molly smirked to herself as he walked down the steps. She'd always thought Rupert was most attractive. Nice that she hadn't lost her touch.

Six riders had to jump off. Jake took one look at the course. For an indoor arena with limited space it was enormous, ending up with an upright of 5 feet 8 inches.

"I'm not jumping Revenge," he said to Colonel Carter.

"Don't be bloody silly, man. There's £4000 at stake."

"I don't care. It's too much to ask an inexperienced horse. He jumped a beautiful round earlier. Let's leave it at that."

The Colonel looked thunderous.

"Only tell how good he is if you have a go."

"He's had a tough week."

Molly's face was twitching. "I think you're being very foolish, Jake. I've just been talking to Rupert Campbell-Black, Bernard, and he said he'd certainly jump Revenge against the clock."

"All the more reason for not," snapped Jake.

"Quite right," said Fen crossly. "He's a young horse; set him back months if he lost his confidence."

"Really Fenella," said Molly, "no one asked your opinion."

"He'll be sixth anyway," said Jake. "That's £500. I said I'd train him my way. You'll have to lump it."

Rupert rattled everyone by setting a virtually unbeatable time of 29.3 seconds.

"Such a good rider," said Molly to Colonel Carter and, lowering her voice, "You've no idea what sense he talked."

No one could beat Rupert's time. Ludwig was a second slower, Lavinia had a fence down, Humpty couldn't catch him, nor could Hans Schmidt.

"I think that's £4000 in the bag," said Rupert to Billy. "I might even take the girls to Annabels."

Jake felt sick. Looking at the six jumps he wondered how the hell he could beat Rupert's time. Then, when he came to the rustic poles, where everyone else had gone around the wall, he cut in from the other side, jumping the fence sideways as he turned. The crowd gave a shout and, suddenly aware of a knife-edge finish, bellowed him home. He cleared the last fence and looked at the clock. He'd done it. A fifth of a second faster than Rupert. He hugged Sailor, who gave three huge bucks, nearly unseating him. The crowd went mad.

"Well done, my friend," said Ludwig, clouting Jake on the back. It was his biggest win yet. Everyone—except Rupert, Molly and Colonel Carter—surged forward to congratulate him.

The arena was now pitted with holes. Several women in fur capes and ball dresses carrying ribbons and the huge silver cup walked out, tiptoeing to avoid any droppings as the winners came in, Jake riding Sailor and leading Revenge. The Princess smiled and said she'd been following Sailor's career and she was sorry she hadn't got any Polos, and hadn't Revenge jumped well? Jake felt very happy.

Back in the collecting ring the Yuletide spirit was relentlessly reasserting itself. Two Welsh cobs were being harnessed to a sleigh which was being loaded up with Christmas trees by a man in a red coat. Helen's old admirer, Monica Carlton, in a tricorn hat and a frock coat, was putting on a false moustache.

The band played "All The Nice Girls Love a Sailor," as Sailor cantered the lap of honor under the spotlight, as proud as a butler with the family silver. Jake went deliberately slowly, knowing that Rupert would have difficulty holding Belgravia.

"For Christ sake, get a move on," snarled Rupert, cannoning into him.

"It's all very well," thought the Colonel darkly, "Jake gets £4000 plus £250 out of that. I get a measly £250."

Rupert came out of the ring, looking at his watch. Tiffany Bathgate would be at the apartment in half an hour; he'd better step on it. Then he glanced across the collecting ring and his blood froze, for, picking her way towards him, very pale but unspeakably beautiful, a fur coat hiding any trace of pregnancy, was Helen. As usual, she made everyone else look commonplace. Rupert was off Belgravia in a second, handing him to Marion, taking Helen in his arms.

"Darling, I'm so sorry. It was all my fault," she said.

"No, it was mine," said Rupert, holding her against him, his brain racing.

Looking down, he saw how the fox fur coat set off the red hair and the huge eyes that were already filling with tears.

"I missed you so much," she said, "I nearly went to the apartment and waited for you as a surprise."

Rupert felt dizzy with horror. That would have been a fine welcome for Tiffany Bathgate and Dopey.

"What would you like to do?" said Rupert, his ingenuity working overtime. "There's a party, if you're not too tired, then we could have some supper."

Anything to keep her away from the apartment until the coast was clear.

"I'm a bit tired, but I don't want to be a party pooper."

"I'll just go and see what Billy's plans are," said Rupert. "Have a word with Malise. And here's Humpty and Ivor. I won't be a second."

"Hello stranger," said Humpty, kissing her. And as they all gathered round to welcome her, she suddenly realized how nice they were and how wrong she'd been to build them up as obsessed, insensitive monsters.

Rupert went over to Billy, who had just bought himself a triple whisky for the bar.

"Helen's arrived."

"I saw. Fine mess you've got yourself into. I don't know why you're looking so cheerful."

"I love my wife," said Rupert blandly. "Look, you must divert those schoolgirls. Take them out to dinner, explain that Helen's turned up."

"Why the fuck should I? I *must* talk to Lavinia."

"The party'll go on for hours. She'll be much more receptive after a few drinks. Look, I'll pay. But I promised Tiffany a night out (and in) so be a love and give them a whirl, and tell Tiffany to keep herself on ice for the next time."

Billy looked mutinous.

"You don't want to ruin my marriage," pleaded Rupert,

Billy sighed. "OK, I'll intercept them, then take them straight back to wherever they are staying and come on to the party."

Billy was knocked sideways by the smell of warm scented flesh, newly washed hair and radiantly expectant youth. The two girls were bitterly disappointed, and also well below the age of consent. In the end Billy was too kind to dump them. He gave them a fancy dinner with lots of champagne, most of which he drank himself, and when he saw Tiffany dolefully looking at her gold watch, said,

"It wasn't an excuse, honest. Helen really did turn up."

"You will give him my phone number won't you?" she said.

Back at Olympia, lights had been turned out in the stables. Horses dozed in their stalls. A Christmas drunk was running up and down pinching hay out of Belgravia's hay net distributing it among horses that didn't have any.

The party was soon well under way. This year Humpty was acting as host; everyone turned up at his trailer with bottles. Predictably Driffield arrived with a bottle of Airwick.

"Thought you needed it Humpty," said Driffield, splashing whisky into his glass. "Place smells like a wrestler's armpit."

Heavy drinking stepped up the high jinks. For his officious behavior during the week, the collecting ring steward was dumped in the water trough. Later a pretty waitress from the Olympia Bar, well primed by the rest of the British and German teams, asked Humpty if she could actually meet Porky Boy. Only too happy to show off his favorite asset, a blushing Humpty led her off to Porky Boy's stall, followed at a safe distance by the other riders. The waitress looked into the stall first.

"Oh dear," she said, turning to Humpty, "he seems to have shrunk." Rushing forward to defend his beloved, Humpty discovered to his horror that instead of Porky Boy, one of the grey Shetland ponies that had pulled Snow White's wedding coach was calmly devouring Porky Boy's hay. For a second Humpty was speechless.

Then he exploded. "Who's stolen Porky Boy?" he bellowed. "Someone's stolen my horse. Don't you all laugh at me. I'm going to call the police."

He was just dialing 999 in the nearest telephone booth when suddenly Porky Boy emerged from behind a bank of wilting poinsettias, looking very put out at being deprived of his supper. Humpty jumped on the horse and chased Rupert, Ludwig and Hans around the stands and into the arena. Ivor Braine was happily getting drunk with Wishbone, the sandy-haired Irishman.

"Get it done, lad, it'll do thee good," Ivor was saying, as he filled up the Irishman's glass.

Dudley Diplock was grumbling to Malise about the fact that they no longer televised the presentation of the prizes.

"It's what the public likes to see."

But Malise wasn't listening. He was looking at Helen Campbell-Black, who was being pinned against a pile of straw bales by Monica Carlton, who was still wearing her moustache and tricorn hat.

"Excuse me." said Malise and went over to rescue her.

"Oh shove off, Malise," said Monica. "I get little enough chance to talk to this exquisite creature."

"So do I," said Malise. She looks ill, he thought, and supposed it was the tired last months of pregnancy.

Fortunately Monica soon got sidetracked by the pretty waitress.

"Are you OK?" Malise asked Helen, slightly lowering his voice.

"Fine," she said brightly.

"I like to take a fatherly interest in the wives of my team," he said in what he knew was an unnaturally hearty voice.

"I wish Rupert would take a fatherly interest in our baby," said Helen bitterly.

"It's probably jealousy," said Malise, "and apprehension. He sees the looming challenge to his own identity and privacy. I know I felt the same, but I became positively doting once they arrived."

"I sure hope so," sighed Helen.

They watched Lavinia and Count Guy, arm in arm, working their way through the crowd towards them.

"Pity she's chucking herself away on that frog," said Monica Carlton.

"I didn't know," said Helen, startled. "Is it serious?"

"I think so," said Malise.

"Oh, poor Billy," said Helen in distress. "I don't think Lavinia would have been quite right for him, but then I don't think anyone would be special enough for Billy."

"Might just be the making of him," said Malise. "He's too soft, too protected by your husband, drinks too much, too."

"We're just going," Lavinia said to Helen, adding fondly, "Guy doesn't like parties over here because he hates not being able to talk Fwench, but I just wanted to intwoduce him."

"Ah, *la belle Helene*," said the handsome Count softly.

He took Helen's hand, pressed it to his lips, then gazed into her eyes.

"Everyone speaks of your beauty, but none did you the justice. Now I understand why Rupert keep you hidden away."

"When's your baby due?" said Lavinia rather pointedly.

And when Helen told them, Guy, not appearing to mind in the least not talking French, proceeded to express amazement that Helen was still so slim, and launched into a long dissertation on what she ought to say, and how his aunt Hortense had just had her sixth child, and how he hoped Helen would come and stay in his chateau when the next Paris show was on.

"Must go and have a word with Jake Lovell," said Malise.

"I thought you wanted to *aller*, Guy," said Lavinia petulantly, "We're getting married," she told Helen.

"Oh I'm so pleased for you both."

"Come *on* darling," said Lavinia, dragging the reluctant Guy away. Nearby, Wishbone was trying to sell Humpty an Irish horse.

"But who's he by?" Humpty kept saying.

"Ah," said Wishbone, smiling engagingly, "who would you like him to be by?"

Malise found Jake in a corner talking to Hans and Ludwig. Beside them Fen had fallen asleep on a hay bale.

"That's a very good horse of yours, Jake," said Malise.

"Vitch von?"said Hans Schmidt, "Zay are both top hole."

"Revenge," said Malise. "You ought to be thinking of him in terms of the next Olympics."

"Not enough mileage." said Jake flatly.

"I disagree. I saw that horse when he was carting Annie Buscott all over the place. The improvement's been remarkable."

Jake blushed slightly.

"Olympics aren't till September," said Malise.

"What about Sailor?" said Jake quickly.

"Great Nations' Cup horse, not sure if he's Olympic stature. No, don't look boot faced. I know how you feel about Sailor, but his wind isn't that good, and in a high altitude country like Colombia he won't be very happy. Africa's a great horse too, but I notice she likes soft going more and more these days. I only discovered this evening that Revenge is owned by your father-in-law."

"Taking my horse's name in vain," said Colonel Carter, who'd been eavesdropping. "Think he's got Olympic potential?"

"Well I certainly wouldn't rule him out."

"What are you going to do with him now?" Colonel Carter asked Jake. He'd had enough to drink to become bullying.

"Turn him out for a couple of months. He needs a break."

"Well don't leave him out too long," said Malise. "He needs the experience; but I congratulate you, Jake, he's a credit to you. So's she." He looked down at the sleeping Fen. "Been watching her in the practice ring. Living with you full time, is she now?"

Jake nodded.

"She'll be knocking on the front door herself in a few years' time," said Malise.

Jake made sure Fen was asleep, then said, "She's a little cracker."

The party dragged on. Wishbone and Ivor were singing "Danny Boy" when Billy finally arrived at two in the morning. Rupert buttonholed him immediately. "Everything OK?"

"Fine," said Billy. "I've delivered them safely back. You can go home now." He helped himself to the last four fingers of whisky with a trembling hand.

"How was little Tiffany?" asked Rupert.

"Upset; but not nearly as much as me. I've just seen Lavinia necking in the street with Guy de la Tour. She's certainly down for the Count."

"So will you be if you keep on drinking. Helen and I are off. Come with us."

"Did Lavinia say anything?" said Billy.

Rupert looked at him straight. "Yes, I'm afraid she said she and Guy are getting married. Look, I'm sorry, but you can do better than her any day, Billy."

As Billy was leaving he bumped into Malise.

Seeing Billy's face, Malise said, "Why don't you come back to my flat for a cup of coffee?"

"Terribly kind, but I think I'd rather be by myself."

"Are you sure? Where are you going?"

"Don't know really—bit of a shock—I was going to ask her to marry me, you see, when this Guy suddenly turns up."

He was very drunk, but despite the awful haircut and the missing front teeth, he had a stricken dignity. Tenners were falling out of his overcoat pocket. Malise gathered them up.

"My fancy dress winnings," explained Billy.

"I'll look after them for you," said Malise. "Come on, where are you staying?"

"Addison Gardens, with Rupert."

As they passed the men's lavatory, they could hear Ivor supervising Wishbone being sick. "Get it oop, lad, get it oop. It's all right as long as tha' knows the way it's going."

"I'll walk you up there."

"Please, I'd rather be alone," said Billy.

"All right," said Malise. "Look, Lavinia's a nice girl, and I can't imagine she and Guy will last very long, if that's any comfort to you. But I honestly think you can do much better than that. As Helen said earlier, you're special."

Billy shook his head. "I loved her, but I suppose they'd have been frightful in-laws. Good night."

It was bitterly cold outside. Programs, food wrappers, streamers, old number cards and wisps of straw were whipped around his feet by the icy wind.

"In the bleak mid-winter," Billy sang, "frosty wind made moan."

His voice broke and tears poured down his cheeks as he set out unsteadily in the direction of Addison Gardens.

*B*ack at the Mill, good as his word, Jake turned his horses out for a rest. It pleased him to see them really enjoying their grass, even Revenge dropping his belly like an old hunter. In February a program was announced for Olympic possibles. The riders mustn't overjump their horses and they must take part in the Olympic trials at the Bath and Wells Show and Crittleden in June. The probable team would then be chosen for a trial over the huge, demanding fences at the Aachen

Show in Germany in July, after which the Olympic team—four riders and a reserve—would finally be selected.

Officially, the Olympic Committee told Jake, they were interested in both Sailor and Revenge. Unofficially, Malise rang Jake and asked him if, in the event of one of the other riders, say Rupert, being selected without a decent horse, would Jake be prepared to jump Sailor and lend Revenge to Rupert. The answer was an extremely curt negative. If Revenge made sufficient progress to be selected, over Jake's dead body would he let anyone else ride him, particularly Rupert. Malise apppreciated his sentiments and reported back to the Olympic Committee, who felt somewhat differently. Colonel Roxborough, the Chairman, Master of the Westerham, a bronze medalist before the war, who'd never moved an inch to get any of his five wives, was not the only member who felt Jake was behaving in a thoroughly unsportsmanlike fashion. After all, Belgravia and Mayfair, who'd both been overjumped, were not as good as they used to be, and Macaulay, after a dazzling start, had suddenly lost form altogether.

The Committee was heartened, however, by Billy Lloyd-Foxe at last hitting top form. Trying to forget Lavinia, avoiding parties where he might bump into her and cutting down on his drinking, he had concentrated on his horses with dramatic results. The Bull, and often Kitchener, were in the money at every show they went to, and both were regarded as Olympic possibles.

Among the other possibles were Humpty, Driffield, Ivor Braine and Lavinia de la Tour, who had married Guy in March. Billy managed to be abroad for the wedding, but sent them a king-size comforter as a wedding present, adding a wry little private note for Lavinia: "If I can't spend the rest of my life on top of you, at least my present can."

As a newlywed, no doubt subjected to endless demands by Guy, Lavinia lost form. It was agony for Billy to see her with Guy on the circuit, but he found his heart didn't ache quite so much if he was beating the hell out of both of them.

In March, while Rupert was driving from Dortmund to Vienna, Helen went into labor. As his van was snowbound on a mountain road, no one managed to contact him for thirty-six hours. Flying straight back to Gloucestershire he found that Helen had nearly died after a long and very difficult birth, and that the baby was in the intensive care unit. Seeing her paler than her white pillow, her red hair dark with sweat and grease, Rupert was overwhelmed with remorse. How could he have done this to her?

"I guess Nanny was right about good child-bearing hips. I'm sorry, darling," he said, taking her hand.

Not a single word did she reproach him, but he saw the hurt in her huge eyes and knew that his absence would be held against him later. As he sat with her in her private room, various doctors came and talked to him, and nurses popped in to have a gaze. Actually the nurse in charge was frightfully pretty, but after three hours Rupert was rigid with boredom. He turned on the television but when he looked around and saw that Helen was crying he turned it off.

He was delighted to have a son, particularly after his smooth and expensive G.P. friend, Dr. Benson, had turned up and assured him that both child and mother should pull through.

"But I really think you should stick around for a bit, Rupe. She's had an awful time and kept calling out for you all the time."

"I appreciate your advice," said Rupert coolly.

"You can do better than that," said Benson, equally coolly. "You can act on it, unless you want Helen to wind up in a bin."

Rupert rang Billy and told him he wouldn't be coming to Vienna and would he bring back Rupert's horses.

"What's the baby like?" asked Billy.

"Got red hair, so we know it's Helen."

Then Rupert sat down and wrote letters putting baby Marcus Rupert Edward down for St. Augustine's and Harrow. Looking at the tiny baby, with its sickly face like a howling lemon and bracken-red stubble of hair, it seemed impossible that he would ever attain such heights.

In the evening Rupert went home to Penscombe and slept for fourteen hours, but after that he scrupulously visited Helen every day. She seemed pathetically grateful for the attention, but was distressed that she was unable to breastfeed.

"What the hell does it matter?" asked Rupert. "I thought you wanted your figure back."

He was further irritated that Helen had struck up a friendship with another mother named Hilary Stirling. In her early thirties, Hilary denied her good looks by wearing no makeup and pulling her dark hair into a bun. A passionate supporter of the Women's Movement, a braless, undeodorized vegetarian with unshaven legs and armpits, she had just had her second baby, Kate, named after Kate Millett, by natural childbirth—"A wonderfully moving experience," she told Helen.

Hilary's husband Crispin, who appeared to do everything in the house—cook, clean *and* look after Germaine (their first child)—had also been present at the birth. He was very earnest, with long thinning hair and a straggly beard, and came to visit Hilary in the hospital with Germaine, now aged eleven months, hanging from his neck in a baby sling. Helen thought him extraordinarily unattractive, but at least, unlike Rupert, he had been there being caring and supportive.

It suddenly seemed to Rupert that every time he came to see Helen, bringing bottles of champagne, gulls' eggs, smoked salmon and armfuls of spring flowers from the garden that Hilary was sitting on Helen's bed, breastfeeding her disgusting baby and flashing her goaty armpits.

Helen thought she was wonderful.

"She's a very talented painter. Look at this sketch she did of me this morning."

"Looks as though you've been peeling onions."

"Oh Rupert, don't be silly. She's very clever too; got several degrees."

"And every one below zero," snapped Rupert.

In between visiting Helen he had not been idle. He worked the novices and kept up his search for an Olympic horse, which included dining with Colonel Carter and even forcing himself to flirt with the appalling Molly.

After two weeks Helen was allowed home and baby Marcus was installed in Rupert's old cradle, newly upholstered in white frills, in his beautiful buttercup-yellow nursery, next to Rupert and Helen's bedroom. Rupert's old Nanny, fetched at Rupert's insistence had already settled in to look after him and slept in the room on the other side.

Rupert thought this was insane.

"How can Billy and I wander around with no clothes on if Nanny's two doors down? Billy might easily come home plastered and wander into her room by mistake. The baby ought to be on the top floor with Nanny, like Adrian and I were."

"But I'd never see him," protested Helen. "I want him near me. You can't expect poor Nanny to stagger down two flights of stairs every time he cries."

Helen grew stronger physically, but sunk into post-natal depression. She had radar ears; every time a lamb bleated out in the fields she thought it was Marcus crying and raced upstairs. Rupert had the lambs and ewes moved to another field out of earshot. But Helen was still impossibly jumpy. Rupert was hustling her to sleep with him again and was furious when, egged on by Hilary, she refused. A power struggle, too, was developing between her and Nanny. If Marcus cried in the night, often they met head-on over the cradle. Nanny insisted on putting Marcus in long white dresses and refused to have anything to do with disposable diapers. She also wanted a strict routine—you had to show the baby early on who was the master. Helen believed that babies should be fed on demand and cuddled a lot. If they couldn't sleep you took them into bed with you, whereupon Nanny launched into horrific tales about ladyships in the past who'd done the same thing and suffocated their babies.

One day when Rupert was away Marcus wouldn't stop crying, his frame wracked, his little lungs bawling the house down. How could such a tiny thing make so much noise?

"Leave him. He'll exhaust himself," insisted Nanny.

Helen, terrified of losing Marcus, and utterly fed up with this whiskery old bag hanging over him and calling all the shots, summoned the doctor.

Dr. Benson, who was more than a little in love with Helen, was delighted to confirm her fears: "Baby's hungry; needs more food."

Afterwards there was a stand-up row and Nanny packed her bags.

Terrified of Rupert's wrath, Helen called Hilary, who offered only praise.

"Best thing you've ever done. Don't let that M.C.P. talk you round."

Later, Rupert walked into the nursery to find Helen changing a diaper and, with a look of horror, walked out again. With a hand that trembled slightly, Helen powdered Marcus, rather clumsily put the disposable diaper on him, tucked him into his cradle and gave him a kiss. With a gurgle of contentment he fell asleep immediately, obviously not missing Nanny.

Rupert was waiting outside.

"Why the hell are you doing that? Is it Nanny's afternoon off?"

"I fired her this morning."

"You what," thundered Rupert, "Where is she?"

"Gone."

"You sacked Nanny without asking me?"

"Its nothing to do with you," said Helen, losing her temper. "You're never here, never take any interest in Marcus."

"Balls. I haven't been away from home for more than a night since you had him."

"You've only been back three weeks," screamed Helen, going into her bedroom.

"You turned her out, just like that?"

"She's out of date."

"She was my Nanny and my father's before that. We're healthy enough. Can't be much wrong with her."

"Why don't you put her in the antiques' fair then? I'm not having her upsetting Mrs. Bodkin and, anyway, Hilary figures for successful parenting. . ."

"Don't you quote that bloody dyke at me. Successful parenting, my ass, and who's going to look after the baby now?"

"He's called Marcus, and I am. Most mothers do look after their children, you know. I don't want Marcus growing up caring more for Nanny than me, like you did."

"And how d'you intend to get away? It's Crittleden next week, Rome the week after."

"Tory Lovell takes her baby with her."

"Christ, you should see it. Trailer festooned with diapers, Tory shoving pablum into some bawling infant, who spits it all out, then bawls all night, keeping every other rider awake."

"Well, I'll stay home then," sobbed Helen.

Suddenly from next door there was a wail.

"Go and see to him," snapped Rupert. "Now aren't you sorry you sacked Nanny?"

Fortunately Billy chose that moment to arrive back from Vienna, trailing ribbons, bringing Rupert's horses and panting to see the new baby.

"What a little duck," he said, taking a yelling Marcus from Helen. "Isn't he sweet? Look at his little hands. No, shush, shush sweetheart, that's no way to carry on, you'll upset your mummy."

Amazingly, the next minute, Marcus shut up, gazing unfocused at Billy, enjoying the warmth and gentle strength.

"Isn't he a duck? he said again.

"You'd better take over as Nanny," said Rupert with a slight edge in his voice. "Then we won't have to fork out for an ad in *The Lady*."

Helen thought for the millionth time how glad she was Billy hadn't married Lavinia Greenslade. He was such a comfort.

"You will be godfather, won't you?" she said.

Billy blushed. "Of course, although I'm not sure I'll be able to point him in a very Christian direction. Who else have you asked?"

"Only my new friend Hilary so far," said Helen, shooting a defiant glance at Rupert. "I can't wait to have you two meet. I'll know you'll enjoy her."

Every night for the next week they were woken continually by Marcus crying, driving Rupert to frenzies of irritation.

"That's my night's sleep gone," he would complain, then drift off to sleep two minutes later. Helen would get up, feed Marcus, soothe him to sleep and lie awake for the rest of the night.

In April Billy and Rupert set off for Crittleden, leaving Helen and Marcus alone in the big house, except for one of the girl grooms, whom Rupert had insisted sleep in. Resentful of Rupert, Helen poured all her love into the delicate little boy. Thank goodness Hilary only lived a few miles away, so they spent alternate days together, discussing books, plays, paintings, their babies, and inevitably, Rupert.

Jake Lovell was having his best year yet. His horses couldn't stop winning. Revenge, brought in from grass, fat, mellow and almost unrecognizable, was now fit and well-muscled again. Even Jake realized his Olympic potential, but in four years' time.

Tory and Fen, however, were widly excited when a form arrived for Jake asking him to fill in his measurements for an Olympic uniform, which included a blazer and trousers for the flight and the opening ceremony. Aware that forms had been sent to all the other possibles, Jake had no intention of tempting Providence by returning the form until his selection had been confirmed after Aachen. He was appalled when he discovered that Tory, with her usual efficiency, had filled in the form and mailed it.

Despite this tempting of Providence, the first Olympic trail at the Bath and Wells Show went well. Both Sailor and Revenge jumped accurately and were only beaten by a tenth and a seventh of a second against the clock by The Bull. Humpty was fourth, Driffield fifth, Ivor Braine sixth, Rupert a poor seventh, not even getting into the jump-off. The rest were nowhere.

Before the second trial in June at Crittleden, Jake was a good deal more edgy. Colonel Carter was never off the telephone, throwing his weight around, trying to organize Revenge's career, until Jake lost his temper and told the Colonel to get stuffed.

More sinister, Jake noticed an unfamiliar missel thrush singing in the willow tree nearest the stables the day before they were due to leave for Crittleden. Jake chased it away, but it came back and went on singing. When he lived with the gypsies a missel thrush had sung all day outside the caravan of the old gypsy grandmother. One day she was in perfect health, the next she had died. Jake believed in omens. All day he worried about the children, Isa and little Darklis, who at thirteen months had grown into the most enchanting black haired, black-eyed gypsy child, the apple of Jake's eye.

He even went and fetched Isa from the playgroup himself. He didn't tell Tory of his fears. They had decided not to bring the children to Crittleden as Jake and Fen needed a good night's sleep before the trial and children around might be distracting.

"Are you sure you don't mind not coming?" Jake asked Tory.

"I can watch you on television," she said. "Anyway I'd be so nervous for you, I'd wind you up. I know you're going to make it."

Jake hated leaving them all. Whenever would he get over this crippling homesickness every time he went away? As they left on the hundred and fifty mile drive it was pouring with rain and the missel thrush was still singing. It was even wetter and colder at Crittleden. Jake and Fen spent a lot of time blocking up holes in the horses' stables.

On the way to the Secretary's tent to declare for the next day, Jake bumped into Marion, fuming as usual with Rupert.

"He's only got Mayfair in the running now. He used the tack rail on Belgravia so much, one of his legs went septic, so he's off for a fortnight. Rupert's talking of using electrodes on Mayfair; the horse is a bundle of nerves."

"And Macaulay?" said Jake.

"Sold to an Arab Sheik. So he's off to some Middle East hellhole, poor sod. You know what that means?"

"Yes," said Jake bleakly. "He'll throw the Sheik's son and heir once too often and end up in the stone quarries. Can you get me the address?"

Marion said she'd try, but Rupert had been very cagey about this deal because Helen, who was in an uptight state, might be upset if she found out the horse had gone.

"Not that she's showing any interest in anything except Marcus at the moment."

Jake shook his head. "Why d'you stay with Rupert?"

Marion shrugged. "I guess I'm hooked on the bastard, and at least I can make the lot of his horses a little easier."

All the next day the rain poured down like a waterfall. The riders put up the collars of their mackintosh coats and shivered. As he finished walking the course, Jake was accosted by a reporter from the local evening paper.

"This is the toughest course ever built at Crittleden, Jake. Anything to say?"

Jake kept walking. "I'm sorry I can't talk to you before a class."

"But I've got a deadline," wailed the reporter. "Arrogant sod," he added furiously.

But Jake didn't hear, and when he passed Humpty and Driffield he barely nodded, trying to cocoon himself, to get a grip on his nerves. He found Fen holding Revenge and Sailor—three drowned rats. Sailor, who loathed the cold, looked more miserable and hideous than ever.

"You OK?" he asked Fen.

She nodded. "What's the course like?"

"Not OK," said Jake. "Dead and holding. It'll put five inches on all the fences.

Smug in the covered stands after a good lunch, the Olympic Committee smoked their cigars and waited. Jake, who had a latish draw, watched one rider after another come to grief, which did his nerves no good. He noticed that the dye of his cheap red coat was running into his breeches. If he survived this ordeal, he'd bloody well buy himself a mackintosh coat.

Only Porky Boy and The Bull went clear. Revenge went in at number 20 and, despite having to carry extra weight because Jake was so light, he jumped strongly and confidently, with only a toe in the water for four faults. Jake felt passionate relief that he wouldn't have to jump again.

Rupert went in next, jumping a very haphazard clear, and came out looking none too pleased; he was followed by Driffield, who, despite Olympic-level bellyaching beforehand, had only four faults.

Sailor looked even more fed up as Fen took off his rug. But he nudged Jake in the ribs, as if to say, "I don't like this any more than you do, so let's get on with it."

"I heard Rupert saying it's like a skating rink in the middle on the far side of the rustic poles," said Fen, "so jump to the right."

"Yes sir," said Jake, trying to stop his teeth chattering.

"Your breeches look like a sunset," said Fen.

"Hope that's not symbolic of my career," said Jake.

Sailor was cold and it took him the first four jumps to warm up. He gave Jake a seizure when he rapped the double very hard. But fortunately, though the pole trembled, it didn't come out of the cup and Jake managed to steer clear of the skating rink at the rustic poles. Although Jake was aware what a tremendous effort Sailor had to make at each fence, carrying so much lead, he completed the course without mishap.

Jake's heart filled with gratitude. What horse could be more gallant? As he patted him delightedly and gave him half a packet of Polos, he wondered if subconsciously he was holding back Revenge because he *so* wanted to take Sailor to Colombia.

"Keep him warm and under cover," he said to Fen and went off to check the jump-off course. He found all the clear-round riders having a frightful row with the Crittleden judges.

"For Christ sake," said Rupert, "we've gone clear. Isn't that enough for the buggers? It's like jumping out of quicksand."

"Porky Boy might easily slip," said Humpty.

"It's a bitch of a course," agreed Billy.

But the judges were adamant, the Olympic Committee wanted them to jump again. This time Porky Boy had three fences down, Rupert and Driffield two and Jake and Billy one each.

"Can't ask us to go again," said Billy, grinning at Jake. "At least that's a grand in each of our pockets."

"Sailor's finished," said Jake. "Couldn't even jump over a pole on the ground."

Billy nodded. "Don't worry, they're not that crazy."

But once again the Olympic Committee, or rather Colonel Roxborough, who had once won a bronze medal, wanted a duel to the death.

"Seems a bit extreme when Jake's horse is carrying so much lead," protested Malise. "They really are ghastly conditions."

"Could be just as ghastly in Colombia," said the Colonel. "Are we conducting an Olympic trial, or are we not? You couldn't divide a gold medal."

Malise had to go down and tell Billy and Jake they had to jump again. He must not transmit the grave doubts he felt.

I'm retiring Sailor," said Jake.

"Then you'll scupper your Olympic chances," said Malise. "Just take it very slowly."

Sailor was too exhausted even to look appalled as Jake rode him through the driving rain back into the collecting ring. Jake couldn't bear to watch Billy, but he heard the subdued cheers as he rode out with twelve faults.

Rain was dripping in a steady stream from Malise's hat as he walked up to Jake.

"Now I mean it, take it really slowly."

"He's got no bloody choice after what you've put him through," snapped Fen.

Malise knew he should have slapped her down, but she was speaking the truth.

Jake hated having to ask Sailor to do it. He felt like a murderer as he cantered slowly into the ring. Tory must be watching at home and worried too. If only that bloody missell thrush had shut up. The driving rain was making visibility almost impossible.

"I'm sorry, boy, I'm sorry." He ran a reassuring hand down Sailor's dripping grey braids.

There were only seven fences. Sailor managed the first and second, but the ground was so churned up that he slipped on take-off at the third, the wall, and sent all the bricks and nearly himself flying. It was like riding on a kitchen floor after you've spilled hot fat. Frightened now, Sailor knocked down the oxer and rapped the upright, which trembled, but as in the first round, didn't fall. Perhaps they were in luck after all. Somehow he nursed Sailor over the rustic poles; now he was coming down to the combination. By some miracle, despite a nasty skid, he cleared the three elements. Now it was only the parallel. Ears flattened against the rain, tail swishing in irritaion, Sailor looked for a second as though he was going to stop.

"Go on, baby, Go on," muttered Jake.

Sailor made a mighty effort, then, threw himself with a groan over the fence.

Only eight faults. They had won. Despite the deluge, the crowd gave him a tremendous cheer as Jake pulled Sailor to a walk, patting him over and over again. Then just in front of the selector's box, like some terrible nightmare, Sailor seemed to stop, make an effort to go on, then physically shrink beneath Jake and collapse in the mud. Jake, whose good leg was trapped beneath him, took a couple of seconds to wriggle free. Scrambling up, covered in mud, he limped over to Sailor's head, cradling it in his arms. Sailor just lay there. Then he opened his wall eye, tried to raise his head, gave a half-choked nicker and his head fell back.

"Sailor!" whispered Jake. "It's all right sweetheart. You'll be OK in a minute. Where's the vet?" he howled, looking around frantically at the horrified blur of the crowd.

The next minute the vet ran on the course through the torrent of rain, carrying his bag.

"Quickly; it must be his heart; do something," pleaded Jake.

The vet opened Sailor's eye and shook his head. "I'm afraid I can't. He's dead."

"He can't be," said Jake through pale trembling lips. "He can't be, not Sailor," and suddenly, to the crowd's horror, his face crumpled and they realized it was tears mingling with the rain drops.

"Sailor," he sobbed, kneeling down, putting his arms around Sailor's neck, "don't die, please, you can't die."

In an instant the immaculate Crittleden organization swung into gear. The tractor and trailer were chugging through the mud from the collecting ring and the arena party ran on, putting eight-foot screens round Jake and the horse, and the loudspeaker started belching out music from South Pacific.

The crowd stood stunned, not moving. Colonel Roxborough descended from the stands, Malise ran in from the collecting ring, but Fen got there first, flinging her arms round Jake and Sailor, cuddling them both, sobbing her heart out too.

"Any hope?" asked Malise.

The vet shook his head. "Heart attack I'm afraid."

Fen turned round. "It's your fault," she screamed at Malise and Colonel Roxborough, "your bloody fault. Jake didn't want to jump him. Now what have you proved?"

Malise went up and put his hand on her shoulder. "Awfully sorry, very bad luck, might have happened at anytime."

"Don't touch me," hissed Fen, shaking him off. "You're all murderers."

Malise went over to Jake, who was still cradling Sailor's head in his arms, crying great strangled sobs. "It was the missel thrush," he kept saying over and over again. He seemed almost deranged.

"Come on Jake," said Malise gently. "Bloody bad luck, but let's get him out of the ring.

It took three of the arena party to pull Jake off, and the rest of them to get Sailor into the trailer.

Half the crowd and all the grooms were in tears. The riders were visibly shaken. The organizers were in a tizzy about who'd won.

"It's in the F.E.I. rules, Jake wasn't mounted when he left the ring," said Grania Pringle, who was about to present the prizes.

"Then Billy's got to get it," said Colonel Roxborough. "Let's get on with it, get people's minds on to something more cheerful. Bloody good thing it happened today. Just think if he'd collapsed in Colombia. That's what Olympic trials are for."

Grania Pringle turned on him, her beautiful make-up streaked with tears. "Bloody well shut up, Roxie. Don't be so fucking insensitive."

As the tractor came out with its grizzly burden Billy, near to tears himself, rode up to Jake: "Christ I'm sorry, of all the ghastly things to happen. We all knew how you felt about him. But I'm not taking first prize, Malise. Jake won it, he must have it."

"Very kind of you, Billy, but we have to abide by the rules."

He looked at Jake. It was hard to tell now which was downpour or tears. The rain had washed all the mud from the white shrunken face.

"Bastard," he spat at Malise, and turned in the direction of his lorry.

Suddenly he turned back. "Where are you taking Sailor?" he demanded.

"Don't worry your head about that," said Malise. "Get out of those wet clothes."

"You're not taking his body away for cat food."

"He won't go for cat food," said Malise reasonably. "They'll take him to the Hunt kennels."

Jake shot him a look of pure hatred. "As if that were any better. Take him to my van."

Fen dried Revenge off and fed him, while Jake loaded the two novices into the van. She couldn't bear to watch them loading Sailor, so she went and called Tory to tell her they were coming home. As she came out of the telephone booth, Malise was waiting for her. She was about to walk past him when he said, "Look, I know how you both feel."

"I should doubt it," said Fen coldly. "And don't try telling Jake it's only a horse. He loved Sailor more than any human." She added suddenly, with a wisdom beyond her years, "He felt they were both ugly, both laughed at, both despised and rejected. Together they were going to show the world."

Malise looked at her thoughtfully. "He's very lucky to have you. Can't you stop him driving in this state? It's simply not safe."

"You didn't worry too much about Sailor's safety, did you?" snapped Fen. "So I don't think you're a very good judge. And in this state, which you put him into, all he needs is Tory."

Jake didn't speak a word on the way home. Fen found it unbearable the way Revenge kept nudging Sailor's body, waiting for his wise old friend to scramble, grumbling, to his feet and tell him not to worry. They reached Crittleden at midnight. Jake drove the van straight around to the orchard. The rain had stopped, leaving a brilliant clear night. Moonlight flooded the dripping apple trees and the grave which had already been dug for them by the next-door farmer. He stayed to help them unload Sailor, which was a good thing, as he was stiff and cold now, and terribly heavy. It was so bright you could see the flecks on his fleabitten coat, his mane still neatly braided. Jake wrapped him in his white and maroon rug and patted him goodbye. Jake's face was set and expressionless as he covered the body with earth, pressing it down neatly. Later, when he'd unloaded and settled the other horses, he made a cross and put it on the grave.

By a supreme effort Tory managed not to cry in front of him, and when they finally fell into bed around four o'clock he just groaned, laid his head on her warm friendly breasts and fell asleep.

Next day he spent a long time digging up wild flowers to plant around Sailor's grave. Outwardly he appeared calm, but Tory knew he was bleeding inside. In the afternoon Malise called. Jake refused to talk to him.

"How is he?" asked Malise.

"All right," said Tory, "but he won't talk about it."

"Well it might cheer him up to know he and Revenge have been selected to go to Aachen. Probably he's suffering from shock. He'll be OK in a day or two."

He called again two days later. "Just confirming Jake and Revenge are available for Aachen."

"Well, its a bit awkward," said Tory.

"Let me speak to him."

"I'm afraid he doesn't want to talk to you. And he's completely gone off the idea of going to the Olympics."

"But that'd give him an interest, best possible therapy," said Malise. "He can't deprive his country of a horse like that."

Colonel Carter was less reticent. He called repeatedly, complaining about Jake refusing to take Revenge to Aachen and poor Tory, who had to field the calls, received a torrent of abuse.

"It's preposterous. Fellow's a milksop, blubbing in the ring, suppose he's lost his nerve."

For once Tory lost her temper. "Don't you realize they've broken his heart?"

The village sent a wreath to put on Sailor's grave. Letters of sympathy poured in. "We all loved him," wrote one woman. "To us Sailor was show-jumping." "I'm sending you my pocket money," wrote one little girl. "I expect the other horses are missing him, and you might like to buy them some Polos."

On the Thursday morning after Sailor's death Fen, having spent two hours on the novices in the indoor ring, was just grabbing a quick piece of toast and marmalade, and dashing off an essay on Mercutio before racing off to school, when Wolf started barking frenziedly and she heard the sound of wheels on the bridge. Going out, she found a plump blonde with a sweet round face and two tough-looking men getting out of a horse trailer.

"Yes?" she said.

They all looked faintly embarrassed, then the girl said, "I'm Petra, Rupert Campbell-Black's new groom. We've come for the horse."

"What horse?"

"Revenge."

Whimpering, Fen bolted back upstairs to wake Tory and Jake. Jake, unable to sleep, had only dropped off with the aid of a strong shot of belladonna at six o'clock. He came down zombie-like, eyelids swollen, eyes leaden with sleep, wearing only jeans. Looking at his sticking-out ribs, Fen thought how much weight he'd lost recently.

"What did you say?"

"They've come for Revenge."

"Don't be bloody silly," said Jake, going to the open back door. "Bugger off, all of you."

The girl went very pink. "We were told you'd been told."

"What?"

"That Rupert Campbell-Black bought Revenge yesterday."

Jake went very still. "Are you certain?"

She nodded, pitying him. Jake had long been one of her heroes.

"I don't believe it," snapped Jake. "Just one of Rupert's silly games. I'll go and call Bernard."

The Colonel was out. Molly answered, hard put to conceal her elation.

"Bernard's been trying to get through to you for three days, Jake."

"Is it true?"

"Yes. Rupe's been after Revenge for months."

It was "Rupe" now, was it? Jake leant against the hall table, suddenly dizzy with hatred.

"I'll buy him. Offer him to me."

"I hardly think you can top Rupe's offer."

"How much?"

"Forty-five thousand pounds," said Molly maliciously.

"You're crazy. He'll ride that horse off its feet in six months."

"Well, that doesn't really matter, now that Bernard's got the cash," said Molly. "Anyway, I'm sure Rupert won't. He's taking him to the Olympics. Bernard's set his heart on that. We tried to talk to you last night to say the deal had finally gone through, but you wouldn't come to the telephone. Oh, Bernard's just come in. Have a word with Jake."

The Colonel picked up the telephone. "'Fraid its true, Jake. Had the feeling you were a bit chicken about the Olympics, bit out of your depth really. He who dares wins you know. Campbell-Black's man enough to have a go."

"He's a sadist," said Jake.

"Rubbish, he's a brilliant horseman with a lot of experience, not fair to Revenge to hold him back."

Jake hung up and called Malise.

"Rupert's told me. I tried to dissuade him, but the deal had gone through. I'm awfully sorry, Jake, but there's not much I can do. It's Carter's horse."

Jake got dressed and went out to the yard, to find Fen standing outside Revenge's stall with a 12-guage in her hands and Wolf snarling beside her.

"Keep away from that door," she hissed. "This is our horse. If you lay a finger on him I'll blast you full of lead."

"You've been watching too many Westerns, love," said the taller of the two men, but he backed away slightly.

Jake strolled across the yard. "Put that gun down, Fen."

"No! he isn't their horse to take."

"I'm afraid he is," he said. "Bernard's sold him to Rupert."

It was too much for Fen. Revenge was her baby, the one she'd changed from a nervous wreck to a loving, happy and willing horse. She dropped the gun with a clatter and rushed up to the men.

"Please don't take him away," she sobbed. "We lost Sailor last Saturday, please don't take away Revenge too."

"I'm sorry, love, I know it's hard, but orders is orders."

Jake turned to Tanya. "Go and get Revenge."

It took only a few minutes to put one of Rupert's rugs and a halter on Revenge. Jake went to the book they kept in the tackroom, describing each horse's likes and dislikes, and the training and the feed he'd been getting, and which of Jake's medicines he needed. Numbly he wondered whether to give it to Rupert. It would certainly help the horse. Then he thought, sod it, and, tearing out the page, he crumpled it up and threw it in the bin.

It gave him a terrible pang to see how merrily and confidently Revenge bounced up the ramp of the trailer, thinking he was going to a show. He'd been such a devil to load when he'd arrived. He looked worth every penny of £45,000 now.

Jake went up and stroked him and gave him a handful of oats. It gave him an even worse pang to think how Revenge would react when he got to the other end and didn't find Fen to welcome him. He couldn't look as the trailer drove off over the bridge, through the fringe of willows.

Africa was the first to notice Revenge's absence. She'd been look- ing for Sailor since Jake came back, leaving her manger after a quick mouthful, coming to the half-door with a puzzled expression on her black face and calling out for him. Now that Revenge was gone too she was irritated and nervy, circling her stall, picking up straw, letting it hang from her mouth like the village idiot. Jake went up and put his arms around her neck, fighting back the tears. "I miss them too," she seemed to be saying with her wise kind eyes, "but you still have me; please love me because I'm the one who always loved you best."

And suddenly Jake felt ashamed. Africa, the goodest, truest, gentlest of them all, and he'd been neglecting her recently, because Sailor and Revenge seemed so much more important. He went into the tackroom, looking at the rows and rows of ribbons. Across the yard in the sitting room, lovingly polished by Tory, were all his silver cups. The place of honor had been given to the one he'd won at Olympia with Sailor. Then he'd been king of the castle, now he was at the bottom of the heap again, with only Africa and half a dozen novices to his name. He looked up at the cupboard on the opposite wall where, well out of reach, he kept all his poisons: belladonna, henbane for galls, hemlock, and the ground-down toadstools, which if sparingly administered could cure colic or purge a sick horse to recovery.

In an old silver snuff box he kept warty caps. One spore of the fungus would attach itself to Rupert's throat, giving all the symptoms of consumption, but causing death in a few weeks. It was a nice thought. But he preferred to beat Rupert in other ways.

He went upstairs to Fen's room, noticing the threadbare landing carpet. Tory was desperately trying to comfort her. Poor little Fen, first Marigold, then Revenge. He put a hand on Tory's cheek and stroked it. She looked up startled, blushing at the unexpected tenderness, relieved he wasn't as shattered as she'd expected.

"Fen," he said, "I've got an idea. I think its high time Africa had a foal."

Fen didn't react. She just lay there, slumped, her shoulders heaving. "And it's high time you had your own horse," he went on. "Think I've found one for you. She's only five, and roan, not a color I like, but her mother was a polo pony, so she turns on a sixpence and she jumps like a cricket already,"

Almost blindly Fen reached out for Jake. "It's so terribly, terribly kind of you," she sobbed, "but it's no good. I can't stop thinking about Revenge.

The more Rupert rode Revenge the better he liked him. He'd never sat on such a supple well-schooled animal. It was like playing a Stradivarius after an old banjo. They clicked the moment he got on the horse's back. It was easier for Revenge to carry Rupert's 170 pounds than Jake plus two unmoveable lead weights. The horse also loved jumping against the clock. He had already won one class at the Royal Highland, where he had trounced all the other possibles. Now he was in Aachen with the probables, for the final trial, and attracting a huge amount of interest from the world's press. How would Gyppo Jake's horse go with Rupert over such huge fences?

Rupert, in fact, had received a lot of flak. After Sailor's tragic death the public felt it was very unfair on Jake that the other horse he'd spent so much time on should be snatched from under his nose. As soon as Marion heard that Rupert had appropriated Revenge she handed in her notice, properly this time, then went straight to Fleet Street and told them exactly how much Rupert had paid for the horse, an offer the frightful Colonel couldn't refuse, and then went on to give them some choice tidbits about the cruelty of Rupert's training methods. The *News of the World* felt the material was too hot to print but *Private Eye* had no such scruples. Rumors were rife.

No one could get any comment from Jake on the subject, so the reporters beseiged Rupert.

"Well, I'll concede Jake Lovell's a good trainer," he said diplomatically, "but the horse needed an experienced rider on his back. Winning's about taking chances. Jake wasn't even prepared to take the horse to Colombia. As for the cruelty charges, they're too ridiculous to discuss. Horses won't jump if they don't want to."

And now it was the eve of the trials and Rupert knew perfectly well that if Revenge beat the rest of the international field as well as the English probables tomorrow and was picked for Colombia, people would conveniently forget how the horse had been acquired. Helen was so wrapped up in little Marcus that she hardly appreciated the furor. Rupert had hoped she might leave Marcus with Mrs. Bodkin and fly out to Aachen, but she was still looking desperately tired and she didn't feel quite confident enough to leave him.

Rupert, however, was finding consolation in his new groom, Petra, who he had nicknamed Podge. He was glad Marion had gone; he was fed up with her tantrums and her beady eyes following him all the time. Podge, on the other hand, with her chunky body and legs, though not as upmarket or as handsome as Marion, had a nice smooth skin and was always smiling, and she adored the horses, almost more than she worshipped Rupert. Naturally Revenge was homesick at first; any horse coddled as Jake's were would feel the draught when he left the yard. But Podge had made a huge fuss over the horse and after a few days of kicking his stall out and spurning his food he had settled in.

It was the eve of the Aachen trials and, having seen the horses settled, Rupert and Billy took a taxi back to their hotel. There was something about a hotel bedroom that made Rupert want to order a bottle of champagne and a beautiful girl to drink it with.

"What shall we do tonight?"

Billy pushed aside Rupert's clothes which littered both beds, and collapsed on his own bed.

"Go to bed early. I'm absolutely beat."

"Ludwig's having a barbecue at his house."

"I don't want a hangover tomorrow."

"But just think of all that Kraut crumpet." Rupert went to the window looking down the tidy village street, then said casually, "Thought I might take Podge."

"Oh for Christ's sake leave her alone. You know how it screwed up your relationship with Marion. Pity there isn't a Gideon bible, then I could read you the seventh commandment all over again."

"Well I am not getting much joy out of my wife at the moment. She's temporarily closed, like the M4."

Billy put his hands over his ears. "I don't want to hear. You know I adore your wife."

The telephone rang. Rupert picked it up.

"Hello darling. I was just talking to Billy about you." Next moment the lazy smile was wiped off his face.

"It's Marcus," sobbed Helen. "He's been hospitalized. He can't breathe, he's gone purple in the face. Oh Rupert, I know he's going to die. Please come back."

"I'll be on the next plane. You're at Gloucester Hospital? Don't worry, darling, he'll pull through, the Campbell-Black's are very tough."

He rang Malise in his room, who came over straightway.

"You must go back at once."

"I'm sorry. Helen's in a frightful state."

"Hardly surprising. They're terrifying, these illnesses of little children. I remember going through them with Henrietta and," he paused, "with Timmie. I hope everything'll be all right. Give Helen our love and sympathy."

Rupert was lucky to get a plane at once and reached the hospital by midnight. He hadn't bothered to change; he was still wearing boots, breeches and a tweed coat over his white shirt and tie.

"My name's Campbell-Black," he said to the receptionist. "My wife came in this afternoon with our baby, he's called Marcus. He may be in the operating room."

His hand shook as he brushed his hair back from his forehead. The girl looked down her list, wishing she'd bothered to wash her hair that morning. She remembered Rupert from earlier in the year when he'd caused such a stir when Helen had the baby.

"Marcus's in the children's ward on the fourth floor."

The elevator was occupied with some patient coming back from the operating room. Rupert ran up the stairs. The nurse met him in the passage.

"My son, Marcus Campbell-Black," he panted, "he was brought in this afternoon."

"Oh yes." With maddening lack of haste the nurse went back into her room to check the chart,

"He's in Room 25."

"Is he, is he," Rupert choked on the words, "going to be all right?"

"Of course he is. He had an attack of croup."

"What's that?"

"No one quite knows why it comes on. The baby goes blue and can't breathe. Parents invariably think he's swallowed something and is choking to death. All he needs is to inhale some moisture. We're keeping him in the humidifying tent for tonight. Dr. Benson says he'll be as right as rain tomorrow."

"Are you all right?" she asked looking at Rupert's horrified face. "It must have been a terrible shock for you. Mrs. Campbell-Black will be so pleased you've come back. She was very upset, but Dr. Benson's given her something to calm her down. Can I get you a cup of tea?"

And she brought me all the way back for this, thought Rupert, in the middle of the final Olympic trial. In Room 25 he found Marcus lying happily in a huge cellophane tent. Helen was sitting on the edge of the bed wiggling Marcus' toes. She got up and ran to Rupert.

"Oh I'm so glad you came. I was so frightened. I thought he was going to die."

Rupert patted her shoulder mechanically. Nanny would have recognized croup, he thought darkly. Behind her on the bed he could see his son and heir pinkly gurgling, digging his pink starfish fingers into his blanket.

"Look," said Helen fondly, diving under the tent and holding Marcus up in a sitting postion, "he can hold his head up now. Don't you want to cuddle him?"

"I'm sure he ought to be kept quiet," said Rupert.

He listened while she poured out her worries and tried not to contrast the innocent fun he'd been having in Aachen, getting slightly tight with Billy at Ludwig's barbecue, with the terrifying world of children's illness and the dark claustrophobic intensity of Helen's love.

"I am sorry I brought you back," she said. "I was so terrified you might find him dead. I needed you so badly. I'm sorry I've been offish lately, but it must be worth coming all this way just to see him. He's so cute, isn't he? Do you think he's grown?"

"I need a drink," said Rupert. At that moment Benson walked in.

"Hullo Rupert," he said heartily. "You must have been worried stiff, but, as you can see, he's all right. Nothing to worry about. You need a drink? Come on, I'm sure Matron's got something tucked away."

Benson obviously wanted a heart-to-heart. The head nurse only had sweet sherry, but at least it was alcohol. Immediately Benson launched into the subject of Helen.

"Bit worried about her. Only twenty-four. Very young to cope on her own with a big house and a young baby. She misses you, you know."

"I miss her," said Rupert somewhat briskly, "but Christ, she won't come to shows with me. I got her a marvellous nanny and she promptly sacked her. I asked her to come to Aachen. I've got an Olympic trial tomorrow. I'll have to fly back in the morning."

Benson looked pained. "So soon?"

"I do have a living to earn."

"I know," said Benson soothingly. "I do think it would help if you could get a nanny, a young cheerful girl, who Helen wouldn't feel threatened by. Then in time she'd feel confident enough to leave Marcus."

"She needs a holiday."

"Best holiday she could have would be for the baby to get well and strong. But I'm afraid all the indications are that he's going to be an asthmatic."

"Christ, are you sure?"

"Pretty certain. We'll do some tests while he's in here. And you know that's not a condition helped by the mother's anxiety. With any luck he should grow out of it, or at least be able to handle it as he gets older."

Rupert drained the glass of sherry, making a face.

"Want another?" asked Benson.

Rupert shook his head. He felt absolutely shattered. He had been up at five that morning.

"What's your schedule?"

"Well the trial's tomorrow, then the International in London, then, if I'm picked for Colombia, a brief rest for the horses before we fly out."

"And after that you could take her and Marcus away for a long holiday?"

Rupert shook his head. "Virtually impossible in the middle of the season. Horses lose their precision if you rest them too long."

Benson nodded. "Appreciate your problem. I've got patients on the tennis circuit. Has she got a friend she can stay with?"

Rupert thought of Hilary. He guessed she had been stirring things up.

"Not really. I'll have to find her a nanny. Can I take her home this evening?"

"Good idea. The child's in no danger now. Do her good."

Helen was aghast when Rupert told her he'd be flying back in the morning. She lay in the huge double bed, with that pinched defiant look of roses touched by the frost in December. Then, as Rupert joined her, she lay back, staring at the ceiling wanting to be soothed and comforted and told she was being splendid.

Rupert comforted her in the only way he knew, by trying to make love to her. After a few minutes she started to cry.

"Christ, what's the matter now?"

"I'm too worried about Marcus. I can't switch off, and you're going back."

"Darling, the trial's tomorrow afternoon."

"Horse, horse, horse." She was suddenly almost hysterical. "Surely Marcus is more important than a horse trial?"

It was a debatable point, thought Rupert, but he merely said, "Benson says there's nothing to worry about."

Rupert left at nine o'clock and ran into bad weather, arriving only just in time to walk the course. Once again he contrasted Podge's lovely smiling welcome with Helen's set martyred face as she'd said goodbye that morning.

"How's Marcus?" asked Podge. "Oh, I'm so relieved that he's O.K. We was all so worried. Revvie and I missed you. He was restless last night so I slept in his stall—'spect I look like it."

"Lucky Rev," said Rupert. "He looks in the pink anyway."

"He's great, on top of the world. You'll just have to sit on his back."

What a contrast to Marion, thought Rupert.

For the first time in his life he was suffering from nerves. It must be tiredness. He longed for a stiff drink, but Podge had made him a large cup of strong black coffee instead. He knew the world's press was watching as he rode into the ring.

His fears were groundless. Revenge jumped like an angel, literally floating over the vast fences. After the trial the selectors went into a huddle. Elated, almost sure of a place, Rupert went off to call Helen. He carefully spent five minutes asking how they both were before telling her Revenge had come first, beating even Ludwig, going like a dream and muzzling any critics.

"I'm very glad for you," said Helen in a tight little voice.

"Who's that in the background?" said Rupert.

"Hilary and the kids," said Helen. "She's driving Marcus and me home from the hospital and staying over night. She's being so supportive."

As he got off the telephone, a German reporter accosted him:

"Meester Black, it is unusual for zee English to beat zee Germans in this country, no?"

"No," said Rupert coldly, "I think you're forgetting the last two world wars," and stalked off.

Feeling utterly deflated, he went back to the stable where an ecstatic

Podge was chattering to Revenge as she settled him for the night.

"Didn't you do well, darling? It's Colombia here we come. We'll have to make you a sun hat to keep off the flies."

"Don't count your chickens," said Rupert, checking Revenge's bandages.

"You really look tired," said Podge, then, blushing, added, "I bet you didn't eat last night, nor this morning. I made you a shepherd's pie for tonight. It's not very good and I'm sure you'd rather go out with Billy."

Rupert pulled the half-door behind him:

"I'd much rather stay in, right in," he said softly, drawing her towards him, "and I absolutely adore shepherd's pie."

"Oh we can't," squawked Podge, "not here in front of Rev."

"Want to bet?" said Rupert, pushing her against the wall.

Jake Lovell heard the news on the tackroom wireless as he was filling in the diet sheets. Fen, who was cleaning tack, didn't dare look at him.

"After a successful trial in Aachen, Germany," said the announcer, "the following riders and horses had been picked for the Olympics in Colombia. Charles Hamilton and Porky Boy, Billy Lloyd-Foxe and The Bull, Rupert Campbell-Black on Revenge." Fen gave a gasp of horror. "Brian Driffield on Temperance with Ivor Braine as reserve."

Fen went over and put her arms round Jake. "I'm so, so sorry," she said. "It was you who made him a great horse. Rupert just had to get on his back."

Molly Carter, delighted that Revenge had been selected, felt a trip to Colombia would be in order.

"We must give a celebration party for Rupert and Helen before he leaves. 'Phone him up, Bernard, and fix an evening he's free, and then we can invite everyone else. And do ask him about hotels in Bogota, and say to make sure we get tickets to watch Rev."

Colonel Carter got off the telephone, magenta in the face. "Most peculiar. Rupe says Revenge belongs to him now, and there is no possible way he's coming to any party."

"Oh Bernard," snapped Molly. "You know what a tease Rupert is. He must have been joking. I'll call him up."

"Rupert," she said archly, two minutes later, "Bernard must have got the wrong end of the stick. We want to give a little celebration party for you."

"Well you can count me out," said Rupert curtly. "I never mix business with pleasure and you and the Colonel were strictly business, believe me."

"You can say that?" splutter Molly. "After all we've done for you?"

"Yes," said Rupert. "Go and spend your forty-five grand on buying a few friends. It's the only way you'll get them," and hung up.

Billy couldn't believe he'd been selected for the Olympics. For days he floated on a cloud of bliss. He felt sorry for Lavinia—not being picked, but it would make things much easier in Colombia if she wasn't there to upset him.

All the team members had been much too superstitious to fill in their clothes measurement forms, so there was a last-minute panic to get the uniform in time. Rupert made a terrible fuss about the clothes.

"I am *not* going to wear a boating jacket with a badge on," he said disdainfully, throwing the Royal blue Olympic blazer across the room.

Billy didn't care. He was so enchanted to be in the team, he'd have worn a grass skirt if necessary.

The only blot on the horizon was the tension in Rupert's marriage. Billy didn't like Hilary one bit. He thought she was bossy, strident and disruptive, and having a very bad effect on Helen. She was always around the house these days, breastfeeding her baby in the drawing room, or shoveling brown rice down little Germaine. Despite disapproving of Rupert's stinking capitalist habits, she had no compunction about drinking his liquor or using his washing machine all day. You couldn't get a pair of breeches washed these days for revolving diapers.

The excuse for Hilary's presence was that she was doing a painting of Helen. Like the sketch she had done before, she made Helen look the picture of victimized misery—Belsen thin, her face all eyes, tears streaking her wasted cheeks. Rupert, who, like most rich people, detested free-loaders, grew so irritated that, after half a bottle of whisky one night, he crept in and painted a large black moustache and a beard on the picture, with a balloon coming out of Helen's mouth saying: "Monica Carlton had me first."

Billy fell down laughing, Helen was absolutely livid. Hilary merely looked pained, assumed a They-know-not-what-they-do attitude and started another painting. So Rupert achieved nothing.

One evening when she was giving Marcus his late bottle, Billy tackled Helen.

"Angel, I don't want to interfere but I think you ought to come to Colombia."

"I can't leave Marcus."

"Well, bring him."

"He's too little. He'd never cope with the climate."

Billy tried another tack: "I know Rupe seems very tough on the outside, but he needs the clapping, most of all from you. He's too proud to plead, but I know he's desperate for you to go. Hilary could look after Marcus."

Helen cuddled Marcus tighter, a look of terror on her face: "When Marcus had croup the other day and I thought he was dying I made a pact I'd never leave him."

"You do have a husband as well."

But Helen wouldn't be persuaded.

The last show before the Olympics was the Royal International. Rupert and Billy left The Bull and Revenge to enjoy a well-earned rest in Gloucestershire and drove up to London with Kitchener and Belgravia and a handful of novices. On Wednesday Billy and Kitchener won the King George V Cup, an all-male contest and one of the most prestigious in the world.

The following evening, while the women riders were competing for the Queen Elizabeth Cup, the entire British team, except Rupert, who had other unspecified plans, went out on the town together. They started in a West End pub called the Golden Lion. Ivor, Billy and Humpty had all bought rounds of drinks and were deliberately hanging back to see if they could make Driffield put his hand in his pocket.

"That's mine," said Billy as the barman tried to gather up the second half of Billy's tonic. "I'm hoping someone is going to buy me the other half."

Looking pointedly at Driffield, he put the tonic bottle into his breast pocket. He was still coming down to earth after yesterday's win. Everyone was hailing and congratulating him on that and getting picked to go to Colombia. Looking around the bar, he was aware of some wonderful girls in summer dresses eyeing him with considerable enthusiasm. He wished he could ask one of them out. It was a glorious July evening. The setting sun was lighting up the dusty plane trees in the square, the door of the bar was fixed open and people were drinking in the streets,

"I'm thirsty, Driff," he said.

"I'm thirsty too," said Humpty.

"I didn't know you were thirty-two," said Ivor, surprised. "I thought you were only thirty, Humpty."

"I was saying I was thirsty, Driff," said Billy, winking at the others.

He flicked his still-lit cigarette end in the direction of the open door, but it missed and landed in the lap of a girl in a cyclamen pink dress who was sitting on a bench nearby.

"Oh Christ!" Billy bounded towards her. "I'm frightfully sorry," but as he leaned forward to remove the cigarette end, the tonic from the bottle in his pocket cascaded forward, all over her dress.

"For God's sake look what you're doing," said her companion.

"Oh Hell," said Billy, "I'm dreadfully sorry."

The girl burst out laughing. "It really doesn't matter; it'll dry in a sec. It's so hot it's nice to have an impromptu shower."

Billy looked into her face and his heart skipped several beats. She was certainly one of the prettiest girls he'd ever seen. She had smooth brown skin with a touch of pink on each high cheek bone, slanting dark brown eyes, a turned-up nose, a mane of streaky tortoiseshell hair and a big mouth as smooth and as crimson as a fuschia bud. Her pink dress showed at least three inches of slim brown thigh and a marvelous cleavage.

Billy couldn't tear his eyes away. "I'm most awfully sorry," he repeated in a daze.

"It couldn't matter less," said the girl, highly delighted at the effect she was having on him.

Billy pulled himself together. Getting out one of Rupert's blue silk handkerchieves, he started to wipe away the ash, but it all smeared into the tonic.

"Oh dear, that's much worse. Look, let me buy you another dress."

"There's no need for that," snapped her campanion. He was about thirty-five, with a pale sweating face that was even more rumpled than his grey suit.

"Then let me buy you a drink—both of you. What would you like?"

"You've caused quite enough trouble already," the man said. "Why don't you buzz off?"

"Don't be beastly, Victor," said the girl in her sofy husky voice. "We'd *love* a drink."

The man looked at his watch. "We'll be late. The table's booked for nine and they don't like to be kept waiting."

"They'll wait for me," said the girl blandly.

"Anyone would," said Billy. "Have a quick one."

But the man had got to his feet. "No thank you *very* much," he said huffily.

"I must have a pee," said the girl. "You go and get a taxi, Vic."

There was a great deal of Ally Ooping and badinage from the rest of the riders as Billy waited for her to come out. What would Rupert do in the circumstances, he wondered. Probably accost her and get her telephone number, but he couldn't do that with the frightful Victor hovering.

As she came out he caught a heady new waft of scent. She'd teased her tortoiseshell hair more wildly and applied more crimson lipstick. He wanted to kiss it all off. Perhaps that luscious mouth would pop like a fuschia bud. He took a deep breath. "I don't mean to be presumptuous but you're the prettiest girl I've ever seen."

"That's nice," she said.

"My name's Billy Lloyd-Foxe."

"The great show jumper," she said mockingly. "I know. You won the King's Cup yesterday."

He blushed scarlet. "I'd adore to see you again."

As she smiled he noticed the gap in the white slightly uneven teeth, the raspberry pink tongue of the good digestion.

"You will," she patted his cheek with her hand. "I promise you. Oh look, Victor's managed to get a taxi, how extraordinary." She ran out into the street and he hadn't even asked her name. If Rupert had been here he would have lynched him. On the other hand, if Rupert had been here, the girl would have gone off with Rupert instead.

Billy spent the rest of the week at the International feeling horribly restless, praying the girl from the Golden Lion might turn up. After Lavinia, he'd vowed he'd never let another girl get under his skin, and here he was miserable as all get out. Even in the excitement of setting out for Colombia he was unable to get her out of his mind.

In the weeks leading up to the Olympics, Jake Lovell sank into deep depression. Then, unable to face the razzmatazz and hysterical chauvinism of the actual event, he flew off to the Middle East to try and find Macaulay. He had located the Sheik, but when he got there, after a lot of prevarication, he discovered that Macaulay had indeed blotted his copy book by savaging the Sheik himself and had been sold less than six weeks ago to a dealer who kept no records and couldn't or probably didn't want to remember where Macaulay had gone.

Jake went to the British Embassy, who were very unhelpful. With a big oil deal going through, they didn't want to rock the boat. After repeated nagging, they sent Jake to Miss Blenkinsop, who ran a horse rescue center in the capital, and, as far as Jake could see, was a constant thorn in the authorities' flesh, as she waged a one-woman battle against appalling Middle Eastern cruelty and insensitivity towards animals.

Miss Blenkinsop was a gaunt sinewy woman in her late fifties, totally without sentimentality, and with the brusque, rather desexed manner of someone who has always cared for animals more than people.

She gave Jake a list of sixty-odd addresses where he might find the horse.

"Hope your nerves are strong, you'll see some harrowing sights. Arabs think it's unlucky to put down a horse, so they work them till they drop dead, and they don't believe in feeding and watering them much either. Horse has probably been sold upcountry. You've as much chance of finding him as a needle in a haystack but here are all the riding schools and quarries, the most likely spots within five miles of the city. I'll lend you one of my boys as interpreter. He's a shifty little beast, but he speaks good English, and you can borrow my car if you like."

For Jake it was utter crucifixion. He was in a bad way emotionally anyway, and he had never seen such cruelty. Like some hideous travesty of Brook Farm Riding School, he watched skeletons, lame, often blind, frantic with thirst, shuffling around riding school rings, or tugging impossibly heavy loads in the street or in the quarries, being beaten until they collapsed, and then being beaten until they got up again.

For five days he went to every address Miss Blenkinsop had given him, bribing, wheedling, cajoling for information about a huge black horse with a white face, and one long white sock. No one had seen him. Sickened and shattered, he returned every night to his cheap hotel where there was no air conditioning, the floors crawled with cockroaches and drink was totally prohibited. As the coup de grâce, on the fifth night, he couldn't resist watching the Olympic individual competition on the useless black and white hotel television. As Billy rode in, the picture went round and round, but sadistically it held still for Rupert and Revenge, who produced two heroic rounds to win the bronze. Ludwig got the gold on his great Hanoverian mare, Clara, Carl Kennedy, the American number one rider, got the silver.

Black with despair and hatred, Jake went up to his cauldron of a room and lay on his bed smoking until dawn. He had nearly run out of money and addresses. Today he must go home empty-handed. Around seven he must have dozed off. He was woken by the telephone:

It was Miss Blenkinsop: "Don't get too excited, but I may have found your horse. He's been causing a lot of trouble down at the stone quarries." She gave him the address.

"If it is him, don't bid for him yourself. They'll guess something's up and whack up the price. Give me a ring and I'll come and do the haggling."

At first Jake wasn't sure. The big muzzled gelding was so pitifully thin and so covered in a thick layer of white dust as he staggered one step forward one step back, trying to shift a massive cartload of stone, that it was impossible to distinguish his white face or his one white sock. Then the Arab brought his whip down five times on the sunken quarters, five black stripes appeared and with a squeal of rage, Macaulay turned and lunged at the driver, showing the white eye on the other side.

"That's my boy," thought Jake with a surge of excitement. "They'll break his back before they break his spirit."

Miss Blenkinsop had a hard time making the Arab owner of the quarry part with Macaulay. Although vicious, he was the strongest horse they'd ever had and probably still had six months' hard labor in him, but the price the hideously ugly Englishwoman was offering was too much for him to refuse. He could buy a dozen broken-down wrecks for that.

When Jake took Miss Blenkinshop's trailer to collect him, Macaulay was too tall to fit in, so Jake led him very slowly back through the rush hour traffic.

Macaulay twice clattered to the ground with exhaustion, and several times they narrowly missed death as the oil-rich Arabs hurtled by in their huge limousines. But Macaulay displayed no fear, he was beyond that now, but most touchingly he seemed to remember Jake from the time he treated his lacerations after Rupert's beating-up in Madrid. When Jake came to fetch him, his lacklustre eyes brightened for a second and he gave a half-nicker of welcome.

That night, after he had made the horse as comfortable as possible, Jake had supper with Miss Blenkinsop. She drew the curtains and produced an ancient bottle of Madeira. After two glasses Jake realized he was absolutely plastered. After Arab food, the macaroni and cheese she gave him seemed the best thing he had ever eaten.

Jake always found it difficult to express gratitude, in case it was construed as weakness.

"I don't know how to thank you," he finally mumbled.

"Don't bother," said Miss Blenkinsop. "Do something about it. Spread the word when you get back to England. We need cash not sympathy, and a law banning the exporting of all horses to the Middle East."

"If I can get Macaulay back on the circuit," said Jake, "the publicity for you will be so fantastic, the money'll start flooding in."

"He's in a very bad way. Think you'll be able to do it?"

Jake shrugged. "He's young. My grandmother cured a mare with a broken leg once, bound it in comfrey and she went on to win four races. I'm going to have a bloody good try."

For a second he stared at his glass, miles away, then he said, "I had a horse called Sailor once. He was near death when he arrived, but he did pretty well in the end."

When Jake and Macaulay got back to England, the news that Great Britain had won the team silver medal, Billy clinching it with a brilliant clear, didn't upset him very much.

Kings, they came home. After a gruelling thirty-hour journey from Colombia to Stanstead Airport, The Bull and Revenge, accompanied by Tracey and Podge, had a good night's sleep at Colonel Roxborough's place. Next day they drove the horses in the van to Heathrow to meet Rupert and Billy. They had quite a wait because of scenes of hysterical excitement at the airport. Press and television cameras were everywhere; police had to keep back the huge crowd. Britain hadn't notched up that many medals at Colombia not to be very proud of her show-jumping bronze and silver.

At last they all set off for Penscombe around four o'clock in the afternoon in high spirits, sharing several bottles of champagne on the way. Tracey was soon laughing like a hyena. Only Podge was sad. In a couple of hours she would have to give most of Rupert back to Helen, but there'd be other shows, she tried to tell herself. Outside Cirencester, Rupert was stopped for speeding by a policeman, who solemnly got out his notebook, then asked for their autographs. Every time people saw their van with the lettering "Rupert Campbell-Black and Billy Lloyd-Foxe, Great Britain" they started cheering. Even Rupert was thrown by the welcome as they neared home. As they entered Chalford there were crowds all along the route, cheering, waving British flags and holding up placards saying "Well done Billy and Rupert." "Three cheers for Bull and Revenge."

Rupert looked at Billy. "Shall we ride home?"

Billy nodded, too moved to speak.

The horses were still tired, but delighted to be out of the van in familiar territory.

They were cheered all the three miles home, Rupert and Billy riding in front, followed by Tracey and Podge in the van, tooting victory salutes on the horn. Two miles out Henrietta, one of the junior grooms, arrived with an ecstatic Badger and Mavis, with red, white and blue bows attached to their collars. Billy scooped up Mavis on to the saddle in front of him, where she ecstatically licked his salty face. After that The Bull had to guide himself home because Billy needed one hand to clutch Mavis and the other to wipe his eyes. The Bull didn't care. With garlands of flowers around his massive neck, he must have put on ten pounds between Chalford and Penscombe with all the carrots and sugar that were fed him along the way.

To Rupert, Penscombe had never looked so lovely as on that golden September afternoon, with the valley softened and blurred by a slight blue mist, and great pale cream swathes of traveller's joy. There was the weather cock glinting on Penscombe church. And suddenly towards them came the village band, sweating in their red tunics, playing "Land of Hope and Glory" somewhat out of tune.

"This is really too much," said Billy, half laughing and half crying, as the band shuddered to a straggly halt in front of them and turned around, striking up "Rule Britannia" to lead them in. The village was decked out like a Royal Wedding, every house had put out the flags, a huge streamer stretched across the village street saying "Welcome home our Four Heroes." Photographers ran along the pavement, snapping as they went. By the War Memorial the mayor was waiting for them. Shaking them both by the hand, he read a speech of welcome that Revenge tried to eat. Rupert was looking everywhere for Helen. Can't even bother to come and meet me, he thought, savagely.

And suddenly, there she was on the pavement, in a yellow sleeveless dress, holding Marcus in her arms, looking apprehensive and not at all sure of her reception. In an instant Rupert was off Revenge and kissing her passionately, but not too hard in case he squashed Marcus, and the photographers went crazy.

"Show us your medals, Rupe," they yelled.

So Rupert, ultra-casual, got them out of his hip pocket and hung them round Marcus's neck, But when he tried to pick up the baby and cuddle him, Marcus arched his back rigidly and started to yell, so Rupert handed him back to Helen. Helen looked up at Rupert incredulously. She'd forgotten how beautiful he was, even after a long drive and an even longer flight. As he came through those hysterically cheering crowds, laughing and joking, he seemed like a god again. It was only just coming home to her, the magnitude of his achievement.

She picked up the bronze and the silver medals and examined them wonderingly.

"You made it, you honestly made it. Oh Rupert, I missed you so much," and suddenly she knew she was speaking the truth. She realized she'd really kept him at a distance since she got pregnant, and maybe it was her fault.

"Did you?" said Rupert, his face suddenly serious.

"Horribly. Can we really try and spend some time together, and make a go of it?"

Rupert kissed her again. He felt ridiculously happy.

"As long as you give Thrillary the bullet."

Helen looked disapproving, then giggled. "We're not quite so close. She is a little bossy."

"She's more of a male bloody chauvinist pig than I am," said Rupert.

Next day, after all the excitement, Billy was ashamed to find himself overwhelmed with a feeling of restlessness and anticlimax. After checking the horses, he decided to give himself a day off and spent most of the morning opening his mail. As a result of his silver medal, there were countless offers of free feed, tack, rugs, breeches. A van manufacturer was offering him a large sum of money to do a press campaign. Several television companies were waving fat fees to make films of his life.

"I shall have to turn professional," he told Miss Hawkins, their secretary, half-jokingly.

Perhaps the depression was caused by the fact that everyone in the world seemed to have written to congratulate him—except that wonderful girl he'd seen at the Golden Lion. He hoped each letter might be from her, but as he didn't know her name he couldn't identify her anyway. For the thousandth time, he kicked himself for not being more forceful at the time.

"Some man from the *Daily Post* called Jamie Henderson's written to ask if he can come down and interview you," said Miss Hawkins. "I pencilled in next Sunday. I thought you could take him up to the pub for lunch, as he's coming all the way down from London. It's the only day you've got really. You'll be off to Athens, Portugal and Germany the next day."

She was highly delighted Billy was for once getting as much attention as Rupert. "His Lordship still in bed?" she went on in surprise. "Are those two having a second honeymoon?"

When his depression didn't lift in the days that followed, Billy thought it might well be due to the fact that Rupert and Helen suddenly seemed to be madly in love again. Helen had agreed to get a nanny; Rupert had agreed to come home more often, and for them to do more things together. Billy was happy that they were happier, but it only emphasized his own isolation. What was the point of being a conquering hero if you didn't make any conquests?

The Sunday Jamie Henderson was due Billy rose early because it was so hot, worked all the horses that needed it, then hacked The Bull out because it was such a beautiful day. The stream at the bottom of the valley was choked with meadowsweet, and as he rode home he could hear Badger howling at the church bells.

As part of their new togetherness campaign, Helen and Rupert were just leaving to go out to lunch with Marcus as Billy walked in through the front door.

"We'll be at the Paignton-Lacey's," said Helen, "so you and this pressman will have the house to yourselves. There's no need to go out for lunch. There's cold chicken and potato salad and I've washed a lettuce. All you've got to do is pour French dressing over it. And don't leave the butter in the sun," she added.

"This baby needs more luggage than a horse," said Rupert, going out to the car with a blue plastic potty seat in one hand, a box of disposable diapers in the other and several bottles under his arm. "One never gets enough to drink at the Paignton-Laceys."

Billy took the carrycot from Helen and put it in the back. As he waved them off to the accompaniment of Marcus yelling and Vivaldi on the car radio, Rupert looked at him and raised his eyes to heaven.

Billy had a bath and put on a clean shirt and a pair of jeans; he was nervous, he never knew what to say to reporters. Sitting outside with a jug of Pimms, he read the Sunday papers, which were still full of Olympic news. There was a nice picture of him in the *Sunday Express,* and a piece in the *Telegraph* with a headline about Rupert's shadow coming out of the shadows. He was pleased about that too. He took off his shirt; might as well try to top up his Olympic tan.

In no time at all he seemed to have finished the jug. The valley looked even more beautiful now. The apples were reddening in the orchard, the dogs panted on the lawn, insects hummed in the Michaelmas daisies. September was such a lovely month; why wasn't there someone here to share it with him?

He watched an emerald green Volkswagen pause on the road running along the top of the valley towards Penscombe. He looked at his watch; Jamie Henderson was late.

The door bell rang, followed by a frenzy of barking. Then a voice said, "All right, down. I'm a friend, not a foe."

Billy went into the hall. After the dazzling sunshine it took a few seconds before he could distinguish the figure in the doorway. Dressed in white hotpants and a red shirt, her hair streaked by the sun, her long long legs and body rising up to the wonderful breasts like a trumpet, stood the girl from the Golden Lion.

"I've brought you some freesias," she said. "they should have been Sweet Williams."

Billy opened his mouth and shut it again.

"I must be dreaming," he said slowly. "Please don't make me wake up."

She came towards him and gave him the gentlest pinch on his bare arm. "You're awake all right. Didn't I promise we'd meet again?"

"I know, but I never believe in good fortune. Come through to the kitchen and I'll get you a drink. I made a jug of Pimms, but I drank it all waiting for some boring reporter who's supposed to be interviewing me for the *Daily Post.*"

"That's me."

"I don't expect he'll take long. What did you say?"

"That's me - Janey Henderson."

"Oh my God, our secretary put down Jamie. I was expecting a fella. Are you really a journalist?"

She nodded and turned her palms towards him. "Look, I've got ink on my hands."

He got an apple, some cucumber and an orange, and started chopping them up. Janey admired the broad mahogany back.

"You're very brown. I suppose that was Colombia. Congratulations by the way, I watched you on the telly."

"Wasn't me, it was The Bull. I was so shit-scared my mind went a complete blank. He just trundled me round. Just get some mint." He stepped out of the kitchen window, raided the herb bed and came back.

"Look, I can't believe this. Are you really a journalist?"

Janey grinned. "Rather a good one." She took the mint from him and started to strip off the leaves and put them in the jug.

"Oh dear," said Billy. "Should I have heard of you?"

"Not really, if you don't read the *Post* regularly. They want me to do a big piece on you."

"I don't read enough," said Billy apologetically. "Helen, Rupert's wife, is always accusing us of being intellectual dolts."

"You can read the instructions on a Pimm's bottle and that's enough for me."

"Shall we go outside?"

Janey considered. She didn't want to get flushed and shiny.

"We can pull the bench into the shade," said Billy.

"They wanted me to bring a photographer but I said it would cramp my style." The way her eyes wandered over his face and body when she said it made him feel hot and excited.

She sat in the shade, Billy in the sun. They talked about The Bull.

"Honestly, I worship the ground he trots on," said Billy. "He's such a trier and he's got such a beautiful mouth."

"So have you," said Janey.

Billy didn't know what to do with his mouth now.

"Is it true that you're thinking of turning professional?"

Billy nodded. "I've had my shot at the Olympics, so there's no excuse really not to. I can't go on living with Rupert forever. I'm 27 now."

"Don't you find it difficult, the three of you?"

"Easy for me; must be hard for them sometimes."

"They don't mind you coming in late, bringing back girls?"

"Haven't been many of them lately."

Janey looked at him until he dropped his eyes.

"What about Lavinia Greenslade?"

Billy filled up her glass before answering.

"I was very cut up when she married Guy. But at least I had something to get stuck into with the horses. Since we split up, I've had my best season."

"Are you getting over her?"

Billy ate a piece of apple out of his Pimm's. "Yup. I got over her in the Golden Lion about six weeks ago."

"It was six weeks three days to be exact."

Billy sidled down the bench and took her hands. "I didn't know how to find you. Every time anyone interviewed me in Colombia, all I wanted to say was that I'd got a message for the girl in the Golden Lion (you look a bit like a lion), would she please come back. I spent more time thinking about you than worrying about the next day's rounds."

Then an awful thought struck him. "You're not married or anything, are you?"

Janey shook her head. "The ash came out of the dress, by the way."

Reluctantly, Billy let go of her hands. "Do you interview lots of people?"

"Robert Redford last week, Mohammed Ali the week before that." Billy felt quite faint with horror.

"You didn't meet *them* first in a pub?" he asked.

They finished the Pimms and they talked and talked. Billy had never felt such a strong sexual attraction to anyone. She was so glowing and she had a special way of swivelling her eyes and gazing up at him from under her eyelashes that made him quite dizzy with longing.

It was so hot they had lunch it the kitchen. At first he sat opposite her, then he came and sat beside her.

"Do you have hundreds of brothers and sisters?"

"Yes. I'm the youngest. They're all married. My mother despairs of getting me off the shelf."

"That's ridiculous. How old are you?"

Janey paused for a second. "Twenty-four."

Neither of them ate much lunch, but they finished one bottle of Muscadet and started on a second.

"I hope this piece is going to be O.K.," sighed Janey. "My shorthand keeps misting over. How long have you lived here?" she asked.

"Since I was twenty-one, although before that I used to come here sometimes in the school holidays. I adored the place even then. If Rupert and I had fights, I used to wander off down the valley. There's a secret glade with a pond where I used to look for the kingfisher."

"What's he like?"

"Rupert? Oh marvellous. I know him so well it's like a marriage."

Janey put the top on her pen and, put her notebook away. "What's his own marriage like, off the record?"

"Very happy," said Billy firmly. He knew journalists, they were always trying to catch him out over Rupert.

"Must be under terrible pressure, now she's got a baby and can't go everywhere with him, with girls mobbing him wherever he goes."

"They've got it worked out, and if you met Helen, she's so stunning no one would want to wander from her. Anyway, it's always a honeymoon whenever he comes home."

Somehow he wanted to convince Janey that marriage to a show-jumper wasn't impossible.

"Can we go and see The Bull?"

"Can you ride?" said Billy, gathering up the fruit from the Pimm's jug.

"I've tried, but I can't stay on when they start running."

Billy grinned. "I'll teach you."

They seemed to have spent an awfully long time over lunch. The sun was already dropping, shining into their eyes. The Bull was delighted with the Pimm's fruit.

"Why don't we go and look at your secret glade?" said Janey.

"All right," said Billy. "Let's leave your notebook in the tack-room. You're not going to need it."

There wasn't a breath of wind, but the great heat of the day was beginning to subside; smoky-grey ash trees seemed to shiver in the stillness. The cows were lying down and the young horses in the big field were trying to crowd into the shed to get away from the flies.

As they walked up the fields their hands occasionally brushed. Janey felt the corn stubble bristling against her sandals. As the path narrowed she moved in front. Billy admired the length of her smooth tanned legs. The softness of her upper thighs, beneath the white shorts, made his throat go dry.

"I always come up here when I am very happy or when I am very sad—when I was dropped from the British team, when I was picked for the Olympics."

Janey gave him another sidelong glance and picked a blackberry. "Which do you feel now?"

"Not sure. That's up to you."

She didn't answer. They had dropped down now to a little spring, crowded with forget-me-nots and pink campion, which had almost dried up.

Unlike me, thought Janey, who could feel herself bubbling between the legs.

They came to a gate. On the right was a mossy old wall, skirting a poplar grove.

"Hell," said Billy, looking down the path. "It's overgrown with nettles. You'll get stung," he added, as Janey clambered over the gate. "I'll carry you."

"No," squeaked Janey, pulling away from him.

If only she'd stuck to her diet last week and been down to her target weight of a hundred and twenty pounds, she'd have let him. But a hundred and thirty was too heavy; he'd rupture himself.

"We'll go back," Billy said reluctantly.

"No," said Janey. "I need to see this enchanted glade where you seduced all those Pony Club groupies and Lavinia Greenslade."

Billy, construing this as a rejection, was suddenly cast down. She was just coming here so she could get some good quotes. Janey ran down the path. Thirty yards down on the left she found a willow-fringed pool with its green banks completely secluded in the green gloom. She'd forgotten how much nettles hurt. "Ow, ow, ow," she moaned, collapsing onto a bank, tears stinging her eyelids, white spots jumping up on her brown legs.

"Oh angel," said Billy, "you should have let me carry you. Your poor beautiful legs. Let me get some dock leaves."

He picked a handful, green and smooth, dipping them in the pool.

"Christ it hurts," said Janey through clenched teeth.

He lay down on the bank beside her.

"There," she said pointing to the outside of her calf of her right leg and the inside of her ankle.

"That's better, a bit higher."

Billy, crooning with contrition, moved the dock leaves up to her knees.

"I shouldn't have let you come down here."

"Oh yes you should," said Janey softly, "bit higher."

His hand had reached the inside of her left thigh now. His fingers were so gentle, she could feel the damp cool of the dock leaves against her burning red legs.

"Higher," she whispered.

As though acting on their own, Billy's fingers crept up, and dropped the dock leaves as he met a fuzz of damp pubic hair dividing round the skimpiest of pants. He looked up, and found her smiling at him through her tears.

"Enter these enchanted woods, you who dare," she said mockingly, "Go on, that's the only way you can cure the hurt."

"Oh Christ, Janey," he muttered, feeling the liquid between her legs. The next minute he had moved up the bank beside her, putting his arms around her, and kissing her almost reverently, and she was kissing him back, her tongue expertly caressing his tongue and the inside of his lips. His hand found the wonderful generous breasts, with the nipples hard as hazelnuts, and he felt her draw in her stomach as his hand crept downwards. She had exactly the right amount of flesh on her. Her hands were caressing his bare back, her fingers burrowing in his hair.

"Jesus," he said to himself incredulously, "this amazingly beautiful girl really wants me. Oh please God don't let me botch it up by coming too quickly."

He undid the buttons of her shirt with trembling hands and buried his face in the billowy cleavage, breathing in her scent.

"My nettle stings at the top still need a bit more attention," Janey said, with of gasp of laughter, so he slid his hand underneath her pants, finding her clitoris, which was as hard as her nipples.

"Oh please go on, please please," she moaned, then shuddered and gave a long contented sigh, and he felt her throbbing to stillness.

"Come inside me, I want you," she said a moment later.

"Not yet." His experience of outdoor screwing was that one always got worried about keepers crashing through the bracken and came too quickly. But she wouldn't listen to him, sitting up with her breasts tumbling, undoing his belt with practiced skill. Jeans were really hell to get out of, he thought, like getting a woman out of a girdle, and his cock stuck out through the hole in his pants, so he had difficulty getting them off too.

After all her London lovers, Janey suddenly realized what a marvelous body Billy had, with the broad shoulders, flat stomach and the incredibly muscular buttocks and thighs from riding so much.

"God you're strong," she said.

Billy laughed. "You should try Rupert. When he squeezes a horse with his legs you can hear it groan."

"I'll never last a second," he warned, as he was sucked into the warm spongy whirlpool, feeling her gripping him, feeling her hands caressing his buttocks, moving with him.

"I'm sorry, I can't help it, I've got to come."

For a few seconds he lay on top of her feeling the delicious warmth. Then he rolled off, pulling up a handful of grass to wipe her dry.

Janey grinned. "I hope there aren't any nettles in it."

"Are they still murder?"

"Much better. I'm beginning to understand about the pleasure-pain principal. Maybe de Sade had a point."

He brushed a green beetle out of her hair. "Sorry I came so quickly."

"I should have been offended if you hadn't. Wouldn't have said much for my sex appeal. Anyway I'd already come once when you were stroking me, so I could afford to be generous."

Billy looked down at his flaccid cock. "A bad workman blames his tool," he said.

He lit them both cigarettes to keep off the midges. Janey lay on her elbow, looking at him through half-closed eyes.

"How come you sell yourself so short when you're such a mega-star?"

Billy shrugged: "I've always hunted in pairs with Rupe."

"So?"

"No one's likely to look at me when he's around, so he usually gets the girls."

"That's not what I heard." Janey combed her hand through his black chest hair. "I think you're stunning."

"And I don't meet many girls like you. I didn't want to rush my fences."

He put out a hand to bracket one of the brown breasts. "You're so beautiful." He felt his cock rearing up like a kite: "I think I might hit better form this time, or are the midges eating you?"

"I'd much rather something else ate me."

Billy looked at her lascivious face, mascara-smudged under her eyes, crimson lipstick kissed away. Slowly she edged up the bank, until her bush was level with his face.

"Oh," she murmured, as he rolled over and got to work, "Oh sweet sweet William, this is definitely the lap of honor."

Billy laughed and carried on.

By the time they set off back to the house a huge red setting sun was spiked on the poplar copse like a balloon about to pop. Pigeons flapped towards the wood.

"Helen and Rupert are back," said Billy. "Come and say hello."

Janey shook her head. "I must get home."

"But you can't," he said appalled. "You've only just come."

Janey giggled. "You can say that again. I'm not up to meeting anyone at the moment. Anyway, they're virtually in-laws."

"You can't just go." Billy looked like a small boy left behind by his parents the first day of prep school. "I'm going to Lisbon tomorrow," he went on. "We haven't talked about anything. Why don't you come with me?"

"I've got to work."

"Will you write to me? I'll be back for the Horse of the Year Show on the first of October."

"I'll be back from America about the third or fourth. You can leave a number with the Features desk."

"Please don't go. I can't bear it."

"It's been so perfect," she said. "I don't want to come in and make polite conversation, I must get back to London and write it all down before I forget."

"Not all of it."

"No, the glade's our secret. See you at Wembley."

And with that he had to be content.

He couldn't go straight into the house. He walked around in a daze, watching the sun set and the stars come out. He couldn't believe it, just as when he was a small boy he couldn't believe anyone as dazzling as Rupert could choose him as a friend.

He walked into the kitchen to find Helen rather ostentatiously clearing away the remains of lunch and heating a bottle for Marcus.

"I'm sorry Helen, lunch was marvelous."

"Badger didn't think so. He's just thrown up most of the chicken and potato salad on our bedroom carpet. You left the fridge door open and the butter in the sun. Are you in love or something?"

The next day they set off for Portugal, Greece, then Germany, then back without a break for the Horse of the Year Show at Wembley. It was the longest four weeks of Billy's life. When he couldn't get Janey on the telephone he nearly flew back. He discussed her endlessly with Rupert.

"You know I'm hopeless at playing the field. I want to marry her."

Rupert looked thunderstruck. "You can't marry her. You don't even know her."

"I've spent a whole day with her."

"You haven't even screwed her yet?"

"I have too," said Billy sulkily, "and it was marvelous."

Rupert looked even more disapproving. "Then she's just a whore, going to bed with you on the first date. It wasn't even a date. She came to interview you, wormed it all out of you. You wait until the piece appears in the *Post*. 'Billy Lloyd-Foxe is not only a silver medalist, he also gets the gold in the sack'."

"Oh fuck off," said Billy furiously. "Why d'you reduce everything to your own disgusting level?"

25

*T*he moment Billy got back he called the news desk at the *Post*, to be told Janey was still away. Her interview with Jack Nicholson had taken longer than expected—Billy wondered miserably what form it had taken—and she was expected back sometime that week.

Now it was the fifth day of the Horse of the Year Show and there was no sign of her. He must have passed the competitors' board fifty times a day in the hope of a message. His fears that she'd only been nice to him because she wanted some good quotes were multiplied when he talked to Joanna Battie and Dudley Diplock.

Did they know her? he asked.

"'Course I do," said Joanna. "She's the *Post's* star writer, hanggliding one week, going into battle in a tank the next, interviewing Prince Charles the next. Pretty high-powered stuff."

"Very pretty," said Billy.

"Very," said Dudley with a wolfish laugh. "Puts out, by all accounts. Fleet Street claims she got to the top on her back."

"On her front," said Joanna. "Janey's much too liberated to accept the missionary position."

Billy felt quite sick. "Are you sure?"

"Well, let's say she's a bloody good journalist and, like most of them, she's not too particular how she gets her information. They pay her well. I reckon she's on twenty thou a year, don't you Joanna?"

After a sleepless night, Billy talked to Rupert as they exercised the horses. Rupert was reassuringly outraged.

"For God's sake! Remember the things they've said about you and me in the past, even implying we're a couple of fags. You know it's all fairy tales. They make it up to excite themselves. Christ, Revenge is sluggish. I'm going to have to nail up his stall during the day to stop the public stuffing him with goodies."

At that moment Humpty Hamilton came waddling past in a pale blue quilted vest. "Hi, Sweet William," he said and waddled on, roaring with laughter.

Next to come by was Driffield. "Hullo great lover," he sneered. "Seen the *Daily Post?*"

Finally, as Billy was handing The Bull back to Tracey, Lavinia rode into the practice ring. "Hullo, Sweet William," she said, an acid note creeping into her voice. "You *have* made a conquest."

Heart thumping, Billy ran to the news stand.

"Hi, Sweet William," said the man behind the counter, handing him a copy of the *Post*. "You've boosted my sales so much this morning you can have it for free."

Billy retired behind a pillar. Janey's piece was in the middle, opposite the leader page, with a huge heading. "Sweet Sweet William" and a picture of Billy taken from an extremely flattering angle.

"When I went to see Billy Lloyd-Foxe," Janey had written, "I took him a bunch of freesias. They should have been Sweet Williams, since he is easily the nicest man I have ever met." Then there was a lot of guff about his Jean Paul Belmondo looks, and his clinching the team silver and winning the King's Cup. Then it ended:

"We all know of his sympathy for animals, his brilliant horsemanship, and his ability to smile even in the bitterest defeat. Last year he admits he was heartbroken when his long-standing girlfriend, Lavinia Greenslade, married French heartthrob, Guy de la Tour. Since then the only female in Billy's life has been Mavis, his blond mongrel, who follows him everywhere, bestowing a slit-eyed expression of marked disapproval on any lady intruder.

"Billy lives with Helen and Rupert Campbell-Black, and his soothing easygoing presence must be a great help in sustaining a somewhat volatile marriage. But Billy, with characteristic modesty, says he owes everything to Rupert (including money, he adds with a smile). He also has the highest praise for his chef d'equipe, martinet Malise

Gordon, and of course The Bull—who eats the fruit out of the Pimm's jug—with whom he jumped a final clear in the team event to clinch the silver for Britain. He may only have got a silver, but he's got a heart of gold. I haven't heard a bad word about him on the circuit. After seven hours in his company, all I can say is please give me back my heart, Billy. The *Daily Post* offices are open to accept parcels twenty-four hours a day."

Billy read it incredulously over and over and over again. It was a love letter. He rushed to the telephone. There was still no answer at Janey's apartment. The features desk said she'd gotten back last night and was racing to finish the Nicholson piece and had probably switched off her telephone. Billy couldn't bear it. He had to see her. He told Rupert he was going into London for a couple of hours.

"Well don't be too long," said Rupert, grinning. "You're obviously better in the sack than I thought. And what's this about my 'somewhat volatile marriage'? What does 'volatile' mean—that I'm always out on the tiles?"

Billy took a taxi to Janey's. It was a long time before she answered. Compared with her glamourously tawny appearance before, she looked pale and black under the eyes and rather unadorned like a sitting room the day after the Christmas cards are taken down.

"Billy," she said, "how lovely to see you." She didn't sound as though it was at all.

"I'm sorry to barge in, but I've missed you like hell."

She backed away nervously. "Darling, I'm terribly sorry, I can't stop. The office wants Jack Nicholson by tomorrow lunchtime, so I'll have to work all night."

"Surely you can stop for five minutes."

"I can't, honestly. I've got complete brain freeze, I've just got to crack it."

"The piece you wrote about me, it was so kind, and ludicrously flattering."

She smiled, looking suddenly more like the Janey who'd come down to Penscombe. "Did they run it today? They must have held it back for the Horse of the Year. I filed the copy weeks ago."

And perhaps she feels quite differently about me now, thought Billy. He was dying to ask about Jack Nicholson. Instead he said, "It's the last night tomorrow. Will you hve dinner with me afterwards?"

"I don't know. I'm supposed to be dining with some MP as a preliminary interview. What time d'you finish?"

"About eleven, But I'm off to Washington, New York and Toronto on Monday, and I must see you."

"You must go now, but I really will try and make it tomorrow."

"I'll leave a ticket at the gate. Janey, I love . . ."

But she'd shut the door on him. Billy was filled with black despair. She hadn't seemed pleased to see him, dismayed in fact, and rather guilty and not looking him in the eye. If she'd filed the copy weeks ago, she was bound to have met someone else in America.

Back in her apartment, Janey Henderson felt equally suicidal. Her vanity wouldn't allow her to explain to Billy that she'd already been home for forty-eight hours on a crash diet in order to look ravishing for him on Saturday night. He'd caught her at the worst possible moment—she'd been writing and hadn't dressed or had a bath or used deodorant for two days. Her body had that rank smell of fear and sweat that always drenched her when she was wrestling with a piece. She was convinced her breath smelled from her all-meat diet. She hadn't shaved her legs since she'd last seen him, her hair was filthy, she was sure she had dandruff and she couldn't meet his eyes because he'd caught her with unplucked eyebrows and no makeup. Also her ginger cat, Harold Evans, had been sick in the bathroom that morning and she hadn't had time to clean it up. The apartment was a mess because her cleaning woman had walked out while she was away and the neighbor who'd come to feed Harold Evans had failed to change his litter box—hardly a lover's bower.

Janey knew she ought to go back and wrestle with Jack Nicholson. Instead she reread the proof of the piece on Billy. She had actually lied to him and had only telephoned the corrections through last night. It really was rather good, and he looked so gorgeous in the photograph. He'd looked even more gorgeous just now. He must have masses of girls after him. She musn't seem too keen. She'd lusted and lost too often over the last ten years. She was in fact twenty-nine. That was another lie she'd told Billy. Would he ever trust her when he found out?

Janey Henderson came from a respectable upper-middle class family. Her father had been in advertising, her kind easy-going mother had stayed at home, brought up the children and encouraged them to have careers, but never taught them how to do anything around the house. Janey, the baby of the family, had been the most successful. She possessed a strong sex drive which led her into trouble, but was bourgeois enough to be paranoid about being talked about. Used to adoration at home, she expected it from her lovers and in order to keep them happy she would tell lies and, when they got angry, she tended to move on to another one, who could be fooled for a few weeks that she was absolutely perfect. Her father doted on her and, if she had any troubles with landladies or bills or angry bosses, she'd run to him. In the old days he had always bailed her out, but since his advertising agency had folded in the economic collapse of 1973 he suddenly found himself very short of money.

Janey Henderson was attracted to power. As a journalist, she had racketed around and met endless stars. She had mixed with the rich and famous and longed to live like they did. She was a good, if sloppy, writer, an inspired listener who was able to sift out the minutiae that mattered. A teenager in the swinging sixties, she had enjoyed the fruits of the permissive society and benefited in her career from the rise of the women's movement. She had also watched her girlfriends trying to do their own thing, raising their consciousness and their husband's blood pressure, finally walking out on these husbands and then being absolutely miserable as single parents. At 29, Janey realized there was nothing one needed more than a good man. She wanted to settle down and have children. She had seen Rupert's beautiful house and assumed that servants and land and unlimited Pimms were all normal perks of a show-jumper's life. Janey also longed to be a more serious writer. If she married Billy, she could be more selective, producing one piece a month instead of two or three a week, and even writing books.

Janey Henderson pondered on these things. The sight of the blank page in the Olivetti and the mess in the apartment brought her back to earth. There was no MP to be interviewed tomorrow night. If she had to hand in copy at lunchtime, she reckoned it would take her till late evening to clean the place up and make herself look ravishing.

Harold Evans was weaving furrily around her ankles demanding lunch. "I must take you away from this squalor, Harold," said Janey, picking him up. "How would you like to live in Gloucestershire?"

Back at Wembley Billy was inconsolable, despite the fact that Rupert had good news of a possible sponsor. "He approached me to test the water. I said you'd need at least £50,000 a year to stay on the road."

"What a lot of money—what does he make?"

"Cat food."

"The Bull won't have to eat it, will he?"

"No, but he might have to change his name to Moggie Meal Charlie or something."

"Christ, what's this sponsor like?"

"Oh, frightful, thatched hair, jangling I.D. bracelets, frilled duck-egg-blue evening shirts, firm handshakes, fake American accent, and calls you by your Christian name every second sentence."

"What's his name?"

"Kevin Coley. Rather suitable under the circs. Puts a lot of himself into his products."

Billy grinned. "What's in it for him?"

"Social mountaineering. He's made his pile and now he wants upmarket fun and some smart friends. He thinks you have tremendous charisma."

"Glad someone does," said Billy gloomily. "He won't much longer if The Bull goes on knocking down fences."

"I think you should talk to him," said Rupert. "Fifty grand a year's not to be sniffed at. Your mother's not likely to croak for at least twenty years. And I thought you wanted to marry that girl?"

"After today I don't think she'll have me."

Billy was sure that Janey wouldn't turn up the following night. Even his horoscope was ambiguous: it warned Pisces subjects to watch out for fireworks, and make travel plans in the evening.

It had been the Germans' Wembley. Hot-foot from the Olympics and their double gold, they had jackbooted their way through the week, winning every big class except the *Sunday Times* Cup which had gone to Rupert. On the last night the crowd was really hungry for a British victory. The big class was the Victor Ludorum, a two-round competition in which riders with double clears jumped off against the clock for £6000. Rupert jumped clear in the first round and so did Billy, although he was very lucky. The Bull rapped every fence and had the upright swinging back and forth like a metronome on *lente,* but he didn't bring it down and the crowd went wild.

They had given him and The Bull a colossal welcome whenever he'd come into the ring that week. But each time Dudley Diplock had announced them as "that great Olympic combination—Billy Lloyd-Foxe riding The Bull" the little horse had raised two hoofs at the commentary box and knocked up a cricket score. He was tired after a long season. Tonight, however, he felt more bouncy. "You've got to win," Billy urged him, "to impress Janey, if she comes."

Now Billy sat in the riders' stand, biting his nails, watching Rupert jump his second round. Revenge was also a bit tired. He flattened twice and had eight faults at the combination and a brick out of the wall. As he came out of the ring, Rupert patted Revenge consolingly, determined to refute any charges of cruelty, knowing the television cameras were still on him.

Billy met him in the collecting ring.

"Just wait till I get this bugger back to his stable," said Rupert. "I'm going to beat the hell out of him."

"He's had a long year," protested Billy. "Think how well he did in the *Sunday Times* Cup." He did hope the honeymoon between Rupert and Revenge wasn't over.

As he mounted The Bull to warm him up over a couple of practice fences, he could hear Dudley Diplock waxing lyrical over "Ludwig's second clear".

Billy felt desperately low; Janey was obviously not coming. His mind was a complete blank. He couldn't remember the course, or how many strides there were between any of the fences. The Bull clouted the practice fence.

"For God's sake pick your bloody feet up," snapped Billy with unusual irritation. The Bull looked martyred and limped a few paces. As Billy turned him to jump it again, he heard a voice calling:

"Hullo, William."

And there she was. Her lovely hair all tortoiseshell blonde and lion-like as it had been at Penscombe. She was wearing a black and grey striped silk rugger shirt with a white collar and very tight black velvet trousers.

Billy found it impossible to wipe the silly grin off his face as he trotted across the collecting ring towards her. "You made it! God, that's wonderful! And you look bloody marvelous. Was the MP furious you ditched him?"

"Livid."

"I don't blame him."

"I hear Rupert's out already," she said. "I've just passed a stand absolutely hung with whips, spurs, boots and strange leather devices, exactly like a tart's boudoir. I don't know *what* you get up to in show-jumping, really I don't."

Billy laughed.

Janey patted The Bull. "I'm sorry I was a bit offish yesterday, I'm always awful when I'm working."

"Did you finish the piece?"

"Yes." She shot him a sly look. "It wasn't nearly as complimentary as the one about you."

"Number 43," shouted the collecting ring steward. "Where's number 43?"

"I can't get over the fact that you're really here," said Billy.

"Number 43."

"Billee, they're calling you!" shouted Hans Schmidt.

"For the last time, number 43."

"I think they're calling you," said Janey.

Billy came down to earth. "Oh my God, so they are. Don't move I won't be long."

"I want to watch you."

"Stop coffee-housing," said Rupert, "and get into the ring."

"Oh thank goodness. Rupe, this is Janey. Will you get her a drink and look after her till I get back?"

"How d'you do?" said Janey. "I hear you had two legs out of the combination. It sounds awfully rude."

"Oh please," Billy prayed as he rode into the ring, "don't let her fall for him."

He must concentrate. But joy seemed to surge along the reins and The Bull bounced round the course rapping nothing and the crowd went berserk as Billy pulled off the only British double clear.

"Well done," said Janey, who was sitting in the riders' stand with Rupert clutching a large vodka and tonic. "You were marvelous, and you get a bigger ovation than the Rolling Stones." She giggled. "I asked Rupert who that fat man in the ring with a tape measure was.

He said he's the course builder. I asked him how did he know he was coarse. You do have the *most* extraordinary terminology in show-jumping. What on earth's a rustic pole?" She'd obviously made a hit with Rupert, who generally didn't like people taking the piss out of the sport.

There were six riders in the jump-off. Three Germans, Wishbone, Count Guy and finally Billy. Ludwig went first and jumped a very fast clear. From then onwards there were no clears until Hans Schmidt came in.

"Look at his stride—twice as long as The Bull's," said Rupert.

Hans incredibly knocked two seconds off Ludwig's time, cutting every corner.

"Billy won't make it?" asked Janey.

"I don't think so. The Bull simply isn't fast enough."

Hans came out, a broad grin on his round face. "Beat zat," he said as Billy rode into the ring.

"And here comes Billy Lloyd-Foxe on The Bull, our Olympic Silver medalist riding for Great Britain," said Dudley, trying to be heard over the cheers.

"Must be hell having to jump while you're taking a shit," said Janey.

The cheers continued as The Bull circled, his fluffy noseband like a blob of shaving cream, cantering along on his strong little legs, bottom lip flapping, ears waggling, taking in the applause. Billy gave him a pat. He was a mediaeval knight jousting for Janey's hand.

"If he wins everything'll be all right and he'll ask me to marry him," said Janey, crossing both fingers. As the bell rang the cheering started; as he rose to the first fence it increased, and it increased in a steady crescendo as he cleared each fence, riding for his life. As he turned for the last two fences, the double and then the huge wall, Billy glanced at the clock, realizing he was in with a chance. The cheer rose to a mighty roar as the whole crowd rose to their feet as one to bellow him home. The Bull was over the double and hurtled over the wall, nearly crashing into the side of the arena, before Billy could pull him up.

The crowd of ten-thousand turned to the clock. Billy turned around, putting his hands over his eyes. As he took them away a mighty roar took the roof off. He had won by a tenth of a second. The scenes that followed were worthy of a cup final. People were leaping over the stands into the arena, rushing forward to cheer and pat The Bull. Spectators were throwing hats, cushions, hand bags into the arena.

Rupert looked at Janey and saw all her mascara had run.

"Wasn't he wonderful?" she said.

"You do love him, don't you?"

She nodded, getting out a handkerchief.

"Well, mind you look after him."

Billy and The Bull got another deafening round of applause as they came into the ring to collect their ribbon. Then the band played "Little White Bull," and The Bull, very smug after all the attention, bucketed around the ring twice, deliberately keeping within the circle of the spotlight. Afterwards Billy came up to see Janey. "You were so wonderful," she said. "I've never been so proud in my life. What an absolutely sweet horse he is."

From all sides people were congratulating Billy, but he had eyes only for Janey. "Look, I've got to go back into the ring for the personality parade. Will you be all right? How did you get on with Rupert?"

"Great, but he's not nearly as attractive as you."

Billy blushed. "He must have been pulling his punches."

The cavalcade that brings the Horse of the Year show to an end must be the most moving event in the equestrian calendar. Among the celebrities were little Stroller and two of the police horses who'd displayed exceptional bravery during a bombing raid, followed by ponies, hacks and hunters, the heavy horses and, finally, the Olympic team. Then Malise, not without a tremor of emotion in his voice, read out Ronald Duncan's beautiful poem: "To the Horse," and Janey found herself in floods of tears again. What a wonderful dashing, romantic, colorful world she was moving into, she thought, after three large vodka and tonics on an empty stomach.

As Billy came out to the collecting ring, a man came up to him who he instantly recognized from Rupert's description as Kevin Coley.

"Bill Lloyd-Foxe," he said, pumping him by the hand. "Kev Coley." Billy was almost blinded by his jewelry.

"I think Rupe's spoken about me."

"Of course," said Billy, trying not to laugh. "He was *most* impressed."

"So was I, by tonight's win. Great stuff, Bill, great stuff. I'm ready to talk terms. Why don't we have dinner together?"

Billy's heart sank. "Well, actually, I've got someone with me."

"Bring her too," said Kev expansively. "My wife Enid's up in the stands. The girls can chat while we talk business." Suddenly they were interrupted by an old lady, tears pouring down her face. "Oh Mr. Lloyd-Foxe, I read in the paper you were thinking of turning professional. You won't sell The Bull, will you?"

Billy smiled. "Of course not."

"I've bought him some Polos." She got a dusty packet covered in face-powder out of her bag.

"Gosh, that's terribly kind of you," said Billy.

"Don't you worry your head, ma'am," said Kevin Coley. "If Bill turns professional, he'll never have to sell The Bull."

Billy found Janey in the trailer repairing her face. Tracey had already hung the ribbons up on the string across the wondow.

"Darling, I cried my eyes out—it was so choke-making." She mustn't hug him too hard or her new trousers might rip.

"Sweetheart, do you mind if we go out to dinner with a man who wants to sponsor me?"

"No, yes I do. I want to be alone with you and see the conquering hero come." Putting her hand down, she touched his cock.

Suddenly Billy realized that if he married this wonderful girl, he could sleep with her every night for the rest of his life.

"We can do that later on," he said. "It just means that if I pull this deal off, I can ask you to marry me."

Rupert came in in a dark suit, smelling of aftershave.

"I hear you've met up with Medallion Man," he said, then in an undertone to Billy, "Do you mind frightfully saying that I had dinner with you all tonight if Helen asks you? I'm sure she won't."

"Where are you off to?" said Billy.

"Well, do you remember a little unfinished business called Tiffany Bathgate?" and added, as Billy looked disapproving, "and anyway, I thought I'd make myself scarce in case you and Janey wanted to use the trailer later."

At four o'clock in the morning Billy lay in Janey's arms in the double bed in her apartment. They had just made love and he was thinking how beautifully she kept the place. There were clean dark-blue sheets on the bed, and three bunches of freesias on the bedside table had driven out any smell of cat. What a glorious talented creature she was.

"Ouch" he said, trying not to wake her as Harold Evans kneaded his stomach.

"Billy," she said, "there's something I've got to tell you. Promise you won't hate me for it?"

Billy's heart sank. The lovely irridescent soap bubble was about to burst. "I'm 29, not 24," she went on.

Billy started to laugh with sheer relief. "Is that all? I wouldn't have minded if you'd said forty-four. Are you sure you won't find it tough to marry a younger man?"

Billy found himself very nervous about telling Helen he was getting married. Rupert had been no problem. In fact Rupert and Janey both experienced passionate relief that they enormously liked but didn't fancy one another; they were too alike, perhaps. And Rupert, having set up the sponsorship which enabled Billy to marry Janey and start his own stable, felt he had masterminded the whole affair, which mitigated any jealousy.

Nothing would happen in a hurry anyway. Billy would have to find somewhere to live and, although it might be difficult to go on being partners if Billy were a professional, Rupert was sure they could work something out. Although it would be a struggle financially, Rupert wasn't prepared to turn professional until he'd had another stab at a gold medal in four years' time.

Helen, however, was shattered when she heard the news. Without Billy the precarious balance of their marriage would surely be destroyed. He was so sweet to Marcus and he could always jolly Rupert out of a bad mood by making him laugh. Nor did the two women really take to each other. After Billy and Rupert returned from their American trip, Billy brought Janey down for the weekend. Each woman was set back on her heels by the glamour of the other. Janey never expected Helen to be that beautiful. Helen didn't expect Janey to be that sexy. Janey had never worn a bra and her clothes were always a little too tight, because she kept falling by the wayside on her diets, and her shirts and dresses were always done up a button too low. Helen's were always buttoned up to the neck. After six years in Fleet Street Janey was virtually unshockable and during dinner that Friday she arrived kept both Rupert and Billy in stitches, providing a wildly inaccurate low-down on the sex life of leading public figures.

Helen had taken great trouble to cook a superb dinner: crab pancakes in cheese sauce, gigot of lamb, and the most perfect quince sorbet. It was a good technique if one wanted to establish a reputation as a brilliant cook, reflected Janey, to serve very small helpings as Helen did, so everyone wanted seconds. Janey, not having eaten all day, was starving, and had thirds of everything, praising like mad. Everyone drank a lot. Janey got happily tight.

How nice, thought Rupert, to find a woman with such an appetite. He'd never admired Lavinia, she was a drip. Janey was fun and tough. She would be good for Billy.

Between Helen and Janey there was also professional jealousy. Janey asked Helen about her novel. Helen said it was coming on very very slowly.

"I'm a scholar, you see, and I'm not prepared to put up with anything second-rate."

"Why don't you try journalism?" asked Janey.

Helen said she didn't really feel she could bring herself to do anything like that. She'd never read the *Post,* but she'd heard it was very sensational.

Janey registered the snub and said that, in her experience, writers who were any good wrote.

"I've got a book coming out in the spring," she said, "a collection of interviews. I just got the piece I did on you in at the end, darling," she added to Billy.

She and Billy were so in love they couldn't keep their hands off each other. Helen wistfully tried to remember the time when she and Rupert were like that. The attempt at a second honeymoon after the Olympics had not lasted very long.

Marcus was brought down and admired and fed. How can such good-looking parents produce such a hideous baby, thought Janey. But, realizing it would endear her to Helen, she asked if she could give Marcus his bottle.

"Billy tells me you're getting a nanny."

"Well, a girl," said Helen. "It'll mean I can spend more time with Rupert." She must try to like this self-confident, sexy creature. "I'm so pleased you're getting married to Billy," she said when they were alone. "He's so darling, but he's kind of vulnerable too. You will look after him, won't you?"

"Funny, Rupert said the same thing," said Janey. "I actually hope *he's* going to look after me."

Everyone else thought Janey was marvelous; the dogs, the grooms, Marcus, Miss Hawkins, Mrs. Bodkin, for whom Janey left a five-pound note. There was a bad moment, however, when Janey was changing for dinner on Saturday night and couldn't be bothered to go down the hall to the john. Instead, she got a chair and was crouching over the basin having a pee when Helen walked in to turn down the beds. Helen was shocked rigid and even more annoyed that Rupert thought it was funny. Janey, sensitive as a radar, realized Helen didn't approve of her.

"She's a bit lined skirt and petticoat, or half-slip as she'd call it, isn't she?" she said to Billy. "I bet she makes love in long rubber gloves."

Billy laughed, but he refused to bitch about Helen.

"We really must look for a house very soon," said Janey.

Rupert persuaded Helen to give a party at Penscombe for Billy and Janey. As she'd done up the house so beautifully, he said, it would be nice for everyone to see it, and they hadn't had a party since their marriage. She wouldn't have to do any work. They'd get in caterers, and as the drawing-room wasn't big enough for dancing, they'd rent a tent. The party would be held in the middle of December just before the Olympia Christmas show, so all the foreign riders would be in the country.

There were frightful arguments over the guest list; all the show—jumping fraternity had to be asked.

"But not Malise Gordon, or Colonel Roxborough. I don't want any grown-ups," said Rupert.

"Oh, we must have Malise," protested Helen. "He's so civilized."

"He wasn't very civilized when Ivor Braine took the wrong course in the Nations' Cup last week. If he comes, he'll start telling me to go to bed early because I've got a class next year."

"You ought to ask him," said Billy. "He'd be awfully hurt."

"Oh all right, but I'm not asking Jake Lovell. His fat wife wouldn't get through the door."

By the time they'd included Janey's Fleet Street friends and most of the celebrities she had interviewed, who knew Rupert and Billy anyway, as well as all Rupert's smart friends, the number was up to 300. Rupert flipped through the final selection.

"I've slept with practically every woman on the list. Gives me a feeling of *déjà vu,*" he said to Billy.

"You haven't slept with Hilary."

"*She's* not coming!"

"Bloody is. According to Mrs. B she's been around a lot recently."

Rupert, furious, stormed off to find Helen.

"Either that woman doesn't come to the party or I don't."

"All your friends are coming," said Helen. "I don't see why I shouldn't have *one* of mine."

"She'll bring that disgusting baby, and start whipping out a triangular tit in the middle."

"Hilary is not just a good painter, she's a highly intelligent concerned human being."

"Crap," said Rupert. "All right, I'll ask all the grooms then."

"You can't," said Helen aghast. "They can never hold their liquor."

A week before the party, while Rupert and Billy were in Amsterdam, the au pair, Marie-Claire, slipped on the yellow stone steps in the hall and landed painfully on her coccyx. The next day Hilary slipped carrying Germaine but managed to keep her balance. Helen suddenly decided to carpet the hall and the stairs a pale avocado green to go with the pale pink and green peony wallpaper. The carpet men worked overtime, the dogs sat in a martyred row on the ticktacked underfelt, and everything was finished and tidied away by the eve of the party when Rupert and Billy were due home.

Helen had just got Marcus to sleep when they arrived and woke him up with all the din of barking, neighing, shouting and the banging-down of trailer ramps. Why the hell did they make so much noise? She had to spend a quarter of an hour soothing and rocking Marcus back to sleep and went downstairs to the kitchen just as Rupert was coming in through the back door. There was snow in his hair.

"Hello darling," he said, kissing her. "You all right? I see the tent's up. Everyone's coming, the Germans, the French team, the Italians, all the Irish—it's a complete sell out."

"Go and get a drink. There's a surprise for you in the hall," said Helen.

Rupert went out—there was a long pause. The new carpet was so soft, Helen didn't hear him come back. His face was expressionless.

"Do you like it?"

"I didn't know Marcus could be that sick," said Rupert. "That carpet is exactly the color as regurgitated Heinz peas and bacon baby food. What the fuck have you done?"

Helen bridled. "It's called pistachio."

"Pissed-tachio after everyone's spilled red wine over it tomorrow night," said Rupert.

"It was a death trap," snapped Helen.

"Pity your friend Hilary didn't fall down it more often. That's Cotswold stone you've just covered up!"

"Those steps were dangerous. Marcus'll be walking in a few months."

"He'll walk right out of the house when he sees that carpet."

"Well, everyone thinks it's very pretty," Helen's voice was rising, "Mrs. Bodkin, Marie-Claire."

"That's only because you pay them. Who else? Thrillary I suppose. Expect it's her idea; matches her complexion."

It was, in fact, a great party. Rupert and Billy mixed a champagne cocktail to start off with, which, with one and a half hours solid drinking before dinner, got everyone plastered. Janey, looking sensational in see-through black, was such a hit with all the foreign riders that Billy put her on a leadline and, screaming with laughter, towed her around after him. Their happiness was totally infectious. Even Driffield couldn't find anything to grumble about.

Only Helen, in priceless ivy green silk, a boat-shaped neckline showing off her slender white shoulders, seemed tense. She was not a natural hostess and she was only too aware of all the Biancas and Granias and Gabriellas of Rupert's past. Nor could she bear to see drink rings spreading like a million Olympic symbols on her furniture, and cigarette ash and wine stains on her new carpet.

Rupert tried to persuade her to enjoy herself. But once dinner was over, he felt he could relax his duties as host. People knew where they could get a drink. From then on he was seen coming off the dance floor with one beauty after another.

Hilary arrived late. Armed with a carrycot, she marched down the hall, sending international show-jumpers flying, and up the stairs.

"Straight up to my wife's bedroom," said Rupert sourly.

Next moment Helen went past with a baby's bottle.

"Is that for Hilary?"

"Marcus is crying."

"You should have sent him to Mrs. Bodkin. Where the hell's Marie-Claire?"

"She disappeared into the shrubbery with one of the French team two hours ago and hasn't been seen since," snapped Helen. "I told you the drink was too strong."

Upstairs, Helen collected Marcus and went into the bedroom, where she found Hilary combing her hair.

"Oh, you look beautiful," she gasped.

Hilary had been to the hairdresser and had her dark hair set in wild snaky curls around her face. She had rouged her cheekbones and kohled her eyes and was wearing a red and black gypsy dress with a flounced skirt and hooped earrings.

"I never dreamed you could look so wonderful," Helen said in genuine amazement.

"I wanted to prove to your bloody husband I wasn't a complete frump," said Hilary. "I've even shaved under my arms." She held up her arms, showing not a trace of stubble, "And I absolutely hate myself."

"Well, I sure appreciate you," said Helen.

Hilary, drenching herself in Helen's Miss Dior, said, "How's it going? Sounds wild enough."

"I'm not great at parties."

"Rupert shouldn't subject you to them. What did he say about the carpet?"

"He hated it."

Why did the conversation always return to Rupert? wondered Helen.

The excitement had stepped up when they went downstairs. Ludwig was blowing a hunting horn, Billy, plastered and blissful, was necking on the sofa with Janey, Mavis curled up beside them, looking resigned.

"Come and dance, Helen," said Humpty Hamilton, who was wearing one of Rupert's tweed caps back to front.

"You haven't met Hilary, have you?" said Helen.

At that moment Rupert came off the dance floor with a ruffled blonde.

"Evening," he said to Hilary without any warmth.

"Doesn't Hilly look lovely?" said Helen.

Rupert looked her up and down. "Rather like one of Jake Lovell's relations."

Next moment a very drunken Hans staggered up and bore Helen off to dance. "What a beautiful place you have 'ere Mees Helen, what a beautiful woman you are," he sighed. "Lucky Rupert."

In front of them in the crepuscular gloom, she could see Count Guy, wrapped like a wet towel around Marie-Claire. So it was that member of the French team, she thought, wondering if she ought to stop them.

"Poor Laveenia," Hans shook his head. "I'll bet she weesh she marry Billee now. But what a beauty he's got heemself, what a beautiful girl."

"Yes, she's very nice."

"Did you know Ludwig's geeving Billee a horse as a vedding present? A very good one, Mandryka."

Count Guy's arm was up to his elbow down Marie-Claire's dress. Really she couldn't be a very suitable person to look after Marcus, thought Helen. Over in the corner she saw Hilary dancing with Malise. They were talking intently. That was good; they'd get on together.

The party ground on. The local MFH, trying to find his way home, drove over the hedge. Podge was sick in a flower bed. Helen was dancing with Billy, his hair all over the place.

"It's a wonderful party, Angel. I can't tell you how grateful I am. You've made Janey so welcome, she can't get over it. I say, there's Hilary doing the tango with Ludwig. She's looking really very sexy this evening, and you know I'm not her greatest fan."

Billy went back to Janey. As an excuse to escape from the party for a second, Helen decided to check if Marcus was OK. There were wine stains all over her beautiful carpet. Why couldn't they all go, so she could get the place straight again? In the hall Rupert was talking to Hans and a couple of Italians. When he'd drunk too much, he seldom betrayed it, but his eyes tended to glitter. Now they were like sapphires under a burglar's flash light.

"Where are you going?" he said, not turning round.

"Just to check Marcus."

"If he doesn't shut up, I'll come upstairs and ram a cricket stump up his arse."

Quivering with rage, Helen fled upstairs. How could Rupert say terrible things like that, just to get a laugh, when Marcus was so darling? Despite the din, he was still fast asleep.

Whoops and yells from downstairs made her rush out onto the landing. Hanging over the stairs, she heard Rupert saying to a rather pale Podge, "Go on darling, go and get him."

"Mrs. C-B won't like it."

"She'll have to lump it."

Podge opened the front door. Helen could see a flurry of snowflakes and she was gone.

"You can't Rupert," said Janey, half-laughing. "Don't be a sod, not on Helen's new carpet. It's taken quite enough punishment as it is."

Helen went back and turned off Marcus's light. What could they be talking about? She powdered her nose and combed her hair. Oh God, she was tired. If only she could go to bed and read *Mansfield Park*. Then she heard more cheers and a commotion downstairs. For a minute she thought she must be dreaming, for there was Revenge in the hall, and Rupert was jumping onto his back, riding into the drawing room to colossal cheers and screams of laughter. Blazing with fury, she ran down the stairs.

"What the hell are you doing?" she screamed. Over the laughter no one heard.

"Twenty five pounds you can't jump that sofa," said Count Guy.

"Done," said Rupert and the next moment he'd cleared it, narrowly missing the chandelier.

"Rupert," screamed Helen, "what are you doing on that horse?" Everyone suddenly went quiet.

"No party's complete without Revenge," said Rupert, and popped him back over the sofa.

"Get him out of here," she screamed hysterically. "Out, out, out!"

"All right," said Rupert, but as Revenge came into the hall, unnerved no doubt by the occasion, he crapped extensively, which was greeted by a howl of mirth.

"I think he's trying to say he doesn't like your new carpet," said Rupert. Helen gave a scream of horror and fled upstairs, throwing herself down on her bed, sobbing her heart out. How could he do this to her, how could he, how could he?

Malise met Hilary at the bottom of the stairs. They had already had a long discussion about the Campbell-Black marriage and knew whose side they were on.

"Go to her," said Malise. "At once. I'll see someone clears up the mess."

Hilary found Helen a sodden heap on the bed. "I can't bear it, I can't bear it. Why does he humiliate me like that?"

"I don't know, dear," Hilary stroked her hair. "He's a monster, as I keep telling you. You're exhausted. Take a couple of Valium and go to sleep. I'll help you get undressed."

Just as she had got a still sobbing Helen out of her clothes and was fetching her nightgown from under the pillow, Rupert walked in.

"Get out," he said to Hilary. "I might have guessed you'd be here."

"I've just given your wife a couple of sleeping pills. Now leave her alone."

"She can't go to sleep. She's the hostess."

"You stop being a hostess after something like that. How could you do that to her? You're the most uncaring man I've ever met."

"It was a joke and for a bet," said Rupert tonelessly. "All the mess's been cleared up. There's not a mark on the carpet. Now get out."

"Please stay," sobbed Helen.

"I'm not leaving till you fall asleep, dear," said Hilary.

"Oh for Christ's sake," exploded Rupert, storming out of the room.

Helen, surprisingly, was so exhausted she fell asleep almost immediately. Hilary stayed a few minutes, folding up Helen's clothes and tidying the room and her own appearance. Switching off the light, she quietly closed the door, then, moving down the landing, checked first Marcus and then Kate. Out on the landing she found Rupert, waiting with a glass in his hand. His hatred was almost palpable.

"They're all asleep, no thanks to you," she said.

Downstairs the band was playing the Post Horn Gallop. Rupert stooped to pat Badger, who was trembling. He hated rows and was rising like a soufflé out of one of the Jack Russells' baskets.

"Why do you drool over that dog and neglect Helen? What's she ever done to you?"

Rupert stood up. "She was perfectly happy before you came along and started breastfeeding her this feminist crap."

"That's not true. She was nearly dying when I first met her, and you weren't even there."

"I happened to be trapped in one of the worst blizzards of the winter; not much I could do about it."

"You grumble that she has no friends, and then when she finds one you insult her. You always treat me as though I don't exist."

"Perhaps you don't. I detest women that come on like Supergirl, and you detest me," he said coming towards her, breathing in the hot feral sweat of her body, "because your wimp of a husband couldn't even satisfy a hamster."

"Don't you dare say anything against Crispin," screamed Hilary.

"You have to go around poisoning other people's marriages," Rupert went on. "Well, bloody well stay away from Helen."

"She needs a few allies."

"Not like you she doesn't." He was taunting her now. "I know what your game is. You liked undressing her, didn't you? She's beautiful, isn't she? And you've been running after her as fast as your unshaven legs can carry you, you bloody dyke. Well, she won't enjoy it, she's not very keen on that sort of thing."

Next minute Hilary had slapped him very hard across the face. Without a thought Rupert hit her back, even harder. She burst into tears and, somehow, a second later she was in his arms and he was kissing her, forcing her mouth open. Frantically, she struggled, flailing her fists against his back, so much broader and more muscled than

Crispin's. Suddenly she relaxed, mouth separating, and was kissing him back even more fiercely.

"I hate you," she sobbed.

"You don't. You want me like hell. You've wanted me ever since you saw me at Gloucester Hospital. That's why you've been smarming over Helen all this time."

"You're a brute."

"Of course." He took her hair and yanked her head back so he could kiss her again. Fingers splayed on her back, his thumbs caressed her shaven armpits. "That's a great improvement," he said softly. "It was getting so long you could have braided it."

He drew back the landing curtain. The snow was three inches thick on the window ledge and still coming down.

"We mustn't," she said, pulling away from him. "It's so unsupportive."

"Not nearly as unsupportive as you're going to be," he whispered evilly. "I'm going hunting tomorrow. Get rid of Crispin after lunch. He can take Germaine tobogganing for an hour or so."

*U*nable to face the hassle of a big wedding, Billy married Janey in Gloucester Registry Office at the beginning of January, thus forfeiting the large number of wedding presents which are so useful to a couple setting up house. Rupert was the best man. Helen was disappointed that they didn't even bother to have the marriage blessed in Penscombe church, but Billy felt, that first year with Janey, that the gods were blessing him anyway. Never had he been so happy.

Just before they married, Janey negotiated a fat deal with the *Post* that she would write a series of racy interviews around the world, which enabled her to travel with Billy on the circuit, all expenses paid. From Antwerp, to Paris, to Madrid, to Athens, to Madison Square her portable typewriter gathered airline stickers as she talked to Presidents, rock stars and distinguished tax exiles.

Often there were tensions when she had to file her weekly piece. A sweating, tearful teeth-gritting Janey bashing away at her typewriter in some foreign hotel bedroom wasn't conducive to Billy getting any sleep before a big class. Nor did Janey, hopelessly unpunctual, endear herself to other members of the team by making them always late for dinners and parties. Billy was too besotted to notice. His horses were going well. Mandryka, the dark brown Hanoverian Ludwig von Schellenberg had given as a wedding present, upgraded himself incredibly quickly and was showing all the makings of being as great a horse as The Bull, or Moggie Meal Al, as he was now renamed. Billy winced, but not much. At £50,000 a year from Kevin Coley it was worth wincing for. Anyway he was still the same Bull in the stable.

In fact, in that first year of marriage Janey and Billy were extremely rich. Janey's salary, plus expenses, plus Billy's steady winnings, plus Kevin's sponsorship, added up to nearly £100,000 a year. And although Billy was always buying Rupert drinks and gave Helen his winnings for housekeeping (when he hadn't spent them celebrating), gas, electricity, telephone and heating bills at Penscombe were invariably picked up by Rupert.

When they were in England, Billy and Janey lived with Helen and Rupert and muttered vaguely about househunting. In the end it was again part of Rupert's colossal generosity toward Billy that he let them have Lime Tree Place, an enchanting but dilapidated 17th-century cottage on the Penscombe Estate which had just become vacant, on condition they pay for fixing it up. Planning permits had to be obtained to extend the kitchen and build on a dining room, two more bedrooms and a nursery. Janey hoped to have a baby almost immediately. In time, they would turn the mouldering moss-encrusted outbuildings into stabling for a dozen horses. Helen came down to the cottage and talked a lot about closet space and knocking down walls, and, inspired by the beauty of Penscombe, Janey felt there was no need to spare any expense.

For Janey and Billy that first year seemed effortless, because at home they were backed up by Helen's clockwork domestic routine which ironed Billy's breeches, washed his shirts, remembered to get his red coats from the cleaners, and by Miss Hawkins, who saw that Billy's entry forms were sent off and bills were paid and appointments put in the diary.

For Janey's liking, they had spent rather too much time with Kevin and Enid Coley, who flew out to several of the foreign shows and were always hanging about at Wembley, Crittleden and Olympia.

Billy made excuses for Kevin, saying he was merely proud that Billy's horses were going so well and particularly that Moggie Meal Al came second in the European championships in Paris. And if Kevin did tell Billy how to ride and Malise exactly how to run the British team, Billy felt Malise was perfectly capable of taking care of himself. Janey was rather less tolerant. As a wedding present the Coleys gave them a vast china poodle lifting its leg on a lamp post. Janey wrote Enid a gushing letter of thanks and put the poodle in the cellar.

There were also too many invitations to visit Château Kitsch, as Janey called Kevin's mock tudor castle in Sunningdale, where there was lots of horseplay and one was likely to be pushed into the heated swimming pool at any moment. But on the way home they enjoyed lots of giggles about the electric toadstools that lit up on either side of the drive at night, and the huge luminous Moggie Meal Cat symbol outside the front door which winked and miaowed when you pressed the door bell, and the button in Kevin's den which had merely to be pushed for the entire leather-bound works of Dickens and Scott to slide back to reveal a bar offering every drink known to a man.

Janey, reared in Fleet Street, could drink even Billy under the table. Looking out of the window one evening, Helen saw them coming up the drive hysterical with laughter, as Billy pretended to lift his leg on every chestnut tree.

"Billy's being Kevin's china poodle," explained Janey. "Christ my feet are killing me. We ran out of gas and had to walk from Stroud."

Helen had mixed feelings about Janey. In the end you couldn't help liking her. She was fun and marvelously iconoclastic about showjumping, but she was a bit too easy to talk to. Any secret confided would be around Penscombe and Fleet Street in a flash. And Janey was so messy, wandering around the house with her cat, Harold Evans, riding like a parrot on her shoulder, eyes screwed up against the cigarette smoke, spilling ash and leaving a trail of dirty cups and, after midday, glasses.

Helen, so fastidious, couldn't bear the fact that Janey kept filching her perfume and makeup and borrowing clothes. There was an embarrassing occasion when Helen and Rupert were away for the weekend and Janey borrowed one of Helen's dresses to go out to dinner with the Coreys and split it, not even down the seam, so it was beyond repair.

Even worse was the time Helen came downstairs, ashen, because her mink coat, given to her by Rupert on their second anniversary, was missing. She was about to call the police when Janey suggested they look around the house first.

"Isn't this it, bundled up in the downstairs bathroom?" Janey announced rather casually two minutes later. "Mrs. Bodkin must have brought it down for refurbishing—ha ha, that's a joke—or something."

It was unfortunate that Janey had left three candy wrappers and a program for a Michael Frayn play that had been on in Bath in the pocket. Helen was very upset, but too nice to shout at Janey. Instead she went to church and asked God to make her more tolerant.

Occasionally Janey cooked, but made such a mess in the kitchen that it took Helen twice as long to clear up afterwards, and she wished Janey wouldn't take books out on her library card, read them in the bath and forget to return them, or even worse, lose them abroad. Helen had never kept a library book too long, and always renewed them.

In a way, Billy and Janey's presence helped Rupert and Helen's marriage. Rupert tended not to be so intolerant if the others were there, but in another way the newlyweds' happiness showed up the flaws.

Rupert was wildly jealous of the love Helen lavished on Marcus. "I'm so enjoying him," she kept saying. ("As though Marcus was a quadruple vodka and tonic," said Janey.) He was also envious of the relaxed hedonistic relationship Billy had with Janey. When had Helen ever got tight with him, when had they last been hysterical with laughter? He heard the giggles and gasps of pleasure issuing from their bedroom. Mrs. Bodkin was always finding empty bottles under the bed.

Janey, Helen thought, brought out the wrong things in Billy. She encouraged him to drink more, bet more, always dine out rather than eat at home. Billy, more emotional and physically less strong than Rupert, couldn't cope with such excess.

The blatant sexuality of the relationship unnerved Helen too. Billy and Janey were always sneaking off to bed. You only had to look at Janey's washing on the line. Mrs. Bodkin's mouth disappeared in disapproval at the black and scarlet crotchless panties, the cut-out bras, the G-strings, garter belts and fishnet stockings. Janey, careless and thoughtless, left her vibrator in their unmade bed where it was found by Mrs. Bodkin.

"Billy's got a bad back. It's for massaging his spine," explained Janey airily. Mrs. Bodkin was not convinced; Janey was a minx.

Helen and Janey's attitudes to each other were ambivalent. Janey was jealous of Helen's beauty. Helen even looked gorgeous in a bath cap, and Billy would never say a word against her. Helen, spurred on by Janey's fame and journalistic success, started working on her novel again.

"She talks as though she's writing *Hamlet*," grumbled Janey. It irritated the hell out of Janey that Helen was always slightly dismissive of Janey's journalism. She never commented on Janey's pieces even if they were spread across two pages of the *Post*. Even when she produced her much-praised interview with Kissinger entitled, "You're only as good as your last peace," Helen only said, when pestered, that she didn't feel Janey had quite captured the full weight of Kissinger. It was part of her puritan upbringing that you must never praise if you didn't admire.

"She doesn't mean it bitchily," Billy kept protesting.

"Oh she does, Buster, she does," said Janey grimly.

Helen, in fact, was jealous of Janey for being so sexy. Occasionally she worried that Billy, Rupert and Janey spent so much time abroad together. Rupert did little to dispel this fear. It diverted any suspicions she might have had about him and Hilary.

Show-jumping and Rupert changed during the mid-seventies. As the sport became more popular and sponsorship increased, so did the prize money. Before, the show-jumping season had lasted from April to October; now, riders could jump all the year round and, because of the number of indoor evening shows, they were kept busy by night as well as by day. When he started in the sport, Rupert would buzz off to Argentina to play polo, or go racing at Longchamps or skiing at Klosters. Now show-jumping had become an all-consuming passion. Always on the circuit, he was jumping his horses so hard he wore them out in a year or so and, as a result, was endlessly searching for new ones. If he was at home he was training horses or selling them on. Horses took over his life, so determined was he not to turn professional.

Podge travelled with him, adoring, satisfying his physical needs, suffering but not sulking if something better took his fancy. And on the rare occasions he was back in Gloucestershire, there was Hilary, ranting, cantankerous and insatiable, but exerting a horrible fascination over him.

After the party for Janey and Bill, Helen retreated into herself, becoming more and more houseproud, "spending her time rubbing female fingerprints off Rupert," said Janey. Helen spent a great deal of money on clothes and at the hairdresser, and did a lot for charity. Hilary didn't help the marriage. For her own good reasons, she kept urging Helen to walk out on Rupert.

"You are a talented writer, inhibited by a fascist pig—virtually a one-parent family. What support does he give you looking after Marcus?" she demanded.

"Unlimited funds," Helen had to admit truthfully.

"Our parents' generation sacrificed their careers for marriage," went on Hilary. "You musn't make such sacrifices. It is impossible to be happily married, a good mother and have a career."

Helen hoped she was a good mother. She was certainly an adoring one. Marcus was walking now and his first word was "Mummy." And he had several teeth. He had grown into a beautiful child, shy, with huge solemn eyes, and a riot of Titian curls which Rupert was always urging Helen to cut. Marcus was wary of Rupert, who was not amused by jammy fingers on clean white breeches, or by the fact that Marcus screamed his head off if ever Rupert put him on a horse. Calm and sunny when his father was away, Marcus picked up the vibes from Helen and became whiney and demanding on his return.

Another bone of contention was the dogs. Having read the articles in *The Guardian*, Helen was terrified Marcus would catch some obscure eye disease from them. She wanted them kept outside. Rupert flatly refused. The dogs had been there before she had, he pointed out coldly. In fact, since Marcus was born, he reflected, the dogs were

really the only ones pleased to see him when he came home. Both he
and Helen festered inside with a sense of grievance.

Billy was saddened by the increased deterioration of Rupert's marriage, and discussed it at length with Janey. One hot evening at the
end of July, on the eve of their departure for Aachen they lay in bed at
Penscombe sharing a bottle of Moët.

"How on earth," said Janey, "can anyone as beautiful as Helen be
so uptight? If I had those kind of looks . . ."

"You do," said Billy, snuggling up against the spongy cushion of
her bottom, feeling for her breasts.

"D'you think I'd look nice with my hair up, like Helen?" asked
Janey.

"I'd rather you shaved your bush."

"D'you think they'll split up?"

"No. I think underneath they still love each other. Besides,
Helen's too scared of the outside world, and Rupert doesn't believe in
divorce. Marriage is for children, and having someone to run your
house. You get your fun elsewhere."

"I hope you don't feel like that!"

"No," said Billy, sliding his hands down over the smooth folds of
her belly.

Janey pressed her stomach in. "I must lose weight. Do you think
he's gone off her physically?"

"Hard to tell. He nearly killed an Italian diplomat who made a
pass at her a couple of years ago. She's one of his possessions; he's very
territorial."

"Do you think he's good in bed?"

"Cock like a baseball bat. Used to bat bread rolls across the room
with it when we were at school."

"Lucky Helen." Janey sat up, excited at the thought.

"Am I big enough for you?" asked Billy anxiously. Janey climbed
on top of him, holding on to the brass bedstead, causing frightful
creaking. "Quite big enough. Look how good I am at rising at the
trot."

*H*ilary, in fact, was Rupert's first serious affair since he had met
Helen, and it was a complete love-hate relationship. Despite her pro-
testation that all men were beasts, Hilary herself was an animal in
bed—insatiable, almost a nymphomaniac. She didn't bath enough,
she was a slut, she had a bad temper, and Rupert had to keep kissing

her to shut her up, and later cut her nails himself to stop her lacerating his back. He detested her hypocrisy in still going on being a friend of Helen.

It was the one affair about which he never boasted to Billy, knowing how appalled Billy would be. Making love to Hilary was like eating a pork pie when you were desperately hungry, then discovering by the date on the discarded wrapping that it should have been eaten a month before.

"If you ever breathe a word about this to Helen I'll throttle you," he frequently warned her, and she knew he wasn't joking. This, however, did not prevent her rocking the boat. The night before Rupert was due to leave for Aachen he'd stood her up and she had rung up Penscombe in a rage, screaming at Rupert on the telephone. Rupert, who was in bed with Helen at the time, reading his horoscope in *Harpers,* held the receiver to his ear for a minute, then said calmly, "Have a word with Helen about it. She's just here." And Hilary was forced to pull herself together and issue an impromptu invitation for Helen and Rupert to come to a dinner party in three weeks' time, which meant she had to go to all the expense of giving one.

Hilary, despite her ranting, was mad about Rupert and grew increasingly strident as he showed no inclination to walk out on Helen. Part of the fascination for him was they saw so little of each other, perhaps a couple of hours a month.

Hilary was sure she could nail him if they had a little more time together. While Rupert was in Aachen at the end of July, she flew out to Germany leaving the children with the long-suffering Crispin. Her excuse was that she needed to be alone to paint. After Aachen, Rupert sent Podge home with Billy and the horses, saying he was off horse-hunting and would be home in a day or two. He had been very short-tempered with Podge all week, because he felt guilty and nervous about Hilary coming out. Together he and Hilary drove to a hotel in the Black Forest, chosen by Hilary. Their stay was a disaster. Having screwed her, Rupert found it a nightmare to have to make conversation to her at dinner, or walk with her in the forest, or be greeted by her carping, rather common voice when he woke in the morning. After forty-eight hours they had a mighty row and returned home on separate planes.

Podge, meanwhile, had returned home twenty-four hours earlier with Billy and Janey to find England in the grip of a drought. Day after day the sun blazed down; young trees and flowers withered; Penscombe's green valley turned yellow; the streams dried to a trickle; leaves were turning. In Gloucestershire people were forbidden to water the garden or wash their cars and there was talk of water rationing.

When they got back Janey and Billy collapsed into bed for sixteen hours to get over the journey. But Podge and Tracey still had to get up at six next morning after four hours' sleep because the horses had to be looked after. When a telephone message came through that Rupert was coming back that evening, Podge redoubled her efforts. Usually, to reestablish his ascendancy as master of the house and the stable, he came home in a picky mood, criticizing everything she'd done and then biting her head off for sulking. By late afternoon, the relentless heat showed no sign of letting up. Most of the horses were inside to avoid the flies, and were let out at night. Arcturus, a grey Irish-bred stallion, was Rupert's latest acquisition. He showed potential, but had blotted his record by jumping sloppily at Aachen. Wearing only a black bikini and espadrilles, her sweating hair in a pony tail, Podge chattered away to him as she brushed his dappled coat.

"Bugger off sweetheart," she said, as Arcturus nudged her lovingly in the back. "Your master's coming home tonight, and he'll want you looking lovely. Hope he's cheered up and not cross with us any more, Arcy. You didn't mean to hit that last triple, and I didn't mean to bugger up the map-reading on the way out. He can be 'orrible, Arcy. If he wasn't so lovely when he was being lovely, I don't s'pose we'd put up with the 'orrible bits.' "

"I don't expect you would," said a voice behind her, "but I'm in one of my lovely moods today."

Arcturus jerked up his head as Podge jumped out of her skin, dropping the brush and going crimson. "I didn't know you were coming back till this evening," she muttered.

"Obviously not, or you'd be properly dressed."

"Sorry." She picked up the straw brush and attacked Acturus's already gleaming flanks again. "But it's been ever so 'ot."

"You look very fetching," said Rupert, pulling her pony tail. "I just don't want Phillips getting ideas." Phillips, the undergardener, had an unrequited crush on Podge. "You're my property," added Rupert.

Podge was filled with a happiness so intense, tears stung her eyelids.

"Hey," said Rupert, giving her pony tail another gentle tug, "you don't seem very pleased with me."

"I am, I am." She brushed away the tears with the back of her hand, leaving a smear of dirt across her face. "I just thought you were cross with me, and if I got everything perfect for when you got back, you wouldn't be."

"Everything looks fine," said Rupert. "I'm going to change. Finish off Arcy and then we'll walk up the fields and see Gemini's foal."

He sauntered off, followed by Badger and two of the Jack Russells.

Podge's hands shook as she filled the haynet and Arcturus's water bucket. Then she shot up to the loft and frantically washed her face. Oh, that awful muddy smear down one side. And she'd wanted to wash her hair before he got back. It must still reek of Billy and Janey's chainsmoking on the drive home. She had a frantic shower, twice washing under her arms and three times between her legs, and making herself sneeze by shaking on so much talcum powder. She'd just pulled on a faded orange T-shirt and skirt which clung to her wet body when she heard Rupert yelling from downstairs. As she came backwards down the ladder of her attic flat Rupert was waiting, sliding his hands up under her skirt, this thumbs biting into her plump bottom.

"Don't," she shrieked.

He was wearing nothing but a pair of old jeans and he smelt of an expensive French aftershave which she couldn't pronounce. Suddenly she had difficulty breathing.

"Not here," she gasped. "What about Phillips and Mrs. Campbell-Black?"

"In London. Come on. Why'd you change? You looked sexy in that bikini."

"Too fat," muttered Podge, pulling on gumboots.

"What the hell are those for?"

"Adders," muttered Podge. "Phillips killed one by the tennis court last week. And nettles and thistles."

As they walked up the scorched fields, Rupert carrying the Hasselblad camera he'd won in Aachen, the chestnut trees were raining down orange leaves, the thistles were turning to kapok, and the little copse of hornbeams Rupert had planted earlier in the year had already died. There were huge cracks in the ground. In the distance they could hear the jangle of a fire engine.

"If we don't get some rain soon, we're going to be in trouble," said Rupert. "Going'll be murder at Crittleden."

The nettles on the way down to Billy's secret pond, which used to reach to four feet and close over the top, were shrunk to a pathetic eighteen inches and no threat to Podge's legs today. The pond was almost empty. Sweat was running in rivulets between Podge's breasts and down her sides. She felt her heart pounding.

"Which horses are you taking to Rotterdam?" she asked.

"You asked me that five minutes ago. You're not concentrating," Rupert said mockingly. As they reached the bottom of the path, he took her hand and turned right.

"Gemini's in the oak meadow," said Podge quickly.

"We'll go and see her later," said Rupert. "I've got more pressing plans for you. He put his arm around her waist, then moved it upwards, till his hand squeezed her left breast. "Very pressing." Then he let her go.

They reached the stream that ran down the valley with water

meadows on either side It was greener here, the stream that ran down the valley with water meadows on either side was choked with figwort and forget-me-not. A circle of ash trees formed a sun trap. No one could see them from the road.

"What happens if someone walks across the fields?"

"Private property. I'll have them for trespassing," Rupert raised his hand and smoothed the sweat from her face. "I've missed you, Podge," he said gently. "Get your clothes off."

An expression of doubt flickered in her eyes, but she took off the orange T-shirt, so her breasts fell out full, pointed and sloping downwards.

"Lean against that tree," said Rupert, adjusting his camera for the light.

Instinctively, Podge put her hand up to loosen her hair.

"No, leave it tied back. I want to see the expression on your face."

"I haven't any makeup on."

"Suits you. Put your arms above your head and lean back against the trunk. Beautiful. Christ, you've got gorgeous boobs. Now turn sideways. Keep your arms up, lovely." He took another picture, then came over, running his hands over her breasts, then kissing her. He tasted of toothpaste and animal health and wonderful digestion. Putting her arms around him, Podge kissed him back so violently, they nearly toppled over.

"Steady," he whispered. "I haven't finished yet."

He undid the drawstring of her skirt and she stepped out of it, then he pulled her pants off. The mouse-brown bush was flattened and he ran his hands through it to fluff it up. Then he spread the pink lips. A shiny snail's trail was trickling down both thighs.

"All right, keep your legs apart. Don't be shy, sweetheart. If you knew how fantastic you look. Now turn around. Don't tense your bum up. Relax." She heard two more clicks. She waited, clinging on the ribbed surface of the tree, throat dry, heart crashing against her ribs. Then she felt a warm hand on her back. Rupert wasn't even sweating.

"Lovely arse," he said softly, running his fingers down the cleft before he came to the sticky warmth between her legs.

"Christ," he said, his hand like a burrowing ferret. "You are the most welcoming thing."

He thought of Hilary's tantrums, of her vacuum-cleaner kisses, her sharp teeth and scraping hands. He thought of Helen's cool distaste and he compared them with Podge's estatically grateful gentleness.

"Why don't you take *your* clothes off?" she said, turning round and kissing him passionately as she fumbled with the zipper of his jeans and then his underwear. Then, sinking to her knees, she buried her face in the blonde hair of his groin, sucking him as pleasurably as a child with a lollipop.

"Steady sweet. I don't want to come yet."

As he turned to remove his trousers, she seized the camera. "Now it's my turn to photograph you!"

Giggling hysterically, she photographed him as he was turning, then caught him again as he was coming towards her half-laughing, half-angry.

The next moment he'd caught up with her, pushing her down on the grass, parting her legs and kissing her damp bush. She writhed, tensed, gave a gasp of pleasure and came. So blissfully quickly, thought Rupert. Recently, Hilary seemed to come later and later, like the Christmas postman. He turned over, lay back and pulled Podge on top of him, feeling her muscles, so tight but so oily, gripping him, breasts swaying like party balloons when the front door opens. Really, she was gorgeous.

The sun had disappeared behind the ashwood by the time they had finished, sated with pleasure and exhaustion. Podge rinsed herself out in the stream, startling several minnows. As they walked home up the sun-drenched valley, Rupert picked grass seed out of her hair.

"There isn't time to see Gemini's foal," he said. "I've got to go and give the prizes at Cheltenham Flower Show."

They were greeted in the yard by Tracey and Phillips. "Mrs. Campbell-Black's just called from London," said Tracey. "I couldn't find you. Will you call her back?"

"Just been up to Oak meadow to photograph Gemini's foal," said Rupert coolly.

"That's funny," muttered Phillips, bitter with jealousy, to Rupert's departing back. "The grass was so poor, we moved them up to Long Acre this morning."

Rupert went off to Rotterdam two days later. The day before he was due back Helen drove into Cirencester to shop and bumped into Hilary in the market, crossly buying cheese for the dinner party she'd been forced into giving the following night.

"Rupert is going to be back, isn't he?" she demanded. "Not that he's a great asset at dinner parties, always making fascist remarks and falling asleep. But I've got ten smoked trout and I don't want my numbers messed up."

Helen, who found herself increasingly irritated by Hilary, said you could never be sure with Rupert, but she thought it'd be ninety-nine percent certain.

"Well, make sure he's there," said Hilary. "No, about an inch more Brie, please."

Hilary had realized by the time she got back from the Black Forest how much she was going to miss the excitement Rupert provided in her drab life. She must get him back. It would be too cruel if he didn't turn up tomorrow night.

Leaving her, Helen popped into the drugstore to pick up the rolls of film she'd found lying on Rupert's dressing table. He'd actually taken some of Marcus last time he was back and she was dying to see them. Mr. Wise, the pharmacist, had gone out and hadn't checked the photographs as he normally did. He always liked to look through the Campbell-Black's folders; they often contained pictures of famous people and interesting places abroad.

Stuck in a holiday traffic jam on the way back to Penscombe, Helen couldn't resist looking at the photographs. That was a gorgeous one of Marcus, but she wished Badger wasn't licking his face, and a lovely one of the rose bower, and a rather boring one of the Jack Russells and Arcturus. Why must Rupert always photograph animals? That was lovely of the herbaceous border, and the valley, how yellow it was now. That must be Gemini's foal. She'd finished one folder and shook the photos out of the next. The first thing she saw was a plump topless girl. Mr. Wise must have given her the wrong set of photographs. Here was another one of her full length, legs apart, in the most disgustingly provocative pose. Helen looked closer, and stiffened. The girl looked like Podge. She looked at four more pictures, all disgusting. Yes, they were definitely Podge. The next one, taken at an angle, half cut off the man's head, but the rest of him looked decidedly familiar. The next, also naked, was definitely Rupert, full frontal and roaring with laughter.

A second later Helen had rammed the Porsche into the car in front with a sickening crunch. She banged her head hard and the front of the car buckled up like the face of a bulldog in a cartoon film.

"Why don't you look where you're going?" yelled the driver of the car in front. He found Helen crying hysterically, trying to collect the scattered photographs before anyone could see them.

Rupert flew in from Rotterdam around six the following evening, tired but once again victorious. He'd left the grooms to bring back the horses. Phillips met him at the airport in Helen's Mini and gleefully told him that Mrs. Campbell-Black had banged up the Porsche that afternoon. Serve the bastard right, he thought, as he saw Rupert's look of fury. Shouldn't go down in the woods with Podge.

Helen walked up and down her bedroom, wondering how the hell to tackle Rupert. By some miracle, in four years of marriage, she'd never actually caught him being unfaithful. She'd suspected other women—Marion, Janey, Grania Pringle, several of Rupert's exes, but never in a million years Podge, with her fat legs, her cockney accent and her plain homely face. It had come as a terrible terrible shock, Helen couldn't stop shaking. It was so revolting too, taking photographs of her in one of their own fields, where anyone might have walked past. She wished she had a girlfriend to pour her heart out to, but Janey was still on the way back from Rotterdam with Billy and, anyway, Janey wasn't safe. She thought of calling Hilary, but Hilary would just say, "I told you so." She still had a blinding headache from yesterday's accident in the Porsche and a huge bruise on her forehead.

The usual frantic barking told her Rupert was home. For once, instead of going to the stables, he came straight upstairs into the bedroom.

"I hear you banged up my car. Are you all right?"

"Perfectly, thank you." Helen gazed out of the window, quivering with animosity, refusing to look round.

"How the hell did it happen?"

"I was in a jam, looking at some of your photographs just back from the drug store." She swung round, handing him the folders. "They're kind of interesting. Have a look."

Casually Rupert picked them up. When he was feeling trapped, his eyes seemed to go a darker, more opaque, shade of blue and lose all their sparkle.

"I thought I'd taken some nice ones of Marcus. That's good, and so's that, and there's a gorgeous one of Badger, and Arcy. Christ, he's a good-looking horse. Pity you shut your eyes in that one." He gave a low whistle. "Who's that?"

"You know perfectly well," screamed Helen. "It's that slut, Podge."

"Phillips must have borrowed my camera. God, she's got quite a shape on her."

"It was you who took them," hissed Helen, "and your hand is remarkably steady, which is more than can be said for Podge's when she took photos of you."

Rupert flipped through the photographs, playing for time.

"Who's that headless chap? Got a cock like the Post Office tower."

"It's yours," said Helen in a choked voice, "and I guess you can't deny the fact that the next one is you."

"I'm afraid it is," said Rupert. Then he committed the cardinal sin of starting to laugh.

Helen lost her temper. "How dare you go to bed with her!"

"Who says I've been to bed with her?"

"Don't be ridiculous. And I suppose Janey and Billy know all about it. How could you, how *could* you?"

Rupert scratched his ear, looking at her meditatively. "Do you really want to know?" he said softly.

"Yes, I bloody well do."

"I fucked her because she was at home when I got back and she wanted me."

Helen flinched.

"And she's a bloody miracle in bed."

"And I'm not, I suppose?"

"No, you are not, my pet. If you want the truth, you're like a frozen chicken. Fucking you is like stuffing sausage meat into a broiler. I'm always frightened I'll discover the giblets."

Helen gasped, unable to speak.

"You never react, never display any pleasure, never once in four years of marriage have you asked for it. If I want you, I have to sit on the street with a begging bowl, and I'm bloody fed up with it. Everytime you part your legs a degree, you behave as if you're bestowing a colossal favor. It's not your fault. Your bloody mother instilled it into you. 'Behave like a lady at all times.' My God."

Helen gazed at him, too stunned to say anything, just watching him strip off his clothes in front of her, down to the lean, beautiful sun-tanned body that was so terribly reminiscent of the photographs. For a terrifying moment she thought he was going to pounce on her, but he merely went off into the shower, to emerge five minutes later dripping and rubbing his hair dry with a big pink towel.

"Have you got the message?" he said. "I don't get my kicks at home so I get them elsewhere."

"You've got to fire her," whispered Helen through white lips. "I can't go on meeting her, knowing this, having seen those disgusting pictures."

"What's disgusting about those pictures? Kodak obviously enjoyed them. She's got a nice body and, what's more important, she's not remotely ashamed of it. You could pick up a few tips from her."

He went into his dressing-room and got out his dinner jacket and a white dress shirt.

"Where are you going?" Helen asked numbly.

"Out to dinner. It's Hilary's dinner party, remember? You insisted I should be back on time."

No one could dress quicker than Rupert when he chose.

"You can't go out to dinner after this," Helen whispered in bewilderment.

"Why not? The drink's free. It's much better than staying here and listening to the hysterics that you're about to give way to any minute. I don't like having books thrown at me and that scent bottle's dangerously large. Don't you think you'd better get changed too?" He was frowning in the mirror now as he tied his tie.

"Aren't you even going to apologize for you and Podge?"

Rupert flicked the bent tie expertly through the gap. "Why should I apologize for your inadequacies?"

Now he was brushing his still damp hair with silver brushes, back over the temples, and in two wings over the ears. He picked up his jacket. "Don't bother to wait up for me. I'll tell Ortrud, or whatever her name is this week, you've got a migraine."

Helen simply couldn't believe that he could treat an act of such magnitude so lightly. And the terrible things he had said. Was she really that awful in bed? Was it all her fault? The moment he'd left she threw herself down on the bed sobbing her heart out. Not for the first time she wished she hadn't put Marcus's nursery next to their bedroom. Within seconds there was thumping on the door and cries of "Mummy, Mummy." Helen gritted her teeth. Where the hell was Ortrud? The thumpings grew more insistent. "Mummy, why are you crying?"

Helen put on her dark glasses and opened the door. Marcus almost fell inside. He was wearing blue and white striped pyjamas and clutching a stuffed purple skunk Rupert had brought him from Aachen.

"Mummy crying," he said doubtfully.

Helen picked him up, revelling in his newly bathed softness.

"Momma's got a sore head." She banged her hand against her temple, then the skunk's head against he window. "Mummy go bang in car. That's why she's crying."

Marcus seemed to accept this. Helen looked nervously for the thin trickle of mucous from his nose that always heralded an asthma attack (usually triggered by Rupert's presence) but there was no sign.

"Story," said Marcus pointedly.

"I can't face it," thought Helen. "Ortrud," she screamed down the stairs. But Ortrud, on hearing that Helen would be staying in, had pushed off to the Jolly Goat in Stroud to meet her friends.

Rupert, having vented his wrath on Helen because he felt so guilty, was not enjoying Hilary's dinner party. Hilary, despite her arbitrary comments to Helen about even numbers, was delighted he had come alone.

"What's the matter with her?" she asked.

"Migraine," said Rupert tersely.

"You mean a row," said Hilary out of the corner of her mouth. "Have some of Crispin's elderflower wine to cheer you up."

Rupert looked around dismissively at the bearded husbands looking self-conscious in dinner jackets. If it hadn't been Hilary and Crispin's wedding anniversary they would have refused to dress up. Everyone except Rupert brought presents.

Hilary put him on her right at dinner. There wasn't even a decent looking woman for him to flirt with or make eyes at across the table. The dinner was disgusting—smoked trout, then jugged hare of all unbelievable things in August. With Hilary's slovenly cooking it was probably jugged hairs as well.

"What's the matter? You're not your usual dazzling self," said Hilary in a low voice, letting her hand brush against his as she passed the red currant jelly. Rupert didn't return the pressure.

"What's really the matter with Helen?" she asked. "She was all right yesterday."

"She's all wrong now," said Rupert. He turned to the German woman with braids round her head on his right.

"It must be a lonely life working with horses," she said to him.

"No," said Rupert. "It's very overcrowded."

What an idiot he'd been to shit on his own doorstep. He'd have to fire Podge now, and Arcy and the other horses who were absolutely devoted to her would be upset at the height of the season. Grooms weren't hard to find, but ones as good as Podge virtually impossible. Why the hell, too, had he ever embarked on an affair with Hilary? She revolted him now. She insisted on lingering hours over coffee: "I hate breaking up the ambience."

Rupert grew increasingly restless as the dwindling candlelight flickered on the shiny unpainted faces. The woman on Rupert's right went off to the bathroom. Crispin was out of the room making more coffee, no doubt caffeine free. Hilary's lugubrious paintings glared down from the walls. Hilary could bear it no longer.

"Helen's found out about *us*, hasn't she?"

Rupert's eyes narrowed. "Who?"

"*Us*, you and me of course."

Rupert laughed. "No, about someone else, actually."

"I don't understand."

"Helen found out I was knocking off someone else."

"A long time ago?"

"No ten days ago."

Hilary gasped. "You bastard, you rotten bastard," she hissed. "I don't believe you."

"What are you two looking so secretive about?" Crispin appeared at their side. "Sorry I was so long dear, I was changing Germaine. More coffee Rupert?"

Rupert looked at Crispin's hands. He bet he hadn't washed them. "No thanks." He got to his feet. "I must go. Been a lovely evening, but I got up at four o'clock this morning and I don't like to leave Helen too long."

He never minded in the past, said Hilary to herself furiously. "Why don't you call up? She's probably fast asleep. Pity to break up the party."

"What party?" said Rupert, so only she could hear him. "Our particular party is over, my darling."

"What happened to your Porsche?" asked Crispin, watching Rupert curl his long legs into Helen's Mini.

"Helen had an accident yesterday," and he was gone.

He was home by a quarter to twelve. Ortrud's light was on, so was

Podge's over the stables. Probably the whole household knew he'd gone
out after a screaming match with Helen. He wandered down to the
stables. It was still impossibly hot. A full moon upstaged the crowded
stars. The horses were moving restlessly. Arcturus came to the half-
door. Rupert gave him a carrot he'd pinched from Hilary's crudité dish
on the way out.

"Wish I was a stallion like you," he said.

Arcy rolled his eyes and took a nip at Rupert, who cuffed him on
the nose.

"One day when you're famous," he told the horse, "you'll be encouraged to fuck any mare you like. Why can't I?"

Rupert knew Podge would be waiting up for him, but he went
straight back to the house. He didn't fancy sleeping in the spare room.
It was supposed to be haunted and he wasn't tight enough not to
mind.

After finally settling Marcus, Helen had had a bath, bathed her
eyes, washed her hair and put on the plunging black silk Dior nightgown Rupert had given her for Christmas but which she had never
worn because she had no cleavage. Now she lay in bed without the
light on, with the moonlight pouring in through the windows. As
Rupert tiptoed past the door she called out to him. He entered cautiously, waiting for abuse, his hair gleaming as silver as one of his hair
brushes.

"I'm sorry," she said in a choked voice. "It's all my fault."

Rupert, completely wrong-footed, was unbelievably touched.

"I understand exactly why you went for Podge," she went on.
"I'm hopeless in bed. It's just my upbringing that makes me so dreadfully inhibited, but I love you so much. I can't bear the thought of
losing you. I'll try and make as many overtures as Rossini." She was
trying to make a joke, but her voice cracked. Rupert sat down, pulling
her against him.

"No, it's my fault," he said, stroking her bare arms. "I'll get rid of
Podge tomorrow, pay her off so you never have to see her again. I
suppose it's my upbringing too. Fidelity wasn't the family's strong
point, but I love you."

"I'll go and buy black sexy underwear like Janey and read sex
books and learn how to drive a man to the ultimate of desire."

"You do already. Have I ever not wanted you? I just got tired of
trying to fuck someone who didn't want me."

That night Tabitha was conceived.

Gradually Billy and Janey got their cottage in shape. And although Billy drew the line for the moment at a swimming pool or a tennis court, the place seemed to have every other luxury.

"If I have a fantastic season and you write your arse off, we should be straight by the end of next year, give or take a few bottles of booze," Billy told Janey when they moved in in October. But he never expected the bills to be quite so astronomical. Having no wedding presents, he and Janey had to buy everything from garlic crushers to washing machines. Billy's mother was very rich and could have helped out. But she didn't like Janey, who described her as an old boot with a tweed bum, or, in kinder moments, as "the Emperor Vespasian in drag". Mrs. Lloyd-Foxe had the big nose and thick grey curls that look better on a man. She thought Janey was tarty and agreed with Helen that Janey wrote sensational things in the paper. Last week Janey had written about her marriage, giving rather too many intimate details. Most people including Billy thought it was very funny. Mrs. Lloyd-Foxe did not.

"How's dear Helen and darling little Marcus?" she asked every time she called Janey, knowing it would irritate her.

Mrs. Lloyd-Foxe had daughters who seemed to produce babies with the ease that chickens lay eggs. It was up to Janey, her mother-in-law implied frequently, to produce a son as soon as possible. "Then there'll be a little Lloyd-Foxe to carry on the line."

Helen, feeling slightly sick, but much happier after her rapprochement with Rupert, was thrilled she was having having another baby. Janey wanted to be pregnant too and hadn't taken the pill since she'd been married to Billy. But each month it was just the same. She went to see her doctor, who said it was too soon to worry and suggested she get her tubes blown.

"You've also been racketing around the world a lot," he told her. "Why don't you stop work for a bit, play house, look after Billy and get in a nesting mood? Try to confine intercourse to the middle of the month between your periods."

Janey in fact, was bored with traveling around. She was fed up with living out of suitcases, interviewing pop stars and heads of state. She wanted to stay at home and watch the lime trees around the cottage turn yellow and go out mushrooming in the early morning.

There was also the matter of her expenses, which were colossal, and which had very few bills to back them up because Janey had lost them. There had been too many dinners for ten at Tiberio's or Maxim's, with Janey and Billy treating the rest of the team. The *Daily Post's*

show-jumping correspondent, jealous of her turf being invaded by
Janey, had ratted to the sports editor about unnecessary extravagance.
The editor, Mike Pardoe, nearly had a coronary when he saw the total
and summoned Janey from Gloucestershire.

Pardoe had once been Janey's lover. As she looked at his handsome
watchful, wolfish face, Janey thought how much nicer Billy was.

"These expenses are a joke," said Pardoe. "How the hell did you
spend so much money in Athens? Did you buy one of the Greek
islands?"

"Well, the copy was good. You said so."

"It's less good recently. Most of it seems to have been written with
your pen dipped in Mouton Cadet from a hotel bedroom. I want you to
come back to Fleet Street where I can keep an eye on you and put you
on features I need. You're a good writer, Janey, but you've lost your
edge."

"I want to write a diary from the country, rather like *The Diary of
a Provincial Lady*," protested Janey.

"Who the hell's interested in that?"

Janey was livid. She looked at Pardoe's fridge, laden with booze,
and the leather sofa on which he'd laid her many years before, and
which had just been upholstered in shiny black. She didn't want to go
back to that wild, uncertain pre-Billy existence, where you shivered on
the subway platform on the way to work in the dress you'd worn the
night before and everyone knew you hadn't been home.

She went off and lunched with a publishing friend and told him
she wanted to write a book on men and where they stood at this moment in the sexual war. "I'm going to call it *Depatches from the Y-Front*."

"Good idea," said the publishing friend. "Make a nice change
from all this feminist rubbish pouring off the presses. Take in the lot:
divorcees, adulterers, house husbands. Is the post-permissive male better in bed? Make it as bitchy, funny and as contentious as possible. I'll
give you a £21,000 advance."

Tight after lunch, Janey went back to Pardoe and handed in her
resignation. "You'll be back," he said. "If you ever finish that book,
which I very much doubt, I might serialize it."

"I doubt it," said Janey, "because you'll certainly be in it, and
you'll be too vain to sue."

Janey was not that worried about how long she'd take over the
book. Her father had supported her mother. Why shouldn't Billy support her? Billy came back from Hamburg to be told Janey had resigned, but was being paid a huge advance.

"I'm going to be a proper wife, like Helen," she went on.

Billy said he preferred improper wives and, although he liked the
idea of her living in the woodcutter's cottage, like Little Red Riding
Hood, he did hope too many wolves wouldn't turn up dressed as

grandmothers. He was also slightly alarmed that, along with the £50,000 bill from the builders, there was a tax bill for £10,000. Suddenly there didn't seem to be anything to pay it with.

"Give the bills to Kev," said Janey airily. "That's what he's there for."

But all worries about money were set aside with the excitement of moving in and the furniture looking so nice on the stone floors and lighting huge log fires in the living room and cutting back the roses and honeysuckle which were still in flower and darkening the windows. Then there was the bliss of waking up in their *own* bed in their *own* room, looking through the lime trees at the valley. How could they not be happy and prosper in an enchanted bower like this?

Janey missed Billy when he started going off to shows without her, but she was enjoying getting settled, and it was heaven not having to get up at five o'clock in the morning to drive off over mountain passes or break down on icy roads. The winter that followed was very cold, and the wind whistled past their doors straight off the Bristol channel, but Janey merely turned the central heating up to tropical and thought idly about her book. The muse must not be raped; she must be given time to yield her secrets.

Rupert missed them both terribly when they moved out. All the fun seemed to have gone out of the house. He was making heroic attempts to be a good husband and Helen was trying equally hard to be more sexy. But when you were feeling sick and heavy with pregnancy, it wasn't easy. Badger missed Mavis most of all and spent days down at the cottage whenever Rupert was away. When Rupert arrived to fetch him, he would lie in front of the fire in embarrassment with his eyes shut, pretending that because he couldn't see Rupert he wasn't there.

As an ingratiating gesture, Janey invited Kev and Enid Coley to her first dinner party. The huge china poodle was unearthed from its home in the cellar, dusted off and put in a place of honor in the living room. Unfortunately Janey had sprayed oven-cleaner all over the inside of the stove the day before and forgot to wash it off, so when she removed the duck from the oven the kitchen was flooded with toxic fumes and the duck was a charred wreck, the size of a wren. Everyone screamed with laughter and Billy was sent off to Stroud to get Chinese take out. Just as well perhaps. When Billy checked the mustard Janey'd put on the table, he discovered it was the horses' saffron anti-fly ointment.

"Janey's very attractive," commented Enid Coley on the way home, "but I'm not sure she's a homemaker."

By the time Christmas came, things were very tight. The Bull bruised a sole before the Olympia show and Billy didn't have a single win with the other horses. He sent a Christmas card to his bank man-

ager and decided he'd have to tap his parents, who'd invited them
down for Christmas.

"Only for a couple of days," Janey told Mrs. Lloyd-Foxe firmly.
"We can't really leave the horses."

The visit was not a success. Janey, who always left shopping until
the last moment, was forced to spend an absolute fortune on Christmas
presents, which shocked Billy's frugal parents, who gave them a hideously ugly piece of family silver instead of the check they had anticipated.

The Lloyd-Foxes lived in a house called The Maltings, which was
so cold that Janey couldn't bring herself to get up until lunchtime, and
then only to hog the fire. Billy's mother was not tactful. She came back
incessantly to the subject of babies. It was so sad at bridge parties not
to be able to boast of a little Lloyd-Foxe baby in the offing. She was so
pleased dear Helen was being sensible and having a second child.

"I'll iron Billy's shirts for him," she said, coming into the bedroom and picking them up off the floor. "I know how he likes them,
and I'll make you an apple pie to take back to Gloucestershire. He so
loves sweets."

"She'll get it in the kisser if she doesn't shut up," muttered Janey.

Out of sheer irritation Janey left her room in a mess, with the fire
on, and didn't bother to make the one bed they'd slept in, out of the
two single beds. Billy was the only form of central heating in the
house. At noon and six o'clock, Janey listed toward the vodka, and
Billy's mother's jaw clenched. She was very tired of cooking and she
could have done with a little help and praise from Janey. Finally, on
Boxing night, Billy asked his father for a loan.

Mr. Lloyd-Foxe hemmed and hawed and said it had been a bad
year with the squeeze and, although he had twenty thousand to spare,
he had divided it between Billy's sisters, Arabella and Lucinda.

"I feel they need it more than you and Janey do, as you're both
working."

Janey didn't even bother to kiss her mother-in-law goodbye, and
it was only after they'd left that Mrs. Lloyd-Foxe discovered Janey had
painted the letter "L" out of the sign saying The Maltings on the gate.

After Christmas the bills came flooding in. Billy, who'd never
paid a gas or telephone or electricity bill in his life, had no idea they'd
be so high. He also read his bank statement, which was infinitely more
scarlet after Janey's Christmas shopping.

"Did you honestly spend £60 on the cushion for my mother?"

"Pity I didn't hold it over the old monster's face," said Janey.

The tax man and the builders were also hustling for payment.
Another shock was that the £21,000 advance on the manuscript was

divided into three: £7,000 on signature, £7,000 on delivery and £7,000 on publication.

"How soon do you think you'll deliver?" asked Billy.

The original date had been March, but Janey, who'd only made a few random notes, said there wouldn't be a hope before the summer, which meant that autumn publication was impossible.

Janey had no idea either of the astronomical cost of running and traveling a string of horses, nor was she any good as a back-up team. She kept forgetting to post entry forms, which meant Billy drove 200 miles to a show to find he wasn't eligible to compete. Often fast talking got him in, often it didn't. Billy was one of the best riders in England, but he was not a natural jockey like Rupert. He had to work at it and keep schooling his horses to get really good results. Nor did Janey understand Billy's temperament, that he lacked self-confidence, and needed to be kept very calm before a big class. Rows and requests for money sapped his concentration. He needed to distance himself, and with a lovely wife in a warm bed at home, he tended to spend less time in the indoor ring at night and to get up later in the morning.

In March he came home from a long three-week trip abroad. He'd missed Janey desperately and deliberately called her at Southampton to say he'd be home in time for dinner, adding, rather plaintively, that he hadn't eaten all day. As he settled the horses at Rupert's, a marvelous smell of boeuf bourgignon drifted out of the kitchen and he wondered if Janey would be cooking something nice for him. As he came up to the front door he tripped over a pile of milk bottles. The place stank of cat, not stew, and as he took the last finger of whisky to the sink to fill the glass up with water, he found it full of dirty dishes. The dishwasher was broken, explained Janey; and the man hadn't come to fix it yet. As he went back into the drawing room, he noticed drink rings on the Georgian table Helen had given them as a wedding present. The place looked rather as Penscombe used to before Helen came and tidied it up. Somehow, these days, mess got on his nerves. He had had a bad week, hardly in the money at all. He tried to ignore the pile of brown envelopes unopened on the hall table. There was no more whisky, only vodka, but no tonic.

"Drink it with soda water."

"I'm starving."

"I'm sorry, darling. I forgot to get anything in, and it was too late by the time you rang. Let's go out."

"Too bloody expensive. I'll have some cornflakes."

Billy's stomach was churning painfully. He wondered if he were getting an ulcer. He'd had an early start in the morning. He went upstairs; the cupboard was bare; there was nothing in his drawers.

"Have I got any clean shirts or breeches?"

"Oh Christ," said Janey, clutching her head, "I left them in the laundromat in Stroud. The washing machine's busted too."

"What time do they open?"

"About 8:30."

"I've got to leave at six."

"I'm sorry, darling, truly I am. Look, give me your breeches and shirts and I'll wash them by hand. Then we can dry them in front of the fire and I'll get up early and iron them."

"It's all right. I'll borrow some from Rupert. I'm only away for a couple of days this time."

"I'm desperately sorry," said Janey, suddenly catching sight of two unposted entry forms in her out-tray and shuffling them under a pile of papers "I'm going to mix you a nice drink."

After two glasses of vodka and soda which didn't taste so bad after all, Billy felt fortified enough to open the brown envelopes.

"Janey darling," he said five minutes later, "we shall simply have to pull our horns in. These bills are frightful. We don't need a swimming pool. We simply can't afford the deposit, or even less to pay for it when it's finished."

Janey pouted. "It'll be so nice for you to flop into the pool when you come back from shows."

"There's only about three months a year warm enough to do that in Gloucestershire."

"I've been trying to economize. Mrs. Bodkin's got the flu, and I took her a bunch of daffodils without leaves today, because they were cheaper."

"But we haven't been really living it down, have we? There are five half-eaten cans of cat food gathering mold on top of the fridge and Mavis really doesn't need half a chicken every day. She's getting awfully fat."

"Well, Badger often drops in for lunch. You know how Helen starves those dogs."

"I think we ought to cut down Mrs. Bodkin to half a day a week," said Billy regardless of Janey's frown. "And give up Miss Hawkins. You could do my fan mail."

"Do your fan mail?" said Janey, outraged. "What about *my* fan mail?"

"Just for a little, till we get straight."

Janey started to get angry and hysterical. "I've got to finish this book. It's got to be handed in by July. I haven't got time for anything else. I'm writing every day. I get up at eight and I've only just finished this evening. Stupid not to grab inspiration when it takes you."

She didn't point out that most of today had been spent drinking coffee, and later whisky, with one of the builders. After all, she rationalized, she had to get the blue collar view for her book somehow.

"I know darling," said Billy soothingly. "All I'm saying is that we must not do any more to the house at the moment."

"Go to Kev," said Janey, emptying the last of the vodka into his glass. "Kev will provide, the great ape. I'm going to make you some scrambled eggs." She went toward the kitchen. "I say," she popped her head around the door a moment later, "Helen gave me a chapter of her novel to read today."

"Any good?"

"She can't write 'Bum' on a wall. She said, 'Janey, I want you to be real honest with me,' which meant she wanted me to lie convincingly. She told me a much funnier thing today. She's got frightfully thick with the new vicar and evidently when Rupert flew back from Geneva for the night last week he found the vicar holding a Lenten meeting in the drawing room, with everyone including Badger meditating with their eyes shut."

Billy laughed. "Rupe told me."

He wandered into the kitchen, trying not to notice the mess or the way Janey threw the eggshells into a huge box, where they joined about a hundred other eggshells. That must account for the odd smell. He picked up a jar of coffee on the dresser and looked at the price. "Christ, coffee's expensive. I'm going to drink whiskey in future."

Janey came and put her arms round him: "I do love you," she said. "Don't worry about money, I've got a lovely bottle of St. Emilion."

After three huge vodkas and a bottle of St. Emilion the problem didn't seem so bad. Billy would ride with panache, Janey would write like a maniac while he was away. They would soon get out of their mess.

Spring came, more longed-for then ever after the hardness of the winter, and the woods were filled with violets, anemones, primroses and bird song. Janey thought about new clothes. The wild garlic made her feel homesick for drunken lunches in Soho. She knew marriage to Billy was far more precious and durable but she missed the jokes and the gossip. She lived on the telephone to her mother. She was finding it increasingly difficult to buckle down to her book. She was used to the weekly deadlines of journalism, the steady fan mail, people coming up to her at parties and saying, "You were a bit near the knuckle last week."

In the country there was no second mail delivery, no *Evening Standard,* no FM Radio; she found it difficult to get used to the slow rhythms. Gloucestershire was a soporific county and she found herself falling asleep in the afternoon. She had her fallopian tubes blown which was not really painful, but affected her more than she expected. She sank into despondency and to pre-menstrual tension was added post-menstrual depression when she found she wasn't preganant.

The bills got worse. Janey's tax bill came in and Billy realized that, as her husband, he was liable for an extra £15,000.

Every time Janey went shopping, wherever she looked baby clothes seemed to be mocking her. She seemed to be alone in a world of mothers. She took her temperature and wrote it down on the back of a Christmas card every day, and Billy was supposed to leap on her when her temperature went up. But invariably she mislaid the card or Billy wasn't there on the right day.

In May Helen gave birth to a daughter, whom they called Tabitha. Rupert was present at the birth, and although to Helen he seemed to spend more time making eyes over his white mask at the pretty nurses and seeing how all the machinery worked, at least he was there. And from the moment he set eyes on Tabitha and she opened the same Cambridge blue eyes as his, Rupert was totally enchanted. She was indeed the most angelic baby. She gurgled and laughed, and, almost immediately, she slept through the night; and, if she woke, it was Rupert who got up without a murmur, displaying a sweetness and patience Helen had never seen before.

Where Rupert was concerned, it was the great love affair of the century. Here was someone he could love unstintingly, and who adored him back. Later her first word was "Daddy," and, when she took her first steps, they were toward Rupert. And almost before she could walk she screamed to be put on a pony, and screamed even louder when she was lifted off. Rupert would do anything for her, bathing her, playing with her for hours, watching her as she slept, plump, pink-cheeked, blond and ravishing in her crib. Delighted at first with Rupert's delight, Helen gradually became irritated by it and drew even closer to Marcus, who couldn't understand, at two, why his father didn't dote on him and bring him presents and cuddle him on his knee. As a result, when Rupert wasn't around he would punch and pinch little Tab and fill her crib with toys. One day Rupert caught him trying to suffocate Tab with a pillow and give him a back-hander which sent him flying across the room. Two hours later, Marcus had one of his worst asthma attacks. He recovered, but by that time Rupert had moved on to another show.

The christening upset Janey very much. She was a godmother, but it was such a tribal affair, such a ritualistic celebration of fertility. All the Campbell-Blacks were there in force, going into ecstasies over such a ravishing baby. Mrs. Lloyd-Foxe sent Tab a beautiful silver mug. Janey got drunk afterwards and spent all night in floods of tears. Billy was in despair. "We've only been married a year and a half, darling. I'll see a doctor. It might be my fault."

30

All the riders were now revving up for the World Championship which was being held at Les Rivaux in Brittany in July. Only six British riders would be selected to go. Considering Billy a certainty, Kevin Coley had reserved a big tent at Les Rivaux and was intending to make a party of it, flying out all his important customers for a gala.

As it was only May, Billy wasn't too worried about qualifying. He was bound to hit form soon. The Bull had gotten over a virus complaint and was back on the circuit. Another key event, from Kevin Coley's point of view, was Westerngate, a big show in the Midlands towards the end of May. The Moggie Meal factory was just a few miles outside of Westerngate, and Kevin Coley had a tent at the show, where all his senior staff were expected to turn out in their best clothes and mingle with important customers.

The highlight of the day for all of them was to meet Billy and watch his horses, Moggie Meal Al, Moggie Meal Kitch (Kitchener) and Moggie Meal Dick (Mandryka), jumping. They were also keen to meet Billy's beautiful and famous wife Janey, whom many of the wives had thought a scream when she wrote in the *Daily Post*.

Westerngate was about eighty miles north of Penscombe. Billy was expected to be on parade all three days of the show, and Kevin and Enid Coley were naturally disappointed that Janey was working on Thursday and Friday, but were very much looking forward to seeing her on Saturday for lunch.

"Do I have to come?" grumbled Janey.

"It is important," urged Billy. "They're our bread and butter."

"Bread and margarine if you ask me. I hate to leave the book," she lied, "when it's going so well."

"I'll come home on Friday night and collect you," said Billy, "and we can drive down in the morning. But we'll have to leave early; I've got a novice class around eleven-thirty."

On the Monday before the show Billy had gone to Kevin to ask for an advance of £20,000 to keep some of his creditors at bay. Kevin thought for a minute. "Yes, I'll help you out, Billy."

"That's terribly kind of you," said Billy, heaving a sigh of relief.

"It isn't kind, it's fucking generous. But I'm not going to help you out that much. I'm only going to give you £2,000 or you'll lose your hunger."

Billy's heart sank.

"You'll have to win the rest. Cut down on the booze and lose some weight. It's a tough world. I'm counting on you for the World

Championship. I've booked that tent for Les Rivaux so you'd better start winning and qualify."

Billy wished Kevin hadn't booked the tent; it was tempting providence.

Bad luck seemed to pursue him. He had such a hangover at Fontainebleau, he forgot to check to see that Tracey had screwed in Kitchener's studs. Kitchener went into the ring and promptly slipped on take-off, putting him out for the whole season, which left Billy with only The Bull and Mandryka. Janey was sympathetic when he rang, but she was four days late with her period, and cocooned in secret expectations.

On Wednesday night Billy came home from Fontainebleau and found Janey had put three pairs of breeches and four white shirts in the washing maching with one of her scarlet silk scarves, so they came out streaked red like the dawn. Billy was very tired or he wouldn't have hit the roof.

"I can't think what you're worrying about. I'm not complaining," Janey shouted back at him, "and I've ruined a perfectly good scarf. I've been so busy, you're lucky to have your shirts washed at all. Why don't you go out and win something, then you can afford to send them to the laundry."

Billy felt that terrible clawing pain in his gut that was becoming so familiar these days. A large glass of whisky seemed the only answer.

Going upstairs in the faint hope of finding some clean shirts, he saw instead the beautiful new iron headboard on the spare-room bed.

"Where did that come from?"

"I bought it weeks ago."

"And paid for it?

"Not yet." Janey didn't meet his eyes.

"Why d'you buy bloody beds when I can't afford boots?"

"Why don't you buy cheap vino instead of paying £3 a bottle? Why are you always buying drinks for people, giving them the shirts off your back, even if they are streaked red like the dawn? As I said, why don't you win something? I'm fed up playing second fiddle to a string of bloody horses."

Billy went back upstairs. When she got into bed, he was lying under the covers wearing pyjamas buttoned up to the neck. Even though his face was turned to the wall she caught a waft of bad digestion and drink fumes.

"Billy," she said apologetically. He didn't answer, but she knew he was awake. Nothing, however, could dent her happiness. She was eight days late. She woke up in the night and Billy was so still she thought he'd committed suicide, so she woke him up in a panic and, half-asleep, he instinctively put his arms around her, forgetting the dreadfulness of the row.

He left before she woke in the morning to go to Westerngate, but returned on Friday night in better spirits. The Bull had come in second in a big class, so perhaps his luck was turning.

Janey was delighted: "Who beat you?"

"Jake Lovell of all people. He's back on the circuit."

"Who's he?"

"You know Jake. Oh, I'd forgotten. You probably never met him. He was a definite for the Colombia Olympics with two top-class horses. Then one had a heart attack at Crittleden. Appalling bad luck. Should never have been jumped. And then Rupert set his heart on the second."

"And got it, no doubt," said Janey. "He always gets anything or anyone he wants."

"Yes, he did. It was Revenge actually. Belonged to Jake's step-father-in-law. Rupert made him an offer he couldn't refuse; left Jake without any horses. Now he's really back on form. I'm glad. I always felt bad about that business."

Cheered up by Billy's second, they got mildly tight together. "I'm so pleased you're coming tomorrow," said Billy. "They're all dying to meet you. I want to show you off."

Janey didn't feel like being shown off. She felt fat and bloated; perhaps it was the first stirrings of pregnancy. In anticipation of maternity, and to cover the bulges, (she was ten days late now), she was wearing one of Billy's streaked shirts and nothing else.

"Do you like short hair?" she said, pausing at the *Daily Mail* fashion page.

"I do on Mavis. Can I shave your bush tonight?"

It was all rather erotic. Billy'd bought her a porn magazine to read and laid her on a towel on the bed and used a razor and masses of soap and hot water. Wincing in case he nicked her, she read a story about a Victorian maid and her boss, which was too absurd for words and full of misprints and anachronisms, which she kept reading out to Billy:

" 'I want to lock your bunt,' said the vicar, his hot six rearing up." But it soon had her bubbling over inside; the libido was an awfully bad judge of literature, Janey decided.

"Christ, you look fantastic," said Billy as he rinsed away the last soap and hairs. Janey peered at herself: "Rather like an old boiler chicken."

"It'll be fantastic going down on you. Did you ever allow any of your other boyfriends to do this to you?" asked Billy as he leapt on her. " Can we play for a long time?"

Janey, however, having come quickly herself, wanted to get it over with. She was suddenly tired and wriggled frantically trying to bring him to the boil and then exciting him with a story of how Pardoe took her in the back of the Jaguar one summer night.

Janey fell asleep immediately afterwards. Billy lay awake and
fretted. Mandryka had put in a nasty stop yesterday. He must get to
Westerngate early and sort it out. Janey woke up in the morning with
a hangover, feeling Billy's prick nudging her back, his hand stroking
her shaven flesh.

"What time ought we to leave?"

"Ten at at the latest. I haven't declared and I promised Kev we'd
be there for pre-lunch drinks."

Janey didn't want sex but, to get herself in a more receptive
mood, she fantasized she was a schoolgirl in a gym tunic, being seduced by a very strict headmaster in a dog collar. Next moment the
headmaster's wife walked in and they both decided to have her.

"Shall I tell you a story to excite you?" asked Billy.

"I'm fine," said Janey who was deep in headmasters. "Nearly
there."

The next moment pleasure flooded over her. She longed to go
back to sleep.

"You look so fantastic," said Billy, "how about soixante-neuf?"

Janey couldn't face a huge cock down her throat. "I can't Billy,
not with a hangover. Please stay inside me. I want to feel you coming."

Afterwards they both fell asleep. When they woke it was five
minutes to ten.

"What are you doing?" said Billy when he went into the
bathroom five minutes later.

"Washing my hair."

"But you can't, we've got to leave *now*."

"You'll just have to drive a bit faster, or go without me."

"I can't," he said aghast. "They're expecting you. Your hair looks
fine. It's only a show. It's you they want to see, not your hair."

"I know what they'll say, 'Not as attractive as her photograph,
nothing to look at in the flesh'," snapped Janey, who was now upside-
down, head in the bath, rubbing in shampoo. "I do have a public
image to keep up. It was you who wanted bloody sex." They didn't
leave until after eleven.

"Revving up is actionable," hissed Janey, coming out of the house.

"So is being an hour late," snapped Billy.

"And my fringe has separated."

Billy didn't feel a striped rugby shirt with a rather dirty white
collar, flared jeans and an old denim jacket were suitable, but he didn't
complain as he would have had to wait another twenty minutes. Ran-
cid with ill temper, they drove all the way to Westerngate with Janey
trying to do her face, snapping at Billy every time he went around a
corner. Traffic was terrible. They were held up for thirty-five minutes
by a couple of gays unloading some carpet into an antique shop on
Broadway High Street.

Billy kept looking at his watch. "Kev's going to flip his lid. I'm going to be too late to declare." His stomach was killing him.

They arrived at half-past one. Billy went straight off to try and find the secretary, leaving Janey to park the car in the sponsors' car park. There was the Moggie Meal tent. There was the awful cat winking on the flag. Oh God, here was Kevin Coley coming towards her, wearing a suit the color of a caramel cup cake. He looked simply livid.

"Hi Kev," she said casually. "The traffic was awful."

"Where the hell is Billy? He's been late once too bloody often and they've put their foot down. They've closed the declaration. They're already walking the course. That means he'll probably be dropped for the Royal and for Aachen, and it's too bloody near the World Championship."

"He's gone to talk to the stewards now. They'll let him in. The crowds have come to see The Bull."

"Don't you bank on it. Everyone's been waiting for you too. We held lunch until a quarter of an hour ago. It's not bloody good enough."

It was with great difficulty that Janey stopped herself shouting back at him. Matters were hardly improved when Billy turned up, abject with apologies, and said they were going to allow him to jump, and he had better go and walk the course.

"See you later darling," he said to Janey. "Go and have some lunch."

Face set, she ignored him.

Keven Coley took her arm, none too gently. "You'd better come along to the tent and repair some of the damage. And smile, for Christ's sake. You're being paid for it."

In the tent they found customers and staff stuffing themselves with roast beef and lobsters. Most of them were already tight. Kevin clones were everywhere with thatched hair and lightweight and light-colored suits. The wives also all seemed to wear beige or pastel suits. Many wore hats on the back of their heads with too much hair showing at the front and high heels which kept catching on the raffia matting and sinking into the damp earth beneath.

Enid Coley, in a brown checked suit and yellow shirt with a pussy-cat bow, was not the only one who looked disapprovingly at Janey's jeans and rugby shirt. "I don't care, I don't care," thought Janey. "I'm eleven days late, and I'm going to have a baby." The little Coley children or the Sprats, as Billy called them, were rushing around being poisonous. "I'll never let my children grow up like that," Janey thought to herself. Kevin put her between two directors' wives who were eating strawberries and cream.

"The gardens aren't as good as the ones at Buckingham Palace," said one.

"No," said the second, "although I didn't really notice the ones at Buckingham Palace the first time I went."

Next moment Helen walked into the tent looking like a million dollars in an off-white canvas suit and dark brown boots.

"I'm really sorry I couldn't make lunch, You did get the message, didn't you? But with young kids it's so difficult to get away," she said to Kevin and Enid who looked as though they'd been kissed under the mistletoe.

Enid, pink with pleasure, took Helen on a tour of the more important clients. Helen was so nice to all of them. Then suddenly she saw Janey and her face lit up.

"Janey, how lovely. I didn't know whether you'd be able to get away."

"We were just saying the BSJA ought to get together and buy you a bra, Janey," said Enid Coley.

Later Janey sat in the riders' stand with Helen watching the big class. She had been pleased with her rugby shirt and jeans until she saw Helen's suit, which was French and cost at least £300. When they had walked through the crowds earlier all the men had stared at Helen, so Janey had taken her dark glasses off, so people could see her sexy slanting eyes, but they still looked at Helen. So she took off her denim jacket to show off her splendid bosom, but they still looked at Helen. Why the hell couldn't Billy be as rich as Rupert, so she could afford decent clothes? She was still furious with Kev who was sitting on her other side. In the next-door stand he had booked seats for all his frightful clients, who clapped and shrieked when riders fell off, and cheered before rounds were finished, and stood up and took pictures all the time to the rage of the people sitting behind them.

"Isn't Kev hell?" she whispered to Helen. "I bet he streaks his chest hair."

"I think he's charming," said Helen in surprise.

Billy's stomach was killing him, like a giant clenching a huge fist in his gut. The only answer, as Kevin was safely in the riders' stand, was to nip into the bar for a couple of quick doubles.

"Those hangover pills you gave me aren't doing much," he grumbled to Rupert when he got back to the collecting ring.

"I should think not," said Rupert. "They're for backache. D'you know, I really think Tab is very bright. She smiled at me today. They don't usually smile till three months."

"Lucky you. Janey's not smiling at me."

Suddenly Billy thought of the shaved bush under those jeans and, overwhelmed with lust, he waved at Janey. Janey ignored him.

It was a tough course. Ludwig went clear. Two Americans, just arrived and accustoming themselves to European fences in anticipation of the World Championships, went clear. The usual mighty roar of applause went up as Billy and The Bull rode into the ring. All Kevin's guest stood up to take photographs.

"My husband may not be the most successful, but he's certainly the most popular rider in England," said Janey, shooting a venomous look at Kevin, who was tugging at his goal-post moustache and twisting his I. D. bracelet.

"Come on Billy, Come on The Bull," yelled the crowd. They too refused to adopt Moggie Meal Al.

"I can't bear to look," said Janey, and didn't, continuing to talk to Helen about straight-legged jeans.

Billy was clear and jumping beautifully until he came to the penultimate fence, when a great cheer went up from the Moggie Meal contingent and distracted The Bull, who jumped the wing instead of the fence and, catching his front leg, went head over heels. The Moggie Meal supporters let out piercing shrieks and started clicking their cameras frantically.

Billy was unhurt and managed to hang onto the reins, getting up and running like mad after a thoroughly rattled Bull. Nearly crashing into a flag, Billy picked it up and waved it in mock fury at The Bull who backed away in terror. Billy started to laugh, threw down the flag, snatched up a handful of grass and gave it to The Bull, reducing the crowd to fits of laughter. Vaulting on to The Bull's back, he cantered out of the ring, grinning broadly.

"That's two grand up the spout," thought Janey. "I don't know what he's got to look so cheerful about."

Billy came into the stand, kissed Helen hello and sat down between her and Janey.

"Sorry Kev," he said.

Janey caught a waft of whisky and hoped it didn't reach Kevin. After two minutes, Billy got to his feet.

"Who'd like a drink?"

"Not for me," said Kevin Coley pointedly.

"Nor me," said Helen standing up. "I must go and call Bergita."

"That's what I call a real lady," said Kevin as Helen made her way along the row, thanking everyone for getting up.

"As opposed to me," muttered Janey to herself crossly.

"Pity she doesn't come to shows more often. But then she's such a caring mother," Kevin went on.

Janey looked stonily down at the collecting ring, where a black-haired rider was walking towards a girl groom with long mousy hair, who was leading a large grey horse.

"Who's that? He's attractive," she said to Billy.

"That's Jake Lovell," said Billy. "I was telling you about him last night. And that groom's his sister-in-law, Fenella Maxwell. She won a novice class this morning and she's only sixteen. She's bloody good. Jake's trained her really well. Isn't she pretty?"

"She's certainly a most attractive young lady," said Kev.

"I'm surprised you can tell for the zits," said Janey.

"Miaow," said Kevin.

"Oh, go eat your own product," snapped Janey.

She went downstairs to the john. She really must stop being a cow. Glancing at her reflection under the flourescent lighting, she thought how awful she looked, piggy-eyed and shadowed. She did hope she wasn't going to be one of those women who felt sick for nine months. As she sat on the toilet she felt the sudden cold on her shaven bush. Just to convince herself she slipped her finger between her legs, then pressed it against the white glossy lavatory wall. She couldn't believe it. She reached further into her vagina, pushing against the neck of the womb. She pressed the white wall again. It was unmistakeable, a second dark red fingerprint. She gave a groan, tears spilling out of her eyes. She was wracked with despair. Oh God, the red badge of discouragement. It was so ironic. Before she was married, the red fingerprint was all she craved; she'd been so terrified of getting pregnant all the time. Now she knew why it was called the curse, the curse of not having babies. She leaned against the wall and cried and cried.

Twenty minutes later she came out of the bathroom, huddled behind her dark glasses. Kevin was waiting outside. "Where the hell have you been? Billy was looking for you. He's just about to jump Moggie Meal Dick. He told me to tell you. What's the matter?" He lifted off her dark glasses.

"Why are you crying?"

"Nothing, it's nothing."

"Worried about money?"

Her lip trembled. "I thought I was pregnant. I was ten days late, you see. I've just discovered I'm not."

"Been trying long?"

"About eighteen months. Since we married really."

"May not be your fault."

Janey gave a bitter laugh. "Billy's mother thinks it is."

Kevin looked at her thoughtfully.

"Enid's got a first rate gynecologist. I'll tell her to give you a ring."

Mandryka got four faults and was out of the running. Rupert was first, Jake Lovell second. It was noticed that both men stared stonily ahead, not exchanging a single word, as they lined up for their ribbons.

Helen drove Rupert home. "I really do think Janey should look after Billy better. All his boots need heeling. He was wearing a filthy shirt and Kevin said she made him really late today."

Rupert shook his head. "There's no doubt William has made a marriage of inconvenience.

31

*B*illy went abroad again. He was very loath to leave Janey when she was so depressed, and also to miss the opportunity of sleeping with her in the middle of the month when she was at her most fertile. He was tempted to fly back for the night, but he simply couldn't afford it. Janey promised him she'd try not to worry and concentrate on her book.

Concentration was not easy. The tax man dropped in and so did the builders, both wanting money. Janey explained that Billy was away and that she wasn't entitled to sign checks unless he was here, but fear came in great waves. The days were so long too. She got up early, which meant she was starving by midday, and started eating. Having worked until six in the evening, she was shattered and ready to dive into a quadruple vodka. Evenings yawned ahead.

She went to see Helen and grumbled how bored she was. Helen suggested she do something for charity. Why didn't she join the local Distressed Gentlefolk's Committee? Janey went sharply into reverse, saying that that would be carrying coals to Newcastle, and she was only bored because she had so much work to do.

The third day after Billy left, Janey tried and failed to write a chapter on schoolboys. She didn't know any schoolboys; all her brothers were older. She ought to go to Eton or Harrow and talk to some, but research took time and was invariably expensive.

She wrote down all the men she'd been to bed with, rather too many of them, hoping this might give her inspiration. It didn't. Then she tore the list up in case Billy found it and was upset. The house looked awful. She went from room to room trying to find a free table space. She'd written in the bedroom and the kitchen and the living room and even the dining room, and left them all in a mess—everywhere except the future nursery. She was not going in there; it made her cry.

The garden looked so pretty, full of hollyhocks and roses, and the honeysuckle hanging heavy on the warm June air. The lime trees were in yellow flower, filling the air with sweet heady scent. The lime tree bower is my prison, she thought to herself. She looked again at her contract and trembled. 70,000 words, it said. She hadn't really produced any of them, and her publisher kept calling and saying he'd be only too happy to come down and discuss what she'd already done.

She wished she were in Athens with Billy. It was no good trying to work. She'd go out and weed the front garden. Mavis sat, aggrieved and shivering ostentatiously, behind her. Going outside meant walks not weeding. Harold Evans came out and rolled in the catmint, Mavis gave half-hearted chase, and Harold shot up a tree, tail flushed out like a toilet brush.

After half an hour Janey peered in at the kitchen clock. Two minutes past six. Hooray, it was cocktail time. She went in and poured herself some vodka. An inch up the glass, two inches? Oh well, it was mostly ice. She couldn't be bothered by lemon, but splashed in some tonic.

God, what a wasted day. She tried to think about men in a two-career family. Not easy really. She and Billy could do with a wife each to look after them. She looked around the kitchen and shuddered at the mess. She'd really clean up before Billy came home. She picked up the paper. There was a brilliant piece by one of her rivals, which depressed her even more. At least there was a movie on television to cheer her up.

She heard the sound of voices, but it was only two farm laborers going past the gate, tired and red from the sun, returning home to supper and a pint of beer perhaps, because they'd earned it. How lucky they were. The despair of another wasted day overwhelmed her.

After three vodkas, she was starving. She made an herb omelette with six eggs, throwing eggshells into the cardboard box which she still hadn't emptied. She meant to share the omelette, which turned into scrambled eggs, with Mavis, but Mavis didn't like the herbs, so Janey ended up eating the whole thing. The boring pan had stuck; she'd clean it later. She ran her hands through her hair, a snow of dandruff drifted down. She hadn't washed it since Westerngate. God, she was going to seed. She bolted all the doors, and having poured herself another vodka, she was just about to turn on the television when the door bell rang. Who the hell would call at this hour of the night? It was bound to be some rapist out in the woods. She'd ignore it. Mavis was barking her head off and the bell rang again. Terrified, she unbolted the door and opened it an inch on the chain.

"Who's that?" she said, peering through the gap. Next moment she was assailed by Paco Rabanne.

"It's me, Kevin."

She could see his medalion catching the light.

"Come in," she said weakly. "I thought you were a rapist."

Relief gave way to panic. Which was the least sordid room to take him into?

"I'm working," she said, heading for the living room. "I'm afraid I only tidy up before Billy comes home."

"So I see," said Kevin.

The drawing room faced north and was cold. There were dead flowers, the skeleton of a three-month old fire, coffee cups and dog and cat plates. Janey shivered.

"Let's try the kitchen."

Kevin followed her, wrinkling his nose. He looked quite amazing in a black velvet suit with a white silk shirt slashed to the navel, three medallions and his blonde hair newly washed.

"You look different," she said.

"I've shaved off my moustache."

"That's right," muttered Janey fuzzily. "It's right that a goal-post moustache should come down in summer."

"I've just left your husband in Athens this morning. I had to attend a function in the area. Thought I'd look in."

"How is he?" said Janey, her face brightening.

"Bit choked. Maggie Meal Al seems to have lost his confidence since he hit the wing at Westerngate. Moggie Meal Dick keeps four-faulting."

"Which one's he?"

Kevin frowned. The frown deepened as he saw the mess of cups and dirty milk bottles, the sink full of dishes.

"I've been working so hard," Janey explained again.

Kevin looked pointedly at the half-full drink, still with unmelted ice cubes.

"What would you like to drink?" she said.

"A dry white wine please."

"Well, be a duck and get it from the cellar. I must go to the john."

Upstairs she looked at herself in despair. Her hair looked like a gollywog, her face was red, her eyes tiny from drinking and lack of make-up. Old trousers and a shrunk T-shirt made her bum and her boobs look huge. Scraping a washcloth under her armpits, spraying her crotch with scent, she slapped on some liquid foundation and failed to pull a comb through her tangled mane. She went to the typewriter and wrote: "Men shouldn't drop in," with one finger.

Downstairs, Kevin, up from the cellar, was holding a bottle and looking boot-faced. "I gather you don't like our wedding gift."

Janey turned green. "Oh, no, no, no! We just put it there because er, Billy's mother came to dinner and she had a poodle which, er, died, and we thought she'd be upset." She shrugged helplessly. It had been worth a try.

Then there was the hassle of finding a corkscrew and a clean glass, and then a basin that wasn't full to wash a dirty one in.

"Why d'you buy Whiskas instead of Moggie Meal?" said Kevin, looking at another of Harold's plates gathering flies.

"I'm sorry, Kev. I know I'm a lousy wife, but I'd just learned the names of Billy's horses when you changed them all, and the village shop's run out of Moggie Meal. I get so bombed when I'm writing and I haven't eaten all day."

Kev raised an eyebrow at the remains of scrambled egg in the pan.

"How's the book going?"

"All right. I've gotten to married men."

"Based on Billy?"

"Billy's too nice. Most married men I know are like babies—into everyone."

She wondered if he used a curling iron as well as a blow dryer, and had got that butterscotch-smooth tan out of a bottle. He was in good shape though, his flat stomach emphasized by the big Gucci belt.

She was dying to get herself another drink, but he was only a quarter way down his. Kevin didn't drink much; it made his accent slip. She felt mesmerized by his flashing gold cufflinks and medalions.

"Don't you get frightened when you're here alone?" he asked.

"I've got a panic button wired up to Rupert's house, and a burglar alarm, but since Harold kept setting it off I gave up using it."

Kevin got up and walked around the kitchen. "This place is a mess and you look frightful. I'd never allow Enid to let herself and our place go like this."

Janey felt livid. She got up and poured another drink, but nothing came out. "It helps if you unscrew the top of the bottle," said Kevin.

"Do you honestly think," Janet said furiously, "that if you walked into Solzhenitsyn's house he'd be dusting or putting cups in dish washers or making chutney? You bet there's a Mrs. Solzhenitsyn playing the Volga boatman to calm his nerves and bringing in the samovar and caviar snacks every ten minutes, and typing his manuscript, as well as keeping his house clean. Christ!"

"Enid looks after me."

"You bet she does! Because you're so jolly rich she doesn't have to work. She doesn't have a money problem in the world, any more than Helen does. So they can spend all day washing their hair and waxing their legs and thinking about getting your underpants whiter than ever."

"My mother went out to work, and she cleaned the kitchen floor every day."

"So what?" snapped Janey. "She wasn't a writer. Writers think about writing all the time, not cleaning, and if they're worried about money all the time they can't write."

"It'd be better," said Kevin, "if, instead of writing rubbish about the opposite sex which makes you restless, you scrapped that book and spent more time looking after Billy. He looked like a tramp in Athens,

breeches held together with safety pins, pink shirts, dinner suit covered with stains, holes in his shoes." He picked up a pile of envelopes,
flipping through them. "These envelopes should have been posted
weeks ago. You're a slut," he went on, turning to face her, "and you're
overweight. If you were my wife, I'd send you straight off to a fat
farm."

"Ridiculously bloody expensive," said Janey, blushing scarlet.
"I'd rather buy a padlock for the fridge. I am trying to write a book."

"You drink too much. So does Billy. It's impairing his judgement. If he's not careful he won't be selected for the World Championships."

"I expect he's fed up with being hassled by you."

"That's not the way you should talk to your husband's sponsor,"
said Kevin, getting to his feet and putting down his half-finished
drink. "Well, I'm off."

Janey was shaken. She was so used to rows with Billy ending up
in bed that she couldn't cope with the progression of this one.

"Aren't you going to finish your drink?"

"No thanks. Get some sleep, and when you're sober we'll do some
straight talking."

"It's hardly been crooked talking this evening," said Janey sulkily,
following him unsteadily to the door. In the doorway he turned, shoving
his fist against her stomach, just a second before she hastily pulled it in.

"God, that zipper's taken some punishment! I'll come back on
Thursday and take you out to dinner," he said.

It was all Billy's fault, thought Janey as she shaved her legs three
days later, for telling Kev to drop in on her. Beastly jumped-up creep.
The bath looked as though a sheep had been sheared, not a follicle of
superfluous hair was left on her body. Her bush had started to grow
again like a badly-plucked chicken, so she'd even shaved that too. She
hadn't had anything except three grapefruit and two bottles of Perrier
since she'd last seen Kevin. She'd cleaned the house and washed her
hair and painted her nails and rubbed body lotion in all over, even into
the back of her neck. She couldn't tell Billy about Kev because he
hadn't called, which boded ill too. He always called if he won.

Oh well, she'd be a good wife, and nice to Billy's sponsor and at
least Kev would be useful for her chapter on arrivistes. Janey detested
Kevin Coley, but she cleaned the bedroom most thoroughly of all,
putting roses on one bedside table and the Moggie Meal Sponsored
Book of Pedigree Cats beneath the bible on the other. She felt much
thinner but her nerves were jangling from so many diet pills. Nothing
was going to happen tonight, she kept telling herself, but she hadn't
felt so jumpy since she'd gone to Wembley for her first date with Billy.
Kev hadn't said what time he was coming. Probably he had high tea
and would arrive at five.

He turned up at eight. When she answered the door he said, "Sorry, must have come to the wrong house," and turned back down the path.

"Kevin, have you been drinking?"

He turned, grinning. "Is it really you? You look quite different from the lady I saw three days ago." He stared at her for a minute. "Wow," he said, sliding a hand round her waist. "You look delightful, quite the old Janey."

For a second he fingered the spare tires above her straining white trousers. "You could lose a few more pounds without missing it, but you're on the way and the place smells fresher too."

No one, reflected Janey, could smell anything except Paco Rabanne.

"I'm only coming out with you to research my chapter on married men," she said.

He had a buff-colored Mercedes. Frank Sinatra's "Songs for Swinging Lovers" was belting out of the tape machine. Christ, he must be old to like that kind of music, thought Janey. That brushed-forward hair must cover a multitude of lines. The village boys, idly chatting and guffawing in the evening sun, stared as they passed. "That'll reach Mrs. Bodkin and probably Helen by tomorrow," thought Janey.

"Lovely properties," remarked Kev as they drove along, "lovely old Cotswold places."

He was wearing a white suit and black shirt and a heavy jet medalion. You'd get a black eye if he kept it on in bed, Janey was appalled to find herself thinking. Interesting that he'd made such an effort for her. Beyond seeing that his suits were reasonably well cut in the first place, Billy didn't think about clothes. He was without vanity; that was one of the things she loved about him.

Kev took her to a very expensive restaurant in Cheltenham. The menus had no prices, and although he showed off and was very rude to waiters, snapping his fingers, complaining the wine wasn't cold enough and sending food back on principle, they treated him with undeniable deference.

"How do you keep so fit?" she asked, looking at his waistline.

"I exercise a lot. Enid and I have joined the country club. You have to be elected. I play a round of golf whenever feasible. I jog on weekends. I exercise with weights in the morning."

Janey giggled. "Do you swing Enid above your head?"

"Don't be silly," said Kevin coldly.

For the first course Janey lapsed and had huge fat pieces of asparagus dripping in melted butter.

"Naughty," chided Kevin. "At least 300 calories."

"I don't care," said Janey, lasciviously taking an asparagus head in her mouth. "I'll go back to grapefruit tomorrow."

Kevin had melon and left the maraschino cherries, followed by steak, well done, with runner beans and green salad. Janey noticed he left the spring onions. She felt a great weariness, probably because she hadn't had enough to drink. She was fed up with talking about product attributes and growth potential. Then suddenly when she thought the evening was beyond redemption, he ordered another bottle of Sancerre, and some of his cronies came over, who were plainly impressed by Janey.

"I'm taking care of her while Billy's abroad," said Kev, and winked.

Suddenly Janey was enjoying herself. There was nothing like the high that went with the possible beginning of an affair. Kev kept looking at her, holding her eyes a second longer than necessary, as though he was caressing her. He was so tough, and positive, and knew exactly where he was going.

"D'you want to go somewhere and dance?" he said as he signed the bill.

She shook her head, ashamed of the hopeless desire that was sweeping over her. As they left the restaurant she swayed and he caught her arm.

"Sorry Kev. Don't ask a girl to drink and diet."

It had been a clear hot day, followed by a dewy short night. They'd been haymaking. The fields had that mingled honey scent of mown grass and drying manure. As they drove home she said, "You'll be the first man since Billy."

"So I should hope."

"It'll be like losing one's virginity all over again."

Kevin put a perfectly manicured hand on her thigh. The diamond in the center of the thick gold ring on his fourth finger glittered in the moonlight.

"I've wanted you since the first night we met, but you've always been so bloody superior."

"Not a lady like Helen?"

"You're a snob. She'd never have sneered and put me down the way you have."

"I'm sorry. I suppose I hated Billy being dependent on someone else."

He removed one of the two bracelets on her right wrist and threw it on to her lap. "and don't jangle."

"You jangle enough," she said.

When they got back to the cottage Mavis followed her round like a disapproving duenna. Kevin went to have a pee. Janey went into the kitchen. It was so hot she opened the fridge and, getting a piece of ice out of the tray, ran it over her tits to make the nipples stand up. Then she poured herself a huge drink to steady her nerves. The next minute

Kev walked in and took it from her and poured it down the sink. "You don't need that sort of booster any more," he said.

I hate him, she said to herself. He's everything that darling Billy isn't.

Mavis, who'd done sterling service as a hotwater bottle all winter, was outraged when Kevin tried to shut her out of the bedroom.

"She always comes in," protested Janey.

"Not anymore she doesn't," said Kevin, booting her with his foot.

"You would get on well with Helen," sighed Janey.

"I don't approve of pets in bedrooms. Ouch!" howled Kev as Mavis bit him sharply on the the ankle.

It took all Janey's self-control not to giggle. There were no band-aids in the house, but finally Kev, stripped except for one of Billy's handkerchieves tightly bound around his ankle, climbed into bed.

"I hope your alarm clock works," he said. "I've got a meeting in Bristol at 9:30."

Janey looked at him through half-closed eyes. "Are you sure you don't want to send me back because I'm not room temperature?"

She put her hand on his cock which was inching upwards and was about to add that in terms of growth potential he was not bad himself, but she didn't think he'd be amused. He made no comment about her shaved bush until afterwards.

"You do that?"

"No, Billy."

"Relationship still very alive then?"

"Yes," said Janey.

It was very nice to be made love to by someone so scented and powdered, but all the perfumes of Arabia couldn't conceal the feral whiff of the jungle killer. Beneath his civilized trappings, Kev was a thug as ruthless as Rupert.

She was ashamed of betraying Billy by sleeping with Kev in their bed. On the other hand, it was bliss not to have to get up and go home dribbling afterwards. Kev had only brought a slimline briefcase with him. Inside was a clean shirt, a toothbrush and toothpaste in a case, and a disposable razor. He's everything that Billy's not, thought Janey once again. Perhaps that's why I fancy him and that's what I really need.

Billy called the next day. Things weren't thrilling. He was missing her. He'd be back on Sunday.

"Did Kev call you? Good. Madryka got a third yesterday, but The Bull's a bit stale. I'm going to rest him next week before the World Championship. How's the book going?"

"Fine," said Janey, who hadn't touched it. She felt guilty but safer. Kev wouldn't let her starve.

"By the way, where were you last night?" asked Billy.

Janey's mind galloped. "I had dinner with Helen."

"That's nice."

Putting down the telephone, she called Helen and suggested they have supper at the local bistro. Before she went out she was fortified by a telephone call from Kev. She'd been waiting all day, wondering if he'd call. She found she couldn't eat anything, pushing her food around her plate.

"You're not pregnant, are you?" asked Helen.

"No, no. I was so disgustingly fat, I took the opportunity of Billy's being away to go on a diet. Now my stomach seems to have shrunk, thank God."

"Don't talk to me about dieting," sighed Helen. "Rupert's given up liquor until after the World Championship. He's lost ten pounds and he looks great but, golly, it makes him mean."

For once Helen unbent a bit. Rupert had bought her a gym tunic and wanted her to dress up as a schoolgirl.

"But I can't. I've got nobbly knees and I'm terrified he's going to start fancying the real thing."

Janey, remembering Billy's tales about Tiffany Bathgate, rather thought Rupert already had.

"I wish Billy'd occasionally look at another woman," she said idly. "It'd be such fun getting him back."

On Saturday morning Janey steamed open their bank statement, then fainted, hastily stuck it up again and went out and bought a pair of white overalls, a white canvas skirt and two striped T-shirts. The weather was so lovely, she lay in the sun. She could always tell Billy she'd been typing in the garden.

Kev came and screwed her on Saturday afternoon. Both of them were sober and the pleasure was even more intense. Janey'd lost eight pounds and was beginning to feel beautiful again. Afterwards they lay in each other's arms.

"Did Billy call?" asked Kevin.

"Yes, not much joy. Sometimes I wish he wasn't such a good loser."

"He's a loser," said Kevin brutally. "Let's make no bones about it. I've got to go now." Janey was appalled at how miserable she felt when Kev said he had to leave.

They had a bath together which made her feel happier. Afterwards she put on her new white overalls which just covered her boobs, and nothing else. Her newly washed hair divided over her brown shoulders. As she made the bed, she instinctively removed hairs, looking for Kevidence, she told herself with a giggle. She persuaded him to have a drink before he went. They were in the living room when they heard a step outside. Janey went to the window. "Oh my God, it's Billy."

"It's all right," said Kev calmly. "Billy told me you were depressed and to drop in to cheer you up. I just happened to be in the area."

Janey patted her hair frantically in the mirror.

"Do I look as though I've just got out of bed?" she asked.

Kev laughed. "You always do anyway."

Billy was absolutely thrilled to see them both. He'd always been worried that they got on so badly and this would certainly make things easier. He looked awful, thoroughly tired out, his hair a tangled mess, eyes blood shot. He smelt of curry and drink.

"How did the last days go?" asked Kevin.

"Bloody awful. The competition's so hot because everyone's over for the World Championship. You're lucky if you get in the money at all. Here's some Arpège for you, sweetheart." He also put down a bottle of duty free whisky.

"Your wife's been on a diet," said Kev. "Doesn't she look great?"

"Sensational," said Billy. "So does the house." He looked around. "Really lovely. You must have worked hard. I'm filthy. I must go and have a bath and change."

"Have a drink first," said Janey, sloshing three fingers of whisky into a glass. She was nervous Kev might have left some of his jewelry in the bedroom. Billy accepted it gratefully; anything to postpone the opening of the brown envelopes and his bank statement. They discussed the World Championships—he would either jump Mandryka or The Bull.

"The Bull—I mean Moggie Meal Al—is a bit stale. I'm going to rest him for the next two weeks."

*T*he gods that had blessed Billy during the first year of marriage seemed to withdraw their sponsorship during the second. The following week Billy rang, jubilant from a show in the South, saying he'd just come first in a big class and won a £5,000 car. He was going to pop up to London in the morning for a ten o'clock appointment with Enid's gynecologist, who'd been making some tests, then pop back to the show, compete in the afternoon, then drive the car straight home afterwards. Tracey would drive the van and, as the car was still being broken in, he was afraid they'd both arrive in the middle of the night.

"But I really feel my luck's turning, darling."

Janey spent the afternoon in bed with Kevin, so she was glad

Billy was going to be late. At midnight the telephone rang. It was from a pay phone.

"Billy!"

"Yes darling."

"Where are you?"

"On the Penscombe-Birdlip road."

"Are you all right?"

"I don't know. I was driving home when a wall jumped out and hit me."

"Christ."

"I'm afraid I was a bit over the limit, and I think the car's totalled."

"Stay where you are," said Janey. "I'll come and get you."

She drove in her nightie, frantic with worry. The first thing she saw was an accordioned pile of scrap metal. God knows how Billy had escaped alive. Then she saw Billy sitting on the wall, singing.

"Billy Lloyd-Foxe sat on a wall,
Billy Lloyd-Foxe had a great fall.
All Kevin's horses and all Kevin's men
Couldn't put Billy together again."

He was absolutely plastered. She must get him home before the police came along and breathalyzed him.

"Billy Lloyd-Foxe sat on a wall," he began again.

"Shut up and get in the car."

She had to help him in; his legs kept giving way. When they got home she helped him upstairs. He collapsed on the bed, white and shaking.

There was a huge bruise on his forehead.

"Must have a pee."

He got to his feet and, staggering towards the closet, opened the door and was about to step in.

"Bill-ee, the other door."

"Oh yes." He took two steps back, one forward, and veered off towards the bathroom.

"I didn't know anyone could pee that long," said Janey when he came back.

"I've done one minute, fifty-five seconds before now. Rupert timed me." He collasped on the bed again. She knelt down beside him.

"What's the matter?"

He looked at her, not focusing. "I went to the doctor."

"And what did he say."

"That it's me, not you. I've got a zilch sperm count. He showed me it under the microscope. Not a tadpole in sight."

He hung his head. "He said we should think seriously about adoption." Janey put her arms around him.

"Oh angel, I'm sorry. But it doesn't matter. Of course we can adopt."

"But I wanted you to have my babies. You wanted one so badly and I can't give you one. Christ!"

She felt desperately sorry for him, but she couldn't help feeling relief in a way for herself, and piss off to his bloody mother. She put him to bed and within seconds he had passed out. He woke with a most appalling headache and went to the doctor, who said he had a concussion as well and he should rest for a week. Billy ignored him. The following morning he set off with Rupert for Aachen.

Janey called Kevin as soon as he'd gone and, feeling disloyal, told him about the car and the sperm count. In a way, she felt she'd been dealt a marked card. She'd married Billy thinking he was a star and the star had almost immediately started falling out of the firmament. That she'd contributed almost entirely to this fall didn't enter her head. She forgot how miserable she'd been bouncing from lover to lover in Fleet Street, waiting desperately for telephone calls, often alone on weekends. She remembered only the fun and excitement. Kevin's propaganda was soft-pedaled but lethal.

"Honey, Billy is simply not macho enough for you. You're like a beautiful lily. You'll only thrive if tied to a very strong stake. He's too weak, too Piscean. He's totally dominated by Rupert. He simply can't cope on his own. He's never going to get himself out of this mess. He's over the top. Everyone's saying so."

By contrast, Kev was so positive, ordering her about, paying restaurant bills with wads of fivers.

Billy called from Aachen. He sounded depressed and slightly tight. "Darling, please don't worry about babies. I promise I'll sort us out after the World Championships. I miss you horribly. I wish you were here."

Janey proceeded to plead with him not to call her until he got home.

"I hate to hear you so down. It really upsets me, puts me off work. I know you'll get in the money soon."

Feeling faintly guilty, Janey then left Mavis with Mrs. Bodkin and flew off to Spain with Kev. Billy was due back on Sunday. She'd be home by Saturday lunchtime. She spent a fortune on clothes and having her hair streaked beforehand. She felt, subconsciously, that if she made the financial situation worse, some kind of confrontation would be triggered off. Kev had never mentioned any permanent relationship, but the affair was certainly heating up.

Billy got home on midday Saturday, his heart like lead. There was no barking. Janey must have taken Mavis for a walk. He had difficulty opening the front door for letters on the doormat. He was so tired, it took him a little while to realize that among them were his own letters and postcards from Aachen. And there was the telegram he'd sent yesterday saying he was coming home early, unopened.

The house was very tidy. Harold Evans weaved furrily round his legs.

But there was no sign of Janey anywhere. He felt faint with horror.

Perhaps she'd been murdered or kidnapped. He poured himself a large whisky and telephone Mrs. Bodkin.

"She's gone away, researching for her book in Norfolk," she said, "and staying with her mother. She's coming home today. I've got Mavis. She's been as good as gold. D'you want to come and pick her up?"

Relief gave way to a dull anger. Mrs. Bodkin looked secretive and overexcited when he arrived, her mouth disappearing in disapproval. She loved Billy, he was as nice a gentleman as you could find, and so thoughtful. But he should never have married that trollop.

After two more drinks back at the cottage, he heard a car draw up.

There was Janey running up the drive in a faded purple T-shirt and cut-off pink trousers. Her tortoiseshell hair was incredibly bleached by the sun (Billy didn't recognize streaking) and she was browner and thinner than ever. His stomach twisted with desire and the pain of his ulcer. All he could think of was how much he'd like to fuck her.

"Darling how lovely! You said you weren't coming back until tomorrow," cried Janey. "Must have a pee."

She didn't look as though she'd been staying with her mother, thought Billy. She never bothered to wear makeup or scent when she went down there.

"I bought you some Norfolk strawberries, darling," she lied. Actually she'd bought them in Cheltenham on the way from the airport in case she needed an alibi. They went back into the house.

"Sweetheart, you look awfully pale," said Janey, suddenly noticing.

"What's happened?"

"I sent you this telegram. You haven't read it."

He turned away, fighting a terrible desire to break down and cry.

Janey opened it with shaking hands. Had he heard something about her and Kev? Smoothing out the paper, she read: "Mandryka broke leg. Had to be shot. Coming home. Love Billy."

She turned in horror.

"Oh angel, I'm sorry." She went over and put her arms round his shaking shoulders. "What happened?"

"It was my fault. He missed his jerk, hit the top pole smack, got caught up in the rest of the poles, and that was that. It was horrible." His face worked like a little boy about to cry. "He was such a great horse. I know he was bad tempered, but he could be so brave."

"Come to bed," she said gently. "I'll take care of you."

Upstairs he rolled on top of her, took her perfunctorily and immediately fell asleep.

"There's no choice," said Billy, facing the ruins of his career next morning. "It's The Bull for the World Championship. At least Kev's keeping away and not breathing down my neck at the moment. Christ knows what he'll say about Mandryka."

He was away the next two days jumping the Grade B and C horses at Crittleden. Janey spent the second afternoon in bed with Kevin where they did more talking than copulating. Billy, said Kevin, had been drunk in Aachen when he jumped Moggie Meal Dick. That was why he put the horse wrong at the fence where he broke his leg. Everyone was talking about it.

He was gone long before Billy got home, giving Janey plenty of time to wash off scent and makeup, get back into her old clothes and be sitting dutifully at her typewriter.

"Good day?" she asked.

"Not bad. Here's *The Tatler*. Rupert gave it to me. There's a picture of Tab and Helen. I think Rupe's bought up every copy."

Billy went upstairs and changed into his dressing gown, secured with his old Harrovian tie; the belt had been lost years ago. As there was no sign of dinner, he poured himself a drink and then started opening the new pile of brown envelopes. He started to tremble. He knew Janey had been depressed about babies and probably needed to cheer herself up, but these bills for clothes were ludicrous. And how the hell could she have spent £50 at the hairdresser? She hadn't even had a haircut. He poured himself another drink and sat down on the sofa.

"Darling, we must talk about money."

Janey, however, was deep in *The Tatler*. "Oh look, there's Mike Pardoe, and there's Rupert's mother. She is amazingly well preserved. She must be over fifty."

Billy tried again. "I've just been through the cancelled checks. The bank says they're going to bounce anything more we submit. Soon I won't be able to feed the horses."

"Oh dear," said Janey in mock horror. "Of course the horses always come before everything else."

"How long d'you think it'll be before the book's finished?"

"How can I tell? Oh, that is a sweet one of Tab, and Helen looks marvelous. She is so *bloody* photogenic. And there's Caroline Manners. What an incredibly plain child."

"You said July last time."

"More likely October."

"So it won't be published this year?"

"Nope. Oh look, Henrietta Pollock got engaged. Poor man."

Billy's heart sank. He was hoping to keep the manager sweet by a promise of £14,000 by Christmas.

He tried again. "We simply can't go on like this. We've got an overdraft of £30,000. We owe the tax man twenty grand and the builders fifty grand and you spend £50 at the hairdressers, and £250 on clothes, expecting me not to notice. D'you take me for a complete fool?"

"Not complete. Pity you banged up the car. Oh, there's Ainsley Hibbert. She's gone blonde. Not a bad guy with her too."

"Janey, have you listened to a word I've said?"

"Yes, I have. We owe rather a lot of money, about £100,000 in fact. You'll have to tap darling Mumsie, won't you? She won't let poor Billy starve."

Billy was having difficulty keeping his temper.

"If the book's not going to be finished yet, could you do some journalism, just to pay the more pressing bills?"

Janey got up. "I must go and put on the parsnips."

"I don't want any dinner. If you honestly think I can eat. . . ."

"It doesn't seem to stop you drinking. Why don't *you* go out and win something? It's awfully boring being married to a failure."

Billy put his head in his hands.

"Why d'you always try and make me feel small?"

"You are small," said Janey. "You told me you'd lost a lot of weight recently."

"For Christ's sake, can't you take anything seriously? If we really try, I know we can get straight."

"Borrow something from Rupert."

"He's pushed himself at the moment."

"Paying for the new indoor swimming pool," said Janey, walking out of the room.

Two minutes later Billy followed her, putting his arms around her.

"Angel, we can't afford to fight."

Janey laughed bitterly. "I should have thought that was the only thing we *could* afford to do."

The telephone rang. Billy went to answer it. "Oh hello. Yes, I see. I quite understand. It was very good of you to let me know. Good luck anyway." Very slowly he put the reciever down; as he turned he seemed to have aged twenty years.

"That was Malise. I've been dropped for the World Championships.

"He wanted me to know before I read it in tomorrow's papers. They've selected Jake Lovell instead."

What, thought Janey, was Kev going to say, stuck with a tent in Les Rivaux and all his male customers revved up for a stag freebie full of Oh la la's?

33

Although there is colossal prestige in being picked for the Olympics, it means competing only against amateurs. The competition the riders wanted to win almost more, therefore, was the World Championship, which takes place every two years midway between Olympic games, and is open to amateurs and professionals alike. The Championships are also considered more of a test of horsemanship, because in the last leg the four finalists must jump a round on each others' horses.

It was with considerable trepidation at six-thirty a.m. on a Tuesday in mid-July that Jake set off with Fen and Tanya for Les Rivaux in the van to take the ferry at Southampton. The van had been loaded up with hay, feed and woodshaving bedding the night before. Tory was to follow later with the car, the trailer and the children. Everything was planned to the last "t"—including a large jar of lemon drops for Macaulay. Even so it turned out to be a nightmare journey. The temperature was up in the eighties. Cow parsley along the edge of the highway had given way to hogweed, holding its flat disks up to a cloudy grey sky through which the sun shone opaque like an Alka Seltzer. Jake drove, Tanya map-read, Fen kept them both supplied with cups of black coffee.

As they neared the coast the sky darkened. At the port Fen lost the horses' health papers and the entire van had to be turned out before she found them where they should have been all the time, with the horses' passports. By now they had missed two ferries and the horses, picking up the vibes of anxiety, were stamping and restless. After a further delay, despite blackening skies and large grey agitated waves, the ferry decided to sail. A storm blew up in mid-channel, bucketing the boat from side to side and throwing Fen's new pony, the young and comparatively inexperienced Desdemona, into such a panic she nearly kicked the stall out.

Fen, having been repeatedly yelled at by Jake for losing the health papers, was further upset by two truck loads of little calves on the boat, mooing piteously with their pathetic faces peering out between the slats. In turn, she went and yelled at their driver for not giving them any water.

Finally, they reached the French port at seven o'clock and set off for Les Rivaux. Jake was going crazy from being stuck behind huge trucks but this was Fen's first trip to France and she couldn't contain a surge of excitement, as the sun came out and they drove past orchards, poplar-lined rivers and a ravishing château, half-hidden by trees, its reflection glimmering in a lake. She was bitterly disappointed that her hero, Billy Lloyd-Foxe, hadn't been selected. He'd bought her a drink at Westerngate; not that that meant much, he'd been buying everyone drinks. But perhaps she might meet a handsome Frenchman at the World Championship who'd sweep her off to his château and make fantastic love to her behind peeling grey shutters. Her dreams were rudely shattered by a loud bang. The van swerved terrifyingly; somehow Jake managed to steer it into the slow lane and, despite frenzied screaming of brakes from all sides, to avoid a crash. They had blown a tire, causing the most frightful traffic jam, which resulted in apopleptic Frenchmen, no doubt missing their dinners, leaning continually on their horns, which did nothing to improve Jake's nerves.

Eventually, just as the tow truck arrived and towed them onto the side of the road, a vast blue van with the familiar emerald green words "Rupert Campbell-Black, Great Britain" on the side, flashed past, blowing its horn and making no attempt to stop and help.

It was three o'clock in the morning, and many more cups of black coffee later, before they finally rumbled into the horse-stall park to find, as a last straw, that two of their stalls had been appropriated by Rupert's horses and a third by a horse belonging to someone called Dino Ferranti.

"He's the American No. 3", said Jake.

Fen loved Jake, despite his hassling her. She knew this kind of mix-up was the last thing he needed before a championship. He was all for putting the horses in other stables and sorting it out in the morning, but Fen, seething with protective indignation, was determined to drag Rupert's new groom, Dizzy, out of bed.

It wasn't hard to find Rupert's trailer although it was parked some way from the others under an oak tree. Every light was blazing and sounds of laughter and revelry disturbed the hot summer night.

Throwing open the door, Fen found Rupert, Ludwig and a languid very good-looking boy with streaked blonde hair, lazy grey eyes, and an olive complexion playing strip poker. Dizzy, wearing only a G-string, was stretched out on one of the bench seats. Another beautiful dark girl was sitting on Rupert's knee, wearing one of his striped shirts and nothing else. Ludwig was down to his underpants, a riding hat and one sock. The languid boy was just in jeans and Rupert who was on the high wagon and smoking a joint, was the only one fully dressed. They were all high as kites, laughing uproariously and half-watching a porno movie on the video, in which a plump redhead was doing unmentionable things to a supine Santa Claus.

Having glanced at the film, Fen went crimson, and looked back at the table, hastily averting her eyes as one of the brunette's breasts fell out of the striped shirt.

"*Bon soir,*" said Rupert. "*Asseyez-vous.* It's 50p in the back stalls."

"Come on honey," drawled the handsome boy in a strong southern accent, his eyes crossing like a Siamese cat. "Come and sit on ma knee."

"No, you come and neck wiz me," said Ludwig, getting to his feet and clicking his bare and socked heels together.

"You're all disgusting," stormed Fen. "And what's more," she said "you and some creep called Dino Ferranti have stolen our stables."

"Aw c'mon, honey, come over here," said the American boy, holding out long sunburnt hands.

"Well, you'd better find somewhere else to put your donkeys," said Rupert. "You haven't met Dino Ferranti, have you?"

"No, nor do I want to," said Fen, losing her temper. "Look," she screamed, waving the papers under Rupert's nose, "*numero quatre-vingt et un, deux, trois, quatre.* It's as plain as the *nez* on *votre visage.*"

"We didn't realize they were your stables," said Dizzy pouting.

"I suppose you're too thick to read, like most of Rupert's grooms."

"Temper, temper," said Rupert.

"You bloody well come and shift them. If you'd had the decency to stop and help on the highway, we'd have arrived at the same time as you and there wouldn't be this stupid muddle. I've never met anyone so deficient in team spirit."

"What d'you want me to do?" asked Rupert. "Start singing 'Forty Years On?' Billy's the singer, and he's not been selected, thanks to your fucking brother-in-law."

Fen didn't respond. She turned and went down the steps.

"All right, if you won't move your horses, I'll let them out."

"Don't play silly games," snapped Rupert. "You'll regret it. Come on Dino, it's your deal."

"Who's that? She's kinda cute," drawled the American boy, taking a swig out of the whisky bottle and handing it to Ludwig.

"Jake Lovell's sister-in-law," said Rupert.

"Wass he like?"

"Hell. He's got a chip or, as my wife would say, a french fry on his shoulder. His lack of charm seems to have rubbed off on her."

Five minutes later Dino lost the round and had to take off his jeans. Getting up to unzip his fly, he looked out of the window.

"Beautiful night," he drawled. "moonlight's bright as day. Look, there's the Big Dipper. Ah don't know if Ah'm imagining things but Ah just saw a grey horse trotting past the window."

Ludwig got unsteadily to his feet and peered out.

"It's Snakepit and zee other horse," he said. "Zee leetle Maxvell ees taken zem avay. You better pull zee thumb out, Rupert."

Dino Ferranti started to laugh. "Well I'll be damned."

In a flash Rupert had tipped the brunette onto the floor and was out of the trailer streaking across the grass in his bare feet.

"Come back," he bellowed to Fen.

Fen trotted on, keeping a safe distance ahead of him. "Not till you promise to get your horses out of our stables."

Despite the month off booze and two miles jogging every morning, Rupert couldn't catch up with her. His language deteriorated.

"Tut Tut," said Fen, "and in front of a lady too. If you don't promise, I'll let them loose in the forest. They need a break. Can't be much fun being owned by a revolting bully like you."

For five minutes, which seemed an eternity to Rupert, she cantered slowly ahead until she was under the dark brow of the forest.

"Well?" she said.

Rupert agreed. "All right, we'll move them. Now give them back to me, you little bitch."

"And have you run me down? I'll take them back and tie them up *outside* your stables."

"I'll sue you for this."

"We could sue you for pinching our stables," and making a wide circle she galloped off, yelling over her shoulder, "I hope you sleep horribly."

For grooms there is no sleeping late. Two and a half hours later Fen had to stagger out of bed to feed and walk the horses. Having not eaten yesterday, after being sick on the boat, she felt desperately hungry. On the way back to the van for some breakfast, she bumped into Humpty's groom, Bridie. After swapping notes about their respective horses, they decided to go and have breakfast together.

"Going's bloody hard," said Bridie, gazing at the ground which was splitting and cracking like a great brown jigsaw. "No sign of rain either; not going to suit Lord Campbell-Black." She lowered her voice. "He's been overjumping all his horses. I saw them at Crittleden last week. They'd just come on from the Royal and from Aachen. Arcturus was lying down in his stall so exhausted I thought he was dead. It was sheer exhaustion. They haven't had a break since January. Arcy can't move unless he's drugged up the eyeballs. When the effect wears off he's in agony."

"Who's Rupert going to jump in the Championship?"

"Snakepit," said Bridie.

Fen groaned. "Trust Rupert to put in a sod."

"Needs two people in the stables, one to groom, one to keep an eye on him. He's got a terrible cow kick. Already killed one of Rupert's Jack Russells."

"Perhaps he won't make the final."

"On current form he can't fail."

They went into the breakfast tent. Fen was piling apricot jam on to her fourth croissant when Bridie asked her if she'd seen Dino Ferranti.

"I met him briefly last night," said Fen coldly.

"Don't you think he's devastating?" sighed Bridie. "Those snake hips and those terrific shoulders, and that angelically depraved face. And he dresses so well."

"He was half-naked when I last saw him," said Fen.

After that the whole story came out.

Bridie looked at Fen in awe.

"You didn't let out Rupert's horses?"

"Yes, I did."

"And rode Snakepit."

"Yes."

"Probably didn't play up because you weren't frightened of him. Mind you, I think Rupert's devastating too. If he lifted a finger in my direction I'd go."

"I wouldn't. I think he's hell."

Four hours later Ludwig and Dino Ferranti, both in dark glasses and both with fearful hangovers not improved by the midday sun, tottered down to the stables to work their horses, and paused at the sight of Isa Lovell, not a day over six, cantering Macaulay round the practice ring.

"O. K. Fen," he shouted in a shrill Birmingham accent, "put it up," and, cantering towards the upright, cleared 5 feet 3 inches without any trouble.

Dino Ferranti had the puffy eyes of the heavy sleeper, but at this moment he couldn't believe them.

"Look at that!"

"I'd rather not," said Ludwig. "With kids zat good, I'm not going to be Vorld Champion much longer."

They stopped and watched for a few minutes, as the child put the horse over several more fences.

"That's the girl from last night," said Dino.

"Ha," said Ludwig. "Mees Maxwell, Jake Lovell's groom. Maybe that's zee horse Jake's going to jump. Looks very familiar. No, it can't be."

"Looks bloody well," said Dino.

Les Rivaux is one of the most beautiful seaside ports in Brittany. The showground is about a mile outside the town, half-ringed on the inshore side by the forest in which Fen had threatened to let Rupert's horses loose. In front lies the sea. On the day of the first warm-up class of the show it lay like a film of mother of pearl on the platinum-blond sand.

"Too many foreigners," said a large English lady tourist disapprovingly, as two Italians nearly fell off their horses at the sight of Rupert's groom Dizzy riding past in a tight turquoise T-shirt and no bra.

Les Rivaux was already swarming with Dutch riders in leather coats, Portuguese with hot eyes and chattering teeth, Argentinian generals, Americans in panamas and dark glasses, all gabbling away in different languages, lending a Ritzy illicit flavor to the show ground. The weather was still muggy and hot and, although the swallows were flying low and the cows lying down, there was no sign of rain to soften the punishingly hard ground.

A large crowd gathered to watch this first event, a small speed class in which most of the riders had entered the horses they would later jump in the World Championship. In the big afternoon class they would jump their second horses.

Rumors had already begun to circulate around the showground that Jake Lovell was jumping one of Rupert's old horses. When Rupert first saw Tanya leading Macaulay and Desdemona quietly around the collecting ring that morning, he stared for a minute at the familiar big black horse with dinner-plate feet and the ugly white face, but made absolutely no comment.

It was a mark of Rupert's nerve that it had no effect on his riding. He continued to bitch at and insult the other riders, which was always his way of psyching himself up before a class, then produced a round that threw everyone else into a panic. Not only was his speed faster than light, but, from the way he had to exert every ounce of brute strength to keep Snakepit on course, the horse was obviously a devil to ride.

Guy de la Tour, the star on whom the French crowd had pinned their hopes, jumped a slower but stylish clear to a storm of bravoes. He was followed by Ludwig, recovered from his hangover, but who, despite Clara's long legs, couldn't catch Rupert. Speed was not Macaulay's strong point; he was too careful and jumped too high. Jake was very happy with a slow clear, putting him in eleventh place.

As the Americans were hot favorites for the Nations' Cup, there was a lot of interest in how the horses would react to a French course. Neither the number one rider, Carl Kennedy, nor the number two, the red-headed Mary Jo Wilson, had found their form yet, and notched up eight and four faults respectively.

Interest was therefore centered on Dino Ferranti, riding a young liver chestnut thoroughbred called President's Man. Dino had never competed in Europe before, but even Fen, who'd had another row with

him in the practice ring because his groom dismantled the upright
when she was about to jump it, had to admit he was a glorious rider.
For the purist, he lounged in the saddle like a cowboy and sat a little
too far back, but he was so supple he seemed made of rubber, and was
able to throw his weight completely off the horse while it was in the
air, yet somehow touch down smoothly as he landed.

Loose mane and long tail flying in the American fashion, President's man loped around the course like a cotton-tail rabbit. There was
consternation and raised eyebrows all round when the clock said he was
three seconds faster than Rupert.

"Well done," everyone said as he came out.

"That's very lucky to win the first class in the show," said
Humpty. "That is a handsome animal. Who's he by?"

"Great, our first win," said Mary Jo, rushing up and hugging
Dino. "That's Rupert second, Ludwig third and Guy fourth."

"Do you mind?" said a shrill voice, barging through the circle of
mutual admiration. "I haven't been in yet."

"*Soixante-six*," called the collection ring steward. "*Numero soixante
six.*"

"*Je suis ici*," shouted Fen, ramming her hat down over her nose
and galloping into the ring. Desdemona was only 14.3, little more
than a pony. Her father was a thoroughbred, her mother a polo pony,
and she was fast and nippy, with amazing acceleration between fences,
but, like her mistress, her courage at this stage was much greater than
her technical skill.

Laughing and joking, Ludwig, Dino, Rupert and Guy had their
backs to the ring all admiring the comely Mary Jo. Suddenly they
heard cheering from the crowd and, turning, saw the little roan mare
flying around the ring. She turned in the air over the stile, whipped
over the double and took the wall at full gallop, clearing it by inches.
Jake put his hands over his eyes as she thundered down towards the
combination.

Looking in wonderment through splayed fingers, he saw her pop,
pop, pop over the three fences like a ping-pong ball. Knocking a tenth
of a second off Dino's time, she had to gallop halfway around the ring
before she could pull up. Pink in the face with elation, she made a
discreet but perfectly noticeable V-sign at the group around Mary Jo as
she came out of the ring. Darklis and Isa were yelling like savages.

Jake bawled her out for "bloody irresponsibility". "You could
have brought her down at any moment." Then his face softened, "but
it was a great round."

They were calling for winners. Fen stuck her nose in the air and
rode into the ring. Dino caught up with her. In a white stock, black
coat and the tightest of white breeches, with her newly washed hair

tucked into a net, she was almost unrecognizable as the angry child who'd barged into Rupert's trailer last night.

"Lady, ah sure underestimated you."

Fen ignored him.

"You look real pretty when you're mad, but ah sure wish you'd smile."

"I will when they give me my ribbon."

"Ah thought you were Jake Lovell's groom."

"So I am, so are Isa and Darklis. We all pitch in. Everyone's everything."

"Are you going to ride that pony in the World Championships?"

Fen patted Desdemona lovingly. "No. I'm too young."

"Thank Christ for that," said Dino looking them up and down. "I guess it's only a matter of time though."

News of Rupert's strip poker party and Fen's moonlight flit with his horses spread around the ground like wildfire, only rivaled as gossip by stories of Billy's drinking and speculation as to whether Jake's horse, now registered as Nightshade, was really Macaulay. Then an Italian rider found a bucket of bran in his horse's stables, not put there by any of his entourage, and immediately everyone started panicking about sabotage. Security was tightened up all around. The Americans and the Germans hired security guards with dogs. Even Rupert went so far as employing a man to sleep all night outside Snakepit's stall.

"Terrified Fen'll let him out again," said Dizzy.

"I bet you wouldn't have taken him," she added to Fen, "if you'd known what a sod he can be—only equalled at the moment by his master. I don't know what the hell's the matter with him."

Rupert was missing Billy. In every major competition he'd ever jumped Billy'd been there to fool around with, bounce ideas off and talk out problems. Rupert was too proud to go to Malise for advice. He'd lecture him and then be irritated if Rupert didn't follow the advice. Helen was too ignorant and not basically interested.

Hyped up to a peak of physical fitness, Rupert longed to swim in the sea, but thought it might put his eyes out for the Nations' Cup tomorrow. He longed for a drink, but he'd vowed not to touch a drop till the championship was over. French girls mobbed him, if anything, more than English ones, but he was finding easy lays less and less satisfactory, and Helen's arrival tomorrow would put the kibosh on that. He was also livid with Helen for not bringing out the children. Lavinia de la Tour had offered them the run of Guy's château thirty miles away, but Helen was too nervous about French food and water and rabid dogs and the effect of the heatwave on Marcus's delicate skin. Tab, who Rupert was dying to show off, Helen felt, was too young.

Rupert had never suffered from nerves before, but he didn't want to ride Macaulay in the final. He'd watched the gypsy rabble of the Lovell gang—those beautiful children with their frightful Birmingham accents and their fearlessness swarming all over Jake's horses, polishing and braiding them up, kissing them, playing around their feet as though they were big dogs. He'd never seen horses so relaxed or children so happy. He compared Marcus's cringing terror and he vowed Tab would never grow up like that.

He was drawn to Dino Ferranti, whom he'd met while jumping on the Florida circuit, as he was drawn to Ludwig, as the rich, beautiful and successful are invariably drawn to one another.

Dino reminded Rupert a little of Billy. They were both easygoing and had the same sense of the ridiculous. But at twenty-six, Dino was tougher and more ambitious. He was vainer than Billy too, with his pale silk shirts, his beautiful suits, his expensive cologne and his ash-blond hair that fell perfectly into place, however much he ran his hands through it. But beneath that almost effeminate langour, Dino had a will of iron and a physical strength like Rupert that allowed him to be in the thick of a party until five o'clock in the morning, but still able to wipe the smile off the opposition the next day.

Dino's grandfather had been an Italian immigrant who loved messing around with flowers and had started a small perfume factory. He invented a scent called Ecstasy, which became as famous and enduringly popular as Joy, Arpège or Chanel No. 5. His son, Paco, had a shrewd head and capitalized enough on his father's inventions to become a millionaire, President and founder of Ferranti, Inc., which made all kinds of scents, colognes, soaps and aftershaves, which sold worldwide. Later he diversified and started an engineering business. His three elder sons all went dutifully into the company. But Dino, his favorite, the youngest and most beautiful, rebelled. From an early age he was only interested in horses, riding his own ponies and, even though he was beaten for it, his father's race horses. Assuming he would grow out of this obsession, Paco let his son ride as much as he liked, feeling deeply relieved when Dino reached six feet by the time he was seventeen and would obviously be too tall for a flat-race jockey. At six foot two, he was too tall for a jump jockey and turned instead to show-jumping, but there was no way he could make big money out of the sport in America. His brothers complained he always smelled of the stables and flew off to further the cause of the Ferranti empire whenever he came home.

Deciding to cut his losses, Dino enrolled at an East Coast University to major in business economy. When he took his freshman exams, his papers were exemplary until the last exam, when such was his despair, he staggered in dead drunk in a dinner jacket just as everyone was picking up their pens. Waving a half-empty gin bottle, he proceeded to offer it to other shocked and frantically shushing candidates, before passing out at his desk.

Such was the brilliance of his other papers, all straight A's, that the examiners overlooked such a lapse. Dino was elected president of next year's class. Paco was so delighted that the day Dino was due to come home for the vacation a plane landed on the campus airstrip—Paco's reward for his son's success.

Dino promptly flew home, kissed his mother, and having thanked his father, asked for a private word in the library.

"Dad, business isn't for me."

Paco was astounded. "But you're doing so well."

"I didn't want to embarrass you by having a Ferranti fail, and I guess I hate losing too, but I don't want to spend the rest of my life in an office. You've got other sons to do that. I'm going to jump horses."

Paco sighed: "Still, still, why can't you do both?"

"Because horses need you twenty-four hours a day, just as a successful business does. I'm a great rider, I know it. I want to be up there competing against the best in the world. It is the only life I want to lead."

"Are you asking or telling me?"

"Telling," said Dino gently. "If you're prepared to help me, I'll be eternally grateful. If not, I'll make it on my own."

"You can't make a living out of it."

"In Europe I can." He saw the sadness in his father's eyes. "I'm not a loser. I won't starve. I'd never forgive myself if I didn't try."

Paco looked at his favorite son reflectively. "All straight As—all but one when you were loaded. I never guessed how much you were hating it. That takes guts. Maybe you'll make a go of it. I'll make a deal with you. I'll help you out for the first five years so you can stay in the States."

Five years later, almost to the day, Dino arrived in Les Rivaux.

The World Championships start with a Nations' Cup. The twenty riders who jump in this event who have the least faults go through to the next leg, which consists of three gruelling individual competitions. The four riders who average out the least faults in these go through to the final. A compulsory rest day follows. Then the final takes place in which each of the four riders jump his own horse, and then, in turn, each of the other three riders' horses.

Great Britain had patchy fortunes in the Nations' Cup. Rupert produced two dazzling clears on Snakepit. Humpty, trying to impress a new sponsor, jumped disastrously with over twenty faults in both rounds. Driffield went clear, then went to pieces in the second round. Jake had eight faults in the first round, then went clear.

The Americans jumped brilliantly; so did the Germans, putting them first and second, with the British a poor third. This meant four American riders, four Germans, Rupert, Jake, Wishbone, Piero Fratinelli, the Italian No. 1, a couple of Mexicans and, to the ecstasy of the French crowd, Guy de la Tour, went through to the semi-final.

By the third and final competition of the semi-final Ludwig and Rupert were so far ahead on points that they virtually only had to stand up to get into the last four. The class consisted of ten enormous fences, with a jump off against the clock. Rupert got eight faults, Ludwig twelve, which ensured them a place in the final. Dino went clear. Only Jake and Count Guy were left to jump.

"It'll be you, me, Ludwig and Guy," Rupert said to Dino as he came out of the ring. "One from each country, very suitable."

Jake was so incensed by Rupert's contemptuous assumption that there was no likelihood he would make the final that he was prepared to carry Macaulay over the fences if necessary.

"You must win this class, even to qualify," said Malise, giving Macaulay a pat as Jake rode off into the ring.

Macaulay was obviously determined to give all his supporters a heart attack. Fooling around, pretending to shy at the crowd, bucking and getting up to all sorts of antics between fences, he nevertheless went clear, kicking up his heels as he came out in a sort of equine V-sign.

Everyone got out their calculators, trying to work out whether he was in or not. In came Guy, who was ahead of both Dino and Jake on points. Laughing, handsome, he was turned on by a big crowd, particularly of his own people. He could feel waves of love and admiration like a hot blow dryer.

Coming up to the penultimate fence, a huge upright which had unsettled everyone except Macaulay, Guy's spectacular black gelding, Charlemagne, gave it a mighty clout. Everyone held their breath, but the pole stayed put. Alas, Guy made the mistake of looking around, like Orpheus, and the Eurydice he lost was his place in the championship. His concentration snapped and he put Charlemagne wrong at the combination. The horse hadn't enough impulsion to get far enough over the first element and demolished the second and the third. The crowd groaned. All around the course riders and their retinues were frantically doing sums on their calculators.

"It's worse than math exams," grumbled Fen.

Next moment Malise came up to Jake, with a barely suppressed expression of delight on his face.

"You're in," he said.

Americans were crowding around Dino, punching him on the arm.

"We're in, we're in."

No one dared show any elation in the face of such bitter French despair. Financially and, from the point of view of national morale, it was essential that the host nation had at least one rider in the final. The crowd was too stunned to clap. The commentator was too stunned even to translate into English his announcement that Rupert, Dino, Ludwig and Jake would go through.

Dino and Jake decided not to jump off. They wanted to rest their horses for the final. They rode into the ring together. Twenty thousand francs could be divided between them, but not the huge vase that went to the winner. It looked just like an urn.

"Oh my God, we can't exactly break it in half," said Dino.

"You better keep it, Jake. I'm sure it's to put your ashes in."

Hell, thought Rupert, I'm going to have to ride that black bugger after all.

*I*t was one thing to get through to the final but quite another to have to think about it for the next two days. Ludwig was lucky. The German team liked each other, ate, drank, sightsaw, sunbathed and worked their horses together. All were firmly rooting for Ludwig. A German victory was all that mattered. Dino received the same support from the American team.

Malise sighed and wished he could unite the British in the same way. But Rupert, Humpty and Driffield were all individuals motivated by self-interest and ambition and frantic jealousy. Nor could you expect any solidarity from Jake Lovell, a loner who liked to keep to himself at shows. At earlier shows Billy had kept everyone sweet, particularly Rupert. Now that he was gone tempers and hatreds flared up. Humpty was in despair, knowing that his newly acquired sponsors would be far from happy he hadn't made the final. Rupert and Jake made no secret of their mutual animosity. It was ironic, thought Malise, that they would get more kick from finishing in front of the other than winning the championship.

Determined to create some sense of union, however, Malise insisted that the entire team and their wives, including Fen, go out to dinner that night to celebrate having two British riders in the final. Tomorrow was a compulsory rest day, so it didn't matter if they suffered a few hangovers.

Jake promptly refused on the grounds they couldn't get a babysitter. Alas, they got back to their hotel to find the patron's wife, who had given them frightful rooms on a noisy main road, had suddenly discovered from the evening paper that she was harboring a potential

World Champion. Nothing, she insisted, was too much for Monsieur Lovell. She and her husband would immediately move out of their quiet bedroom overlooking the courtyard, so Jake and Tory could have the double bed and ensure two good nights' sleep before the great ordeal.

All this was overheard by Malise who was staying at the same hotel. Perhaps, he asked, Madame would be prepared to babysit tonight?

To Jake's fury, Madame was only too 'appy. Darklis and Isa would have dinner in the kitchen and watch *The Sound of Music* on television. It is arguable whether Monsieur or Jake felt more like strangling Madame at that moment.

By the time their rooms had been sorted out, Fen, Jake and Tory were the last to arrive for dinner. The restaurant at the end of the town took up the entire ground floor of an eighteenth century château on the edge of an estuary. Gleaming virginia creeper jacketed the walls and threatened to close the shutters. Pale crimson geraniums cascaded into the khaki water.

"Smell that wine and garlic," sighed Fen ecstatically. "Oh, cheer up Jake. At least it'll be a change from hamburgers and Mars bars."

Malise, suntanned and elegant in a cream linen suit and dark blue spotted tie, and Colonel Roxborough, sweating in grey flannel, rose to welcome them. But not before Rupert had turned to Humpty saying, "Here come Prince Charmless and the two ugly sisters."

"Rupert," implored Helen, blushing scarlet. "Hi Jake. Congratulations. I was so excited when I heard you were in."

"As the actress said to the Bishop," said Rupert. "You're priviledged, Jake. You must be the only thing that's excited my dear wife in years. I certainly don't."

Helen had arrived at Les Rivaux after a long, long detour to visit some cathedral, so she had missed seeing him go through to the final. They'd had a row because she refused to sleep with him, insisting she must wash her hair before dinner.

"That's not true. I'm over the moon about you making the final. It's just marvelous to have two British riders there."

"Must be difficult for you, Helen. Do you support us or the Yanks?" asked Humpty.

"Particularly when you see Dino Ferranti," said Humpty's wife, Doreen. "He's out of this world."

"Come and sit down," said Malise. "You go next to Doreen, Jake, and Fen go between me and Rupert, and Tory go on Rupert's other side."

"Tory's going to need a long spoon," said Fen, glaring at Rupert.

"*Touché,*" he said, and laughed.

"What's everyone going to have to drink?" said Colonel Roxborough. Still on the wagon, Rupert?"

"Only till Saturday. Then I'm going to get legless. Christ I'm
starving."

He looked across at a side table where a waiter was slicing up a
long French loaf with a bread knife. "Just imagine that that was one's
cock," he said with a shudder.

Thinking she must make some attempt at conversation, but feeling eighteen and a fat deb again, Tory asked Rupert how Tabitha was.

"Fine," said Rupert and proceeded to totally ignore her, talking
across to Colonel Roxborough about Count Guy's *débâcle* and staring at
a luscious brunette at a table nearby.

Jake longed to rescue Tory but he was trapped by Doreen
Hamilton. Insulated by successive waves of exultation and apprehension at making the final, he looked at the slice of lemon in his gin and
Schweppes, counting the pips, I will win, I won't, I will. Must have
the best of three. There were two pips in Mrs. Hamilton's lemon, I
will, I won't. Despondency struck. Then he looked across at Colonel
Roxborough's glass, two slices, two pips on the top, he bent his head,
three on the bottom, which added up to an uneven number. Relief
overwhelmed him; he would win.

Doreen Hamilton looked at him oddly. "What *are* you doing?"

Jake grinned. "Counting lemon pips. Odd numbers, I win, evens
I don't."

"That's cheating. You start with an odd, so there's more chance of
ending on an odd. Tell me," she lowered her voice, "how is Macaulay
going to behave when Rupert gets on his back."

"Very badly I hope."

Rupert was making no secret of the fact that he found the company boring.

Doreen's incessant chatter gave Jake plenty of opportunity to look
around. Helen, with her sadness and red hair, reminded him of autumn. He noticed the rapt expression on Malise's face as he talked to
her. So that was the way the wind blew. She'd be much happier with
Malise, thought Jake. He'd look after her, but he was far too upright
and old-school-tie to make a play for her.

"Soupe de Bonne Femme." Driffield was looking at the menu.
"What's Bonne Femme?"

"Good woman," said Rupert. "Of absolutely no interest to anyone."

At last the food, and several bottles of wine, arrived.

"I'm sure this octopus comes out of a tin," grumbled Driffield.

"I wish I'd chosen hors d'oeuvres like you, Fen," said Humpty,
looking disconsolately at his piece of *paté* the size of a matchbox.

"I must say I'm terribly hungry," said Fen, spearing an anchovy.

Rupert was eating mushrooms. He glanced up and caught Fen looking at him. "A franc for your thoughts."

"I was hoping one was poisonous."

For a second he stared straight into her eyes, and suddenly it was as though he was putting a spell on her.

"You're going to be a knockout in a couple of years," he said, lowering his voice.

Almost matter-of-factly, as if he were examining a horse, he ran an appraising finger down her cheek. She winced away, aware of the bumpiness of her complexion.

"Those spots would go with regular sex, and you'd lose that puppy fat," he said. "You ought to come and work for me. I'd let you ride in all the senior classes. You're ready for it. That was a stunning win at the beginning of the week. Jake's holding you back."

"Like Revenge, I suppose. I don't forget so quickly," she said, her colour mounting.

"Revenge won two medals," he said. "I'm quite serious. You and I'd make a great team, in bed and out."

He was speaking almost into his buttonhole, so none at the table except her could hear.

"What about Helen?" hissed Fen. "I suppose she doesn't understand you."

For a minute the candlelight flickered on the predatory cold, unsmiling face. Then he laughed, making him human again.

"On the contrary, I don't understand her. She uses much too long words."

Fen gave a scream of laughter. Then, as the smile faded and he went on staring at her, she was appalled to feel her stomach curl, overwhelmed with a squirming helpless longing for him.

Her plate of hors d'oeuvres was taken away, hardly touched.

Humpty looked reproachful. "What a waste!"

Nor could she eat her chicken Kiev.

Jake, deep in conversation with Doreen and Colonel Roxborough about other people's horses, had also drunk a great deal more than he'd eaten. Suddenly he glanced down the table and saw little Fen staring at Rupert. She was curiously still. He'd seen that look in frightened mares confronted by stallions, terrified yet sexually excited. He'd felt the same terror, without excitement, when Revenge was taken away from him. Rupert was not going to take Fen.

He stopped eating his steak, fingering his knife. Helen had noticed it too. Suddenly she stopped talking to Malise about Proust.

"It's like asking me to go over to the Russians," Fen was saying furiously, "and futhermore, I don't like the way you treat your horses."

"You've absolutely no idea how I treat my horses. You just listen to gossip."

"You're only sucking up to me because you think I'll be so overwhelmed by your glamour I'll give you a lot of tips about how Jake rides his horses."

But it was the helpless snapping of courtship.

Desperately Helen turned to Tory. "What's the name of the horse Jake's riding in the final?"

"Christ, she ought to know," thought Fen. "She's married to a finalist."

"He's called Nightshade," mumbled Tory nervously.

"But in the stable we call him Macaulay," said Fen.

"How weird," said Helen. "Rupert had a horse called Macaulay once, named after me. Macaulay was my maiden name."

Rupert's face was a mask.

"It's the same horse," said Fen, slowly spitting out every word.

"It can't be," said Helen bewildered. She turned to Rupert. "He died of a brain tumor. You said he did."

"I did not," said Rupert in a tone that made Fen shiver.

Everyone was listening now.

"I sold him to that Sheik Kalil, who bought half a dozen horses a couple of years ago."

"And you bought him from Kalil?" Helen asked Jake.

"No," said Jake flatly, "I found him in the stone quarries."

"He was pulling a cart loaded with bricks," said Fen, "and he was starving. They don't feed horses out there, or water them, just drive them in the midday sun till they collapse. Then they whip them till they get up again."

A muscle was flickering in Rupert's cheek.

"You've been listening to fairy stories again," he said to Fen.

"We've got photographs," hissed Fen, her fury fuelled by guilt and anger because she found him irresistable. "Jake saved his life. I know you all sneer at all the medical knowledge he picked up from the gypsies, but it bloody well works. And it worked on Macaulay. He was just skin and bone held together by weals. He could hardly walk. It's taken Jake two years to get him right."

Helen looked appalled. "Is this true, Rupert?"

Rupert shrugged his shoulders. "How should I know? If you're prepared to accept any cock-and-bull story. I run my stable on a very tight budget and I can't ensure every horse I sell on is going to be mollycoddled for the rest of its life."

"You sold him to the Middle East," said Fen, knocking over her wine glass as she jumped to her feet. "You must have known what would happen. You ought to be bloody well ashamed of yourself."

Bursting into tears, she fled out of the restaurant.

There was a stunned silence. Rupert picked up his knife and fork and went on eating his steak.

"What's up with her?" said Driffield, looking at the desserts on the menu.

"Perhaps she's eaten something that doesn't agree with her," said Ivor.

"Adolescent girls," said Colonel Roxborough. "Up one moment, down the next. Overemotional. My daughter was like that. It's their age. How old is she?" he asked Tory.

"Sixteen," muttered Tory, staring at her plate. She detested scenes and she felt desperately sorry for Fen, but need she have gone quite so far?

"Probably tired," said Malise.

"Needs a good night's sleep," said Doreen Hamilton comfortably.

"Needs a good screw," said Rupert.

He hadn't noticed that Jake had got to his feet and limped down the table until he was directly behind Rupert.

"What did you say?"

Rupert didn't turn his head. "You heard."

"Yes I heard." Jake's black eyes glittered like deadly nightshade berries, his face ashen against the tousled black hair.

"You leave her alone, you bastard."

"You're hardly in a position to call me that. At least my parents were married to one another, in church too, unlike yours."

"Rupert," exploded Malise.

"You leave my parents out of this," hissed Jake. "I'm warning you, keep away from her."

"Why?" drawled Rupert. "Have you got the hots for her? If you read your prayer book you'd realize that sort of thing's very frowned on. Thou shalt not covet thy wife's sister and all that."

The next moment Jake had grabbed Rupert's shirt collar with one hand and snatched up the bread knife from the side table with the other.

Jerking Rupert towards him, he held the knife against Rupert's suntanned neck.

"Keep your foul mouth shut," he hissed. "If I catch you putting one of your filthy fingers on her, I'll run this through you, you fucking sadist," and very slowly he drew the blade across Rupert's throat. No one moved, no one spoke. Everyone's eyes were mesmerised by the knife blade flickering in the candlelight.

Then Helen gave a strangled sob.

"Jake," said Malise quietly, "give me that knife."

"It's all right Colonel Gordon," said Jake, without looking in his direction. "This time it's a warning, Rupert, but you heard me, you stay away from her. Next time you won't get off so lightly."

He threw the knife down so if fell across Fen's red wine stain, giving an illusion of spilt blood, then limped out of the restaurant.

"Are you all right?" gasped Helen.

Rupert sprang to his feet, ready to give chase. But Malise was too quick. Leaping up, he blocked Rupert's path.

"No," he said sharply. He might have been speaking to a rabid dog about to pounce. "Stay—here. It was *all* your fault."

Rupert looked at him incredulously.

"That man has just tried to kill me."

"There's a simple remedy to that," said Malise. "Don't wind him up."

"Bloody bad form," said Colonel Roxborough. "Fellow can't hold his drink. Let's have some brandy. Think we all need it."

"I want some *crêpes suzette,*" said Driffield.

Rupert sat down, his face absolutely still.

Malise looked round. "None of this is to go any further than this table. We don't want the press getting hold of it. Rupert was simply taking trouble to be nice to Fen; she overreacted because she's protective about Macaulay. Jake overreacted because he's protective about both her and the horse. Isn't that true, Tory?"

Blushing scarlet, Tory mumbled that Jake was probably uptight about the final and she better see where he'd got to, and thanking Malise for a lovely dinner, she stumbled out of the restaurant, knocking over a chair as she went.

"Tory the elephant packed her trunk and said goodbye to the circus," said Rupert.

Fen didn't stop running until she got to the stables. It was dark now, a huge full moon with a smudged apricot-pink face gazed down at her reproachfully. How could she have let herself go like that?

She went straight to Macaulay's stall. He was enchanted to see her and nuzzled her pockets enquiringly as she sobbed into his solid black neck.

"Oh Mac, I'm sorry. I should never have said all those awful things. Malise'll never pick me for the team now."

Gradually her sobs subsided as Macaulay stood in silent titanic sympathy.

"You're such a duck," she said in a choked voice. "Please buck that pig off the day after tomorrow."

She heard a step outside. Jake, Malise, Rupert? She couldn't talk to anyone. She melted into the dark of the box behind Macaulay. The top half-door was stealthily opened. Behind Macaulay's stalwart frame she couldn't see who it was. Then she heard the clank of a bucket being lowered, hitting the water bucket. Then the door was shut and bolted.

"Hell." She was locked in for the night.

Next minute the ever-greedy Macaulay had shot towards the door and she heard the sound of munching. Desperately she snatched the bucket from him.

"No, Darling, you mustn't eat it. We don't know what it is."

Snorting with exasperation, Macaulay pursued her round the box. Suddenly the top half of the door was opened again.

"Who is it?" she said in terror.

"What the hell are you doing here?" said Jake.

"Talking to Mac."

"Disturbing his beauty sleep more likely. You OK?" he added more gently.

"Yes, but look what someone's put in his stall." She held up the bucket.

Jake lit a match and then whistled. "Jesus Christ!"

"What is it?"

"Beet, unsoaked," he said grimly. "Someone's trying to nobble him."

"Rupert," said Fen.

Jake shook his head. "He's still in the restaurant. Might be one of his supporters, but I don't thinks it's Rupert's form. Too easily traced, and he's just longing for a chance to make me look silly in the final. More likely some Kraut fanatic or one of the Yanks. Brits don't nobble Brits. All the same, we'll have to take turns to sleep outside the stall. I'll stay here tonight. You go back and share our double bed with Tory."

"You ought to get a decent night's sleep."

"I'm so bloody tired I'd sleep on a bed of nails."

Back in their hotel, still wearing a pale grey silk petticoat, Helen Campbell-Black removed her makeup with a shaking hand, turning her head to catch different reflections in the three-sided mirror. Rupert was already in bed, watching a tape on the rented video machine of Clara jumping. Every so often he froze the film so he could study the angle of Ludwig's body or the position of his hands. Each jump was played over and over again. Then he got up and strolled naked across the room, changing the tape to one of Dino jumping President's Man in Florida. The horse was young and inexperienced, giving each fence at least a foot, because he hadn't yet learned to tuck his legs under him. Manny, as Dino called him, would need much more riding in the Final. Rupert could see Dino carefully positioning him at each fence. Pity there wasn't any film of Hopalong jumping Macaulay.

As Helen picked up a different jar to remove her eye makeup she caught a glimpse of Rupert in the mirror with his back to her. He must have lost ten pounds. He'd always had a marvelous physique, but now he was trimmed down to a leaner, even more muscular hardness. He seemed to burn with excess energy and restlessness. I must be married to the most desirable man in the world, she thought despairingly, so why do I feel so undesiring? Since the affair with Podge, she'd tried so hard to make advances, to be more imaginative, but it was as though he pressed the freeze button on her each time, turning her to stone, robbing her of any spontaneity.

Was he attracted to Fen, she wondered, or had he just been baiting Jake? She knew Jake pulling a knife wouldn't put him off in the least. Malise had dismissed the incident as a drunken brawl, but she was frightened by the obsessive black hatred in Jake's eyes.

She delayed coming to bed as long as possible, praying that Rupert might fall asleep. But when she finally came out of the bathroom, he had turned off the television and was lying on the bed, looking at the latest photographs of the children she'd brought from England. He flipped past the ones of Marcus with hardly a glance, but examined every angle of Tab's sweet pink face. Perhaps Tab would be the one female in his life he could love unstintingly without despising her or himself.

"Take your nightdress off," he said without even looking up.

Helen sighed and complied.

Rupert pulled her towards him, not even bothering to kiss her. I'll be so dry inside, she thought in panic, and he's so huge it's going to hurt. Instinctively her mind and her body went rigid. His cock reminded her suddenly of the grey stone gargoyles jutting, hard and ugly, out of the walls of the cathedral.

"What's the matter?" Rupert prised her legs open with his hand.

"Jake pulling the knife, I can't get it out of my mind."

"What aspect of it?" he said mockingly. "Were you turned on by such a macho display on Jake's part, or the thought of being a rich widow?"

"Oh stop it," sobbed Helen.

"Or were you jealous of Fen?"

"She's only a child," gasped Helen, as fingers moved up inside her. "It's not fair."

"To her or you?" said Rupert. "Look, do you honestly think I'm going to flirt with a fat pustular schoolgirl for any other reason than to rile Hopalong Chastity? And I certainly succeeded. None of the Lovell contingent'll get any sleep tonight."

"And what about Macaulay?"

"You never bothered about him when I had him. And solicitude now seems a bit out of place."

He took her then. Helen lay back, quite unable to participate. It was over in a couple of minutes and she was certain he'd been thinking about Fen.

Tense and miserable, she knew she should drop the subject, but she couldn't help warning Rupert to stay away from Fen. Jake was obviously unbalanced about her. When he didn't answer, she thought he was really taking in what she said. It was five minutes before she realized he was fast asleep.

Rupert was right. None of the Lovell contingent slept. Fen, lying on one edge of the bed, couldn't stop thinking about Rupert. "My only love sprung from my only hate," she whispered to herself, as Helen had whispered five years earlier. Tory lay on the edge of the other side. She was worried about Jake. A row like that was the last thing he needed before the final. She felt even more guilty that she was suddenly racked with jealousy of Fen, her baby sister who was growing more beautiful every day. Rupert, who had never treated Tory with anything but contempt, had really taken trouble to charm Fen, and she too had seen the black hatred in Jake's face when he held that knife to Rupert's throat. She tried to tell herself that Jake was fiercely protective of anything he owned, particularly his family. She tried to suppress the thought that Jake was falling in love with Fen.

Jake, after an hour's deep sleep, was woken by the barking of the rotweiller guarding Ludwig's horses. Hatred of Rupert, churning around and round in his head, prevented him dropping off again. Next morning, despite all Malise's stipulations, the story of the knife incident was all around the show ground.

Grooming the horses next day, Fen found she had never been the recipient of so much attention. The public flowed by to get a glimpse of a possible future champion. Suddenly every German, American and English groom rider seemed to have time to stop and gossip, and ask her how she and Macaulay were getting on, what he was like to ride, what sort of temperament he had. Watching the Lovell children swarming all over him, they could be excused for thinking he was as mild as an old sheep.

Dino Ferranti rolled up about midday.

"Hi." he said.

"Buzz off," said Fen, applying the body brush with more vigor.

"That is a cute horse, and you sure have a cute ass when you're grooming him. How's he feeling today?"

"Just fine," snapped Fen.

"I really like him. Jake's smart; doesn't jump him that often, does he? Pulls him out for the big event. I never heard of him before this week."

Fen turned, pink from exertions and anger. "Don't smarm over me just because you want information about Mac. I'm not telling you anything about him."

"Honey, you're over-reacting. I admire your boss. How'd you like to have dinner with me tonight?"

"No thanks."

"We won't mention Macaulay once, right. I just need an attractive girl to help me relax."

"Why should I help you relax? You're the opposition."

He really is attractive, she thought reluctantly, lounging against
the door, with that wide untroubled smile and the marvellously relaxed elongated body. He shook his head.

"You ought to get out. There's more to show-jumping that the
inside of a tack-cleaning bucket. You ought to have some fun. Anyway," he added slyly, "I am just dying to hear what happened last
night. Did Jake really pull a carving knife on Rupert? You must be the
most fought-over girl in France."

"Shut up," hissed Fen, blushing to the roots of her sweating hair.
"I don't want to discuss it. Now please go away."

Later in the day all the finalists tried to relax. Leaving Helen to
visit the house in which Proust spent his childhood, Rupert went racing with County Guy and Lavinia, and had three winners which
seemed a good omen. The copy of the *Evening Standard,* specially flown
in for Patric Walker's horoscope, also predicted Scorpios would have an
exciting and successful weekend. So he felt he could legitimately relax.
The German team swam and sunbathed together. The Americans took
a plane to Paris and went sightseeing. Jake took Tory, Fen and the
children for a picnic in the Brittany countryside, finding a perfect
place shaded by a glimmering silver poplar copse by the side of a
meandering river. Tory and Tanya slept, the children swam and made
daisy-chains with Fen. Jake wandered off with binoculars, revelling in
the wild flowers and butterflies. He found a very rare orchid, stocked
up on the medicine cupboard and also, to his joy, discovered a clump
of tansy, so he had a fresh lucky sprig to put in his left boot for tomorrow.

Night fell. Jake and Tory were safely in bed at the hotel. In a
sleeping-bag outside Macaulay's stall Fen took her position with Lester
the teddy bear. It was quiet and very hot. All she could hear was the
occasional stamp of a horse and the sound of Rupert's bodyguard pacing up and down outside Snakepit's stall. The indigo sky was overcrowded with stars. Too many, like my pimples, thought Fen. They
suddenly seemed to have doubled. It must be her period coming, perhaps that was why she was so jumpy.

Now she was alone she could think about Rupert—and Dino. She
was in such a muddle. Jake had kept her so busy over the past three
years that truthfully there had been no time for men in her life, except
for her long-distance crush on Billy Lloyd-Foxe. Now she was assailed
by all kinds of longings and despairs. If only she were Helen, able to
roll up at the championship tomorrow with gleaming hair, bathed, in
a beautiful uncreased dress after eight hours sleep. She hated Rupert,

and Dino, who had only asked her out because he wanted to pump her, but it made her realize how much she was missing by devoting herself so exclusively to horses. If only she felt tired. She stiffened as a step approached. Then she caught a waft of scent. It was Dino.

"Couldn't sleep. No point in jumping rounds in my head, so I just came by to check no one's been after Manny."

"They haven't," said Fen.

"D'you want a drink?" He produced a flask from his pocket. "It's only bourbon. I've only had two drinks all evening. Christ, I'd like to get looped. May I talk with you for a few minutes?"

He slid down the stable wall beside her so his long legs were bent at an acute angle. In the faint light, she could see the perfect profile.

"Are you nervous?"

He nodded. "Sounds kinda girl scout, but I don't want to let the team down—they've been so great—or the horse, or my Daddy or Mumma. They were great, too, to back me. I guess none of us needs the money like Jake. How come he hates Rupert so much?"

Fen explained about the bullying at school and the barrage of insults and the annexing of Revenge and the cruelty to Macaulay.

"Guess that's enough to be going along with," said Dino, handing her his bourbon flask. He noticed with a flicker of encouragement that she didn't bother to wipe the neck before she drank.

"Jake's terribly torn," explained Fen. "He wants to beat Rupert so badly, but he's crucified at the thought of what it might do to Macaulay's confidence having Rupert on his back again. It must be hell, like going to a wife-swapping party on one's honeymoon."

Dino laughed: "Yeah, that just about sums it up. I'm kind of ambivalent about Rupert too. I really like the guy. He makes me laugh, but that was before I met his wife."

"What about her?" Fen tried to sound casual.

"Well, she's so beautiful, I mean seriously beautiful. The way he carries on with girls. They were coming out of his ears on the Florida circuit, and boy, they threw themselves at him. I figured he'd made some kind of marriage of convenience to some dog. Then I had dinner with them this evening. I mean, how could you cheat on that? Christ, I'd never let her out of my sight, and he treats her like shit, putting her down all the time. I was appalled. Doesn't she have anyone on the side? She could get anyone."

"I've never heard anything about other men. I think she's too frightened of Rupert, and so are the men. One of the Italian team kept her too long on the dance floor once and his hands started to travel, and Rupert hit him across the room."

"That figures—like Hamadryad baboons."

"Like what—"

"Huge baboons that live in the desert in Abyssinia. They're more interested in fighting off other male baboons than in screwing their wives. In fact they neglect their wives when there's no one to fight off. I'm telling you, I'm going to be in Britain for Crittleden and I am going to make one hulluva pitch. She doesn't deserve that kind of treatment."

"I wonder if Jake's getting any sleep," said Fen.

"Shouldn't guess so. It's like Henry V on the Eve of Agincourt. I better go get some insomnia. Night, honey, this time tomorrow we'll be bombed on euphoria or despair."

Lying awake at the hotel, Jake looked at his watch—three o'clock. Within fourteen hours he'd know if he'd pulled the mightiest from their seats. His good leg ached because it hadn't been relaxed with sleep. He kept breaking out in a cold sweat at the thought of riding Snakepit. He knew he wasn't strong enough to hold him. If he fell off and wrecked himself, there wasn't anyone to ride the horses. He also knew Tory had been awake all night beside him. Thank God she knew when to keep her trap shut.

"Tory," he said, reaching out for her.

"Yes." She put her arms round him. "Do you want to talk, or turn on the light and read?"

She could feel him shaking his head in the darkness.

"It's going to be all right. Horses always go well with you. You're going to win."

"I wish I was riding Sailor."

"He'd have looked after you, but he might have looked after the others a bit too well. Macaulay hasn't got such a conscience."

She slid her hand down the empty hollow of his belly and touched his cock.

"Would that help?"

"It might, but I won't be much use to *you*."

"I don't need it." The bedsprings creaked as she clambered down the bed, then he felt the warm soft caress of her lips and the infinite tenderness of her tongue. Because he knew she liked doing it, there was no hurry, no tension.

"I was so right to marry you," he mumbled.

Tory was filled with an overwhelming happiness. In the eight years of their marriage, he'd probably paid her as many compliments, but when they came they were worth everything. She felt bitterly ashamed that she had wasted so much emotion being jealous of Fen.

Rupert got up and dressed.

"Where are you going?" said Helen.

"For a walk. It's too hot. I can't sleep."

"Oh darling, you must rest. Shall I come with you?"

"No, go back to sleep."

A quarter of an hour later he paused beside Fen, her long hair fanning out, already slightly damp from the dew, teddy bear clutched in her arms. He toyed with the idea of waking her, but she needed sleep. He'd put her on ice for a later date. As he pulled the sleeping bag round her, she clutched the teddy bear tighter, muttering "Don't forget to screw in the studs."

When he let himself into the van Dizzy hardly stirred in her sleep, smiled and opened her arms. Rupert slid into them.

Ludwig von Schellenberg had such self-control that he willed himself into eight hours' dreamless sleep.

World Championship day dawned. There were a couple of small classes in the morning to keep the rest of the riders happy, but all interest was centered on the four finalists. Each stall was a hive of activity; braiding and polishing and everyone giving everyone else advice. It was hotter than ever. In the trailer Jake watched television, trying to steady his nerves, and wondered if there was any hope of keeping down the cup of tea and dry toast he'd had for breakfast. Tory was frying eggs, bacon and sausages for the children (it didn't look as though anyone would have time to cook them a decent meal before the evening) and at the same time ironing the lucky socks, breeches, shirt, tie and red coat that Jake had worn in each leg of the competition. The new tansy lay in the heel of the highly polished left boot. Jake had seen one magpie that morning, but had been cheered up by the sight of a black cat, until Driffield informed him that black cats were considered unlucky in France. Milk cartons, cans, and eggshells in the garbage bucket were beginning to smell. Fen was studying a German dictionary:

"It doesn't give the German for 'whoa'. You'll have to fall back on *Dummkopf, Lieberlein* and *Achtung*."

"Or *Auf Wiedersehen*," said Jake, "as Clara bucks me off and gallops off into the sunset. By the way, remember that red T-shirt you wore when Revenge won at Olympia?"

"I've got it here," said Fen.

"D'you mind wearing it this afternoon?"

Fen did mind very much; it was impossibly hot and she'd got very burnt yesterday, and the red T-shirt would clash with her face. But it was Jake's day, she mustn't be selfish.

"Of course not," she said.

Jake was encouraged by the number of telegrams. British hopes obviously rested with Rupert, but Jake had generated an enormous amount of good will. People were obviously delighted to see him back at the top again. There were telegrams from the Princess and one from the Colonel of the Regiment at Knightsbridge Barracks, who'd somehow discovered that their old horse Macaulay had ended up with Jake. The one that pleased him most was from Miss Blenkinsop in the Middle East. He knew that she, as much as he, enjoyed the sheer pleasure of showing the world that he could succeed with a horse Rupert had thrown out. Every time Macaulay won anything, he'd religiously taken ten percent of the winnings and sent them to Miss Blenkinsop for her Horse Rescue hospital. If he won today, she would get £1,000.

If he won. "Oh my God," he said, and bolted out of the trailer through a crowd of reporters towards the outside lavatory where he threw up his breakfast.

"Why don't you bloody well go away?" shouted Fen to the reporters. "You know you won't get any sense out of him before a big class."

In the end they had to be content with interviewing Darklis, who sat on a hay bale, smiling up at them with huge black eyes.

"My Daddy's been thick four times this morning. He doesn't theem to like French food. I love it. We've had steak and chips every single night."

At last there was the course to walk, which made Jake feel even worse. It was far bigger than he'd imagined. The water jump was wider than the channel. The heavy thundery blue sky seemed to rest on the huge soaring oxblood-red wall, and Jake could actually stand underneath the poles of the parallel.

Malise, walking beside him, winced at the French marigolds, clashing with purple petunias and scarlet geraniums in the pots on either side of each fence. How could the French have such exquisite color sense in their clothes and not in their gardening?

A couple of English reporters sidled up to them. "Did you really pull a knife on Rupert, Gyppo."

"Bugger off," said Malise. "He's got to memorize the course. Do you want a British victory or not? That's tricky," he added to Jake, looking at the distance between the parallels and the combination. "It's on a half-stride. The water's a brute. You'll get hardly any run in there. You'll need the stick."

"Macaulay never needs a stick," said Jake through frantically chattering teeth. The sheer impossibility of getting Snakepit, let alone President's Man, over any of the fences paralyzed him with terror.

Rupert walked with Colonel Roxborough, wearing dark glasses but no hat against the punishing Brittany sun. He seemed totally oblivious of the effect he was having on the French girls in the crowd. The German team walked together, so did the Americans. Count Guy, in a white suit made by Yves St. Laurent, was the object of commiseration. Over his great disappointment now, he shrugged his shoulders philosophically. At least he didn't have to jump four rounds in this heat and his horses would be fresh for Crittleden next week.

In the collecting ring Ivor Braine had been cornered by the press and was telling them in his broad Yorkshire accent that he was convinced Jake had been brandishing a knife because the steaks were so tough.

"I wish Saddleback Sam had made it," said Humpty for the one thousandth time.

Driffield was busy selling a horse at a vastly inflated price to one of the Mexican riders.

"Wish it was a wife-riding contest," said Rupe. "I wouldn't mind having a crack at Mrs. Ludwig, although I would draw the line at Mrs. Lovell."

Once again he wished Billy were there. He'd never needed his advice more, or his silly jokes to lower the tension. Obviously drunk at ten o'clock in the morning, Billy had already called to wish him luck.

Rupert had asked after Janey. Billy had laughed bitterly: "She's like a wet log fire, if you don't watch her all the time,she goes out."

Next week, reflected Rupert grimly, he was going to have to take Janey out to lunch and tell her to get her act together.

Despite the lack of a French rider in the final, all the publicity had attracted a huge crowd. There wasn't an empty seat or an inch of rope unleaned over anywhere. Malise sighed. If there was a British victory, all the glare of bad publicity over the feuds between riders might be forgotten. He watched Rupert, cool as an icicle, putting Snakepit over huge jumps in the collecting ring. Jake was nowhere to be seen, probably being sick again.

At two o'clock each of the four finalists came on, led by their own band. Ludwig came first to defend his title on the mighty Clara, yellow brow-band matching the yellow knots in her braids. Her coat was the color of oak leaves in autumn, her huge chest like a steamer funnel. Unruffled by the crowd, her eyes shone with wisdom and kindness.

Then came Dino on the slender President's Man, who looked almost foal-like in his legginess. The same liver chestnut as Clara, he seemed half her size. Dino lounged totally relaxed in the saddle, like a young princeling, his olive skin only slightly paler than usual, hat tipped over his nose, as though he was taking the piss out of the whole proceedings.

Then Rupert, eyes narrowed against the sun, the object of whirring video cameras and cheers from the British contingent, not shifting in the saddle as the plunging eyerolling Snakepit shied at everything and fought for his head.

And finally Jake, his set face as white as Macaulay's, who strutted along pointing his big feet, enjoying the cheers.

Like a council of war, the four riders lined up in front of the President's box, the bands forming a brilliant scarlet and gold square behind them. Les Rivaux can seldom have produced a more breathtaking spectacle, with the flags, limp in the heat, the scarlet coats, the plumes of the soldiers, the gleaming brass instruments, the grass emerald green from incessant sprinkling, the forest which seemed to smoulder in its dark green midgy stillness and in the distance the speedwell-blue gleam of the sea. The bands launched into the National anthem, each crash of cymbal and drum sending Snakepit and President's Man cavorting around in terror. Macaulay and Clara stood like statues at either end of the row.

Fen, body aching from grooming, fingers sore from braiding, her red T-shirt drenched with sweat, waited for Macaulay to return to the collecting ring. She was far more nervous than usual. She had a far bigger part to play. With the three other grooms she would spend the competition in the cordoned-off part of the arena and change Jake's saddle on to each new horse. Nearby was Dizzy, braless and ravishing in a pink T-shirt, her newly washed blond hair trailing pink ribbons. One day I'm going to look as good as her, vowed Fen. Then she had another look at the vast fences. How absolutely terrifying for Jake. The field emptied, large ladies bustled around with tape measures, checking poles for the last time.

"I've bet £100 on Campbell-Black," said the Colonel in an undertone to Malise. "I reckon it'll be a jump-off between him and Ludwig, with the American third and Lovell nowhere. He simply hasn't got the nerve."

Helen, seeing the riders in their red coats, was reminded of he first day she met Rupert out hunting.

"Dear God," she prayed, "please restore my marriage and make him win."

Tory, in the riders' stand, with Darklis and Isa, prayed that Jake would win.

"I wonder when Daddy's going to be thick again," said Darklis.

Then a hush fell as in came Ludwig. As he rode past the President's box and took off his hat, the rest of the German team, who'd all been at the champagne, rose to their feet, shooting up their hands in a Heil Hitler salute, to the apoplexy of Colonel Roxborough who went as scarlet as his carnation.

The only sound was the snort of the horse, the thunder of hoofs and the relentless ticking of the clock. Girding her great chestnut loins, a symbol of reliability, Clara jumped clear.

Malise lit a cigar. "At least we know it's jumpable," he said.

Dino came in, talking quietly to the young horse.

"That's a pretty horse," said Malise.

"And a pretty rider," thought Helen, who was sitting near him.

Being so much slighter, President's Man seemed to go twice as fast. Dino's thrusting acrobatic style and almost French elegance and good looks soon had the crowd cheering. He also went clear.

Then came Rupert, hauling on the plunging Snakepit's mouth, heating him up so he fought for his head all the way around. By some miracle of timing and balance, he too went clear, and Snakepit galloped out of the ring giving two colossal bucks and nearly trampling a crowd of photographers under foot.

"God help those who come after," sighed Malise.

"I'm not taking a penny less than £30,000," said Driffield.

Fen gave Macaulay a last minute pat and a kiss.

"Good luck. Remember you're the greatest, and remember what you've got to avenge."

Jake looked suddenly grey. "I can't go in."

"Yes you can. You're doing it for Macaulay and Miss Blenkinsop."

"I'm going to throw up."

"No you are not. Keep your mouth shut and off you go."

"*Numero Quatre*," called the collecting ring steward irritably.

Jake rode into the ring, obviously quite untogether. He might never have been on a horse in his life. He had the first fence down, and the second he took completely wrong, so Macaulay stumbled and nearly came down on the hard ground. Then he hit the third.

"Twelve faults." thought Tory in despair.

"He's blown it," drawled Dino.

"Oh my God," said Fen. In anguish she watched the tenths of seconds pirouetting on the clock as Jake pulled Macaulay up to a standstill, stroked his neck, spoke to him and started again.

"Can't even ride his own horse," said Rupert scathingly. "It was a freak he got to the final anyway."

"He's bound to get time faults," said Colonel Roxborough.

Jake set off again in a somewhat haphazard fashion and cleared the rest of the ten fences, but never really connected all the way round, notching up three and one half time faults.

He shook his head as he rode up to Fen.

"A great start, huh?"

"Competition's young, you wait," she said, giving Macaulay a lemon drop. Then, when Jake had dismounted, she removed the saddle, which had to be put on Snakepit, the horse Jake was riding next.

"You've got three minutes to warm him up," she said looking at her watch.

"Needs cooling down if you ask me."

Ludwig's groom came over to collect Macaulay, who went off looking very put out, turning his head continually to gaze back reproachfully at Jake. Jake went up to Snakepit, who flattened his ears and rolled his eyes.

"Now you'll get your come-uppance," Dizzy hissed at him.

In the roped-off arena Macaulay did several wild jumps, nearly unseating Ludwig. He didn't like the discipline of the German rider. He went into the ring, a mulish martyred expression on his white face.

"Look at the old moke," giggled Fen. "Isn't he lovely?"

Despite the disapproval, however, Macaulay gave Ludwig a good ride and went clear.

"Interesting what the horse can do when it gets a proper rider on its back," said Rupert.

Dino went in on Clara. He was very nervous and gave Clara very little help, but each time he put her wrong she was so well trained she got him out of trouble, rising like a helicopter off her mighty hocks.

Jake didn't want to watch Rupert on President's Man. He was getting acquainted with Snakepit. He spent several minutes rubbing his ears, smoothing his sweating lathered neck, talking to him softly and giving him pieces of sugar. Faced with the challenge of a new horse, he was too interested to be nervous.

Next minute he was up, determined not to hang on the horse's mouth. He went on talking to him. Snakepit was so short in front it was like sitting on the edge of a cliff, a cliff that might crumble any minute and turn into an earthquake. He rode quietly round for one of the two minutes left, stroking and still talking, then put him over a jump, letting him have his head. Suddenly Snakepit seemed to sweeten up.

"What d'you reckon?"

"Very good," said Fen. "Must be a nice change for him, like a weekend on the Riveria after working in a factory."

Cheers from the ring indicated Rupert had gone clear on President's Man, urging him on by sheer brute force and driving power. The horse, however, was upset.

Jake rode Snakepit into the ring. Snakepit tugged at the bridle and found no one hauling him back, so he stopped pulling and gave Jake one of the easiest rides in his life.

As they came to the upright Jake, out of sheer nervousness, hooked him up a stride too short, but Snakepit, revelling in his new-found freedom, made a mighty effort and cleared the fence easily.

"Bloody hell," said Rupert. "He'd have stopped if I'd done that to him."

"Looks a different horse," said Malise in a pleased voice. Having insisted that Jake was selected, he was desperate for him to ride well.

The Colonel grunted. "Still going to win my bet."

At the end of the second round everyone was clear except Jake, who was on fifteen and one half faults. The crowd was beginning to get bored. They wanted trouble, crashes, upsets and falls. It was Ludwig's turn to ride Snakepit.

"I vas in two brains vether to ride heem. I've got a vife and children," said Ludwig to Jake, "but after zat round, I doubt if I'll have any trouble wiz him."

Snakepit, however, thought otherwise. He didn't like the harsher more rigid style of the German, who, like Rupert, wouldn't give him his head. He deliberately knocked down the upright and kicked out the second part of the combination.

Rupert had no trouble going clear on Clara.

Jake, who was warming up President's Man, couldn't resist having a look at Dino on Macaulay.

"The American chef d'equipe told him to give Mac a good whack at the water," said Fen gleefully, "and Dino's neglected to take off his spurs too."

"Jesus, it's like riding a charging elephant," muttered Dino to himself. "Hasn't he got any brakes?"

Macaulay lolloped crossly into the ring, with a mulish expression on his face. "I'm not a seaside donkey giving rides," he seemed to say, as he ran out at the upright. Then, having been given a clout with the bat, he jumped it but proceeded to bring the wall tumbling down.

"Joshua at the battle of Jericho," said Fen.

Coming down to the water Macaulay ground to a halt, then jumped the small brush fence with no effort at all, landing with a huge splash in the middle of the water, absolutely soaking Dino. Then he put his head down and started to drink. The crowd, particularly the Lovell children, screamed with laughter.

Dino finished the course and rode out grinning. "I did not expect an impromptu shower," he said to his team mates.

"That round's probably lost him the championship," muttered Fen. "He's a good loser."

President's Man was frightened, puzzled and muddled. Having been broken and trained by Dino, he'd seldom carried other riders on his back. But now he liked the gentle hands and the caressing singsong voice of the man on his back. Trying to imitate Dino's acrobatic style, Jake managed to coax a beautiful clear out of him.

"Bloody hell," said Dino, shaking his head. "You'd figure Manny'd want to avenge me after what Macaulay did to me."

It was the start of the last round. The excitement was beginning to bite, the crowd had woken up.

"This is a gymkhana event," grumbled Colonel Roxborough. "I'd never have let my Baskerville Boy go in for this."

"Rupert's on zero, Ludwig's got eight faults, Dino eleven, Jake fifteen and a half, but he's got the easiest round to come," said Malise, who was busy with his calculator.

Ludwig rode in first on President's Man. The young horse was really tired and confused now. He had jumped his heart out for three clears; he'd had enough. Like Snakepit, he preferred the gentleness of his last rider. Despite brilliant tactics from Ludwig, he knocked up eight faults.

"Glory alleluia," said Fen, rushing up to Jake as he mounted Clara, "Ludwig's got half a fault more than you now."

Riding Clara was like driving a Lamborghini. With the slightest touch of the leg she seemed to surge forward. Jake had never known such acceleration. He felt humble to be riding such a horse. The crowd was growing restless again. With three clears under his belt, Rupert was obviously going to walk it.

"Oh dear, oh dear," said Fen with a total lack of sympathy. "Snakepit's carting Dino."

Snakepit, thoroughly over the top, galloped around the ring, taking practically every fence with him, notching up twenty-four faults.

"Actually he did bloody well to stay on," Fen conceded, as Snakepit carried Dino unceremoniously out of the ring.

"I think I've won my bet," said Colonel Roxborough.

"Looks like a British victory," said Malise, wishing he felt more elated.

"Rupert used to own that horse," said the Colonel smugly. "He'll find him a piece of cake."

Macaulay thought differently. Rupert had decided not to warm Macaulay up. The horse had already jumped three rounds and anyway, when Rupert had gone up to him, Macaulay had promptly flattened his ears, given a furious squeal of rage and recognition and struck at him like a cobra. Rupert only just jumped out of the way in time.

"Don't look," said Fen to Jake. "It'll only upset you. Concentrate on Clara."

"I think Rupert needs our help," said Colonel Roxborough.

Humpty, Malise, Driffield, Colonel Roxborough, Dizzy and Tracey all stood around Macaulay's head, holding on to his bridle for grim death as he stood at the entrance to the arena.

They blocked Macaulay's view as Rupert got onto his back, but he knew instantly. He seemed to tremble in terror, his ears glued to his head, his eyes seemed all whites in a white face.

But with six of them hanging on, he could do nothing.

"In you go," said Colonel Roxborough. "Good luck."

They all jumped away as Macaulay shot forward. The moment he got into the ring, he went up on his hind legs, huge feet shadow boxing, his white face suddenly a mask of malevolence. Then he came down.

"Oh look," said Fen in ecstasy. "He's not going to fail us."

Taking no notice of Rupert's brutally sawing hands, Macaulay went into a rodeo act, bucking and bucking and cat-jumping and circling in the air, frantic to get Rupert off.

"He ought to join the Royal Ballet," said Fen.

Ivor's mouth was open so long a fly flew in. Even Driffield stopped selling his horse.

"Do something," said Helen frantically to Malise. "He's going to kill him."

"With any luck," muttered Fen.

"Dear God," said Jake in misery, "I should never have subjected Macaulay to this."

It was amazing Rupert stayed in the saddle so long. Macaulay's mouth was bleeding badly now, bits of red foam flying everywhere. It was quite obvious to the crowd that the great black horse, like a maddened bull, had only one aim in life—to get the rider off his back.

Rupert plunged his spurs in and brought his whip with an almighty thwack down on Macaulay's quarters.

"You can't shift me, you black bugger," he said through gritted teeth.

"Oh la la, quelle domage," said Fen happily. *"Oh, bien fait Macaulay."*

Dino shot her a sidelong glance. "You're being kind of unsporting," he drawled as a final maddened buck sent Rupert flying through the air. It was lucky he let go of the reins. A second later Macaulay had jammed on his brakes and swung round in pursuit. Rupert had never run so fast in his life. As he dodged behind the wall Macaulay followed him, squealing with rage, teeth bared. The crowd was in an uproar.

"Stop him," screamed Helen. "Someone do something."

Rupert had shot into the oxer now, hiding behind the brush part, peering out from a lot of sky blue cinerarias like Ferdinand the Bull. Macaulay was too angry to be thwarted. He cantered around to the other side, where Rupert was only protected by a large pole, and went for him, darting his head under the pole, only missing by inches.

Rupert ran out of the oxer, belting towards the combinations, taking refuge in the third element, which was a triple only two hundred and fifty yards from the collecting ring.

"I don't know why he doesn't take up broad-jumping." said Fen. "He'd certainly qualify for the Olympics."

Malise strode up to the French chief steward.

"You must send in the arena party to head him off," he said.

"And get them keeled," said the steward. "He is still within the time limit."

The squeak of the elimination hooter went off at that moment, making everyone jump out of their skins. Macaulay was prowling round and round the triple, darting his head at Rupert, tail swishing furiously, quivering with rage.

"That horse doesn't seem very keen on Rupert," said Ivor Baine.

"Hardly surprising," said Humpty. "It used to belong to him."

Four *gendarmes* entered the ring, gingerly fingering their pistols. Macaulay turned, revving up for another charge. Rupert snatched up one of the poles. It was extremely heavy. As Macaulay advanced, Rupert brandished it at him.

The collecting ring steward rushed up to Jake. "I theenk Meester Lovell, you better go and collect your horse."

At that moment Macaulay reared up, striking at Rupert, only missing him by inches, knocking the pole from his hands.

Rupert backed away; he had no protection now.

Jake walked into the ring, a small figure, totally insignificant without a horse.

"Watch this," Fen said to Dino.

As Macaulay turned to go in for the kill, Jake put his fingers to his mouth and whistled. Macaulay stopped in his tracks, looking wistfully at Rupert for a second, then, turning, trotted back across the arena, nickering with pleasure, nudging Jake in the stomach, licking his face. The crowd, having been frozen with terror, suddenly burst into a huge collective roar of laughter.

"Well done," said Jake softly and, not even bothering to take hold of Macaulay's bridle, he walked out of the ring. Macaulay trotted after him, giving him great sly digs in the ribs as if to say, "Didn't I do well?"

Malise turned to Colonel Roxborough. "Even the ranks of Tuscany could scarce forbear to cheer."

"I've just lost a hundred and we've lost the championship. I don't know why you're looking so bloody cheerful."

"Tarry a little," said Malise.

Rupert came out of the ring, his face like marble. Helen rushed forward. "Darling, are you all right?"

"No I am bloody not," spat Rupert, pushing her out of the way. "I'm going to object. That was deliberate sabotage on Jake's part."

The reporters surged forward, clamoring for a quote.

"What are you going to do, Rupe?"

"Lodge an objection. That horse should be put down instantly. It's a total delinquent. Jake put it in deliberately to fuck me up."

He was so angry he could hardly get the words out. The collecting ring was in an uproar.

Malise elbowed his way to his side.

"I'm going to object," said Rupert.

Malise shook his head. "Can't make it stand up. Macaulay's no more difficult a horse than Snakepit. He was all right with all the other riders. He's like a lamb with the Lovell children."

"Well, Jake trained him to do it then. He tried to kill me the other night, and he tried to kill me now."

The reporters were avidly writing down every word.

"The competition isn't over, Rupert," said Malise, lowering his voice. "Jake's still got to ride Clara."

"To hell with him," snarled Rupert. "If the jury won't accept an objection, I'll have the law on him for attempted murder." And he stalked off in the direction of his van.

Jake rode Clara into the ring, holding his hands up high, sitting very straight in the saddle, trying to copy Ludwig's style of riding.

"It seems a shame to ask you to beat your master," he said.

"Oh Clara, please do a cleara," said Fen.

The crowd had witnessed near tragedy and then high comedy. The commentator had to put everyone back on course. Ludwig had sixteen faults after four rounds, Dino had thirty-five; Rupert Campbell-Black had been eliminated. Jake, after three rounds, was half a fault less than Ludwig. He could not afford a single fence down if he was going to win. He kicked Clara into a canter. Over the first fence she sailed, over the second, over the third. She gave the parallel a clout but the bar didn't budge. Ludwig, smoking frantically, stood with his back to the arena, the rest of the German team giving him a running commentary.

Fen, eyes tight shut, was silently moving her lips.

"What are you doing?" asked Dino.

"Asking God to help Jake," said Fen, not opening her eyes.

"Rather unfair to Jake," said Dino. "I guess he can do it by himself."

Malise suddenly turned to Driffield. "For Christ's sake stop selling that horse and come and watch this."

Alone in the ring, it was as though Jake was in another world. He was only conscious of the joy of riding this beautiful, beautiful horse, thinking he could clear the stands, even the Eiffel Tower, on her. He turned for the water.

"Come on *Lieberlen,* or *Dummkopf,* I forget which it is."

Clara took a great leap, happy to have an expert on her back. Jake was aware of the blue water going on for ever and the anxious upturned faces of the photographers. But he had found the perfect stride and was safely over. The crowd couldn't forebear a cheer, then shushed themselves. The three elements of the combination, then the huge triple and he was home. Overcome with nerves, he made Clara take off too early at the first element. She only just cleared it so he turned her to the left at the next element, giving her room for an extra stride and placing her perfectly at the last element.

He was over.

"Magic riding," raved Malise. "Oh come on, Jake."

Unable to restrain itself, the crowd broke into a huge roar. The triple seemed to rush towards him. He lifted the mare up and up. The poles flew beneath him.

"That'll do," he thought in ecstasy. "I'm World Champion."

All around the thunderously cheering arena Union Jacks were waving as he rode out of the ring, patting the gallant mare over and over again.

"He won," screamed Fen, hugging Tory and then flinging her arms around Dino and kissing him.

Dino taking advantage, kissed her back, "That's almost worth only coming in third," he said.

All the British team except Rupert were going mad with excitement. Malise and Colonel Roxborough were throwing their hats in the air. Jake came out of the ring and slid off Clara into Tory's arms. For a second they clung to each other, not speaking. He could feel her hot tears on his cheek and the thunder of congratulatory hands raining down on his back.

A magnum of champagne was thrust into his hands. He opened it and soaked everyone around, then they all had a swig.

There was no sign of Malise or Rupert. They were closeted with a member of the international jury, Rupert shouting in only too fluent French and Malise trying to pacify him. But there was no case, said the Frenchman. There was nothing in the rules about not putting in a difficult horse. Macaulay plainly hadn't liked Rupert, but he'd behaved with all the other riders, and Snakepit certainly hadn't been an easy ride for anyone, except Jake. Jake was undeniably the winner and they'd better get on with the presentation. Muttering that he was going to report Jake to the B.S.J.A., Rupert stormed out of the tent.

"Where are you going?" said Malise.

"Not back into the ring to get the booby prize," snarled Rupert.

"My dear boy," said Malise gently, drawing him aside, "I'm sorry, It was bad luck. You've had a great disappointment and probably a very frightening experience."

"Balls," said Rupert. "I've been robbed."

"You must have beaten Macaulay up several times for him to go for you like that."

"He was my horse. What fucking business is that of anyone's?"

"The R.S.P.C.A. for start, and the F.E.I., not to mention the B.S.J.A. It won't do your image any good, nor will a lot of sensational stuff about selling Macaulay to the Middle East, and him starving and ending up in the stone quarries."

"If you believe that story."

"I do," said Malise, "and it could ruin you. The press is longing to get you, and you know what the British are like about cruelty to animals. It'll take a lot of guts, but go back into the ring and keep your trap shut. Bet you'll get a lot of marks."

Back came the bands, but this time the four horses were too tired to be disturbed by the drums and the cymbals. Ludwig shook Jake by the hand. "Well done, my friend, well done."

"Clara was the best trained horse. You should have won it," said Jake.

"You fought back from a terrible start; zat is more important."

Dudley Diplock ran up to Jake. "Seuper, absolutely seuper," he cried, giving Macaulay a wide berth. "Can I interview you immediately after the presentation?"

Rupert rode in last. The crowd gave him almost the biggest cheer in sympathy. He was handsomer than Robert Redford, he had jumped three spectacular clears and certainly most of the women in the audience had wanted him to win.

Jake rode forward, leaving the other riders lined up behind him, and removed his hat as the band played the National Anthem. His hair was drenched with sweat and there was a red ring on his forehead left by his hat. In a daze he was given numerous ribbons, so you could hardly see Macaulay's white face. There also was a purple sash, which clashed with Jake's scarlet coat, and a huge laurel wreath for Macaulay's neck, which he tried to eat. Then, to Jake's intense embarrassment, one beautiful girl after another in matching green suits came up and presented him with prize after prize: a gold medal, a Sèvres vase, a Limoges tea set, a silver tray, a huge magnum of champagne, an enormous silver cup and, finally, a check for £10,000.

There was nothing except one ribbon and a much smaller check for the others.

"Can't we each have one of those girls as consolation prizes?" said Dino.

Even when Prince Philip came up and shook him by the hand, Jake was too euphoric even to be shy and managed to stumble a few sentences out. Aware that the place was swarming with photographers and television cameras, Macaulay resolutely stuck his cock out and refused to put it in again.

"Just like Rupert," said Fen.

As Jake came out of the ring he was cornered by Dudley Diplock. "May I personally shake Macaulay by the hoof. How the hell did you get him to do it?" he added, lowering his voice. "I've been waiting ten years for someone to give that shit Campbell-Black his comeuppance. The whole show-jumping world will club together and give you a medal."

Gradually it was dawning on Jake that most people seemed more delighted Rupert had lost than he had won. After the television interview with Dudley, which was not very articulate but so full of euphoria and gratitude to Macaulay and Tory and all the family and Malise that it charmed everyone, Malise joined them. Neither he nor Jake were demonstrative men, but for a second they hugged each other.

"You were brilliant," said Malise in a strangely gruff voice. "Sorry I didn't get to you earlier but I've been with Rupert. He wanted to object."

"Nothing to object about," said Dudley.

"Quite," said Malise. "But that's never deterred him in the past. Fortunately they weren't having any of it. But he has been badly humiliated, so I think the less crowing about that side of it the better. Come on," he added to Jake, "everyone's waiting to talk to you."

"Who?"

"The world's press for a start."

"I want to ride Mac back to the stable. I've got nothing to say to them. I won. Isn't that enough?"

Malise looked at him. Was there a flicker of pity in his eyes? "It won't have had time to sink in," he said, "but thing's are never going to be the same again. You're a superstar now, a world beater. You've got to behave like one."

On the way they passed Helen Campbell-Black; she was crying. Both Malise and Jake hoped that Rupert wasn't going to take it out on her. As they fought their way into the crowded press tent, ecstatic English supporters, stripped to the waist, including Humpty, Ivor Braine and Driffield, were already getting plastered.

"Fucking marvellous, you beat the bugger," said Driffield, thrusting a glass into Jake's hand, while Ivor overfilled it with champagne.

"Three cheers for the champion," said Humpty. "Hip hip hooray."

Everyone joined in. The noise nearly lifted the roof off.

"Lovell for Prime Minister," yelled an ecstatic British supporter. Opening another magnum, he sprayed the entire press conference with champagne.

Jake was carried shoulder-high to the table with the microphones. He collapsed into a chair as he was bombarded with questions. He answered the foreign ones through an interpreter.

He was extermely happy, he said, but very, very tired. One didn't sleep much before a championship. He'd won because he was very lucky. Macaulay was a great horse, perhaps not in the class of any of the other horses, but he had been rested all year. Clara was the best trained horse, she didn't knock down a single fence, she ought to get a special prize.

"What about Macaulay?"

Everyone was still clamoring for information about the horse.

Jake said carefully that he'd always admired him, and when Rupert sold the horse on, he'd tracked him down and bought him.

"Did you deliberately put him in to sabotage Rupert?" asked *Paris Match*.

Jake caught Malise's eye. "Of course not. I'd no idea how he'd feel about Rupert."

"Did you know Rupert had sold the horse because he was vicious?" asked Joanna.

Jake looked up, the sombre black eyes suddenly amused. "Who's vicious," he said, "Rupert or the horse?"

Everyone laughed.

Later a celebratory party went on until four o'clock in the morning, but Rupert and Helen gave it a miss and flew home.

Soon all that was left of the World Championship was a few wheel tracks and a bare patch at the corner of the collecting ring, where all week ecstatic grooms had snatched up handfuls of grass to reward their successful charges as they came out of the ring.

A week after the riders came back from the World Championship, Billy went up to London to speak at the Sports Writers' Association Lunch. If they'd known I was going to be dropped, they probably wouldn't have asked me, he thought wryly. Janey needed the car to go shopping ("Only food from the market, it's so much cheaper," she added quickly), so she dropped Billy off at the station. He couldn't face *Horse and Hound,* it'd be too full of the World Championship, so he bought *Private Eye,* which always cheered him up, except when they were foul about Rupert. As he sat on the station platform he read a marvellous story about a member of the Spanish Royal family's sexual perversions, and another, even more scurrilous, about a trade union leader and a pit pony. Then his heart stopped beating. The next story began:

"Ex-slag-about-Fleet-Street Janey Henderson, sacked from *Daily Post* for the size of her expenses, is now trying to write a book about men. Despite encyclopedic knowledge of the subject, Janey felt the need for further research and recently returned from four days in Marbella with loathsome catfood tycoon, Kevin Coley. Meanwhile her amiable husband Billy Lloyd-Foxed (as he's known on the circuit) is forced to turn a blind drunk eye. Coley is his backer to the tune of £50,000 a year."

Billy started to shake. It couldn't be true, it couldn't—not Janey. She'd always laughed at Kev. *Private Eye* got things wrong; they were always being sued. He read it again. The words misted in front of his eyes. He didn't even hear the train come in. The ticket collector tapped him on the shoulder. "You want this one don't you, Billy?"

"Yes, no, I don't know. No I don't."

Running, pushing aside the people coming off the train, he rushed out of the station, flagging down the first taxi. "Take me home."

"All right, Mr. Lloyd-Foxe."

No one was there. Janey was still out shopping. He pressed the LR button on her telephone to find out the last number she'd rung. It was Kevin Coley's at head office. Hating himself, he looked in her top drawer. Janey had started a letter which she'd crumpled up:

"Darling Kev, I won't see you today, so I'm writing. God I miss you, I'm just coming down to earth after Marbella. Can't you think of somewhere nice and far to send Billy?"

He gave a moan of horror. His legs were trembling so much he could hardly stand. The bottle clattered against the glass and the whisky spilled all over the carpet. He drained it in one gulp, then he ran all the way to Rupert's. He found him in the yard, selling a horse to an American. One look at Billy's face and Rupert said to the buyer:

"Sorry, I've got to go. If you're interested in the horse give me a ring later." And, putting a hand on Billy's shoulder, he led him inside. As soon as the door was shut behind them Billy said:

"Did you know Janey was being knocked off by Kevin Coley?"

"Yes."

"How the hell?"

"Helen saw them lunching together in Cheltenham, and Mrs. Bodkin's been gossiping. And Mrs. Greenslade said in Les Rivaux that she saw them coming off a plane."

"It's all over *Private Eye*. Why the hell didn't you tell me"

"I thought Janey'd come to her senses," said Rupert, pouring him a large drink. "Christ, if you'd have told Helen every time I'd had a bit on the side she'd be back in America. Probably doesn't mean a thing to Janey. She's just a bit bored."

"With one bounder, she was free," said Billy miserably. "She's been so cheerful in the last three weeks. She was so down before, I thought it was because the book was going well. It must have been Kev. What the hell do I do?"

"Punch him in the nose."

"I can't at £50,000 a year. Very expensive bloody nose."

"Find another sponsor."

"Not so easy. I'm not the bankable property I was two years ago."

"Rubbish. You're just as good a rider. You've just lost your nerve." Rupert looked at his watch, "aren't you supposed to be making a speech in London?"

Billy went white, "I can't."

"You bloody well can. Don't want to back out on that. They'll say you've really lost your nerve. I'll drive you up."

Billy somehow survived the lunch and making his speech. Paranoid now, he imagined all the audience there looking at him curiously, wondering how he was coping with being cuckolded. The journalist in the front row had a copy of *Private Eye* in his pocket.

Even worse, that evening he and Janey had to go to some dreadful dance at Kev's golf club in Sunningdale. Billy didn't say anything to Janey. He had a faint hope, as he had when he was a child, that if he kept quiet and pulled the bedclothes over his head the nasty burglar might assume he was asleep and go away. Janey, he noticed, didn't grumble at all about going, as she would have done once, and looked absolutely ravishing in plunging white broderie anglaise.

She was easily the most beautiful woman in the room. All the men were gazing at her and nudging Kev for an introduction. Billy wondered how many of them had read *Private Eye* and proceeded to get drunk.

Enid Coley was made of sterner stuff. Having tried to fill up Janey's cleavage with an orchid and maidenhair fern wrapped in silver paper, which Janey rudely refused to wear, she waited for a lull in the dancing. Then she walked up to Janey, holding a glass of wine as though she was going to shampoo her hair, and poured it all over Janey's head.

"What the hell d'you think you're doing?" demanded Billy.

"Ask her what *she's* been doing," hissed Enid, "Look in my husband's wallet, and you'll see a very nice picture of your wife. Since you've been away she's been seducing my husband."

"Shut up you foul-mouthed bitch."

"Don't talk to me like that. If you weren't so drunk all the time, you might have done something to stop it."

Taking Janey, dripping and speechless, by the hand, Billy walked straight out of the golf club. It was not until they were ten miles out of Sunningdale that she spoke. "I'm sorry Billy. When did you know?"

"I read *Private Eye* at the station."

"Oh, my God. Must have been terrible."

"Wasn't much fun."

"Beastly piece too. I wasn't sacked from the *Post*. I resigned."

Billy stopped the car. In the light from the street lamp Janey could see the great sadness in his eyes.

"Do you love him?"

"I don't know, but he's so macho and I'm so weak. I guess I need someone like him to keep me on the straight and narrow."

"He's hardly been doing that recently," said Billy. "Look, *I* love you. It's *my* fault. I shouldn't have left you so much, or let us get into debt, or been so wrapped up in the horses. It must have been horrible for you, with no babies, and struggling to write a book on no money.

I'll get some money from somewhere, I promise you. I just don't want you to be unhappy."

On Monday Kevin Coley summoned Billy. "I've had a terrible weekend. I haven't slept a wink for worrying," were his opening words.

"I'm so sorry. What on earth's the trouble." asked Billy.

"I knew I had to break the news to you that I can't go on sponsoring you. My only solution is to withdraw."

"Pity your father didn't do that forty years ago." said Billy.

Kevin missed the joke; he was too anxious to say his piece. "The contract runs out in October and I'm not going to renew it. You haven't won more than £3000 in the last six months. I'm losing too much money."

"*And* fucking my wife."

"That has nothing to do with it."

"Then I tried to hit him," Billy told Rupert afterwards, "but I was so pissed I missed. He's talking of sponsoring Driffield."

"Oh well," said Rupert, "I suppose one good turd deserves another."

Winning the World Championship had transformed Jake Lovell into a star overnight. Wildly exaggerated accounts of his gypsy origins appeared in the papers. Women raved about his dark mysterious looks. Young male riders imitated his deadpan manner, wearing gold rings in their ears and trying to copy his short tousled hair style. Gradually he became less reticent about his background and admitted openly that his father had been a horsedealer and poacher and his mother the school cook. Sponsors pursued him, owners begged him to ride their horses. His refusal to turn professional, his extreme reluctance to give interviews (I'm a rider not a talker) all enhanced his prestige. The public liked the fact that his was still very much a family concern, Tory and the children helping out with the horses. Fen, under Malise's auspices, won the European Junior Championship in August, and, although still kept in the background by Jake, was beginning to make a name for herself.

Most important of all, Jake had given a shot in the arm to a sport that in Britain had been losing favor and dropping in the ratings. The fickle public likes heroes. The fact that Gyppo Jake had trounced all other nations in the World Championship dramatically revived interest in show-jumping.

Wherever Jake jumped now, he was introduced as the reigning World Champion, which was a strain because people expected him to do well, but also increased his self-confidence. For the rest of the year, and well into the Spring, he and Macaulay stormed through Europe like Attila the Hun, winning every grand prix going. Two of his other novices, Laurel and Hardy, had also broken into the big time. Laurel, a beautiful timid highly strung bay who started if a worm popped its head out of the ground in the collecting ring, was brilliant in speed classes. Hardy, a big cobby grey, was a thug and a bully, but had a phenomenal jump. Both were horses the public could identify with.

But it was Macaulay they really loved. While other riders were forced by their sponsors to call their horses ridiculous, constantly changing names, Macaulay remained gloriously the same, following Jake around without a lead like a big dog, nudging whoever presented the prizes and responding with a succession of bucks to the applause of the crowd.

In November Jake was voted Sportsman of the Year. Macaulay came to the studios with him and excelled himself by sticking out his cock throughout the entire program, treading firmly on Dudley Diplock's toe and eating the scroll that was presented to his master. For the first time the public saw Jake convulsed with laughter and was even more enchanted.

Enraged by his humiliation in the World Championship and the appalling publicity he received over selling Macaulay to the Middle East, Rupert decided to pull up stakes for a couple of months. Loading up six of the best horses, he crossed the Atlantic and boosted his morale by winning at shows in Calgary, Toronto, Washington, and Madison Square Garden.

Helen had always sighed wistfully that her parents had never had the opportunity to get to know their grandchildren. Rupert took her at her word. Flying the whole family out, plus the nanny, he dumped them in Florida with Mr. and Mrs. Macaulay while he traveled the American circuit and "enjoyed himself" as Mrs. Macaulay pointed out sourly. Staying with her parents with the two children shattered one of Helen's illusions. Even if things got too bad with Rupert, she could never run home to mummy any more. The whole family was glad to get back to Penscombe in November.

Two weeks after Rupert left for America, Billy had gone on a disastrous trip to Rotterdam where he had fallen off paralytically drunk in the ring and sat laughing on the sawdust, while one of his only remaining novices cavorted around the ring, refusing to be caught. The English papers had been full of the story. Billy got home to find that Janey had walked out, taking all her clothes, her manuscript, Harold Evans and, and worst of all, Mavis. Billy had stormed drunkenly round to the apartment were she was living with Kev and tried to persuade her to come back. She had goaded him so much, and become so hysterical, that finally he'd blackened her eye and walked out with Mavis under his arm.

A week later he received an injunction from Janey's solicitors saying he was violent and ordering him to stay away. Next day, The Bull, who'd been lackluster and off form for weeks, had a blood test. Not only was he anemic but he'd picked up a virus, said the vet, and should not be jumped for three months.

Billy took refuge in the bottle, selling off his novices and pieces of furniture to quiet his creditors, and to buy more whisky, refusing to see anyone. He also sacked Tracey because he couldn't afford to pay her any more. She refused to go. No one else should be allowed to look after The Bull. She'd live on her dole money, she said, and wait until Billy got his form back.

Rupert was shattered, when he got home, to find Billy in such a state. Typically, whenever he'd spoken to Rupert on the telephone in America, Billy had pretended things were all right and he and Janey were ticking along. Now sitting in a virtually empty cottage, surrounded by empty bottles, he had gone grey and aged ten years. Immediately Rupert set about a process of, as he called it, re-hab-Billy-tation, ordering Helen to get Billy's old room ready at Penscombe, packing Billy off to an alcoholics' home to dry out and searching for a new sponsor.

Helen, while sorry for Billy, could not help being secretly delighted. She had never really approved of Janey. Now with Billy back in the house, they would have fun together like the old days.

But it was not the same. It was like sending your son off all youthful, glorious and confident to the wars in his plumed uniform, and having him come home in the royal blue suit and red tie of the wounded, hobbling around on a stick. Billy talked incessantly about Janey, Mandryka and his failures. He didn't drink any more. He was quiet, sad and pathetically grateful. Helen once again marvelled at Rupert's kindness and gentleness.

One evening in early December, when she'd been talking to Higgins the gardener, Helen heard shouting from the indoor ring. Peering around the door, she found Billy walking around on Bugle, the willful eight-year-old bay thoroughbred Rupert had picked up in America. Unable to get a tune out of him, Rupert had handed him over to Billy. Now he was haranguing Billy because of his reluctance to take Bugle over a line of fences all well over five feet high.

Billy was shivering like a whippet on a cold day. "I simply can't do it yet, Rupe," he groaned. "Give me a few more weeks."

"Get moving and get over those bloody jumps," howled Rupert. "This is not a holiday camp."

"Oh Rupert, don't force him," Helen began.

"And you can bugger off," said Rupert, turning on her furiously.

Helen retreated to the drawing-room and tried to read the *Times Literary Supplement*. Twenty minutes later Rupert walked into the room, ashen and trembling even more than Billy.

"What's the matter?" asked Helen in horror.

Rupert poured himself three fingers of neat whisky which he drained in one gulp.

"He jumped them," he said. "He jumped them beautifully and all clear, half a dozen times. I'm sorry I shouted at you, but I just can't afford to show him how scared I am for him in front of him."

The problem was finding Billy a sponsor. Janey's departure, the failure of the horses and the heavy drinking had been so widely publicized that Billy would have to show himself in the ring, sober and successful, before anyone would come forward.

"You can ride for me for the rest of the year," said Rupert.

"I have my pride," said Billy, "and I've bummed quite enough off you and Helen."

Billy made his comeback at the Olympia Christmas show, not the best occasion to return, with the merrymaking and hell-raising and the memories it evoked of both Lavinia Greenslade and Janey. All the other riders and grooms were very friendly and welcomed him. But he knew behind his back they were saying how much he'd aged, that he'd lost his nerve and would never make the big time again.

Never had he been more desperate for a drink than half an hour before the first big class. Rupert, who'd been watching him like a warden, marching him away from the bars, had just been called away to do a quick television interview. Tracey was walking Bugle around the collecting ring. Inside the ringside bar Billy could see Christmas drinkers knocking back doubles, slapping each other on the back, guffawing with laughter. Surely one drink wouldn't hurt, one quick double to steady his nerves. If he was this strung up, he'd transmit his fears to young Bugle. Rupert gave him pocket money now. Easing his last fiver out of his breeches pocket, he was just going into the bar when a voice said, "Hello Billy. How lovely to see you back."

For a second he didn't recognize the plumpish but ravishingly pretty girl, with the long light brown hair tied back with a black velvet ribbon, like the young Mozart.

"It's Fen. Fenella Maxewll. How are you?" Stepping forward, she kissed him on both cheeks. "Are you in the next class?"

He nodded.

"So am I. Malise has persuaded Jake to let me jump. I'm absolutely terrified."

"Makes two of us," said Billy, still staring at her.

"Rupert says you're riding a super new horse."

"Yup, he's super all right. Whether I'll be able to get him around is another matter."

Suddenly they were surrounded by a group of ecstatic teenagers. "It's Fen," they screamed pushing Billy out of the way. "Can we have your autograph? How's Desdemona?"

As she signed their books, with a new and rather flashy signature which she'd been practicing during the long trips in the van, she saw Billy sidling away.

"Here," she said to the teenagers, "Don't you want his as well?"

The teenagers looked enquiringly at Billy, then politely handed him their books.

"Who's he?" muttered one of the teenagers, as she wandered off, examining Billy's signature more closely.

"Billy someone," said her friend, also examining the autograph. "Didn't he used to ride The Bull?"

"He's the best rider in England," Fen shouted after them.

Billy shook his head ruefully. Fen tucked her arm through his. "I told you it was high time you came back," she said. "Let's go and walk the course."

The course seemed enormous. Billy sat in the riders' stand clutching a Coke and wondering how the hell the riders could coax their horses over such enormous fences. To Rupert's intense irritation Jake Lovell jumped a beautiful clear on Macaulay, so did Fen on Desdemona.

"That stable simply can't put a foot wrong at the moment," said Malise. "High time you were back to redress the balance, Billy."

Despite the heat and stuffiness of the arena, Billy began to shiver. He could feel his white shirt drenched beneath his red coat. In the old days there had been excitement and nerves, not this cold sickening sensation of leaden nausea. Could everyone see? As he mounted Bugle he noticed two young riders with Jake Lovell haircuts, swapping stories. Once they had looked up to Billy and would certainly have watched him jumping on a new horse. Now they nodded briefly, carrying on with their conversation.

He jumped one practice fence and, nearly falling off, left it at that. Oh God, they were calling his number. Rupert's face swam in front of him.

"I think I've got a sponsor interested. A Victor Block from the Midlands. He's the Cutie Cup Millionnaire, makes bras and corsets. You may have to change Bugle's name to Cutie B Cup, but he's worth a lot of bread and he's up in the stands, so don't have three stops at the first fence."

"If I ever get to the first fence," said Billy in a hollow voice.

"For Christ sake, hurry up, Billy," snapped the collecting ring steward. "Don't spend so long in the bar next time."

As he rode into the ring panic assailed him. He should never have agreed to ride. The saddle was hard and unfamiliar, his legs felt cramped and powerless, refusing to meet the leather and blend into it, his hands on the reins were numb and heavy, without any flexibiity. In the old days he'd fallen into the rhythm of any horse's stride. Now he humped along like a sack of cement.

"And here comes Billy Lloyd-Foxe on Dougall. Se-uper, absolutely se-uper, to see you back, Billy. Let's all give Billy a big hand."

The applause, albeit tentative, unnerved the inexperienced Bugle. The first fence loomed up higher and higher. Desperately Billy tried to balance himself, hands rigid on the reins, interfering with the horse, pulling him off his stride. Bugle rapped the pole; it swayed but didn't fall.

"Oh God," groaned Tracey, her nails biting into her palms. "Oh don't let him be over the hill."

"Is this the guy you want me to sponsor?" asked Victor Block. "Doesn't look like much to me."

"You wait," said Rupert, trying not to show his desperate anxiety.

Bugle approached the second fence battling for his head. Billy felt the horse steady himself, judge the height, rise into the air and, making a mighty effort, twist over the fence.

"Forgive me," said Billy in wonder, sending up a prayer of thankfulness.

Now his hold on Bugle's neck was relaxed, the bay's pace increased, covering the churned-up tan with long lolloping strides. Suddenly Billy felt the blessed sustaining confidence start to come back. Fence after fence swept by. He was riding now, helping rather than hindering. Bugle was jumping beautifully. His heart swelled in gratitude. He was oblivious of the cheering gathering momentum. He took off too far away from the wall, but it flashed oxblood red beneath him and Bugle cleared it by a foot.

"What a horse, what a horse." He had to steady him for the last double and nerves got to him for a second, but he left it to Bugle to find his stride. Over and clear. A huge roar went up.

Billy concentrated very hard on Bugle's perfect black braids to stop himself breaking down as he circled the horse before riding him out of the ring. On the way he passed Guy de la Tour smiling broadly.

"Well done, *mon ami*, well done," and riding up to Billy he shook him by the hand, and then, leaning over, kissed him on both cheeks. The crowd broke into a great roar of approval. Billy the prodigal had returned.

Mr. Block turned to a jubilant Rupert. "Happen you're right, I'll sponsor him. But I'll have to organize the money side, so he can get on with the riding."

In the jump-off Jake went fastest, with Rupert second, Guy third and Fen fourth, and Billy, anxious not to hurry a young horse, was fifth. As Jake rode back into the ring to collect his ribbon and cup, followed by the rest of the riders, Rupert turned to Billy.

"I had to get you back on the circuit," he said. "One of us has got to break the run of luck of that murdering gypsy bastard."

All runs of luck come to an end. After a brilliant March in which he swept the board in Antwerp, Dortmund and Milan, Jake rolled up for the Easter meeting at Crittleden, a ground which had never really been lucky for him since Sailor's death. It had rained solidly for a fortnight beforehand and the ground was again like the Somme.

In the first big class Macaulay, who was probably a bit tired and didn't like jumping in a rainstorm, slipped on take-off at the third element of the combinations. Hitting the poles chest on, he somersaulted right over. Jake's good leg was the padding between the ground and half a ton of horse. Spectators swear to this day that they could hear the sickening splinter of bones. Without treading on Jake, Macaulay managed to scramble immediately to his feet and shake himself free of the debris of wings and colored poles. Most horses would have galloped off, but Macaulay, sensing something was seriously wrong, gently nudged his master, alternately looking down at him with guilt and anguish, and then glancing over his shoulder with an indignant "Can't you see we need help?" expression on his mud-spattered white face.

Humpty Hamilton reached Jake first.

"Come on, Gyppo, up you get," he said jokingly. "There's a horse show going on here."

"My fucking leg," hissed Jake through gritted teeth and fainted.

He came around as the ambulance men arrived. Normally a loose horse is a nuisance at such times, but Macaulay was a comfort, standing stock still while Jake gripped onto his huge fetlock to stop himself screaming, looking down at Jake with the most touching concern. He also insisted on staying as close as possible, as Jake, putty-colored and biting through his lips not to cry out, was bundled into an ambulance.

Fen had taken one look at the casualty department at Crittleden Hospital and called Malise, who was in London.

"Jake's done in his good leg," she sobbed. "I don't think a local hospital should be allowed to deal with it."

Malise agreed and moved in, pulling strings, getting Jake instantly transferred to the Motcliffe in Oxford, where the X-rays showed the knee cap was shattered and the leg broken in five places. The best bone specialist in the country was abroad. But, realizing the fate of a national hero rested in his hands, he flew straight home and operated for six hours. Afterwards he told the crowd of waiting journalists that he was reasonably satisfied with the result, but there might be a need for further surgery.

Tory managed to park the children and arrived at the hospital out of her mind with worry just as Jake came out of the operating room. For the first forty-eight hours they kept him heavily sedated. Raving and delirious, his temperature rose as he babbled on and on.

"Were any of his family in the navy?" said the ward sister, looking faintly embarrassed. "He keeps talking about a sailor."

Tory shook her head. "Sailor was a horse," she said.

"When can I ride again?" was his first question when he came round. Malise was a great strength to Tory. It was he and the specialist, Johnnie Buchannan, who told Jake what the future would be when Tory couldn't summon up the courage.

Johnnie Buchannan sat cautiously down on Jake's bed, anxious not in any way to jolt the damaged leg which was strapped up in the air.

"You're certainly popular," he said, looking around at the mass of flowers and get-well cards that covered every surface of the room and were waiting outside in sackfulls still to be opened. "I haven't seen so many cards since we had James Hunt in here."

Jake, his face grey and shrunken from pain and stress, didn't smile. "When can I ride again?"

"Look, I don't want to depress you but you certainly can't ride for a year."

"What?" hissed Jake through bloodless lips. "That'll ruin me. I don't believe it," he went on, suddenly hysterical. "I could get up and discharge myself now." He tried to rise off the bed and remove his leg from the hook, gave a smothered shriek and collapsed back, tears of pain and frustration filling his eyes.

"Christ, you can't mean it," he mumbled. "I've just bought two new horses and employed another groom. I've got to keep going."

Malise got a cigarette from the packet by the bed, put it in Jake's mouth and lit it.

"You nearly lost the leg," he said gently. "If it hadn't been for Johnnie, you would never have walked again, let alone ride. Your other leg, weakened by polio, would never have been able to support you on its own. You've got to get your good leg sound again."

Jake shook his head: He didn't mean to sound ungrateful. "It's just that it's my living. This'll ruin me."

"It won't," said Johnnie Buchannan. "If it knits properly, you'll be out of here in five or six months and can conduct operations from a wheelchair at home. If you don't play silly games, and take the physio side of it seriously, you could be riding again by this time next year."

Jake glared at them, determined not to betray his despair. Then he shrugged his shoulders. "All right, there's not much I can do. You'd better tell Fen to turn all the horses out. They could use the rest."

"Isn't that a bit extreme?" said Malise.

"No," said Jake bleakly. "Who else can ride them?"

For a workaholic like Jake, worse almost than the pain was the inactivity. Lying in bed hour after hour, he watched the leaves slowly breaking through the pointed green buds of the sycamores and the ranks of daffodils tossing in the icy wind, and fretted. He had no resources. He was frantically homesick, missing Tory, the children, Fen and the horses and Wolf the lurcher. The anonymity of the hospital sickeningly reminded him of the time when he had polio as a child and his mother seldom came and visited him, feeling too guilty perhaps for never bothering to have him inoculated.

A fastidious, reserved and highly private person, he couldn't bear to be totally dependent on the nurses. He was revolted by the whole ritual of blanket baths and bedpans. Lying in the same position, his leg strapped up in the air, he found it impossible to sleep. He had no appetite. He longed to see the children, but with the hospital eighty miles from home, it was difficult for Tory to bring them often, and when she did, Jake was so ill and tired and weak he couldn't cope with their exuberance for more than a few minutes, and was soon biting their heads off. He longed to ask Tory to come and look after him, but he was too proud, and anyway she had her work cut out with the children and the stable.

The Friday morning after the accident Fen had been to see him. Such was his despair that he had been perfectly foul to her and sent her away in tears. Wracked with guilt, he was therefore not in the best of moods when Malise dropped in during the afternoon, bringing three Dick Francis novels, a bottle of brandy and the latest *Horse and Hound*.

"You've made the cover," he told Jake. "There's an account of your accident inside. They say some awfully nice things about you."

"Must think I'm finished," said Jake broodingly. "Thanks anyway."

"I've got a proposal to make to you."

"I'm married," snapped Jake.

"It's about Fen. If you're grounded, why don't you let her jump the horses?"

"Don't be bloody ridiculous. She's too young."

"She's seventeen," said Malise. "Remember Pat Smythe and Marion Coakes. She's good enough. What she needs is international experience."

"I don't want her overfaced. Anyway she's daffy. She'd forget her own head if I wasn't there to tell her what to do."

"It's not as though your horses were difficult," said Malise
"Macaulay dotes on her. She's ridden Laurel and Hardy, and Desdemona's been going like a dream."

"No," said Jake, reaching for a cigarette.

"What is the point? You've brought all those horses up to peak
fitness and you've got two grooms who need wages. Why throw the
whole thing up and just lie here worrying yourself sick about money?
Let her have a go. She's your pupil. You taught her. Haven't you got
any faith in her?"

Jake shifted sideways, giving a gasp of pain.

"Pretty grim, huh?"

Jake nodded. "Can you get me a drink?"

Malise poured some brandy into a paper cup.

"It'll give you an interest. She can call you every night from wherever she is."

"And where's that going to be?"

Malise poured himself a drink, to give himself the courage to
answer. "Rome. Then she can fly back for the Royal Windsor, then
Paris, Barcelona, Lucerne and Crittleden."

"No," said Jake emphatically.

"Why not?"

"Too young. I'm not letting a girl her age abroad by herself, with
wolves like Ludwig, Guy and Rupert around."

"I'll keep an eye on her, I'll personally see she's in bed, alone, by
eleven o'clock every night. She needs a long stint abroad to give her
confidence."

"How's she getting to Rome? In Rupert's private jet, I suppose."

"Griselda Hubbard's got a van that takes six horses. She can easily
take two or three of yours."

"Griselda Hubbard," said Jake outraged. "That's scraping the
barrel."

"Mr. Punch has turned into rather a good horse," said Malise.

"But not with Grisel on him. Fen's far better than her."

"Exactly," said Malise. "That's why I want to take her."

Back at the Mill Fen was battling with blackest gloom and trying
to cheer up Macaulay. It was nearly a week since Jake's fall, but the
horse still wouldn't settle. He wouldn't eat and at night he paced his
stall. Every time a car came over the bridge, or there was a footstep in
the yard, he'd rush to the half-door, calling hopefully, then turn away
in childlike disappointment. Since Jake had rescued Macaulay from the
Middle East they hadn't been separated for a day. Fen had tried to turn
him out with the rest of the horses, but he'd just stood shivering by
the gate in his New Zealand rug, asking to be brought in again. Poor
Mac, thought Fen, and poor me too. She'd thought about Dino Fer-

ranti so often since the World Championship, hoping so much that she'd bump into him on the circuit this summer. And now Jake had ordered the horses to be turned out, and there'd be no going abroad, and she'd be stuck with taking Desdemona to a few piffling little local shows.

A rather attractive journalist whom she'd met at Olympia had called that afternoon and asked her if she'd like to sail over to Cherbourg for a big party on Saturday night. She'd had to refuse, just as she kept having to refuse dates and parties because there was always some crisis cropping up with the horses. And now that Jake was in the hospital she had ten times as much responsibility. She'd been up all last night with Hardy, who, having gorged himself on the spring grass, suddenly developed a violent attack of colic. Brought into the stable, he had promptly cast himself and been so badly frightened when he couldn't get up that Fen had had to call the vet. It was some compensation this morning that a recovered Hardy, instead of taking his usual bite out of her, had butted her gently with his head and then licked her hand in gratitude.

Added to this, Jake had been perfectly bloody when she'd visited him in the hospital. She knew he was suicidal or he wouldn't have been so awful, but it was difficult to make allowances sometimes. And, finally, it was Sarah, the new groom's third night off that week. She was very good at her job, Sarah, and extremely attractive, with long black hair which never got greasy and a flawless creamy skin which never got pimples. She was also quite tough. She had turned down a job with Guy de la Tour because it was underpaid. You were expected to work twenty-four hours a day, seven days a week, and the only compensation was being screwed by Count Guy when he felt like it. Instead she had taken a job with Jake.

"Your brother-in-law," said Sarah, "may be moody, and prefer four-legged creatures to anything on two legs, but at least he pays properly and gives you plenty of evenings off."

"Not if you're family, he doesn't," thought Fen gloomily, as she watched Sarah, dressed up to the nines, drive off to a party in her pale blue sports car.

Once again, Fen repeated Dino's words, "There is more to life than the inside of a tack-cleaning bucket!" She was fed up with bloody horses. She wanted some fun.

A delectable smell of chicken casserole drifted out from the kitchen. Looking at her watch, she was surprised to see it was half past nine. Inside she found Tory stacking up a pile of envelopes. She had spent the evening cancelling shows and wondering what bills to pay first.

"Poor lovie, you look shattered," she told Fen. "Let's have a drink before dinner."

"Can we afford it?" said Fen, looking at the bills.

"I think so," said Tory. "At the moment anyway. It just infuriates me that, having paid for all that foreign stabling in advance, we won't be able to use it."

Having opened a bottle of red wine and filled two glasses, Fen slumped in the armchair. Although it was the end of April it was still cold. Wolf the lurcher, who was missing his master even more than Macaulay, leapt onto Fen's knee for comfort.

"Poor old boy," said Fen, cuddling his shivering shaggy body.

"How's Mac?" said Tory, draining the broccoli.

"Still off his feed. His whole routine's been disrupted. Ouch," she screeched, as Wolf, hearing the sound of a car on the gravel, leapt off her knees, scratching her thighs with his long claws. Next moment he'd opened the back door and rushed off barking frantically into the yard.

"Who the hell could that be?" said Fen.

"Wolf obviously knows him," said Tory. "He's stopped barking."

"May I come in?" said Malise.

"Oh hell," muttered Fen," he'll think we've eaten and stay chatting for hours."

"Hello," said Tory, going crimson with her usual shyness. "You've come at the right time. We've just opened a bottle." She filled up another glass.

Malise sat down at the long scrubbed table, enjoying the warmth, admiring the children's paintings and the newspaper photographs of the horses on the cork board, alongside this year's already substantial number of ribbons for which there was no longer space in the tackroom. He looked at the pile of envelopes.

"You've been busy."

"Cancelling shows," said Tory. "Hoping we might get some of our money back. Why don't you stay for supper?" she stammered. "We've got masses."

"I'm sure there isn't enough," said Malise.

"Tory always cooks for five thousand and it's always marvelous," said Fen.

Malise suddenly realized he hadn't eaten all day.

"Well it'd be awfully nice."

"It's only chicken," said Tory apologetically.

"I'll get it out," said Fen. Typically Tory, she thought, as she got four huge baked potatoes and a large blue casserole out of the oven.

"Nice kitchen," said Malise as he put butter in his baked potato. "How's Macaulay?"

"Devastated," sighed Fen. "He even misses shows. Every time the telephone rings in the tackroom he starts cantering around the field."

"This is excellent, Tory," said Malise. "I hadn't realized how hungry I was. By the way, I've just been to see Jake."

"Oh how kind. How was he?"

"Pretty miserable still, frustrated, bored."

"And still in a lot of pain?" asked Tory.

"Yup, but at least I gave him something to take his mind off his leg. You'd better get the horses in tomorrow, Fen. He's agreed you can jump them."

"Poor Jake," said Fen. "I drove over to see him this morning. He looked awful. What did you say?" She stopped with a piece of carrot on the way to her mouth.

"He's going to let you ride the horses."

"Where?" stammered Fen.

Malise laughed. "Rome, Paris, Windsor, Barcelona, Crittleden, Lucerne just for starters."

Fen opened her mouth and shut it again. Then she turned to Tory, "Is this true?"

Tory laughed and hugged her. "If Malise says so, it must be."

"But we can't afford it."

"Of course you can. You'll be jumping as a member of the British team, so those expenses'll be paid, and if I'm anything to go by, you'll be in the money very soon."

Fed looked at him incredulously. "Thank you," she said in a choked voice. Then, jumping to her feet and falling over Wolf, she ran out into the yard, muttering that she must go and tell Macaulay.

"Oh please God, forgive me," she prayed as she buried her face in Macaulay's neck, "I didn't mean it when I said I wanted to give up show-jumping."

The following day Fen loaded up Macaulay in the trailer and drove to Oxford. Without asking anyone's permission she unloaded him in the Woodstock Road and rode him across the emerald-green, billiard-table-smooth hospital lawn and, cavalierly trampling a bed of dark red wallflowers underfoot, banged on the window of Jake's room.

Jake, sunk in the depths of gloom, thought he was hallucinating when the great white face with the white eye peered through the glass at him. Fortunately it was a slack period. Matron was at lunch, patients were resting and comely Nurse Wutherspoon, who was a show-jumping fan, pushed Jake's bed so it was flush to the open window. The reunion touched everyone. At first Macaulay couldn't quite believe it, pressing her face against Jake's shoulder, nickering in ecstasy, then licking his pyjama jacket and his face with a great pink stropping tongue. For a minute Jake couldn't speak, but at last his face took on some color as he fed Macaulay a whole pound of grapes and a bar of chocolate and an apple. Word soon spread around the hospital, a crowd of nurses had soon gathered in the room to pat and even take photographs of the World Champion. They were thrilled to see the delight on Jake's face. They had all been worried about his slow recovery and his black depression. In the middle the matron walked in and everyone melted away. Fortunately she was also a show-jumping fan.

"We really don't allow visitors out of hours, Mr. Lovell, but I suppose we can make an exception in Macaulay's case."

After twenty minutes Fen put Macaulay back in the trailer and came back to talk to Jake thanking him over and over again for letting her go, promising to call him every night.

"When are you off?"

"Friday morning. Grisel's collecting me."

She saw him again once before she left, on the way home from a day trip to London. He was so busy giving her last-minute instructions, he didn't notice she never took the scarf from her head.

"Rome's tricky," he said. "You'll find the fences coming off the corners very fast and at dusk the trees around the arena throw shadows across the poles which make it very easy to make mistakes. Macaulay's eyesight's not brilliant. If you're in any doubt, don't jump him. You won't like Rome, lots of wops with machine guns pinching your bottom. Don't carry money or your passport in your bag, the muggers are frightful, and put any winnings in the hotel safe at once."

"If there are any," said Fen in a hollow voice.

"I gather Billy Lloyd-Foxe is back on the team too," said Jake. "If you have any problems, go to him rather than Malise. He has to ride the horses. He knows what he's talking about."

"I've been very wicked," said Fen when she got back to the Mill three hours later and found Tory in the kitchen darning Fen's lucky socks. "I've bought three pairs of trousers, three shirts, two dresses and a bikini. I promise I'll win it all back. And I passed a poster of Janey Lloyd-Foxe in the subway, telling me to read her every week in the *Daily Post,* so I drew a moustache on her and wrote 'bitch' underneath."

"I hope no one saw you," said Tory in alarm. "Let's see what you bought."

"And I went to the hairdresser," said Fen casually. "I covered it up with a scarf, because I thought Jake might freak out. It's gone a bit flat." She removed the scarf. Tory just gaped at her. Fen had gone out that morning with dark mouse hair trailing almost to her waist. Now it was streaked white blond and no longer than two inches all over her head. Tendrils curled round her face and down to a point at the nape of her neck. She had been on a crash diet for the last ten days since she heard about the trip, and now weighed no more than 110 pounds. As a result of so many salads, the pimples had gone for good, the new hairstyle emphasized the emerging cheek bones, the brilliant slanting aquamarine eyes and the long slender neck.

"I'm sorry," Fen hung her head, "but I thought it would be easier to manage like this."

Certainly it won't keep men at a distance, thought Tory. Malise was going to have his work cut out as a chaperone. Suddenly, with a flash of equal pain and pleasure, she realized that Fen was no longer a child, a little sister. Almost since this morning she'd grown up into a beauty.

"It's gorgeous," she said in awe. "The hair's heaven."

Fen grinned with relief.

*F*en had seldom met anyone she disliked more than Griselda Hubbard. Having told Fen to be ready at 5:30, she rolled up while it was still dark at 4:45 just as Fen was feeding Desdemona and Macaulay. Refusing to come in for a cup of coffee, she sat drumming her fingers on the wheel of her vast eight-gear van, looking at the immaculate stable yard as though it were a pigsty, forcing Fen into a complete panic and sabotaging all her down-to-the-last minute organization. Macaulay loathed getting up early at the best of times. There was no way you could hurry him over his breakfast or Sarah over blow-drying her hair.

"It'll dry all crinkly if I leave it," was her only answer in reply to Fen's frantic pleas.

"What on earth's that?" said Griselda, as Fen installed a huge jar of lemon drops, taking up a large corner of the very limited cupboard space.

"Macaulay's reward if he jumps well."

"You're optimistic," said Griselda dismissively. She was bull-terrier solid rather than fat, with huge fleshy thighs stretching a maroon track suit, and a hard face with short-permed dark hair, small beady eyes, and more than a suggestion of moustache on her upper lip. She might have been any age between thirty and forty-five, but in fact was only twenty-eight.

"I am not sitting next to her," muttered Sarah.

Georgie, Griselda's girl groom, as thin and wiry as Griselda was solid, had a pointed nose, watery blue eyes and a long beige braid down her back. There was a lot of fuss about loading. Griselda had four horses, with her star Mr. Punch on the outside.

"I'm not having that brute next to Punchie," she said as Fen started to lead Macaulay up the ramp.

"He wouldn't hurt a fly," protested Fen.

"Punchie is not a fly," said Griselda, "and that's not what Rupert Campbell-Black says. Put Desdemona next to Punchie."

"Desdemona gets scared. It's easier if she's between Mac and Hardy and Mac goes in first."

"Look, if you hitch a lift with me," said Griselda, "you abide by my rules."

Handling the monster van like a man, Griselda calmly knocked down two of Tory's carefully nurtured lilac trees on the grass by the gate. Fen shivered for Desdemona and Macaulay's safety as Grisel overtook van after van on the highway. She got to the ferry two hours early, which meant lots of hanging around. Fen insisted on feeding her horses at the docks, which, to Griselda's intense irritation, had Mr. Punch and the rest of her horses clamoring for their lunch too. To upset Fen, there was the inevitable truck load of bewildered thirstily bleating little calves. The driver said they were destined for the pot.

"Why can't they bloody kill them in England?" said Fen.

"E.E.C. Regulations," said the driver.

"Don't be so sentimental," said Griselda. "You eat meat, don't you?"

When they were at sea they had lunch in the restaurant. Grisel ordered a huge steak. "I need my fuel. I'm the only one doing any work."

Fen, who was starving, ordered a grilled sole, which seemed less bloodthirsty. The moment it arrived Grisel made a point of asking her to go down to the hold and check the horses.

Throughout the three-day journey she treated Fen with even more contempt than the grooms, insisting she map-read, then hitting the roof when Fen gazed out of the windows at the pink and white apple blossom and, wondering how she would put Desdemona at all the fences that flashed past, twice navigated Grisel on to the wrong highway.

Every sixty miles or so Griselda ordered Sarah or Fen to make her yet another cup of strong black coffee with three spoonfuls of sugar.

Jake always stopped to water and graze his horses on the way. Griselda believed in pushing on. "We'll never make Fontainbleau by nightfall if we bugger around blowing them out with grass. Who'd like a lemon drop?"

"They're Macaulay's," snapped Fen.

"He'll hardly get through all those. No wonder he's so pudgy."

"Certainly likes her pound of flesh," muttered Sarah to Fen, "although why she should want any more flesh defeats me, the ugly cow."

Finally, two days later, with the Ave Maria ringing out all over the city, they drove into Rome. Fen was knocked sideways by the beauty of the churches, the statues, the lakes reflecting the yellow and turquoise sky and the great hump-backed dome of St. Peter's. The streets swarmed with people parading up and down, gossiping and showing off their new clothes. The traffic was terrifying. Griselda, however drove the van on undaunted, on the principle that if she crashed into a Ferrari it would come off worse. Sarah, sitting by the window, was the object of repeated wolf-whistles.

"I always feel I'd like to end my days in Rome," she said smugly.

"Probably will if Griselda doesn't drive more slowly," said Fen. "Oh look at that beautiful park over there." Through the gap in the houses she could see a rustic amphitheatre circled with umbrella palms.

"That's the show ground," said Sarah. "It's supposed to be the most beautiful in the world."

The stables, part of a military barracks, were splendid, with big roomy stalls enabling the horses to look out into the yard.

"There's Snakepit and The Bull," said Sarah. "So Rupert and Billy are already here."

Fen suddenly felt nervous and wondered what they'd think of her new hair.

"Hullo," said Dizzy, coming out of Snakepit's stall. "We flew out. We were lucky. Have you had a frightful journey?"

"Marvelous," lied Fen because Griselda was in ear-shot.

"Where is the team staying?" Griselda asked Dizzy.

"The Apollo, just around the corner."

"Well I'm off," said Griselda. "I expect you'll want to settle your horses, Fen. Can you carry my bags to the taxi line, Georgie? And mind you sweep out the horse area, and clean up the living area."

"Bitch," said Fen, glaring at Griselda's solid departing back, with Georgie running after her, buckling under the heavy suitcases. "We're getting home some other way," she added to Sarah, "even if we have to carry the horses."

Having examined the box stalls for sticking-out nails and jagged edges of wood, they put down wood shavings and fed and watered the horses. Macaulay, however, had a more pressing need. Dropping down, folding like a camel, he rolled and rolled.

"God, I'm so tired. I could sleep on a clothes' line," said Fen.

"Where shall we have supper?" said Sarah.

"There's a nice trattoria around the corner," said Dizzy.

"Can I come with you?" asked Fen.

"No you can't," said Driffeld, who'd been checking his horses. "You're staying at the Apollo with the team and you'll be expected to dine with them too. Come on, we'll share a taxi."

"Pay for it, you mean," said Fen under her breath, knowing Driffeld's meanness. "You can sleep in the hotel room alternate nights, and I'll sleep in the van," she said apologetically to Sarah.

"Malise won't put up with that," said Driffeld. "You've made the grade now, dear, and you'll have to behave like one of us."

The Hotel Apollo was a sprawling yellow villa, its stuccoed walls peeling. The walls of the lobby were decorated with friezes of Apollo in various guises, cavorting with bathing nymphs, bemused maidens and hairy-legged flute players. There was a rackety elevator, but Fen preferred to climb a huge baroque staircase to her room on the second floor, which turned out to be the height of luxury.

Meanwhile downstairs in the bar, Malise, hiding his disappointment that Helen hadn't made the trip to Rome this year, was giving Billy and Rupert a pep talk.

"I need your help, chaps," he said with unusual heartiness. "Fenella Maxwell's not eighteen yet. Tory and Jake are in a panic she's going to get seduced by some wop. I promised them we'd keep a close eye on her."

"Tory's overreacting," said Rupert. "I can't actually envisage Fen having to fight them off."

"Poor old Jake," said Billy, looking down at his glass of Coke. "Bloody bad luck when he'd just battled his way back to the top."

"I must send him a Please-Don't-Get-Well card," drawled Rupert. "He tried to kill me last year, remember?"

"Pity he didn't succeed," said Driffeld nastily.

Billy thought wistfully of the old days when pre-dinner drinks were the nicest part of the day, to celebrate or cheer you up after a lousy round. You'd start with a pint of beer because you were thirsty, and after that several large whiskeys, with increasing merriment in anticipation of some exotic food, heightened by plenty of wine and several brandies afterward. Life had seemed framed in a halo, studded with buttercups. Now all meals had a terrible sameness, with people getting sillier or more aggressive. The first wild agony of losing Janey had given way to a dull numbing loneliness. He had become aware of the appalling similarity of the show-jumping circuit, the faceless bedrooms, the endless traveling. Before, it had been redeemed by hell-raising with Rupert, or living it up with Janey. Everywhere he went he was reminded of her and the good time they had had, and every night he watched the other riders ring home to check up on their families and report the latest success. He had no one to call now, no one who gave a damn if he won or lost, except his creditors, who he was gradually paying back. The money from each small win was sent to Mr. Block, who kept what was necessary for Billy's livelihood, took his cut and passed the rest on to the tax man. In fact, if he could get back on form and notch up about five really good wins, he could discharge the whole debt. Once Janey filed for divorce, Billy's mother, making no secret of her relief, had come to his aid, not giving him a huge sum, but enough to settle the most pressing bills. Rupert had been wonderful. Looking across at him, a fond father showing photographs of the twelve-month-old Tabitha to Malise, Billy felt a wave of passionate gratitude for his support and kindness. Never once had Rupert tried to persuade him to have a drink, as other people did constantly.

Malise's voice broke into his thoughts.

"Hope you don't mind coming here again too much," he said in an undertone. "I'm fond of this place, even if it is a bit quaint."

Billy smiled. "Of course not." That was all part of the act, to be cheerful, never to show the cracks in his heart.

He pointed to one of the more grotesque figures portrayed in the frieze round the walls of the bar.

"What did that poor chap do?"

"Raped Apollo's mother. He was pegged down so birds could peck continually at his liver."

"Sounds like mine in the old days," said Billy.

"Another Coke?" asked Malise.

"No, I'm fine," Billy looked across at Griselda Hubbard, massive in a red track suit. What a disgusting ugly pig she was, and already badmouthing poor little Fen.

"She's a hopeless map-reader and kept making the most ridiculous fuss about stopping to graze and water the horses. If I'd listened to her we'd still be in France. Jake's mad to let her ride the horses, she's so soft. They'll be walking all over her in a week or two, and she's no sense of hierarchy, treats her groom like an equal, even a superior. She'll have both her and the two horses tucked up in her hotel bedroom watching the telly at any minute."

"I hope we can get English food here," grumbled Driffeld, brandishing an empty glass and looking around, hoping someone would buy him a drink.

Rupert was discussing declining television viewing figures with Malise. "They ought to sack Dudley, he's such a pratt. What we need on the circuit is someone every little pony-mad girl can identify with. It's the pony-mad girls that make up the audiences and bring in their parents."

"What about Fenella Maxwell?" said Malise.

"Well, if she shed about twenty pounds, most of which is pimples."

"Hello," said a shrill voice.

Everyone turned around.

"Mamma Mia," said Billy.

"Christ," said Rupert. "You *have* grown up."

Fen stood staring at them, eyes widened like a faun, bleached sea-green shirt tucked into bleached sea-green Bermuda shorts, espadrilles on the ends of her long smooth brown legs. Her spiky blond hair was still wet from the shower. Not a pimple spoiled her smooth brown cheeks, only a faint touch of blush. She looked like a wary but very beautiful street urchin.

"Oh God," thought Malise, "how am I going to chaperone *that* in Rome?"

As it was late, they went straight in to dinner. Ivor Braine and, amazingly, Driffeld made concerted efforts to sit next to Fen. Ivor gazed at her with his mouth open. All of the team members except Griselda, who was obviously feeling upstaged, were incredibly nice, asking her about Jake's leg and the horses and how the glamorous Sarah was settling in. The waiters, flashing teeth and menus, kept filling up her glass with Chianti. Not having touched a drop since she'd started dieting, she suddenly felt very light-headed.

"I'm starving," she told Driffeld. "I don't think I could ever look at a grapefruit or a lettuce leaf again."

"I'm going to have fettucine," said Grisel sourly, "followed by *abbacchio al forno*."

"What's that?" said Ivor.

"Roast baby lamb, cooked whole," said Griselda, watering at the mouth.

"Probably one of those lambs that came over on the ferry," thought Fen savagely. "Bloody carnivore." Suddenly she felt less hungry.

"What's *ucelletti*?"

"Little song birds roasted on a spit," said Grisel. "They're very good."

"God, this is a barbaric country," said Billy. "I'm surprised they don't casserole all those stray cats hanging round the street."

"Not enough meat on them," said Rupert.

Next moment a messenger arrived at the table with two telegrams for Fen. One was from Jake and Tory and the children. When she opened the other she gasped and went bright scarlet, but didn't manage to shove it back into the envelope quickly enough to stop Driffeld reading it.

"'Congratulations'," he read out, "'and good luck. Look forward to seeing you this summer. Dino Ferranti.' Consorting with the enemy, are we? You could do a lot worse for yourself. Evidently his father's as rich as Croesus."

"It's nothing," stammered Fen. "We just met briefly at the World Championship. I wonder how he discovered I'd been selected."

Rupert was looking across at her with a dangerous glint in his eyes. "The sly fox," he said "must have been working overtime at Les

Rivaux. As well as making a play for you, he was running like mad after Helen."

"Not nearly as much as Macaulay was running after you," began Driffeld, then stopped when he saw the blaze of anger on Rupert's face. "Sorry, dangerous subject."

"Dino," said Rupert, leaning over to fill up Fen's glass, "even pursued Helen when we were in America. While she was staying with her mother, he was evidently never off the telephone, pestering her to go out with him."

Fen felt her happiness evaporate. Seeing her face, Billy said quickly, "Never met Dino. Can't imagine him pestering anyone. He sounds far too laid back."

Dinner seemed to go on for hours. Fen found she couldn't finish her spaghetti.

"Is Billy all right?" she said to Driffeld in an undertone. "He seems to have lost all his sparkle and his hair's even greyer than it was at Olympia."

"Hasn't really had a good win since then," said Driffeld. "Malise is only keeping him on the team for sentimental reasons."

"He's still so attractive."

"Who is?" asked Rupert. Throughout dinner his eyes had flickered over Fen. He was the only man she'd ever met who could stare so calculatingly and without any embarrassment, as though he was a cat and she a bird's nest he was going to raid in his own good time.

"No one," she said quickly. She turned to Ivor. "Tell me about your new horse. Is he really called John?"

"I think you've lost your audience, Ivor," said Rupert five minutes later. Fen had fallen fast asleep, her head on the red raffia table mat.

Three days later Fen had reached screaming pitch. The week had been one succession of disasters. She remembered Jake warning her that his first show with the British team had begun catastrophically, but nothing could have been as bad as this. She didn't even dare call him at the hospital.

On the first day she'd entered Desdemona for a speed class for horses who had never jumped in Rome before. The little mare had gone like a whirlwind, treating the course with utter disdain, sailing over fences she couldn't see over, whisking home in the fastest time by a couple of seconds. Fen was so enchanted by such brilliance she promptly jumped off and flung her arms round Desdemona's neck, to the delight of the crowd.

The British team was less amused.

"You berk," said Rupert, as starry-eyed she led Desdemona out of the ring, "you've lost yourself a grand."

"But she won," gasped Fen.

"She may have done, but you disqualified her by dismounting before you left the ring."

"Oh my God," said Fen. "Oh Des, I'm sorry. I didn't think. What on earth will Jake say?"

"Shouldn't tell him. Least said, soonest sewn up," said Ludwig cheerfully, who, as the new winner, rode grinning into the ring to collect his prize money.

In the big class later in the day Fen made two stupid mistakes, putting Macaulay out of the running. Then on the second day in the relay competition, because Rupert always paired with Billy and Ivor with Driffield, Fen was stuck with a very reluctant Griselda.

"I'll show her," fumed Fen as she waited on Desdemona, holding her hand out ready for the baton as Griselda cantered up to them after a clear and surprisingly swift round on Mr. Punch. Desdemona, however, had other ideas. Mr. Punch had nipped her sharply several times on the trip out and, at the sight of him thundering down on her, she jumped sharply out of his way, making Fen drop the baton.

"What dreadful language," said Rupert, who was standing nearby, grinning from ear to ear. "What a good thing all those nice Italian spectators can't understand what Griselda's saying to Fen."

Determined to redeem herself in the big class in the evening, Fen rode with such attack that when Macaulay decided he didn't like the jump built in the shape of a Roman villa and started to dig his toes in, Fen shot straight over his head, covering herself in bruises.

Yesterday Malise had organized some sightseeing. They went to St. Peter's and saw the statue of St. Peter, with his foot worn away by the kisses of the pilgrims.

"I came here with Janey," Fen overheard Billy saying to Rupert. "I swore that by the end of our life together I'd have kissed her more than the pilgrims had kissed that foot. Perhaps that's why she pushed off." He was trying to make a joke of it, but Fen could sense his despair.

Being superstitious, all the riders wanted to visit the Trevi fountain.

"Isn't it beautiful?" said Fen, admiring the bronze tritons, the gods and goddesses, the wild horses and the leaping, glistening, rushing cascade of water.

"Only thing missing is Rossano Brazzi," said Driffield.

"Who's he?" asked Fen.

"He was in *Three Coins in the Fountain*. Christ, you must be young. Do you think," he added, looking at his loose change, "an Irish penny would work?"

"No, it's bad luck," said Rupert, chucking in fifty lira. "I expect you'll sneak back at dusk and fish that out, Driffield."

Fen threw in ten lira.

"Please, Fountain," she prayed, "when I come back, let it be with a really nice man who loves me as much as I love him."

Opening her eyes, she found Billy beside her. He had also tossed a coin into the fountain, watching it floating down to land on the bronze and silver floor. His lips were moving, his face haggard, his hair even greyer in the sunlight.

"He's wishing he'll come back to Rome with Janey," thought Fen. "Oh poor, poor Billy."

Back at the show in the afternoon, she hadn't fared any better. And now she'd been packed off to bed at eleven o'clock, with soothing reassurances from Malise that she was not to worry, she'd soon find her feet and to get a good night's sleep. How could she possibly sleep with all that din and merrymaking in the streets below?

Her mood was not helped by the fact that Sarah and Dizzy had been asked out by two American tennis stars over for the tournament which ran concurrently with the horse show. Both grooms had come and used Fen's rooms to bathe and wash their hair and change, and had gone off in raging spirits looking gorgeous.

Fen went out on the balcony. Here I am in the most beautiful city in the world, she thought, with the spring in its green prime, with the streets and parks filled with lovers kissing, holding hands, necking in traffic jams, lying on the grass. Everywhere she went, gorgeous Italian men, with hot dark eyes, followed her, wolf-whistling and pinching her bottom, but Rupert and Billy and Malise chaperoned her so fiercely she wasn't allowed near them. Only that evening at a cocktail party she'd met a fantastic-looking French tennis player who was just asking her out to dinner when Rupert came up and told him to piss off.

"What's that you say?" asked the Frenchman.

So Rupert told him in French, even more forcibly, and the Frenchman had gone very white and backed off. That was another thing. Rupert had made terrific verbal passes at her at the World Championship, but now he was treating her as though she was a very boring nine-year-old child he was expected to look after. And tonight no doubt he and Billy had gone off on the town.

She knew she ought to undress and try to sleep. But it was so hot and stuffy she stayed on the balcony watching the lights twinkling in the grounds of the Villa Borghese. Even the moon was wrapped in a gold lurex shawl of cloud, as though she was going out for the evening.

"Nothing in excess," Apollo's motto, was carved over the door at the entrance to the hotel. I'm obviously not going to get a chance even to have anything in moderation. Fen thought sulkily.

"Please Apollo," she pleaded, "I promise I won't be excessive. Just let me have a bit of fun." As if in answer to her prayer, the telephone rang. Fen sprang on it. "*Buona Notte.*"

"Hi," said a soft voice, "is that Fen?"

"Who's that?" she sqeaked, her heart hammering.

"It's Dino, Dino Ferranti."

Fen sat down very suddenly on the bed.

"Hello, hello," he said when she couldn't speak. "Fen."

"Yes," she stammered. "Oh how blissful to hear you."

"I sure missed you baby. Did you get my telegram?"

"Oh yes. It was so sweet of you, how did you know?"

"I've had my spies out. How are you getting on?"

"Not great, I haven't won a thing."

"Don't worry, it's a helluva course. Has Rupert been leaping on you?"

"On the contrary, they're all treating me as though I was a typhoid carrier."

"This is a godawful line," said Dino.

"Where are you?"

"In Rome."

"Rome!" She knew she should be cool, but she couldn't keep the squeak of delight out of her voice.

"Just dropped by to look at a horse. I'm flying out tomorrow. I guess it's late, but you wouldn't like to come out, would you?"

"Oh, yes please."

"I'll pick you up in half an hour."

She'd never washed her hair or bathed so quickly. Thank God she hadn't worn her new pink dress or her pink shoes yet. She'd been saving them for a special occasion. "Everything in excess," she told her radiant reflection as she sprayed duty free scent bought on the boat everywhere: in her shoes, behind her knees and ears and on her bush.

She hoped Dino wouldn't be turned off because she'd cut her hair. She wished she had time to paint her toenails.

She decided not to take the elevator, she was bound to run slap into Malise, and instead crept down the huge staircase, clinging onto the bannisters for support. Her knees kept giving way. In two minutes she'd see Dino.

Blast! There were Rupert and Driffield in the lobby, appearing to be examining some expensive sweaters in a glass case. She shot back upstairs, peering through the bannisters. Hell! They were still there. She'd just have to brazen it out. Why shouldn't she go and have a drink with Dino? She reached the bottom of the stairs and was just tiptoeing across the marble floor to the front door when Rupert and Driffield turned round, both doubled up with laughter.

"What's the matter?" asked Fen, walking past them, her nose in the air.

"April fool." said Rupert.

Ignoring them, Fen walked on.

Catching up, Rupert tapped her on the shoulder. "April fool."

"I don't know what you're talking about."

"I sure missed you, kid. This is Dino Ferranti."

Fen looked at him, bewildered.

"Is he here already? Where is he?"

Rupert looked down at her, his eyes narrowed to slits, that mocking cruel smile on his beautiful face.

"In America, as far as I know."

"He's not," said Fen patiently. "He's in Rome. I've just talked to him on the telephone."

"And he's come to look at a horse and all the British team are treating you as if you were a typhoid carrier."

The color drained from Fen's face.

"It was you," she whispered.

"Sure was. Don't you think I've picked up quite a good Yank accent from my wife?"

Fen looked at him in horror. "You bastard. How could you?"

Rupert shrugged. "New girl's tease." He ruffled her hair. "Come on, I'll buy you a drink."

"You bloody won't," and, bursting into tears, she ran back upstairs. As she panted, sobbing, up to the second floor Rupert came off of the lift.

"Come on, it was a joke."

"Not to me, it wasn't." She fled down the passage, but as she scrabbled desperately in her bag for her key Rupert caught up with her.

"Angel, I'm sorry. I didn't realize it would upset you that much."

"Go away," she sobbed. "I hate you."

"Shush, shush," he said, taking her in his arms. "You'll wake Grisel from her ugly sleep."

"Stop it," she said, hammering her fists against his chest as the tears spilled down her cheeks. But he was far too strong for her.

Next moment he was kissing her quivering mouth. For a second she clenched her teeth together. Then, suddenly aware of the warmth and vitality, she melted and began to kiss him back. Her hands against her will crept up over the powerful shoulders, her fingers entwining in the sleek thick hair.

"What the hell are you two doing?" said a voice.

Fen nearly went through the ceiling. Rupert didn't move.

"What does it look as though we're doing?" snapped Rupert.

He stopped kissing Fen, but still shielded her in his arms. "Look, Malise, this is entirely my fault, not Fen's. I enticed her out as a practical joke, pretending to be someone else. Then I followed her upstairs and—er—forced my attentions on her."

"She didn't appear to be putting up much resistance," said Malise coldly.

"That's my irresistible charm," said Rupert. Letting go of Fen, he opened her door and gave her her bag which had fallen on the carpet. "Go to bed, darling. I'll sort this out."

Malise, in a dinner jacket, had been to the theater. Rupert and he glared at each other.

"Well," said Rupert softly, "what are you going to do about it?"

"Nothing, this time," said Malise, "but you can thank your lucky stars, albeit interpreted by Patric Walker, that I caught you outside the bedroom. If this happens again I'll leave you off of the team for the rest of the year."

Rupert looked unrepentant. "She's so adorable it's almost worth it," he said.

Billy, who'd forgotten to declare for the following day and had just returned from the show offices, was absolutely livid when he heard what had happened.

"You rotten sod," he shouted at Rupert. "Didn't you see the way her little face lit up when that cable arrived? She's obviously mad about him. How could you do such a fucking awful thing to her? You don't understand anything about people's feelings. You're like a bloody boy scout in reverse. You have to do a bad deed every day," and he walked into his bedroom, slamming the door. Immediately he dialed Fen's number.

"If that's Rupert you can bugger of."

"It isn't. Are you OK?"

"Perfectly," said Fen in a choked voice.

"Do you want a shoulder to cry on?"

"And get into more trouble with Malise! No thank you very much," said Fen with a stifled sob, and hung up.

By morning misery had hardened into cold rage against Rupert. How could she have betrayed Jake and let herself kiss him back like that and, even worse, enjoyed it? She was a nymphomaniac virgin. She went out to work the horses, boot-faced, with dark glasses covering her swollen eyes.

Malise came down to watch her, asking her to come and have a cup of coffee with him afterwards.

Perhaps he'll even send me home, she thought miserably.

But Malise merely wanted to tell her that she hadn't been picked for the Nations' Cup tomorrow. Ivor Braine had pulled a back muscle, so the team would be Rupert, Billy, Driffield and Griselda.

Hanging her head, Fen reminded Malise of a snowdrop.

"I'm sorry I've been so hopeless."

"You haven't. You won that class the first day."

"You don't want to send me back because you've made a ghastly mistake?"

"You have the self-confidence of a snail," said Malise. "You obviously don't rate me as a chef d'equipe if you assume I'd select someone who was no good."

Fen sprinkled chocolate on her cappucino.

"Wherefore rejoice," she said moodily, "what conquests brings she home?"

"Oh, you will. Look, you're a very very good rider; better, dare I say it, even than Jake when he jumped that first earth-shattering double clear on Sailor at Madrid. But it's all strange. Macaulay's strange, you haven't got Jake to mastermind your every move. Griselda's bitching, Rupert and everyone else are letching."

Fen flushed and bit her lip.

"Rupert really wouldn't do for you," he said. "I realize he's attractive. But Helen's had so much of that to put up with, and you know how Jake detests him."

"I didn't want—it wasn't like that," stammered Fen.

"I don't want excuses," said Malise, "Rupert accepts full responsibility, but that doesn't alter the fact that you shouldn't have been out of your room, in a party dress, an hour after you'd been sent to bed. Now, d'you want to come and have a look at the Sistine Chapel?"

There were two big classes that afternoon. The first a knock-out competition, the second a Puissance, sponsored by one of Italy's leading car manufacturers.

"Macaulay's in a foul mood," Sarah told Fen when she got to the show ground. "He's just sulking in his stall."

"He's fed up with not winning," said Fen. "I'm going to jump him in the Puissance."

Sarah looked horrified. "Are you sure that's wise? Jake's never jumped him in a Puissance, and high-jumping really isn't his forte. The ground's absolutely rock hard."

"I don't care," said Fen. "Get him ready."

That evening when she got back to the hotel Fen called Jake.

"I suppose you've won a class at last," he said sourly, "or you wouldn't be calling. How's Macaulay?"

"Wonderful. Actually I've got good news and bad news about him."

"For Christ's sake. He's all right, isn't he?"

"Well the bad news is I entered him in the Puissance."

"You what!" Even at a thousand miles away, she quailed. "But the good news is he won."

For two minutes Jake called her every name under the sun. Then he asked, "How high did he jump?"

Fen giggled, "Seven foot two, easy peasy. He could have gone higher, and, oh Jake, he was so delighted to be in the money again. You know how he adores winning. He bucked after every jump and insisted on doing two laps of honor and ate the President's carnation. But he's really well," she added hastily. "I hosed down his legs myself and put on cooling linament, and I'll walk him around in an hour or two, but it really bucked him up."

"How much have you won?"

"Well, I haven't worked it out yet; you know my math. About £3000 I should think. But the best news is I won a little car as well, so I'll be able to whizz you around all over the place when you come out of the hospital. How are you anyway?"

Jake didn't want to talk about himself, but she could tell by the sound of his voice how thrilled he was.

40

There was a cocktail party at the British Embassy that night, and for once the team wasn't under Malise's ever-watchful eye. A complimentary ticket from the Minister of the Arts to hear Placido Domingo as Otello at the Teatro dell'Opera had been too much for him, but he'd had tough words with the team beforehand.

"This is the first Nations' Cup in the series. If we win it'll be a colossal boost to morale. So there's to be no heavy drinking and I want everyone in their rooms by midnight. You'll be the only one completely sober," he added to Billy, "so I'm relying on you to look after Fen and see she's in her own bed and not Rupert's by eleven o'clock."

Billy shook his head. "If you honestly think Rupert'll take any notice of me."

Rupert arrived at the party in a new suit—pale blue and made for him by one of Italy's leading couturiers, who normally only designed clothes for women, but who had succumbed because he rightly felt Rupert would be such a good advertisement for his product.

Anyone else would have looked like a raving queen, thought Billy, particularly wearing an amethyst shirt and tie. But such was Rupert's masculinity, and the enhanced blueness of his eyes, and the lean broad-shouldered length of his body, that the result was sensational.

All the girls at the party were falling over themselves to offer him smoked salmon and asparagus rolls, and fill up his glass with champagne.

"They're all convinced I'm an American tennis player," he said, fighting his way through the crowd to Billy. "I've already been complimented three times on my backhand and my serve. The only thing I want to serve here," he said, lowering his voice, "is Fenella Maxwell."

"Oh for Christ's sake," snapped Billy.

"She wants it," said Rupert softly. "She was like a mare in season last night. Besides I've a score to settle with Hopalong Chastity."

"Poor sod's in the hospital with a smashed leg. Isn't that enough for you?"

"William, he's tried to kill me twice, once with a knife, once with Macaulay. I intend to get my own back."

He glanced across the room to where Fen was talking to the Italian Minister of the Arts, who was about three times her age. She looked pale and tired.

"Look at her being letched over by that disgusting wop. I'll just make her jealous by chatting up those two girls over there and I've got her on a plate."

"Your conceit is unending. Christ, I wish I could have a drink."

"Those two look as though they might have some dope at home. Come on."

The girls were certainly very pretty—one blonde, one redheaded.

"You must be tennis players," giggled the redhead. "You look so incredibly healthy."

"No," said Rupert unsmiling.

"What do you do then?"

"I ride horses," said Rupert; then, after a pause, "Extremely successfully."

The conversation moved on to marriage.

"Billy is separated and gloriously available," said Rupert. "I am married and ditto."

"Doesn't your wife mind?"

"No."

"Does she work for a living?"

"No, nor does she smoke, drink or fuck."

The girls laughed uproariously. Billy turned away. Outside it was dusk. A stone nymph in an off-the-shoulder dress reclined in the long grass, against a blackening yew tree. Fireflies flickered around a couple of orange trees in tubs. Water from a fountain tumbled down grey-green steps between banks of pale lilac geraniums.

I can't bear it, he thought miserably, and toyed with the idea of

asking Fen to come and have dinner with him alone. She didn't look
very happy, particularly now the blonde was obviously making time
with Rupert. She and her friend were secretaries at the Embassy, the
blonde was saying, they loved the life in Rome.

Her redheaded friend joined Billy by the window.

"I'm sorry about your marriage," she said. "I'm separated myself.
No one who hasn't been through it knows how awful it is."

Billy mistook the brimming tears of self-pity in her eyes for pity
of his own plight.

"When did you split up?" he asked.

"Six months ago," she said, and she was off.

Fifteen minutes later they were interrupted by Driffield, looking
like a thundercloud.

"Crippled lame," he said in disgust. "Horse can't put his foot
down. Vet's just had a look; thinks it's an abscess." He grabbed a glass
of champagne from a passing tray. "Where's Malise?"

"Gone to the opera."

"Bloody fairy."

"My God," said Grisel, joining them. "That means Fen will have
to jump. That's all we need."

"She jumped bloody well this afternoon," said Driffield.

"I'd better go and tell her," said Billy. But, glancing across the
room, he saw she'd disappeared. He tried the other rooms, fighting his
way through the yelling crowd, then he tried the garden, hearing
laughter from behind a rose bush.

"Fuck off," said a voice as he peered round. Two elegant young
men were locked in each other's arms.

Fen's coat wasn't in the cloakroom. Yes, said the attendant, a girl
in a pink dress and pink shoes had just left with the Minister of the
Arts. He assumed she was his daughter.

"She isn't," said Billy bleakly.

"Lucky chap," said the attendant.

Billy returned to Rupert and told him what had happened.
Rupert, who'd already drunk a bottle and a half of champagne, shrugged his shoulders. "Oh well, she won't come to any harm with him.
He looked past it. Anyway these 'ere," he jerked his head in the direction of the two secretaries, "look very accommodating. We'll all have
dinner, then go back to their place."

"I don't want to," protested Billy. "I must find Fen."

"She'll go back to the hotel early," said Rupert. "She heard Malise's pep talk. She was as contrite as anything this morning."

At dinner the girls got sillier and sillier, and Billy's despair
deeper. Back at their apartment, he went into the bathroom to have a
pee. The spilled talcum powder, the chaos of makeup, the tights and
pants dripping over the bath, the trailing plant gasping for water and

the half-drunk gin and tonic reminded him poignantly of Janey. He longed to go back to the hotel. The redhead was pretty, but it was obvious she would much rather be in bed with Rupert. "Your friend's a live one, isn't he?"

On the walls of her room were posters of Robert Redford and Sylvester Stallone. The bed was very narrow.

"I don't usually do this on the first night," she said slipping out of her pale yellow dress with a slither of silk. Her body wasn't as good stripped; her breasts drooped like half-filled bean bags.

"I'm awfully sorry," Billy said later, looking down at his flaccid, lifeless cock.

"Don't you find me attractive?" said the girl petulently.

"It's because you're so beautiful you've completely overwhelmed me," lied Billy. "And I've got a big class tomorrow, which never helps."

With his hands and his tongue he had given her pleasure, but, rejected by her husband, she needed confirmation that men still found her irresistible. Billy could feel her being "frightfully understanding," but he could imagine the whispering round the Embassy tomorrow.

"My dear, he couldn't get it up at all. No wonder his wife walked out."

By a quarter to twelve Rupert was ready to go home too.

"We'd love tickets for tomorrow," said the blonde as they left. "You will call, won't you?"

"I nearly couldn't perform," said Rupert in the taxi. "She just lay back stark naked on the bed and said, 'Come on Campbell-Black, let's see if you're as good as they all say you are.' Must be hell to be impotent."

"I hope to God Fen's back," said Billy.

But to his horror her key, No. 88, was still hanging at the reception desk.

"Jesus," said Rupert, "there's Malise getting out of a cab. Go and tell him about Driffield. I'll get the key and whizz up and wait in her room. You join me when the coast's clear."

"Good opera?" Billy asked Malise.

"Magical," said Malise. "I cried nonstop through the last act."

He didn't even seem to notice that the hall clock said half past twelve.

"First Edition's unfit," said Billy. "Vet says it's an abscess."

"Hell," said Malise. "Fen'll have to jump. Does she know?"

"We didn't tell her," said Billy, "in case we raised her hopes and you wanted Driff to jump Anaconda."

Malise shook his head. "Macaulay's the better bet. You saw Fen safely into bed, did you?"

Billy nodded, blushing slightly. "Must be asleep by now."

"Good man. I'll tell her in the morning."

—

With a growing sense of outrage Billy and Rupert sat in Fen's room, Rupert drinking weak brandies from Fen's untouched duty free bottle, Billy drinking one disgusting cup of black coffee after another.

At three-thirty they heard a commotion outside.

"*J'ai perdu mon clef,* key, you know, what St. Peter, the one with the kissed foot had in abundance," said a shrill voice, "so if you'd be so very kind as to let me into my room."

In a flash Rupert was at the door, where he found Fen and a sleepy-looking maid in a dressing-gown.

"*Grazie,*" he said to the maid and pulled Fen inside. "What the bloody hell have you got to say for yourself?"

Fen's hair was tousled, her brown skin flushed. Her eyes glittered, red-irised and out of focus. She was wearing an exquisite grey silk shirt which just covered her groin and carrying her pink dress.

She gave a low bow.

"*Buona notte, senors,* or should it be *buon journo,* I forget. I sheem-hic-to have got myself into the wrong room." She backed toward the door.

"Come here," hissed Rupert. "Where the hell have you been?"

"Do you really want to know? I've been having fun. When in Rome, get done by the Romans." She opened the door into the passage, swinging on the handle.

Rupert caught her by the scruff of the neck, marched her back into the room and sat her down on the bed. Then, locking the door, he pocketed the key.

"Now come on. Out with it."

Fen looked at them owlishly. "I've been out with the Minister of the Arts, such charm and such finesse. He said I was a work of art myself and he bought me thish lovely shirt from Pucci."

She stood up, pirouetted round and collapsed onto the bed again.

"And I regret to tell you I lost my virginity. And it's no point going to look for it at the Loshed Property Offish, it's gone for good. One should be in the hands of an eckshpert the first time, don't you think? 'I jumped seven foot two this afternoon, so it's but a tiny leap into your ancient four poster, Mr. Minister,' I said."

Billy felt a great sadness.

"You little slut," said Rupert slowly. "You just picked him up and went to bed for a 60,000 lira dress."

"Better than nothing, which I'd have got from you two. Anyway," said Fen, suddenly furious, "if I'm a slut, what the hell d'you think you are, going to parties, picking up awful typists, and all those horrible things you said about Helen? How you can behave like that when you've got a beautiful wife, and lovely children? You're the most immoral man I've ever met."

There was banging on the next-door wall. Someone shouted in German.

"Oh shut up," said Fen, banging back again.

Her eyes lit on the brandy. "I want another drink."

Billy got to his feet. "You've had enough," he said flatly. "Come on, get to bed. I'll help you undress."

Fen swayed away from him. "No, no, I can't be undressed twice in an evening." Then she swayed back towards him. She stood on tiptoe trying to kiss him, but the effort was too much for her. She collapsed back on the bed and passed out.

"It's not funny," said Rupert.

"I know it isn't," said Billy.

"What the hell are you doing?" said Rupert, as Billy started unbuttoning the grey silk shirt.

"Shame if she puked over her Pucci," said Billy.

"Lovely body," said Rupert. I suppose we can't take advantage?"

"No we can't," said Billy, tucking her into bed.

Through nightmares of pain and torture—they must be acupuncturing her brain with red hot pokers—Fen could hear bells. They must be ambulance bells, taking her to the hospital to die.

But it was the telephone. She reached out, dropped it and picked it up.

"Morning Fen, sorry to wake you," said a brisk voice. "Have you had a good night?"

"Yes," she croaked.

"Congratulations anyway on your first cap. Driffield's out. You'll be jumping today."

"I what?" stammered Fen in horror.

"Makes you speechless, does it?" Malise laughed. "See you down at the stables in about an hour. Then we can put Macaulay over a few practice fences."

Fen put the telephone down and groaned. She got up, rushed to the bathroom and was sick.

"Why doesn't someone turn down those bloody bells?" she croaked. "They can't be Christian to make a din like that."

Her breeches, which she'd taken to the launderette yesterday, were still hanging over the balcony. She winced with pain as she opened the shutters. The sunlight hit her like a boxing glove. She staggered back to the bed and, picking up the telephone, dialed Billy's number.

"Billy, it's Fen—I think. Get me an ambulance."

He laughed. "Is it that bad?"

"I've never known pain like it."

"I'll be with you in a couple of minutes."

He found her white and shuddering. "Here lies one who's name is writ in Krug," she moaned. "Take me to the nearest pharmacia and tell me the Italian for Alka Seltzer. I've got to jump, Billy. More likely to jump over that balcony."

"Drink this. It's disgusting, but it should help." He handed her some Fernet Branca in a tooth mug.

"Ugh, it is disgusting. I'm going to throw up."

"No you're not. Keep your head up, take deep breaths."

"Do you think there's any hope of the arena party going on strike?" said Fen.

Billy looked at the bruises on her thighs, wondering if they were the result of amorous pinches from the Minister of Arts. Fen seemed to read his thoughts and blushed. "I got them falling off Macaulay."

She was not helped by a sudden heatwave hitting Rome. As she tottered the course beside Billy three hours later, the temperature had soared into the nineties. The sun seemed to be beating personally down on her head. There was no shade. The colored poles danced before her eyes.

"Where did you go last night, Fen?" said Griselda bullyingly as they examined a vast wall.

"I don't remember the name, but I had shellfish," said Fen faintly.

"Hum," said Griselda in disbelief.

"This course is designed to make riders think every inch of the way," said Malise, as they examined the huge water jump floating with water lilies, known as the bidet. "It's going to take very accurate jumping. The stile's only four and a half strides before the combination. Macaulay'll probably do it in four, Fen. Are you feeling all right?"

"Fine," said Fen, clinging onto the wing of the fence. "It's just the heat."

"Poor kid, suffers from nerves as badly as Jake," thought Malise, looking at her green face.

Eight teams came out for the Nations' Cup. Fen, after yesterday's triumph, got a rousing cheer as she rode in the parade flanked by Rupert and Billy.

The playing of each National Anthem seemed to go on for ever.

"It's you, not our gracious Queen, that needs saving today," said Rupert out of the corner of his mouth.

Great Britain's fortunes were varied. Rupert jumped an effortless clear which brought more rousing cheers—even from the most partisan crowd in Europe.

Waiting, pouring with sweat, teeth chattering, wondering whether to be sick again, Fen felt too ill even to be pleased that Griselda had nearly fallen off at the bidet and had notched up twelve faults. She came out furiously tugging Mr. Punch's head from side to side.

Britain was in third place when Fen went in.

"Go for a steady clear," said Malise. "I'd like to drop Grisel's round."

Fen felt like a Christian after the Roman emperor had made that terrible thumbs-down sign of death. Alone in the ring, under those towering stands which had just become a sea of faces, she could feel the lions stealthily padding towards her.

Macaulay, who always felt a great responsibility for the rider on his back, understood that Fen needed help. Watching his earnest white face appearing over each jump, Billy realized he was taking Fen round. He was about to take five strides after the stile, then changed to four, bouncing easily over the combination, but causing Fen to lose a stirrup. Slowing fractionally so she could find it again, he rounded the corner. For a minute Fen looked perplexed, then she turned him sharp right towards the huge yellow wall. A million times afterwards she relived that moment. She seemed to hear a shout from the collecting ring, but it was too late. Gathering Macaulay together, she cleared the wall, then looked round for the next jump in bewilderment. In front a triple was facing backwards with a red flag on the left. Excited officials were waving their arms at her; the crowd gave a groan of sympathy. And suddenly it dawned on Fen—she'd taken the wrong course.

Head banging, fighting back the tears, white-faced, she cantered out of the ring.

"Fucking imbecile," said Rupert.

"You've ruined our chances," said Grisel, her mouth full of hot dog.

Fen slid off Macaulay, loosening his girths, giving him his lemon drops, whispering, "I'm sorry, I'm sorry," over and over again.

"Bad luck," said Sarah, "you were going so well."

Malise came up. "I hope that won't happen in the second round," he said bleakly.

"I must not cry, I must not cry," said Fen, and fled to the john where she was sick for the fifteenth time that day.

On her return she found everyone more cheerful, particularly Mr. Block, Billy's sponsor, who'd flown out to watch the Nations' Cup. Billy and Bugle had gone clear, bouncing over the fences like a Jack-in-the-box. At the end of the first leg the Germans were in the lead, the Italians second, and the English and the Swiss tying for third place.

Fen couldn't face the riders' stand. She sat on an upturned bucket, under the thick canopy of an umbrella pine, with her head in her hands. Macaulay, led by Sarah, came up and nuzzled her.

"Poor old boy," said Fen listlessly. "It's bloody hot."

Macaulay looked longingly as an ice-cream seller came by.

"Oh get him one," Fen told Sarah. "He deserves it."

At that moment Rupert came up, keeping his distance because Macaulay promptly rolled his eyes and stamped his foot threateningly. "I hope you'll know better in future than to get plastered and seduced by geriatric wops," said Rupert viciously.

Already the sun was beginning to slant sideways through the pines, throwing treacherous shadows across the fences, particularly the parallel.

On his mettle, Rupert jumped just as brilliantly in the second round. He was unlucky to hit the second pole of the parallel and notch up four faults. He came out in a furious temper.

"Horse was going superbly, but he simply couldn't see what he was jumping at the parallel. I'm going to object."

Nor did the Germans or the Italians fare any better. The unaccustomed hot weather and the punishing course was tiring them all out. Grisel finished her second hot dog and rode off into the ring.

"How the hell can she stuff herself like that before a class?" said Fen.

"Her nerve ends are so coated with fat they don't function properly," said Sarah. "Oh whizzo, she's fallen in the bidet. Look at her covered in water lilies."

"You're being very unpatriotic," reproved Billy. "She is jumping for Britain."

He put a hand on Fen's forehead. "Are you feeling any better?"

"Not after that frightful fiasco."

He shrugged. "Happen to anyone."

Having fallen off, Griselda went on to notch up a further four faults.

"Just get around this time. That's all that matters," said Malise, as Fen went in. She had never felt so ill in her life.

"Keep the white flag on your left, keep the white flag on your left," she said to herself over and over again.

Somehow she got over the first seven fences, including the bogey parallel. But as she approached the combination a child at the edge of the crowd let go of her gas balloon and, with bellows of misery, watched it float out like a spermatozoa just in front of Macaulay. For a second he glanced at it, confused, put in a short stride, found himself under the fence and took a colossal cat jump which nearly unseated Fen. Losing her reins, but clutching on to his mane for dear life, she managed to stay on as he cleared the second element, but her foot went straight through the iron. His last huge leap over the final element completely unseated her and she went crashing to the ground, but, with her foot trapped, was dragged bumping horribly for several yards before Macaulay, realizing what had happened, jammed on his brakes.

Two officials ran up and disconnected her. Blood was pouring from her nose onto her white shirt, tie and breeches. Staggering to her feet, she looked dazedly round for Macaulay.

"I must get back on, got to finish."

There he was, looking apologetic and worried. His white face seemed to come towards her and go away. Stumbling over to him, she tried to clamber on, but at 17.2 it was like climbing the Matterhorn.

"Give me a leg up," she screamed to the steward. "I'll run out of time."

The stewards, in broken English, told her she mustn't jump and looked desperately around for the first-aid man. Just as he came running on, she somehow managed to get her foot in the stirrup and heave herself up, blood still streaming from her nose.

Heedless to the cries to stop, she turned to the last row of jumps.

"Get her out of the ring," said Billy, as white as his shirt. "She'll kill herself."

The crowds were screaming in horror. Fen had lost so much blood it seemed that she was dressed all in red. Somehow she cleared the next two fences. She looked around, bewildered and swaying. There was only the oxer left. Fortunately Macaulay took charge. He could see the collecting ring and he wanted to get back there as soon as possible. Trotting briskly round the oxer, with Fen clinging round his neck, he carried her carefully out of the ring.

Malise, Billy and Rupert rushed forward.

"It's only a nosebleed," muttered Fen into Macaulay's blood-soaked mane. "You were right about there only being four and a half strides between the stile and the combination." As they lifted her off she fainted.

"Get an ambulance," said Billy in anguish, "We must get her to the hospital. I'm going with her."

"Don't be so fucking silly," said Rupert and Malise in unison. "You've still got to jump."

41

*T*hey decided to keep Fen in the hospital overnight. After they'd cleaned her up, it was decided she was only suffering from a severe nosebleed and concussion. Later, when Billy turned up to visit her, he found her in a clean white nightgown, slumped in bed, red-eyed, with her swollen face turned to the wall.

"Fen, it's me, Billy."

"Is Macaulay all right?"

"Blooming. I saw he got his five lemon drops. I've brought you these."

He held a bunch of yellow roses in front of her face.

"Thanks." She hunched up her shoulders, pulling the sheet up over her eyes. Billy put the roses in the sink and sat down on the bed.

"How are you feeling?"

She looked round, her eyes swollen with crying, her lips puffy and bruised where she'd hit the ground, her face covered in bruises.

"Terrible. It's very kind of you to come and see me, but I want to be on my own."

"Just wanted to see if you were all right."

"Perfectly," she snapped.

Billy got to his feet. As he reached the door she gave a strangled sob. Billy sat down again and took her in his arms.

"I'm so ashamed," she wailed, burying her face in his shoulder. "Such an awful thing to do. But I was so fed up with being chaperoned and everyone treating me like a baby. In fact, a baby would behave with more responsibility. Getting eliminated twice in a Nations' Cup, I've let you all down: Macaulay, Jake, Malise, all the team, Great Britain."

"Fen," Billy stroked her hair, "can I tell you something?"

"No, I want to talk. I lied to you last night. I was just boasting because I was drunk and fed up. Umberto, that's the Minister of the Arts, was awfully sweet, but his boyfriend died two months ago and he misses him terribly. All he wanted to do was to talk about him. He did the talking. I was listening, and you tend to drink a lot when you're listening. He didn't lay a finger on me except for kissing my hand. But when I got back Rupert was so bloody censorious, just assuming I'd been behaving like a whore, after all he'd been up to—and I was jealous of you fooling around with that beastly redhead—I just lost my temper. But I promise I didn't sleep with him."

For a minute Billy couldn't speak for relief.

"So you're still intacta."

Fen nodded dolefully. Suddenly she realized Billy was still wearing boots and breeches spattered with her blood. He'd taken off his white tie and exchanged his red coat for a dark-blue sweater with a hole in the elbow, but he'd forgotten to take off his spurs.

"You came straight from the show. You shouldn't have bothered. I'm sorry about your breeches."

"Fenella," said Billy gently, "if you'd keep your trap shut for one second, I've got something for you."

He put his hand in his pocket, then dropped a ribbon and a little silver model of the she-wolf suckling Romulus and Remus.

"W-what's this?"

"We won."

"But how could we? Grisel was on twelve and I was eliminated."

Billy grinned. "The Germans went to pieces and I jumped another clear."

Fen opened her mouth and shut it again; then she flung her arms around his neck. "But that's wonderful, *and* with Mr. Block watching. Oh I'm so, so pleased."

"Malise is going around like the Cheshire cat that's just wolfed the canary."

Fen picked up the ribbon: "Is he still livid with me?"

"On the contrary. He now thinks you were very brave to jump at all. Rupert told him you'd swallowed a bad oyster last night and soldiered on because there wasn't anyone else to jump."

"Rupert did?" said Fen incredulously. "That was extraordinarily kind of him."

Billy laughed. "Rupert loves winning, so now Malise thinks you've been very plucky."

"I haven't," muttered Fen. "I've been an idiot." She looked at the ribbon again; it matched the spattered blood. "I had no part in getting this. I don't deserve it."

"You deserved the one at the beginning of the week which Ludwig got, so this one makes up for it."

But the tears were starting again.

"Angel, please don't cry." He pulled her into his arms again, letting her tears drench his shirt. He was so warm, so comforting and rocklike, she couldn't bear him to go.

A nun came in, saying time was up and Fen ought to rest.

Billy looked up. *"Duo momenti, grazie."* He turned back to Fen. "I'll come and collect you tomorrow morning."

"Could you bring me some clothes to wear, preferably a hairshirt?"

"And tomorrow night I'll take you out to dinner and treat you like a grown-up."

A very pale, subdued Fen came out of the hospital next morning. Billy brought her some clothes, but what he'd thought in his haste was a dress turned out to be a cotton nightgown with the pink panther on the front. Her lips and nose were still swollen and blackened.

"Don't look at me, I'm so ugly."

The nuns bundled her bloodstained clothes into a paper bag. "I hope we don't get arrested," said Fen.

"I'm afraid the taxis are on strike," said Billy, putting his arm through hers, "so we'll have to bus back to the Villa Borghese."

"Ooch," said Fen, as a passing Italian pinched her bottom.

The bus came crashing along, fighting for survival in the surging thrusting jam of cars.

"It's illegal to hoot in Rome," said Fen.

"Bad luck for owls," said Billy, as they fought and pummelled their way into the bus. For at least ten seconds they were separated, then Billy fought his way back to her.

"You OK?"

"I need a pencil sharpener for my elbows, and I've been goosed by six men."

"You mean geesed."

The bus doors closed, shooting another ten people into the body of the bus and ramming Fen against Billy. She arched away from him in embarrassment, but it was no good, the crowd pushed her forward again and she lost hold of the bus strap, cannoning into his arms, which closed round her.

"I'm going to complain to Sardine's Lib," she mumbled in embarrassment.

"I'm not," said Billy. "Relax."

Looking up, Fen saw the tenderness in his eyes and looked away quickly. But once again there was something so comforting and solid about him that she let herself relax for the rest of the ride, praying he couldn't feel her heart hammering.

"He loves Janey," she told herself furiously. "He's just being kind."

The rest of the day seemed to pass in a dream. Everyone except Griselda was incredibly nice. Malise let her jump Desdemona in a small class to get her nerve back and was highly delighted when she came in fourth. With a sense of unreality, she sat in the riders' stand beside Mr. Block to watch the Grand Prix, which ended up with a jump off between Piero, Rupert, Ludwig, Wishbone, Billy and Griselda. Billy, galvanized by yesterday's double clear, seemed to have got all his old fire and confidence back. Riding as though he'd got a spare neck in his pocket, he knocked three seconds off everyone's time. Rupert was second.

"Why the hell did I bring you back when all you do is beat me?" grumbled Rupert as they rode into the ring.

Back at the stables everyone was beginning to pack up. Griselda watched Georgie working and grumbled, "I've got a bloody trek home, being misdirected by that stupid Maxwell child. Let's hope Malise has learned his lesson and leaves her off of the team."

Billy, who was hosing down Bugle's legs, looked up angrily. "She's already selected for Paris and Lucerne."

"Oh Christ, don't say I've got to put up with her for the rest of the month. I must get Malise to make other traveling arrangements for her."

Rupert, who was feeding popcorn to Snakepit, looked across at Billy and raised his eyebrows.

Billy nodded.

"He already has," said Rupert. "I've sold a couple of horses this week, so we're taking her back."

"What about Sarah?" said Griselda in tones of outrage.

"Very pretty," said Rupert. "She can have my bed in the trailer any time, as long as I'm allowed to share it with her."

Griselda looked absolutely furious. "The sneaky little thing, she's actually made other arrangements without telling me. Who's going to share the gas and pay for the tolls? Trust her to pull a fast one without telling me."

"She doesn't know she's coming with us yet," said Billy sweetly, "but knowing how much you and Georgie like the van to yourself, I know she wouldn't like to cramp your style."

"Well, on your heads be it if she misroutes you into Rumania," said Grisel crossly.

Billy said goodbye to Mr. Block, who was flying back to London.

"Well done, lad," he said, pumping Billy's hand. "I'm highly delighted with the way things have gone. We're on our way."

Then Billy found Malise. "Look, I know I ought to foot the bill for dinner tonight, and I'm very happy to, and I'd really like to be with you all, but I thought I'd take Fen somewhere quiet," he blushed. "I think she needs cheering up."

Because he knew she was ashamed of her battered face, Billy took Fen to a little dark cave of a restaurant where they sat in an alcove away from everyone else. She was still feeling fragile, so he ordered her a plain rice risotto with a bit of butter and parmesan, and fed her spoonfuls as though she was a little girl.

"I'm so proud of you," she said for the hundredth time. "But this isn't much of a celebration for you, me off my feed, and both of us drinking Coke."

Billy put his hand over hers and it felt so right he left it there.

Afterwards they wandered through the cobbled streets of Rome, past shadowy ruins and floodlit fountains, until they found a secluded stone bench to sit on and Billy kissed her very very gently on her poor sore mouth.

"I'm so glad you didn't go to bed with that wop last night."

He ran his hand down her cheek. It was such a relief not to have to duck her head out of the way so he shouldn't feel her pimples.

"Oh Billy, I've had a crush on you since I was thirteen."

"On me?" he said amazed.

"Yes, millions of girls have as well, but you're too modest or too nice to realize it. It's the general consensus that Rupert's for flings, but you're the one they want to marry. Not that I'm proposing or anything," she added, blushing furiously.

Billy kissed her again. She was not quite sure what one did with one's tongue, so she copied him.

"You're so sweet," he murmured, "but I'm too old and battered and bitter for you. You don't need third-hand goods."

"Rubbish," protested Fen. "What about antiques, they're third- and fourth- and fifth-hand, and they're infinitely more precious than anything new."

They walked back to the hotel through the warm scented night, Fen's espadrilles crunching on the gravel.

As he opened her bedroom door for her he said, "I'll knock on your door in twenty minutes when the coast's clear."

Frantically Fen bathed and brushed her teeth and sprayed on scent. Despite the warmth of the night she couldn't stop shaking. If only she had bigger boobs. Janey was so gloriously topheavy. She looked at Lester the teddy bear and turned his face to the wall. "I don't want you to be corrupted."

Overwhelmed with shyness, conscious of her swollen face, she turned off the lights before she let Billy in to the room.

"Do you think we'll ever find the bed?" he said, as he drew her, frantically trembling, towards him. "Hey, hey, there's no need to be frightened."

"That's what they always say about adders. Look, I know I'm not as sophisticated, or as beautiful, or as witty, or as clever, or as sexy as Janey. Anyone would be a letdown after her."

"Hush," he said stroking the nape of her neck. "Who's making comparisons?"

"I am, because everyone you go to bed with must remind you of her, and it must hurt."

Billy found the bed and pulled Fen down beside him.

"It's certainly not hurting at the moment. You're the one it might hurt."

"I've ridden for so long, I don't think I've got a hymen any more. I've never been able to find it."

Her little hands were tentatively moving over his chest.

"Still scared?" he whispered. Then, when she didn't answer, he kissed her upper lip. "I'll take things very very slowly. We've got all night."

He was thinking so much about not rushing her, or scaring her, that he hardly worried about his own performance. But he felt an amazing happiness when her hands traveled cautiously down his stomach and she said: "Oh feel, isn't it lovely, and so strong, like the leaning tower of Pisa? Is it nice if I run my fingers round the rim?"

"Bliss," mumbled Billy.

"And does that hurt?"

"If you stroke them gently like that, it's heaven."

She was so excited that neither of them ever discovered whether she had a hymen or not. Twined round him like a monkey, riding him so lightly, she exhorted him to please go on, go on. In the end he forgot to be gentle, driving into her with all his strength.

"Oh it was magic, magic," she whispered afterwards.

"Are you sure? Are you really sure?"

"Didn't hurt at all," she said, snuggling into his arms.

"Look," said Billy, "the British flag is creaking up the pole."

Suddenly she heard him singing, slightly shakily, "God save our gracious Queen, Long live our Noble Queen," until there was furious banging on the wall.

Fen gave an ecstatic sigh. Billy's singing again, she thought.

To Billy the following weeks came as a revelation. While Janey had exuded sex appeal, he always had the feeling that, although she enjoyed sex, it was more for her own gratification and her own ego. He was never irresistible to her. With Fen he felt he held the key to paradise. She quivered with excitement whenever he touched her. She wanted to touch him all the time, she adored everything about him and everything he did to her was perfect. She was the most unselfish person he'd ever been to bed with, always thinking of his pleasure before her own, massaging his back when he was tired, happy to stroke and caress him for hours.

They talked horses endlessly, but unlike other riders, she was prepared to spend ages discussing how his horses might be improved, not permanently waiting to engineer the conversation on to her own.

Having stabled Macaulay and Desdemona at Fontainebleau, they stayed an extra day there, wandering through the forest and enjoying a magnificent French dinner in the evening to make up for not being able to eat anything except risotto in Rome. Then they flew home to take Laurel and Hardy, and a couple of Billy's new horses bought by Mr. Block, to Windsor. Then on to Paris, Barcelona and finally Lucerne, where at each place the British riders were invincible. Bugle was jumping brilliantly, so were Desdemona and Macaulay. It was also perfectly apparent to the rest of the team what was going on between Fen and Billy.

"You beat me to the post," said Rupert ruefully, but he couldn't help being glad to see Billy so happy.

Malise, turning a blind eye, was delighted too. He was very fond of Billy and had hated to see him so down and lacking in confidence. He was also thrilled by the success of the team. Billy and Fen were obviously madly in love. They were discreet in public, but you only had to see the way he carried her bags for her and she turned to him for advice, and how they drifted together and always seemed to be echoing each others thoughts and laughing at private jokes. Fen had cheered up

the team too. Humpty had replaced Griselda for Lucerne, and he and
Ivor and Driffield were all mad about Fen. She was their team mascot,
and as a team they had never been more united. They had not lost a
Nations' Cup this year.

Fen lay in a bubble bath. The boom of the champagne cork rever-
berated off the steaming walls of the bathroom in their hotel at Lucerne.

"To your first Grand Prix," said Billy, filling up a tooth mug and
handing it to her.

"I can't drink the whole bottle," protested Fen as Billy put down
the toilet seat and sat on it, watching her.

"What's the matter?" he said. "Aren't you glad you've beaten
everyone?"

"I feel like the end of the holidays."

He came and knelt down beside her, soaping her breasts and kissing her damp neck.

"Sweetheart, it's only the beginning. We may be going home,
but I'll be seeing you at Crittleden next week, and then at the Royal
and the Royal International."

Fen looked down. The soap was beginning to disperse the bub-
bles.

"I know, but it won't be the same."

"It'll be even nicer, I promise. Come on; we'd better buck up.
Malise wants to leave to go out to dinner in twenty minutes."

She didn't tell him that that afternoon a telegram had arrived at
the hotel for him from Janey, congratulating him on yet another double clear in the Nations' Cup. Rupert had torn it up before Billy saw it.

"Last thing he needs at the moment, and don't you go telling
him either," he'd said to Fen.

She hadn't said anything, but it terrified her. Throughout the last
month Fen and Billy had avoided talking about Janey. She was like a
broken ankle that didn't hurt if you didn't walk on it.

As well as her Grand Prix money, Fen, as leading lady rider of the
show, had won a full length fur coat. She disapproved passionately of
fur in principle, but when Billy had dried her after her bath, she
couldn't resist putting it on as a dressing gown, feeling the silk lining
caressing her hot naked body.

Billy stopped in the middle of tying his tie and came towards her.

"God, that's sexy. Just looking at you gives me a hard on."

He took her face between his hands. She was so beautiful. All the
bruising and swelling had gone.

"You don't realize what you've done to me," he said. "Given me
back my faith in life. I never believed I could wake up in the morning
again with such a ridiculous sense of excitement."

Fen parted the fur coat, so she could feel his cock nudging against her belly button. She laid her head against his chest.

"I'm not saying this to make you feel old, but I've never had a real father. My own father died when I was eight, but he divorced Mummy long before that and Colonel Carter was a twerp and, although Jake's been wonderful, he's *not a cuddler,* too austere. Apart from dogs and horses, you're the first thing I've ever been able to love."

Looking down, Billy realized he must never never let her be hurt.

"I know I'm cradle-snatching, but I can't help it," he muttered into her hair.

Anxious to get back to Tabitha, Rupert flew home to Penscombe after the Lucerne Grand Prix. Over a year old now, Tab could walk several steps, but usually crawled forward with a curious sideways gait like a crab, with one leg sticking out. She was wearing blue pajamas; the top had fallen off one shoulder. She was so enchanted when he walked through the door at first she could hardly get a word out.

"My darling angel," said Rupert, extracting her from a swarm of excited barking dogs and holding her above his head until she crowed with laughter. She was so pink and blonde and beautiful.

"Daddy's brought you lots and lots of presents."

The best present for Tab was obviously seeing her father again. She snuggled up to him like a kitten.

Helen came into the hall warily, holding Marcus by the hand.

"Hullo darling," she kissed him. "Had a good trip?"

"Great. Billy's really back on form. Christ, he's jumping well."

"I'm so glad. Not back on the booze, is he?"

"No, no. He's utterly bombed on Perrier and love."

"Love?" said Helen surprised.

"Little Fenella Maxwell. Best thing that ever happened to him."

"But she's not eighteen yet, just a child."

"So's he. She mothers him like an old mare. They're really sweet together, and at last he's got someone who can talk to him about horses."

Unlike me, thought Helen bitterly. "I'm having lunch with Janey tomorrow," she said.

After the 400-mile drive from Lucerne, Billy and Fen stayed near the coast and took a lunchtime ferry the next day. The grooms had lunch. Billy booked a berth for three hours and took Fen to bed, dreading the separation ahead as much as she was. They reached Gloucestershire about sunset. It was one of those magical evenings when they had both the lorry windows open and the air was heavy with the scent of elder flowers and wild roses.

Fen sat glued against Billy, hand on his thigh, any pretence that they weren't having an affair abandoned. It was only ten miles to Penscombe now. Once there she would borrow one of Rupert's trailers and drive Macaulay and Desdemona on to the Mill, arriving about midnight.

Tracey was fast asleep on one of the bunk beds. Sarah was emptying out the fridge. Billy and Rupert's horses were beginning to stamp and whinney as they recognized he familiar scents of home.

"Will you do me a great favor?" said Billy, staring fixedly at the road ahead. She could feel how tense he was.

"Of course."

"Will you stay the night with me at the cottage and I'll drive you back in the morning?"

Fen was almost speechless with happiness. Billy needed her, he really needed her. She reached up and kissed his cheek. "I was wondering how on earth I was going to drag myself away from you this evening."

"I rang Mrs. Bodkin from Lucerne and told her to clean the place up and make the bed. I'm a big boy now. I can't go on living with Helen and Rupert for ever, and anyway," he looked at his watch, "I haven't fucked you for at least seven hours. Will you mind a few of Janey's things lying around?"

"Not if you don't," said Fen.

She called Tory from Rupert's tackroom. "I've got as far as Rupert's. I'm utterly wiped out. Helen's asked me to stay the night. Do you mind awfully? Billy, or someone, will drive me back in the morning."

"I'll be punished for lies like that," she said to herself as she put the telephone down.

It was dusk by the time they'd settled the horses. All that was left of the day was a saffron glow on the horizon. Billy, who knew the path along the edge of the woods, led the way holding her hand, with Mavis racing in front chasing rabbits. The night was so warm they could smell the honeysuckle and syringa a hundred yards away.

"What an adorable place," said Fen in ecstasy. "Gosh you're lucky to live here."

In the gateway Billy put his arms round her, holding her like a balloon that might float away at any moment.

"It's all right," she said softly. "I'm here to look after you."

As he opened the front door, Mavis shot ahead, squeaking with excitement. He turned on the light and went into the kitchen, dumping the bags. Fen followed him. "It looks lovely," she said.

"Mrs. B.'s been working fantastically hard," said Billy. "Christ, I wish we could have a drink."

"I'll make some coffee," said Fen, picking up the kettle.

"Are you hungry?"

She shook her head.

"Then let's go to bed. I need to lay you and the ghost."

Fen went into the hall. Behind the door opposite, she could hear excited squeaking and scrabbling.

"Mavis must have shut herself in."

She opened the door and switched on the light, then gave a gasp of horror. In front of the fire, thin, beautiful and menacing in a black sleeveless T-shirt and the tightest black leather trousers, stood Janey.

"Hello Fen," she said with a twisted smile. "It's been amazingly kind of you to look after Billy in my absence, but I'd like him back now."

Fen gave a sob and turned on her heel, going slap into Billy coming out of the kitchen.

"You look as though you've seen a ghost."

"No, I've seen a real live person. Go into the other room and see."

As she fled down the garden path she heard Billy calling her to come back, but she kept on running along the woodland path. Once she stumbled and fell, cutting her hands but not even feeling the pain. She didn't stop until she reached Rupert's front door. It was open. The dogs surged forward, barking. Rupert came out of the kitchen, a large whiskey in one hand, a letter in the other.

"Hullo duck. Had a tiff?" Then he saw her dirty grazed hands and her stricken face. "Angel, what's the matter?"

"It's J-Janey, she was waiting for us at the cottage."

"Fucking hell, how did she get in?" He led Fen into the kitchen and poured her a large drink.

"I don't want anything," Her face crumpled.

"Oh sweetheart, I'm sorry. He won't take her back."

"He will, I know he will. He only had me as a stop-gap."

"Rubbish, I've never seen him happier."

"I can't bear it, I simply can't bear it."

Helen, who'd been tucking the children in, heard the commotion and came downstairs. Walking into the kitchen, she found a blonde in Rupert's arms.

"Oh I do beg your pardon," she said with heavy sarcasm. "I didn't mean to interrupt."

"Don't be stupid, it's Fen. That bitch Janey's come back."

Fen turned to Helen. "I'm so sorry to bother you," she sobbed, "but I didn't know where else to go."

The telephone rang. Still with one arm around Fen, Rupert picked it up.

"Yes, she's here. Well, not brilliant. What the fuck's going on? Good, see you. He's coming over," he said replacing the receiver. "Now dry your eyes and have that drink."

Billy was over in ten minutes. Rupert left them alone. Fen looked up, her eyes spilling over with tears. "Oh Billy."

"Darling Fen," he drew her towards him, "I never dreamed in a million years she'd come back."

"You must talk it over with her. She's still your wife."

"I don't know if I want her back. I'm so much better without her."

"There's something you should know. Janey sent you two telegrams, one in Paris and one in Lucerne. Rupert tore them up."

Billy digested this. Then he said bitterly, "That was only when I started winning again. Janey likes hitching her wagon to a star. Whether she'll be so amused by a star on the wagon, I doubt."

His hold tightened on her. "I'll go back and have it out with her. Will you stay here? Rupert'll look after you and I'll come and see you in the morning. I just want you to know you're the sweetest thing I've ever been lucky enough to meet in my life."

Meanwhile Rupert went out onto the terrace and found Helen watching the stars come out, the faint reflection of the half-moon mingling with the water lilies strewn across the lake.

"How the hell did Janey know Billy was coming home tonight?"

"Well, I may have told her. I don't think I did. I had lunch with her yesterday. She was wearing Billy's Old Harrovian tie. I certainly told her Billy was real happy with Fen."

Rupert turned on her in fury. "You did what?"

"Well she was so worried, she said it was so much on her conscience. Billy being on his own and drinking and doing so badly."

"She knew bloody well he was doing well, she sent him telegrams."

"Then she looked really sad, and said she did hope some day he'd find someone nice—so I told her about Fen."

"She was fishing, you stupid bitch."

"Rupert, please, don't talk to me like that."

"You've only done Billy the worst turn ever. He'd just struggled out of the quicksand; now you've pushed him back again."

At that moment, Billy came out on to the terrace.

"Will you look after her?"

"You should be doing that!" snapped Rupert, "and kicking out that slut."

Rupert stayed up half the night talking to Fen, who was almost crazy with grief.

"I'm sorry to be so boring but I love him so so much. I saw her. I knew she wants to come back, and she's so winning, and Billy's too straight not to let her. It's funny, I wanted to fall in love so badly—but I never dreamed it would hurt so much."

Helen couldn't sleep. Why did Rupert always have more time for other people—Fen, Billy, Tab—than he did for her? On the other hand she knew she was being punished.

"Dear God," she prayed, "what have I done? I told Janey about Fen, not because I wanted to reassure her, but because I wanted to put her down."

Next day the rain came, stripping off the last pastel frivolity of the blossom, segretating the fluffy white heads of the dandelion clocks, bowing down the cow parsley, muffling the cuckoo, and turn-ing every show ground into a quagmire. Fen was permanently soaked to the skin, always cold, shivering with misery, particularly at night without Billy to love and warm her. Lester, the teddy bear, was rein-stated and soaked with tears, like her pillow, as, night after night, she cried herself to sleep. By day, work was the only anodyne. She begged Malise to excuse her from the huge nine-day show at Aachen on the grounds that Billy would be on the team, probably with Janey in tow. Instead Malise left Billy out, giving him a few weeks' sabbatical to sort out his marriage. Billy, after all, had turned professional and was no longer eligible for Los Angeles, and Malise was determined to get his Olympic squad into shape in plenty of time. Fen, Rupert and Ivor Braine were certain to be part of the team. The fourth place he still hoped to keep open for Jake if his leg mended in time.

Fen tried to hide her heartbreak from Jake when she visited him in the hospital on her return from Lucerne.

"Look what we won," she said brightly, tossing a canvas bag full of ribbons onto the white bedspread.

Jake took one look at her face.

"Who is it, that bastard Campbell-Black? I said it would happen. I'll bloody kill Malise when I see him."

Fen went over to the window, fighting back the tears.

"It wasn't Rupert at all, it was Billy."

"Billy!" For a minute Jake was dumbfounded. "What happened? you're not . . .?"

"No, nothing like that. Janey came back."

"Christ. I suppose the bitch found out he was going well and didn't want to miss out."

"Something like that."

Jake loved Fen, but so angry was he with Billy and Janey, and so horrified to see Fen's haggard face, that he took it out on her. He hated himself. He wished he had words to comfort her, but he just wanted to hit out at a world that seemed so manifestly unfair to both of them.

Fen let him rage until he'd run out of reproof and expletives, then collapsed sobbing on the bed.

"I couldn't help it, Jake. I didn't mean to fall in love."

Jake patted her shoulder. "Sorry I came on so strong. I just hate you being hurt. Should never have let you go."

"Haven't you ever been in love or hurt by a woman?"

"Never—by a woman." (Not since his mother had committed suicide, anyway.)

"Not even Tory."

"Tory couldn't hurt a fly."

Gradually the ribbon board filled up in the kitchen, as one show followed another—Aachen, Calgary, Wolfsburg. Funnily enough, it was Rupert who saved her in those first weeks. In the evenings abroad he wouldn't let her slink back to the van to cry her eyes out, but dragged her to dinner with the team. In his mind she was a part of Billy, and therefore to be protected, cherished, and occasionally bullied. He had never really had a woman friend before. Women in his book were to be pursued, screwed, and discarded. Repeatedly he was on the brink of taking her to bed, because he wanted to and he thought it might blot out the pain, then some rare altruism stopped him.

Fen was confused. Accustomed to hating Rupert, she now discovered in him an unexpected gentleness, particularly in the way he talked about Tabitha.

Billy tackled Rupert the moment he came back to England.

"How's Fen?" was his first question.

"I took her to dinner last night."

"With the team?"

"No, by myself."

"What the bloody hell for?"

"She needed cheering up."

"What form did the cheering up take—horizontal?"

"She wanted to talk. She's still mad about you."

"Oh God," said Billy, trying not to feel pleased.

"But the only way out of this stupid impasse is for her to find someone else."

Billy was appalled how much the thought upset him, but he said, "You may be right."

"Damn sure I'm right. Particulary if you persist in this bloody-fool belief that Janey's the best thing for you."

Billy wasn't sure. The night he'd got back to the cottage and found Janey there they had screwed all night, blotting out all feelings of guilt and remorse. Next day, he'd insisted on driving Fen, white, silent, stunned, back to the Mill, feeling her disintegrating in his arms as he said goodbye to her, saying he'd always adore her—which was a different word than love.

When he got back Janey'd been through his wallet and found Fen's photo and was in hysterics.

Billy tried to reason with her. "I never looked at another woman the entire time we were married. Then you file for divorce. I was trying to get over you."

"Why didn't you come around and murder Kev?"

"I'm not like that. I missed the only time I took a slug at him."

"Was she better in bed than me?"

"She was different," said Billy tactfully.

"Did you screw her in our bed?"

Billy shook his head.

"But you were coming back to."

"Look, you'd have thought I was a frightful drip if I hadn't."

Billy had changed, thought Janey. The red face, the sour whisky breath had gone. He was brown, lean, well-muscled, tougher, more irritable, but infinitely more attractive.

"You mustn't see her any more," said Janey, pouring herself another glass of vodka, hardly graced by tonic.

"How can I not see her? We're on the same team. If I worked in an office, or was an engineer or an architect, I could try and find another job in another part of the country, but show-jumping's the only thing I can do. I was totally impotent after you left me. She picked me up from the gutter. She gave me back my confidence, my nerve, my sexuality. I've won £20,000 in the last month."

"What d'you want me to do, ask her to move in?"

"I'm just trying to say it isn't as simple as that. You can't just waltz out of my life for nearly a year and expect things to be exactly the same."

"I've finished my book," said Janey. "*The Post* is going to serialize it. They've offered me £30,000. And the publishers have commissioned another one, so you won't have to struggle quite so hard darling."

She's not listening, thought Billy in despair, she never listens, except when she's on to a good story.

Hysterical scenes followed. Janey steamed open letters, counted the Kleenex—"Perhaps she's used one"—examined the hairs in the bath: "That's thicker and curlier than mine."

"That's pubic hair for Christ sake," said Billy.

Janey's attitude was totally irrational. On endless occasions she had deceived him, betrayed him, made a fool of him, but it was part of her abyss of insecurity that she simply couldn't believe that he wasn't sneaking off to see Fen when he got the chance.

Nor was it just her insane jealousy of Fen; she was paranoid about the rest of the world. What did Billy's mother, Helen, Rupert, Malise think about her behavior? Janey liked a place in the sun and a lot of spade work would be required to win back these people's approval.

Everyone was laying bets that the reconciliation wouldn't last.

Fen didn't see Billy again until the Crittleden meeting at the end of July. Rupert had warned her that Janey was coming, so in order to upset herself as little as possible, Fen arrived only just in time to walk the course for the big event, the Crittledon Gold Cup, worth £15,000 to the winner. She found the show ground in an uproar. Always with an eye to publicity, Steve Sullivan, who owned Crittleden, had introduced a new fence which all the riders considered unjumpable. Called the moat, it consisted of two grassy banks. The horses were expected to clamber up the first bank, along the top and halfway down the other side, where they were expected to pop across a ditch three foot deep, on to the second bank, which they again had to scale, ride along the top and down the other side. Here they had to jump a small three-foot rail a couple of strides away.

Worried that all the show-jumpers might load their horses up in their vans and drive ten miles down the road to Pripley Green, where there was another big show taking place, Steve Sullivan had only put up details of the Gold Cup course an hour before the competition. When the riders saw the moat was included, all hell broke loose.

"I'm not jumping that," said Rupert.

"Nor am I," said Billy. "That ditch is three foot deep. If a horse falls in, it'll put him off jumping water for life."

"It's a very gentle slope down," protested Steve Sullivan. "It's not slippery. They'll jump it easily, won't they, Wishbone?" he added, appealing to the Irishman.

"Sure. I can't see the thing giving much trouble," said Wishbone.

"There," said Steve. "I took my old mare across it the other night. She jumped it without turning a hair."

"She's due to be turned into cat food at any minute," snapped Rupert. "Doesn't matter if she breaks a leg. These are top class horses. I'm not risking £100,000 for a bloody moat."

He went off and complained to Malise who came and examined the course.

"Seems perfectly jumpable to me, acceptable hunting fence."

"These aren't hunters," said Rupert.

Billy conferred with Mr. Block.

"I haven't spent eight months getting Bugle right to have him smash himself up in one afternoon. D'you mind if I pull him out?"

"Do what you think is best, lad," said Mr. Block. "Don't like the look of it myself. First hoss'll be all right, but once the turf gets cut up, it'll be like a greased slide in the playground."

Steve Sullivan's sponsors, Fuma, the tobacco giants, however, had put a lot of money into the competition and wanted a contest. The telephones were jangling in the main stand. Steve suggested putting up a big wall which the riders could jump instead, as an alternative to the moat.

"Not a fair contest," said Rupert. "Walls aren't the same as banks."

"Handing it on a plate to a little horse," said Humpty. "Little horses only need two strides between the bottom of the bank and the rail."

Count Guy declared the moat *vraiment dangereuse*. Ludwig agreed: "It ees your Eenglish obsession with class, haffing a moat, Steve. Where is zee castle, zee elephant and zee vild-life safari park?"

Steve Sullivan was sweating. He'd never faced a mutiny before. The riders were all standing grimly on the bank, hands on their hips.

Fen, meanwhile, had been quietly walking the rest of the course. It was a matte, still day, overcast but muggy, the grass very green from the recent storms. Midges danced in front of her eyes. Finally she reached the moat and stood banging her whip against her boots, looking at them in disapproval, hat pulled down over her nose.

All those grown men, including Grisel, making such a fuss, she thought. It was a tabby cats' indignation meeting. Rupert walked up and kissed her. "Hi, angel, you've arrived just in time to join the picket line. We're going to give Steve his come-uppance."

The riders went into a huddle.

Fen stood slightly apart. She caught sight of Billy. For a second they gazed at each other. He noticed how thin she'd got, her breeches far too large, her T-shirt falling almost straight down from collar bone to waist. Fen moved quickly away, stumbling into a fence, sending the wing flying. As she picked herself up, she heard Rupert say to a man from the B.B.C. "OK you're on. We'll all jump."

Fen fled back to the collecting ring under the oak trees where she found Desdemona being walked around by Sarah.

"What's happening?" she asked.

"Bloody storm in a challenge cup," said Fen. "We're all going to jump, but, from the nasty gleam in Rupert's eye, I know he's up to something."

"You'd better ring Jake."

"No, he's bound to tell me not to jump."

The crowd seethed with rumor and counter-rumor. They had seen the riders gathered around the moat. This was about the most testing competition of the year. Many of them had traveled miles to watch it. The arena nearly boiled over with excitement and a huge cheer went up as Rupert, the first rider, came in. Theatrically, with much flourishing, he took off his hat to the judges and cantered the foaming, plunging, sweating Snakepit around and around waiting for the bell which was waiting for the go-ahead from the television cameras.

He was off, bucketing over the emerald green grass, jumping superbly, clearing every fence, until he came to the moat.

"He'll show them how to do it," said Colonel Roxborough.

"I think not," said Malise bleakly.

The entire riders' stand rose to their feet, holding their breath, as Rupert cantered up to the huge bank, then at the last moment, practically pulled Snakepit's teeth out and cantered round it, ignoring the shouts of "wrong way," and cantering slowly out of the ring.

There were thirty-five horses entered for the class. The next twenty riders deliberately skipped the moat, or retired before they reached it. For the first few rounds the crowds scratched their heads in bewilderment, then, as they realized they were witnessing a strike, the deliberate sabotaging of a class, their bewilderment turned to rage and they started to catcall, boo and rhythmically clap. In the Chairman's box, with its red carpet and Sanderson wallpaper, Steve Sullivan was having a seizure.

"Bastards, bastards! All led by the nose by that fucker Campbell-Black."

Malise watched the spectacle with the utmost distaste.

"Behaving like a bunch of dockers and car-workers," said Colonel Roxborough apoplectically, who, without realizing it, was slowly eating his way through a bunch of grapes in a nearby Lalique bowl.

"Can't you put the screws on Billy, Mr. Block?" pleaded Steve.

"I troost Billy's joodgement when it comes to hosses," said Mr. Block. "There'll be another class next week."

Malise went down to the collecting ring. Billy, having followed the other riders' example, had just come out of the ring, to loud booing from the crowd. He avoided Malise's eye.

Only Driffield, Ivor and Fen, of the British riders were left to jump.

"You're making complete idiots of the judges and the crowd," said Malise furiously to the British squad. "If you don't like the course don't jump it, but don't resort to these gutter tactics. D'you want to kill the sport stone dead?"

With £15,000 at stake, Driffield was sorely tempted.

But then Count Guy and Ludwig both went in and retired, and who was he to argue with the experts? Dudley Diplock was in despair in the B.B.C. commentary box. Telephones were ringing on all sides.

"Can't we just go back to tennis?" he pleaded into one receiver. "Or motor-racing or cricket? There must be a county match somewhere."

Another telephone rang. "You sit tight, Dudders," said the sports editor. "It's a bloody good story, the news desk has been on to say, 'Be sure to interview Campbell-Black afterwards. He seems to be the ringleader.'"

Driffield retired.

"Your turn now, darling," said Rupert to Fen. "Jump as far as the bank. Don't worry about the crowd—only Italians throw bottles—and then retire. The B.S.J.A. can't suspend all of us."

Jake lay in his hospital bed, waiting for a telephone call. He had checked with the switchboard five times. The operator was a friend of his. They had given him a direct line, but no telephone calls had come through. He was livid with Fen. Perhaps she's seen Billy—he'd caught a glimpse of him walking the course—and had been too distracted to ring. And now she was obviously going to join the strike organized by Rupert. The moat looked very dangerous. He'd be furious if she did jump, furious if she didn't. He got the bottle off the bedside cupboard and poured himself a large whisky into a paper cup.

The nurses gathered round the bed. "We've just heard on the radio that they're all on strike."

"Poor old Dudley," said Jake, and couldn't help laughing, even though the Matron had just walked into the room.

"Well this is simply the blackest, most extraordinary day in show jumping," said Dudley desperately, "and here comes Fiona, I mean Fenella, Maxwell, on Esmerelda, I mean Desdemona, a really super little mare, who's been jumping brilliantly all summer. I wonder if she's going to strike like the other riders."

The crowd was in an uproar, booing, yelling, screaming.

"Jump, jump, jump," they yelled, stamping their feet in the stands and slow-handclapping.

"All this must be upsetting to any horse, particularly a young horse like Esmeralda. Now what's Fiona going to do?" said Dudley.

Fen raised her whip to the judge, then took one look at the mass of jeering yelling faces. The next minute a beer can landed at Desdemona's feet.

"If you'd stop making this ghastly din," she screamed at the faces, "I'd like to try and jump this course."

Only a handful of spectators heard her, the rest thought she was hurling abuse and stepped up the catcalling. Another beer can landed at Desdemona's feet. Fen turned, shaking her fist.

"Is she going to be all right?" said Billy in anguish.

"I'm sure she's tough enough to cope," said Janey, shooting him a furious glance.

Fen could hardly hear the bell. Fueled by rage, stroking Desdemona's neck, she set off. Over the wall, over the oxer, over the parallels, over the rustic poles, over the road jump, just avoiding two more beer cans, then over the gate. She rounded the corner, away from the collecting ring, riding towards the moat, but instead of circling it like the other riders, she dug her heels in. Desdemona bounded up the grassy hillock. The first thing the riders saw were her roan ears, then her face and her forelegs arriving on the top.

"Bloody hell," snarled Rupert.

"Traitor," thundered Grisel.

"Blackleg," said Driffield.

"Scab," said Humpty.

"She'll get the £15,000," said Driffield in anguish.

"She's not over yet," said Billy.

"Stupid exhibitionist," said Janey. "Serve her right if she kills herself."

As Fen reached the top the crowd went silent. As the little mare trotted along the top, picked her way fastidiously down the other side and paused above the water, Fen allowed her to have a good look.

"Constitutes a stop," said Grisel.

"Didn't take a step back," said Billy, as Desdemona bounded gaily across to the other bank, slightly unseating Fen, who had to cling onto her mane as she scrambled up and over the other bank. By some miracle she came down the other side collected and popped easily over the rail. For a second the crowd was totally silent; then they let out a huge heartwarming cheer.

"Bloody marvelous," said Billy. "Oh well done, pet."

Rupert and Janey turned on him in unison. "Whose side are you on?"

"The side of guts and great horsemanship," said Billy sulkily.

"You little beauty," whispered Steve Sullivan.

The Colonel ate the last black grape, pips and all. "If that girl doesn't go to Los Angeles it's over my dead body."

"I agree," said Malise.

"Se-uper, absolutely se-uper," shouted Dudley from the commentary box. "Oh well done Felicity, brilliantly ridden."

Jake suddenly found he was clinging on to Matron's hand as, with a huge roar, that grew to a crescendo, the crowd cheered Desdemona home. In a businesslike manner she cleared the rest of the jumps. "What a fuss about nothing," she seemed to be saying and cantered out of the ring with a buck and a whisk of her tail.

Jake turned to Matron, grinning from ear to ear. "Christ, did you see that? Have a drink."

"You know you're not allowed alcohol in the hospital, Mr. Lovell."

"To hell with that," said Jake, reaching for another paper cup with a shaking hand and pouring the remains of the whisky into it.

"Oh well, cheers," said Matron, tapping her cup against his.

"No one speak to her," ordered Rupert.

"Send her to Coventry," said Janey.

As Fen came out, a crowd, noticeably short of other riders, swarmed round her. Desdemona disappeared under a deluge of patting hands.

Sarah fought her way towards them.

"Oh Des, oh Fen, oh well done. I was so scared." She wiped away the tears. "No one will ever speak to us again."

Fen looked up at the riders stand and saw the rows of stormy faces looking down at her.

"Picket line looks fairly grim," said Fen flippantly. "Coventry, here we come." But her heart sank.

"Bloody hell," said Billy, getting to his feet, "Don't be so petty."

"Sit down," thundered Rupert.

"Don't you dare speak to her," squealed Janey furiously.

Ignoring the cries of protest, Billy walked down the stone steps, vaulted over the collecting ring rail and fought his way to Fen's side.

"Well done, beauty. Showed us all up."

Fen started, turned pale, gazing down at his dear familiar face with the turned-down smiling eyes and the sun catching the greying hair. She wanted to collapse off Desdemona into his arms.

"Oh Billy," she croaked, "I miss you."

He didn't have time to answer.

Dudley Diplock came rushing up, brandishing a microphone. The crowd separated to let him pass, deferring to television, then, gathering behind him, waving at the cameras, trying to get into the picture. Journalists crowded around. "Good for you, Fen."

Another huge cheer came from the ring. Fen swung round in the saddle. Wishbone had jumped the bank, but had the stile down. Fen was still in the lead. Ivor was about to go in.

"If you can jump it, Fen," he said adoringly, "reckon I can have a go."

After that the rest of the riders jumped the moat without mishap.

Hans Schmidt jumped clear on his new horse, Papa Haydn, and in the jump-off was a tenth of a second faster than Fen. But, although he got the £15,000 and the cup, he removed the oak-leaf wreath of victory from Papa Haydn and put it round Desdemona's neck. The crowd roared their approval.

"I take zee money," he said, kissing Fen, "but you take zee laurels."

She was cheered around two laps of honor.

Dudley collared her again. "What made you jump it despite the other riders?"

Fen grinned. "I don't like a lot of men telling me what to do. I think they behaved like a bunch of drips."

"Fighting talk," said Dudley. "You're not worried you've made yourself very unpopular?"

Fen shrugged. "They could have jumped it if they'd wanted to."

"Jake told you to have a go, did he?"

"I didn't call him," confessed Fen. "I was terrified he'd tell me not to. Sorry Jake," she said into the camera.

"I'm sure you all know," said Dudley, "that Fiona's brother-in-law, World Champion Jake Lovell, is in the hospital recovering from a nasty broken arm."

"Leg," said Fen gently.

"Leg, and we all wish you better, Jake, and hope to see you back soon. This must be the best possible pick-me-up."

"That deserves another drink," said Matron. "We seem to have exhausted your whisky, Mr. Lovell. I think I've got a drop of brandy in my office."

Janey had been drinking all day and, when she and Billy got back to the van she headed straight for the vodka bottle.

"Why the hell did you insist on rushing up and congratulating her in front of all the press and television cameras?" she asked.

"What *will* people think?" said Billy, trying to make a joke.

"They'll think you're still having it off with her."

"They will if you go on yelling like this."

"I suppose you were making a date with her in that brief poignant moment."

"I was not."

"Or saying how much you missed her."

"I merely told her she jumped well. She deserved it. I hate packs ganging up because they haven't got enough guts to savage someone on their own. I did it many years ago to Jake, and I've been bitterly ashamed of it ever since and I'm not going to do it again."

"I suppose you fancied her like mad when you saw her."

He looked at her face, red, shouting and featureless with rage.

"Oh for Christ's sake," he snapped, "you buggered off for nearly a year."

"I knew it wouldn't be long before you threw that in my face again."

"I'm not," said Billy wearily, "but if I can forget about Kev why can't you forget about Fen?"

"I left Kev because it was over, because I was bored with him. You were in full flood with Fen. How do I know it's over, that you don't lie beside me at night hankering for her boy's body?"

Billy filled up the kettle from the tap and turned on the gas. He was so slow lighting a match that he nearly blew his eyelashes off. Even the gas ring was against him. He was tired, he was hungry, he longed for a drink. He was depressed by the knowledge that Bugle could have jumped the moat and he'd have been fifteen grand richer. None of this would matter if Janey would meet him one tenth of the way.

"How do I know it's all over between you and Fen?" She burst into noisy sobs.

Billy went over and hugged her.

"You'll have to trust me; it's you I love, always have loved. I shacked up with Fen because I was dying of loneliness and you won't help either of us by regurgitating her memory every five minutes."

"I know," sobbed Janey. "I don't know why you put up with me."

A new syndrome, which Billy imagined Janey'd pick up from Kev, was the mood of sweetness and light, followed by heavy drinking, followed by the hurling of abuse and china, followed by flagellating herself into a frenzy of self-abasement. Billy found it exhausting. He'd had a shattering year. He sometimes wondered if his shoulders were broad enough to carry both their problems. Holding her heaving, tearful, full-blown body, breathing in the vodka fumes, Billy looked out of the window at the Crittleden oaks against a drained blue sky and was suddenly overwhelmed with longing for Fen, for her merryness, innocence and kindness. She'd looked so adorable today, flushed and defiant, with her wary greeny-blue kitten eyes, waiting for the others riders to turn on her. The whistling of the kettle made them both jump.

"_H_ow many miles to Coventry?" sighed Fen,
"Threescore miles and ten.
Will I get there by candlelight?
Yes—but don't come back again."

It was the last night of the three-day East Yorkshire Show. Fen lay in bed with Lester the teddy bear slumped beside her, listening to the rain drumming on the roof of the van. Sleep had evaded her again, and even the new Dick Francis had failed to distract her. She put it down and reached for her diary with the tattered photograph of Billy tucked in between September and October. He was laughing, his eyes screwed up against the Lucerne sun.

Next week was Wembley. It had been a desperate six weeks for Fen. After Crittleden, as good as their word, the British riders had sent her to Coventry. At every show she went to, people who'd been her friends cut her dead or deliberately turned their backs. She knew Rupert was behind it. He'd gone out of his way to be kind to her after she'd split up with Billy, and she'd defied him publicly and humiliatingly, which had been a terrible blow to his ego. As the majority of riders were either frightened of Rupert or jealous of Fen's meteoric rise, they were only too happy to follow his lead.

Things were not all Campbell-Black, however. Jake's leg was mending at last; he was expected to be out of the hospital soon after Wembley and riding by the spring. And if the Crittleden victory had enraged the riders, it had enchanted the public. The press were all on Fen's side. Overnight the telephone started ringing, with newspapers, magazines and television stations clamoring for interviews. Invitations flooded in for her to speak at dinners, open supermarkets, address pony clubs, donate various items of her clothing to raise money at charity auctions. Everywhere she was mobbed by autograph hunters. Her mailbox was full of fan mail from admiring men and little girls, who wanted signed photographs or help with their ponies.

For a public hungry for new idols, Fen fitted the bill perfectly. With her slender androgynous figure with its suggestion of anorexia, jagged cabin-boy hair, and gamin, wistful, extraordinarily photogenic face, she was a true child of her time. Just as the public was drawn to Jake because he was mysteriously enigmatic, they loved Fen because she couldn't hide her feelings. She was either furious or suicidal or ecstatic, and her naturally friendly nature endeared her to everyone.

Fen was flattered by the fame and adulation, but all her energies were centered on the horses; all she cared about was Billy.

The horses were going superbly, except for Hardy who was growing more ungovernable. He was too strong and fly and ever since he'd run away with her at the Royal and Lancaster early in the month and jumped right over two rows of girl guides sitting quietly by the ringside, Fen had been frightened of him, and he knew it. If he got any worse, he'd be a serious danger to Jake when he tried to start riding again.

The horses occupied her more than full time, and it was only on the endless drives, or when she fell into bed, usually long after midnight, that she allowed herself to think of Billy.

Rumors filtered through on the groom Mafia that all was not well in the Lloyd-Foxe household. Tracey told Dizzy, who told Sarah, who told Fen of endless rows into the night, of Janey opening Billy's suitcase on the highway and throwing all his clothes out of the window, because she thought he was driving too fast, of Janey storming out of a B.S.J.A. party because she heard Fen was coming, of Billy looking white and strained and uncharacteristically snapping at the grooms.

So Fen lived on the crumbs of hope. She knew Billy would make every effort to save his marriage, but she couldn't help counting the days to Wembley in October, when they would all be under the same roof for a week.

The following evening a very tired Billy arrived home from the Lisbon Show. It was the first show to which Janey had not accompanied him since they got back together. She had stayed home to write a piece on international polo players for the *Post*. At first Billy found it a relief to be away from the rows and the hysterics, but it was not long before the old demons started nagging him. He had forgiven Janey totally for going off with Kev, but he couldn't stop the sick churning fear which overtook him when he called home and she wasn't there. He hated the idea of her being closeted with some handsome polo player. He remembered how she'd first interviewed him. He could hear her now:

"In the last chukka, how amazing! You *are* brilliant, and what amazing right arm muscles. Let me feel them. You have to be so brave to play polo."

He and Rupert had reached Penscombe as a great red September sun was falling into the beech wood. The trees had hardly started to turn, but there was already a ring of lemon-yellow leaves around the mulberry tree in the center of the yard and a wet leaf smell of autumn in the air. Having supervised the unloading and settling-down of his horses, Billy decided to walk the half-mile home through the dusk. He needed a few minutes to prepare himself for Janey. What sort of mood would she be in? Would she have missed him? Would she have ransacked his drawers, frenziedly searching for evidence? He dreaded Wembley next week because Fen's presence would trigger more abuse.

Dew was already whitening the grass, the blue smoke from a hundred bonfires was blending with the damp vapors rising from the stream at the bottom of the valley; the golden dahlias in the front garden were already losing their color in the fading light. The sick feeling of menace overwhelmed him once more. There were no lights on in the cottage.

Oh God, where was she? She knew he was coming home this evening. He broke into a run, slipping on the wet leaves and the mud. He banged the gate noisily behind him. That should give the polo player a chance to leap for his breeches. He *mustn't* think that. Next moment Mavis hurtled down the path, greeting him in ecstasy. The front door was open. Janey must have gone out in a hurry. Despairingly, he dropped his bag on the yellow flagstones in the hall, so he had two hands free to stroke Mavis's joyful wriggling body.

"Billy, darling is that you?" called Janey.

Overwhelmed with relief, he could only croak out, "Yes."

"I'm in the living room."

He found her sitting at her typewriter wearing only his sleeveless vest and a pair of scarlet panties.

"I thought you weren't here," he muttered.

She got to her feet and ran to him.

"Oh, darling, I'm sorry. The piece was going so well, I couldn't be bothered to put the light on."

"You'll ruin your eyes," said Billy. "Sorry to interrupt. Why don't you keep on working?"

"Course not, now you're back. How did you get on?"

Billy unzipped the carry all, produced a handful of ribbons and chucked them down on the table.

"Brilliant," said Janey, sorting them out. "Two firsts, three seconds, a third, a fourth and two fifths."

"The first was the Grand Prix, and there's lots of loot, a lovely kitchen clock and a television set and a very obscene china bull with a huge cock. I left it at Rupert's. I'll bring it down in the morning."

Watching her poring over the ribbons, her breasts falling forward, strands of bush escaping from the red satin panties, Billy felt his cock rising and wished he didn't always want her so much. Sex had not been brilliant lately because Janey had so often fallen asleep drunk, but if they could avoid a row before they went to bed, he might get to screw her tonight.

Janey looked up, misconstruing the expression on his face.

"Sorry I look so awful, but I took Mavis for a walk in the woods at lunchtime and my trousers got drenched, so I took them off and couldn't be bothered to find any more."

"You look lovely."

"I've been a good little wife," Janey went on. "There's a casserole bubbling in the oven. I've ironed all your shirts; not very brilliantly, I'm afraid; some of the collars curl worse than Mavis's tail, and I've got your dinner jacket back from the cleaners."

Billy was pleased she was in high spirits; then he felt a lurch of fear. The last time he'd seen her in this manic mood, that floating-on-air, inner-directed radiance that had nothing to do with him coming home, was when she was starting her affair with Kev. He desperately wanted a huge drink to blot out the terrors.

Janey read his thoughts. "Let's have a drink."

He followed her into the kitchen, which looked amazingly tidy. Janey got down two glasses and, instead of reaching for the vodka for herself, got a carton of orange juice out of the fridge. Filling the glasses, she handed one to him.

"Aren't you drinking vodka?"

"Nope. I've got something to celebrate."

"You've sold the book in America?"

"Nope, I'm coming off the booze for a few months." She chinked her glass against his. There was no mistaking the sparkle in her eyes. Billy couldn't bear to look at her any more. He went to the dresser and started flipping though his pile of mail.

"Seven and a half months, in fact," said Janey.

"What?"

"That's the time I'm giving up booze for,"

"Whatever for?" said Billy wearily.

"I'm going to have a baby."

Billy dropped the pile of letters.

"Your baby," said she softly. "Our baby."

"How d'you know?" he muttered. There had been so many false alarms.

"James Benson confirmed it today."

"Is he sure?"

"Absolutely."

Billy turned incredulously.

Then she ran to him, flinging her arms round him, burying her face in his shoulder.

"Oh Christ," he said, "how wonderful. Oh Christ, how wonderful. Where can I hug you that I won't hurt it?"

"Anywhere you like. It's only six weeks old."

"Why didn't you tell me you were going to Benson?"

"I didn't want you to get too excited. I told myself if I could manage to keep my trap shut until I'd had the test it'd be all right. It's like you not drinking until all the bills are paid off."

"They are now. Lisbon wiped out the lot. Oh angel, I'm so happy."

"Are you sure?" she said in an uncertain voice. "You don't f-feel," she stumbled over the word, "I've done it to trap you into staying with me?"

She took his face in her hands and found it was wet with tears.

"I was so miserable about the low sperm count," he muttered. "I felt such a shit not being able to give you a baby. Oh darling, I'm so happy. It's the best news I've ever had. Can we call my mother and tell her? She'll be beside herself."

"D'you think?" asked Janey doubtfully. "She hasn't paid the subscription to my fan club for a long time."

"Course she will."

"Oh, and I told Helen," said Janey. "She called this afternoon, and I was so excited I had to tell someone."

"Was she pleased?"

"Ish. You know Helen. She said, 'It'll be a real positive experience for you, Janey. After all, you're still just at prime child-bearing age.' The silly cow."

Billy grinned. "I still can't take it in. God, it's wonderful."

The telephone rang. Billy leapt on it.

"Hi. Guess what? Oh, you know," he said, sounding a little deflated. "Helen must have told you. Isn't it? I haven't come down to earth yet."

"Rupert is terribly pleased," said Billy as he put down the receiver. "He wanted to bring a magnum of Krug over, but I said it'd be wasted on us, so he suggested some extra strong grass that Guy had sold him."

Janey giggled. "No, that's all behind us. We're responsible parents-to-be now. Let's go and have a fuck instead."

Fen and Sarah arrived at Wembley just before midnight on Sunday. Fen was utterly shattered. She hadn't eaten or slept properly for weeks. Jake could help only so much by remote control. She'd had a bad fall from Hardy yesterday and her back still ached. The very thought of jumping the four horses all week in big classes that went on late into the evening filled her with exhaustion.

Next morning, on her way to declare, she looked through the red curtains and saw Billy walking the course for a novice class. He was wearing old green cords and a tweed coat and laughing at some crack of Rupert's. He looked so happy and carefree and so much younger. Her heart twisted with longing. I'm not cured, she thought in panic. In the secretary's tent she found Humpty and Griselda, who both turned their backs on her. Oh God, how long was this stupid pantomime going on?

Early in the evening, when she was least expecting it, she bumped into Billy. He was very friendly, but shifty somehow, not meeting her eyes and firing questions about Jake and the horses, asking after Laurel twice and congratulating her in a hearty, most un-Billyish way. He seemed almost in a hurry to get away from her, which left her uneasy and depressed.

She wandered down to the stables. Macaulay's top door was shut to stop his adoring public feeding him and tugging souvenir hairs out of his mane. She slid into the box and shut the doors quickly behind her. Macaulay nickered with pleasure but didn't get up, so she sat down on the straw beside him, stroking his mane, still crinkly from the afternoon braids.

There were two classes that evening—a fancy dress pair relay and then the *Sunday Times* Cup, worth £10,000. She hadn't entered the relay because she was scared no one would want to be her partner. Outside she heard shrieks of laughter. Standing up, she peered through the crack in the stall and saw Billy and Rupert teetering past wearing fishnet stockings, three-inch heels, and coats and skirts with coconuts heaving in their sweaters. Then they were gone, and next door she could hear Sarah getting Hardy ready for the *Sunday Times* Cup. Fen sighed and sat down beside Macaulay again. She was just nodding off when she heard hoofs clattering outside, and an excited voice saying:

"Guess what? Gossip, gossip, gossip," It was Dizzy.

"What?" said Sarah, coming to the door.

"Where's Fen?" asked Dizzy.

"In the van, I think. I haven't seen her for some time. Come on, out with it."

"Janey Lloyd-Foxe is pregnant."

Fen's hand tightened convulsively on Macaulay's mane.

"Jesus," said Sarah, "When did you find out?"

"Well Count Guy, Billy, Rupert and Driff were all declaring. And Count Guy was ribbing Billy, saying he'd heard some *très interessant* rumors, and Billy went all scarlet and pleased and admitted Janey was having a baby. Count Guy was tickled pink of course. He didn't like Billy being separated from Janey, in case he started running after Lavinia again. Anyway, they were busy congratulating each other when bloody Driffield said, 'Who's the father, Kevin Coley?' The next minute Billy let him have one on the jaw—wham—sending Driff flying across the tent. Then Billy jumped on Driff with his hands round Driff's neck, howling, 'Take it back you effing bastard,' and other pleasantries."

"Golly," said Sarah.

"Rupert and Count Guy dragged Billy off and Driffield said he'd get Billy suspended."

"'No, you won't,' said Rupert. 'There's nothing in the B.S.J.A. rules about eliminating a competitor before an event, only during.'"

Both grooms started to giggle.

"Anyway," Dizzy went on, "Malise made Driffield apologize. Driff said it was only a joke and Billy, Rupert and Guy turned on their booted heels and stalked out undeclared and had to come back five minutes later when Driffield had gone. So it looks as though Driff, not your poor boss, is going to be the next candidate for Coventry."

"Christ," said Sarah, "Fen'll go bananas when she hears. He must be mad about Janey to punch Driff. I'm glad someone has at last; he's such a poisonous little toad."

"I thought Billy couldn't have kids," said Dizzy. "Do you think it is Kev's?"

Like a sleepwalker, Fen came out of Macaulay's stall.

"Fen," gasped Dizzy, backing into the patiently waiting Arcturus. "We didn't realize you were there."

"Obviously not," said Fen, "or you wouldn't keep Rupert's horse hanging around in the cold. All you bloody well do all day is gossip."

Not even bothering to close Macaulay's door, she walked unsteadily away from them. "Billy's going to have a baby," she muttered over and over again through trembling lips. She had no idea where she went, but she ended up in the van, locking the door behind her.

A few minutes later she heard pounding on the door.

"Fen, it's Sarah, they're walking the course."

"I don't care," sobbed Fen. "Leave me alone."

"Please, I'm sorry about your overhearing everything, but Hardy's all ready and I know you wanted to jump him in this class."

"Go away for Christ's sake."

"Let me in. I want to look after you."

Fen didn't answer. She lay on her bed, sobbing convulsively, shuddering like a palsied dog. She couldn't cope any more. There was no future, nothing, nothing. The light had gone out at the end of the tunnel; both ends were blocked up; there was no hope. "Oh Billy, oh Billy," she groaned.

Then she heard someone fiddling with the door handle, then voices, then more fiddling and the door was forced open and the inside of the living area was flooded with light.

"Go away," Fen screamed. "I can't take it. I simply can't take it."

Then she saw a man's figure framed in the doorway.

"Billy," she croaked in an insane moment of hope. "Oh Billy."

"Afraid not, sweetheart," drawled a voice. "You'll just have to put up with second best."

It was Dino Ferranti.

Fen slumped back on the bed. "Leave me fucking alone."

"You can't fuck alone. It's a physical impossibility," said Dino, sitting down on the bed and drawing her close to him. "There honey, hush, hush." He stroked her hair, damp with tears, feeling her drenched shirt and jersey against him, horrified by the fragility of her body.

"I love him so much I don't know what to do."

"Hush, don't try to talk." Gradually he managed to calm her.

"What am I to do?" she repeated shakily.

Dino pulled off a piece of paper towel, dried her eyes and held out another piece for her to blow her nose with.

"There are still twelve riders to jump before you. You're gonna get dressed and jump that course."

"I am bloody not."

"Sure you are. Just figure if this had happened in L.A. You couldn't just not jump. Every round's a dress rehearsal for that day, right?"

"Los Angeles is ten months away," snapped Fen. "I'm having difficulty getting through the next five minutes."

She was shivering violently now.

Dino poured her a glass of brandy.

"Have a slug of this."

"I don't want it."

"Yes, you do. Open your mouth." He almost forced it down her throat.

"Bastard," said Fen, but she drank it.

"Now get out of those clothes," Like a father, he removed her shirt and tie, which were streaked with lipstick and mascara.

"That's my lucky shirt and tie," moaned Fen, covering her breasts with her arms.

"Haven't brought you much luck today," said Dino. "Try another combination." He held out a clean shirt for her.

"I am *not* going to jump," said Fen mutinously. "Not on Hardy. He's a nightmare and I haven't walked the course."

"You've got time to watch the last three rounds," said Dino. "Come on, put your jacket on and borrow my dark glasses."

"I hate you," said Fen. "I truly, truly hate you."

For a moment, as he stood behind her while she checked her appearance in the mirror, she was struck by the contrast between her waiflike figure, white face and swollen eyes, and Dino, brown as peanut butter, ridiculously elegant in a black silk shirt and pale grey suit. He'd streaked his hair pale grey since she'd last seen him.

"Talk about Beauty and the Beast," she said.

News of Janey's pregnancy and Billy punching Driffield had spread rapidly round the showground.

Fen came out of the van to find the place swarming with reporters. Dino despatched them ruthlessly. No, Fen couldn't speak to anyone, nor could she sign any autographs. With his arms around her, he forced a gangway through the crowd.

"Who's that with her?" asked the man from the *Express*. "Face is familiar."

"Think he's an actor," said the girl from the *Mirror*.

By some miracle they had time to watch a couple of rounds.

"Watch the wall," warned Sarah. "There've been a lot of mistakes there, and the combination's on a funny stride. People have been taking three strides, then changing their minds and asking the horses to take off too early, then hitting the third element."

"I suppose you know *all* about it," snapped Fen at Sarah.

"I'm awfully sorry, Fen," said Sarah in an undertone. "I'm so glad you made it."

"I wouldn't have," said Fen, casting a venomous glance at Dino, "if Mussolini here hadn't come jackbooting round. Why can't I go into a decline in peace?"

Mary Jo Wilson, the number-one American girl rider, auburn-haired and extremely attractive, was in the ring. She took a brick out of the wall and had a pole down at the second element, then crashed through the third. The crowd gave a groan of sympathy.

"What did I tell you?" said Dino. "Hi Mary Jo," he shouted as she came out of the ring.

"Dino," her face lit up. "I didn't know you were in Europe."

"How many clears?" Fen asked Sarah.

"Only four."

Dino removed his dark glasses from a protesting Fen.

"But my eyes are still red."

"Just fantasize you're a white rat."

She rode through the cherry red curtains into the brilliantly lit arena. "And here comes Fenella Maxwell," said Dudley Diplock in ecstasy. "Hot from her brilliant second in the Crittleden Gold Cup, on Hardy."

The crowd, who'd been bitterly disappointed when Fen hadn't been at her appointed place in the class and had assumed she'd scratched, gave a cheer of delighted surprise.

"Bloody unfair," grumbled Grisel. "Why should they waive the rules for her?"

"Because she's a star," said Billy. "She's the one they've come to see."

It is the mark of a great athlete that the mind can transcend adversity, and somehow heighten the performance. After two shaky jumps, which had her fans gasping and nearly stripped the paint off the poles, Fen clicked into automatic pilot. Hardy, given his head and showing his true quality, went clear. The crowd went beserk. Their idol hadn't failed them. Crittleden wasn't just a flash in the pan.

"Thank God I didn't walk the course," said Fen as she came out. "I'd have been so terrified I'd never have crossed the starting line."

"You screwed up at the first two fences," said Dino.

"Don't come on like Jake," said Fen icily. "I'm going back to the van."

"No you're not," said Dino, catching her by the scruff of her neck. "You've got to jump off."

He took her into the riders' stand to watch the first rounds. From all sides people hailed him.

"Where are zee horses?" asked Hans Schmidt.

"Arriving the day after tomorrow. I might jump Manny in the Victor Ludorum."

At that moment Billy's number was called. Behind Fen and Dino, Janey Lloyd-Foxe was holding court, looking ravishing in a red wool Laura Ashley smock.

"You'd think she was eight months pregnant," muttered Fen savagely. Janey was talking to Doreen Hamilton, speaking more slowly than usual so Fen could hear every word.

"Yes, Billy is absolutely over the moon. The night I told him he couldn't sleep for excitement. It's going to be a terrific incentive to his career. He says he's jumping for two now. He's treating me like glass. Won't even let me pick up a duster."

"Never been her forte anyway," said Fen to herself, her knuckles white where she clutched her whip.

"When's it due?" asked Doreen.

"June. Billy'll be at the Royal and the International, but he says he'll probably cancel both."

The jump-off course was a blur before Fen's eyes.

"Oh here comes my darling," said Janey as Billy, the first to jump off, cantered into the arena, a huge grin spread across his face. "Don't you think prospective fatherhood suits him?"

Dino put a hand on Fen's knee. "Ignore her," he said. "She's only trying to wind you up."

Bugle put in an incredibly fast time. Janey went into noisy ecstasy.

"Never seen him ride before," said Dino. "He's bloody good. No one's going to be able to cruise after that."

He was right. Both Ludwig and Wishbone clocked up slower times. In came Rupert to the usual ecstatic schoolgirl screams. The whole of the pony club stand, hopeful of losing their virginity in such a glorious cause, rose to their feet to cheer.

"Extraordinary that someone so good-looking should be such as bastard." said Dino. "Like a blackbird singing the most exquisite song and dumping on you at the same time. Jesus, look at that acceleration. He ought to have starting gates."

As Snakepit stampeded the course, the jumps hardly seemed to exist. He skimmed them effortlessly.

"He's improved a whole lot since the World Championships," said Dino as Rupert thundered home two seconds faster than Billy. "Pow, you can't help admiring him."

"I can, only too easily," said Fen.

Joyously raking his hand down Snakepit's steel-grey braids, Rupert shot out through the red curtains, sending Hardy flying.

"Why don't you look where you're going, you clumsy oaf?" snarled Fen.

"Because I don't like what's in my way," snapped Rupert, "and if Svengali Lovell can tell you how to beat that time, I'm a Dutchman."

"Unfair to Dutchmen," Fen shouted back over her shoulder. "Some of them are rather nice."

"Remember, if you're going too fast, accelerate," Dino called after her.

Suddenly Fen remembered Rupert in Rome sneering at Grisel's and her disastrous performances in the Nations' Cup, saying that women always crack under pressure.

"To hell with Rupert," she said to herself, "to hell with Janey Lloyd-Foxe and her beastly baby. If I'm going to commit suicide this is as good a way as any."

Having bowed briefly to the Princess in the Royal box, she turned Hardy around and thundered through the start at a gallop. Hardy, who was used to being checked all the time and fighting for his head, was puzzled for a minute, then rose to the challenge. Over the first fence she was up on Rupert's time, throwing herself over, her hands nearly touching Hardy's noseband. Over the parallel bars and, with an amazing flying change, she jumped the gate almost sideways.

God, thought Dino suddenly terrified, she's taking me literally. Scorching over the upright, bucketing over the walls, Fen was already looking ahead to the combination. She was coming in too fast; she was going to crash. She knew a terrifying moment of fear, then Hardy took over and executed a trio of perfect jumps and hurtled Fen through the finish. From the earsplitting cheers of the crowd who had risen to their feet she knew she had beaten Rupert's time. The problem now was stopping. At the side of the arena a bank of blue hydrangeas came to meet them. Hardy skidded to the right, sliding along on his back legs for five seconds before coming to a halt.

Fen sauntered out of the ring, pleased that for once even Dino seemed shaken out of his customary cool.

The next moment Ludwig clapped his hand on her back.

"Brilliant. I haf never seen a round like zat."

Count Guy followed suit, and suddenly all the British riders, except Rupert and Grisel, were shaking her hand and hugging her. She was home from Coventry at last.

Was it all worth it, wondered Fen, as she accepted her ribbon from the Princess, and her huge silver cup sparkling even more dazzlingly as it reflected the exploding flashbulbs? Was it worth the lack of sleep, the setbacks, the heartbreaks, for this moment of glory? She admired the Princess's ankles in flesh-colored stockings as she walked back to the Royal box. Then there was a terrific roll of drums which nearly sent Snakepit and Rupert into orbit, leaving a gap between Fen and Billy who was third. Turning, Fen looked him straight in the eye. With a supreme effort, far greater than winning the cup, she managed to smile. "I'm so pleased about your baby," she said.

Then, before he had time to answer, the arena was plunged in darkness and Fen and the dappled grey Hardy were illuminated by the spotlight. She was aware that no one was leaving, there was no crashing of seats or banging of exit doors, or feet running down the concrete steps, just a long silence followed by the most almighty cheering, and, as the bank struck up "Red Roses for a Blue Lady," everyone started singing and clapping in time. Then the other riders filed out and she was alone and spotlit in the ring, sending Hardy into his wonderful, effortless, long striding gallop, and the crowd cheered so loudly that she went round again. Billy may not love me, she thought, but they do. Why can't I go on riding around this ring for the rest of my life?

Dudley captured her in the collecting ring, brandishing his microphone like a furry black lollipop.

"Se-uper, absolutely se-uper. You sorted out the girls from the boys today," he roared with laughter. He'd had too many in the whisky tent. "And Harvey went se-uperly. You *must* be pleased."

"He did, and I am."

"Must be a cert for L.A. now."

"You can't look beyond tomorrow with horses," said Fen.

"Must be difficult to choose between him and Esmeralda."

Fen looked broodingly at Dudley for a second.

"*She's* called Desdemona, and *he's* called Hardy, and why don't you remove your silly hat when you're talking to a lady, Dudley, or, knowing you, you probably think I'm a gentlemen."

Oh Christ, she thought, I shouldn't have said that.

Out of the corner of her eye, beyond the Shetland ponies and the famous ex-racehorses who were lining up for the personality parade, she could see a pack of reporters hovering. Dudley was flapping around saying goodnight to the viewers and reminding them to switch on tomorrow for the Puissance. Fen tried to dive behind a baker's truck but the reporters were old hands. Next moment they'd ringed her like a lasso, blocking her escape on all sides.

"What d'you think about Billy Lloyd-Foxe's wife having a baby?"

"I'm very pleased for him."

"Nothing else to say?"

"If it grows up like Billy it'll be a wonderful child."

"But not like Janey?"

"I didn't say that." Fen looked desperately round for help. "I hardly know Janey."

"You were very fond of Billy, weren't you?"

"It's difficult not to be," said Fen, bursting into tears. "He hasn't an enemy in the world."

All she could see was their avid searching eyes and their frantically scribbling pens.

"Why can't you leave me alone?" she sobbed.

A shadow fell across the notebooks.

"Pack it in," said Dino coldly and, taking the couple nearest Fen by their coat collars, he yanked them out of the way. "Bugger off and fuse your own typewriters with your lousy copy. You heard what the lady said—leave her alone."

44

*B*ack in the van Dino peered unenthusiastically into the fridge. "One black avocado, half a can of beans, a pork pie that ought to be on superannuation. You have two alternatives," he said to Fen, "you can cry yourself to sleep, right, or come out to dinner with me. I'm starving."

"I'm not hungry and I ought to call Jake."

"Sarah called him. He said what the hell were you doing risking Hardy's neck, then exhausting him showing off in that double lap of honor."

Fen pulled a face. "And that's all the bloody praise I get."

Dino took her to an Italian restaurant off High Street, Kensington, which stayed open late. Outside Fen could see dusty yellowing plane trees fretted by raindrops and lovers under pulled-down umbrellas hurrying to catch the last bus. Imprisoned in Wembley, with its heat, airlessness and tensions, she'd forgotten an outside world existed. At the next table a couple were holding hands. Taking in the merry din, the bottles of chianti, the photographs of the Colosseum on the wall, the solicitous waiters, Fen was reminded of the night in Rome with Billy, when her face was all bruised and he'd fed her risotto with a spoon. She wanted him so badly it took her breath away.

"What are you thinking about?" demanded Dino.

"That I ought to be in the intensive care unit, not wasting your money."

"It is *my* money," said Dino, grabbing the menus, "I'll order for you."

"Grapefruit bolognese'll do me fine," said Fen, emptying half a glass of wine in one gulp.

"How come you speak Italian so well?" she said when he'd finished ordering.

"Because I'm Italian I guess."

"You're American."

"Only by adoption. I'm just a simple lousy Latin lover at heart."

"Why have you streaked your hair grey?"

"Well, hearing you were heavily into older guys like Billy, I figured I stood more of a chance if I looked more mature. Besides," he grinned, "I thought it suited me."

"It does," admitted Fen. "You look too bloody glamorous for words, but it's too early to make jokes about my broken heart."

Dino put a suntanned, beautifully manicured hand over hers. "How come you didn't acknowledge my telegram?"

"I wasn't sure it was from you."

"It said it was, didn't it?"

"You don't know the terrible thing Rupert did to me in Rome." Just for a second his hand tightened painfully on hers.

"No not that," said Fen. "I'd been packed off to bed ludicrously early and was sitting there, dying of boredom, when Rupert rang up pretending to be you and asked me out to dinner."

"Did you go?"

"Did I? I've never got bathed, washed my hair and dressed quicker in my life. Then I found Rupert and Driffield killing themselves at the bottom of the stairs."

Dino looked half smug, half sympathetic.

"That was a lousy trick. Were you disappointed?"

"Shattered. After that I thought the telegram was probably one of Rupert's vile little practical jokes too, so I never wrote and thanked you."

"If you had I'd have been over much sooner."

"And I might never have got involved with Billy. D'you think I'll ever get over him?" she added dolefully.

"Sure you will. Just stick around."

The waiter arrived with their first course, half a dozen mediterranean prawns each and a huge white bowl of mayonnaise, strongly flavoured with garlic.

Dino ordered another bottle, and started stripping the prawns with incredible dexterity, then dipping them in the mayonnaise and passing them to Fen.

"Mm, they actually are delicious. Do you undress women as expertly?"

"Far more expertly, and I don't pull their heads and legs off either."

Fen paused for a minute, thinking how amazingly attractive he was, if you liked that sort of thing, she told herself hastily.

"Did you ever get Helen Campbell-Black into bed?"

Dino grinned. "We had lunch several times, but she never had more than one course and left half of that because she was always wanting to rush me off to some art gallery. I said, 'Honey, I am not into culture, I'm only into sex.'"

"You didn't manage to divert her into some large double bed?"

He shook his head. "She was running scared the whole time. Whenever I put my hand on her back to guide her across the road, she shot into the oncoming traffic. If you try anything further a burglar alarm goes off."

"In Rupert's van?"

"No, in her head. She's so beautiful you want to gaze and gaze, but I guess she's like a Ming vase, beautiful but empty."

"Goodness, I've eaten all those prawns," said Fen.

"Good girl." Dino ran his hand down the inside of her arm, caressing her gently, almost abstractedly as if she were a dog. "Funny, I fancy you. I always have."

Fen jumped away. "You mustn't say things like that. I'm not ready for propositions."

"Wasn't a proposition. Just a statement of fact."

"Even though I'm not beautiful like Helen."

Dino looked at her meditatively. "You could gain some weight," he said, "but you'll do."

Fen noticed he was beginning to squint slightly. He must be desperately jet lagged.

"How's Manny?"

"Awesome, much better than me. He's grown so much and filled out. He was winning a lot earlier in the year. Then my daddy had a cardiac arrest in July. He's better now, but I was off the circuit for some weeks."

"Why have you suddenly come over here at the end of the season?"

"To work with this guy whom I reckon is the best coach in the world. I'm going to stable the horses at his barn for a few months, take in a few shows in Europe, then have a stab at the World Cup in April. Then back to the States for the run up to the Olympics. I guess I want a gold as much as you do."

"Who is this coach? Do I know him?"

"No one knows him very well. He's kind of unapproachable." Dino smiled confidingly. "Actually, I fancy one of his jockeys. I figured if I was living there with permanent access, I might stand a better chance."

Fen slumped in her chair, utterly deflated. She looked down at the tiny lamb cutlets that had just arrived and removed the blackened sprig of rosemary that lay across them. She was utterly heartbroken over Billy, but no girl likes an attractive reboundee whipped from under her nose before she's even had a moment to try and rebound on to him. It would have been useful to have Dino in England if anyone asked her to bring a man to a party or to some official dinner. Moodily she poured too much salt on to the side of her plate, watching it turn green in the mint sauce.

"No, I don't want any more to drink," she said sulkily. "I've got a class at nine tomorrow."

Dino took no notice and filled up her glass.

"Did you meet this girl on the circuit?" she asked.

"Last year at the World Championship."

Fen glanced up suddenly and was amazed how much he was laughing.

"Jesus, you're thick, Maxwell. You may win trophies at shows but you've got the perception of a blind worm."

"I don't understand," stammered Fen.

Dino took her hand again, turning it over, gently tracing the heart line with his thumb.

"I saw Jake this afternoon. He figures you've done a fantastic job, but it might help to have another guy around the barn to jump some of the horses. In return he's going to help me with Manny when he comes out of the hospital."

Fen suddenly felt near to tears again. "So he thinks I can't cope?"

"On the contrary, he thinks you're too good to waste. He wants a gold for you too. He's only helping me because he knows there's no way I can beat you."

Fen sat on Jake's hospital bed a fortnight later. "It is absolutely infuriating," she grumbled, "but the entire household, Tory, the chilren, the grooms, the horses, even Wolf are madly in love with Dino Ferranti. It's a good thing you're coming home next week to restore normality before they all defect to America with him."

She got up and wandered restlessly round the room, looking at the inside of the hundreds of get-well cards, eating grapes, trying not to be upset by Jake's hisses of pain as, with contorted sweating face and gritted teeth, he battled on endlessly bending and stretching to strengthen the muscles of both broken and wasted legs. She couldn't help noticing how fragile and lacking in muscle they looked and wondering if he would ever ride again, let alone make the big time.

"The physiotherapist warned you not to overdo it," she said reprovingly.

"Physiotherapists aren't interested in medals," said Jake.

"Tory's planning a surprise Thanksgiving Dinner for Dino, so he won't feel homesick," Fen went on. "Sarah is actually putting on makeup first thing in the morning for the first time in history. Any minute Desdemona will start curling her pink eyelashes. I can't think why he has to be so bloody charming all the time. Goodness you've got a card from the Princess, you are a star. Are you looking forward to coming home next week?"

"Of course," panted Jake, leaning back for a second against the bedstead.

"We're all longing to have you," said Fen.

Neither statement was strictly true. Jake, having dreamed of nothing but getting out of the hospital for five months, was now thrown into a blind panic at the thought of facing the outside world. Learning to walk again was really taking it out of him—falling all the time, dragging himself up again, black with despair that neither of his legs would ever be strong enough to support him and terror whether he'd ever have the guts to get on a horse again.

Night after night he dreamed of tumbling poles and colossal horses crashing from great heights onto his legs, splintering them to smithereens, and woke sobbing and screaming until some night nurse arrived to calm him down. After his early animosity, he felt an almost slavish gratitude to the nurses and the Matron, who had all taken such a personal pride in getting him right. When they weren't too busy on the wards, particularly at night, they would spend hours talking to him and he found himself unbending as he never did at home or with the other riders. There was one blonde nurse for whom he had a special fondness, Miss Wutherspoon, who brought him fresh eggs from the country and always popped in to show herself off, radiant and scented, before she went out on dates. Jake supressed a faint suspicion that she might return his interest. Desirable nurses were not attracted to bad-tempered cripples like himself.

Finally, he didn't feel up to running the stable, driving miles to shows, raking the country for new horses. He longed for the children but didn't know if he could cope with the decibel level of their shrill demands, or with the doglike devotion of good, shiny-faced Tory, heaving her bulk around the Mill as she waited on everyone.

All he wanted to do was to spend two months soaking up the sun on some Hawaiian beach with Miss Wutherspoon in a grass skirt ministering to his every need. He was glad Dino was going to be there to shoulder some of the responsibility.

Fen, on the other hand, was in a muddle. Having run the place virtually single-handed for five months, she was close to collapse, but she had been buoyed up by her hopes of Billy and by the feeling that she was being indispensable and splendid. Now Dino had moved in and taken over at least half of the reins. Everyone seemed happier and she couldn't help being jealous. She felt she'd been demoted from senior to freshman and next week when Jake came home she'd be back in kindergarten.

She was irritated by the way everyone deferred to Dino. She couldn't fault him as a worker. Despite the very late hours he kept, he got up at six like everyone else and spent at least seven or eight hours in the saddle working not only his own horses but all of Jake's novices. He had funny ideas about feeding his horses, arriving with a trunk full of vitamins and additives, but he was out of bed in a flash if there was any trouble with a sick horse in the night.

And, despite his languid playboy image, he was amazingly domesticated. Fen nearly fainted one evening when she came home from an interview in Birmingham with A.T.V. to find him ironing his shirts.

"What are you doing?" she asked in amazement, "Tory can do those."

"Why the hell should she? She's exhausted."

Fen watched the expert way he slid the iron along the folds of the blue silk sleeve into the cuff. "Where d'you learn to do that?"

"At college. All the money went on the horses. I couldn't afford to send them to the laundry. I hate wrinkled shirts, so I figured I better learn to iron."

"You'll make a wonderful wife someday," said Fen.

At that moment Darklis appeared round the door in a pink nightgown, looking disapproving.

" 'Lo Fen. We saw you on T.V. Are you coming, Dino? You promised to read *Green Eggs and Ham*. Dino's going to take me to Disneyland," she added to Fen. "Come on, Dino."

"I'll be up when I've finished," he said, refusing to be bullied.

In the hall Fen met Tory wearing a dressing gown, pink from a hot bath.

"I've just left Diana Ferranti slaving over a hot iron," said Fen.

"Isn't he marvelous?" sighed Tory. "I had a blinding headache and he just took over. He's cooking supper too. Gosh, it smells good. So nice to have a man who can tell the difference between rosemary and basil. Jakey wouldn't notice if you gave him dog biscuits."

"I'm beginning to think Dino's more interested in Basils than Rosemarys, anyway," said Fen pointedly.

She went out to the barn to check the horses. It was a very cold starry night. An early frost had polished the cobbles in the yard and starched the golden willow spears which rustled under foot and already clogged the stable gutters. As she adjusted a rug here and checked a water bucket or bandage there, Fen brooded on Dino's deficiencies. In some painful way he reminded her of Billy. But while Billy was like a dog, loving, dependant, enthusiastic, Dino was feline, cool and detached. He was far tougher and more critical than Billy. He saw Fen's faults only too clearly.

Only last week he caught her shouting at Sarah for giving Hardy, who was supposed to be on a diet, the wrong feed. When he told her to stop, she started shouting at him instead, whereupon he calmly bundled her into a stall and shut the door on her till she cooled down.

"How can I have any authority with the grooms if you take the piss out of me all the time?" she complained furiously afterwards.

"They have to humor and nurse you before big classes, so bloody well treat them properly at home."

Most irritating of all, despite saying how much he fancied her during dinner after the *Sunday Times* Cup, he hadn't lifted a long sun-tanned finger in her direction since he arrived at the Mill. Perhaps living in such close proximity had put him off. Not that she cared a scrap; she was still hopelessly hooked on Billy. But she was irked that girls with soft caressing American accents always seemed to be calling Dino up and twice since he'd been living there he'd disppeared in his car after work and not returned until dawn was breaking. Occasionally Fen cried herself to sleep and wondered if Dino, who occupied the blue room at the end of the passage, ever heard her as he tiptoed past to bed.

All in all, for a man who was supposed to be staying in England because of her, he was behaving in an odd way. Standing in Des-demona's stall, ruffling her coat which had thickened from being turned out during the day, Fen gave her the last peppermint.

Looking out of the half-door she saw a small pale sliver of new moon curling itself round the weathervane. Turning a coin in her pocket, she sighed, realizing there was no point wasting a wish on Billy any more.

"Please moon," she said, "give me a gold."

A week later Jake came home. It was a perfect October afternoon with all the trees turning against a rain-heavy navy blue sky. There was not a speck of dust anywhere in the barn or an inch of tack unpolished. Only Dino's horses and four of the novices who were still going to shows were in their stalls. The rest of the horses were out in the dif-ferent fields that checkered the hill behind the stables.

But they sensed something was up. They had been restless all day, snapping and shrieking at each other, not settling down to serious grazing, hanging around the gates. Only now, just before Jake was due, had they all galloped off out of sight to join Macaulay, Africa and Africa's foal, who were grazing in the top field. Darklis and Ira weren't back from school yet, although a huge banner saying, "Welcome Home, Daddy," which they'd painted with Sarah and Dino's help, hung from the two largest willows across the gateway. Above the mur-mur of the mill stream Fen heard the sound of a car on the bridge. Sarah darted into the yard. Then Wolf, who'd also been jumpy all day, gave an excited bark, As the car drove into the yard he leaped forward, scrabbling hysterically at the paint with his paws.

"Welcome home," cried Fen, running forward. "Steady boy." She caught Wolf's collar before opening the car door. "You don't want to send your master flying."

But when he realized it truly was Jake, Wolf remained motionless for the several seconds as though he'd been stunned. Then he put back his head and let out a series of spine-chilling howls. Jake noticed tears were coursing down the lurcher's rough brindled cheeks.

"Come on boy," said Jake gently as the dog crept forward, laying his head on his master's knee, tail rammed between his thin trembling legs, as though he couldn't believe such a miracle. No one spoke as Jake stroked Wolf's head over and over again, smoothing away the tears. Then, as he struggled out of the car, Dino went forward to give him a hand.

"Hi," he said. "It's so good to have you home. Even the sun's come out to welcome you."

Jake nodded, face impassive, not trusting himself to speak.

"Come inside and rest, darling," said Tory.

"I want to see the horses.."

"You must take it slowly," she pleaded. "Today's been such a strain."

"Pass me my crutches," snapped Jake.

"Here they are," said Fen.

As he stumbled painfully across the cobbles, slipping and once falling to his knees, Fen was about to rush to help him.

"Don't," said Dino sharply, grabbing her arm.

He tried not to show how shocked he was by Jake's appearance in the sunlight. Grey with exhaustion, desperately thin, he'd had to make two extra holes in his belt to keep his trousers up.

"Oh God," said Fen, as he stumbled again.

"He's got to do it on his own," said Dino.

After what seemed an eternity he reached the gate, leaning on it, gasping, to recover his breath, Laboriously he managed to open it and stagger inside, leaning back against it for support. The field sloped up to the skyline, dotted only by a few orange chestnuts and lemon yellow ashes. Not a horse in sight. Jake put his hand to his mouth and whistled. There was a long pause. He was about to whistle again when suddenly over the brow of the hill they came—black, dark brown, chestnut, bay, grey, roan. Some of them jumped over fences from nearby fields, thundering down the hill, manes and tails flying. It was like the last furlong of the Derby as they hurtled towards Jake. Hardy came from the back, elbowing, nipping, shoving the others out of the way, squealing jealously. Already plump from their rest, they had never moved faster in the height of their fitness as they stampeded the gate.

"They'll kill him," whispered Sarah.

"They're going to crush him to death," cried Tory in anguish.

"Get him out of there," urged Fen, "Oh Dino, do something."

But miraculously, about ten feet away, they jammed on their brakes and, although the ones behind cannoned unceremoniously into the leaders, they all slithered to a halt, not even touching the tips of Jake's shoes. They stood there, gazing at him goofily. Then, with a thunder of nickering, they edged forward and with the utmost gentleness started to nudge and nuzzle his face, his hands and his coat, occasionally getting jealous, flattening their ears at each other and giving each other a nip or a squeal. Hardy, true to character, licked Jake all over with his tongue, then gave him a sharp nip on the sleeve of his coat, just to show he was still boss.

"I've never seen anything like that before," said Dino, looking down and seeing tears pouring down Fen's cheeks. Finding her hand in his, he gave it a gentle squeeze. Fen looked down, started, blushed scarlet and snatched her hand away to wipe her eyes.

"Someone's missing," said Sarah.

"It's the big fellow, said Dino.

Next minute they saw Macaulay standing on the crest of the hill, like Bambi's father. Jake gave another whistle and the next moment Macaulay came crashing down the hill like an out-of-control steam roller, so fast that all the other horses parted in self-preservation to let him through. When he reached Jake, he chased all the others away with enraged squeals, instantly returning to press his great white whiskery face against Jake's. Jake put his arms round Macaulay's neck, clinging on for support, his shoulders shaking.

"D'you think he's OK?" said Fen in dismay.

"Leave him," said Dino. "He's best alone with the horses."

*H*aving dreaded Jake's return, Fen found it easier than she'd expected because he and Dino got on so surprisingly well. Dino was unruffled by Jake's black moods and biting sarcasm, and didn't take them personally.

"The guy's in a lot of pain," he kept telling Fen, "Got to get his act together. He needs to boss people around a bit to regain his self-respect."

Together they worked on the horses, and on Hardy and Manny in particular, with Jake giving orders, stumbling around the yard, first on two crutches, then one, and by the end of November walking with a stick. He also plugged relentlessly away at the exercises. Dr. Buchannan was delighted with his progress and said with any luck he'd be riding by February.

At night after supper, instead of collapsing in front of the television, Jake and Dino would talk over a bottle of wine until they dropped. Dino asked most of the questions, but while Jake gave Dino the benefit of all his gypsy secrets and remedies, Dino was able to counter with information on the latest medical and dietary break-throughs in the States. Soon all Jake's horses were taking extra vi-tamins. "They all rattle as they go past," said Fen crossly.

Dino also encouraged Jake into a new régime to get him back into peak condition. Fen was staggered to see Jake, who seldom man-aged more than a cup of the blackest, sweetest coffee for breakfast, actually sitting down to slices of apple, dried apricot, prunes and sticks of carrot, followed by one of Dino's multivitamin cocktails.

"All the same, Dino's just picking Jake's brains," said Fen indig-nantly, as she dried the dishes one evening. "You wait till America gets the team gold and Dino the individual. Then you'll be sorry."

"Don't be mean, Fen," said Tory gently. "Dino's doing it for Jakey's sake as well. He looks so much better and does him so much good to feel needed."

Fen was also finding Jake's criticism very hard to take. After all, she'd made more money than he ever had during the last year and she was fed up with Dino sticking up for Tory. She was only helping out tonight because Dino'd given her hell for treating Tory like a slave.

"You all just leave her with the dishes. Why the hell doesn't Jake buy her a dishwasher?"

"But she's quite happy," protested Fen.

"You talk as though she was some retarded kid in a mental in-stitution."

Dino had been particularly touched by Tory's surprise Thanksgiv-ing dinner.

"Where'd you get this pumpkin pie recipe?" he said, amazed. "It's better than they make at home."

Tory went very pink. "I called up Helen Campbell-Black," she stammered.

Fen and Jake looked at her increduously. She must adore Dino to seek advice from the enemy camp.

The only thing that cheered Fen up during those weeks was her own increasing success. She had two good wins at home shows. All the papers regarded her as a sure bet for L.A. Her fan mail increased. She was expected to have instant opinions as magazines called daily asking her for her views on men, clothes, and dieting. Hardly a day passed without some journalist coming down to Warwickshire to interview her. You couldn't walk past a magazine rack without seeing her face peering out; Fen was not conceited by nature but she couldn't help brooding on the admiration of the outside world, compared with the distinct lack of reverence with which she was treated at home. Jake and Dino believed there was a job to be done and she was there to get on with it.

One afternoon in late November Fen and Sarah had been working out, getting Desdemona and Macaulay fit for Olympia next month. As they rode into the yard they found Dino, who'd just had a strenuous session in the indoor ring, cooling off Manny in the yard.

Next minute Tory came out of the kitchen door, her hands covered with flour.

"Oh Dino, someone called Mary Jo rang. She's staying at the Dorchester. Can you call her?"

"Sure, I'll do it now." He handed the horse to Louise, his groom, and walked into the house.

"Lucky Mary Jo," sighed Sarah.

"Who's she?" asked Tory. "She asked after Jake's leg and sounded awfully nice."

"Mary Jo Wilson, I should think," said Fen, sliding off Desdemona. "The American girl wonder. Lots of red hair tucked into a bun and perfectly tied stocks, with diamond tiepins, and a white carnation in her buttonhole. Too bloody toney for words, if you ask me. I'm sure she rides side-saddle in bed."

"But jolly attractive in a Helen Campbell-Black sort of way," said Sarah, not without malice. "Dino obviously likes redheads."

"Well, she sounded sweet," repeated Tory, without any malice at all.

Dino came back. "Sorry it's short notice," he said to Tory, "but I won't be in for dinner tonight."

"Shall I keep something hot for you?" said Tory.

"I'm sure Mary Jo's doing that already," snapped Fen, then immediately wished she hadn't.

Dino shot her a sour look. "It'll make a nice change," he said evenly and went off to supervise Manny's feed.

"Why are you so foul to him, Fen?" said Tory reproachfully.

"Because he's so bloody swollen-headed."

"His head's not the only thing that'll be swollen when he sees Mary Jo," said Sarah with a giggle.

"Don't be disgusting," snapped Fen.

She felt impossibly bad-tempered, particularly when Dino came back in time for breakfast the next morning, spent all day yawning and was so untogether Hardy had him off three times.

A week later Dino took his horses off to a show in Vienna where there was a World Cup qualifier. Fen was so certain he'd taken Mary Jo that she rang up the Dorchester, to be told that Miss Wilson had checked out the morning Dino had left and wasn't expected back until December 12th, the day Dino was due home. Fen spent the next few days imagining Dino waltzing round and round a Viennese ballroom to the Blue Danube with Mary Jo in his arms.

Dino returned as expected on the 12th after a very successful show. Manny had obviously improved dramatically under Jake's tuition. He had qualified for the World Cup, won a big class on the third night and come second in the Grand Prix. Jake was delighted. That's what he gets a kick out of, thought Fen. He really likes improving horses at home better than jumping them at shows.

Dino bought toys for the children, silk scarves for the grooms, a beautiful black sloppy sweater for Tory, which covered all her bulges and a new bit which they were all raving about on the continent for Jake. But nothing apparently for Fen. That's because I was so horrible before he left, she thought miserably. It was a very cold night. The water trough was already frozen and a thin sheet of ice lay over the cobblestones. In the tackroom she found a drooping Louise hanging up Dino's tack which she'd been cleaning on the drive home.

"You must be exhausted, poor thing."

Louise nodded. "Sure but it was a great show. You always feel less bushed when you win."

Fiddling with the striped handle of a body brush, Fen casually asked.

"How did Mary Jo do?"

"Not bad," said Louise, as though it was the most natural thing in the world for Mary Jo to have been with them. "She's having problems with Melchior. He keeps kicking out fences, but Balthazar jumped real super and qualified for the World Cup. She's worried she won't make the team for L.A., particularly as Dino must be a dead cert now. But the competition's so hot and she's twenty-six already and by the next games she'll probably be tied up with babies. Pity she can't come down here for a week or two and work with Jake, not that the American coaches aren't great, but Jake does have the edge with difficult horses."

"I can't think why he doesn't apply for the job as American chef d'equipe," snapped Fen and, chucking down the body brush, she stalked out into the bitterly cold night, wandering around in a sweater and jeans, oblivious of time and temperature. Tory's voice brought her back to reality. In the kitchen she found Dino, changed into a grey cashmere sweater and grey cords, drinking a large whisky and soda and telling Tory about Vienna. Ribbons and photographs were spread out all over the pine table.

"It's so beautiful. We went to one cemetery where all the great musicians are buried: Beethoven, Brahms, Haydn. The most moving thing of all was Schubert's grave. Look." He handed the photo to Tory. "On the headstone they've carved a picture of him arriving in heaven and an angel putting a laurel wreath on his head—because no one recognized his genius on earth."

"Unlike you," said Fen acidly. "Everyone appreciates you, Dino."

"Not everyone." Dino's face was expressionless, but he quickly gathered up the photographs.

"Lovey, you look frozen," said Tory. "Have a hot bath. I'm just off with Isa to see Darklis' play. Dinner's in the oven. Goulash and baked potatoes. And there's an apple pie if you want it."

Jake was away in Ireland for two days to look at some horses. It had been regarded as a great step forward that he felt well enough to go. Fen, however, couldn't face dinner alone with Dino and Louise.

"Thanks." She walked through the kitchen. "I'm not hungry at the moment. Wish Darklis tons of luck."

In her bedroom she slumped on her bed. Fighting tiredness and misery she drew the blue and white gingham curtains. The tops were still off the shampoo and conditioner she'd used to wash her hair for Dino's return; the wet towel was still on the bed, the hair dryer plugged in. Despite switching on the fire she couldn't stop shivering and decided to have a bath. She'd just stripped off when there was a knock on the door.

"Who is it?" she grabbed the wet towel.

"Me." Dino came into the room, shutting the door behind him.

Fen turned away towards the mirror. "I'm about to have a bath."

"I've fixed you a drink." He put a large vodka and tonic down on the dressing table.

She sat on the dressing-table stool, thin bare shoulders rising out of the dark red towel, slanting eyes suspicious.

Dino noticed the plugged-in hair dryer.

"Going out?"

She shook her head. "My hair was dirty."

The room was warming up now. Why couldn't her teeth stop chattering?

"I've got a present for you," said Dino, easing a black square box out of his hip pocket and opening it. Fen gasped as he took out a gold chain, with an F exquisitely set in pearls and emeralds on the end. He hung it round her neck, fumbling over the clasp, with hands that were not quite steady.

"Well," he said.

Looking up at his reflection, she noticed his suntan was fading and the Siamese-cat eyes were squinting slightly as they always did when he was very tired.

"It's lovely," she whispered, fingering the F. "It's the loveliest thing anyone's ever, ever given me. I'll never take it off. Thank you so much. I thought," her voice shook, "you'd deliberately forgotten me because I'd been such a bitch."

She stood up to turn around, but Dino gripped her bare arms, dropping a slow infinitely measured kiss on her left collar bone. Suddenly her stomach started to curl and a pulse to beat insistently between her legs.

"How could I forget you?" he said ruefully. "I never think of anything else." He was nuzzling at the side of her neck now, softly kissing the lobes of her ears. "And quite frankly if I don't unzip my fly and climb inside you soon I'm going to end up in the funny farm."

"Truly? You're not just being kind?"

"Kind? Christ, I've backed off enough."

He turned her around. She gazed up at him, troubled, trembling. "I'm not sure, Dino. I've been so hurt, I've only got a little bit of heart left."

"I've got more than enough heart for both of us. I won't hurt you, sweetheart. I'm going to make you better."

Slowly he drew back her clenched arms which were holding the towel up and put her hands round his neck. Beneath her fingers she could feel the power of his shoulder muscles.

"Go on, kiss me," he whispered.

As she tentatively put her lips up, he kissed her back so gently she thought she'd faint with joy, kissing first her top lip then the bottom, then sliding his tongue between her teeth. One hand was cupping her left breast now, moving slowly and lovingly, the harbinger of pleasure.

"Darling little Fen, tell me what turns you on."

"You do," she moaned. "Oh please go on."

But as he pulled her down on the bed and began to kiss her in earnest, sliding his hand over her body, she caught a glimpse of Billy's photograph beside the bed. Then she thought about Janey and then about Mary Jo Wilson, who last night had been lying beside Dino submitting, no doubt ecstatically, to the same expert caresses. She couldn't stand it. This time she wanted a man who was all hers, who she didn't have to share.

Violently, she pulled away from him.

"Hey, what's the matter?"

"You are. You're so bloody promiscuous, smarming all over me one minute, then rushing up to London at the drop of a telephone receiver to push off to Vienna with Mary Jo. Guess who's coming for Dino? You bet your sweet life Mary Jo is."

For a second Dino's hand clenched on her shoulder. Then he looked around the room at the posters of Snoopy and the china horses and Lester the teddy bear and the pyjama case in the shape of a camel, and then at the tattered photograph of Billy Lloyd-Foxe in the leather case.

"You're still a kid, aren't you?" he said bitterly. "I guess you're just about adult enough to sleep with an old teddy bear like Billy Lloyd-Foxe."

"Bastard," hissed Fen, and the next moment she'd slapped Dino's face very hard. "Just shut up about Billy."

Dino shrugged. "And you hit out just like a kid. Unfortunately, I happen to be a grown-up. I had my twenty-first birthday five years ago and I've got the appetites of a normal guy. If you think I'm going to remain celibate while you keep putting another battery in the stupid flashlight you're carrying for Billy you've got another thing coming."

"It's not a stupid torch," screamed Fen. "You're just like Rupert and Jake. None of you understand the meaning of the word love."

"All I can promise," said Dino, "is that I want you more than any girl I've ever met, but I'm a hedonist, not a medieval knight keeping myself pure for some unobtainable lady love, nor do I like sleeping alone. The central heating in this house leaves a lot to be desired. So if you won't put out I'm going to find my entertainment some place else."

And with that he left her. The next minute she heard his car door bang and the crunch of wheels on the gravel. Bursting into tears, she threw herself down on the bed.

46

*T*he next few days were awful. Fen and Dino hardly exchanged a word. Fen got up before dawn. Dino changed his routine, got up after lunch and spent his evenings working the horses in the indoor ring. It seemed impossible in such a small house that they could avoid meeting. Dino was polite but unsmiling.

On Friday morning Fen, Dino, Louise and Sarah were due to get up at 3:30 a.m. for a 4:30 departure for a show in Amsterdam. On the Thursday before that the *Sunday Express* sent a photographer and a reporter down to the Mill to interview Fen. In the evening she had to go to a dinner at the Savoy where she was being nominated for one of the Sporting Personality of the Year awards. The organizers were sending a car for her, which, at the end of the evening, would whizz her back to Warwickshire to catch three hours sleep before leaving for Amsterdam.

The *Sunday Express* reporter was a charming middle-aged roué who thought Fen was gorgeous and buttered her up to mountainous heights in the hope of possible indiscretions. After lunch cooked by Tory, the photographer took pictures of Desdemona and Macaulay from flattering angles, as they were still a bit pudgy from their six week's rest, and later photographed the stables and the house and the kitchen, with Tory cooking and Fen pretending to fill in entry forms against a background of ribbons.

"I'm thinking of getting a secretary to cope with all my fan mail," said Fen, who'd had three glasses of wine at lunch.

"I'm not surprised," said the *Express* reporter. "Every little girl in England dreams of being like you."

"I hope to Christ they don't behave like her," said a voice, and Dino wandered in, unshaven, yawning, bloodshot-eyed and poured himself a large whisky.

"Is that your breakfast?" snapped Fen.

"No, the first one was my breakfast," said Dino. "Hi," he added to the reporter and wandered off in the direction of the stables.

"That's Dino Ferranti, isn't it?" asked the reporter, refilling Fen's glass. "Good-looking, despite the stubble. More like a rock star. He your latest?"

"Hardly," snapped Fen. "He's working with Jake. Honestly, if I were cast away on a desert island I'd rather be propositioned by the gorillas."

"You'd be wasting your time," said Dino coming back into the room. "Gorillas are mostly gay. Anyone seen this week's *Horse and Hound*?"

"And don't bloody eavesdrop," said Fen, "Let's go into the sittingroom. We'll be more private."

It was already dark when she waved goodbye to them. Outside, the van was waiting, already filled with gasoline, water and human and equine supplies. She'd better step on it. The car was picking her up at five thirty. Sitting at the kitchen table she found Dino, Tory and Sarah checking the list of what they were taking to Amsterdam. Fen looked at her message pad—A.T.V., *Woman's Own* and Malise Gordon had called. Picking up the telephone, she suddenly noticed black fur all over her pale pink angora sweater which was drying on a towel.

"Bloody hell," she said, dropping the receiver back on its cradle.

Tory looked up, alarmed. "What's the matter?"

"My pink sweater, I've got to take it tomorrow and you can't even keep the bloody cats off it."

Dino looked up from a pile of horses' health papers.

"Knock it off." he said softly. "Tory's cooked lunch for your press admirers, which you haven't even had the manners to thank her for. She's done all our ironing for tomorrow and seen everything's back from the cleaners, as well as providing enough food for us for a month. She doesn't exactly have the time to police your pale pink sweater," he really spat out the Ps, "against marauding tom cats."

Fen lost her temper. "I ran this bloody stable single-handed for five months and now I don't get any proper back-up," she screamed and stormed out of the kitchen. Ten minutes later she was back with dripping hair: "Who's been using my hairdryer?"

"I did," said Tory apologetically, "on Darklis."

"Well you've blown the fuse. How am I expected to dry my hair?"

"Why don't you go stick your head in the oven," said Dino, "and preferably don't light the gas? You're getting much too big for your £500 boots. We all know you're England's answer to show-jumping and the role model for the entire schoolgirl population and we're fed up with it. You know perfectly well you wouldn't speak to Tory like this if Jake was here."

"*Were* here," screamed Fen, "*Were* here. 'If' takes the subjunctive," and she stormed out of the room again.

"Oh dear," said Tory, in distress, gazing out at the last orange rays of sunset. "Oh dear, oh dear."

Fen was in such a rage that she went off to London without saying goodbye to anyone. She wore a black, backless taffeta dress she'd bought in Paris last summer and never worn, with high-heeled black shoes, black stockings and Dino's necklace at her throat. As she walked into the pre-dinner cocktail party, which was choc-a-bloc with every sporting celebrity, commentator and journalist you could imagine, a few heads turned in her direction. She went to talk to Dudley Diplock, propped up against the fireplace, who was already three sheets to the wind and gave the room the benefit of her back view. The dress was so low it almost gave her a cleavage at the back. When she turned around five minutes later everyone was gaping at her.

"What does F stand for?" asked a famous tennis player.

"Fuckable," said Fen sweetly.

"You can say that again," said the tennis player as everyone laughed.

Soon the journalists were hovering round her. They kept asking her about Billy and Dino, but she cracked back that she was married to her career and had no intention of getting a divorce. She had a good deal to drink and had some difficulty negotiating even the short walk into the dining room. She found herself sitting between a famous soccer player with permed blonde hair and a fake suntan, named Garry, and an Olympic shotputter whose arm muscles bulged through his dinner jacket, whose stomach folded over the table and who lifted Fen above his head to loud cheers when she complained she couldn't see the Princess.

The first course, because most people were in some sort of training, was prosciutto and melon, which Garry the soccer player thought too outré for words.

"You got a boyfriend?" he asked Fen.

"Nope."

"Fort as much. Riding an 'orse is a subsitute for sex."

"What an original thing to say," said Fen politely, moulding her uneaten roll into pellets and chucking them at Dudley.

"Stands to reason. Funny thing, most of them look like 'orses, but you don't."

"You're talking garbage," said the shotputter.

"Why don't you come home with me?" said Garry the footballer. "Wife's staying with her mother. I'd give you more fun than an 'orse."

"You reckon?" said Fen.

Suddenly all the flashbulbs exploded as the photographers clustered round a late arrival, a tall, dark, very broad-shouldered man wearing a dirty bomber jacket, a dark blue shirt, no tie, jeans and sneakers. He was extremely good looking in a brutal, suntanned, heavy-eyelidded way, and appeared not remotely embarrassed to be the only man in the room not wearing a dinner jacket. The plane from Rome was late; he hadn't had time to change.

At the sight of him the convoy of waitresses, rushing in like some musical comedy act, nearly dropped the massive oblong silver plates of beef they were bearing aloft. One comely brunette was so excited she gave the shotputter five slices of beef as she gazed entranced. Others dived for the kitchen and within seconds six plates of prosciutto and melon were pressed on the new arrival from all sides, followed by several very large glasses of rum and soda, which he lined up in a row in front of him, laughing all the while, showing beautiful big white teeth with several gold fillings. In the mat of black chest hair hung a gold St. Christopher medal.

"Who's that?" said the shotputter.

"Enrico Mancini," said Fen. "The fastest man on earth."

"Certainly be'aves like it," said Garry disapprovingly. "I don't like racing drivers. Fink they're God's gift. Not much skill in driving round and round the same track."

He's coarser looking than Rupert, thought Fen, watching Enrico Mancini joking with a couple of television commentators, but he behaves with the same certainty that he owns the earth. He was forking up prosciutto very fast now, his eyes raking the room for women or cronies.

"Lovely beef," said Fen. "I don't know how they cook it on such a large scale."

She took a big slug of red wine and, looking across at Enrico Mancini, found he was staring at her. Christ, he was taking the skin off her face. She looked hurriedly away, then glanced back five seconds later. He was still staring, gazing with peculiar intensity through a pot of yellow chrysanthemums. Her beef had lost all its appeal. She took another slug of wine. Putting her elbow on the table, it slid off as though it was greased. When she looked back again he'd moved the flowers and was smiling at her, lounging lazily in his chair. Then he blew her a kiss. Fen blushed, then found herself smiling.

"Eat up your beef, Fenella," said the soccer player. "You'll never get to Los Angeles that way."

"No thanks. I'm full," said Fen, putting her knife and fork together.

"Shame to waste it," said the weightlifter, forking up the slices of beef. Dudley Diplock swayed over to have a chat, launching into a long story about Colonel Roxborough.

"How wonderful," said Fen after five minutes, when it was obvious some response was expected.

"I said he'd had a stroke," said Dudley.

"Oh dear, I'm sorry. I misheard you. Who did you say?"

"Colonel Roxborough, but he's expected to pull through."

Fen could see Enrico Mancini writing a note on the back of a place card.

"I reckon you've got a good chance of getting the woman's award tonight," said Dudley.

"How dreadful for the family," said Fen, who thought they were still on Colonel Roxborough's stroke.

"The award, Fen! If you do, we'll have a chat on camera immediately afterwards. Good luck."

"Thanks Dudley." said Fen. Her glass seemed to be full again and someone had brought her a large brandy and the pretty brunette waitress, with some disappointment, Fen thought, was handing her a card.

On the back of the place card saying Enrico Mancini he had written, "Will you come out with me afterwards?"

Fen looked up. Enrico was still staring at her with that knowing, speculative supremely confident smile. He raised his eyebrows. Fen shook her head, mouthing: "I can't".

"Black or white," said the waitress.

"White, no, sorry, I mean black."

"Must go to the toilet, " said Garry.

Fen had broken off some frosted grapes and was putting them in her bag, wrapped in a paper napkin, for Darklis and Ira, when she felt a warm hand traveling the length of her back, lasciviously fingering her spine.

"There is no such word as 'can't,'" said a husky Latin voice and, spinning round, she saw Enrico had taken the empty seat.

He had eyes the color of molasses and an incredibly sensual mouth like one of his own rubber tires. I wonder if he changes it after three laps when it gets worn out with kissing, thought Fen with a giggle.

"Why d'you laugh?" he said softly, "I don't find you funny."

"I don't find you funny either," stammered Fen. "I'm just nervous."

"With good cause," said Enrico. "You won't escape. I have wanted you for a very long time."

"About an hour," said Fen, looking at her watch.

"No, no, I see you on television in May in Rome and Desdemona, when you beat my friend Piero Fratinelli. His father makes my car. Then later you fall off Macaulay and got on again with the concussion. I said I must meet this girl. She is not only beautiful but brave. I am more attracted by courage than beauty in a woman. You and I will be magnificent in bed."

"You saw me in Rome?" said Fen amazed.

"Of course. That ees the only reason I come here tonight. They told me you'd be here. Shall we go?"

"We can't," said Fen.

His eyebrows were so black and his hair so thick and his face so strong and commanding. Oh heavens, thought Fen in panic, how can I not go to bed with him?

"Why not?"

"Well, it's a bit rude, before the speeches and the awards."

"I will give you my own personal award," said Enrico, staring at her breasts. "Much better than some stupid prize."

"Besides I've got to go straight back to Warwickshire at eleven o'clock. I'm leaving for Amsterdam at four-thirty."

Enrico looked at his massive digital watch, pressing nobs. "How many miles?"

"More than a hundred and twenty."

"At night that takes me one hour and ten minutes, no more. We leave London at three. That gives us four hours if we leave now. Not long but quite long enough for the first time, which should be brief, passionate, exquisitive and leave one hungry for the next."

Fortunately there was a roll of drums and it was announced the awards would begin in two minutes. Fen staggered off to the ladies. She looked pretty abandoned; her hair was all over the place. Overwhelmed by frantic excitement, she tipped half a bottle of Diorissimo over her body and wandered back to the table to find Garry having a frightful row with Enrico for taking his seat. Fen collapsed into hers as the lights dimmed. Garry, who was even more drunk than Fen, was removed, complaining bitterly to a chorus of shushes. Enrico poured Fen another glass of wine.

"What does hedonistic mean?" she asked the shotputter.

"Haven't a clue."

"Nor have I, but I think I'm about to be it."

She hardly heard a word of the speeches as, in the dim twilight of their corner, she felt Enrico's hand running all over her back, firm warm powerful hands with splayed fingers and pudgy balls to the thumbs. Now they were inching around underneath the front of her dress.

"You mustn't."

"I must," he said, leaning across her to stub out his cigar.

"Ouch," squealed Fen as he bit her shoulder.

Now his free hand was moving downwards, slipping into the cleavage of her buttocks. She leapt away as the lights blazed on. The Princess, to thunderous applause, was presenting the award for the male personality of the year to yet another famous soccer player, who was saying he was "absolutely over the moon, definitely" and holding up his prize like a football cup.

When the Princess started reading out the female nominations Enrico started kissing Fen. Enjoying the frantic swordplay of tongue and saliva, she could feel the stubble on his cheeks. He had a zoo-like unwashed smell. He was just like a stallion. Unheeding, she kissed him back. His hand was between her legs now. If the lights hadn't blazed on again she had a feeling he would have taken her there and then in that dark corner.

The huge cheers seemed to be getting louder. Someone was tapping her on the shoulder.

"You've been nominated," whispered the shotputter.

"Fuck off," growled Enrico.

Fen wriggled away just as the spotlight found her.

"Come here," said Enrico.

Next moment there was a burst of cheering and Dudley Diplock was crying, "Well done, Fen. Go on. You've won."

Everyone seemed to be helping her through the tables as she frantically straightened and pulled down her dress and wiped away the mascara, smudged under her eyes.

"Oh she's crying, bless her," said a fat woman, "She's only eighteen and so unspoiled."

Fen fell up the stairs and was picked up by Dudley.

Fen clutched the trophy, which was a model of a silver pen writing on a silver page. Finally the deafening cheers were silenced. Fen took the microphone, grinning fatuously.

"Honestly I had no idea. I can't tell you how knocked out I am. Thank you, sports writers, for this stunning award. It was due to the horses. I've just got good ones and my brilliant brother-in-law, Lake Jovell," no, that wasn't right, "I mean Luke Jovell," she opened her hands despairingly, "I'm sorry, I'm a bit over the top. It's the excitement and all your wonderful hospitality."

Everyone laughed and cheered.

Dudley collared her for an interview but all she could think about was being in bed with Enrico. At the table she could see him waiting, fingers drumming impatiently. He was not a man who would be kept waiting very long.

As she left she tapped one of the B.B.C. minions on the shoulders.

"Could you tell the car that's supposed to be taking me back to Warwickshire that I won't be needing it."

"Right ho, dearie."

"Should I call home? They're expecting me back by one o'clock."

"No," said Enrico.

His flat was all white, with pile carpet thick as a hayfield, huge white sofas and walls lined with mirrors. Everywhere there were photographs of Enrico, winning races or being photographed with Presidents and Kings.

"This is small place," he said, adjusting the dimmer switches. "In Rome I haf really nice apartment."

In the drawing-room he took off her dress, then her stockings. Then he turned the spotlights on her, so that she was reflected a hundred times in the mirrored walls, as though taking part in some vast orgy. She wished her face wasn't so pink and weathered compared with her slender white body. As first she covered her breasts and her bush with her hands, but she was too drunk really to mind.

"I'm awfully out of practice," she mumbled. "Can we have a long warm-up first?"

Enrico shook up a bottle of Moët Chandon, then opened it, spraying it all over Fen's body, into every crevice. Then he picked her up and carried her into the bedroom where, on a huge oval bed, he proceeded very slowly and thoroughly to lick every drop off until Fen was a squirming, ecstatic bundle of desire. God, he had a cock like a salami. A lot of junk is talked about the size of the male member having no importance in sex. And when a man is as magnificently endowed as Enrico, and as skillful in manipulation, and of such unquestionable sex appeal, and the girl in question is as well lubricated as one of Enrico's engines, the result is bound to be ecstatic. For Fen it was the most glorious hour of her life. "Talk about a one night stunned," she muttered afterwards.

Hazily she looked at the clock beside the bed, red eyes flickering like hers. "My God, it's a quarter to three. We must go," she said, leaping to her feet.

Enrico put out a hand. "Stay with me. Give Amsterdam a miss."

"I can't. The van's loaded. The tickets booked. I must go."

Enrico leaned over, kissing her and running his hand down her body.

"You are like little schoolboy, no? Next time I bugger you."

"Not sure," muttered Fen wriggling away. "I *must* be home by four."

The motorways were deserted. She was almost more turned on by his handling of his Ferrari and the subdued dragon roar of its engine. He didn't seem to be driving fast at all and it was only as he overtook other night flyers that she looked at the speedometer and realized they were travelling at more than 120 m.p.h. They didn't talk. One big hand rested between her thighs.

How long would she be in Amsterdam, he asked, and where was she staying? He would be in New York when she got back, but he would be back in London for the last day of the Olympia show when he would come and watch her. She was to leave some tickets at the box office.

He had her home by five past four; it would have been four o'clock if he hadn't spent five minutes parked on the bridge, with the engine growling, leisurely kissing her goodnight, his tongue tickling her epiglottis.

"'appy treep, my darling," he said as he dropped her off at the front gate. Thank God Jake's still away, thought Fen. As she walked up the path, high heels crunching on the frozen grass, the owls were hooting and the dog star was just sinking in to his kennel behind Pott's meadow.

All was activity in the stable ward. She could see Sarah, Louise and Tanya putting on bandages and tail guards, changing rugs. In the van Tory was making a last-minute check.

She crept unnoticed into the kitchen and went slap into Dino, still wearing the same check shirt, jeans and sweater he'd had on when she left. He plainly hadn't been to bed and was absolutely white with anger.

"Where the hell have you been?"

"I haven't been to hell at all, rather the reverse." She realized she was still tight. "I've just been finding out what hedonism is and I do agree it's much better than celibacy."

For a second, she thought he was going to hit her.

"Why the fuck didn't you call? All the kids, Tory and the groom saw you winning the award. They were so excited they had a bottle of champagne ready to welcome you when you got back. Not that you looked as though you needed it from the way you fell up the stairs. Then you just disappear. Don't even bother to tell the car you didn't need it."

"I did. I told a B.B.C. minion."

"Probably pissed like you. Anyway he never passed on the message. No one got any sleep or knew whether to load up the horses. We were all worried stiff."

Enrico, thought Fen dreamily, was stiff but not worried.

The grandfather clock in the hall struck the quarter hour.

"We're leaving in fifteen minutes," said Dino.

"I'll be ready. Don't worry."

At that moment Tory came in. "Oh Fen, where have you been?"

"I got diverted," said Fen, weaving joyfully towards the door, "Highly diverted. I'm sorry to have caused so much trouble."

Never had her bed looked so inviting. She'd only had time for a lightning shower and a change when she heard the van revving up. Bloody hell, Dino was just doing that to wind her up. Sweeping the entire top of her dressing table into a carryall and throwing Lester on top, she fled downstairs.

*I*t was not an "appy treep". Fen's hangover descended like a million thunderbolts just as they reached Southampton. The crossing was frightful and she spent the entire time commuting between the hold, where she comforted a terrified Hardy until the gasoline fumes overcame her, and the ladies' room. Her face, as a result of Enrico's stubble, was blotched like salami.

Dino, Louise and Sarah were blisteringly unsympathetic, went off to a huge lunch and didn't even buy her a brandy to steady her stomach. As the van, which seemed so pedestrian after Enrico's Ferrari, steadily ate up the miles she was overcome by the depression that goes with extreme tiredness. It had all been a dream. She should never have let Enrico take her to bed on the first night. She would never see him again. It was eleven o'clock when they reached Amsterdam; midnight before the horses were stabled and fed and they reached the hotel. Louise was sleeping in the van, Sarah, Fen and Dino in the hotel. Dino pointedly carried Sarah's suitcase but not Fen's. The manager came out to welcome them in perfect English: "Miss Maxwell, Mr. Ferranti, you must be very tired. Would you like something to eat? We can make some sandwiches."

"I'd sure appreciate a drink," said Dino, stretching after the long drive. "We'll be down in a minute."

The porter took them upstairs. He reached Fen's room first and threw open the door. Fen was knocked sideways by the most heavenly scent. She could hardly get inside for the flowers—roses, gardenias, stephanotis, banks and banks of freesias and hyacinths. It was like suddenly coming out of a freezing cold night into a heated conservatory.

"How gorgeous," she gasped.

"My God," said Sarah, "he must have denuded every flower shop in the low countries. Who on earth are they from?"

Fen took a card out of the tiny envelope lying on the bed.

"Adorable Fen, you were magnificent, I die till Monday week, all my love E."

"I say," said Sarah, snatching the card.

"Don't," screamed Fen, trying to snatch it back and keep the silly grin off her face.

"Who the hell's E?" asked Sara. "Prince Edward, Edgar Lustgarten, Ethelred the Unready, Edward Fox, 'Enry Higgins, Eamonn Andrews? Go on, who is he? Who is E?"

"I'm not going to tell you," said Fen, "My trap is shut."

Dino appeared at the door, "If we're going to catch the restaurant before it closes . . . Christ."

"Fen has a new boyfriend," giggled Sarah. "His name begins with E."

"Stands for excessive, extravagant and extremely silly," snapped Dino.

"No, it doesn't," said Fen, putting a freesia behind her ear and waltzing around the room. "It stands for 'edonism."

Throughout the show Fen jumped atrociously. Her mind was simply not on the horses. She couldn't eat, she couldn't sleep at night, she inhaled the heavy scent of the flowers which brought back the powerful disturbing image of Enrico. No man had any right to be that attractive. He had discovered erogenous zones she didn't kow existed. She kept looking at her watch, surprised that only a minute had passed.

On Saturday night he telephoned her from New York. The manager brought the telephone to the table where she and Dino and Louise were having a very scratchy dinner, attempting to celebrate Dino's win in a big class that evening. The connection was awful.

"I cannot wait to have you in my arms, *cara*," said Enrico and proceeded to tell her all the unmentionable things he was going to do to her when they met again until Fen was surprised the telephone didn't turn blue. Fen turned redder and redder, acutely aware of Dino listening in stony silence.

Fen got an earful from Jake when she got home. Even though they arrived back after midnight he had her up at the crack of dawn the next morning, insisting she jump a new and extremely difficult novice round the indoor ring, with her arms folded, stirrups crossed and reins knotted. She fell off four times and ended up on the floor screaming at Jake.

"You're not going to make a bloody fool of yourself at Olympia," he said.

"I suppose Tory and Dino have been telling tales."

"They didn't need to. One of the Olympic scouts was in Amsterdam. He said if Jesus Christ had ridden that donkey into Jerusalem the way you were riding Laurel and Hardy all week he deserved to be crucified."

The end-of-term jollities of the Olympia Christmas show were lost on Fen this year. Parties were held every night in vans and trailers. Dino went to each of them with a different girl and deliberately got drunk. Fen went to none because she wanted to look beautiful for Enrico, which was difficult with the long hours and the airlessness of Olympia and because sleep, when she finally got to bed, again evaded her because of the din outside.

Gossip circulated as usual. Rupert Campbell-Black had acquired a new wonder horse from America called Rock Star, which was reputed to have cost him two hundred thousand dollars. His marriage on the other hand was in trouble. Helen had managed to do her Christmas shopping without visiting Olympia once. The Lloyd-Foxes, by contrast, were blissfully happy. Janey had embarked on a book on postnatal depression called *The Blues of the Birth*. Jake's leg was mending but no one thought he would make Los Angeles. Fen was showing a dramatic loss of form, so was Dino Ferranti. Wishbone had placed in every class.

The days crawled by. Not eating properly, Fen was appalled that she was getting pimples again. Not knowing where she was staying, Enrico sent flowers to her care of the B.S.J.A. tent and lots of giggling ex-debs carried them down to Fen's van, which now, according to Dino, looked like a hearse.

At long last it was the final day of the show and Enrico was due that evening.

"What d'you think?" said Fen, teetering on one of the bunks in the trailer so she could see her bottom half in the mirror opposite. She was trying on a new pair of breeches, specially made for her in white sharkskin.

"Brilliant," said Sarah who was cleaning Hardy's bridle, "I've never seen anything so sexy. They make your legs go on for ever, but you *must* wear panties underneath.

"No, it'll ruin the line."

"It'll ruin your reputation if they split."

Fen bent down, straining the breeches to the limit, and extracted a riding coat from the tissue paper in the cardboard box.

"Now what d'you think of these together?" she said triumphantly when she'd shrugged her way into it. The coat was dark purple instead of the regulation black or midnight blue, lined with rose pink silk, tightly fitting and only just skirting the top of her hip bones. It made the perfect foil for the white breeches.

Sarah whistled. "You'll never get away with that. It's a bum freezer. Colonel Roxborough will have another stroke."

"You wait," said Fen. "I bet it starts a trend. Everyone'll be wearing them in a few months."

"Not if you've got a bum Griselda's size," said Sarah.

"But it does look sexy!"

"Incredibly. But you look more like a page in *Figaro* than a show jumper, and I don't think the B.S.J.A. will like it."

As long as Enrico does, that's all that matters, thought Fen. "I still think you ought to wear underpants," said Sarah, "what else did you get?"

Faintly embarrassed by such extravagance, Fen produced a pale blue jumpsuit with zippers everywhere and a pair of matching pale blue leather boots.

"Gorgeous," sighed Sarah enviously. "You must have blown your entire year's winnings. Goodness, I must go and get Hardy ready."

Fen's new clothes caused an instant sensation, setting every photographer snapping and all the riders wolfwhistling, except Dino and Grisel who both looked extremely disapproving.

"Playing Buttons in the Christmas pantomime?" was Dino's only comment.

Just as she was walking the course for the last class of the show, in despair that he wasn't going to turn up, Enrico arrived and caused an even bigger sensation. Wearing a red shirt, a black coat with a huge astrakhan collar and half an inch of stubble on his chin, he was accompanied by a girl and a man. The girl, deeply tanned with her streaked blond hair scraped back into a bun, was wearing huge gold hoop earrings and the sort of long squashy fur coat destined to put her straight on to the hit list of the Animal Rights Movement. The man, also blond, was wearing dark glasses, a pale blue jump suit identical to Fen's and carrying a pale blue handbag.

Hell, thought Fen, that means I can't wear my jump suit tonight—we'd look like hers and hers. Enrico, who had found the seats Fen had left for him at the box office, was making a lot of noise settling in. All the fresh-faced pony club girls, the horsey ladies and the fathers with three whiskys under their belts, were looking at him in amazement.

"Look, there's Enrico Mancini," said Rupert, "Who's that bird with him?"

"Anna-Fabiola Caraccio," said Dino. "She's a friend of Mary Jo's; and with them is that fag designer, Ralphie Walcott."

E for Enrico, thought Dino. That was it. That explained the booming exhaust he'd heard on the bridge. He watched Fen go crimson, giving Enrico a fleeting wave and mouthing that she'd be over to see him as soon as she'd jumped the first round.

Damn, damn, damn, damn, thought Dino, his heart twisting with misery.

For once Fen was glad she was drawn first. Even though she'd hardly taken in the course when she walked it, she managed to transmit her elation to a rather jaded Hardy who went around without touching a fence to the noisy delight of the crowd. Hardly bothering to pat him, Fen threw her reins to the waiting Sarah and ran off. Dino, watching from the riders' stand, saw Fen mounting the steps, her spiky blond hair gleaming, turning every head in those shiny tight white breeches. He saw Enrico getting up and kissing both her hands and her lips and then, because the people behind were complaining they couldn't see Driffield jumping, sitting down and pulling Fen onto his knee.

"I thought you weren't coming," said Fen.

"Carissima," purred Enrico sounding rather like one of his own engines, "the traffic was terrible, all those stupid peoples looking at the lights. Then we have to wait in line at the entrance. Ralphie 'ere 'ad his 'andbag searched. 'Ave we missed a lot? That was a beautiful round, you look so sexy in those trousers." He ran his hand up her inner thighs till it came to rest on her crotch.

Noticing disapproving glances from all round, particularly from the Royal Box, Fen wriggled away.

"We're going to a party," said Enrico. "Don't change. Just come like that. Can you leave now?"

"Not really," said Fen, feeling flustered, "I've got another round to jump and I might be in the jump off."

"Give it the miss," said Enrico, putting his hand back onto her groin.

"I can't, really," said Fen thinking of the money she'd spent that morning. "Too much at stake."

"Don't be seely, Enrico," said the beautiful girl. "Haff some self-control. You wouldn't stop in the middle of a Grand Prix."

"Those trousers—they turn me on so much," complained Enrico.

Wishbone had just come in but no one sitting near Fen and Enrico was watching him at all. Crimson with embarrassment, Fen escaped back to the riders' stand.

"Vroom, vroom," teased Rupert. "You are flying high. Enrico's got an even worse reputation than I have."

Dino, having kicked Manny with unaccustomed viciousness as they went into the ring, jumped appallingly and knocked up so many faults that he didn't even qualify for the second round. Only sixteen riders went through. Fen, going first, went clear again. Instantly she went off to placate Enrico. She was appalled to find him creating yet another disturbance, infuriating everyone by coming out in the middle of Billy's round.

"You have finished, no," he demanded.

"No, I'm terribly sorry, not yet. I should be through in about three-quarters of an hour but I've got jump off and then change."

"Don't change a theeng. I want you like that," said Enrico, stopping to give her a lingering kiss.

"For Christ's sake get a move on, Rico," snapped Ralphie, who was still trapped in the row and being told from all sides to sit down.

"You go on to the party," said Fen. "I'll meet you there."

"Ees better," said Enrico. "Give her the address, Ralphie."

"Are you sure it's not smart and I can wear this?" asked Fen.

"*Si,*" said Enrico, hand on her crotch again. "Come and come and come as you are."

In a turmoil Fen went back to the collecting ring. The second round over, the arena party rushed on with brushes to smooth the tanbark. The band played carols.

"Oh come all ye unfaithful," sang Rupert.

"Where's Dino?" said Fen. Looking at the jump-off course, she suddenly felt nervous and uncertain, needing his advice.

"Disappeared somewhere," said Sarah. "He seemed terribly choked up about his round."

Fen cantered Hardy around the collecting ring, trying to get him on his toes. It was like sitting on a log. For once he wasn't even fighting for his head. As her number was called, she saw Dino go into the riders' stand. He was wearing a suit, his hair wet from the shower. He must be angry if he didn't even come and wish her good luck. There was £10,000 at stake.

Going first, her only answer was to put in such a fast clear she'd frighten the others into making mistakes. There was no doubt Hardy was exhausted. For once she had really to push him on for all her worth. She cleared the first four fences without too much difficulty, then pulled him too sharply into the triple. Unable to make it, and to avoid crashing into the wing, he ran out. Yanking him back, she rode straight at the jump from three yards away and just cleared it. Only the combination was left, but Hardy was all to pieces now. He took off too early at the first element and Fen had to hurl herself forward in a supreme effort to keep her weight off him and not jab him in the mouth. Alas the effort was too much for her new breeches. As she flew through the air she was aware of a dreadful ripping sound and the sharkskin split right down the back. There was nothing she could do, she was going too fast. She had to jump the remaining two elements. splitting the breeches further each time until her entire backside was exposed with no long coat to cover it.

As she whipped through the finishing line the entire riders' stand stood up cheering. The crowd was in an uproar, half drunken guffaws, half wails of embarrassment and sympathy. The photographers had no such scruples and rushed forward, an excited, snapping, leaping pack. Frantically tugging Hardy to a standstill in front of a bank of pink chrysanthemums, Fen put her hands down to assess the damage and, encountering so much bare flesh, clapped her hands over her eyes, leaving Hardy to trot round the ring, reins flapping.

Next moment the course builder was rushing towards her with a coat. But Dino was to quick for him. Vaulting over the hedge of red poinsettias in front of the rider's stand, he sprinted across the ring, captured a somewhat bewildered Hardy and, tearing off his grey jacket, put it round Fen, leading her sobbing out of the ring.

Reporters converged on them from all sides.

"Great viewing," said Rupert who was about to jump and was laughing his head off. "Now I know why that fence is called the combination. Nanny used to wear bloomers that split up the back like yours."

"Fuck off," snapped Dino.

Pulling Fen off Hardy, whom he left to Sarah, he hustled her through the crowd. Before she knew it she was back in the trailer.

"Stupid little fool," he yelled, slamming the door behind them. "Why the hell didn't you wear underwear?"

Fen looked at him aghast, her eyes full of tears, not even able to speak. So he answered for her.

"Because you wanted to excite the hell out of your new boyfriend, right. Well, he's no bloody good for you, I can tell you here and now."

"How d'you know."

"Used to screw an old girlfriend of mine. Gave her crabs in fact, just proving that Latins are lousy lovers."

"That's not funny," sobbed Fen.

"I'm amazed he asked you out a second time," he went on furiously. "Fuck'em and forget'em, that's his motto. Bloody Mafia thug. Do you honestly think he's the way to get over Billy? Couldn't even wait for you to finish your class, could he?"

"He had to go to a party."

"You bet he did, and by the time you get there he'll have picked up another bit of trash."

"You're just jealous," screamed Fen, "because he's so attractive."

Fighting to control his temper, Dino took a deep breath. "All I'm saying," he added in a calmer voice, "is that the guy is bad, mad, stupid, cruel and insensitive. But if you insist on finding that out for yourself, don't come whining to me when he ditches you. Now you'd better get changed. You must be fifth and you've got to collect your money."

"I am not going back into that ring."

"Don't be such a drip. Go back in and laugh it off, and that mob'll eat out of your hand. You've bared it, now you've got to grin. And then we're going home."

"I'm bloody not," said Fen. "I'm going to join Enrico at that party. Then I've got a broadcast at the television studio first thing tomorrow morning. I'll make my own way home."

There was a bang on the door. It was Louise.

"Fen, Sarah says they're waiting for you."

"I'm not coming, and you can get out," she added to Dino. "I want to change."

"You need to change," said Dino brutally, "back into a decent human being. You were a really sweet kid when I first met you. I wonder whatever happened to her."

"Get out," screamed Fen, "out of my life."

As soon as he'd gone she gave way to tears. Horrible man, how dare he say those awful things. She couldn't wait to reach Enrico to be soothed by his admiration and distracted from her misery and humiliation by his lovemaking. But what the hell could she wear? Her breeches were only fit for the bonfire, she couldn't turn up in the same jump suit as Ralphie. She only had a pair of black jeans and a white shirt, and she was far too drained to wear white. Rifling through Sarah's drawer, she unearthed a black T-shirt. It'd have to do. She'd settle for looking pale, interesting and understated. Enrico had liked her in black last time.

She knew she ought to have gone back into the arena. She ought to call Jake and to check that Hardy was all right, but all she could think of was getting to that party before Enrico whizzed on to another one. She didn't believe Dino. She was sure he was jealous, but he'd sewn a whole seed packet of doubts.

The repeated hammerings on the door distracted her. Party eye makeup only seemed to emphasize the tiredness of her eyes. She now had three pimples instead of two and makeup failed to disguise them. Obsessed that her breath might smell because she'd eaten so little recently, she cleaned her teeth until her gums bled, then cheered herself up by making a Dracula face in the mirror.

Outside the trailer she went slap into a swarm of reporters, who peppered her with questions about Dino, Enrico and her breeches. Without Dino it was almost impossible to throw them off and she was forced to run out of Olympia into the homegoing crowd who all stared and pointed at her. With so many Christmas parties around, it was impossible to find a taxi. Not knowing London well, Fen started to walk in the direction of Eaton Square, which was the address Ralphie had given her. It was bitterly cold. Half an hour later, frozen stiff, her feet blocks of ice in her high-heeled shoes, she reached Knightsbridge and found a cab.

She hardly had time to cover her red nose and her three pimples, which had reappeared, when the cab pulled up. Her heart sank when a spectacular but utterly stoned girl opened the door. Her bright pink hair matched her trousers. Her sequinned waistcoat only just covered her nipples.

"Hi," she said vaguely.

"Is Enrico here?"

The girl gave a silly laugh. "Somewhere he is, come in."

Having repaired her face as best she could, Fen went into a big dimly-lit room. People with glazed expressions were having off-center conversations. Everyone was very dressed up and glamorous. Fen recognized several well known actresses. Two women were necking in a corner, a man in a ballet skirt and a tweed coat was asleep on the sofa. There was no sign of Enrico.

She found him in the next room, in a corner, with Anna-Fabiola on his knee, one hand inside her shirt, the other under her skirt half way up her thigh. He was talking to two other girls. Heart hammering, Fen walked over:

"Hullo Enrico."

"Fenella." At least he dropped Anna-Fabiola and came towards her. For a minute she was wrapped in warm masculine reassurance as he held her to his chest. But she could also smell stale sweat and there was garlic and whisky on his breath when he kissed her.

He let her go and led her back to Anna-Fabiola, who smiled vacantly. The two girls who'd been vying for his attention looked at Fen as though she was something the cat couldn't even bother to bring in. She desperately needed a drink.

"What happened to your breeches?" said Enrico. "I wanted to 'ave you like that."

"They split in the jump off," said Fen miserably. "In front of ten thousand people. It was awful."

But Enrico wasn't interested. He was talking to Ralphie who'd just wandered over with his jump suit undone almost to his crotch to display a pink, hairless chest. In the end Fen was forced to find her own drink. When she came back Enrico had undone all the buttons of Anna Fabiola's shirt and was playing with her breasts.

"Isn't she lovely?" he said to Fen. "Wouldn't you like to play with her too?"

With a sob Fen turned away. Suddenly she wished she was going home in the van with Dino and Sarah, home to reality and sanity. She was exhausted, sober, desperately in need of comfort and bitterly aware that she was looking her worst and couldn't compete with any of the girls hanging around Enrico. She was amazed when he followed her, taking her upstairs and opening and shutting several doors before he found an empty bedroom. There was no lock on the door.

"We can't" said Fen aghast. "Someone might come in."

"Let's hope they will," said Enrico. "You are very sexy, *cara*, you need to be shared."

Next moment he was undressed, lying on his back, his chest matted with black hairs like an ape, his cock rising like some grotesque Italian pepper-grinder. The smell of unwashed body assailed her as she knelt over him. She suddenly remembered Dino's warning about crabs. When Enrico seized her head, forcing it down she nearly threw up.

"Go on, little school boy, you make love to me this time."

His hand was fingering her bum crack. Appalled, she wished she could ram her tail between her legs, like Wolf. It was all horrible, there was none of the ecstasy of the last time. She longed to run away but she had nowhere to go. There were no trains to Warwickshire at this hour. Anyway she had to do the broadcast. There was a bang on the door. Fen snatched the sheet around her. It was Ralphie and Anna Fabiola.

"Come and join us," said Enrico, holding out his arms.

Leaping out of bed, Fen snatched up her clothes and fled past them. She spent the night shivering on a tiny sofa in some maid's room which actually had a lock on the door. All she could think about was getting back to the Mill to tell Dino what a fool she'd been.

Somehow she got herself together and to the B.B.C. by ten o'clock in the morning. It was a children's program; she couldn't let them down. She was met by a very embarrassed producer who said that, as Doctor Seuss was in town, they'd had to completely re-schedule the program and very sadly wouldn't be needing her after all. Of course she'd be paid all expenses and her fee and she must come another time; they'd be in touch. Fen knew perfectly well he was lying, that he'd seen the story and the photographs of her breeches splitting in all the morning papers and was terrified she might corrupt the young.

All the way home on the train Fen died of shame as she huddled behind dark glasses, coat collar turned up, watching businessmen glued to and glazing over her photograph. The headlines were predictable: 'Bottoms Up' said *The Sun,* 'Cheeky Fen' said the *Mirror,* 'What an Ass' said the *Daily Post.*

Tory met her at Warwick station looking very red-eyed. Fen thought it was because she'd been behaving so badly.

"I'm sorry I didn't ring," she stammered. "I meant to, I was so choked about my breeches splitting. When did the others get back?"

"About three in the morning," said Tory, starting up the Land Rover.

Wolf in the back crept forward wagging his tail and putting his rough face against Fen's cheek. At least she had one friend. For a mile or so they didn't speak. It was a mean grey day. The only colour came from the last red beech leaves and the blond grasses edging the road.

"Was Dino in an awful mood?" mumbled Fen.

There was a pause.

Then Tory said, "He's gone."

"Gone?" said Fen, "Where?" Suddenly she felt as though she'd jumped out of a plane and her parachute wasn't opening.

"Back to America."

"But he can't have," whispered Fen.

"He left this afternoon, loaded up the horses and everything."

"But whatever for?" said Fen, aghast.

"He didn't say," said Tory, bursting into tears.

"Did he—did he leave any message for me?"

"Only to say he'd probably see you in Los Angeles."

"Nothing else."

"He gave me a dishwasher" sobbed Tory. "It arrived half an hour after he left."

*B*ack in November that same year Helen Campbell-Black sat in James Benson's waiting room, flipping through the houses for sale in *Country Life,* and idly wondering how much Penscombe was worth. Glancing at her gold watch, she decided there wasn't really time before her appointment to rush to the john for yet another quick clean-up. It seemed ludicrous, after having two kids, that she was still desperately embarrassed by anything down there. She shifted slightly on the leather sofa. The irritation was really awful and not helped by worrying about it all the time. Outside the waiting room a group of starlings, ravenous after a week of hard frosts, were jostling each other around the bird feeder. A thrush darted forward, warily grabbing a crumb that had fallen on the starched white grass and carrying it off to the safety of a nearby ash tree. Helen admired his speckled breast and bright eyes.

"What a beautiful woman," thought the nurse as she showed Helen into the consulting room. If there was one patient likely to make Dr. Benson flout the Hippocratic oath, it was she. He always insisted on seeing Helen the last appointment before lunch, so he could spend more time with her. And although he was supposed to be a friend of the husband's, he never referred to him in any other way than as "that shit Campbell-Black."

This morning's examination did nothing to revise Dr. Benson's opinion, but as he ushered Helen back to her chair his face was as bland as ever.

"I'm afraid it isn't just a rash," he said. "It's the clap."

"I beg your pardon."

"The clap. Gonorrhea."

For a second he thought she was going to black out.

"What!" she gasped.

"Gonorrhea," he said gently.

"But I can't have, I mean, I haven't, I wouldn't sleep with anyone but . . ." her voice trailed off.

"I'm sure not, but, whatever you've heard to the contrary, it really doesn't come from train lavatory seats."

"So in fact . . ." she began.

"When did you last have intercourse with Rupert?"

She tried to pull herself together, trying to remember. "About two weeks ago."

"That was probably it, although it could have lain dormant longer. Don't worry. It's easy to cure."

Helen started to cry. Benson went to the built-in bar and poured her a large brandy. It was several minutes before she could bring herself to drink it, as though she was terrified of contaminating the glass. Dr. Benson longed to take her in his arms and comfort her, but he could still hear his secretary typing outside.

"I can't believe it," Helen said in a choked voice. "I feel so polluted, and where can Rupert. . . ?"

"Have got it from?" Benson shrugged. "Some quick fling on a trip abroad." Then, seeing the anguish in her face, "You know—far from home, missing you, needing to celebrate a victory. Won't have meant a thing to him. He'd better come and see me the moment he gets back. He'll have to be off sex for a bit too."

"I can't believe it," Helen said again, gazing into space, shaking violently.

Benson was staggered. He only saw a reaction like this when he told parents their children had some fatal disease or had to break the news to a patient that they had cancer.

"You'll need a series of penicillin injections. Nothing to worry about," he turned to his desk. "And I'm going to give you tranquilizers and some sleeping pills to tide you over the next few days. Cheer up. It happens to the best people."

"I feel so contaminated," whispered Helen. "How could Rupert do it?"

"Probably didn't know. Come on, we'll organize the shots and then I'll buy you lunch."

Helen had to wait until late the following night to confront Rupert, but the entire household was aware something was up. The grooms, Mrs. Bodkin, Charlene the Nanny, all knew that Mrs. C-B had gone off to see handsome Dr. Benson and come back whitefaced, had locked herself in her bedroom and given way to hysterical sobbing.

"Didn't touch any lunch or dinner," said Charlene, the Nanny. "Didn't even come and say goodnight to the children."

"Might be hysterectomy, might be cancer of the womb," said Mrs. Bodkin in excitement.

"Might be another baby," said Dizzy, "which means she can't walk out on His Nibs for another nine months."

"If it is, I'm off. I'm not looking after three children," said Charlene. "What d'you think it'd be like working in public relations?"

Rupert got back from Hamburg about nine o'clock. He realized something was up when Helen didn't come down and say hello, although far off were the days she'd charged down the stairs to fling herself into his arms. He dumped his bag in the kitchen.

"All dirty washing," he said to Charlene, who had positioned herself at the kitchen table, as being the best place to hear any excitement, and was reading the *Daily Mail* and eating a yogurt.

"Look what I bought for Tab," said Rupert, proudly producing an exquisite German doll in national costume. "According to the instructions on the box she does almost everything except say 'Oooh' at the moment of orgasm."

"Beautiful," said Charlene. "What did you get Marcus?"

"Sweets," said Rupert blandly. "I must have left them in the van. I suppose I better give them to him in the morning."

Bastard, Charlene said to herself.

"Where's Helen?"

"In her room."

"She all right?"

"Not in a carnival mood."

"Know what it's about?"

"She's been a bit jumpy all week. Went to see Dr. Benson yesterday and came back in a frightful state."

"Oh dear," said Rupert pouring himself a large whisky, "I'd better go and see her." Then his eye was caught by a recipe in Helen's writing entitled: Prawns and Kiwi fruit in Pernod-flavored Mayonnaise. Getting out his fountain pen, he wrote "Oh please not."

Charlene giggled, so Rupert proceeded to tell her how his new horse Rock Star had gone. "He really is world class. If I can't get a gold with him I might as well retire."

When he went upstairs an hour and several whiskys later he found the bedroom door locked.

"Let me in."

"Go away," screamed Helen.

"I'll break the door down, or shoot it out if you'd prefer."

After a long pause she unlocked it.

"Christ, you look as though a train's hit you." He'd never seen her so ill.

"I went to James Benson yesterday."

"So I hear. Are we expecting quads?"

"Don't you dare be flip," she hissed. "I've got gonorrhea."

"Really," drawled Rupert, his dark blue eyes suddenly taking on that opaque look. "You must be more careful who you leap into bed with in future."

"Stop it, stop it," screamed Helen. "You know perfectly well I haven't slept with anyone but you."

"I don't know that at all," said Rupert coldly. "I see little enough of you and your extreme reluctance to come on any of my trips abroad would rather suggest the contrary."

"You bastard," screamed Helen. "You caught it from one of your disgusting whores."

"Oh come on. You've got absolutely no proof. I've certainly got the clap. I was treated for it in Hamburg—those German clinics are like Sainsburys on a Saturday morning—but I caught it from you."

"Don't put that number on me. I've never looked at another man since I married you."

"What about Dino Ferranti?" said Rupert softly. "He's been in England for six weeks."

"I haven't been near Dino or anyone else," screamed Helen. "You gave it to me and you know it. I'm leaving you and I'm taking the children."

"You can take Marcus," yelled Rupert, "but if you lay a finger on Tab I'll fight you in every court in this country."

This was the final straw. Maddened, Helen tried to lash out at him, but Rupert dodged back and only the ends of her long colorless nails caught his cheek. The next moment the door opened.

It was Marcus, red hair ruffled, eyes huge with terror, pyjama-top falling off.

"Thtop thouting Daddy, pleas thtop thouting."

Tabitha toddled in after him, wearing only the top half of her pyjamas, diaper discarded.

"Daddy, Daddy," she squealed in delight, running towards him, "Daddy home," then seeing blood on his face, "Daddy got a hurt."

"Poor Daddy's indeed got a hurt," said Rupert, pulling a couple of tissues out of the box on Helen's dressing table to stem the bleeding. Then, gathering Tab up in his arms, he walked out of the room.

"I'm beginning to think you and Badger are my only fans."

Helen, with a superhuman effort, pulled herself together. "Daddy has cut himself shaving," she explained to Marcus. Everyone loved everybody, she went on. She was absolutely fine. Anything to ward off an asthma attack. But thin mucus was trickling from his nose, a sure sign that one was on the way. He was having difficulty breathing. Oh God, it was her fault for locking herself in her room and not coming to say goodnight. He must have heard her crying.

"Relax, Marcus, please."

Soon she had laid him face down across her lap, tapping his frail ribs with cupped hands to force the mucus out of the bronchial tubes as the physiotherapist had taught her. He had swallowed so much phlegm that eventually he threw up all over her and the carpet. By the time she had got him to bed and calmed him down, read him a story and cleaned up the mess it was long after midnight.

The light was on in Rupert's dressing room. On the bed she found Rupert fully dressed, stretched out fast asleep with the sleeping Tab in his arms. Photographs of Rock Star were scattered all over the bed and the floor. In their blond beauty and their carefree abandonment, they were so alike. When Helen tried to take Tab back to her own bed the child went rigid in her sleep and clung on, so Helen left them.

Back in her bedroom she wearily took a couple of valium and tried to think rationally about her marriage. She was trapped, trapped, trapped. She longed to leave Rupert, but where could she go? Certainly not home to her parents. The tensions of those two months in Florida last summer had finished that, and how could she ever afford Marcus's colossal medical bills in the States? And if she walked out, taking the children, they would have to give up so much: Penscombe, the valley, the swimming pool, the camp up in the woods, the tennis court, the horses, the skiing, the jet set existence, the fleet of servants, not to mention the library and the pictures, which they would probably appreciate later. All this for life in a one-bedroom flat. Janey at least had a career and could support herself; Helen had nothing. Her novel, to be honest, was merely a series of jottings. She poured everything out in her journal, sometimes leaving it around in the hope that Rupert might read it, and realize how unhappy she was. But he only read Dick Francis and *Horse and Hound*. Maybe he was as unhappy as she was and only bullying Marcus to work off his frustrations.

Yet she was only twenty-seven. Was this emotional dead-end really all there was to life? Admittedly there were times of comparative contentment when Rupert was away, which was, after all, eleven months of the year, interspersed with periods of desperation like the present, when he humiliated her publicly by chasing other women, and now giving her the clap.

She was only twenty-seven. She longed for love but, having been married to Rupert for six and a half years, she felt she had become what he kept telling her she was: boring, prissy, brittle and frigid. He had so sapped her self-confidence that she didn't think she'd ever be able to hold another guy. She knew she attracted people like Malise, Dino and James Benson, but was sure they would all lose interest once they got her into bed.

—

Zonked by the valium, Helen didn't come down until eleven o'clock the next day. She found Marcus devouring German chocolates, candy wrappers everywhere.

"Where did you get those?" she said furiously.

"Daddy bought them for me."

Helen went storming into the tackroom. "You've given Marcus candy."

"You're always reproaching me for not giving him presents. The one time I remember I get it in the neck."

"You know the kids aren't allowed to have candy except after lunch. How can I bring them up when you spend your time undermining my authority?"

"What authority? Producing a whining, sickly little milksop."

"That's because he's terrified of you."

The marriage limped on for a few more weeks. Helen continued to paint the house different colors, spending fortunes on wallpaper and fabrics. "One day I'm going to wake up and find I've been completely reupholstered in Laura Ashley," grumbled Rupert.

As Dr. Benson had predicted, Helen and Rupert recovered from the clap. Rock Star continued to sweep the board and provide a powerful new interest for Rupert, achieving almost a walkover at the Olympia Christmas Show.

The following Sunday, the last before Christmas, Janey and Billy lay in bed reading the papers.

"Christ," said Janey, "Have you seen this?"

"Hell," said Billy. "D'you think it's true?"

"I'm sure, and checked for libel, or they wouldn't risk it. Helen's going to flip her lid."

The Campbell-Blacks were having roast beef for Sunday lunch, Rupert was just carving second helpings when he was called away to the telephone. Helen cleared away the children's plates, helping them to apple pie and cream, and then settled down with the Sunday papers to wait until Rupert got off the telephone. She picked up the *Sunday Post*. What an awful rag it was, but you couldn't help reading it. Some starlet called Samantha Freebody was naming her lovers on page six, the little tramp. Helen read about the antics of several deviant vicars and lascivious witches, then turned to page six and froze, for there, confronting her, was a large picture of Rupert lying on a beach in bathing trunks, eyes narrowed against the sun, glass in his hand, palm trees in the background.

"One of my most thrilling affairs," Samantha Freebody had written, "was with international show-jumping ace, Rupert Campbell-Black. I was filming in Portugal and he came out for five days as part of the British show-jumping team. We met at a party. I was swept off my feet by his blond, blue-eyed good looks, and his air of tremendous selfconfidence. He'd had a good win in the show ring that day and, having met me, was keen to keep on riding all night. At first I resisted his advances. I didn't want to appear cheap. But a tide of champagne and euphoria swept us down to the beach and at two o'clock in the morning we made passionate love under the stars, until the warm waves washed over us. For the rest of the five days we were inseparable, loving each other all night. By day I would go and watch him in the ring. After five days we decided to end our idyll. He had other shows to go on to. I had to finish my movie. He was married, his wife expecting her second baby. It was only fair to give him back to her, but I really enjoyed the novelty of our naughty, racy lovemaking."

"Can I get down?" said Marcus for the second time.

"May I?" said Helen automatically, getting up and lifting Tab out of her high chair. "Go and watch television, darlings."

Upstairs she locked herself in the bathroom and threw up and up and up. Rupert was waiting as she came out.

"What on earth's the matter? You sound like Jake Lovell before a big class."

"Look at this," croaked Helen, handing him the paper.

Rupert skimmed through it without a flicker of expression. "Load of rubbish, don't believe a word of it."

"The dates tally. You were in Portugal just before I had Tab."

"Just ignore it," said Rupert. "That girl's publicity mad."

"I don't understand you," screamed Helen. "You go berserk if anyone criticizes the way you ride."

"I ride for a living. That's what matters. I don't fuck for a living."

"Could have fooled me. She obviously does."

"I wonder how much she got," said Rupert, picking up the paper again.

"Aren't you even going to sue?"

"What's the point?" Rupert shrugged, "If you leave mud to dry, you can brush it off. What did you do with the roast beef? I want a second helping."

"You can honestly eat having read that?" said Helen, appalled. "And how am I supposed to cope? Mothers sniggering at the playgroup. Mrs. Bodkin, Charlene and the grooms all talking their heads off."

"I'm sure they'll enjoy it enormously."

"How can I ever hold my head up in the market again?"

"Ask them to deliver," said Rupert.

Matters were not improved a week later when a leading columnist in the *Sunday Times* took Samantha Freebody to the cleaners for naming names:

"How must Rupert Campbell-Black's unfortunate wife and children feel?"

The answer was much, much worse. Everyone who hadn't seen the original piece in the *Sunday Post* rushed off to the library to read it. A couple of days later Janey rang up Rupert to wish him a Happy New Year.

"And for God's sake hide *Private Eye*," she went on. "You've been nominated White's Shit of the Year."

"Thank God it's the new year now," said Rupert. "Apart from buying Rocky, last year wasn't the greatest of years."

In the evening Rupert found Helen in the drawing-room writing letters. He wished she wouldn't always wear her hair up these days like a confirmed spinster.

"Applying for a new husband?" he said.

Helen gritted her teeth and didn't answer.

Rupert crossed the room and kissed the nape of her very clean white neck. "I'm sorry I gave you the clap and went to bed with Samantha Freebody. I am totally in the wrong. There is absolutely no excuse. But the more you reject me and take no part in what I do the worse it becomes. Come on, get up."

The sudden unexpected overture totally disarmed her.

"There, there," he said, drawing her against him, "it's all right. Shall we have another try? I'm going to cancel the next two shows and take you abroad. Charlie Masters has offered us his house outside Nairobi. We can lie in the sun and I'll give you the honeymoon you never had."

"And I will heal me of my grievous wound," quoted Helen sadly.

"Grievous womb?" demanded Rupert. "You been to see Benson again?"

Helen shook her head, smiling faintly.

"That's better," said Rupert. "It seems an awfully long time since you smiled."

"What about the children?"

"They're not coming," said Rupert firmly, "nor are the dogs, just you and me on our own. And I'll start off tonight by taking you out to dinner."

The door bell rang. It was Janey. Billy had gone to some evening show in Warwickshire and she was at loose ends.

"Come and have a drink," said Rupert. "Helen and I are having a rapprochement."

"About time," said Janey.

She was full of gossip and in high good humor. Evidently Fenella Maxwell had gone into a complete decline since Dino Ferranti walked out. Fen didn't seem very good at holding men, she added with satisfaction. Janey had lapsed in her resolution to give up drinking while she was pregnant, but at least she had cut down and was only drinking wine.

Helen could hardly believe her ears half an hour later when she heard Rupert saying to Janey, "Why don't you come out to dinner with us." She went upstairs and sat on her bed in a rage for ten minutes. Then she steeled herself to be tolerant. After all Janey *was* on her own.

Downstairs she found Tabitha had invaded the drawing-room, reducing the place to chaos. Every ornament had been moved, Janey's handbag had been upended and a flotsam of bus tickets, old telephone numbers, defunct mascara brushes and dirty combs lay scattered over the floor. Then she started screaming for sweets and for Daddy to read her a story. On being told Daddy was going out, the screaming redoubled. Picking her up under one arm, Rupert took her upstairs for Charlene to sort out.

Rupert hadn't bothered to make a reservation, but as usual the best table in the restaurant became available straight away. Everyone was staring and nudging: "Look who's just walked in. It is, isn't it? He's even better in the flesh." Helen wished she had washed her hair.

"Where are you going for your second honeymoon?" asked Janey.

"Kenya," said Helen.

"Some golfing friends of my parents have just gone there on Safari. They're called Dick and Fanny, can you imagine!"

Janey could always make Rupert laugh, thought Helen with a stab of envy.

"Have you heard the latest Samantha Freebody story," Janey went on, squeezing lemon on her smoked salmon. "Billy bumped into her at the opening of some sports center last night. He was going to cut her dead when she accosted him and said: 'You've got a hole in your sweater!' and Billy replied quick as a flash, 'You've got a hole between your legs, but the difference between us is I don't write about my hole all over the *Sunday Post*.' She's so publicity mad, the old slag heap, Billy says she'd turn up for the opening of an envelope."

Somehow by bringing the whole awful business into the open, Janey was making things much better, thought Helen. Now she was attacking Rupert.

"You're a monster to Helen. You treat her appallingly."

"I don't remember you treating Billy all that well in the past," said Rupert coldly.

"That was only once. I just needed to prove that Billy was really the only man for me. I'm with him for keeps now."

Janey was being real nice, thought Helen, so upfront and supportive. It was such a novelty to be talked about and defended and argued over that Helen drank more than usual.

While they were having coffee she went to the bathroom.

"All right?" they both said solicitously when she came back.

"Rupert's just suggested that Billy and I fly out to join you in Kenya for one of the weeks," said Janey.

"But, but, I thought it was supposed to be a honeymoon," stammered Helen.

Rupert didn't quite meet her eyes.

"All honeymoons should be spent in duplicate," said Janey. "Helen and I'll come if you and Billy promise not to talk about horses."

Charlie Masters' house, a few miles outside Nairobi, was perfect. Open balconied, it had papyrus walls, leopard skins on the floor, a vast sunken bath, comfortable beds, and a fleet of smiling African boys who could not only cook but didn't turn a hair at any outlandish English antics.

The garden, lushly crowded with jacaranda, flame trees and a sweet smelling tangle of herbaceous plants, also contained a tennis court and a swimming pool ringed with palm trees. All around lay the bush and Helen had the feeling that the house was only here by the courtesy of nature and any minute the jungle might take over. From the start the holiday was a disaster. With Billy and Janey around, she and Rupert never had a moment to themselves. Billy and Rupert played tennis and swam all morning, followed by more tennis and swimmng, followed by a large dinner, more drinking and a trip around the Nairobi night clubs. Billy was drinking again, not to excess, but on vacation he reckoned he was justified in coming off the wagon.

Helen, exhausted and emotionally bankrupt, wanted to sleep, be cherished and made love to in the gentlest way and to talk through her and Rupert's problems. She tried to persuade Rupert to dine alone with her, but the others seemed always to come along too. She was deeply embarrassed too the way Rupert and Billy wandered around the garden with no clothes on, their cocks wiggling like those rubber devils that hang from driving mirrors. She was sure Janey only wore a bikini because she was pregnant. Helen worried too about the children—well, mostly Marcus—and insisted on telephoning home every day from the local post office, which was extremely time-consuming and irritated the hell out of Rupert.

As soon as Rupert and Billy hit Kenya, people discovered they were there and old friends started calling up and inviting them to parties. Newspapers wanted to interview them, Kenyan television wanted to send down a crew. The alacrity with which Rupert welcomed every diversion made it obvious that he didn't want to get away from it all in the least.

After one long boozy lunch, when Rupert and Billy had gone out on safari, Helen unbuttoned slightly to Janey.

"I simply don't know what to do. Our marriage is in smithereens. Rupert simply doesn't want to spend time with me. I feel everything I do gets on his nerves."

Janey poured herself another glass of wine. "Want one?"

Helen shook her head. "Oh all right, just a small one."

They took their glasses out onto the terrace. A shower of rain had rinsed the earth, a rainbow arched over the jacaranda trees.

"I think you're too subservient," said Janey. "I mean Billy was lovely but pretty casual before I took off with Kev."

"Billy was always very caring," said Helen.

"But he was always happy to booze with his chums rather than come home to me. Why don't you try making Rupert jealous? He was jolly broody over Dino Ferranti. Even talked to Billy about having your telephone tapped."

Helen looked amazed. "He had no cause. There was nothing between Dino and me except a few lunches."

"Ho," said Janey. "Rupert is aware how fragile a thing possession is. He can't imagine anyone having lunch with anyone else's wife without evil intent. He thinks everyone is like himself."

"But what can I do? We can't go on like this."

"Don't shove off until you've found someone else. If you're going to be virtually a single parent, why not get paid for it? If you left Rupe you wouldn't be able to buy dresses like that, or do the house over every two years. It's very cold outside the marital cage."

It was so oppressively hot that they retired to Janey and Billy's bedroom. Sitting on the bed, Helen appeared to let off a huge fart. Crimson, she jumped to her feet. "That wasn't me."

Janey laughed. "You've sat on my vibrator."

Helen took a slug of wine.

"If your sex life's so good," she said, "why d'you need a vibrator?"

"Oh they're lovely," sighed Janey, "and they do jazz things up. Billy's wonderful, but not absolutely infallible."

Outside the crickets were shrilling their permanent burglar alarm, the frogs croaked in lazy lechery.

Janey peered at her smooth brown face in the mirror. "God, I look like a hag. Look at all these wrinkles."

"You haven't got any," said Helen, "and now you've given up smoking, you won't get all those little lines around your mouth."

"I'm bound to get them as punishment for all the men I've sucked off," said Janey ruefully.

Helen turned away, shocked. What an appalling thing to say.

She'd only sucked Rupert off once and been so revolted she'd never done it again. She realized in despair what light years sexually she was behind Janey. She must try and catch up. Blushing even further, taking another huge gulp of wine and gazing at the eyeless African mask on the wall, she asked. "Do you, do you really enjoy doing that to men?"

Janey shrugged. "Well, it's an acquired taste. Whisky and dry martinis don't taste very nice the first time. It's all right if you swallow it fast. I said to Billy the other day, 'It's a pity one can't have it with tonic, or better still with ice and lemon!' The trouble with sex is that all sorts of things are wildly exciting in fantasy, but no good when they happen. I get frightfully turned on by the thought of being buggered, even whipped. But when darling Billy tried it I didn't like it at all."

That night they all went to a party which continued in a state of rampage and carousal until eight o'clock in the morning. Neither Rupert nor Billy felt like playing tennis the next morning, so they lazed around the pool.

Helen was wearing dark glasses, a large hat to prevent her freckles spreading and a lime green bathing suit. She's so thin now, she's really better covered up, thought Janey critically.

Every day Janey'd start on another diet, and abandon it by lunchtime, when Rupert opened a bottle and the smell of Abdul's cooking drifted out from the kitchen. But her skin was turning as golden as a peach. She was four months pregnant, and Billy liked her plump anyway.

Helen, having finished yesterday's *Guardian,* was reading *Crime and Punishment* with effort. Janey was reading *Vogue.* Billy was flipping through a pornographic novel, skipping until he came to the sexy parts. Jomo, the African boy, was steadily but unhurriedly sweeping up jacaranda petals and bird droppings. Morning glory spread in a sapphire haze over the tennis court wire, vying with the sky in blueness.

"Have you ever tried that?" said Billy, handing the book to Rupert.

"Once in Solihull during the Royal."

"Let me see," said Janey.

"No you can't," said Billy, "or you'd go back to bed for the rest of the morning. And you've only got a week to get brown."

"Billy never finished *Histoire d'O,*" said Janey, peeling a piece of loose skin off her heel. "He kept having to take me upstairs between pages."

Rupert got up to pour himself a drink, broad-shouldered, bronze and rippling fit as any of his horses, thought Janey. She lifted her thighs slightly off the mat so the flesh fell downwards and they looked thinner.

"Bikinis are awfully stupid things," said Janey. "You look as though you'd got one on when you take it off."

"Take it off then," said Billy idly, not looking up from his book.

Janey encountered a searching look from Rupert.

"All right," she said and removed her bikini. Her breasts had a soft honeyed ripeness, her round belly swelled like a fig and her bush was shaved, leaving her as smooth as a pink billiard ball. Helen, rigid with shock and envy, couldn't take her eyes off her, Billy looked up and found Rupert staring at Janey with an erection like a steeple. Next moment Billy found he had an erection like a steeple too.

"Christ, it's like a cathedral city round here," he said, rolling over and returning to his book.

Without turning his head, Rupert said to Helen, "Take your bathing suit off too."

"I can't. I burn so easily."

"Use plenty of oil," said Janey, her breasts moving as she handed Helen the Ambre Solaire.

"I'm fine," snapped Helen.

"Take it off," repeated Rupert, with a distinct edge to his voice.

"No! What would Jomo think? It's all right for Janey, she's a guest. I'd never be able to look Abdul in the face again either when I discussed desserts."

She turned back to *Crime and Punishment* and read a whole page without taking in a word. Abdul seemed to take an enormously long time clearing up ashtrays and taking orders for drinks.

I can't do it, I can't, thought Helen in panic, I can't take my clothes off in front of them and besides, said an inner more truthful voice, my boobs aren't as good as Janey's.

Janey didn't bother to dress for a late lunch, which started with salad Niçoise. A large piece of tuna fish fell on her left breast. Rupert removed it with a spoon. Everyone, including Abdul, giggled immoderately, except Helen, who was a tight knot of embarrassment inside. Realizing this, Billy tried to persuade Janey to get dressed. But the atmosphere was getting more and more highly charged.

"I'm going to have a siesta," said Janey, who'd been exchanging lingering glances with Rupert. Inside, seeing her flushed face and bloodshot eyes, she felt irritated at how awful she looked and wondered how she could have flirted so much with him.

The next minute Billy had come up behind her, catching her oiled breasts in his hands, kissing the back of her neck, slipping his hands between her legs, which seemed even more oiled.

"Christ, you're excited," he said.

Instantly they were on the bed, not bothering to close the windows or the door.

Helen went into her bedroom next door. Despite the oppressive heat, she was trembling violently. She could hear Janey's cries and moans and hastily shut the window. Rupert came in, red-faced and hard-eyed.

"God it's hot in here. Why the hell have you shut the window?" Opening it, he paused for a few seconds, listening to Janey and Billy, a half-smile on his face. Helen was desperate for him to make love to her gently and tenderly, not because she really wanted it, but because she'd seen the intense, predatory way he's suddenly started looking at Janey. She'd die if he had an affair with her.

"Rupert, I do love you."

"Why don't you show it then?"

"It's so hard when you're so angry with me."

"Oh for Christ sake," he walked out slamming the door.

He returned when it was dark and Helen was changing for dinner, grabbing her irritably. Helen shrunk away. "I've just taken a bath and the Mountleys are coming to dinner."

"So the Campbell-Blacks aren't coming, hurrah, hurrah. Why the hell did you ask them?" Then answered for her, "Because they've already asked us twice and you can drop literary names all evening."

Professor Mountley was in his fifties, an American who taught English Literature at Nairobi University. His English wife, a little younger, was a show-jumping groupie.

"She knows even more about my bloody horses than I do," said Rupert.

Rupert mixed white ladies and they all sat on the terrace, looking at the green pigeons and the enormous stars and listening to the rustle of night creatures, frogs bubbling like a cauldron, hysterical chatter of baboons and the water pump sound of approaching lions.

"I'm beginning to understand why evacuee children were so frightened of cows in the war," said Janey.

"Nice to be here," said Professor Mountley, raising his glass to Helen.

"Nice to be still here," said Janey. "I'm sure some leopard is going to gobble me up."

"Did you know warthogs lead exemplary married lives?" said Mrs. Mountley.

"No wonder there aren't any in Gloucestershire," said Rupert.

Rupert and Billy were drinking steadily, Janey only less so because it might be bad for the baby, and she didn't want to get too flushed. After long lovemaking, a sleep, three Alka Seltzers and a bath, she was feeling wonderful. She was wearing a frangipani in her hair and a white ruffled slightly transparent shirt, through which could be glimpsed her rosily sunburnt breasts. Conscious of Billy's adoration, the Professor's admiration and Rupert's blatant lust, she was getting thoroughly overexcited.

Before dinner Helen had gone in and offered her a choice of blue or lime green caftans. Being pregnant, she said, Janey might find them more comfortable. ("Comfortable indeed," Janey had snorted to Billy. "Shapeless and ugly, you mean.") If she wasn't aware of Helen's lack of malice, she'd have thought she was doing it on purpose.

"Billy's been reading all about orgies today," she said to Professor Mountley at dinner.

"Janey!" said Helen furiously.

"We call it group therapy in the States," said the Professor with a nervous laugh.

Soon they were all discussing orgies.

I can't bear it, thought Helen. I wanted a nice civilized evening with the Professor and all everyone can talk about is sex. They were all philistines. Earlier in the week she'd lent Janey her precious copy of *A Hero of Our Time,* and Janey had dropped it in the bath. Rupert was talking to Janey in an undertone. Frantically she tried to lip read what they were saying.

Billy, sensing her distress, patted her arm. "Everything's under control."

The Mountleys left around midnight, when everyone was still sitting round the table. The Professor was very reluctant to go, but Mrs. Mountley had recently become a grandmother and felt things were definitely getting out of hand.

Helen, having seen them off, stood on the balcony breathing in the heady smell of warm earth, frangipani, dust and burning charcoal. Beyond the garden she could see the gleaming eyes of waiting animals. But the animals inside the house frightened her much more. Determined to break the spell, she went back into the dining room.

"Don't know about you, but I'm absolutely exhausted."

Rupert looked up, a long cigar clamped between his white teeth.

"Let's have another drink," he said, getting up and filling everyone's glasses with brandy, "and then let's go to bed," he paused, "together."

Helen laughed nervously. "Together?"

"Sure—why not?"

Janey got up, her eyes glittering. "Do we use your bedroom or ours."

"I'd prefer a home fixture," said Rupert. "And besides our bed is bigger."

He strolled over to Janey and began to kiss her. Frozen with horror, Helen watched him take her pink breast out of the white shirt and gently stroke it, then he unzipped her trousers. Helen shot a panic-stricken look at Billy, to see him watching with fascinated pleasure.

Janey ran laughing into the bedroom. Giving a whoop, Billy followed her. Rupert turned to Helen, holding out his hand.

"Come on, darling, or you'll miss the first act."

Helen looked at him aghast. "We can't, what about the servants?"

"I sent them home hours ago." He grabbed her arm.

At the bedroom door she balked. Billy, already undressed, was sitting on the bed drinking brandy, watching Janey and wearing Helen's sun hat. He was roaring with excited laughter and had a huge erection. Janey was standing in front of the mirror, tossing her hair back, spraying Helen's most expensive scent over her boobs and jiggling them so they caught the light. Helen turned to bolt but Rupert's vice like grip on her arm tightened.

"No you don't. Don't be a fucking spoilsport. We might finally find out what turns you on." Shoving her towards the bed, he turned the key and pocketed it. Turning to Billy, he added, "It's harder than getting Snakepit into the van."

Billy took off the sun hat and turned to Helen.

"Come on lovie, it'll be fun. No one's going to eat you."

"Everyone's going to eat her," said Rupert and pulling down Helens underpants and lifting her dress and her pink silk petticoat, he kissed her bush. As she wriggled frantically away, his hand clamped down on her bottom.

Across the room her eyes met Janey's, which were mocking and slightly contemptuous.

"Come and help me undress her," Rupert said to Janey.

As he peeled off the black dress and the petticoat, Janey undid the pink bra.

"Lovely underwear," she said.

Helen covered her pitifully small breasts with one hand, clasping the other over her bush.

"I can't, I can't," she pleaded to Rupert in panic. "I really can't."

"Don't be so bloody wet," he hissed. "Do you want to make me look a complete idiot. Here she is, all yours," he added and, scooping her up, dropped her on the bed between Janey and Billy. The fastest trouserdropper in the business, next minute he was on the bed beside Janey.

From then on it was a heaving anthill of legs and arms. Helen lay beneath Rupert, her eyes glazed, her hair coming down, as responsive as a corpse, aware that Rupert was fondling Janey's breasts at the same time. Janey, determined to put on a virtuoso performance, climbed on top of Billy, bucking like a bronco, arching her back in pleasure, writhing and wriggling against Rupert's hands.

Then they changed over and, despite shutting her eyes, Helen knew Billy was inside her. He was much solider and heavier yet gentler than Rupert.

"I'm not hurting you, am I, angel?" he breathed in her ear, running his hands over her body. "You're so beautiful, please enjoy it."

Helen didn't respond, lying rigid with horror, her teeth clenched, eyes closed. Billy, her dear, dear friend. How could he do this to her? But Billy was watching Janey bucking on top of Rupert. God she looked wonderful, he was so proud of her, as little cries echoed from her throat.

"I'm coming," said Rupert suddenly, his face contorting.

"So am I," said Janey, screaming and threshing.

She might be faking thought Billy, but it's a lovely performance, and next moment he'd shot into Helen. Looking down he saw two tears welling out of her closed eyes and coursing down her cheeks.

"Don't cry, angel, please don't."

More tears welled.

"Oh Christ," he thought, "We shouldn't have forced her." He rolled off, gathering her against him. Rupert gave Janey a long, long kiss, then as he eased out of her said in an undertone, "See if you can get Helen going."

"Move over," Janey said to Billy, pushing him to the left of the bed. "Our turn now." She trailed her fingertips up Helen's thighs. Helen gave a moan of terror, shrinking away from Janey, eyes darting frantically for a way of escape. But, like bookends, Rupert and Billy blocked her exit.

"No, no, no," she sobbed, as Janey's insistent fingers started burrowing inside her, as she felt Janey's breasts flopping on her stomach and Janey's tongue on her breasts.

"Jesus," Billy muttered to himself, "I'll be off again in a minute."

"Please don't be frightened, Helen," whispered Janey as she caressed and stroked. "We're all having such a good time, we want you to enjoy it too."

I can't go on forever, thought Janey five minutes later. No wonder Rupert complains she's frigid. She needs twenty-four hours defrosting. Rupert, bored with a spectator role, crawled down the bed and entered the slippery warmth of Janey from behind, so he could watch Helen. She looked like a martyr at the stake. Putting his hand around, he found that, despite Janey's ministrations, she was as dry as a marathon runner's throat.

She's useless, he thought.

Suddenly, with Rupert behind Janey, Helen saw a way of escape. Shoving Janey to the left, she wriggled away from her and, before any of them realized it, had jumped off the bed and stumbled across the room. In Rupert's pocket she found the key.

"Come here," he snarled.

For once she was in luck. In his excitement Rupert hadn't locked the door properly. Crying hysterically, she managed to slip out, slam the door and turn the lock, just as he crashed against it. She longed to run away into the night, but out on the terrace the moon had gone in and the trees were as black as ink. She heard the dry cough of a leopard and decided to settle for the third bedroom instead. There were no sheets on the bed. Huddled under the counterpane, gazing unseeingly at the bookcase, she shuddered until dawn. If her sleeping pills hadn't been in the bathroom cupboard, which could only be reached by going through the bedroom, she would have taken an overdose. Any minute she expected an enraged Rupert to appear and drag her back to the torture chamber.

But the others were enjoying themselves.

"The grown-up has gone to bed now," said Janey.

"All hands on dick," said Rupert, filling up the glasses.

Playing games of their own, they carried on till morning.

*C*alling home the next day, Helen discovered that Marcus was in bed with tonsilitis and a temperature of 103. She was riddled with guilt that she felt so relieved there was a really good excuse to fly straight home by herself.

In recent months the tonsilitis attacks had been getting closer together. The antibiotics were having less effect and Marcus was look- ing so waiflike that Helen accepted James Benson's recommendation that he should have his tonsils out at once.

"They're as big as billiard balls. Marcus'll be much better off without them. It won't cure the asthma, but all the illnesses he's hav- ing as a result of the infected tonsils are pulling him down. There's a very good man at the Motcliffe in Oxford. He'll only be in four or five days."

"Can I go in with him?"

"I honestly don't recommend it. You've been under a lot of strain recently." Privately Benson thought he'd never seen her look so ill. "Leave him with experts who see this operation fifty times a week."

"You're saying I'm no good as a mother," said Helen, beginning to shake.

"No, no," said Benson reassuringly. "I'm saying you're too good."

"It's certainly been a stressful year. D'you think that's making his asthma worse?"

Benson shrugged. "Probably. Children are like radars, Marcus must realize how unhappy Rupert's making you."

Thank God we didn't take the kids to Kenya, thought Helen with a shudder.

"Rupert wouldn't want me to go in with him."

"Well don't. By all means come and visit him during the day, but go home and get a good night's sleep every night."

The night before Marcus was due to have his tonsils out at the beginning of March, Helen and Rupert went to a big ball in London to raise funds for the Tory Party. It was the sort of invitation that Rupert would normally have refused, but, surprisingly, he was rather a fan of Mrs. Thatcher, the new Prime Minister, and felt she needed every bit of help if the Tories were to stay in power.

"You wouldn't be able to afford to have Marcus's tonsils out privately if the Socialists brought in a wealth tax."

They went to the ball in a very grand party with several ministers and their wives. Helen found the evening a nightmare. Hollow-eyed, thinner than ever, her black ball dress had had to be taken in yet again. She knew she was putting a damper on the evening, but all she could think about was Marcus in his white hospital bed and the surgeon's knife going into his little throat in the morning. All around her every table seemed filled with ravishing, chattering women flirting with bland smooth-haired men. At the same table a bediamonded brunette with a roving eye, who'd already had a long amorous dance with Rupert, was surreptitiously holding hands with one Tory minister while making animated conversation to his wife.

"The whole world's at it," thought Helen in despair.

There was Rupert coming off the dance floor, looking around for fresh talent. Goodness, he was going up to Amanda Hamilton, the much-admired wife of the Minister of Foreign Affairs. Now she was smiling up at him and he was taking her on to the floor. She must be forty, but very attractive in a determined sort of way—driving her husband Rollo on from success to success, knowing everyone, rigidly governed by the social calendar.

Rupert had actually met Amanda Hamilton before, at a party last June, and had promptly asked her out to lunch.

"No I can't," she had repled in her shrill, piercing voice. "Next week's Ascot."

"The week after then."

"No, that's tennis."

Rupert was slightly taken aback until she explained that Wimbledon went on for two weeks and she had to be in her seat on the center court by two o'clock every day.

After that, she explained patiently, there would be a trip to America with Rollo, then Goodwood, and then Scotland.

Now, holding her in his arms in the twilight gloom, as the band played "This Guy's in Love With You," Rupert admired her rounded magnolia-white shoulders. A side door suddenly opened to admit a couple to the dance floor, and Amanda Hamilton's Scotch-mist-soft complexion was briefly illuminated. She didn't duck her head, her unwrinkled, untroubled beauty had no need of dimmer light.

"How was Wimbledon?" asked Rupert.

"Very exciting. He's spoiled, that American who nearly won, but my goodness he can play tennis. I rather admire that kind of drive. It seems odd that no one minds painters or musicians or actors having tantrums, but tennis players, who are, after all, kind of artists, are expected to behave themselves. He's rather like you, in fact. You've had a bad press recently, haven't you?"

"You noticed?" said Rupert.

"Fighting with judges, frolicking with starlets, beating up your horses."

Rupert shrugged.

"D'you beat your wife too? Is that why she looks so miserable?"

Rupert glanced at Helen, who was still sitting frozen, gazing into space.

"What do you think?" he said.

"She looks as though the dentist is filling her back teeth and has forgotten to give her any novacaine."

Rupert grinned.

"I don't think it's funny. Why are you constantly so foul to her when she's so beautiful?"

"She's given me up for Lent."

"Don't blame her with you running after everything in skirts—or trousers—these days. Girls don't seem to wear skirts anymore."

"You seem to have been taking a great interest in my career." His hand was beginning to rotate very gently on her back.

"It amazes me that someone with such dazzling qualities should be quite happy about presenting such an appalling image to the outside world."

"I know what my friends think. Other people don't matter."

Amanda Hamilton shook her head so the pearl combs gleamed in her dark hair.

"One day you might get bored with riding horses and want to try your hand at something more serious."

"Like taking you to Paris?"

"Rollo was saying the other day that one felt rather insulted if Rupert C-B *hadn't* been to bed with one's wife."

Rupert tightened his grip, his hand moving upwards until he encountered bare flesh.

"I'd hate to insult Rollo," he said softly.

"He could do you a lot of good. Have you ever thought of going into politics?"

"No."

"You'd be very good. You've got the looks, the force of personality, the magnetism, the wit."

Rupert laughed. "But not the intellect. My wife says I'm a dolt."

"You've got common sense, and I've heard you're a very good
after-dinner speaker."

"I speak much better during dinner—and to one person, preferably you. When are you going to dine with me?"

"We're off to Gstaad tomorrow. Oh listen, the music's stopped."
She clapped vaguely and turned towards her table.

Rupert grabbed her arm. "Wait. It'll start up again in a second."

"No," said Amanda with gentle firmness, "we've danced quite
long enough. Go back and look after your poor little wife. You must
both come and dine with us when Rollo gets back from Moscow next
month."

"No thank you. I've got absolutely no desire to get better acquainted with your husband."

Amanda smiled and patted his cheek.

"Think about politics as a career. I mean it seriously."

Rupert stared at her unsmilingly.

"*Seriously,*" he emphasized the word, "I'm only interested in getting a gold at the moment."

Two days later Jake Lovell walked down the long corridors of the
Motcliffe Hospital to say hello to the Matron and in some hope of
catching a glimpse of the angelic Miss Wutherspoon. By some stupid
Freudian misreading of the calendar, or perhaps because he was so
anxious to get the go-ahead to ride again, he had arrived for his appointment with Dr. Buchannan five hours early. Dr. Buchannan was
operating, said the secretary, and couldn't possibly see him before four
o'clock.

The day had already been full of omens. It had snowed heavily
since yesterday lunchtime and he and Tory had had to dig out the car
that morning. Two magpies had crossed his path as he was leaving
Warwickshire. An odd number of traffic lights had been green on his
way through Oxford. He'd taken fifty-one strides from the car park to
the front door. There were eleven people in the elevator. His horoscope
said the aspects for Venus were good and this was a make-or-break day.
He hoped to hell it wasn't the latter. He'd had enough of breaks. He
vowed that if Johnnie Buchannan told him he could ride again, he'd
make the Olympic team. The individual event on September 8th was
exactly six months today.

The nurses on the ward greeted him like a long-lost brother.

"My, we *are* walking well. You'll be beating Seb Coe in the 800
metres at this rate."

It was very warm in the hospital. Outside the snow was still falling thickly, blurring the outlines of the trees, laying a clean sheet over the lawn. Orange street lights glowed out of the gathering whiteness. Feeling totally blanketed against reality, Jake asked after Miss Wutherspoon.

"She's having two days leave," said Joan, Miss Wutherspoon's pimply, fat friend, "but she was absolutely furious to miss you. She left you her number in case you felt like calling her at home."

Jake pocketed the number. He had five hours to kill. He might as well ask her out to lunch. On the way to the telephone booth he passed some of the private rooms and heard an unearthly animal screaming like a rabbit caught in a snare. The screams increased, growing more terrible.

Anxious to disassociate himself Jake walked on. Rounding the corner, he was sent flying by what seemed like a bear jumping out of a room at him.

"What the fuck?" he snapped.

Then he realized it was a woman in a huge blond fur coat with tears streaming down her face. She looked half crazy with terror.

"I'm sorry," she stammered. "I don't know what to do. Marcus. Such terrible screaming. Something must have gone wrong."

Jake realized it was Helen Campbell-Black.

"Where is he?" he said over the screaming.

"In there. He's just had his tonsils out. They said not to come till later, but I wanted to be here when he came back from the operating room."

Jake took her arm. "Let's go and see him."

Marcus was still screaming. He was as pale as his pillow; his white nightgown, like a shroud, was splattered with blood. Jake stroked the child's red hair gently.

"He'll go to sleep soon."

"Can't they give him something to stop the pain?"

"He'll just have had a huge shot of morphine. Every time he swallows it must be like an axe on his head."

Gradually the screams subsided into great wracking sobs until Marcus fell into an uneasy whimpering sleep.

"He'll be OK now," said Jake, straightening the sheet.

"Are you sure? W-why did he scream so much?"

"They have to wake them up immediately after the operation to see that everything's all right. We went through the same thing with Darklis and Isa. They were both perfectly OK when they came around later. Darklis was as cheerful as anything, eating ice cream by the evening. When she woke up, she asked, "When am I going to have my tonsils out?"

Helen looked at him stunned, as though only half-listening to what he was saying.

"W-why it's Jake, isn't it, Jake Lovell?" she said slowly. "I didn't recognize you."

"You weren't exactly in a recognizing mood."

Suddenly she jumped out of her skin at the sound of more screaming coming down the corridor.

"Don't worry," he said soothingly. "It's only another child coming back from the operating room. They all sound like that."

Woken, Marcus started crying again. Helen rushed to his side. "Oh please don't, angel."

In a few seconds he'd fallen back to sleep again. They waited for a quarter of an hour. Every noise seemed magnified a thousand times—a car horn outside, a nurse laughing in the corridor, even the snow piling up on the window ledge outside, but Marcus didn't wake up. Jake looked at his watch:

"Come on. I'll buy you a drink."

"I can't leave him."

"Yes, you can. I'll have a word with my friend Joanie. If he makes a squeak they'll call us at the pub and you can rush back."

Outside the snow was still falling—heavy flakes like goose feathers, bowing down the privets in the hospital garden, settling on the collar of Helen's fur coat, forming points on the toes of her tan leather boots, clogging up her eyelashes. Jake walked slowly. It was treacherous underfoot. He couldn't afford to fall, today of all days. They had only got as far as the car park when she broke down again.

"I can't go. I'm sorry."

He led her to his Land Rover, sitting her down on a nose band and a copy of *Riding* magazine. Snow curtained all the windows. All Jake could do was say, "There, there," gently, almost absent-mindedly, patting her shoulder.

Gradually the first wild intensity died down, subsiding into a succession of wrenching despairing sobs.

"I'm so sorry," she kept saying, "I'm such an idiot. Please, please forgive me."

"If we don't both want to die of hypothermia," he said, "we ought to find that pub."

She suddenly realized that he was only wearing a raincoat, his shoes were soaked and his teeth chattering.

"I'm so sorry," she said again in a trembling voice. "I can't go to a pub looking like this."

He handed her her bag. "Well, powder your nose then."

In the pub Jake found Helen a seat by the fire and went off to order triple brandies. Looking in the bar mirror he could see her vacantly gazing into space, twisting her fingers round and round. Christ, he thought, she's the one who ought to be in the hospital. He took the brandies back to the table, holding one out to her. It was a second before she took it.

"I'm a trusty St. Bernard struggling through the snow to bring you sustenance," he said.

She didn't answer.

"Come on, it'll really help."

He noticed how loose her expensive boots were around her legs, and that her skirt was only held up by a brown suede belt, which was on an extra notch. She took a gulp, made a face, choked and then took another gulp. She wished the taste didn't remind her so much of that last night in Kenya.

"Where's Rupert?"

"Gone skiing."

"Needn't have bothered. Plenty of snow here. When's he coming back.?"

She shrugged her shoulders. "Five days—a week."

"And you're left to cope with all this?"

Helen held out thin, shaking hands to the fire.

"I ought to go back." she said restlessly.

"No you ought not. They'll call if he wakes up."

"Poor little kid, he's been so sick," she said. "He was so excited about coming to the hospital. All the presents and everyone for a change bothering about him rather than Tab—except Rupert of course."

"He ought to be in a ward. Other children'd take his mind off his sore throat. Darklis and Isa didn't want to come home."

People kept coming in stamping the snow off their feet. On the other side of the fireplace a couple of undergraduates in college scarves were downing pints of beer. Helen's hair glowed in the firelight; it was the only bright thing about her. Suddenly there were tears trickling under her dark glasses again.

"Oh God,"she muttered in a choked voice.

"Don't worry."

"I haven't got a tissue."

One by one Jake removed all the paper napkins from the nearby tables and handed them to her. The waitress, trying to keep the tables for people having lunch, clicked her tongue disapprovingly as she replaced them.

"Do you want a menu, sir?" she asked, pointedly.

"Yes later, but for the moment, can you get us two more very large brandies?" He gave her a fiver, adding, "Keep the change."

The waitress looked at Helen curiously. Must have been a death at the hospital, she thought. Then she looked at Jake. He was familiar, with his dark brooding eyes.

"Who's that by the fire?" she asked the other barmaid. "What was he in?"

"I think he's got a group. No, he's a show-jumper. I know. He's the one that broke his leg. Dr. Millett was telling us. They thought they were going to have to amputate, but he put up a real fight and pulled through. What's his name, Rupert Lovett, Jack Lovett?"

"Jake Lovell," said the first barmaid.

"Here you are, Mr. Lovell," she said, putting down the brandies on the table. "Can I have your autograph for my niece? She loves horses."

Jake scribbled his name on the back of her order pad and turned back to Helen. He felt a certain academic interest in why she was in such a frightful state. He'd never admired her looks, too thin, breedy and rarefied, and in his eyes she was always contaminated by being part of Rupert. But today he was drawn to her, as he had been drawn to Macaulay, and to all other things terrorized by Rupert.

"He's a beautiful child," he said.

Helen gave the ghost of a smile. "And he's very bright. He's starting to read and he's not four yet."

"Rupert got him on a horse yet?"

"He's allergic to horses."

"Lives in the wrong house, doesn't he? Sure he's not allergic to his father?"

"Rupert thinks he's a wimp," she said bitterly. "Can't wait for him to go away to school."

"Where's he going?"

"St. Augustine's—if Rupert gets his way."

"Christ, don't send him there," said Jake, appalled.

"What was Rupert like at school?" asked Helen.

"Same as he is now—Torquemada."

She looked up with a start of recognition.

"Have you always hated him?"

"For over twenty years."

"He had an awful childhood," said Helen. "His mother didn't really love him."

"A woman of taste," said Jake.

The waitress came up, all smiles now.

"Are you ready to order? And could I have your autograph for our manager's daughter?"

"Steak and kidney pie, chips and cauliflower cheese," said Jake.

"I don't want anything," protested Helen.

"Don't be silly, and bring a bottle of red," he added to the wait-

ress. "You need food," he said a minute later. "I used to try to go
without it until Dino Ferranti converted me. He always said that
seven-eighths of depression is tiredness and lack of food."

"I liked Dino," said Helen. "He was fun."

"We all liked him," said Jake. "Fen misses him like hell, but she's
too proud to admit it."

Then lunch arrived and Jake ate in the way that only really thin
people do. Helen suddenly found she was hungry after all. It was real
steak and kidney pie and there was wine in the gravy.

Jake nodded approvingly: "How's Rocky?"

"Rupert figures he's the best horse he's ever ridden."

"Paid enough for him."

"How's Macaulay?"

Jake's face softened. "He is something else. After Sailor died I
vowed I'd never get so fond of a horse again. But Macaulay really gets
to me. If he could read he'd go around on his own. He's not really a
world class horse, but he's such a trier and he's got so much heart."

"He's not overly fond of Rupert."

Jake grinned. "That's another thing we've got in common."

After a good start Helen didn't manage much of her lunch. Quite
pink now from her thermal underwear, she looked as if she were running a temperature.

"I ought to go back."

"I'll call and check," he said.

When he came back she'd disappeared. He thought she'd bolted
until he saw her shopping bag, with the copy of *The Brothers Karamazov*
and *The Guardian*. When she returned he noticed she'd toned down the
flushed cheeks and tidied the rumpled hair. He knew it wasn't for his
benefit. Just the instincts of a woman who liked looking perfect all the
time.

"He's fine," he said, getting up. "Out like a light still. No one
expects him to wake for several hours." He filled up her glass.

"You have been kind," she said slowly. It was as if she was noticing him as a person for the first time. "Why are you here anyway?"

Jake told her.

She was stricken with remorse. "It's such a crucial day for you.
I'm so sorry. I've been so obsessed with my own problems, I didn't
even think of anyone else. Are you hoping to go to L.A.?"

Jake touched wood. "Yes, if Johnnie Buchannan gives me the
goahead today. I've got just six months to get fit."

"Will you take Macaulay?"

"I'd like to, although potentially Hardy's a better horse. He's been
going well with Fen, but he's still very spooky and erratic. Christ, if
only I had a year."

Looking at him, Helen suddenly saw coming alive that single-minded, driving fanaticism, which had to be there: the fuel of Olympic fire.

"Buchannan warned me I might never ride again. I promised if he mended me I'd bring him home a medal. Fighting talk, huh?"

He stopped suddenly, flushing slightly, hearing his own obsession, wanting to disguise it.

Helen looked at the black hair, the thickly lashed eyes and the thin watchful face. Suddenly she winced and clutched her temples.

"What's the matter?"

"I get this pain. It seems to start as a headache, then becomes toothache, then often reappears as earache."

"Neuralgia," said Jake, "caused by tension."

He felt so sorry for her. She reminded him of a vixen escaping from hounds, lying in the bracken taking a brief panting respite to get her breath back. In a minute she'd be running again, waiting, terrified, for the kill. But Rupert hadn't killed her. He'd totally destroyed her self-esteem.

As they came out of the pub it was still snowing, shortening the visibility, so they could only see the vague outlines of the towers of Oxford.

"Beautiful city," said Helen softly. "Home of lost causes, and forsaken beliefs, unpopular names and impossible loyalties."

"Pretty impossible to be loyal to Rupert," said Jake dryly.

Underfoot it was freezing so hard that he ought to have been more frightened of falling. But he crossed the snow without a slide or a stumble.

Helen was amazed Marcus recovered so quickly. Driving in on the fifth day to take him home, she found him playing with the most exquisite model circus. There were clowns, little dogs with ruffs, a ring master and even a ballerina in a pink tutu who slotted into a cantering horse with a pink plume. All the nurses were gathered round playing with it.

"How darling," said Helen in delight. "Who gave you that?"

"Dake did."

"Dake?" said Helen, puzzled.

"Dake with the sore leg. It's better now. Want to see Dake."

"Who can he mean?"

"Jake Lovell," said Miss Wutherspoon warmly. "He popped in last night on his way back to Warwickshire and brought the circus with him. Marcus was a bit restless, excited about going home. Nurse Tethers, who was on nights, had a very sick child to look after. Jake stayed playing with Marcus for hours."

"How very kind," said Helen. "How very, very kind."

"Mr. Buchannan gave him the go-ahead on Monday evening. I still don't think he's come down to earth."

"Oh I'm so pleased," said Helen, "and he still remembered Marcus."

"Want to see Dake," said Marcus.

51

*T*he winter seemed to go on and on, but at last the snow melted; aconites and snowdrops appeared and Helen watched Rupert's dogs trampling over her crocuses, snapping off their fragile heads, and found she minded less than in other years.

As she went for long solitary walks in the woods, her thoughts strayed far too often to Jake Lovell. Over and over again she got out the road atlas and realized how far he'd driven through the snow to give Marcus the circus. She remembered how embarrassed he'd been by her tears and how cold he'd got sitting in the car, just patting her shoulder.

As she watched the spring emerge with aching slowness she wondered how she could thank him for lunch and for the circus. She didn't want to write in case some secretary opened the letter. He might have told Tory about lunch, but if he hadn't, it might make things awkward. Personal letters were so obvious when they arrived in a private house. She remembered so many arriving for Rupert over the years, usually in gaudily-colored envelopes, sometimes with S.W.A.K. on the back, and how she'd longed to steam them open. Janey, she knew, would have had no such scruples.

Chatting to Janey in the kitchen one day, and leafing through the latest issue of *Horse and Hound,* with a shock of recognition she came across a picture of Jake. The story underneath said he would be making his comeback at the Crittleden Easter meeting and how glad readers would be to see this brilliant but very private rider back on the circuit. He had evidently recovered from one of the worst accidents in show-jumping history and learned to walk by sheer guts and determination. The story went on to praise his staunch close-knit family and to explain that Jake had not achieved the international fame of other British riders because, before the World Championship, he preferred to jump only in this country and get home to his family in the evening. Malise Gordon was quoted as being absolutely delighted. If all went as planned he hoped Jake would be offering himself for selection for Los Angeles.

"Good that Jake Lovell's back, isn't it?" she said to Janey.

"I shouldn't imagine Rupert thinks so." Janey took the magazine from Helen. "I've always thought he was very attractive. All that Heathcliff gypsy passion kept under such perfect control. He's much more self-confident too. I saw him interviewed on TV last night about his comeback and he actually managed to string a sentence together. And, instead of looking sulky and defensive, he was rather cool and detached."

Helen found her voice thickening, as it did when she asked if she could cash a check at the village shop. "Have you ever heard any gossip about other women?"

"No, he's squeaky-clean reputation-wise. You only have to look at Tory to see he hasn't got very high standards."

"I guess he's only interested in getting to the top," said Helen.

"Perhaps," said Janey thoughtfully, "but there's something irresistible about men who are impossibly hard to get, which is not something one can say about your dear husband."

It was strange, reflected Helen, that, after that unspeakably dreadful last night in Kenya, she and Janey could still be friends. Janey had a disarming quality, not attempting to justify or apologize for appalling behavior, which made it possible. Rupert, however, she could not forgive. They both moved around the house not communicating, like goldfish in a bowl.

The week before Easter brought the first sunshine for days. Helen went around the house turning off lights that weren't on, because the rooms were suddenly so unexpectedly bright. Out in the fields she noticed little red buds on the wild roses and larks singing in the hazy drained blue sky, thrashing their bodies like moons against non-existent windows. Perhaps I could escape, thought Helen, listening to the larks' strange whistle; perhaps I too am thrashing against a window that isn't really there.

Next day the vicar came to tea, to talk about raising money for the church spire. Afterwards Rupert walked in from the stables and caught him and Helen praying together in the drawing-room.

"Christ," he said in horror, and walked out again.

The vicar, who had a white beard and stank like a polecat, scrambled creaking to his feet:

"I wish we could make some progress with your husband," he said with a sigh. "I feel he is very troubled."

"I don't think he'd see it that way," said Helen hastily, "but thank you very much."

Carrying the tea things into the kitchen, she found Rupert and Tab eating easter eggs and reading *Dandy* together.

"Flappy Oyster," said Tab.

She shouldn't be eating easter eggs before Easter, thought Helen appalled, but she didn't say anything.

Rupert looked up. "Has your friend from Hollywood gone?"

Burying her head in the dishwasher, as she stacked the cups and saucers, Helen said. "I thought I might come to Crittleden on Saturday."

"The anniversary of your first show," said Rupert. "That's rather touching."

"I'm having lunch with the Godbolds," said Helen, putting all the knives in the wrong way up, "so I can come on afterwards. I also thought I might fly out to Rome for a couple of days."

Rupert looked slightly startled. "Whatever you like," he said.

For the first time in years Helen felt excited and took ages planning what she was going to wear to Crittleden. Despite the lack of sun April had been very dry, so she wouldn't have to wear boots. She settled for a pin-striped suit, a white silk shirt and a charcoal grey tie and a grey derby.

After a lightning lunch at the Godbolds, where she ate nothing, she arrived at Crittleden just as the riders were walking the course for the big class. There was Rupert fooling around with Wishbone and Billy, and there was Jake, still limping quite badly, walking beside Fen. He looked small and preoccupied and very pale. Neither of them were speaking. Fen was only an inch or two smaller than he was.

Jake felt nausea creeping through his stomach as he made his way towards the collecting ring. People nodded and waved and clapped him on the back, but he hardly noticed them. Why the hell hadn't he chosen a smaller show to make his comeback?

A little girl rushed forward for his autograph. "Later," he snapped.

Lack of sleep and food had made him dizzy. Everything seemed unreal. For the past week he'd hardly slept, dozing off, then waking up with the sensation of falling, then lying awake, jumping fences in his head, seeing them growing higher and impossibly higher, as the long hours crept towards dawn and cigarettes piled up in the ashtray.

The sky was getting greyer. He began to shake.

"Are you all right?" said Sarah. "Don't worry. You've been jumping super at home. Mac'll take care of you."

Macaulay tried to knock Jake's hat off to cheer him up and was sworn at for his pains. When Jake was mounted, Macaulay tried again, just a little buck that in the old days would have made Jake laugh— but which today nearly put him on the floor and produced another torrent of abuse. To further shatter Jake's confidence, Rupert was crashing Rock Star over the practice fences, putting him wrong, so he hit his forelegs hard and would be certain to pick them up when he went into the ring. God, he was a beautiful horse, thought Jake, a chestnut stallion showing all the compressed power of his American breeding, with curving muscles like coiled steel cables.

Jake jumped a couple of fences, then, having been nearly sent flying by Rupert, retreated to the outer field desperately trying to get his nerves under control. Suddenly he passed Helen Campbell-Black, looking like a city gent, ludicrously out of place in a pin-striped suit.

"Hi," she said, smiling and coming toward him.

Jake nodded curtly and, circling, rode back to the arena.

Fen was waiting for him: "You're on," she said. "Good luck."

"Good luck," called voices on all sides.

In the old days he had usually been all right once he got into the ring, the nervous tension a necessary preliminary to the class itself, heightening awareness, but that was when his body was fit and flexible, not frozen with fear. Now he was like a child at his first gymkhana. What if he really was jinxed? Sailor had died here. Last year he had smashed up his leg. These things went in threes. What had the fates in store for him today?

Macaulay, aware of his master's terror, heard the bell and suddenly decided to take matters into his own big hoofs. Bucketing towards the first fence, he cleared it easily. Somehow, clinging onto his mane, Jake stayed in the saddle. It was a very hit and miss business. The crowd had their hearts in their mouths all the way around. No one cheered, they didn't want in any way to distract Macaulay, but as he cleared the last triple with a flourish they broke into a roar that seemed to part the grey clouds and bring out the sun, putting a sparkle on everything.

Fen found herself hugging Malise in the collecting ring. "He did it," she gulped, " he really did it. It's going to be all right."

As Jake rode towards the exit, deadpan as ever, the cheers mounted and all the people in the boxes came out on to the balconies to bellow their approval. Helen joined in the applause politely. She felt absurdly deflated. Jake had hardly noticed her and then cut her dead.

"Great round," said Malise.

Jake shook his head. "It was bloody terrible and you know it, but at least I or rather Macaulay got round."

Everyone was congratulating him. It amazed him. They were so thrilled to see him back, but he couldn't take the hero worship and the enthusiasm just yet. He wanted to be alone with Macaulay to thank him. Riding quietly out of the collecting ring he saw Helen Campbell-Black. Aware that he'd snubbed her earlier, he rode toward her.

"Hello."

She looked up: "Oh hi," she said, ultra casual.

There was a long pause.

"He jumped well," she stammered, "I'm so happy for you."

"How's Marcus?" said Jake to the top of her hat.

"He's real fine, so much better. Look, I've been meaning to thank you for ages for lunch and for Marcus's circus. You were so kind driving all that way." She was really jibbering now.

"That's all right," said Jake.

After another long pause she looked up and they gazed at each other.

"I've got your handkerchief too," she said, color mounting in her face, "and Marcus plays with his circus all the time. He just adored you."

Jake said nothing, but went on staring down at her.

Helen put up a trembling hand to stroke the horse's black neck.

"Are you going to Rome?" she asked, desperate for something to say.

"No. Are you?"

"Yes."

"Don't go."

"W-what?" she looked at him in amazement.

"I said don't go. Make some excuse. When's Rupert leaving?"

"Lunchtime, a week from Monday. He's flying over."

"Right. You'll be home in the afternoon?"

"Yes."

"I'll call you there." And he was gone.

Helen was thrown into complete panic. Had she dreamed it? Could Jake really have said that? From that Saturday at Crittleden to the Monday nine days later when Rupert left for Rome, she went through every fluctuation of excitement, worry, terror, and disbelief.

She was completely inattentive at committee meetings and at parties. When the parties were boring she could think of nothing but Jake. Yet when Amanda Hamilton invited them to dinner on Saturday and Helen, radiant in russet taffeta, was courted by two rather handsome Tory M.P.s, she hardly missed him at all. Amanda had been particularly nice to her, soliciting her aid to persuade Rupert to go into politics.

Perhaps if he did, thought Helen, things would be different. He'd be in England most of the time and there wouldn't be any of those punishing three-o'clock-in-the-morning departures, and by using his brain he might have less of a chip on his shoulder about her apparent intellectual superiority.

Rupert was highly relieved that Helen wasn't coming to Rome. Amanda Hamilton was going to be there for the Rome tennis tournament, staying with friends. He was making no progress with Amanda. Like fish pie, he told Billy, she was taking far longer to make than one would expect. Pathological about bad publicity, she even refused to have lunch with him. But she fascinated him more than any woman he'd met for ages, and he was determined to get her into bed before long.

When Rupert's car refused to start on Monday, Helen drove him to the airport. As she drove slowly back to Penscombe, admiring the wild cherry blossom and the pale green spring leaves, she reflected that it was a good thing she'd be out when Jake called just to show she wasn't that eager.

Walking into the house she buried her face in a huge bunch of white lilacs which filled the entire hall with its scent. Marcus rushed out to meet her and show her the pictures of the fair he'd painted at play school.

"Any messages?" she called out casually to Charlene in the kitchen.

"No. Oh I tell a lie, Mrs. Bacon called."

"No one else? Are you sure you didn't go out or into the garden?"

"I've been here all afternoon."

Helen was totally thrown. She wandered restlessly around the living room, moving ornaments, even snapping at Marcus. She tried to read. Half an hour passed. Then Malise called hoping to catch Rupert before he left. Janey called to gossip and the headmistress of Marcus's play group called about their summer tag sale. Helen was uncharacteristically terse with all of them. Then Charlene's mother called and gossipped with Charlene for twenty minutes. Helen couldn't even accuse her of wasting money as it was an incoming call. Perhaps Jake was in a phone booth trying to get through. Unsupervised by Charlene, the children swarmed into the room. The next moment Tab had put jammy fingerprints all over the apricot silk curtains.

"Charlene," screamed Helen, "for God's sake get off the telephone."

Charlene flounced in looking martyred. "It's Gran. She's got cancer of the colon."

"Oh God," said Helen, mortified. "I'm so sorry."

The telephone rang. Helen sprang on it.

"Hello."

"Helen?"

"Yes."

"It's Jake. Sorry I couldn't call before. The class went on and on."

There was a pause. Mindlessly she watched Tab stumping towards the table that held all her favorite ornaments.

"Look, I know it's short notice, but I'm coming your way tomorror. Can we lunch?"

"I don't know. Tab, leave that table alone. *Alone,* I said."

"Shall I pick you up?"

"No." It was almost a scream. *"Tab—I said put it down!"*

"You know the Red Elephant at Willacombe?"

"Yes."

"I'll see you there at one o'clock."

"OK—hey wait."

But he had hung up.

Leaping forward, Helen retrieved a figurine from Tab's grasp. Then, picking up the child, she was suddenly ovewhelmed with happiness, swinging her round and round, covering her with kisses until she screamed with delight.

"Cookies," said Tabitha, sensing weakness.

"Oh, OK" said Helen, "if you really want your teeth to fall out."

Looking at her calendar after a sleepless night, Helen saw to her horror that she was supposed to go to a fund-raising lunch for the N.S.P.C.C. As Vice-President for the local area, she was expected to play a leading part and make a rousing put-your-hand-in-your-pocket speech after lunch.

The President was very put out when Helen called and said she couldn't make it. Charlene had to go to an unexpected funeral, she explained, so she had to stay home and look after Marcus and Tab.

"Surely one of the grooms can do that? I mean, we are expecting you. They're all looking forward to meeting you."

"I'm really sorry, Davina, but I really can't leave them."

"What about Janey Lloyd-Foxe?"

"She's away,"—horrifying how easy she found it to lie—"honestly, I'd never forgive myself if Marcus had an asthma attack. And since we're talking about cruelty to children, I figure my first duty is towards my own kids. I appreciate your help, Davina, but please don't try and run my life," and she hung up.

Looking at herself in the bedroom mirror, she was suddenly elated and amazed by her own defiance. Suddenly, however, panic assailed her. What if Davina called again and got Charlene after she'd left, or if Marcus really had an asthma attack? Whimpering with terror, she called the Red Elephant. Could she leave a message for Mr. Lovell? After a long pause, the manager said there was no table reserved in the name of Lovell, although they had four Mr. Smiths and five Mr. Browns who'd booked tables for lunch. Helen hung up. Perhaps he wasn't going to show up at all.

Mrs. Campbell-Black, reflected Charlene as she listened to Helen singing "I'm in the Mood for Love" in the bath, was behaving in a very odd way. Yesterday she'd unloaded all Badger's cans of dog food from the supermarket into the dish washer and put a box of Tampax in the fridge. Even when she came out of the bath and found Tabitha trying on lipsticks and dropping one on the pale gold carpet she didn't fly off the handle as she normally would.

And now she was walking into the kitchen in a silver jumpsuit and shiny black boots, with her hair trailing down her back in one long red braid.

"You look fantastic," said Charlene in genuine amazement. "Like an astronaut. You ought to go to the moon." (She's over it already, she thought to herself.)

"Do you really like it?" asked Helen.

"Gorgeous. Makes you look so slim. You'll be wasted on the N.S.P.C.C.," Charlene added slyly. And asphyxiate them too with all that expensive perfume, she reflected. Mrs C-B must have bathed in it.

Marcus wandered in. "Mummy pretty. Going out?" His face fell.

"Only to a lunch to make money to help kids who aren't as lucky as you. I must go. I won't be late."

God will smite me down for such terrible lies, she thought.

Terror increased on the drive to the restaurant as she passed two N.S.P.C.C. stalwarts driving like mad in the other direction—late for their one glass of sherry. She glanced in the rear view mirror, hoping she wasn't getting too flushed. She was so nervous, she'd been rushing to the toilet all morning. It would be terribly difficult to go in this jumpsuit; she'd have to take the whole thing off. There was the Red Elephant. She couldn't see Jake's Land Rover anywhere.

He was waiting in the bar, three-quarters of the way through his second whisky. For a minute she thought he was going to kiss her on the cheek, then they settled for shaking hands.

"D'you want a drink here, or shall we go straight in?"

All along the bar sat businessmen gaping, finding her face vaguely familiar, trying to identify her.

"Let's go straight in."

Rupert could never enter a restaurant without turning the whole place upside down and Helen was amazed that Jake slid in so quietly. They reached their table in a corner without anyone recognizing him. There was a bunch of dark purple irises in a royal blue vase.

"It's not considered good form, but would you rather sit with your back to the room?" Jake asked.

Helen nodded.

At her request for a glass of white wine, Jake ordered a bottle and another whisky for himself. Helen found herself quite unable to meet his eyes. It had been so easy to talk before because it had been just a monologue, with her pouring out all her woes. Now, sitting opposite, conversation was incredibly heavy going, like chopping up raw cabbage with a blunt knife.

Marcus was much better. Darklis and Isa were well. Both of them felt it bad form to mention Tory or Rupert. Helen was reluctant to ask Jake about his horses in case she betrayed her total ignorance. Jake felt the same about movies, plays, and books. The weather had been perfect, so that only lasted them thirty seconds. A kindly waiter arrived with the menus. Helen randomly chose whitebait, which she hated, and broiled lamb chops.

She hadn't actually looked him in the face yet. White wine didn't seem to loosen her up at all. Desperate for something to say, she boasted that she'd met half the Tory shadow cabinet at dinner on Saturday, then thought what a fatuous thing to have said. Jake was bound to be wildly left wing. Conversation didn't improve with the arrival of food. There were long silences. Jake, unsmiling, said very little. Helen was beginning to get rattled. Gloom swept over her; she had no charm; she was boring him as she bored Rupert and obviously Dino. She looked down at the silver bodies of the whitebait in their coats of batter and could see their glassy little eyes staring at her.

Suddenly Jake leaned across, took her knife and fork, and put them together and beckoned the waiter: "Could you take the plates away, and bring our next course, but there's no hurry."

"Anything wrong, sir?"

"Nothing. We just weren't as hungry as we thought."

Helen gazed down at her hands, which were frantically pleating the white tablecloth.

"I'm sorry," she mumbled. "What a dreadful waste."

Jake stretched out his hand and very gently began to stroke her cheek. For a second she shied away, then gradually relaxed under his touch.

"There," he said softly, "there. It's all right, pet. I'm just as scared as you are."

"Are you?" she glance up, startled.

"More so, I should think. I was so terrified you'd say no yesterday. I couldn't work up the courage to call you until six o'clock. I hung around the phone booth, steeling myself."

"And I figured you weren't going to call."

"And I thought you'd probably beg off this morning, so I reserved in the name of Smith, and went out first thing, so you couldn't get me."

"And when I got cold feet and called up to cancel and found you hadn't made a reservation, I got in a blind panic because I thought you weren't coming."

They both found they were laughing. Then she told him about the hassle with Davina and the N.S.P.C.C.

"What was *your* excuse?"

"I said I was going to look at a horse. Tory looked at me as though I was barking. We haven't got enough cash for a three-legged donkey at the moment."

"And I left all that whitebait."

"Doesn't matter. Nice treat for the restaurant cats. D'you mind if I smoke?"

As the match flared, she noticed the beautiful passionate mouth with the full lower lip and for the first time realized his eyes weren't black but very dark sludge green to match his shirt.

"Have you really got gypsy blood?"

"Sure. My father was pure romany, ran away back to the gypsies when I was eight. After my mother died I tried to find him and lived with the gypsies for three years before the social security people caught up with me and slapped me in the orphanage."

"What was it like living with the gypsies?"

"Cold sometimes, and always the feeling of being moved on by the cops. But I enjoyed it, I learned a lot. They taught me to recognize a good horse, and treat all nature as a medicine cabinet. Which reminds me." He put his hand in his pocket and produced a bottle of grey-green liquid.

"For you. For neuralgia."

Helen took it wonderingly: "You remembered. What is it?"

"Extract of henbane. Deadly poisonous, neat. Crippen used it to murder his wife."

Helen looked slightly alarmed.

"But that's very diluted. It's a marvelous sedative and a painkiller. Try it, but keep it in a safe place."

Helen was so moved and touched, she had to make a joke out of it.

"D'you eat hedgehogs as well?"

"No," he said coldy, "nor do I tie them on top of poles like your husband."

Oh dear, thought Helen, I've upset him.

Then he said, "Did you know hedgehogs' prickles go all soft when they're with kind people?" and suddenly smiled.

God, he's attractive, thought Helen. "Do you tell fortunes?" she said.

He shrugged. "A little. It's really a con trick. The hand betrays the calling, if it's rough, or pampered, or the nails are bitten. You look more for the face behind the eyes, the droop of the mouth."

Helen held out her hand. Her engagement ring, far too loose, had fallen underside down. For a second the huge sapphires and emeralds on her third finger caught the light, then fell back into place. Jake examined the palm for a second.

"It tells me a small, dark stranger has entered your life."

"You think so."

"I know."

"Is he going to remain there?"

"That's up to you." He ran his finger lightly along the heart line, "Whatever you may think to the contrary, you're extremely passionate."

Neither of them made much headway with their second course, but finding so much to talk about now, they drank their way through a second bottle of wine.

"Were you really intending to ask me out at Crittleden?"

"No, I was far too preoccupied about riding again."

"What changed your mind?"

"I suddenly wanted you like crazy."

Helen blushed. "Ever since you bought me lunch at the pub, I've kept thinking about you. I thought it was gratitude, now I'm not sure."

Jake undid one of the zippers on her jumpsuit: "Pretty. Does this lead anywhere?"

"Only a pocket."

"Nice. I'd like to live in your pocket."

Looking down at his hand at her collar bone, involuntarily Helen bent her head and kissed it, then went crimson.

"I didn't mean to do that," she said, appalled.

"I know you didn't, I willed you to."

Still they lingered, oblivious of the yawning waiters looking at their watches, ostentatiously re-setting tables on either side of them. Seeing her slowly relax, and those huge eyes losing their sadness, Jake couldn't tear himself away. He'd always thought her very over-rated as a beauty. Now she seemed to blossom in front of him—lovelier every second.

In the ladies room Helen was amazed to see her own face. She couldn't believe she hadn't turned into someone else. It took hours to get her jump suit half off and have a pee, she kept undoing the wrong zipper. She realized she must be very tight. She was appalled, looking at her watch, to see it was a quarter of four.

Even in her boots, she was only an inch shorter than Jake. As they walked to her car, he put a hand on the back of her bare neck under her hair, warm and reassuring. It was nice having someone the same size as her. Rupert always dwarfed her.

"I must go back," she said wistfully. "I'm dreadfully late."

As he opened her door he said, "Drive a couple of miles down the road towards Penscombe. There's a little wood on the left. Wait for me there."

The wood was full of primroses and violets. For a dreadful moment she thought she stopped in the wrong place or that he wasn't coming. Then at last he appeared over the hill, stuck behind a trundling farm tractor carrying bales of hay. Taking both hands off the wheel, he raised them in a gesture of despair.

He was out of the car in a second, drawing her into the wood, beech husks crunching beneath their feet. Then, as Helen tripped over a bramble, Jake caught her, drawing her behind a huge beech tree, laying her against the trunk, taking her face between his hands, examining every freckle and eyelash and yellow fleck in her eyes.

"Even Helen of Troy couldn't have been as beautiful as you," he whispered and kissed her very gently on the lips. Helen was glad the beech tree was holding her up. No one had ever melted her in this way. She had no desire to fight him off, just a longing that he would go on holding her forever. But as they broke for breath, some deathwish prompted her to ask,

"It's not because I'm Rupert's wife?"

For a second his face was black with rage, just like the time he'd pulled a knife on Rupert.

"I don't want anything of Rupert's," he said through gritted teeth, his hands biting into her arms until she winced. "Get this absolutely straight. Rupert poisons everything he touches. It's a measure of what I feel for you, that I still want you *despite* the fact you're his wife."

This time he kissed her really hard and she kissed him back, half-longing that he'd push her down and take her on the beech husks. But he led her back to her car, his face shuttered.

"You're not mad?" she stammered. "I've had such a good time today. Living with Rupert makes you skeptical, I guess, so you question everyone's motives."

"Well don't question mine. Where you're concerned they're quite straightforward. I just can't stand that shit having anything to do with you."

He opened the door and, as she got in, leaned over to fasten her seat belt, kissing her briefly on the forehead.

"You know this is only the beginning?"

"Is it?" Helen was overwhelmed by a great happiness.

He nodded. "But we can't afford to rush things. I've got too much to lose."

"You mean Tory and the children."

"No," he said slowly, "I mean you. I don't want to panic you. Drive carefully. I'll call you tomorrow afternoon."

It was a good thing there weren't any traffic cops lurking as Helen floated home. She got lost twice and bought peace offerings of freesias for Charlene and sweets for the children. Really she was going to the dogs in grand style. She came through the door singing with happiness at five past five.

"So sorry I'm late. Lunch went on and on and on. Everyone was going on about sponsored swims and tag sales. What are you having for supper, darlings? Hamburgers and french fries. How yummy."

Normally Helen would have freaked out at junk food, thought Charlene, putting the freesias in water, and she certainly didn't get like that over a thimbleful of sherry.

—

In the evening Charlene went to a wine bar with Dizzy, who this time hadn't gone to Rome.

"Promise promise promise, you won't tell anyone?"

"I promise."

"Goodness," said Dizzy in awe a quarter of an hour later. "I wouldn't have thought the old thing had it in her. Are you sure?"

"Well she certainly wasn't preventing cruelty to children. Mrs. Paignton-Lacy dropped off the minutes for the last meeting on her way home, two hours before Mrs C-B got back."

"Christ," said Dizzy. "Well done her. About time someone gave Super Bastard the run around. I wonder who he is."

"Must be pretty special. She came back floating above ground like the hovercraft. She was never like that after lunching with Ferrantic."

*H*elen sent Charlene and the children out for a picnic the following afternoon so she could talk to Jake without being overheard. But gradually as the minutes ticked by she felt her happiness subsiding like a tire with a slow puncture. Three, four, five, six, struck the grandfather clock in the hall. It was no longer afternoon. The children came home tired and fractious and, sensing her sadness and inattention, fussed even more. Helen looked at the chaos of toys lying around the nursery, counting "he loves me he loves me not" as she put them away. Jake must have forgotten her. Perhaps Tory had kicked up a fuss when he got home and decided the whole thing wasn't worth the hassle.

The evening passed with agonizing slowness. She couldn't settle down to anything. She was appalled how suicidal she felt. She couldn't have got hooked that quickly. This is only the beginning, he'd told her. A small dark stranger has entered your life. How could he hurt her like this? How could he reduce her to such ridiculous uncertainty and despair?

At midnight she took the dogs out for a last walk. As if to mock her, it was the most perfect evening with a gold almost full moon, with a hazy halo of apricot pink. Along the edge of the wood the huge Lawson cypresses rose like cathedral spires, taking on an almost sculptured quality. As she walked across grey shaven lawns, past silent statues, the last of the daffodils gave a flicker of light. The reflection of the moon in the lake was rippled first by a wakeful carp, now by Badger drinking. Her shadow was tall and very black on the lawn. It was so light she could see the blue and green stones in her engagement ring.

Was there after all to be no small escape, no respite from her marriage?

Despairing, she turned back. Glancing up at the golden lit-up windows of her bedroom she could see the rose and yellow silk curtains of the huge four-poster in which she would soon lie alone. As she came into the house the telephone was ringing. After midnight, it must be Rupert. He never had any sense of timing. Steeling herself, she picked up the receiver.

"Helen, can you talk? It's Jake."

She burst into tears. It was a minute before he could get a word in. "Hush, I'm sorry, pet. Please don't cry; it breaks me up. I couldn't call before. Hardy cast himself this afternoon. Had the most frightful colic. The vet's been here ever since two o'clock. He's just finished operating. He'd swallowed a nail and we thought we'd lost him."

"Oh God, that's awful. Is he going to be O.K.?"

"He's still out like a light; but the vet reckons he'll pull through."

"I'm so sorry. You must have been frantic."

"I couldn't get to a telephone. It's in the tackroom and the vet and Fen were in Hardy's stall next door the whole time. Look I can't talk long; the vet's still here, but I must see you tomorrow, if only for five minutes."

"It'll be hard for you to get away if he's still sick. I'll come over your way."

"That would help and, pet, please don't cry anymore."

They met the next day literally for a quarter of an hour.

Jake looked desperately tired; he hadn't been to bed. Hardy was very shaky on his legs, he said, but well enough to bite the vet that morning, so it looked as if he would pull through. Watching his face as he talked about the horse, Helen felt deeply ashamed. He really loves him, she thought, as Rupert was incapable of loving a horse, in fact anything. Last night he must have suffered just as much as she had waiting for him to call, and she'd greeted him with hysterics.

They walked through the beechwoods, breathing in the wild garlic, Wolf bounding ahead and Jake picking up the bluebells the dog had knocked over so Helen could take them home for a few more days of life.

They sat on a fallen log. Helen hung her head, clutching the bluebells. She'd put her hair up today. Jake slowly took out every hairpin so it cascaded down her back in a shining red mass.

"Don't put it up anymore. It reminds me of what you were like before I started to—" he paused—"to know you."

Then he said more briskly, "Look, we've got to get one thing straight. You've been married to a show-jumper for quite long enough to know that things happen with horses, that it's impossible even to say I'll turn up or telephone at a particular time with a hundred per cent certainty."

"I know," she said in a trembling voice, "but I've got so little self-confidence."

"I know that," he said putting his hand under her chin and forcing it upwards: "And I want to give some back to you but only if you give me a chance and realize from the start if I ever don't call you, or don't turn up, it's because I can't. Even though I was demented with worry over Hardy last night, a hundred times I nearly risked it and picked up the phone which would have been madness because at any time Tory could have picked it up in the kitchen. It's difficult enough for us to find time to see each other without complicating things. All right, end of lecture, I'm not going to kiss you because I must have smoked a hundred cigarettes in the last twenty-four hours and I don't want to put you off even before we've got started."

"You couldn't, truly you couldn't." She threw herself into his arms, half crying, half laughing.

He held her for a long time, not speaking, just stroking her hair. Then he said, "I'm off to the Bath and Wells tomorrow for three days. Why don't you drive over? We could have dinner."

"That would be just lovely."

"Or I could book a room in one of the nearby hotels."

He felt her stiffen.

"I don't know."

How could she explain that he was so desperately important to her that she couldn't bear to turn him off? She knew he would lose interest once he realized how hopeless she was in bed.

"Why not?"

"I don't know you well enough."

He laughed. "There's no better way of getting to know someone better."

He called the next day telling her the name of the hotel and what time he thought he'd get there. He didn't mean to bully her, but he felt privately it was vital to bed her as soon as possible. Not just because he wanted her like hell, but because he felt he'd never make any real progress in restoring her self-confidence until he got to grips with her hang-ups. He'd heard gossip that she was frigid. He didn't believe it. Frigid was a gross over-simplification, a term used by men about women who no longer loved them physically. He believed Helen had been very badly frightened but was not frigid.

He wished he could spend hours talking to her, soothing her, making her feel secure. But he had so little time. If he was going to be picked for Los Angeles he couldn't let up for a second. And so he insisted on her meeting him that night at the hotel.

Helen sat alone in her bedroom at dusk. There was no wind. Outside sheep were calling to lambs, baby house martins under the eaves were squeaking peremptorily for their parents to catch insects more quickly. The white cherries shone luminous in the half light. The rank peasant smell of wild garlic in the wood threatened to extinguish the sweet delicate scent of the pink clematis which swarmed round the bedroom window. Her pink running shoes were yellow with buttercup pollen from wandering aimlessly through the fields all afternoon. This time tomorrow she'd be in the bed with Jake.

She had never been so frightened in her life. She wished she could pray, but how could she ask God to help her be better in bed with someone who wasn't her husband? She still hadn't planned her alibi for tomorrow night. Charlene was going out, so she'd have to ask one of the grooms to baby-sit. Always before she'd left a telephone number where she could be reached, but she could hardly give them the number of the Nirvana Motel. And how was she going to smuggle her suitcase out to the car? She'd have to send the children out for yet another picnic.

Even worse, she'd been sitting on her bed trimming her bush with nail scissors when Charlene had walked in with some ironed clothes and Helen had hastily to pretend she was cutting her toenails. Anyway what was the point of trimming her bush when the thing it covered was full of trouble? Over and over again Rupert's words came back to haunt her: "You're just like a frozen chicken. Every time I put my hand down there I expect to pull out the giblets."

And she was so thin now, it would be like going to bed with a broomstick. She had a blinding headache so she took some of Jake's medicine. Gradually the pain eased and she felt calmer. Maybe if he could cure her head he could melt the ice of her frigidity as well.

But it was as if some malignant fate were at work. Just as she was leaving Penscombe the following day, she discovered she'd got her period. She'd been so preoccupied she'd completely forgotten she was due.

She glanced at her watch. It was too late to call Jake at the show. She could ring the Nirvana Motel and leave a message saying she couldn't make it, but that left her with the appalling prospect of not seeing him. She'd have to go, perhaps have a quick drink—he wouldn't want her in this state—and then come home.

It was so hot she wore only a yellow sleeveless dress, yellow sandals and a white silk scarf to keep her hair from tangling. As she drove very fast to meet him, she was so wracked with cramps she hardly noticed the beautiful green bosky evening or the cow parsley frothing along the roadside, or the smell of wild garlic, stronger than ever, like some rampant Dionysian presence pursuing her.

Waiting for Jake, she sat trembling in the hotel lobby, trying to make herself look as inconspicuous as possible. Pretending to read the evening paper, the hall porter watched her idly. You could always tell the first time they came in here, he thought, they never stopped fiddling with their hair, squirting on perfume, glancing in their hand mirrors then fearfully up at the door. Suppose he didn't turn up, supposing someone they knew walked in. He'd seen wives sitting here waiting for their lovers when their husbands walked in with someone else. He had another look at Helen. This one was a looker all right, but she'd go through the ceiling with nerves in a minute. Oh, now she'd dropped her bag all over the floor. He moved forward to help as Helen fell on her knees, frantically scrabbling up credit cards, keys, loose change, and lipsticks. At that moment Jake sauntered through the door, his coat slung over his shoulder. He looked suntanned and happy and not remotely embarrassed.

"Hello, darling," he said, pulling her to her feet, and kissing her on the cheek. "Did the babysitter arrive? I've had the most bloody day at the office. And I'm afraid my father called to say he wants to come and stay next week."

Just like any other married couple, thought Helen in admiration, and she had great difficulty not giggling when he signed them both in as Mr. and Mrs. Driffield.

"No, we'll manage," he said to the porter when he offered to carry their bags up to the fourth floor, adding in an undertone as they got into the elevator, "I'm buggered if I'll tip him for nothing."

When he opened his bag in the bedroom, all it contained was a toothbrush, toothpaste, a bottle of gin and a large bottle of tonic.

"I think that covers all eventualities," he said as he fetched two glasses from the bathroom. Then, seeing the expression of misery on her face, he put them down on the dressing table and took her in his arms trying to still the desperate trembling.

"Pet, please, you look as though you're going to the electric chair."

Helen burst into tears. It was some seconds before she could speak, and then he spoke for her. "You've got the curse."

"How d'you know?" she said incredulously.

"I knew you had it coming. All week you were very edgy and the day before yesterday your breasts were swollen and you had huge circles under your eyes. Fen always says just beforehand is the only time she has decent boobs."

Helen was amazed that he should be so observant. Smoothing her hair very gently behind her ears, he removed her earrings. "Now will you please stop crying. We don't have to do a thing if you don't want to."

He poured half and half gin and tonic into the glasses and handed her one. "You got a pain?"

She nodded.

"Well gin's the best for that. Take a big slug of it. Come on, lie down," he said, removing her yellow high-heeled sandals; "Just relax. We've got hours." He lay down beside her, draining half his drink.

"You don't have to stay," Helen stammered. "You might not want to—if there's no sex."

For a second his face blackened. "What the fuck is that supposed to mean? D'you honestly think I only want you for sex?"

"I don't know. It's all Rupert wants." Somehow the words spilled out before she could stop them.

"How many times," he said wearily, "do I have to remind you I'm not Rupert?"

"I know you're not," she said in a trembling voice, "but it wouldn't make any difference if you were, or if I didn't have a period. I'm no good to you. I'm hopeless at sex. I'm frigid."

"Who said so?"

Despite the heat he could feel the gooseflesh on her arms. She was still shuddering violently, her teeth chattering.

He reached for her glass, making her take a big gulp, and then a second and a third.

"Come on now, tell me all about it." Then it all came pouring out—the humiliations, the taunts, Rupert's always insisting on sex whenever he came home, despite the endless infidelities, then the clap and finally Samantha Freebody.

"That's not all, is it?" said Jake. "What happened in Kenya?"

"How'd you know anything happened?" whispered Helen.

"Second sight. Come on. We can't afford to have any secrets."

He made her take another slug of gin.

"I can't talk about it." she whispered.

"Go on. It'll help, I promise.

So she told him often crying so hard he couldn't hear the words, about the foursome with Billy and Janey.

"Afterwards Rupert made me feel as though I'd let him down, paid him the ultimate insult by not joining in. I couldn't. I'm simply not made that way."

Jake tipped her head back, swept the sodden hair away from her forehead and dried the tears away with his handkerchief.

She heaved a long sigh. "I'm so sorry to bore you."

Jake held her tightly. "Poor baby, poor poor little baby. You did end up in the wrong barn didn't you?"

Her yellow dress had no zipper, so Jake was able to slide it off over her head, before laying her back on the bedspread.

"Still got the pain?"

"A little."

"I'll bring you something for that next time. The gin'll start working soon."

Beneath the coffee-coloured silk petticoat, he could feel her stomach muscles tightly knotted. But gently, as he stroked them with those magic hands that could calm the most frightened horse, she began to relax. She was so tired, after nights of not sleeping, that the singsong voice and the stroking hands and the gin were making her drowsy. Almost before she knew it he had slid off her petticoat and unhooked her bra. Then he was kissing her mouth and, almost in spite of herself she was kissing him back, gently at first, then more and more fiercely, and still his hand continued to stroke her belly.

"You're so beautiful," he murmured.

"I'm so thin."

"No you're perfect."

After Tory's bulk he found Helen's fragility incredibly erotic. For once he felt like a great hunk of man, all-powerful by comparison.

And she looked so unbelievably touching, with her damp cheeks and wide yellow eyes smudged with mascara, and her hair falling in a long red tangle over one shoulder. As he kissed her again, his hand slid downwards caressing all the time, circling the pubic hair then sliding under the pants finding the clitoris, stroking it with utmost delicacy. Helen tensed and then relaxed.

"She's not frigid," he thought in triumph. Slowly slowly like a moth emerging from a chrysalis, she seemed to yield to him. Then she gave a deep sigh of contentment.

After a minute she opened her eyes and smiled.

"Frigid my Christ," he muttered into her hair.

"That was so lovely," she gasped.

"Wasn't it?" He grinned down at her, looking absurdly pleased with himself.

"But you haven't had any sex at all," she said suddenly distressed.

"Doesn't matter. I can wait till next time. It'll be worth waiting for."

The unselfishness, the insight, the kindness put the seal on her love for him.

"That was the most wonderful . . . moment I've ever had," she said.

"For me too," he said kissing the hollows of her throat.

Three days later he had her for the first time in a meadow on the edge of Bifield woods near the old gypsy encampment where his forefathers must often have taken his foremothers. A heavy shower of rain had flattened the grass for them and dispersed the regiments of insects, but it was still very hot. Their lovemaking was rapturous. They fitted perfectly together and despite anything he might say to the contrary to Helen, Jake experienced a feeling of pure triumph: that this was Rupert's wife lying beneath him reduced to a quivering jelly of ecstasy. Once again he had succeeded where Rupert had failed.

—

Meanwhile in Rome at almost the same time Rupert Campbell-Black was experiencing an almost identical moment of triumph as he lay on top of Amanda Hamilton for the first time. Rock Star had had a glorious double clear in the Nations' Cup yesterday, making up for Fenella Maxwell's indifferent form and clinching the victory for Great Britain. Today Amanda was actually missing the final of the men's doubles in order to play mixed singles with him. Full-breasted, narrow-hipped, long-legged, her body was superb for a woman of forty. Only a slight creping on thighs and breastbone betrayed her age. Her string of pearls was still around her neck. In out, in out, superbly in control, Rupert drove her towards orgasm.

Suddenly her face contorted with concentration, then she gave a cry of ecstasy.

"At last."

"My darling," said Rupert smiling tenderly.

"I've suddenly worked it out," said Amanda. "It was *your* cousin, Charlie Cameron, who was married to Rollo's niece-in-law, Antonia Armitage. Before she was married to him she was Antonia Luard."

If it had been any other woman Rupert would have hit her.

53

*F*or the first four weeks Helen and Jake enjoyed an unnatural freedom. Rupert and Fen were traveling abroad with the British team, following the same route from Rome, Fontainebleau, Paris to Lucerne along which, last year, Fen had cavorted so joyously with Billy. Now Fen did no cavorting. She went to bed early, listened with both ears to Malise's advice, worked her horses diligently, but still showed an alarming lack of form. Each day she grew more panicky that she wouldn't be selected for L. A. and would never see Dino again.

In England, however, Jake was on sensational form. Macaulay, blissful to have his master on his back again, was jumping superbly. Hardy, recovered from the operation and still erratic and cantankerous had some brilliant days. Wherever Jake went he annihilated the competition. But he was still nagged by the worry that the selectors had forgotten him because he'd been off the circuit so long. How much would he have to achieve before they began to sit up and take notice?

Almost, but not entirely, taking the edge off his anxiety was his obsession with Helen. Traveling the British circuit, he was away from home three or four nights a week. Sarah was abroad with Fen. Hannah, Jake's new young groom, had a convenient crush on one of the Irish

riders, spending most nights sleeping under haystacks or in the back
of the Irish boy's van. Helen, with a Volvo at her disposal, whizzed up
numerous highways and spend as many nights as possible with Jake,
stretched out in his trailer or on a duvet in the back of the Volvo.
Sometimes they went to hotels. Often, despite Jake's reluctance, Helen
paid. If she had the money, why not? From the moment she committed herself to Jake she felt absolutely no guilt about being unfaithful to Rupert or spending his money.

She did feel guilty about neglecting the children, but she was so
happy whenever she returned, radiant and talkative, and so loaded
with guilt presents, even biscuits for Badger, that everyone flourished.
Helen was blissfully unaware that everyone in the household knew
something was up and were having bets who he was.

On the 28th of May Jake returned to the Mill, having spent three
days at the Great Cheshire Show, where he had won every big class by
day and spent his nights making love to Helen. In three days' time,
which was also the first day of the Lucerne show, the Olympic Committee would announce ten short-listed riders from whom the final five
would be selected in mid-July. Jake arrived home absolutely shattered.
His mended leg ached badly, but that was probably due more to an
excess of sex than show-jumping. As he climbed out of the van, the
sun was setting. Tory ran out of the house to welcome him. He hoped
her elation might be due to the news that he'd been selected, but it
was purely because she was so thrilled to see him. He was so tired, he
kept answering all her questions wrong. As he went into the kitchen,
the children surged forward in their pyjamas to welcome him, hugging and kissing him, bombarding him with questions about the trip.
Realizing he couldn't cope with the din, Tory sent them off to watch
television. Jake poured himself a drink.

"How did Fen do in the Nations' Cup?"

Tory had prayed he wouldn't ask. She didn't want him upset so
soon after he'd got home.

"They dropped both her rounds."

"Shit. What happened?"

"She was in floods of tears when she called. I don't think it was
anything Desdemona did wrong. Fen said it was her fault. She'll probably call you after the Grand Prix."

Jake dropped a couple of ice cubes in his whisky and went out
into the yard, watching the horses being put to bed. Macaulay, having
rolled and wolfed his dinner, was already dragging up the straw, pre-
paring to lie down. Hardy was still restless. It always took him a long
time to settle back, even into his own stall. As Jake progressed down
the line, each horse came to the half-door to welcome him. Tonight for
once they didn't cheer him up. Why hadn't he heard from Malise?

He went into the tackroom.

"Supper," called Tory from the kitchen door.

"Won't be a minute," Jake called back. Next moment he'd picked up the tackroom telephone. As he waited for Helen to answer he noticed the peeling paint on the door. If Charlene answered he would put the telephone down.

"Helen, its Jake."

"Darling." It was worth the risk to hear the ecstasy in her voice. "Where are you?"

"At home. I can't talk. I just want you to know I miss you like hell."

Suddenly he saw Tory appearing in the doorway, "I'll call you tomorrow, bye."

"Darling," said Tory, "I could have made that call for you."

"Think I left my wallet in Humpty's van. I had a drink with him at lunchtime."

"Your wallet's in the kitchen, silly," said Tory. "You *must* be tired. It's so sweet you've got that photograph of me from the color supplement tucked inside it. It's an awful picture. I look so fat. D'you really miss me when you're away?"

"Course I do."

The photograph in fact was part of a feature on show-jumping wives that had appeared in the *Sunday Times* color magazine. On one side of the page were two photographs: one of Tory looking fat, pink and eager, nailing up ribbons in the kitchen, the other of Janey Lloyd-Foxe, managing to look absurdly sexy in a maternity smock. The other side of the page was devoted entirel to a photograph of Helen on the terrace at Penscombe, gazing wistfully down the valley, looking unbelievably beautiful. It was taken before she met Jake and was the reason he had sneaked up to the newsstand last Sunday to scrounge another copy.

In the kitchen Jake thanked God that Hannah, Isa and Darklis were having dinner with them. The children, allowed to stay up because it was Sunday tomorrow, were arguing who was going to sit next to him.

"You can both sit next to Daddy," said Tory, putting a long loaf of garlic bread on the table.

Darklis had painted a picture at school which she showed proudly to Jake.

"It's you and Macaulay at Los Angeles, Daddy."

Both he and Macaulay were standing on the rostrum wearing gold medals, with balloons coming out of their mouths saying "God save the Queen."

"I think you're being a bit premature, but thank you," said Jake.

As Tory served out beef cooked in beer and the children both helped themselves to too many mashed potatoes, and Hannah brandished the ribbons they'd won this week, which tomorrow would be nailed to the cork board, Jake wondered if the last month with Helen was all a dream.

Suddenly the telephone rang. For a mad moment of panic he thought it might be her calling back. It was Malise, from Lucerne.

After two minutes, Tory put Jake's dinner in the oven. After ten minutes, Tory gave the rest of the beef out in second helpings, knowing Jake wouldn't want any more.

"Yes," he said, his back hunched over the telephone, with a curious stillness. "Yes, I see. OK. Yes."

"We're going to need another bottle," said Hannah.

"I don't know if we've got one," said Tory. "What for?"

"To celebrate, or to cheer up."

At last Jake came off the telephone. He looked like a thundercloud. Then he smiled and put his arms round Tory.

"Fen was third in the Grand Prix."

"Oh thank goodness for that," said Tory.

There was along pause. They all waited. "And I've been shortlisted for L.A. He wants me to fly out to Lucerne with Hardy and Macaulay tomorrow."

Tory woke up at four in the morning and, reaching out for Jake, found the bed empty. He was in the study. Cigarettes were piling up in the ash tray. Outside it was already light, blackbirds were bustling importantly across the lawn like clerics in a cathedral close.

"Darling, what *are* you doing?"

"I couldn't sleep."

"Too excited?"

He shook his head ruefully. "Too much to think about."

He'd waited so long for that telephone call, despairing that it could ever come. Now it had and he ought to be overjoyed, but all he could think was that he wouldn't see Helen for at least two weeks. The prospect appalled him.

By morning he had the whole thing in perspective and was quite matter-of-fact when he called her. Helen sounded absolutely shattered and made no attempt to keep the disappointment out of her voice.

"I'm thrilled for you, darling, but we won't be able to have that week in Yorkshire. I can't bear it."

"I'll only be away ten days."

"But that's an eternity and then Rupert'll be back for the Royal and the Royal International. Can I see you this afternoon?"

"It's a bit tricky." He sounded detached, as though he was already in Lucerne, "I've got a hell of a lot to do. We're desperately shortstaffed anyway, with Fen and Sarah abroad and all the papers to get in order."

Being superstitious, he hadn't brought anything up to date in
case he wasn't selected.

"I'll call you later," he said.

Jake didn't get a moment until seven o'clock. Everyone was in the
yard or in the kitchen, so in the end he was reduced to pretending he
needed some cigarettes from the pub. Then the pub pay phone was out
of order, so he had to use the one in the High Street to the fascination
of all the locals. Helen was in a frightful state.

"Sweetheart, I've been frantic. I figured something must have
happened."

"I'm sorry. I've been hellishly busy."

"Am I going to see you this evening?"

"I can't."

"I'll come over to you."

"I haven't had a night at home for days. I've got a hell of a lot still
to do. We're leaving first thing."

Next moment he jumped out of his skin as a neighbor tapped on
the window wanting to congratulate Jake on being short-listed.

"What are you doing in a phone booth anyway?" he asked.

"Ours is out of order," said Jake.

"Come and use ours then."

"I've nearly finished," Jake banged the door shut. "Darling, I'm
sorry, someone banged on the window. Look, I'll call you as soon as I
get to Lucerne."

"I can take a hint," said Helen in a tight voice. "You've only got
time for your bloody horses."

"Don't be a bitch."

"I thought you were different," sobbed Helen, "but you're behaving just like Rupert."

"Hardly surprising, if you carry on like this."

But she had slammed down the telephone.

The locals drinking outside the pub were highly diverted to see
Jake come out of the telephone booth, wander up the street away from
his own car, nearly get run over crossing the street, then wander back
into the phone booth again.

Jake was very restless at dinner, snapping at the children, hardly
eating anything.

"You all right?" asked Tory, as she cleared away.

"I'm sorry." Jake put an apologetic hand on her back. "It's just
nerves I guess."

"And tiredness," said Tory, throwing the remains of his ham and
baked potatoes into the garbage. "You're jolly well going to bed early."

"I will, I promise, but I met Hugh Massey in the street. He says
he's got a video of last year's show at Lucerne. He promised to show it
to me."

"Don't be long," she said.

Pretending to collect his car keys, Jake went upstairs. Darklis caught him in the bathroom.

"Why are you cleaning your teeth, Daddy?"

"Because I got a bit of ham stuck," lied Jake.

In disgust Darklis gazed at her face in the bathroom mirror.

"I don't think anyone will marry me when I grow up."

"I'll marry you, sweetheart," said Jake, dropping a kiss on her head.

"You've already got a woman," said Darklis gloomily.

I've got two, thought Jake wryly.

Helen was waiting in the parking lot of the Goat and Boots, three miles away. She got into his car and they drove half a mile into the country and turned off the road. Helen fell into his arms.

"I'm so sorry, I'm desperately sorry. Please don't ever let me behave like that again. I just couldn't bear the thought of your going away."

"Hush, pet, hush." Gradually he calmed her. "Now," he said, "I'm going to talk and you're going to listen. We've got to face the fact that I'm going to be horrendously busy for the next two months. For one thing we desperately need the cash. Fen's been off form and she needs sorting out. I've still got a long way to go with Hardy. I've got to kill myself to get a place in that team. To be selfish, if I'm not selected I don't want to reproach myself for the rest of my life for having blown it because I didn't work hard enough. I'm not a natural like your husband. Ever since I've been in show-jumping it's been one hell of a struggle to keep going. Fen, the children, the grooms, and most of all Tory, have had to make colossal sacrifices. After that last fall I've crawled back from the gates of hell. But only because they made it possible. I owe it to them all to get to L.A. and I want to go." His voice softened, and he put up his hand to stroke her cheek, which was wet with tears. "Until I met you I thought I wanted it more than anything else. Allow me three and a half months until the Games are over. There, that's the longest speech I've ever made."

"I'll put up with anything," said Helen, in a trembling voice. "I just thought you'd gotten over me."

Jake laughed. "You're like Macaulay, desperate for reassurance."

"That's the difference between us," said Helen slowly. "My marriage is absolute Purgatory. Yours is perfectly OK. We're coming from two different places."

There was a pause. Jake was too truthful to disagree with her.

"Shall I fly out to Lucerne?" she asked with a sudden surge of hope.

"No, I don't want any distractions."

And with that she had to be content.

—

Rupert called the following evening. He was halfway to Lucerne. Rocky, he said, had won the Grand Prix last Saturday.

"How's Fen doing?" asked Helen.

"Disastrously. I can't think why Malise doesn't pack her off back to Junior classes. Mind you, he's really gone off his head now. He's just sent for Jake Lovell. 'Jake Lovell,' I said to him, 'couldn't get a jump in a brothel.'"

Lucerne was a show of mixed fortunes for Jake. Macaulay, who hadn't flown since Jake brought him half starved back from the Middle East four years ago, obviously thought he was being sent back to the stone quarries and completely freaked out on the flight. Sweating as though in the highest fever, his huge body quivering with terror in the tiny crate, his anguished eyes imploring Jake not to desert him, he reminded his master of nothing so much as Helen. It took all Jake's skill and patience to stop him kicking the plane out.

Arriving in Lucerne, Macaulay was pathetically pleased to see such old friends as Fen, Sarah and Malise. He was further comforted to see Desdemona in situ, and dragged Jake halfway across the yard to check if it were really she. Touching her nose, exchanging breaths, Macaulay was still rigid with disbelief. Only when Desdemona reached up to rest her roan face against his still sweating neck, protective and defensive, did he begin to relax. But he never really recovered his form all week.

Bearing in mind that there would be a punishing flight to the Olympics and Macaulay was not all that sound in the wind, and a clean-winded horse was essential for the Los Angeles smog, Jake, after long discussions with Malise, decided to pull him out of the contest. He was heartbroken. Most of all he had wanted to win a medal on Macaulay, but his horses always came first, and Jake was not prepared to put the big fellow through the traumas of another plane journey. He'd already made plans to trailer him home.

Which meant everything rested on the sleek but irritably twitching grey shoulders of Hardy, who was magnificent on his good days, but perfectly capable of dumping Jake or kicking every fence out if he chose. In Lucerne, after a sulky start, he came second in two classes, and jumped an exemplary clear in the first round of the Nations' Cup. In the second he put in a dirty stop at the water leaving Jake sitting in the exquisite model lake with a stream of expletives on his lips and a bridle in his hand, while Hardy cavorted round the ring refusing to be caught. Having learned to duck out of his bridle, Hardy suddenly decided what fun it was, and did exactly the same thing in a speed class the following day.

All this provided wonderful fuel for Rupert, who proceeded to twist the knife on every occasion. Although Fen got very hot under the collar and snapped back at Rupert, Jake refused to rise. He got a quiet satisfaction from the thought of how much better he'd been riding Rupert's wife at home, and a further laugh when the mail arrived one morning and Rupert actually handed him an envelope containing a passionate love letter from Helen. Thank goodness she'd had the foresight to type the envelope and mail it in London.

Finally Hardy put a muzzle on all his critics by coming second to Ludwig in the Grand Prix. But all in all, Jake did not feel the week's adventures had enhanced his Olympic prospects.

After Lucerne, it was back to the Royal in Birmingham, then out to Aachen, then more shows in England and finally Crittleden at the end of July after which the team would be announced.

All this made Jake very uptight and, although he missed Helen appallingly, he had plenty to occupy his mind. Helen, on the other hand, had nothing. She thought about Jake obsessively. His face haunted her dreams. At night she tossed and turned, longing for his hands on her body.

She had even convinced herself Jake would make a much better father for the children, particularly Marcus. Rupert had come home from Lucerne and taken both children to the fair where he had insisted on riding on all the most frightening things. Tabitha adored every minute of it. Marcus was absolutely terrified and ended up being sick on top of the ferris wheel, soaking not only Rupert's trousers but the couple immediately below them, who took it very badly. Rupert returned home in a blazing temper, with Marcus white and shaking and Tabitha in high glee telling everyone what had happened. That evening Marcus had his worst asthma attack ever.

As Helen soothed him to sleep in the early hours of the morning, she found under his pillow one of the little dogs with a ruff from the circus Jake had given him.

"Want to see Dake again," murmured Marcus drowsily, "Like Dake very much."

"Oh so do I, darling," sighed Helen.

A week later Janey gave birth to a beautiful dark-haired boy who weighed seven pounds and happily looked exactly like Billy. They called him Christopher William, soon abbreviated to Christy, and both of them absolutely doted on him.

Watching Billy in his new-found role as an adoring father, Helen brooded all the more on Rupert's lack of interest in Marcus.

On the other hand, she had reason to be grateful to little Christy. As a devoted godmother, she was provided with the perfect alibi. Afternoon or evening, she merely had to tell Charlene she was dropping in on Janey and the new baby. Then, having dumped a bunch of flowers and a glossy magazine and cooed for two minutes, she could rush off to see Jake.

During the Royal Show, she and Jake were able to snatch an afternoon together. Leaving Rupert safely competing in a couple of classes, Jake left Birmingham and drove the fifty odd miles over to Penscombe. Charlene had taken the children to a birthday party, so they had the house to themselves.

Jake was very jumpy. He hated making love to Helen on Rupert's territory. He thought of the Mill with its damp, peeling paint, torn wallpaper and messy homely rooms which had suffered eight years of wear and tear of children and animals. Then he looked at this ravishing house, and the green valley, and the tennis court, and the swimming pool, and the garden in its rose-scented mid-summer glory. The blatant perfection of the whole thing depressed him. And yet, overwhelming all this was his desperate need to see Helen again, and again, though he hated to admit it, the buzz of actually making love to her in Rupert's huge four-poster. He was amazed how passionate and totally uninhibited she'd become.

"I never thought I'd like it that way," she said. "The only problem with soixante-neuf is that neither of you can tell the other how marvelous it is while you're doing it."

"Let's do it straight next time, so you can," said Jake.

Lying on top of her he slowly returned to earth, kissing her freckled shoulders, gently nibbling the lobes of her ears.

Helen, who'd buried her face in the pillow, said in a muffled voice, "Jake—I love you."

There was a long pause, a horse whinnied from the valley, a dog barked in the distance. Then Jake said, "I love you too."

Lying beside her, smoking a cigarette, not worrying about the smell of tobacco because Rupert wasn't due back until tomorrow, he said, "I've never said that to anyone in my life before."

"Not even to Tory?"

He shook his head.

"Why did you marry her then?"

"Because she was rich and she bought me my first horse."

"Didn't you love her at all?"

"Not in the way I love you. As I said, she's been a very good wife, but we're all inclined to take her for granted. Dino brought her out. He really bothered with her, and she adored him."

"Dino was also very fond of me," said Helen, her face suddenly sulky.

Jake sat up and looked down at her, grinning.

"I do believe you're jealous of Tory."

Then, seeing the pain and misery in her eyes, he pulled her into his arms. Clinging to him fiercely like a child begging for a bedtime story to ward off the terrors of darkness, she said, "Tell me about the gypsies."

He settled her into the crook of his arm.

"Well if a woman's unfaithful to her lover he cuts off her ear or her nose, or scars her cheeks, so you'd better be careful. If your wife's unfaithful you tie her to a cartwheel and thrash her, or shave her head."

"Heavens," said Helen nervously, "how primitive."

"Then if you want to marry a girl you send her a spotted hand-kerchief. If she's wearing it next time you meet her, you know she's willing to marry you."

Helen was amazed how much it hurt her to ask, "Did you give one to Tory?"

"Yes. It was very cheap, red cotton. All I could afford at the time. She still keeps it in her jewel case, but it's terribly faded." He looked at his watch. "Christ, I must go."

"Oh please don't."

"I've got a class at seven. I've got to walk the course and it'll take me an hour to get back in the rush-hour traffic. I'll have to drive like hell as it is."

"Am I jeopardizing your career?"

"Yes," he said, kissing her.

Next minute the doorbell pealed and the dogs went into a frenzy of barking.

"Christ, who's that?"

Helen snuggled up to him. "Lie still. It might go away."

The doorbell rang again, the barking increased.

Naked, Helen crept down the passage and, hidden by the clematis which swarmed over the spare room window, peered out. A minute later she was back in her bedroom, giggling. Jake was already getting dressed.

"All I can see is a straw hat."

"Well, you'd better go and re-direct it," said Jake.

Wrapping herself in a big rust-colored towel, Helen went down-stairs.

In the doorway she found two elderly women fanning themselves. One was carrying a camera.

"We thought for an awful moment you were out," said the first, who was wearing the straw hat.

"I was in the bath," said Helen: "Can I help you?"

"We've come to interview you from *Loving Mother* Magazine. Miss Taylor here," the woman in the straw hat waved in the direction of the woman with the camera, "is going to take the pictures."

"Oh my goodness." Helen froze with horror. She remembered they'd called and made an appointment weeks ago. She'd forgotten to put it on her calendar. Suddenly she could feel Jake's sperm trickling down her legs and backed away hastily, ramming her legs together, hoping they couldn't smell all the sex and excitement.

"You'd better come in," she said weakly. "You must forgive me. I had a panic getting Rupert off to the show this morning," she lied.

"Usually I'm so punctilious about these things."

Miss Crabtree gave a jolly laugh. "Oh the needs of the great man must take preference." She stepped into the hall. "What a lovely home."

Helen's mind was racing. How the hell was she going to smuggle Jake out? Then she had a brainwave. "Come on to the terrace, the view's so lovely. Would you like a drink?"

Miss Crabtree consulted her watch. "Well it's only half past four. We'd love a cup of tea."

"Of course, a cup of tea." Helen fled into the kitchen, put the kettle on and rushed up the back stairs, half hysterical with laughter and terror. She found Jake dressed and trying to make his cigarette butt disappear down the toilet.

"Have you got rid of them?"

"No. They've come to interview me about being a devoted wife and mother."

Jake grinned. "They'd better come and interview me."

"Shut up. I've got them safely on the terrace. You steal out by the back door."

Tugging on a dress and a pair of shoes, she flung her arms around his neck. "Call me tonight."

Tearing downstairs, she rang Charlene. She could hear tumultuous party noises in the background.

"Bring the children back at once. Someone's come to photograph them."

"I can't in the middle of tea, and then there's the magician and Tom and Jerry."

"Well bring them back as soon as possible."

They were nearly out of Earl Grey and the only cookies were shaped like animals and topped with different colored icing. All the cups were in the dishwasher which wasn't turned on. She'd have to have a word with Charlene; things were getting awfully slack.

She was just drying the cups when Miss Crabtree wandered into the kitchen.

"It's rather hot out there, so I thought I'd come and help you. They're so lovely and cool, these old houses."

Any moment, thought Helen in panic, Jake would come down the back stairs into the kitchen, and where the hell had Miss Taylor gone?

"How old are your children?"

Helen dragged her mind back.

"Um—four and two."

"What a lovely age."

"They'll be back soon. They've gone to a party. I thought we could talk in peace first."

"I hope you don't mind. Miss Taylor's gone upstairs to find a toilet."

Helen gave a whimper of horror. "Oh dear. I hope there's a clean towel up there."

She was just rushing out of one kitchen door when she heard steps on the back stairs.

"Why don't you go and sit in the drawing-room," she pleaded to Miss Crabtree. "It's awfully cool in there. I'll bring the tea in."

"It might help if you put some tea in the pot," said Miss Crabtree with a jolly laugh, not budging an inch.

Tripping over a truck and an ancient teddy bear, placed on the stair to be taken up to the nursery, Jake fell into the kitchen. To Helen's amazement, he was carrying a bucket and squeegee. She gazed at him desparingly.

"All right, Mrs. C-B," he said putting on a strong cockney accent: "I've finished. I've done all the upstairs winders, even the little blighter on the top landing. Fort I'd swing to my death."

"Oh oh," Helen mouthed ineffectually. "Oh, how much is that?"

Jake scratched his head. "Fifteen pounds," he said. "There's a lot of winders."

Helen got a fiver and a tenner out of the house-keeping pot.

"Here you are. Thank you so much."

Miss Crabtree, who'd taken matters into her own hands, had made the tea.

"Would you like a cup?" she added to Jake. "Cleaning windows in an awfully thirsty business, although . . ." her voice trailed off. He didn't seem to have cleaned the downstairs windows at all.

"No thanks," said Jake. "I'll be off."

"There are quite a few smears here," said Miss Crabtree bossily.

"Only did the top two floors," said Jake; "I leave the bottom to Mrs. Bodkin. When d'you want me again? In a monfs time?"

Helen nodded, not trusting herself to speak.

"Well, cheerio then," Jake nodded to Miss Crabtree.

"I'll see you out," mumbled Helen.

Quite helpless with laughter, they collapsed outside the back door.

"I'd no idea you were such a good actor," she said, as he shoved the money back into the pocket of her dress.

Jake kissed her again. "I'll call you after the class is finished tonight."

In the kitchen Miss Crabtree was joined by Miss Taylor.

"What a lovely house. Where's our hostess?"

"Saying goodbye to the window cleaner. They're awfully un-class conscious aren't they, the Americans? I mean she's just as charming to him as she is to us."

As the day of the last Olympic trial at Crittleden approached, Jake grew more and more nervous. Hardy's off days were fewer and Fen had had some good wins on Desdemona. But equally Griselda Hubbard had hit amazing form, and two short-listed riders, Ralph Naylor and Fiona McFadden, had both jumped brilliantly under pressure at Aachen and several newspapers were agitating for their inclusion in the team. Rupert and Ivor Braine had been so consistent all year, they were virtually certain of a place.

Fen was terribly down because Joanna Battie had written a bitchy piece headlined:"Fen—resting on her Laurel," pointing out that she hadn't had a decent win on Laurel since last year at Wembley, and that Desdemona was too small for an Olympic course. Knowing how desperate Fen was to go, Jake felt almost more apprehensive for her than for himself.

Rupert, on the other hand, was irritated because Helen refused to make up her mind whether or not she was going to Los Angeles. She used the Los Angeles smog being bad for Marcus' asthma as an excuse, but in reality she wanted to see if Jake was selected. If he wasn't she'd stay behind. Rupert, who was trying to persuade Amanda Hamilton to fly out for a few days, wanted a decision one way or the other.

The course for the final trial was unnecessarily huge. There were a number of very unhappy rounds before Jake came in. Grisel was on twelve, Ivor eight. Fen had one stop, because she'd come in too fast, and two elements of combination down. Everyone was grumbling that the combination was unjumpable. Then Jake rode in and proved them wrong by going clear. Thus encouraged, Rupert went clear. But in the final jump-off, Jake really set Hardy on fire on the long run-up to the last fence to score the fastest time.

"Well done," said Fen, desperately trying to be enthusiastic, "you must be picked after that."

Jake shook his head. He was horribly afraid it wouldn't be good enough. They wanted dependability at the Olympics. The selectors locked themselves away. The riders waited and waited for the promised announcement. After an hour biting their nails, Jake and Fen, who were jumping at Stoneleigh early the following morning, decided to push off. If they were selected they'd hear soon enough. If they weren't it didn't matter anyway.

The traffic was terrible. Nobody talked very much. After an hour's delay on the M4 they decided to cut across country. Bored with tapes, Sarah turned on the radio.

Fen looked miserably out at the great rolling cornfields, deepened to red gold by the rain. When would she ever see Dino again, when would she ever be happy? Idly she listened to the eight o'clock news. Mrs. Thatcher, the Prime Minister, would be spending a few days up at Balmoral, staying with the Queen during the summer recess. The Russians had launched another satellite. The unemployed had risen by 20,000 as a result of school dropouts.

"The Olympic Show-Jumping Committee tonight announced their team for Los Angeles," said the announcer.

Everyone stiffened. Fen grabbed Sarah's hand, crossing her fingers on the other. "Oh please, please God."

"The five riders and their horses include: Rupert Campbell-Black and Rock Star, Griselda Hubbard and Mr. Punch," Sarah gave a groan. "Ivor Braine and John." The announcer rustled his notes, "Jake Lovell and Hardy and Fenella Maxwell and Desdemona."

Giving a whoop of joy, Jake nearly drove off the road.

The car behind them was trying to pass and honked furiously.

Speechless, Sarah and Fen hugged each other, then Sarah hugged Jake.

Then they all started shouting at the tops of their voices and bellowing, "California here we come."

Jake drove to the next village where they found a pub and bought a bottle of wine.

"Have one on the house," said the proprietor putting another bottle in the carrier bag. "I've just heard it on the radio. Congratulations."

They pulled up on the edge of a field and drank the Muscadet out of mugs, allowing the horses to graze, and watching the sun set.

"Here's to you," said Sarah, "I'm so proud of you both."

Next moment Fen had stumbled to her feet and was hugging Desdemona.

Jake saw that her shoulders were shaking. He put an arm around her.

"What's the matter?"

"Nothing. I'm just so happy."

"There's no need to cry then."

"I'm going to see Dino again." Half-laughing, half-crying, she rubbed away the tears, streaking her face with grimy hands. "I expect he's got a million other girlfriends by now, but at least I'll get the chance to say I'm sorry."

"Missed him that much have you?"

Fen nodded. "There's never a moment when I'm not missing him. But you wouldn't understand that, never having been in love."

After the team announcement Malise wrote to all the five riders confirming their selection. They would be expected to jump together once more as a team at The Dublin Horse Show, the first week in August, then rest their Olympic horses until they flew them out to Los Angeles at the end of the month.

Leaving Rocky at home to rest, Rupert flew the rest of his Grade A horses over to France for the Deauville and Dinard Shows, and was due home on Monday night. He had been deeply scathing of the rest of the Olympic team.

"A schoolgirl, a cretin, a riproaring dyke and a crippled gypsy. I'll have to carry the lot of them," he told Amanda Hamilton.

Nor was he particularly pleased when Helen decided she would be coming to Los Angeles after all.

Helen sat on the terrace, drinking white wine, breathing in the night scented stock and reading George Herbert in the fading light: "Who would have thought my shrivel'd heart/Could have recovered greenness."

Who indeed? She had never believed, after Kenya, she would ever be happy again, that she would be totally wiped out by love for Jake, that the only person she wanted to be in the world was the second Mrs. Lovell. Not that Jake was showing any inclination to make her so. She knew that he loved her (except in frequent moments of panic) and with that she would have to be content until after Los Angeles.

As Rupert was not due back from Dinard until tomorrow, and Charlene and the children were away for the night, Jake said he might pop in, but only might, she mustn't expect him. On the eve of departure for Dublin, he was frantically busy loading the van. Rupert, taking the easy way, was flying over and letting the grooms do the driving.

Helen hadn't done anything except wash her hair and have a bath earlier. She'd learned superstition from Jake. If she got all dressed up, he wouldn't make it. Watching a half moon sailing like a moth up the drained blue sky, she gave a cry of joy, for there, clearly visible coming along the top road towards Penscombe above the honey-colored stone wall, was Jake's car.

Rushing upstairs to the bedroom, she brushed her teeth, splashed on cologne and jumping into the tub. Holding up the skirt of the yellow dress she'd worn the night he'd first made love to her, and which she knew he liked, she turned the shower hose between her legs, shivering with excitement as the hard jet of water flattened her bush and shot straight up her vagina.

Leaving two dusty footprints in the bath, she jumped out and combed her hair. Since Jake had told her he liked her just as much without makeup, she felt secure enough not to bother with it. Stretching voluptuously, she went to the window, and then stiffened with horror, for there, as usual coming too fast along the road and only moments behind Jake, was Rupert's blue Porsche.

Next minute she heard the crunch of wheels on gravel and the dogs barking and tore downstairs. Opening the door she collapsed jibbering into Jake's arms.

"What's the matter?"

"Rupert's just behind you. I've seen him on the road. What can we do?"

"Nothing," said Jake, his brain racing. "Go and wash that scent off. We have to brazen it out. Pretend I just dropped in."

"Better come out to the terrace," said Helen. "It's getting dark out there and he won't be able to see how we're blushing."

Jake followed her out, running his finger down her spine.

"Anyway if he finds out, he finds out. He's got to know sometime," he said. Helen went very still. Turning round, she looked straight into Jake's eyes. "Has he?" she whispered.

Jake gazed back at her steadily, no shiftiness in his eyes now.

"Yes," he said. "You know he has to sooner or later. It'd just be easier after L.A."

Helen moved towards him. "Do you really mean that?"

"Yes, I think I always have. I just haven't said it."

He only had time to hold her briefly when there was a second crunch on the gravel and more barking.

"I can't face him," said Helen in sudden panic.

"I'll sort him out. Just get me a drink—Scotch, and quadruple, and as soon as possible."

Helen fled to the kitchen, her bare feet making no sound on the carpet.

Bang. Rupert slammed the front door behind him. He was not in a good mood. He'd specially come back to spend the night in London with Amanda and, after two admittedly splendid hours, she'd pushed off to Sussex, saying she had to drive her daughter to some dance.

"Helen," he shouted, "Tab, I'm home. Where the hell is everyone?"

Jake waited on the the terrace.

"Helen," Rupert shouted again more irritably.

"She's in the kitchen," said Jake.

"Who's that?" Rupert came out onto the terrace, then stopped in his tracks looking at Jake with slit eyes. His hair was bleached by the French sun, he was wearing a blue T-shirt, with "I Love L.A." in red letters across the front. Inspiration suddenly came to Jake.

"Beautiful place you've got here," he said. "I'd only seen it from the road."

"There are perfectly good gates at the bottom of the drive. I'm sure you don't need me to show you the way to them," said Rupert coldly.

"I dropped in," said Jake, "on the chance you might be back. I got a letter from Malise this week. I decided as we've both been selected and I want the team gold as much as you do, we stand a better chance if we bury the hatchet, at least temporarily."

He held out his hand.

Rupert, for once at a loss for words, looked down at the hand which was completely steady. He thought of his own humiliation in the World Championship. He thought of Fen defying him at the Crittleden strike. He thought of Jake in the dormitory of St. Augustine's, a terrified little boy, cringing away from the lighted matches. Now here he was waving white flags and offering peace initiatives.

The hand was still there. Briefly Rupert took it.

"All right. I don't trust you a fucking inch, Gyppo, but for the sake of the team gold we'll suspend hostilities till after the games. Then," he added smiling, "I'll smash the hell out of you! We'd better have a drink. Helen," he yelled.

"Yes," said Helen faintly.

"She was getting some ice," said Jake. "Probably hovering to see if I was to be allowed a drink."

"You were lucky to catch me. I wasn't planning to come back tonight at all. What d'you want?"

"Scotch please."

At that moment Helen came through the door clutching a tray with one already poured glass of whisky, the whisky decanter, a second empty glass and the ice bucket. She looked down at them both with terrified eyes, like a rabbit caught in the headlights, not knowing which way to bolt.

"Hi," said Rupert. "We've decided not to kill each other. You've met Helen before, haven't you?"

As Jake took his glass from Helen to stop the frantic rattling, he wondered for a second if Rupert was speaking ironically. Then decided that such was his egotism and contempt for Jake that he couldn't possibly envisage anything between him and Helen. All the same it was a good thing there was *only* Helen's glass, half-full, on the terrace wall.

Jake took a huge gulp of whisky and nearly choked. Christ it was strong, and thank God for that.

Rupert poured two fingers into his own glass.

"I'm giving up after Dublin," he said. "I want ten pounds off before the games."

"I can't afford to lose it," said Jake: "How was Dinard?"

"Bloody good."

"And Rocky?"

"Bloody good too. I keep thinking he's going to jump off the top of the world. I'm scared as hell he's going to peak too early."

In a daze, Helen poured herself another glass of wine. I cannot believe this, she said to herself. Here are two men, who I know detest each other beyond anything, talking not just politely but with enjoyment. Not by a flicker of an eyelid did Jake betray any nerves or the slightest interest in her, he continued to discuss the team, their weaknesses, the strength of the opposition at the games and which riders they had to watch. He asked Rupert's advice on the L.A. climate, and possible breathing and fitness problems. After Dublin, Rupert explained, he was flying Rocky straight out to L.A. to give them both time to get adjusted to the climate. This would certainly give him the edge over the other British riders, who wouldn't be leaving until two weeks later.

If Rupert's in L.A., thought Helen, that'll give Jake and me a whole two weeks. She marveled at his quick-wittedness. She never dreamed he would use the excuse of coming to make peace. She was overwhelmed with gratitude that he had averted a scene. She wished she could remember his exact words before Rupert arrived, but she'd been in such a panic. When he said Rupert would have to find out sometime, did he mean that he was going to commit himself to her and leave Tory, or merely that, by law of misfortune, Rupert would get wind of them sooner or later? She felt sure he had meant the former. Watching his face, dark, intense, growing more shadowed as the sun slipped behind the beeches, Helen could only read one emotion, passionate interest in what Rupert was saying. Bloody bloody horses, she thought, will I ever get away from them?

Jake tried to leave after the second drink. He was already slightly tight and, on an empty stomach, might easily make some false move. He glanced at his watch and put his glass down: "I must go. Sorry to barge in on you like that. Goodbye, and thanks," he added casually to Helen.

Rupert went to the door with him. A desire to show off overcoming natural antipathy, he said, "Like to see the barn?"

"OK," said Jake. "Just for two minutes."

An hour later Helen heard his car drive away and Rupert came through the front door.

"I'm starving. Shall I go and get take-out?"

"I want to be taken out," thought Helen in desolation. She had been so happy when Jake had turned up and now she wasn't sure when she'd see him again, particularly as he was going to Dublin first thing.

She could not resist discussing him with Rupert.

"Wasn't it amazing his coming here?"

"He was certainly impressed by the set-up," said Rupert, picking up his car keys. "Said he'd come to bury the hatchet, bury it in my cranium more likely. Don't trust the bugger an inch. Suspect he came to have a look as much as anything, see if he could pick up a few tips. Asked me the way back to Warwickshire. Hadn't a clue where he was. I told him the Sapperton way. He was so pissed, with any luck he'll run into a wall. Do you want Chinese or Indian?"

The following Friday Helen slumped in total despair at the breakfast table, two hands gaining warmth from a cup of black coffee. She had only heard from Jake once since he'd been in Dublin and that was only a two-minute call before someone interrupted him. He said he'd call back and hadn't. He obviously had cold feet.

"Letter for you, Mrs. C-B," said Charlene, handing her a bulky envelope: "Postmarked Dublin, you better watch out it's not a letter bomb."

Helen was about to tell her not to be nosy, then, recognizing Jake's black spiky handwriting, she tore open the envelope. Inside was folded a large dark blue silk spotted handkerchief.

"That's lovely, Mrs. C-B," said Charlene. "Navy goes with everything."

Helen went white and upended the envelope. There was nothing else inside. The spotted handkerchief—Jake was telling her he wanted her for good.

"She seemed absolutely dazed," Charlene told Dizzy afterwards.

Then she jumped to her feet laughing.

"I'm going to Dublin," she said. "I want to watch—er—my husband in the Aga Khan Cup."

The Aga Khan Cup—a splendid Trophy—is presented to the winning side in the Nations' Cup at the Dublin Horse Show. All of fashionable Dublin turns out to watch the event and every Irish child that's ever ridden a horse dreams of being on the home team one day. For the British, it was their last chance to jump as a team before L.A. All the riders were edgy; which of the five would Malise drop? In the end it was Grisel, who pulled a groin muscle ("shafting some chambermaid," said Rupert) but who'd would be perfectly recovered in time for L.A.

On the Thursday night the British team had been to one of those legendary horse show balls. Unchaperoned by Malise (who was unwisely dining at the British Embassy) and enjoying the release from tension after being selected, they got impossibly drunk, particularly Jake, and all ended up swimming naked in the Liffey. Next day none of them were sufficiently recovered to work their horses.

Jake, who didn't go to bed at all, spent the following morning trying to call Helen from the Press Office. He had huge difficulty remembering and even more dialing her number. A strange bleating tone continually greeted him. Dragging Wishbone to the telephone, he asked, "Is that a busy or the out-of-order signal over here?"

"Sure," said Wishbone soothingly, "'tis somewhere between the two."

"Christ," screamed Jake, then clutched his head as it nearly exploded with pain.

Half of him was desperate to talk to Helen and find out how she'd reacted to the blue spotted handkerchief he'd sent off to her the other day when he was plastered. The other half was demented with panic at what he might have triggered off. None of the telephones seemed to work. Wishbone, who was talking to a man in a loud checked suit, who seemed to know every horse in the show, bought Jake another drink.

"Drink is a terrible dirty ting," he said happily, "but the answer is to drink more of it."

Jake looked at his watch and wondered if he'd ever totter as far as the ring.

"We'd better go and walk the course," he urged Wishbone. "We'll be very late."

"Stop worrying," said Wishbone. "We haven't got a course yet," He jerked his head towards the man in the loud checked suit, who was busy buying yet another round. "He's the course builder."

All in all the British put up a disgraceful performance. A green-faced tottering bunch, they staggered shakily from fence to fence, holding on to rather than checking the spreads, wincing in the blinding sunshine to the intense glee of the merry Irish crowd, who had seen visiting teams sabotaged before.

Ivor fell off at the first and third fences, and then exceeded the time limit. Fen knocked every fence down. Rupert managed to get Rocky around with only twenty faults, his worst performance ever.

Jake, waiting to go in by the little white church, was well aware, as Hardy plunged beneath him, that the horse knew how fragile he felt. "For Christ's sake get around," said Malise, who was looking extremely tight-lipped, "or we'll be eliminated from the competition altogether."

Suddenly Jake looked up at the elite riders' stand, which is known in Dublin as the Pocket. He felt his heart lurch, for there, smiling and radiant, was Helen. She was wearing a white suit, and her hair, which she'd been in too much of a hurry to wash, was tied back by a blue silk spotted handkerchief. His challenge had been taken up.

"Oh good, Helen's come after all," said Malise sounding very pleased and dashing off to the Pocket. "Good luck," he called over his shoulder to Jake.

Concentration thrown to the winds, Jake rode into the ring. Somehow he managed to take off his hat to the judges and start cantering when the bell went, but that effort was too much for him. Hardy put in a terrific stop at the first fence and Jake went sailing through the air. The next moment Hardy had wriggled out of his bridle and cavorted joyously around the ring until he'd exceeded the time limit.

Jake just sat on the ground, sobbing with helpless laughter. When he finally limped out of the ring Malise was looking like a thundercloud:

"There is absolutely nothing to laugh about."

"You don't think he'll unselect us?" said Fen in terror.

Jake shook his head, then winced. But all he could say to himself joyfully over and over again was, She's here and she's wearing the handkerchief.

The Irish won the Aga Khan Cup.

"There's absolutely no point in talking to any of you," said Malise furiously. "But I want everyone, grooms, wives, hangers-on included, to come to my room at nine o'clock tomorrow. If any of you don't show up you're out."

The only answer seemed to be to go on to another, even more riotous ball, where reaction inevitably set in.

"The hair of the dog is doing absolutely nothing to cure my hangover," Fen grumbled to Ivor, as he stepped on her toes around the dance floor. "Really, if Rupert doesn't get his hand out of the back of that girl's dress soon, he'll be tickling the soles of her feet."

The music came to an end.

"I'm going to bed."

"Don't" said Ivor. "I'll have no one to dance with."

"Go and talk to Grisel," said Fen, kissing him on the forehead. She couldn't cope with the frenzied merriment. Nights like this made her longing for Dino worse than ever. She drifted rather unsteadily across the ballroom and out through the side doors, looking for Jake to say goodnight. A couple of Irishmen called out to her, trying to persuade her to come and dance, then decided against it. There was something about Fen's set frozen face these days that kept men at a distance, the way Helen's used to.

She wandered down a corridor and into a dimly lit library which was empty except for one couple. They were standing under a picture light, taking in that intense still way of people who are totally absorbed in one another. They were about the same height. Fen's blood ran cold. She must be seeing things.

The man was comforting the girl.

"Be patient, please, pet."

"It was a crazy idea to come," she said in a low voice. "I can't bear not being able to be with you all the time or go to bed with you tonight."

The man was stroking her face now, drawing her close to him.
"Sweetheart, just let me get Los Angeles over, then we'll make plans, I
promise."

"You really promise?"

"I promise, you know I love you. You've got the handkerchief."
He bent his head and kissed her.

Fen gave a whimper and fled. Forgetting her coat, she ran out of
the building and through the streets, desperate to escape to her hotel
room. Helen and Jake—it couldn't be true. That explained why he'd
been so different recently. Remote and unsociable one moment, then
wildly and uncharacteristically manic the next, and terribly absent-
minded. He'd hardly have minded if she'd fed Desdemona caviar.

Fen had always worshipped Jake and regarded his marriage to
Tory as the one safe good constant she could cling on to and perhaps one
day emulate. Now her whole world seemed to be crumbling. What
about Tory? What about Isa and Darklis? And more to the point, what
the hell was Rupert going to do when he found out? Nothing short of
murder.

55

*E*veryone, albeit a little pale and shaking, was on parade for
Malise's meeting next morning. No one was asked to sit down. Malise,
immaculate as usual, in an olive green tweed coat and a cavalry club tie
glared at them as though they were a lot of schoolboys caught smoking
in the dormitory. Yesterday's blaze of temper had given way to a cold
anger.

"At least we can go to the games knowing we haven't peaked
yet," he said. "I have never seen such an appalling demonstration. You
rode like a bunch of fairies. I doubt if any of you had more than an
hour's sleep beforehand. You've made complete idiots of the selection
committee."

"Three days in the lockup," muttered Rupert.

"And you can shut up," snapped Malise. "Your round, bearing in
mind the horse you were riding, was the worst of the lot. They say a
lousy dress rehearsal means a good first night, but this is ridiculous."

Then he smiled slightly, and Fen suddenly thought what a fantastically attractive man he was for his age.

"Now," he said, "if you can find somewhere comfortable to park
yourselves I'll show you some clips from earlier Olympics."

Refusing a seat Jake lounged against the door so he could look at
Helen, who was sitting in one of the chairs, with Dizzy perched on the

arm. Helen was pale and heavy-eyed with her red hair drawn off her face and tied at the nape of the neck by the blue spotted handkerchief. To Jake she had never looked more beautiful. He felt simply flattened by love. He could hardly concentrate on the clips of straining javelin throwers, and sprinters crashing through the tape and muddy three-day-eventers and Anne Moore getting her silver.

Malise switched off the video machine.

"I don't think I need to tell you much else. If you do get a medal, particularly a gold, it will be the greatest moment of your life, make no mistake about that. And if you don't get that medal because you were not quite good enough on the day, or because your horse wasn't fit, or because your nerves got to you, that's all well and good. But if you can look back afterwards and say I failed because I drank too much, or didn't train or stayed up too late or didn't work my horse diligently enough, you'll regret it for the rest of your life."

"He might be echoing Jake," Helen said to herself.

He looked around at the five riders. "You're probably the oldest Olympic squad we've ever fielded, except for Fen, which means we can offer a wealth of experience, but the heat may get to you. It also means this may well be your last chance of a crack at the Olympics."

He turned to the grooms and to Helen and to Griselda's rather mild father, who was sharing the arm of a chair with Ivor's mother. "I'd like to say the same to the families and grooms and wives for the next month. Try to be totally unselfish. You will find the riders tricky, irascible and demanding. As the competition gets nearer this may take the form of increasing detachment as they try to distance themselves. This you must put up with. They need to keep calm for in this way the horses will stay calm. Don't make unnecessary demands. Wives and families, if they're not coming to L. A., shouldn't expect regular telephone calls. Times are cockeyed. Security will often make it difficult to get to a telephone."

Malise looked over to Jake.

"I'm sorry Tory's not here," he said with a smile, "but she's the one person I know who doesn't need to hear any of this. She's always given you exemplary back-up."

Helen bit her lip. She felt an agonizing stab of jealousy. She must try not to hassle Jake.

"All right, that's all," said Malise briskly, "but I want to come home with two golds."

Having redeemed himself and his country by winning the Grand Prix on Saturday night, Rupert flew Rocky direct to Los Angeles the following day, which would give them both nearly a month to get used to the climate.

Two weeks later he flew back to England on the excuse of having

his Olympic uniform fitted and sorting out business matters, but in
reality to see Amanda Hamilton. He was meeting her at her house in
Kensington. This he regarded as a major breakthrough and also that
he'd been able to drag her down from Scotland in the middle of August
when she should be making shooting lunches for Rollo and entertain-
ing his cabinet colleagues.

As he drove past pavements pastel with tourists and looked at the
expanse of female leg and the briefness of skirts and shorts, Rupert
reflected how strange it was that his sexual energies had become almost
entirely concentrated on Amanda. The fact that she often didn't bother
to dress up or wash her hair or put on makeup when she saw him only
increased his interest. As did the fact that she was always busy with her
children or her committees or Rollo's career and had very little spare
time for him. He'd had to fight every inch of the way. Used to girls
who were only too available, who were always bathed and scented and
dolled up to the nth degree and quivering with anticipation, Rupert
found her an amazing novelty. They knew all the same people and were
governed by the same rules. She was also the first woman he couldn't
bully.

The house in Kensington was burglar-alarmed up to the eyeballs.
Amanda's excuse to Rollo had been Great Aunt Augusta's eightieth
birthday party, which had taken place at lunchtime. Amanda would
spend the night in London and fly north next morning. It was always a
good idea, she explained to Rollo, to pop in on the servants unexpectedly and keep them on their toes.

The servants, a Filipino couple who'd left a member of the Royal
family because there had been too many riding boots to clean, were
very put out at Mrs. Hamilton's arrival. They'd planned to have a party
in the basement that night, but were slightly appeased when Amanda
told them to carry on and that she wouldn't be needing dinner.

After dining in Barnes, which was safe according to Amanda,
because "one never saw anyone one knew in the suburbs," and which
didn't take long because Rupert wasn't drinking, they crept into the
house unnoticed. Downstairs the party was in full swing.

"Will Rollo have me for breaking and entering?" said Rupert
removing his tie.

Amanda didn't laugh. "You know he can't afford any scandal,"
she said putting her diamond earrings in her jewel case. "Is Helen
flying back to L. A. with you next week?"

"Yes," said Rupert. "I think she must have been to some marriage
counselor who's told her to take an interest in my career."

"Good," said Amanda, feeling the earth of the plants by the window. "Why do servants never understand about watering?"

"Why good?" snapped Rupert from inside his shirt.

"You don't want a messy divorce at the moment. You'll go down much better with the party if you have a beautiful and adoring wife."

"I go down brilliantly anyway," said Rupert, leaping on her.

"It does seem rather awful doing it in Rollo's bed."

"Not nearly as awful as not doing it."

Afterwards she lay in Rupert's arms thinking but not telling him how lovely it was to have a whole night together. Against her better judgement she was becoming increasingly fond of him. Rupert was spoiled and perfectly disgraceful but he made her laugh and then of course he was terribly attractive.

"If you get a gold will you retire?"

"Nail my whip to the wall you mean? I suppose so. I can't go on riding horses for ever."

"What are you going to do about Helen? I really do mean it. You don't want a divorce if you're going into politics.

"As long as I can have the dogs and Tab and the house, I wouldn't mind. Helen can have Marcus and the first editions and the Van Dyck."

"Will you promise to think seriously about politics after L. A.?" urged Amanda: "The P. M. was very charmed by you. If Sir William goes to the Common Market there should be a safe seat in Gloucestershire in the Autumn. You can't play around forever. An aging playboy is a pathetic sight," she went on, lying back on the pillow. "Gradually he starts drifting down to girls who are less pretty and instead of making them on the first night it takes three nights, or they decide after one night they don't like him. You're thirty-one now."

"And you think that's going to be my fate?" said Rupert coldly.

Amanda Hamilton looked at the beautiful depraved face and the marvelously lean muscular suntanned body, and her face softened.

"No, not for a long time, but I don't think an unhappy marriage, coupled with an intellectually undemanding career, are doing you any good."

Rupert took her face between hands. "I suppose you'd never think of divorcing Rollo? You and I'd be marvelous together."

Amanda blushed. "I'm far too old for you and there's Rollo's career and anyway we've got four children to educate."

"I'll educate your children," said Rupert. He glanced at the silver-framed photograph on the mantel of Amanda's eldest daughter, Georgina, and was about to say he wouldn't mind teaching her the facts of life one bit, then thought better of it. Amanda didn't like those kinds of jokes.

By now Rupert wanted her again and, getting out of bed, prowled the room looking for novelty. He could take her sitting in that pink buttonback chair, then his eye lit on the huge mirror over the chimney piece.

"What are you doing?" asked Amanda. "That looking-glass is seventeenth century. It was a wedding present from Rollo's grandmother. Been in his family for years."

"I want to see us," said Rupert, gasping under the huge weight of the mirror. He balanced it on the padded arms of the chair which he'd pulled alongside the bed.

"Can you see yourself now?" he asked Amanda.

"Not a thing."

"I'll tip it forward a bit." Rupert piled up pale blue and lilac silk cushions behind the mirror.

"For God's sake be careful," said Amanda, but she was diverted by what she saw.

The old glass was very flattering and gave a dusky warmth to her body and a golden glow to her face. She liked the way her breasts fell and the lovely curve of her waist into her hips.

"Christ, that's marvelous," said Rupert, getting on to the bed behind her. He was so tan it was almost like going to bed with a black man. Fascinated, she watched his long fingers stroking her belly, then sliding into the dark bush.

"Look how beautiful you are," he said softly, spreading back the butterfly wings of her labia. Next moment he had lifted her buttocks and driven his cock into the warm sticky cave of her vagina.

Amanda gasped.

"Nice isn't it?"

Now he was lifting her right leg, holding back the inside of her thigh so she could see the long length of his cock driving into her. It was like an express train going into a tunnel.

Madly excited, Amanda bucked back against him, feeling his fingers stroking her faster and faster.

"Come on darling, come on."

As they both came they were aware of a mighty crash. Amanda gave a shriek as, lurching forwards, the mirror hit the wooden handles of the chair and crashed to the ground in a thousand pieces.

"Now see what you've done," she said furiously. "Rollo will murder me."

Next minute she heard voices. Drunken excited Filipinos were storming up the stairs.

"Move the chair back and get into the bathroom," snapped Amanda, sliding into her nightie.

"All right Conceptione," Rupert heard her saying. "I'm afraid the mirror fell off the wall, the string must have rotted. "Hastily she shoved Rupert's glass of coke behind a cache-pot. "Bring me a broom. No, I'll clear it up. I'm fine, you go back to your party."

Three minutes later Amanda opened the door to the bathroom. "You can come out now."

Rupert could tell she was absolutely livid.

"I'll pay for it," he said.

"The money doesn't matter," she wailed. "Think of the seven year's bad luck."

"What about my gold?" he thought broodingly.

As soon as Jake returned from Dublin, Olympic panic set in. The telephone never stopped ringing with officials, press, tack manufacturers and potential sponsors who'd heard he and Fen might go professional after the games.

Because they were not rich like Rupert they had to keep taking the rest of the horses to shows right up to the last moment. In between there were endless medical tests for both horses and riders and Jake and Fen had to rush up to London to get their Olympic uniforms fitted, then on to Moss Bros. to choose coats and breeches.

Fen was livid she wasn't allowed to wear a dark blue coat. "Black's so hard," she grumbled. "Anyway I'm not going to a funeral."

"You may well think you are," said Jake, "when you see the size of the fences."

Jake was so ludicrously busy he had no time to see Helen, which, despite Malise's strictures, drove her so frantic she even called him at the barn.

"It's me, darling. Why haven't you called? Pretend this is a wrong number and call me back the minute you've got a moment."

It was almost a relief when she and Rupert flew off to Los Angeles, giving him breathing space in which he could concentrate on the job at hand. But if he worked flat out during the day, he still spent his few hours in bed worrying about the future.

Their finances were still in a precarious position. The bank needed the Mill and the stable and Tory's shares as security. The manager was very proud of Jake and his incredible come-back and often dropped his name at the golf club, but Jake knew this amiability would vanish overnight if he got into financial trouble.

Now that he had been picked for the Olympics he was an infinitely more bankable proposition, particularly as half a dozen potential sponsors were pestering him. But he didn't like any of them and he knew they'd cool off if he came home without a medal. Anyway he'd seen the appalling pressures sponsors had on Billy, Humpty and Driffield; having to take days off to open factories and turn up at parties and flatter important clients before a big class. Jake knew he didn't have the easy kind of charm or placid temperament to cope with such an invasion of his privacy. He was terrified of no longer being his own boss. It would be back to Brook Farm Riding School and Mrs. Wilton. If the sponsors owned the horses they might take them away, as Colonel Carter had taken Revenge.

More than anything he wanted to get a gold and beat Rupert. But now just as much he wanted Helen, her cool slender body and the extraordinary white hot passion he inspired in her. When he was with the horses or the family he could switch off and forget about her. But at night the pain and longing came back worse than ever.

But, how the hell could he support two households? If Helen ran off with him Rupert would see she was left penniless. Even if she got a writing job she'd have to hire someone to look after the children (if Rupert let the children go, which was unlikely). And if Jake walked out on Tory he would lose the children, Fen and the Mill, not to mention Tory and her incredible support. He'd have to find another stable and ride for another owner. And how would he divide the horses? Would he get Macaulay's front half, Tory the back?

Finally Helen worried him. She said she was prepared to live on nothing but she'd had six years with Rupert, with cleaning women to clean her beautiful house, nannies for the children, and gardeners to tend those exquisite flower beds, not to mention champagne and flowers at every four star hotel she went to. How would she cope with poverty? She had compared herself to a potted plant, wilting unwatered in a greenhouse, while the rain fell on the sweet earth outside. But how would a hothouse plant fare when faced with the winds and snows of the outside world?

He had tried to discuss this with Helen, but she was so insecure she always misconstrued this as backing off. He had thought none of this through when, tanked up with champagne, he had mailed her the blue silk handkerchief from Dublin.

On the day before he left for Los Angeles, as if in answer to a prayer, he had a telephone call from Garfield Boyson, who owned a huge video empire. Boyson was amiable, intensely tough, a lifetime lover of horses and rich enough not to be worried about money.

"I'm driving through your village at lunchtime," said his crackling voice from a car telephone. "How about a drink?"

"Too busy," said Jake: "We're leaving tomorrow."

"You'll not be too busy for this," said Boyson. "See you at the Stirrup Cup in half an hour."

Sneaking off to take leave of Mrs. C-B, thought Fen sourly, as Jake disappeared without explanation. Village boys stopped to admire Boyson's gleaming Rolls Royce, as his chauffeur nodded in the late August sunshine. Inside the bar Boyson downed a triple whisky and clawed up potato chips. His eyes, almost entirely hidden by rolls of flesh, were shrewd and kindly.

"Hello lad, what'd you like?"

"Tomato juice. I'm working," said Jake pointedly. He lit a cigarette.

"You should give up that habit," said Boyson. "L.A.'s lousy for people with bad chests."

"So I've been told."

"Worcester sauce?" asked the barmaid: "Oh it's you, Jake. Didn't see you come in. How's it going?"

"Spare," said Jake.

The barmaid looked up at the wall where she had proudly hung one of Macaulay's World Championship ribbons.

"Hope we get one from Los Angeles to join it," she said.

Jake turned to Boyson: "Well I'm sure you didn't ask me here to tell me to give up smoking."

Boyson laughed fatly. "I didn't. Sit down, lad. I've watched your career for some time. Admired your guts, the way you fought back. Admire that sparky sister-in-law of yours."

"Men tend to." Unsmilingly, Jake looked at his watch.

"Rupert's right about you," said Boyson. "Said you were as short on charm as you were on inches."

"Thanks," said Jake, draining his glass and getting to his feet.

"Sit down," said Boyson, waving a fat ringed hand. "One thing I don't want is a P.R. man. I'll not ask you to chat up customers and open shops. Just like to make things easier."

"What d'you get out of it?"

"Well not to pussyfoot around. My name in front of your horses. Boyson Macaulay. Boyson Hardy, doesn't sound bad."

"No!" said Jake.

"Wait a minute. For that I'd pick up your bills and your traveling expenses and give you a new van with my name on it. I noticed yours was falling to pieces at Crittleden. I'd even buy you some horses."

"And when we start losing?"

"We'll draw up a watertight three-year contract. All riders lose form, so do horses. I know all that. But you've always worked with second-class horses, making them into top-class ones. I'd like to see what you could do with a horse like Rocky or Clara."

Boyson had ordered more drinks, exchanging Jake's tomato juice for a large whisky. Jake drained it without noticing.

"You'd start ordering me about, expecting me to ride your way."

"I wouldn't. I might argue with you occasionally, but you'd be the boss. I don't expect you to tell me how to run my company."

"What sort of terms were you thinking about?"

"About 75 grand a year, and extra of course for the trailer and any horses."

Jake's brain reeled. This was the real big time, but his face didn't flicker.

"Not much for horses."

"Might be more—if you'd agree to another thing."

"What?"

"I've got a lad of fifteen, nice boy, but I didn't marry his mother, if you know what I mean."

"Only too well. I suffered from the same problem."

"I know. That's one of the reasons I thought you and I might get on. He's crazy about horses, wanted to be a flat race jockey, but he's grown too big. You could do with a third groom in your barn, take the pressure off. He's a good lad; admires you no end; got your picture on his wall; says you're the only rider worth bothering about."

"What if he's no good?"

"He is," said Boyson. "Believe me. His mother died recently. He needs a family."

"I'll think about it," said Jake.

"Go to Los Angeles first. I know you've had a lot of expenses. The barn'll be virtually out of action for a month. Horses may take time to get their form back, so don't worry your head about how you're going to pay for it all. Come home with a medal and we're in business."

"And if I don't?"

"We'll have to think again."

"I don't like bribery, Mr. Boyson."

"Garfield to you, and I don't like failures."

"Why don't you sponsor Rupert then?"

"Because he hasn't kept his nose clean—too many scandals, can't understand it with that beautiful wife."

"And I'm squeaky clean," said Jake getting up.

"Well at least you're discreet," said Boyson. "I haven't been able to find anything on you."

They left England on a perfect day. Tory was helping Fen with her packing upstairs. Jake was in the kitchen checking papers. Sarah had left from Stanstead airport with Hardy and Desdemona two days ago. The horses would be out of quarantine and into their Olympic quarters by the time Jake and Fen arrived.

Tory, going down to the kitchen, found Wolf on the stairs swallowing miserably, knowing he wasn't included.

"Nor am I, darling," she said stroking his rough brindle head. "We'll have to look after each other."

Jake looked out the window at the soft russet stables. The willows round the mill-pond were already touched with yellow, and the mill stream dried to a trickle. Last night he'd watched a rippling arrow of migrating wild geese spread out across the sky. Now the house martins were taking up their positions on the telegraph wire.

"Look at those birds in a row," said Darklis. "What are they doing?"

"They're practicing leaving," said Jake.

Perhaps that's what he ought to be doing. The martins would be gone by the time he came home. With an aching feeling of sadness and anticipated homesickness, he looked at his tawny fields and his stables with the horses looking out of the half-doors, all knowing something was up, except Macaulay, who had turned away sulking.

If only he could have afforded to take Tory and the children. If he accepted Boyson's sponsorship he'd be able to do things like that. Tory wouldn't have to work herself into the ground; she and the kids could have new clothes. Then in his pocket he felt the tansy that Helen had had specially made for him in gold—for luck. He'd given Helen the handkerchief; there was no way he could go back now.

Tory came into the kitchen.

"Fen's ready. You ought to be off soon," she said. "I wish you'd have some lunch. I've made you a quiche, and some sandwiches for the journey. I splurged and put smoked salmon in them."

He shook his head, half-smiling. "We get dinner at the hotel tonight." They were flying at crack of dawn tomorrow. He turned to Darklis. "Go and tell Fen we're leaving in ten minutes."

As soon as she'd gone, he drew Tory close to him, cradling her round, tired, kind, unmade-up face between his hands, smoothing back the lank mousebrown hair she'd had no time to wash.

"Don't," she mumbled into his shoulder. "I look awful. I'm going on a crash diet. I'll be thin when you come home."

He put his arms around her, feeling her comforting solidity.

"I won't expect you to call," she said in a not quite steady voice. "Malise has told me what lines from L.A. are going to be like. Just call if you can, but we'll all be thinking of you."

For a second they clung together. Suddenly he wished she was his mother, wise and everloving, that he could always come back to, even though he was committing himself to Helen. With uneasy premonition he thought this might be the last time he saw her.

"Wish you were coming."

"I wish I was too. Take me next time."

"I love you," he said truthfully and for he first time. He'd just have to sort everything out after the games.

As they went out into the yard he saw she was crying. To distract him she said, "You must go and say goodbye to Macaulay."

Macaulay had his back to the door. As Jake approached he flattened his ears. Jake went into the stall. "I'm sorry, boy—I know how you feel. I'm as disappointed as you are."

"We'll be landing in forty minutes," said the stewardess. "Can I have eight autographs for the crew?"

Fen fled to the toilet, desperately putting on makeup in case, by some miracle, Dino had come to meet her at the airport. When she came back they were still flying across the desert and Ivor was still struggling with the quick crossword in the *Daily Mirror* which he'd started the moment they left Heathrow. Jake seemed increasingly up-tight. Perhaps he was wondering if Helen would meet them.

Suddenly there was Los Angeles and her tiredness seemed to dis-appear as she looked down at the great turquoise expanse of ocean and the platinum blond beaches. She could even see the flecking of the breakers. Now they were flying over a vast checkerboard of streets, houses, gardens and brilliant blue swimming pools, and skyscrapers glittering in the midday sun, and the great network of freeways superimposed like arteries. The horizon was bordered by a thick muzzy browny-grey smog curtain.

Jake fingered his gold tansy, trying to keep his nerves in check. This is Dino's country, thought Fen in ecstasy, I've finally made it.

"I can see Robert Redford and Donald Duck," she screamed lean-ing across Ivor.

"Where, where?" he said, gazing out of the window.

"Go back to your crossword." she said soothingly. "You might even finish it by the time we get through customs."

Customs seemed to take longer than the flight. Outside, the heat from the scorching Californian sun hit them like a knock-out punch.

"We'll be microwaved," moaned Fen.

"We'll never jump in this," said Jake to himself.

Waiting for them, wearing nothing but sneakers, jagged denim shorts and a baseball cap was Rupert. He was so brown he almost made the black ground staff look white.

"Welcome to L.A.," he said mockingly. "As part of Malise's new solidarity drive, and because Big Mal himself is in a meeting, I've come to welcome you all. Security is a nightmare."

"Did the horses travel all right?" asked Jake.

"Eventually. The crates didn't fit, and they had to wait for hours to load, and the flight took thirty-three hours." Then, seeing Jake's look of utter horror, he went on, "but they're all fine and out of quaran-tine. Hardy's already bitten Malise, so he must be feeling OK."

"Can we go straight to the stables?"

Rupert looked surprised. "If you feel up to it."

Fen sometimes wished Jake wasn't quite so conscientious. She was dying for a bath and a change, in case she bumped into Dino.

As they drove along in the car Rupert had rented, not a breath of wind stirred the palm trees.

"Is this the roosh hour?" asked Ivor nervously.

"This is nothing." said Rupert briskly passing a Cadillac on the inside, then nipping around a Pontiac. "Once you've negotiated the freeway in the rush hour the individual competition will seem like falling off a log."

"How far are the stables from the Olympic village?" asked Jake.

"Well that's another slight problem," said Rupert. "About a ninety minute drive on the Olympic bus."

"Shit," said Jake, exchanging looks of horror with Fen.

"I'm lucky," said Rupert, not without a certain complacency. "Helen and I are staying with friends in Arcadia, so I'm only five minutes from the show ground."

"Nice house?" said Fen, aware that Jake was beginning to look really fed up.

"Terribly quiet," said Rupert blithely, "Only thing you can hear at night is the occasional splash as an overripe avocado falls into the swimming pool."

No one could fault the stables. They were huge and airy, with push-button doors, air conditioning in the stalls, and water playing on the roof all day to keep the temperature at 65 degrees. They were also banned to the press. The grooms slept in dormitories overhead.

Sarah, who'd dyed her hair red, white and blue, was thrilled to see them. "The talent is fantastic," she said to Fen. "I've just been asked out by a Mexican rider called Jesus."

Desdemona was even more delighted to see Fen. The horse looked so small in the huge stall. As she cuddled her and checked her for bumps and bruises, Fen, trying to keep her voice steady, asked Sarah, "Has the American team arrived yet?"

"Mary Jo and Lizzie Dean arrived this morning. But Carl Kennedy and Mr. Ferranti," Sarah winked at Dizzy who was looking over the half-door, "aren't due until tomorrow night."

"Hi Fen," said Dizzy. "Evidently Dino's swept all before him this year. Manny hasn't had a fence down in three months. He's hot favorite for the Individual Gold."

"So eat your heart out, Mr. Campbell-Black," said Sarah.

"Don't be unpatriotic, dear," said Dizzy.

Both of them had already acquired golden suntans. Dizzy was wearing Union Jack shorts. They made Fen feel drabber and tireder than ever. At that moment Malise rolled up, svelte as usual in a cream suit and a panama with an old Rugbeian hatband.

"You've made it. Don't hang about here too long. You need some sleep. When you're ready I'll take you back to the Olympic village and we'll sort out your security badges. Better sleep in them. After tomorrow you won't be allowed anywhere without them."

After an hour and a half's drive back to the Olympic village in a non-air conditioned bus, which just dumped them outside the male and female sectors, Jake could see exactly why Rupert had found a house in Arcadia. Having been issued his security badge, which had his name, a photograph, nationality, and the classes for which he was entered, he had to fight his way through the tightest security. It took ages to find his room as the guards on each floor all had to check where he was going. Finally tracking it down, he discovered he was sharing not with Ivor but with two weightlifters, who were fortunately out on the town. Apart from three beds, the room included three small chests of drawers, a closet, a shower, a hot plate and a fridge. He supposed they daren't provide an oven in case someone put his head in it.

He was dripping with sweat, but it wasn't just the heat. Looking outside, he was suddenly aware of the number of security vans prowling around between the scorched yellow lawns with their sprinkling of palm trees, and the helicopters and airplanes overhead, all part of the largest security operation ever mounted in peacetime.

The tough guys with their guns and their German accents at the gate, the bare institutional corridors, the guards seated on every floor, the smell of fear, the anonymity, all unnerved him, and reminded him of the orphanage.

Overwhelmed with homesickness and claustrophobia he started to unpack. Underneath the beautifully ironed shirts and his new red coat, he found a pile of telegrams and good luck cards he hadn't seen. There was also a letter from Tory.

"Darling, I'm missing you almost before you've gone. When you get this, you'll be in L.A. on the way to the greatest adventure of your life. Please don't be scared, and *please* eat properly. Don't worry, remember you're still the World Champion and the greatest rider in the world. Give a kiss to Hardy. The presents are from the children. All my love Tory."

One parcel contained a black china cat with a horseshoe around its neck. The other a toothbrush which had a glass bubble on the end containing a tiny model of Mickey Mouse, and a bell which rang when you brushed your teeth.

One of the telegrams was from Garfield Boyson, another from Eleanor Blenkinsop. Feeling much happier, Jake undressed, showered and fell into his first dreamless sleep in weeks.

"It's too awful," grumbled Fen the next morning. "I'm sharing with Grisel and an enormous lady discus thrower of very questionable sexuality who snored all night. The corridors are swarming with security guards. I could do with one in the room for protection, except there isn't room for the three of us as it is. Grisel is already making eyes at a beefy cyclist in the next room, and on the other side there are three event riders who keep saying 'must go and call Mummy.'" She giggled. Nothing really mattered today except that she would see Dino.

They were cheered up by more telegrams downstairs, although Jake was slightly daunted to find three long, rather hysterical letters from Helen, saying how much she was missing him, and would he make contact as soon as possible. Then they explored the Olympic village. Jake was appalled by the sheer noise and size. There were sports shops, hairdressers, movie theaters, saunas, swimming pools, even a disco, and too many souvenir shops and televisions everywhere. He'd expected a kind of monastic retreat. It was going to be about as easy to distance oneself here as in a monkey house.

Fen was almost more appalled in the souvenir shop to see posters of Dino on sale. In one he had a terrific suntan, looked too ludicrously glamorous for words and was wearing a pale grey shirt. In another he was jumping Manny wearing the U.S. red coat with the sky blue collar. In horror she watched two American girl gymnasts buy copies of both.

"Look" said Jake to distract her, "there's Sebastian Coe."

"And there's Daley Thompson," said Fen in awe.

Then they went to a meeting called by Malise. The plan, he said, was that from tomorrow the team would rise at four in the morning, drive down to the stables and work the horses from six to eight, then leave them to rest during the punishing midday heat. Then the grooms would walk them around to loosen them up for an hour or so in the cool of the evening. During the day the riders' time would be more or less their own, except for the odd meeting or press conference. Beach barbecues, endless parties, trips to Disneyland, Hollywood or Las Vegas were also offered. Malise wanted them to relax, enjoy themselves, stick together and save the adrenalin for the competitions. It was now Saturday. The opening ceremony was tomorrow, the individual competition a week from Monday and the team event the Sunday after that.

That evening, Malise continued, the Eriksons, with whom Rupert and Helen were staying in Arcadia, had invited the British and the American teams to a barbecue at their house. The information threw both Fen and Jake into a panic. Jake was longing to see Helen, but he didn't want a hassle. Dublin had been a nightmare, worrying all the time whether Rupert suspected anything. He didn't want Los Angeles to be a repeat.

Fen, having showered about fifty times, couldn't put on her makeup. She was shaking so much her eyeliner kept leaving her eyelashes and shooting up the lid. She totally gave up on lipstick. She wore new baggy pink-striped jeans with a pale pink T-shirt.

Grisel, who was exchanging even hotter glances with the cyclist next door begged off the evening saying she was still jet lagged. Luckily, after two more stints on the non-air conditioned bus, Malise had rented a car to drive the team around. As the Eriksons' house was only five minutes from the stables, they decided to check the horses on the way to the barbecue. Shadows of palm trees were beginning to stripe the road, but it was still punishingly hot. Even Desdemona seemed listless.

"Probably still suffering from travel sickness," said Malise reassuringly.

Perhaps Dino would be suffering from jet lag too, thought Fen, and wouldn't feel like a party. But next minute she saw Carl Kennedy going past in dark glasses, so Dino must as least have arrived. Frantically she checked her face in the depths of Desdemona's stall.

Outside she met Rupert, who pulled out the seat of her voluminous jeans, peered inside and asked if she was "reduced to wearing Tory's cast-offs," which did nothing to increase her self–confidence.

"Come on," he said. "Malise is champing at the bit. Not that he'll get any dinner before midnight, Suzy Erikson is so disorganized."

As they reached Malise's rented car, Fen said:

"There's Mary Jo."

Mary Jo was wearing a white T-shirt with "Carl Kennedy for President" printed in large blue letters across the front. "Wait," she called out to them. Close up she looked red-eyed and distraught.

"My dear child," said Malise concerned. "What's the matter?"

"It's Dino," she sobbed.

"What's happened to him?" said Fen in horror.

"Manny went ape on the plane. They think he may have been stung by something. It was Dino's plane. He was flying it. He wanted to crash land in the desert, but he was transporting Carl's horses as well and there was the chance he might have killed the lot of them, the terrain was so rocky, so he had to shoot Manny,"

"Christ" said Rupert, appalled. "Surely they could have tranked him?"

"They tried. It didn't make any difference."

"Where's Dino now?" asked Malise.

"Dropped off Carl's two horses and then flew Manny's body back home."

"Who's he riding now?" asked Jake, who was looking absolutely shattered.

"Nothing," sobbed Mary Jo. "That's what makes it so awful. Manny was our star horse, right, but he was really Dino's only horse. His father'd been ill and he was letting the place run down."

"Won't he come to the games at all?" whispered Fen.

"He told Carl he couldn't face it, not after all those years and years of hard work. And he just adored Manny. I tried to call him at his place just now, but his mother said he was too upset to talk to anyone."

"Surely he can ride someone else's horse?" said Rupert "He's easily your best rider."

Mary Jo allowed herself a faint smile.

"Thanks," she said.

"Well almost," said Rupert.

"Dino wouldn't do that to anyone—take their horse off them at this stage, knowing how much work they'd put in."

"Seems crazy to me," said Rupert. "If I was your chef d'equipe I'd put him on one of Carl's horses."

"I'm awfully sorry," said Malise. "I'll write to him tomorrow. It's heartbreaking."

"But extremely fortuitous for us," said Rupert in an undertone, as Mary Jo moved out of earshot to tell Ludwig and Hans.

"That was totally uncalled for," snapped Malise. "Dino was definitely in the running for the Gold."

"Exactly," said Rupert. "We had better go and have some dinner."

"I think I'll go back to the village," said Fen in a high flat voice. "Jet lag's suddenly got to me. After all it is four in the morning in England."

"Oh come on darling," said Rupert. "Come and see this amazing place. They've even got jacuzzis in the dog kennel. A couple of Bloodies and a good steak and you'll feel on top of the world."

"Honestly I'm exhausted," said Fen, who'd gone terribly white.

"Are you sure?" said Jake, who also seemed stunned by the news about Manny, "I'll come back with you."

"No I'll be fine."

Back at the Olympic village Fen had to climb four flights of stairs, because some Ghanaian athletes, who'd never been in an elevator before, were spending all day riding up and down. Despite her talk of jet lag, Grisel, thank God, was not in the room. As she slumped on the bed, Fen felt the Games had lost any importance. If she blew it next Monday, or the following Sunday, what did it matter.

Poor Dino, she kept whispering, oh poor, poor Dino. In a daze she got out her writing case. Donald Duck paper didn't seem suitable, nor a postcard of an athlete running with the Olympic torch. She tore a page out of her diary, headed December—appropriately wintry, some day in the future, when life didn't matter any more.

"Dearest Dino," she wrote, "I just heard about Manny. I can't think of anything to say except I'm sorry. I loved him too. I know what you're going through. I can't think of anything to say about my behavior last winter, except I'm sorry too about that. With all my love, Fen."

Walking down the four flights of stairs again, she mailed the letter before she had time to change her mind.

The Eriksons lived in a beautiful ranch-style house, which had once been an avocado farm, and which was now converted into the most exquisite garden, with clematis, morning glory and bougainvillaea growing up every tree. Behind reared the mountains, snow-capped and often blacked out by thunderstorms or rain storms but seldom affecting the perfect weather in the valley.

Rupert went into the house and kissed his beautiful hostess with whom he had once been on intimate terms. She was wearing a sopping wet yellow bikini and drinking a Margarita.

"Helen's by the pool," said Suzy Erikson. "Have you any idea how many are coming so I can warn Annunciata?"

"Well, the American team isn't coming," said Rupert, "Nor are either of our women riders, although you'd hardly call Grisel a woman!"

Then he told Suzy about Dino. She was shattered.

"Oh poor Dino, and there goes our chance of a Gold. That's tough, that's real tough."

"What is?" said Helen from the doorway.

She was wearing the briefest of dark blue bikinis that she would have thought absolutely shocking eight months ago in Kenya, and a blue spotted silk scarf tying back her hair. It was the first time Rupert had ever known her tanned; it brought out the amber of her eyes and the wonderful slenderness of her body.

"What's tough?" she said.

"Your lover's had an accident," drawled Rupert.

"What d'you mean?" said Helen aghast. "What are you talking about?" She gripped on to the door handle for support, her knuckles whitening. Fortunately Rupert had turned to the bar and was pouring out some Perrier.

"His prize horse threw a fit on the plane and had to be shot—so I'm afraid he's not coming to the Games. Tough, huh?"

"Is he hurt?" said Helen, trying to keep her voice steady.

"Nothing broken except his heart, according to Mary Jo."

Helen, as though sleepwalking, found one of the leather sofas flanking the fire and sat down very suddenly on it.

"Could I have a drink please?"

Her mind was galloping: where was Jake? had he flown home already, without getting in touch? did horses mean that much to him? Her heart seemed to be crashing against her rib cage.

"I guess Manny was insured," said Suzy Erikson examining her backview in the long mirror. "I wonder if I ought to get my bottom lifted."

"Only by me," said Rupert, putting a hand under her buttocks.

"If he's not coming," said Helen shakily, "Fen'll have to jump."

Letting go of Suzy, Rupert looked at her irritably. "Are you that out of touch? Since when did Fen ride for the American team? I'm talking about Dino Ferranti, your admirer, remember? What d'you want to drink?"

"Oh poor poor Dino," said Helen shaking like a leaf at the terrible gaffe she'd nearly committed.

Rupert and Suzy were having drinks by the pool when Jake, Malise and Ivor arrived. Several other handsome golden-tanned Californian couples had also turned up. A splendid blonde was gambolling in the blue-green water. Helen was lying in a hammock still in her bikini. She wanted Jake to see how good she looked.

"Hi Ivor." She got out of the hammock and kissed him. "How was the flight?"

Ivor went scarlet and mumbled something about it being "Joost fine." Then Helen kissed Malise, which gave her the perfect excuse to kiss Jake too. Putting her face against his cheek on the side away from Rupert, she whispered, "I love you" in his ear. The smell of hot flesh, suntain oil and Helen sent his senses reeling.

He was astonished afresh by her amazing beauty. All his doubts fled. How could he ever live without her? He felt as though he was walking straight through the celluloid of a Hollywood soap opera and plucking out the heroine. He had little time to talk to her, however. Malise, who wanted to squash a romance which he had grimly suspected was developing in Dublin, sat down on the hammock and proceeded to monopolize Helen. Ivor was soon frolicking in the pool and roaring his head off playing with the blonde and a large yellow rubber duck. Jake was saved by his host Albie, an English expatriate mad about show-jumping, who seemed to know every horse Jake had ever owned.

More people arrived, all very beautiful. Jake wished Californians weren't so tall; they made him feel like a midget. Rupert, not drinking, was working off his excess energy in mixed doubles on the floolit tennis court.

"You are horribly unchivalrous," grumbled the brunette playing against him, as she leapt out of the way of one of his thunderbolt serves. "Gentlemen are supposed to ease up when they serve to a lady."

Jake would like to have swum but he felt far too pale and puny to take his shirt off in this company, let alone display his scarred and wasted legs. Helen was still trapped by Malise and now, as well, by some film director.

"Must go and see if everything's OK in the kitchen," said Albie. "Come and meet Paul and Carol. He writes screen plays. She acts in them."

Paul and Carol were polite, but obviously much more interested in ensuring that Carol got the biggest part and Paul's screenplay was not tampered with than in the Olympic riders. Others joined them. Jake felt gauche and out of place. This lotusland depressed him utterly, knowing he could never conjure up paradises like this for Helen.

Wandering into the living room, he picked up the latest copy of *Chronicle of the Horse* wondering whether to get a taxi back to the village. Malise didn't look like he'd be leaving for hours and there was no sign of dinner.

"Is the heat getting to you?" said Suzy Erickson, curling up beside him on the leather sofa.

"A little."

"Why don't you swim?"

"I'd rather watch."

"You would, wouldn't you? You're the stillest man I've ever met."

"Besides," he added wryly, "I've got a lousy physique."

Suzy ran her eyes over him. "I wouldn't say that. You've certainly got something."

"An empty glass for a start."

"Let me freshen it."

"No thanks, I've got to get up at four o'clock tomorrow morning to exercise my horse."

"What d'you do after that?"

"Our time is pretty much our own."

"Then I'll come and pick you up and drive you into the mountains."

"The entire team?"

"No just you," she said softly.

"You're making a pass at me?"

"Right. Haven't you heard how up front Californian women are? And I find you very attractive . . ."

"I'm married," said Jake.

"Your wife can't be very smart letting you come over here on your own."

"She would have come if we could have afforded it."

"Feeling homesick, huh?"

Jake shrugged. "A little."

"I'm real good at curing that. I'd really like to spend some time with you."

With a glorious feeling of irresponsibility, Jake looked at the depraved little face with its gleaming catlike eyes, and long dark hair as coarse and shiny as Macaulay's mane. She had changed out of her bikini and beneath the pale beige string vest the curvy body with its high full breasts was perfectly visible. He suddenly thought how nice it would be to take off into the mountains with her, over the hills and far away, and junk all his problems.

"That," he said, "is one of the nicest offers I've ever had, but I've actually come to L.A. to jump fences, not into bed with beautiful ladies. That's my chef d'equipe out there and he's very hot on abstinence."

Suzy laughed. "He hasn't had much success with Rupe."

"Rupert's different. He doesn't suffer from nerves. I've got to distance myself."

"I've got a marvelous shrink, if you've got anxiety problems. He really sorted out Nastase. He claims you've got to be filled with both anger and calm."

"He should start with Hardy, my horse," said Jake, "He's the one like Nastase."

"Suzy," said a sharp voice, "Annunciata wants to know whether you want to start with the Gambetta?"

It was Helen.

"Oh, you tell her. You're so good at that sort of thing."

"No, you tell her," snapped Helen. "People are starving."

When Suzy had left the room Helen brought Jake another whisky: "Lousy hostess. Can't even freshen people's drinks. That woman's a nympho."

"Shame," said Jake. "I thought it was my personal magnetism."

"What did she want?" said Helen quickly.

"To take me to the mountains."

Helen went white.

"And I refused very politely," Jake went on, "because there's only one woman I want to take anywhere. You look so beautiful, it's a shame to spoil it by sulking."

"You were flirting with her."

"I was putting Malise and Rupert off the scent, and you weren't doing so badly on the hammock."

"Where's Fen?"

"Shattered about Dino."

Helen then told Jake about mistaking Dino for him.

"You can't imagine how I overreacted. It was awful. I nearly gave us away."

"How did Rupert react?"

"I'm not sure. If anything I guess he thinks I'm upset because Dino's not coming."

"Well let him go on thinking that. All the same we must be careful." He told her about the possibility of the Boyson sponsorship. "It would go halfway to solving all our problems. But I must keep my nose clean until the contracts are signed."

"But we can meet during the day. Rupert's out so much."

He shook his head. "Too risky. Everyone knows your face over here. The place is swarming with press, desperate for a new angle. I don't want it to be us. You've just got to hack it until after the games."

Helen's lip quivered. "I don't think I'll survive."

"You've got to," he said more sharply than he intended, "there's too much at stake, our whole future."

A shadow fell across them. It was Rupert. Before either of them could say anything he shouted down the hall, "For Christ sake Suzy, can't we have dinner? I'm going to pass out."

"If you want instant guacamole go jump on an avocado in the garden," said Suzy, wandering in waving a three-pronged fork. "There's steak, swordfish, salmon, smoked chicken and red snapper, so you won't go hungry. It'll be ready in two minutes."

"I suppose we could always barbecue Jake," said Rupert.

Jake got to his feet. "You did that once already," he said in a voice that made Helen shiver. "At St. Augustine's if you remember," and he limped out to talk to Malise.

"You were so vile about that guy before he arrived, I knew I'd find him attractive," said Suzy.

Having finally fallen asleep at 3:30 Jake had to get up jangling with nerves and hangover an hour later. Speeding along the fast lane reserved for car pools, Malise, not used to fierce power braking, kept producing appalling screeches like a butchered pig every time he tried to slow down. Even worse, sitting between Jake and Fen, taking up almost the entire back seat, Grisel grimly ate her way through two huge fried egg sandwiches.

As Jake gave Hardy the gentlest of workouts in the already punishing heat, he realized Rupert's horse Rock Star was hardly sweating. And while Jake felt dislocated and woolly headed from lack of sleep, Rupert, despite his late night, seemed utterly together. By leaving ahead of the pack, not only had he acclimatized his horses to the heat and humidity, but also adjusted his time clock as well.

Fen walked Desdemona beside Jake.

"She's very down," she said.

Like her mistress, thought Jake noticing her swollen eyes but making no comment. Ivor was worried about his horse John.

"It's like sitting on a dead log."

All around them other nations were crashing their wringing wet horses over massive combinations on what was plainly very hard ground.

Later in the day Malise called another meeting. Rupert rolled up in a pale blue track suit, like Rock Star hardly sweating after a four-mile jog along the beach.

"The great problem with the Olympic Games is peaking too soon," said Malise. "Now you're in L.A. you feel you must be doing something to prepare yourself and your horse. You see other teams popping their horses over all sorts of different kinds of fences, and think they've got inside information, but you can be sure no one will know anything until we walk the course on Monday week. If I were you I'd concentrate on work on the flat, and jump your horses as little as possible. Let them rest, relax and enjoy yourselves and have fun."

"I'd rather have Fen," said Rupert, who'd also noticed her red eyes.

As they came out of the meeting they bumped into Ludwig and Hans, who'd just been looking at the Olympic swimming pool.

"Did you know it vos specially built for zee Oleempics?" said Hans.

"So was that girl," said Rupert, as a spectacularly blonde and voluptuous Rumanian athlete loped past them without a backward glance. "Bet I can bed her before the games are over."

"How much?" said Ludwig.

"Hundred bucks."

"Done."

The event that saved Fen from utter despair was the opening ceremony that afternoon. Everyone had been cynical about the American hype beforehand—particularly Rupert who made Helen furious with his persistently disparaging remarks. But somehow, despite the Antony and Cleopatra set, the girls in hot pants with their silver balloons, the 85 males bashing away at *Porgy and Bess* on their grand pianos, and the President grinning like a puppet, the whole thing worked.

There was a big row beforehand. Rupert had removed the Olympic badge from his blue blazer and had the trousers narrowed to drainpipe proportions. Fen had shortened her skirt. Grisel had put on so much weight that she kept popping buttons and the skirt of her dress was so stretched there weren't any pleats left. Ivor had typically ordered trousers too small, so the cuffs skimmed his ankles and a blazer so big it hung like a peasant's smock.

"You're all a bloody disgrace, except Jake," snapped Malise. "Let's hope you can lose yourselves among the rest of the British athletes."

After all the razzmatazz, it seemed the athletes might be ignored, but on they came in alphabetical order to tumultuous cheers from the amazingly over-adrenalized and happy croud. There were Mexicans in big hats, and Africans in national costume, and the French incredibly chic in couture-designed clothes, and the English very formal, with the sexes sharply defined.

"You can tell Rupert's been in the army," said Fen, watching his straight-backed march. Jake tried to disguise his limp as much as possible.

"Thank God we're jumping out in Arcadia and not in front of a crowd as big as this," said Fen looking at the endless sea of faces.

Huge cheers greeted China and Rumania and everyone stood up. Then, on a note of crazy informality, the American athletes came on to an earsplitting roar. They all wore tracksuits, so, unlike other countries, there was no division of the sexes. Joyous as otters they swarmed, rowdy and exuberant, in total disarray. All carried cameras and were soon snapping away at one another and the other teams and the stadium, then fighting their way through to the other side of the parade to photograph Mom in the stands.

Even when the black athlete came on carrying the Olympic torch on the last lap, there was doubt whether she'd ever make it, as the U.S. team swayed around her clicking away like pressmen.

"The Marx brothers seem to have taken over," said Rupert.

But finally the torch was lit with the little flame all the way from Greece and, after the endless speeches, thousands of doves of peace fluttered into the blue.

"I hope you'll take note," hissed Fen to Rupert, "and stop bitching at Jake."

Then the beautiful girl singer stood up and started belting out "Reach out and touch" and everyone was breaking formation and kissing each other and shaking hands. Fen found herself kissed by Rupert, and three times by Ivor.

"O Christ, here comes Grisel," said Rupert. "I'm off. One must draw the line somewhere."

"I told you not to wear mascara," said Jake as Fen wiped her eyes.

And suddenly it got to her—the Olympic ideal. Despite the sniping, the commercialism, the chauvinism and the heartbreak, here she was in Los Angeles carrying her own torch for Britain in front of this wonderful, friendly, deeply moved, appreciative crowd.

For a few minutes her misery over Dino and over Jake and Helen was put aside as she realized suddenly the magnitude of her achievement, that at nineteen she'd been picked to ride for Britain. For without all the competitors, there would be no competition. And if there weren't people prepared to lose bravely and with a good grace, there wouldn't be any winner. True greatness was the ability to pick yourself up from the floor.

"Isn't this your best moment ever?" she whispered to Jake. He nodded, too moved to speak.

"It'll be even better when we go home with the team gold, and the gold, silver and bronze in the individual," said Rupert. "Oh look there's my Rumanian," and, shoving through the crowd, he grabbed her. For a second she gazed at him with her slant-eyed impassive Slav face, then the crowd shoved them together, and he was kissing her.

"First base," said Jake, wondering if Helen was looking.

"Ludwig's going to lose that bet," said Fen. "Can't you hear the clang of iron curtains dropping?"

After the ceremonies they met Helen, who'd been watching with the Eriksons.

"Wasn't it wonderful?" said Fen. "You must feel jolly proud to be American."

Tolerant suddenly, because Dino not coming to the games had made her even more aware of the agonies of being in love, she moved aside to introduce herself to the Eriksons and apologize for not being able to make it the other night, leaving Helen and Jake a moment alone together.

"I was watching you the whole time," whispered Helen, her eyes glowing. "Conscious of your every single moment, so proud that you finally made it here after all those setbacks, knowing you'd be thinking of me."

Jake felt once again the great weight of her love.

*T*hey had eight days to kill before the Individual event. It was a bit like being on holiday, knowing war was going to break out any minute. Grisel sweated and became more and more bad-tempered. Fen wilted, Ivor fell asleep on the beach and woke up scarlet down one side of his face. Jake, being dark-skinned, fared better. For the first time in his life he was really brown. Suzy Erikson was never off the telephone. Rupert went water skiing, racing, surfing, pursued Miss Rumania, and played endless games of poker with Ludwig, Count Guy, Carl Kennedy and Wishbone to the despair of their chefs d'equipes who felt that each team should stick together. At every game, honoring Dino's absence, they left an empty chair. But he didn't show up.

Fen kept hearing bits of news of him. There was a huge piece headlined "The Agony of Dino Ferranti" in the *Los Angeles Times* the day after Manny was shot. Carl Kennedy had also spoken briefly to him on the telephone.

"I guess he's still in shock," he said. "I offered him Whittier to ride, but he's just not interested."

Yet countless times a day Fen looked in her pigeon hole at the Olympic village, hoping that among the telegrams and cards from wellwishers there might be a letter from him.

Jake had frightful trouble sleeping in the Olympic village. The weightlifters were so fed up with his chain-smoking that they made him go outside and smoke in the passage. Often he didn't bother to go to bed at all, just stayed up watching television. Once Ivor discovered you could watch cartoons all night, Malise had great difficulty getting him to bed as well.

Malise organized a team trip to Disneyland, and Fen had to hold Ivor's hand when he got scared in the haunted house and during the pirates' battle, and calm him down when he became overexcited after shaking hands with Mickey Mouse. In amazement Fen gazed at the massive overweight Americans, stuffing themselves with hamburgers, hot dogs and ice cream, and exhorting her through capacious mouthfuls to "Have a nice day."

"Have you ever seen people so fat?" she whispered to Jake. "D'you think Grisel's got any Los Angeles blood?"

"No," said Rupert overhearing, "Grisel's far too unpleasant. They remind me more of your wife, Jake."

Just for a second Fen thought Jake was going to spring at Rupert.

"Don't rise," she pleaded, putting a hand on Jake's arm.

Everywhere they went they were mobbed by autograph hunters, mostly Americans who had no idea who they were, but who were obsessed with anything Olympic. Rupert, because of his dazzling looks, his beautiful American wife, and his earlier successes on the American circuit was the one whom they recognized. But not always.

"I know you," screamed a woman with blue hair as they were leaving Disneyland, "you're in television?"

"No, I'm in shorts," snapped Rupert.

Rupert kept up his jogging every morning and was soon joined by Miss Rumania. Progress was obviously being made. After a week he produced a pair of pale blue panties for Ludwig. "That tag inside says 'Made in Rumania'."

"How do ve know?" grumbled Ludwig. "I don't speak Rumanian. It might say somezing quite different, like made in Los Angeles."

"It's Miss Rumania who's being made in Los Angeles," said Rupert.

"Vot is her English like?" asked Hans.

"Non-existent, thank God," said Rupert. "But she thinks our vicked capitalist vays are absolutely marvelous!"

The eight days dragged by. Gradually Hardy and Desdemona seemed to be coming together, as Fen and Jake waited on tenterhooks to see which three British riders would be selected from the five to jump in the Individual. The Americans went on winning medals by the bucketful in every contest and the Star Spangled Banner was played over and over again, the commentators reached new levels of chauvinistic hysteria. They seemed hardly to recognize that other countries existed. There was a hardening of purpose among the British team.

On Friday, to break the monotony, they had a mock competition—two rounds then a jump off. Carl Kennedy riding his dark brown mare, Scarlett O'Hara, beat everyone by five seconds in the jump off.

"Either he's an idiot or that mare is phenomenally fit," said Rupert. "If it's the latter, we're all in trouble."

Hardy, overfresh and full of himself from his long rest, knocked a fence down in the first round, but Jake was very pleased with him. Rocky jumped superbly. Apart from one silly mistake in the jump off, he didn't put a hoof wrong. Desdemona, also in tremendous form, came fourth, sailing over the fences with all her old bounce, somewhat reviving Fen's spirits.

"All right," said Malise. "That's the team for the individual: Rupert, Jake and Fen."

Fen didn't dare look at Grisel.

Arriving at the stables on Saturday, however, Fen found Sarah with a long face. Desdemona couldn't put her near hind down. She must have bruised it.

Fen, Sarah and Jake stayed up all night, poulticing her foot and trying to reduce the swelling, walking her out to test the stiffness under the huge Los Angeles stars. By morning Fen thought she was all right. The British vet and the American national vet thought otherwise, and went into a huddle with Malise. Fen felt her presence was purely incidental.

"She's stiff behind and there's swelling. I think she may have chipped a bone," said the national vet.

"She needs at least a week's rest," said the British vet.

"A week," said Fen, aghast. "That rules out the team event too."

"I guess so," said the American. "I'll have another look on Friday in case you've wrought miracles, but I'm afraid tomorrow is definitely out."

For Fen, who'd been up all night, it was too much.

"Fucking bureaucrats," she screamed. "You don't know a bloody horse from your elbows. Give her a shot of bute. She'll be fine. She's often stiff in the morning."

The American vet, nettled, accused Fen of treating her horse like a machine.

Jake and Sarah took Fen's part, and a very undignified yelling match ensued, listened to with glee by all the surrounding grooms and riders, who were frantically translating for one another.

Finally Malise removed Fen by the scruff of the neck and took her off for a cup of coffee in a quiet corner of the British Supporters Club.

"You must pull yourself together," he told her.

"There's nothing left of myself to pull," sobbed Fen. "Desdemona's OK. She's my horse. I ought to know."

"When you see the course tomorrow," said Malise gently, "you'll understand. You might get by in a Nations' Cup or in a Grand Prix, but Desdemona's forte is speed, not huge daunting fences, which she'd really have to stretch herself to get over. I know you love that pony, but I can't let you ride if you're going to be nervous about pushing her every inch of the way."

"Everyone goes on and on about winning not being important and that taking part's all that matters. I'm not even allowed to take part."

"You've got years ahead."

"But I may never get a horse as good as Des."

"If you don't ruin her tomorrow, you'll probably have a chance of another two cracks at the Olympics on her. How would you live with yourself if you jumped her and lost her for good, like poor Dino?"

At the mention of his name, Fen put her head down on the table and sobbed her heart out. "I've tried, truly I have, I've tried to be cheerful. I've taken Ivor to Disneyland three times. But I did hope to see Dino. We were a bit close once."

Malise patted her shoulder. "I know how you were looking forward to seeing him, and now this. It's wretched."

"Can I fly home?"

Malise shook his head. "That's not part of the deal. You're still reserve. If anything happens to any of the others you'll have to jump their horses. I'll need your help tomorrow to see how the course is riding, to cheer us all up. Grisel isn't any good at that. She'll be sulking because I haven't picked her."

"You must be joking," said Fen. "I've been as cheerful as a corpse the last few months."

"And I need you to look after Jake, keep him calm. I think he's missing Tory?" Malise raised an eyebrow. Fen had the feeling he was fishing.

"Yes," she said. "I'm sure he is."

The same afternoon Rupert went racing with Ludwig and Guy. Jake broke his vow and, submitting to Helen's pleading, drove her into the mountains. Looking for wild flowers he was reminded of the picnic he had had with Tory and the children the day before the World Championship. Then he had found the lucky clump of tansy. Now Helen's gold tansy was warding off evil in the breast pocket of his shirt.

Helen found Jake boringly worried about Fen.

"She's very young. She'll have other opportunities."

"You don't think that when you're young," said Jake, "and she's had such a rotten two years. Losing Billy, then being sent to Coventry, then losing Dino, and his not turning up at the games, and now this. She's very brave, makes very little fuss."

I need you far more than she does, Helen wanted to scream. She was fed up with the entire Lovell family. She was jealous of Fen, and she was fed up with Suzy going on about how attractive Jake was and just assuming that he must be madly in love with Tory not to submit to Suzy's charms.

Not having been alone with Jake for days, she wanted to pour out her troubles. Now she was faced with his total detachment. He seemed to have cocooned himself against the outside world. He wasn't interested in the news, or plays or the concerts she had been to at the Hollywood Bowl, or even how appallingly Rupert was behaving. She failed to appreciate that the sensitivity with which he had listened to her and taken her to bed during the summer had a flip side of terrible nerves and vulnerability to outside pressures before a big class.

Finally, when they collapsed on to the grass, he lay with his head on her belly, not speaking, just gazing up at the snowy peaks against the stormy dark sky, luxuriating in the cool air until he fell asleep. Unable to bear wasting precious time when they could be making love, Helen woke him up.

"Jake, d'you really love me?"

"Of course I do."

"You're not showing it much at the moment."

Jake sat up on his elbow, his eyes deeply shadowed in his tanned face.

"Can't you understand that the emotional cauldron of the Olympics either makes or breaks you? I can't afford distractions." He took her hand and placed it on his breast pocket so she could feel the gold tansy, "But I keep you next to my heart the whole time."

"I hoped I'd inspire you," she wailed.

"You do," said Jake, then, remembering Dublin, "but you also distract me. I don't want to spend tomorrow, when I should be concentrating on winning, worrying that I'm going to slip up or betray myself in front of Rupert."

"Don't you even want me there?"

"Of course I do. Just don't expect me to wave and smile during the day. People say I'm rude and ill-tempered. I just want to go inside myself before a class. If I have to worry whether you're happy it'll be one more pressure."

Seeing her uncomprehending face, he said, "There's so much at stake, our whole future."

"I get so lonely at big classes," said Helen petulantly. "I'm almost glad Mother's coming tomorrow."

She pulled Jake towards her. "Please kiss me, I want you so badly."

But kissing was all he would do, which left her feeling profoundly uneasy. When Rupert had been mad about her in the early days he'd always made love to her before and after and frequently in the caravan in the middle of classes.

—

On his way back from the races that evening Rupert dropped into the Olympic village to collect his mail and found a letter postmarked Perthshire. Ever-cautious Amanda had not used her engraved stationery but she apologized for being "utterly bloody" about the mirror and admitted that she was missing him very much, that they'd all be staying up to watch him tomorrow, and to wish him good luck. She'd be back in London in September.

Equally cautious, Rupert tore her letter up and was about to throw it in the wastebasket when he pieced it together again to see if it were really true. He felt absurdly pleased, and wondered why the hell he'd been playing around with Miss Rumania. He had better go back to Arcadia and get some sleep. They were walking the course at 7:30.

Malise Gordon was not a religious man, but he prayed before the Individual that night. He must try and be a good loser and not make any of the three riders feel too awful if they screwed up, and try and keep them calm without transmitting any of his fears and worries. Ivor had a good horse and didn't usually suffer from nerves, but he lacked fire in his belly. Jake was desperately short of sleep and likely to crack. Rupert was far too confident and Rocky much too fresh. On the right day they were invincible but Malise felt apprehensive. He felt ridiculously touched that Fen had sent him a good luck card with a black cat on it, "To the best chef d'equipe in the world," she had written inside. "We'll live to fight another day, love Fen."

Jake slept fitfully, wracked by half-dreams. It was the opening ceremony and the singer turned into Helen sobbing into a microphone that Jake didn't love her. Then he was in the ring with girths breaking and bridles coming off. Finally he dreamed that Hardy had a heart attack in the ring. Lying there in the blazing sun gathering flies, he suddenly turned into Sailor. Jake woke up screaming, crying his eyes out. The next minute one of the weightlifters was sitting on his bed, patting his shoulder with a huge hand, the other was lighting him a cigarette. Having notched up a silver and a bronze the day before, they could afford to be magnanimous. As it was half past three, they said, there was no point in Jake going back to sleep for an hour, they might as well have a cup of tea and all chat to take his mind off things. Jake would rather have been left alone, but he was touched by their concern.

The weightlifters were dozing off as, with a feeling of unreality,

Jake put on the new socks, the white breeches, the shirt and tied his tie with trembling hands. He was all in white like a bride, until he pulled on the gleaming brown-topped boots, and shrugged his way into the new red coat, with the black velvet collar and the Union Jack on the pocket. The day had actually come, as it came to boys going back to prep school, or to men on death row.

"Good luck," mumbled the weightlifters sleepily. "We'll watch you on the T.V. Sock it to 'em."

"Good luck," said the wrestlers, when Jake collected Ivor. "For Christ's sake look after him."

"Good luck," said the dour security guard at the end of the passage, smiling for the first time since they arrived. "Have a good day."

It was a good thing they started early, for as the sun rose pale saffron gilding the Santa Monica mountains, cars were already jamming the freeways, and a continuous stream of enthusiasts from every nation—but mostly America—clutching a selection of hats, thermos flasks, coolers, beer cans, sandwiches, transistors, and even portable televisions to sustain them during the long day, poured into the show ground. Ticket scalpers were everywhere, and to get to the stables the team had to fight their way through autograph hunters and people peddling Coca-Cola, chewing gum, hamburgers, hot dogs and souvenirs.

"If someone else offers me a poster of Dino I shall scream," said Fen.

By seven o'clock the stands were packed under a hazy dove-grey sky which indicated colossal heat to come. Most of the crowd didn't know one end of the horse from another, but, bitten by Olympic fever, they wanted to see America notch up yet another gold.

At seven thirty the riders and their chefs d'equipes walked the course.

No one else, not even the press, was allowed into the arena. Royalty, however, brooked no such restrictions.

"Morning Dudley," Prince Philip called to Dudley Diplock, who was hovering at the entrance. "Walked the course yet?"

"No, Sir."

"Well come on, come on," said the Prince, striding straight through the cordon of security guards with Dudley hopping after him.

"Look at that crowd," said Ivor in a hollow voice.

"Look at that course," said Jake as he gazed at the fences, whose massive size wasn't remotely softened by a riot of trees and flowers.

"Positively awesome," breathed Carl Kennedy as he looked at the combination. There were two unusual fences, one built with light and dark brown bricks in the shape of a hotdog and another designed like a boat with sails at either end instead of wings, with the horses jumping over the bows.

"Holy Mother, that's a turrible thing," said Wishbone looking at the hot dog.

Even Rupert was curiously silent as they measured and re-measured the distances.

"You've all jumped higher than this," said Malise as they gazed at the massive oxer.

"But not every fence," said Ivor.

Fen suddenly felt overwhelmed with shame that she should have wanted Desdemona to jump this course. It was simply too big and she couldn't see any way Hardy could get around. She felt horribly frightened for Jake. She wanted to be with him to bolster his confidence but Malise told her to stick to the riders' stand and keep her eyes peeled for the first dozen or so rounds and pass back any advice.

Jake, icy cold with chattering teeth despite the heat, kept to himself and talked to no one. He had a very late draw, which was bound to tell on his nerves. Suddenly he longed for Tory and her quiet sympathy and understanding, who didn't mind if he bit her head off. Just as he was going through the security check into the stables he heard a cry and Helen bore down on him. She looked ravishing in white grecian tunic and a big white hat with the blue spotted scarf around the brim. A few yards behind her was a large handsome middle-aged woman with a bulldog jaw.

"Darling," Helen cried, "I've been looking for you everywhere. I just wanted to wish you luck and have you meet Mother."

Jake looked at her incredulously. "What?"

"Meet Mother. I've told her so much about you."

"Don't be so fucking stupid," snapped Jake. "I can't meet anyone at the moment," and turned on his heel.

Helen was stunned. "He's a bit uptight," she told her mother. "You can meet him later."

Everyone crowded into the riders' stand to watch the first round. A hush fell over the arena. A ripple ran through the crowd as the first competitor came in. It was Hans Schmidt—his hat at its usual crooked jaunty angle. Papa Haydn, the dark bay Hanoverian, was totally under control. A groan went up from the German team as he sent the second fence, a double of uprights, never a German forte, flying, then proceeded to hit the third fence and the fourth and, not getting up enough speed, had two toes in the water. Unnerved by such an uncharacteristically bad round Papa Haydn demolished the sailboat and then the hotdog, took a pole out of the massive triple which was sited away from the collecting ring, and hit the first element of the combination, for a final thirty-six faults.

"And him ranked number five in the world," said Wishbone in a trembling voice.

"First competitor nerves," said Rupert.

The strain of waiting for the course to be rebuilt told on Count Guy who came next, and who came to grief at the third fence, managed to clear the water, but was going so fast he couldn't pull up and proceeded to kick out the sailboat, the hotdog, the massive oxer, and the two last elements of the combination. He was followed by a Japanese rider who came in with kamikaze determination to finish the course at all costs, and came out to loud cheers with the amazing total of fifty-five faults. One of the young Irish riders coaxed his ugly brown mare around on twenty-four to produce the best round yet. Dino's replacement, Lizzie Dean, couldn't carry the weight of expectation piled on her and notched up twenty faults.

"It obviously walked better than it rode," muttered Ivor who was as green as one of Suzy Erikson's avocadoes.

The heat blazed down, getting more and more murderous, as Spaniards, Swiss, Italians, Canadians followed one another. If they weren't unhinged by the course, they were distracted by the crowd, who every time anyone cleared a fence uttered yoo hoos and Tarzan howls, and yells of "Keep it up, keep it up."

Ludwig came in and aroused a certain interest when it was announced he had won the Gold at the last Olympics, and had been second in the World Championship. Clara looked a picture of health as she trotted into the ring, long ears flickering to catch the slightest command, intelligent eyes shining, taking in the huge crowd. It was soon obvious that she was on form, as she delicately picked her way around the course, clearing the sheet of blue water by a foot, but managing to slow up and become the first horse to clear the sailboat. The screams and cheers that greeted this achievement, however, completely unsettled her. She rattled the hotdog badly, crashed into the oxer and kicked out the vast triple, finishing up with eight faults. All the other riders clapped sympathetically as Ludwig rode out, ruefully shaking his head. All the same, thought Fen, it's the best round yet. Clear rounds were obviously going to be impossible to come by. She tried to remember exactly how Ludwig had tackled the sailboat so she could tell Jake. As she watched the Mexican called Jesus come hopelessly to grief, she felt sicker and sicker with nerves for him.

Even worse, as Ivor went back to the stables to warm up John, someone moved up beside her and she found herself sitting next to Helen and Mrs. Macaulay.

"This is Jake's sister-in-law, Fenella," said Helen. "This is my Mother."

Fen and Mrs. Macaulay nodded at each other without warmth. Fen wondered if Helen had told her mother all about Jake. Helen looked at Fen's uncommunicative profile.

"Jake seems very uptight," she said. "I tried to have him meet Mother."

"The only person he wants to meet at the moment is his maker."

"He does suffer terribly from anxiety," said Helen.

"He's missing Tory." said Fen. "He tried to call her this morning, but all the lines were busy."

Seeing Helen's anguished face, Fen decided she'd gone too far. I'll go to hell for being such a bitch, she thought, but since Dino hasn't turned up and I'm out of the Olympics I'm in hell anyway, so what does it matter.

"Oh look, here comes Mary Jo," said Mrs. Macaulay. "I'm sorry Helen, but that's my girl. I refuse to root for Great Britian."

For five minutes the huge crowd, who'd been getting up and down all morning, halted their pilgrimage for food and drink, Cheered on by their fervor and hysterical enthusiam, and her own passionate desire to win, Mary Jo and Balthazar went around for four faults, only hitting the hotdog, and going into the lead. Grinning from ear to ear, throwing her hat in the air and catching it like a drum majorette, she galloped out of the ring as the crowd rose as one to applaud her.

Unable to face Mrs. Macaulay's smugness, Fen asked Helen to keep her place and went downstairs to encourage Ivor who was jumping in a couple of rounds. God it was hot. As though you'd gone to sleep and forgotten to switch off the electric blanket. The officials in their coral blazers and white panama hats sweated, colored flags wilted against the snow-topped mountains.

She reached Ivor as a poor little Swiss girl rode past crying her eyes out. Four years of hope shattered by three refusals at the first fence.

Ivor didn't fare much better. Stricken with stage fright, he rode like a novice. Nor was he helped by the announcement that here was Ivor Braine from Great Britain on The John. The crowd, thinking it hysterically funny that someone should name their horse after the toilet, went into guffaws of laughter and cat calls. Offended and throroughly unsettled, John ground to three stops at the hotdog.

"Oh no John, no John no." said Rupert, and went off to crash Rocky around the practice ring, as usual getting Dizzy to arrange the jumps on exactly the wrong stride, so Rocky hit every one and hurt himself.

"Teach him to be careful," said Rupert.

A mighty roar from the arena indicated that Carl Kennedy had gone in and was about to jump.

"Now that's an attractive man," said Mrs. Macaulay. "There's something about American men."

"He's gay, mother," snapped Helen.

Despite being used to the frantic enthusiasm of American crowds, even Scarlett O'Hara was unnerved by the noise. She hit the hotdog, then looked as though she was going clear, but as she sailed over the last element of the combination, the crowd let out such a shout of jubilation that the mare assumed she had finished. It took all Carl's skill to get her straight for the huge double and she toppled the last pole. Still he was second on eight faults with Ludwig.

"Isn't he a prince?" said the girl behind Helen, as Rupert waited to go in, "I saw him on T.V. last night. You have to hand it to the British, they do have class."

Quality in every line, Rocky was easily the handsomest horse in the contest. Under the gleaming amber coat his muscles rippled like serpents, and as he danced into the arena, long ears cocked to the unfamiliar sights and sounds, the blend of explosive power and natural grace was unforgettable.

"For Christ's sake take it steadily," warned Malise.

Rocky was the best horse in the contest, but he had never seen a crowd this big, nor heard so much noise, nor seen so many undulating rows of peaked caps like a wriggling aviary.

His forelegs were sore where Rupert had crashed him over the jumps. His tail switched angrily; he was horribly hot, fed up and upset. As Rupert circled him twice to steady him, he humped his back and fought for his head.

That horse is over-fresh and insufficiently warmed up, thought Fen.

Two minutes later Rupert rode out of the ring with an incredible twenty-eight faults. Everyone in the riders' stand and the commentary box was stunned.

"Talk about the Rocky Horror Show!" said Fen under her breath. Then, horrified by her own lack of patriotism, she shot a sidelong glance at Helen and Mrs. Macaulay and was shattered to see neither of them looking remotely upset.

"Must go and find Jake," she said, getting to her feet.

"Wish him good luck," said Helen. "Don't forget to tell him," she called after Fen.

Wishbone was just about to go into the ring. Nearly forty, he'd had a grueling career, and everyone was taking bets on whether the drink or anno domini would get to him first. Today, despite three large whiskys, the heat didn't seem to affect him or his big bay gelding, Christy Mahon. They too got eight faults.

"Well done," shouted Fen as he came out of the ring, "Bloody good round."

She found Ivor, his face tear-stained, in the deepest of glooms.

"Where's Jake?" she asked,

"In the men's room, throwing up."

"He's got to jump in twenty minutes. For God's sake go and get him."

Jake crouched over the lavatory, gazing miserably at the white bowl. Having had no breakfast and virtually no supper he was only throwing up bile now. He felt dreadful, shaking from head to foot. Oh God, he wished Tory was here.

Someone was rattling the door. It was Ivor.

"You OK, Jake?"

Jake groaned.

"Fen thought this might help." Ivor passed a brandy under the door.

"Take it easy," said Malise's voice. "In a few hours this'll be all over."

"How soon have I got to jump?"

"About four to go."

"Any clears?"

"No—Rupe knocked up a cricket score," said Malise bleakly.

So it all depends on me, thought Jake.

He drained the brandy. Amazingly it seemed to calm his nerves and take the edge off his fears. Outside he found Fen.

"Now listen, they've all come unstuck at the hotdog. I think you ought to come off the corner earlier, giving Hardy a bit more time to size it up and take it in five strides."

"He seems to have got out of bed on the right side. He's only given me one nip today," said Sarah.

Hardy was not a handsome horse, but his chubby dappled quarters and shoulders shone like polished pewter, his tail was whiter than the snow on the mountains, and his braids threaded with red ribbon, were the neatest in the contest.

For a second Jake smiled at Sarah as she plugged both the horse's ears with cotton wool. "You've done a good job on him," he said. "He looks great."

"Good luck," said Fen

"I don't need to tell you this," said Malise, "but all our hopes rest on you now."

Giving Hardy a clap on the rump Jake went off into the tunnel. Fen just managed to take her seat by Helen as Jake rode into the ring.

"This is Jake, whom I was telling you about," Helen said to her mother. "He nearly quit because he had such a bad accident last year."

The crowds were tired. They had already sat through nearly three hours of jumping. They had seen all the Americans go and were already drifting away for their lunch.

It's actually happening, thought Jake, as he cantered towards the first huge fence. Feeling Hardy's irritation at having his natural ebullience curbed, he let him have his head. Hardy bounded over, he cleared the next and the next, and with a whisk of his hind legs flicked over the water with inches to spare. He's in top form, thought Jake joyfully. The sailboat caused him no problems. Following Fen's advice, he then took a very sharp turn off the corner, and taking five strides, rather than everyone's four, gathered sufficient momentum and bounded over the hotdog with ease.

He was the first horse to clear this fence which caused such screams of delight, excitement and hysteria from the crowd that they pierced straight through the cotton wool in Hardy's ears, temporarily unhinging him. Breaking into a gallop he crashed through the huge oxer and sent every brick of the wall flying.

"Shit," said Helen.

"Helen Macaulay," said her mother, appalled.

"I've been Campbell-Black for six years, Mother."

"More's the pity."

Fen decided she rather liked Mrs. Macaulay.

Jake meanwhile had pulled Hardy almost to a standstill, stroking him and balancing him, the same way he had calmed Macaulay in the World Championship.

"Silly bugger's going to get time faults," said Rupert.

"He knows what he's doing," snapped Malise.

Jake kicked Hardy into a canter, and proceeded to bounce over the rest of the course, riding out to deafening applause.

"Well done. Marvelous," said Malise, looking considerably more cheerful than he had ten minutes ago, "You've saved the day. You're on eleven."

Only three rounds followed, two of them hopeless, but British hopes were slightly dashed when a Nigerian on a huge black gelding went around at a gallop with a broad grin on his face. Despite shooting out of the saddle at every fence, and reducing the crowd to fits of laughter, he managed to clear everything except the water and the hotdog.

Malise got out his score sheet. "That's Mary Jo on four, Carl, Ludwig, Wishbone and the Nigerian on eight, and you on eleven, Jake," he said.

Then there was a grueling three hour interval before the second round. Twenty riders went through. Ivor was out, Rupert had just scraped in, Jake was fifth. There would be fewer jumps, but they would be harder.

"Let's go and have some lunch," said Malise.

"I'm going to stay behind and sort out Rocky," said Rupert grimly.

"Must try and keep Wishbone out of the whisky tent," said Paddy his groom. Ivor couldn't speak for despair.

"Rupert was overconfident. You were underconfident. It happens to the best people," Malise told him.

On the way to lunch Jake suddenly swayed, overcome by heat, lack of sleep and food and a large brandy.

"You won't be jumping for at least three hours," said Malise firmly. "Go and have a sleep on Sarah's bed."

"Don't be bloody silly," said Jake, mopping his dripping forehead. "I couldn't possibly sleep."

"Well, lie down then."

Within seconds of stretching out on the tiny bed in the attic rooms over the stables, Jake was asleep.

The second round was much tougher. The temperature was up in the nineties, turning the Olympic stadium into a furnace. The horses, having been warmed up, jumped, and put back in the stables, thought that work was over for the day and couldn't understand why they were being pulled out again. Most of them were already very tired.

Even the vast crowd seemed depleted, as spectators, escaping from the punishing heat, watched the competition on the closed circuit televisions scattered around the halls.

Biting her nails, Fen watched rider after rider fight their way through a forest of obstacles. Ludwig had worked Clara too hard in the interval and the great mare knocked up a cricket score.

Jake, having been woken up, was warming up Hardy as Mary Jo entered the ring. From the arena he could see the stands heaving as the spectators stampeded to get back to their seats and cheer on their heroine. Mary Jo was on four faults. Jake listened to the roars of applause growing to a crescendo, which must have been heard all the way to New York. Then there was a silence, and a terrible groan. Four faults, that meant she was on eight, then the cheers started again, rising and rising once more. He must concentrate on Hardy. Then suddenly there was a deafening bellow, which sent Hardy into a frenzy despite the cotton wool in his ears.

Looking up at the stadium Jake could see hats being thrown in the air, rising up above the back of the stand like popped corn. Unless Carl or Wishbone or the Nigerian went clear, Mary Jo had got her gold. There was no way Jake could catch her. The cheering went on and on until finally Mary Jo came out of the tunnel, wiping away the tears, then disappearing into a shrieking crowd of wellwishers.

Carl Kennedy, on eight, went next and again was unlucky. He was jumping cleanly and steadily when the shadow of a helicopter above fell across the first element of the double making it difficult to judge the distance. The gallant Scarlett O'Hara knocked down both elements, but otherwise went clear. The crowd was in ecstasy, stamping their feet and cheering. Carl was now on sixteen faults with an excellent chance of a silver.

In rode Rupert. It was only by some miracle that he could even get a bronze. He was still in a white-hot rage, determined to go clear and show everyone how the course should be jumped. Obviously terrified out of his wits, eyes rolling, frothing blood at the mouth, Rocky went clear until he came to the triple going away from the collecting ring, when he began to slow down. Rupert lifted his whip. Rocky took off too soon, and sent triple, horse and rider flying. Rupert hung onto the reins and appeared unhurt, but it was several seconds before he could mount the panic-stricken Rocky who, thoroughly unsettled, proceeded to notch up a further eight faults.

"Bad luck," said Wishbone who was waiting to go in. But Rupert ignored him, riding straight past him with a pale dangerous face. Wishbone had had enough whiskys in the interval to give him courage, but rather too many for perfect judgment. He knew it was his last chance at a medal. The Irish didn't have enough riders here to make up a team, but he loved his old horse, and would dearly have loved to go home with a medal, so he crossed himself and prayed fervently to the Virgin Mary as he rode into the ring. The Virgin Mary was listening. Gently she guided horse and rider around the ring. Wishbone jumped like a man inspired, he only had one fence down, putting him into second place.

The crowd erupted. Wishbone had entertained them with his antics for many years now. He was a very popular rider. They cheered and cheered. Ireland had got a silver, but America had the gold and bronze.

"They seem to have completely forgotten that there's still Jake and that Nigerian to jump," said Fen furiously.

"Are you all right?" she said to Jake. "It must be much worse when there's so much at stake."

He nodded, not trusting himself to speak. If he got four faults he got the bronze, if he went clear the silver. That was the message bleakly spelled out. With the crowd making such a din there was no way he could get Hardy to concentrate.

"Take his cotton wool out," he said to Sarah.

"Are you sure?" she said, horrified. "He'll freak out."

Malise came up and gave Hardy a last pat. "They're obviously not going to shut up," he said. "I'd go in. Just trust to your instincts."

If I get a medal, thought Jake as he waited, watching the mouthing ecstatic faces, I'll get £75,000 a year from Boyson. He thought of Tory and the children watching at home. He thought of Helen who he'd been so foul to earlier.

"Go in please," said the ring steward in his coral blazer.

From then on Jake thought about nothing but Hardy. Riding slowly to the center of the arena, he turned to the President's Box, where the President, who loved horses, sat with Prince Philip and Princess Anne, and he removed his hat to the judges, showing the sudden pallor on his suntanned face. Then he spoke to Hardy and

Hardy put one foot forward and bowed low to the Prince and the Princess and the President and the crowd burst into ecstatic, charmed applause. They'd got their gold, they could be generous. There was no way this gypsy and his tricks could beat their Mary Jo.

"Isn't that darling?" said Helen to Mrs. Macaulay.

Jake looked up at the cool snow-tipped mountains beyond the stadium and the great blocks of faces watching him, and calmly he replaced his hat and waited for the crowd to settle.

Gradually the cheering decreased to a sizzle of excitement like fat in a frying pan. Jake touched the Union Jack on his saddle cloth, then the tansy in his breast pocket. Hardy stood as still as a rock for once. He had heard the crowd in all its noise and glory, and it hadn't harmed him.

"Stupid exhibitionist," said Rupert to Ludwig.

"Pity not to have any clears," said Dudley Diplock.

Finally when there was no sound at all except the clicking of cameras and the insect hum of a 100,000 strong crowd trying to be quiet, Jake kicked Hardy into a canter. Niether of them looked a bit tired. It was almost as though they were jumping an exhibition round. As they cleared the first two fences, then the third, then bounded joyously over the water the crowd realized Hardy was enjoying himself and started to cheer and stamp and clap him on.

They really like me, Hardy seemed to be saying as he picked his feet up and really bucketed over the hotdog with a jaunty whisk of his tail.

This is the fence I hated last time, he said slowing up at the oxer.

"You like it this time, listen to the applause," said Jake as Hardy flew over like a swallow.

"He's a bit slow," said Fen, sitting beside Malise on the edge of the riders' stand.

"Yes," said Malise, "But what a round, sheer poetry. Come on Jake."

As if Jake heard them he stepped up Hardy's pace, and came storming over the combination. Now it was the last double.

"I can't look," said Fen. She waited, head in her hands for the sickening thud of poles. She heard a gasp, a long pause, an ecstatic scream from Helen on her right and then a mighty roar of applause.

"He's done it, the only clear," shouted Malise throwing his panama in the air. It fell and was trampled underfoot before he could even be bothered to retrieve it.

The crowd held their breath as everyone calculated. Jake glanced at the clock. He was just within the time. Even if the Nigerian went clear he'd got the bronze. Dropping Hardy's rein on his neck, he raised both hands to heaven in a double salute and rode out through the cheering channel of spectators, grinning from ear to ear.

"Fucking marvelous," screamed Fen, tears pouring down her cheeks, as she hugged Malise, his wet face glistening too in the bright sun.

"This is the most amazing turn up for the books," Dudley Diplock was gibbering from the commentary box, "No one ever thought Gyppo Jake would make it back to the big time. This is little short of a miracle."

"Let's go and congratulate him," said Malise and Fen simultaneously, but Helen was too quick for either of them. Jumping over the row in front, she rushed out and down the steps and, red hair flying, she rushed to meet Jake.

"Oh darling, darling, darling," she said, seizing his hand.

Jake looked down at her. Color in his face now, dazzlingly happy, handsome as never before, all efforts at impassivity gone.

"We did it," he said incredulously. "We really did it," and in the euphoria of winning he bent down and kissed her, and she kissed him back, clinging on to him.

In the riders' stand, trapped by the crowd, Fen's eyes met those of Mrs. Macaulay.

"Your brother-in-law," said Mrs. Macaulay accusingly.

"Yes," said Fen equally accusingly. "My sister's husband."

From the right she saw Rupert, descending on Jake and Helen, looking white with rage. Fortunately at that moment Sarah, in floods of joyful tears, and the rest of the British grooms swarmed round Jake and Hardy. Instantly they were joined by Wishbone and the American and German teams who were all patting him on the back and showering him with congratulations. Count Guy arrived with a magnum of Krug.

From then on everything was a daze. Jake was terribly glad to see Malise looking so happy, and Fen jumping up and down, and he was both pleased and sorry when he heard the poor Nigerian, the last to jump, had been unable to cope with the strain and had knocked up twenty faults, which meant Jake had the silver and Wishbone the bronze.

Everywhere he turned there were photographers and people reaching forward to pat Hardy.

"I can't think why he isn't biting everyone," crowed Sarah. "Now he's a medalist he's obviously turned over a new leaf."

The jumps were cleared and the huge Clydesdales dragged on the winners' podium. Together Mary Jo, Jake and Wishbone rode into the ring, followed by their three grooms. Sarah got a special cheer for her beauty and her red, white and blue hair. Then the grooms took the horses as the riders mounted the podium. Jake found it difficult not to laugh as the girls carrying the boxes of ribbons like flag-sellers came out with their ludicrously stiff wide-apart-legged walk.

He bowed his head as the President's wife hung the silver metal around his neck, touching it immediately, checking it was real. He thought his heart would burst with the wonder of the whole thing. Mary Jo ws crying unashamedly as the three flags climbed up the flagpole and the band played the "Star Spangled Banner." Wishbone had no handkerchief, and had to wipe his red-veined nose on his sleeve.

"Well done," said Prince Philip, shaking them all, but particularly Jake, by the hand. "Only clear round," he added. "You must feel *very* proud."

"Thank you, Sir."

Jake was feeling so dazed with emotion, he was glad to get back to Hardy who was so festooned with long-tailed ribbons he could hardly see out. He wanted to stay with him afterwards but he was swept off to a press conference. By the time the reporters had finished with Mary Jo, Jake had consumed at least a bottle and a half of champagne.

"Pity you didn't get a gold, Jake," said the *Los Angeles Times*.

"Frankly I'm bloody glad to have the silver. Being a gypsy, traditionally I cross people's palms with it. It's the right medal for me." Everyone laughed.

"All the same," he went on, looking at the forest of cameras and notebooks and tape recorders, "It's a pity Dino Ferranti had to pull out, or Mary Jo and I might have been a rung lower."

"Do you think there's any reason you came so high?" asked the *Daily Telegraph*.

"I had a good back-up team," said Jake, and proceeded to thank everyone from the family to Malise, to the nurses and doctors at the Motcliffe.

"What are your plans for the future?" asked the *New York Times*.

"I'm going to call my wife and then go and get plastered."

Dudley fought his way through the huge crowd of fans waiting outside. "Congratulations, Jake. Brilliant, brilliant performance. We've kept a line open for you in the commentary box. We'd like to televise you breaking the news to Terry if we may."

"You may not," said Jake. "One doesn't often call up one's wife to say one's got a silver. Some things should be done in private."

Going into the commentary box, he slammed the door. "Can I put a person to person call through to Mrs. Lovell," he said picking up the telephone.

"Certainly, Mr. Lovell," said the switchboard girl. "Congratulations." He got through incredibly quickly.

"Oh Jakey, oh Jakey," Tory was laughing and crying so much he could hardly hear. "It's so wonderful. You both were so wonderful. The whole village have been here watching it. They've drunk us out of house and home and now they're having the most terrific party. We're all so proud of you."

"Hardy was your baby," said Jake. "You sorted him out for me."

"He jumped so brilliantly, and when he bowed, and the only clear too. Speak to the children."

"How much did you win?" asked Isa.

"Can you take me to Disneyland?" said Darklis.

Jake asked if he could speak to Tory again. "I miss you," he said. "D'you want to fly out for the team event?"

"Oh I'd love to. Can we afford it?"

"I think so now," said Jake.

"Boyson just rang by the way," said Tory. "He said you'd kept your side of the bargain, he'd be keeping his. Oh listen, listen, can you hear?" she said in a choked voice. "They're ringing the church bells, Oh Jakey, it's two o'clock in the morning. No one's asleep. They're cheering and dancing in the street, and the pub's open, and they're ringing bells in your honor, listen."

Across the wires, Jake could hear the faint peal. He was so moved he couldn't talk any more. "I'll call tomorrow," he said. "I love you."

"I love you," said Tory.

"Everything all right?" said Fen as he came out of the booth, wiping his eyes.

He nodded. "Absolutely marvelous. They're ringing church bells."

Perhaps it'll be all right after all, thought Fen.

*T*hey gave him a police car with sirens to get him back to the Olympic village.

"I'm sorry," said Jake at the gates, feeling dazedly for his security badge. "I seem to have mislaid it."

"All right, Mr. Lovell, we know who you are," said the security guard. "Congratulations."

The other British athletes were euphoric.

"Well done," said Sebastian Coe and Daley Thompson, hammering him on the back.

The weight lifters hoisted him shoulder high and carried him around the village, Everyone bought him drinks. Jake looked in the mirror in the little room as he changed to go out to dinner. He found his security badge where he'd left it, around his neck under his shirt.

"You are a superstar," he said jabbing his finger at his reflection, pleased that the two pointing fingers met every time, proving he wasn't drunk. He wished he could go out quietly and celebrate with Sarah and Fen; he didn't want the strain of behaving well. He wished Tory was here to share in the triumph, but he had never known such happiness.

Determined not to betray his devastating disappointment, Rupert was in no mood for a victory celebration. He had wanted to leave show-jumping in a blaze of glory, moving smoothly from the gold medalist's podium into politics and, possibly, Amanda's arms. Now the months of training and abstinence had gone for nothing. And although Rocky had jumped like a pig with chilblains, and Rupert had beaten the hell out of him afterwards, a small voice inside told him it was not Rocky's fault.

When he had got back from Las Vegas with the torn-up pieces of Amanda's letter in his pocket he shouldn't have stayed up half the night talking to people at Suzy's dinner party. He was thirty-one, not eighteen anymore. Finally, letting himself into the bedroom at two in the morning and finding Helen breathing especially deeply pretending to be asleep, Rupert—king of the catnappers—had been unable to sleep himself, lying awake thinking about Amanda.

Now he was expected to go out and celebrate the little jerk's freak silver. Malise had rocketed him after the competition.

"These things happen with horses and the less said about your fuck-up today the better. Now we've got to go all out for the team gold. You've got six days to get Rocky together, and I want you on parade at half past nine tonight."

"What for?"

"To celebrate Jake's silver."

"I've got a previous engagement," said Rupert coldly. "I'm taking Helen and her mother to Ma Maison."

"That's where we're all going."

"Cost a bundle," snapped Rupert. "Hardly imagine the Olympic fund will stretch to that."

"It's already been paid for," said Malise, not without a certain quiet pleasure which he afterwards regretted. "Garfield Boyson rang from England and settled the bill in advance."

Rupert's face took on that curiously dead expression that boded trouble. Garfield Boyson had already approached Rupert, in fact he was the only sponsor Rupert would have been prepared to work with. If Boyson had picked up his bills for the next two years, he would have been able to slack off and only enter the big prestigious competitions, gradually devoting more and more time to politics. And now Jake had pinched the sponsorship from under his nose.

—

"I thought you weren't going to drink until after the team event," said Helen as Rupert, hair still wet from the shower, but already dressed in a grey shirt and white trousers, poured himself four fingers of whisky.

"Hasn't done me much good so far," said Rupert adding a splash of water from the wash basin. "Need something to get me through what's obviously going to be a fucking awful evening."

Helen tried very hard to curb her elation. Rupert had told her Boyson was footing the bill this evening, which meant Jake must have got the sponsorship, which must mean he could now afford to leave Tory and marry her.

"It should be fun," she said. "I've never been to Ma Maison, and Mother's dying to meet the team, and I know Malise will enjoy Mother."

"Should do," said Rupert. "He got enough practice driving tanks in the war."

Helen had her back to Rupert, but her slender right arm was crooked over her back, wrestling with the zipper of her dress which was catching in her hair.

"Let me." Moving towards her, Rupert pushed the newly washed hair aside and pulled the narrow gold zipper up to the nape of the neck. He looked at her reflection in the mirror, breathing in waves of Femme from her warm newly-bathed hopelessly excited body. She was wearing a dress of dark gold silk, high necked, long sleeved, falling at the ankles, and clinging caressingly to every inch of her body. Her hair, long at the back, was drawn up at the sides by two gold combs. For a second, his long fingers clamped her waist, then they shifted up towards her breasts. He relized that, totally untypically, she wasn't wearing a bra or even a petticoat. Feeling her tense and draw away, he tightened his grip.

"Haven't seen that dress. When d'you get it?"

"Ages ago—not for a special occasion—I just liked it."

"I'm sure—you look great in it—almost too great."

"What's that supposed to mean?" she said defensively. "Ma Maison's always crammed with movie stars and you're always accusing me of looking too straight."

"Not this time I'm not." Rupert glanced at his watch. "In fact if we miss pre-drinks we've got time to," he began to pull down the zipper.

"No," gasped Helen, shrinking away from him, almost falling over the dressing table, knocking bottles on to the floor in her desperate haste to get away.

"I'm all made up and ready," she said, trying to make a joke of it, "and I promised Mother we'd meet at 9:30. We can't leave her stranded at the restaurant."

"How's she getting there?" said Rupert. "On her broomstick?"

—

Ma Maison, thanks to Boyson's munificence, had gone whole hog. On the British team table there were silver plates, silver goblets for the never-ending bottles of Krug, white roses and lilies, surrounded by silver leaves, in the silver bowl at the center of the table, with two silver horses on either side rearing up from the silver satin table cloth.

Jake was a awarded a hero's welcome when he arrived. It took him ages to get across the restaurant as people pumped his hand and wanted to touch his silver medal, glinting in the candle light. A group of English actors who'd witnessed his victory that afternoon in Arcadia were now happily getting plastered and insisted he sit down and have a drink.

"Who were those people?" he asked Fen, when he finally reached the British team table.

"Michael Caine, Susan George, Roger Moore, to name three." said Fen.

"Oh. I thought they seemed familiar."

At that moment a beautiful girl came up and, tapping Rupert on the shoulder, handed him a menu and a pen. "Would you very much mind?" She gave him a dazzling smile.

"Not at all," said Rupert picking up the pen.

"Asking Jake Lovell if I could possibly have his autograph?"

Jake was already very tight, cocooned in euphoria, acknowledging the accolades with one part of his mind, but with the other back in the ring jumping every fence, feeling great waves of love for that tricky, brilliant horse who'd finally confounded the critics and come up with the goods.

Fen on the other hand wondered how much longer she could keep going. She'd been up since four, supporting Jake all the way, yet still praying Dino might turn up. Now, looking at Helen shining with happiness, aware that both Rupert and Jake were steadily getting drunk, she was filled with a feeling of terrible doom.

"Can I sit next to you and can we go to Disneyland tomorrow?" asked Ivor.

At that moment Suzy and Albie Erikson arrived to make up the party.

"Darling," said Suzy, kissing Jake on the mouth, "you were just sensational. You've got no excuse to resist my advances now."

Fen shot a glance at Helen. She was looking at Suzy with pure hatred.

"We've just had an earthquake warning," said Albie cheerfully. It's going to start right here at this table, thought Fen.

The waiter poured out more champagne.

"To Jake," said Malise. Everyone except Jake and Rupert raised their silver goblets.

"To Hardy," said Jake half-draining his goblet, then looking across at Helen, his eyes not quite focusing, he raised it to her, blew her a kiss and drained the rest.

Help, thought Fen. "Do you think the course'll be as difficult on Sunday," she asked Rupert, frantic to distract his attention. Glancing around, he saw how wan she looked.

"You OK duckie?"

She nodded. "I'm sorry about Rocky today. You must be heart-broken."

Rupert shrugged. "D'you know who I miss most of all?"

"Billy," said Fen. "I miss him too."

Ma Maison came up with a special menu which Fen had patiently to explain to Ivor.

"Clear soup, that's for Jake's clear round, then Coquille St. Jake a la champagne—that's scallops, then Gâteau Hardy. For God's sake stop gazing at Goldie Hawn, Ivor."

As dinner progressed Rupert's anger channeled into anti-American asides to irritate both Helen and her mother. "The Olympics have become a shambles," he was saying, "a laboratory war between East and West. The Americans have better drugs, better computers to detect minor faults, better shrinks to psych out the athletes. The whole spirit of amateurism has gone."

Mrs. Macaulay, who was discussing property prices with Albie, swelled like a bullfrog. Helen, toying with a piece of coquille, managed to engineer Malise on to the subject of Jake. "Naturally I'm disappointed Rupe didn't get a medal, but if anyone deserved one, it was Jake."

Malise nodded. "It's a fairy tale really, after that terrible fall."

"You're fond of him, aren't you?"

Malise smiled deprecatingly. "He's tricky and cussed, but you have to admire his integrity. Of course he's fantastically lucky in his home back-up."

"Isn't Tory kind of dull?"

"God no," said Malise sharply. "She keeps him calm. I must say I never expected him to get a silver. I thought he'd crack."

"But he didn't, he managed without her," said Helen, kneading her bread into pellets in her agitation.

"She's carried him through the last ten years," said Malise gently.

A diversion had been created on the other side of the table. Joan Collins had arrived and was being embraced by Rupert.

"Helen my dear," Malise lowered his voice, "I've known you long enough to give you a piece of advice. Don't play with fire—particularly Olympic Fire. Cool it—until after the games."

Helen blushed furiously. "I don't know what you mean."

"Yes you do," said Malise gravely. "I've got enough headaches keeping the team together, without you rocking the boat."

Joan Collins, svelte in black lace, was progressing down the table. "Hi Jake, we haven't met, but what a round! I was stuck in the studio, but we suspended shooting to watch the second half. All the Brits went wild."

She turned to Helen. "Darling, how are you?" Then her eyes lit on the gold dress. "You meanie. I had my eyes on that. Saw it at Giorgio's yesterday. Then I found out the price. You're lucky to have a rich husband to pick up the checks. Let me know if you ever get tired of him."

Helen went very still.

"I think she already has," said Rupert. He looked across at Helen, his fingers drumming on the table, "Oh this old thing," he said softly.

"Oh shut up," said Fen. "It does suit her."

Suzy, who'd been flirting outrageously with Jake, got up to go to the john. Mrs Macaulay immediately took her place. Jake found himself getting the third degree. Her big red face seemed to have an extra pair of eyes in the middle of her forehead. Really he must be extraordinarily drunk. As Mrs. Macaulay questioned him about Tory, the children, the yard and the horses it became plain to her that, despite the fact that Jake was obviously plastered and kept calling her Mrs. Campbell-Black, his marriage was a good deal happier than Helen's to that monster who was still badmouthing America.

"The television coverage is utterly one-sided," said Rupert. "American viewers are totally unaware of any foreign competition."

Helen turned to Malise helplessly. "Don't you find L.A. fascinating?" she said. "It's such an eclectic mixture of the functional and the bizarre."

"Don't talk crap," snapped Rupert. Malise frowned. Mrs. Macaulay went purple: "That's no way to address a lady."

"What makes you think she's a lady," drawled Rupert, "Certainly not her parentage."

Mrs. Macaulay rose to her feet. "I won't stay here to be insulted."

"Why don't you go then?" said Rupert.

Only Malise's blandishments, Helen's pleadings and the arrival of the Gâteau Hardy, a splendid ice cream cake in the shape of a gray horse, induced her to stay.

Rupert returned to attacking the American team: "They're all robots, Mary Jo's a robot, Carl Kennedy's a robot, Dino Ferranti. . ."

"He is not," howled Fen.

"Fancy him, do you? So does my dear wife. She is dear, too. At least you earn your keep, she's a parasite."

"Didn't know Helen came from Paris," said Ivor in surprise.

Everyone laughed, for a moment lightening the tension.

"There's a marvelous concert at the Hollywood Bowl tomorrow,"

Helen said to Malise, "and tomorrow they're doing *Hamlet* in Russian. I'd love to go."

"Count me out," said Rupert. "Why not *Black Beauty* in Urdu? The only use for the Hollywood Bowl is to be sick in it."

Fen resisted the temptation to giggle.

"There's a very naughty movie on at the Rialto," said Suzy who, irritated to find she'd been ousted from her place next to Jake, wanted to get back in on the action. "Why don't we all go tomorrow night?"

"My wife is not interested in sex," said Rupert flatly.

Jake had been watching Rupert for some time. His eyes narrowed and his right hand played idly with the knife he'd been given to cut the cake.

"I'm not surprised," he said, "Being married to you."

Rupert looked up. There was a long embarrassed pause. Then Fen said desperately, "Ivor and I are going on a tour of movie star's homes tomorrow. We're going to see Rudolph Valentino's grave, and. . ." Rupert put a hand on her arm "Shut up darling," he said softly. "Jake was talking."

"Why don't you give her a break for a change?" said Jake.

"What kind do you suggest, a broken jaw perhaps?"

There was another awful pause.

"Just because you rode like a costive chimpanzee today," said Jake "and screwed up the chances of the best horse in the class, you don't have to take it out on her." He was quivering like a leopard about to spring.

"Oh dear," drawled Rupert. "We have grown in status since we won our silver medal this afternoon, haven't we?"

"Shut up," howled Jake.

"Been at the human growth hormone, have we?" taunted Rupert. "Little man has had a happy day and is now making a big big night of it. Gypsy, my ass, you're just a little suburban creep whose mother screwed around so much she couldn't remember who your father was."

Jake picked up the knife.

"No," thundered Malise.

Suddenly the whole restaurant had gone quiet.

"You little creep," said Rupert gently. "The only thing I'd use you for is to measure my tennis net."

Helen leapt to her feet, knocking her wine glass over.

"Stop it," she screamed. "Just because you're jealous as hell of Jake, you have to spoil everything."

"St. Georgia to the rescue," said Rupert.

"I'm going," said Helen, "Thank you Malise, I'm real sorry everyone" and she fled out of the restaurant, a shimmering column of metal, cannoning off tables, blinded by tears.

"Aren't you going to cut the cake?" said Grisel.

—

Rupert caught up with Helen outside the restaurant. They stood side by side not speaking, while the doorman conjured up their car. Helen was amazed that Rupert could be so charming when Michael Caine stopped on the way out and asked them to a party the following night.

"Shut up," he snarled on the drive back when she asked him to go slower, "Let me get home in one piece. Then we're going to do some straight talking."

At the Eriksons' house the servants had gone to bed. Drunk though Rupert was, he managed to switch off the burglar alarm, before going into the living room and pouring himself a glass of straight whisky. Helen walked towards the stairs.

"Where are you going?"

"Bed. I've had enough of you for one day." Careful, she told herself, careful. But all those things that Malise and Fen had said earlier about Tory and not rocking the boat had only made her more desperate.

"Come here," said Rupert.

It was not a voice to disobey. Rupert once again had that dead expression on his face that always heralded trouble.

She removed her gold high heels, which would impede a quick get-away, and sank into the white warmth of Suzy's sumptuous sofa.

"You ought to be ashamed of yourself," she said in a low voice. "I guess they had a celebration dinner for you when you won your medal."

"Hey wait a minute. You've got very protective about Jake Lovell lately, haven't you? Embracing him when he came out of the ring, sticking up for him this evening. What's going on?"

Helen took a deep breath, aware that she was pushing a huge boulder towards the edge of a cliff and any minute it might roll over crushing innocent people in its path.

"What's going on?" repeated Rupert.

One of Helen's combs had fallen out of her hair, which flopped forward over her face. Looking at the golden tanned face and the shimmering gold body and the mass of shining hair, Rupert suddenly thought she had never looked so desirable—almost wanton—despite her terror.

"You're looking very good. As I said earlier, you're looking much too good. Don't tell me you've got yourself a man at last?"

"Yes I have," said Helen, goaded.

"Who is it?"

"Jake," whispered Helen, "Jake Lovell."

"What did you say?"

"You heard me."

"Jake Lovell," Rupert began to laugh, totally without mirth. "Are you trying to tell me you've been having it off with that pathetic little cripple?"

"Don't you dare call him that."

"A cripple," Rupert went on, "a warped gypsy cripple. Doing our bit for the disabled, are we? It figures. I suppose, makes you feel good. Money in the collection box on Sunday, a day a month for the N.S.P.C.C., and leaping into bed with a cripple. Mrs. Campbell-Black does so much for charity. You bet she does!"

"You're revolting," screamed Helen, "pulling everything down to your own disgusting level."

"It appears to be you who've done the pulling."

"Even at a time like this, all you can do is to make jokes."

"Oh believe me, baby, I don't think this is funny."

"I love him," sobbed Helen, putting her face in her hands, "and he loves me."

Rupert filled up his glass. Then in an almost calm voice that made Helen's blood run cold, he said:

"How long has this been going on?"

"Since February, when Marcus was hospitalized. I was worried stiff. Jake came in to see the consultant about his leg. He was very caring and supportive. I sure needed it after the Kenya trip." She looked up at him. He stared back, as though daring her to go further. Helen dropped her eyes first.

"So that's why you've been hanging around the circuit like a bitch in heat. How extraordinary. I was barking up quite the wrong tree, thinking you'd be turned on by Janey, wasn't I? Never guessed your particular buzz would be a crippled dwarf."

"Jake is not a dwarf," screamed Helen, "He's five foot seven."

"You've measured him have you—all over?"

For a few seconds he paced up and down the room, trying to calm the rage that kept boiling up inside him.

"And you had to pick the one man who's always been out to get me. Remember when he tried to kill me before the World Championship? He doesn't give a stuff about you, he just wants to score off me."

"He doesn't. He wants to marry me."

The boulder was over the cliff now, crashing down, gathering force.

"Marry you?" said Rupert in genuine amazement, "How?"

"As soon as he can get a divorce."

"And he's going to leave that fat rich cow for you?"

"Yes," sobbed Helen. If she said it, it must be true.

"And presumably that night when I came back from Dinard and he was there jawing about healing breaches and team solidarity, he'd merely come to fuck you—I beg your pardon—make love to you?"

Helen lost her temper. "Yes he had. What about you and Podge, and Dizzy and Marion, and Samantha Freebody, and the one that gave me clap, not to mention all the others? You've never been faithful to me for one minute."

"Oh yes I was," said Rupert, "until you got involved with that snivelling child and refused to come abroad with me. He doesn't give a stuff about you," he went on. "Why did he nearly kill me for saying Tory was fat at Disneyland? Why was he on the telephone to her the moment he won the medal? You're not going to break up that marriage. Anyway what's so special about him?"

"He's a better rider," screamed Helen leaping to her feet, "and he's much better in bed."

The next moment Rupert had hit her across the room. Then he picked her up and hit her again so she collapsed sobbing across the glass table, spilling Rupert's whisky over the white sofa.

"And what the fuck are you going to live on? He's got no money. He can't give you anything but Lovell, baby."

"He's got the Boyson sponsorship," croaked Helen.

"He had," said Rupert gathering up his car keys. "That was on the condition he kept his nose clean. It's pretty snotty now."

"Where are you going?" whispered Helen through lips which were already beginning to swell up.

"To find your lover and beat him up till he sees stars and stripes. Then I'm going to string him from the Hollywood sign by his precious medal ribbon."

"No," screamed Helen, "No please."

But Rupert had gone. Next moment she heard the crunch of his car roaring off towards Los Angeles.

Trembling like a palsied dog she ran to the telephone, and after several false starts managed to get through to the Olympic Village. One of the security guards answered. No they couldn't possibly wake Jake in the middle of the night. He'd gone to bed and he was sharing a room with two weightlifters, both of whom had a competition tomorrow and needed their sleep. There was a "Do not disturb" sign on the door.

"Please," sobbed Helen. "It's his wife. I must talk with him. There's been a terrible accident."

The security man hummed and hawed. "O.K., I'll go and wake him."

It seemed an eternity as she stood watching the remains of the whisky drip onto the oyster carpet, before Jake picked up the telephone.

"Tory darling, what's the matter? Are you O.K? Is it one of the kids?" Helen could hear the terrible anxiety in his voice, which made her cry all the more.

"No it's not Tory, it's me Helen. It was the only way I could have them fetch you." She was so hysterical it was a minute before he could discover what she was trying to say.

"Steady, pet. Calm down. Tell me what's the matter."

"Rupert knows everything. He's suspected us for ages." That wasn't true, but somehow it made a better story. "We gave ourselves away this evening. He's on his way to the village."

"Did he hurt you?"

"No—yes—well a little. I'm O.K., but he says he's going to kill you."

As though in a dream, Jake watched a group of English cyclists, drunk and stark naked except for their security chains, being humored very kindly along the passage by some security guards. For a wild second he wondered whether to seek asylum. There were enough guards on duty even in the middle of the night to protect him from a regiment of Ruperts. But then Rupert would probably go back to Arcadia and kill Helen.

"I'm so sorry," she sobbed. "I didn't mean to shock you. I was so frightened."

"Sweetheart, you must keep calm." It was as though he was speaking to a child and watching himself in a black and white film, cushioned by drink, yet curiously sober. This wasn't happening to him.

"Are you still wearing that gold dress? O.K. well get out of it and change into some day clothes. Pack a bag, put in clothes to last you for a few days, bring your passport and your American Express card, dark glasses and as much spare cash as you can get your hands on. I'll come and fetch you."

"Jake, I'm sorry."

"It's all right, but hurry."

Rupert stormed into the Olympic village twenty minutes later, and was held up by a further ten-minute hassle with the guards, because he was, if not completely drunk, obviously in a very wild, excitable state. Finally they let him through and he proceeded to search every room on the third floor, until he found Jake's. The weightlifters, trying to get their beauty sleep, were not amused to be roused by Rupert, roaring around the room, searching under beds, in the shower, even in the fridge.

Then he looked in Jake's chest of drawers. His passport and his toilet articles were gone, and all his clothes, except his red coat, his breeches, white shirts, ties, and boots, which still hung in the wardrobe. On the chest of drawers were framed photographs of Tory and the children.

60

Rupert returned to the Eriksons' house to find all the lights blazing and the place full of cops. Suzy and Albie, coming in tight and finding doors opened, chairs knocked over, whisky spilled, Helen's room ransacked and the alarm unset, had promptly assumed that they'd been burglarized. Rupert ran upstairs, took in the chaos of clothes, jewels and papers. All his spare cash had gone. He went back to the drawing room.

"There's only been one burglary in this house. Jake Lovell's walked off with my wife."

"Are you sure?" said Suzy in amazement. "He didn't seem remotely keen on her."

"He's a better actor than she is," said Rupert. "It's been going on since February. We've just had true confessions time." He looked at the carpet and the sofa. "Sorry about the whisky."

He was very pale, giving the suntan an almost green tinge, but seemed totally in control.

"Annunciata seemes to have pushed off too," said Albie, wandering into the drawing-room and pulling off his tie.

"Oh no," said Suzy, far more upset than by Helen's departure. "I've got fourteen poeple for lunch tomorrow."

"Only thirteen without Helen," said Rupert grimly.

After the police had gone he told them what had happened. In a way their flip, brittle approach helped him to cling onto his sanity.

"I must say she has been looking sensational since Jake arrived in L.A.," said Suzy, "and she got mad whenever he talked to me. I'm sorry, Rupert. Being bored with your wife doesn't necessarily mean you want someone else to take her off your hands, particularly when it's your worst enemy."

She was amazed Rupert was so calm. She found it rather chilling, perhaps he was still in shock.

Then he said, "Can I use your telephone to ring a few people? It'll be midday Tuesday morning in England now."

"Of course," said Suzy. "Go into the study." She was dying to discuss the whole thing with Albie.

Hell-bent on vengeance like an army scorching the earth, Rupert called Amanda Hamilton in Scotland. Fortunately, perhaps, he got Rollo and explained what had happened. Rollo was most sympathetic and fully appreciated that Jake and Helen might try to seize the children and said it would be perfectly all right for Charlene to fly up to Scotland with Marcus and Tab until Rupert got back from L.A.

"I'm awfully sorry," Rollo said again. "Have a word with Amanda."

Even thousands of miles away Rupert could almost hear Rollo putting his hand over the receiver while he briefed his wife.

Amanda sounded extremely shocked. "Darling, I'm sorry. Are you O.K.?"

"Fine," said Rupert, "but they could have timed it better, with the team competition on Sunday. The press is going to have a field day. That's why I want to get Tab," he paused, "and Marcus, of course, out of the way."

"Did you know yesterday? Was that why Rocky jumped so badly?"

"No," Rupert interrupted her. "That was my fault."

Then he called his secretary, Miss Hawkins, and told her to put a red alert on all credit cards, VISA and American Express, to order the bank to stop all checks and to close all Helen's accounts at Peter Jones, Harrods, Hatchards and Cavendish House in Cheltenham. Anyone at home, he said, particularly Charlene and Mrs. Bodkin or any of the grooms or gardeners, would be fired if they spoke to the press.

He went back into the living room with a grim smile on his face. "That should clip their wings."

Tory, after the victory celebrations, fell into bed at five in the morning, but still couldn't sleep for happiness. After all that struggle, Jakey had got his silver. She'd never seen him as happy as he'd been at the press conference. And now, with the Boyson sponsorship, he'd be able to have the horses he wanted; he and Fen wouldn't have to work quite so hard and he'd have more time with the children, which he'd always longed for, and they wouldn't have to scrimp and worry all the time about where the next penny was coming from. She didn't even feel tired when she had to get up at seven and take the sleepy, grumbling children to school. All day people kept calling to congratulate her and Jake. Flowers and telegrams arrived constantly. The village was in a state of total euphoria, already planning the Welcome Home celebrations.

Tory watched clips of Jake's silver four times on breakfast television, and in Olympic Round-up, *and* played it on the video machine, as she washed up all the glasses from last night. She didn't bother with lunch. She'd been on a diet and lost ten pounds since Jake left.

Singing at the top of her voice, she went to collect the children. Jake would be getting up soon, she thought fondly, with a terrible hangover.

On balance she'd decided not to fly to L.A. By the time she had everything organized it would be Friday. Then, after a night flight, there'd only be half a day before the team event. Then they'd be coming home again. There'd be other occasions.

Her mother had called and Tory'd been so happy she'd forgotten to be cool with her. After all it was a long time since Colonel Carter had taken Revenge away. Surely yesterday's medal proved Jake was the greater rider than Rupert?

She even found time to go and give Macaulay two apples and tell him about his master's great triumph. Housework could go by the board today. It was a beautiful September afternoon. Just a touch of wind ruffled the mill pond and the hanging green willow curtains.

The children were very fractious when she picked them up from School. Darklis had lost one shoe, but at least it was better than two, she said. Isa had been beaten up in the playground for boasting about his father. Tory sent them off to watch television. Suddenly, as she was cutting the fat off the lamb chops for their supper, she felt very tired. She'd have a large vodka and tonic when she'd put the children to bed.

Then perhaps Jake would ring. Another wave of happiness overwhelmed her.

Then she heard the noise of bickering from the living room. Isa, to Darklis' rage, had switched channels to get the Olympic results.

"Mummy," screamed Darklis, "Isa's hitting me."

"Stop it, Isa," yelled Tory.

"I always get the blame," shouted Isa. "Mummy, come quickly. There's something about Daddy."

Shoving the chops under the grill Tory ran into the living room.

"Silver medalist Jake Lovell," she heard in horror "has disappeared from the Olympic village. Not seen since last night, he is alleged by the *Los Angeles Times* to have gone off with Helen Campbell-Black, wife of Rupert Campbell-Black, a fellow member of the British team and a bronze and silver medalist in 1976."

Tory thought she must be dreaming. It couldn't be true. They'd made some mistake. Jake had called her last night and told her he loved her. There was a moth bashing against the television screen.

"What does it mean Mummy?" asked Isa. "Where's Daddy gone?"

"Nowhere darling," said Tory in a strange voice. "It's some mistake. Daddy wouldn't do that."

It was a few seconds before she realized that the telephone was ringing. She rushed to answer it. It must be Jake to say it was a hideous mistake.

"Mrs. Lovell?"

"Yes."

"It's the *Sun* newspaper here." It was that thickened voice again with which they announced trouble or asked difficult questions. "Just wondered if you've got anything to say about your husband running off with Helen Campbell-Black."

"I don't know what you're talking about," said Tory and slammed the telephone down.

The telephone rang again. It was the *Mirror* with the same question. Then it was the *Sun* again. Tory took the telephone off the hook. She started to shake violently.

"Mummy Mummy, the oven's on fire." Darklis, having wandered into the kitchen in search of a cookie, found the neglected chops ablaze under the grill. The frozen peas had boiled down to a green scum.

"Mummy" yelled Isa, starting to cry, "they're talking about Daddy."

Martin Bell, gazing sternly out of the television screen, his light brown curls whipped by the Los Angeles breeze, was confirming that Jake had indeed disappeared from the Olympic village, so had Helen Campbell-Black from the house in Arcadia where she had been staying with her husband. According to the *Los Angeles Times,* who had interviewed the maid, Helen had left after a row with Rupert, directly after a dinner at Ma Maison restaurant to celebrate Jake's silver medal. Malise Gordon, the British chef d'equipe, had appealed to Jake to come back for the team competition.

Tory was brought back to earth by the doorbell. It was a neighbor, Mrs. Irvine.

"I heard it on the radio," she said. "I'm so sorry for you. I'll get the children's supper and answer the telephone. You'll not want to be bothered."

"I'm sure it's some mistake," said Tory.

"The poor little soul didn't seem to have taken it in," Mrs. Irvine told her husband later, "so I got the doctor."

At that moment the door bell rang. It was the local stringer for the *Daily Mail*. After that they came like locusts, with their long-range cameras, trying to get in through the front door, the back door, even the windows, swarming through the village attempting to bribe grooms, neighbours, tradespeople, desperate for information.

Tory tried to put a call through to L.A. but all lines were busy.

"It's a bad dream," she kept telling herself. Jake wouldn't go off like that, not when he'd asked her to come out to L.A. yesterday, not with the team event on Sunday, which meant almost more to him than the individual, and which he knew meant infinitely more to Malise.

Alarmed by her calmness and refusal to accept the facts, the doctor gave her a sedative. It was not that Jake wouldn't leave her, she kept saying, but he'd certainly never leave the horses, or the children, particularly in the middle of the Olympics. It was a belief she had to cling to.

Malise, however, called at ten o'clock. "I'm afraid we know nothing more this end. What I imagine happened was that Jake and Helen may have been having a bit of a fling, at least that's what she told Rupert. Tempers flared. Rupert was absolutely livid at not getting the gold. He'd been simply poisonous all evening, threatened to beat Helen up. She appealed to Jake for help and he probably felt he'd got to remove her somewhere safe until Rupert cooled down."

Malise, reflected Tory, as the truth began to sink in, sounded like a gynecologist telling her she'd had a stillborn baby.

"I'm sure there's nothing to worry about," he went on. "I'm convinced he'll come back for the team event."

But Jake did not come back. The Games were into their second week. The public was slightly bored with tales of derring-do and mega-achievement, they wanted a good scandal. Rupert, his beautiful American wife and her romantic gyspy lover were the perfect answer.

"For just a handful of silver he left him," quipped the *New York Post*.

Everyone who knew Jake and Rupert re-kindled the old feud. Jake had been bullied at school by Rupert and had got his revenge twenty-two years later by trouncing Rupert at the Olympics and then running off with his wife.

It was the same in L.A. as at the Mill. Once the *Los Angeles Times* had featured Helen's row with Rupert and her running off with Jake, the reporters were everywhere. Like some horror army of killer ants they crept through seemingly locked doors, through windows, haunting the Olympic village, the Eriksons' house, the stables and the exercise rings.

Fen, as their prime target, had been absolutely knocked sideways by the news.

"I must go to Tory," she pleaded with Malise on Wednesday morning. "She sounds absolutely terrible now it's really sunk in. The English papers are crucifying Jake. I can't leave her to face it on her own. Let me fly home."

"You can't," said Malise, surveying his shambles of a team. "Unless Jake comes back you'll have to jump Hardy."

Everywhere Fen went people were bad-mouthing Jake. Everywhere the press swooped down on her. Every time she worked Hardy the exercise ring was crowded with photographers and curious on lookers.

Rupert was far less vulnerable. First he was holed up in Suzy's house which was electric-fenced and burglar-alarmed to the teeth. Secondly, you didn't try and interview a man-eating tiger. Rupert was in the kind of eruptive mood that kept even the press at a distance.

"Jake was just doing his bit for Britain," he told Billy on the telephone. "Unfortunately in this case the bit happened to be Helen.

Extraordinary. For seven years she never looked at another man. Then, according to Dizzy, for the last five months no one's been able to see her ears for skirt."

"He sounds terrible," Billy told Janey as he got off the telephone. "Do you think I ought to fly out there? The BBC has offered to pay my fare and give me a fat fee if I'll help Dudley do the commentary for the team competition."

"No, you ought not," snapped Janey. "Rupert's had it coming to him for years. I am not going to be left alone with Christy when he's so little . . . nor," she added to herself "am I going to let you loose in L.A. with Fenella Maxwell."

Twenty-four hours limped by with no sign of Jake. On Thursday morning Fen was working Hardy in one of the big exercise rings. Normally the German team should have been using the ring at this time but they'd willingly swapped over with the British to fox the press and give Fen the chance of a little privacy. It was nearly ten o'clock and the sun was already scorching. Hardy, missing Jake, was edgy and miserable. He had received so much adulation on Monday and Tuesday morning. Now suddenly no one wanted to admire the horse whose master had disgraced a nation.

As she slowly cantered him round on the left rein, Fen pondered the horrors of the last two days. Rumors seethed. Jake and Helen had been sighted in England, in all parts of America, on a flight to Bermuda. Jake had grown a moustache, was wearing a false beard. Helen had dyed her hair blonde, brunette, even cut it all off. Last night Malise had made another stiff-upper-lipped plea on television for Jake to come back: "We will jump as a team and conduct ourselves like gentlemen."

"Is he referring to Grisel?" said Rupert.

Rupert still keeps up the stream of flip remarks, thought Fen, allowing no one to see his black despair and utter humiliation. Malise seemed terribly upset too. Fen herself had been in tears all night. She wished she could help Tory. Bloody Helen Campbell-Black, she thought savagely, not even able to hold off until after the games.

Fen's hair was wringing wet beneath her hat, so was her T-shirt. The reins slipped between her damp hands. Suddenly she was overwhelmed by longing for Dino. She had never needed him more. She could have lain down and slept for a year in his arms. But she mustn't think of Dino or Helen, it only upset her. She must keep calm and psych herself into the right frame of mind for Sunday. Perhaps by some miracle Jake would come back.

"Oh Hardy, where's your master?" she sighed.

In the distance she could see the German team riding down from the stables in a cloud of dust to take over. She must make herself scarce before the press turned up. This afternoon, she thought wearily, she had to take Ivor to Disneyland again.

Catching her not concentrating, Hardy gave a whinny and a great nicker of joy and carted her across the ring.

"For God's sake, you disobedient bugger," screamed Fen, hauling ineffectually on his mouth, "where the bloody hell d'you think you're going?"

Hardy ground to a halt. Fen glanced up and gasped. For there, holding Hardy's dark blue sweat rug, tall and golden as a Lombardy poplar in autumn, stood Dino Ferranti.

"Hi, Hardy baby," he drawled, putting up a not altogether steady hand to stroke the dappled face. "I'm real glad you haven't forgotten me, just as I'm real glad your mistress's language is as lousy as ever."

Dino had had a long and very trying nine months, but everything was compensated for when he looked up and saw the expression of incredulous bewildered delight on Fen's face, which left him in absolutely no doubt about how she felt.

"You've gone blonde again," she muttered.

"I know. I didn't seem to score with grey hair."

"Oh Dino, Dino," and she tumbled off Hardy into his arms, and he kissed her so fiercely she had no doubt of his feelings towards her.

"Oh I love you," she bleated incoherently. "I've missed you. I've been so so miserable."

"Me too," he groaned. "Oh Christ darling, we've been so dumb."

As he held her tight, she could feel how much he was trembling and how his ribs stuck out beneath the blue denim shirt.

"You've got so thin," they both said simultaneously, and then started to laugh. Next moment Fen's laughter had turned to tears.

"It's so awful."

"I know. I'm real sorry, sweetheart." He took her face in his hands, kissing her forehead and her nose and the tears spilling out of her eyes before he found her mouth again.

"No, no," she protested, when at last he freed her. "It was so awful for you about Manny. Did you get my letter?"

"There was so much mail and I was so unglued I didn't even get around to looking at it until this morning. Hell, I needed you so badly. But I guess I couldn't handle seeing you again in case you were still mad at me, or didn't feel the way I did. So I chickened out and went home to lick my wounds. Then I heard about Helen and Jake taking off. I figured you might need me as much as I needed you, right, so here I am."

"Oh I'm glad," said Fen burying her face in his chest. "I was so aching to see you, it was the only thing that drove me on to get selected. I thought I'd die when Mary Jo said you weren't coming. You won't ever disappear again, will you? Life's so awful when you're not there."

"You try getting rid of me." He was about to kiss her again when he said, "Ouch."

Hardy, irritably trying to tell them they were hopelessly neglecting a silver medal winner, had nipped Dino on the shoulder.

Then all three jumped violently as a rousing chorus started bellowing, "Vy vos zey born so beautiful, vy vos zey born at all."

Swinging around, they found the entire German squad sitting on their horses laughing their heads off. "And about bloody time too, my friends," said Ludwig.

At the entrance to the stables the inevitable jackal pack of reporters was hovering.

"Heard from Jake?"

"No," snapped Fen.

"How's Tory bearing up?"

"Haven't talked to her today."

"Where's he gone?"

"I don't know."

Oh the bliss of having Dino there once more to get rid of them.

"Go on, get out of here. Fucking get off our backs," he said, hustling Fen and Hardy through the gates.

"Dino, Dino Ferranti," said one of the reporters with quickening interest. "You stayed at Jake's barn last fall, didn't you? What sort of guy was he?"

"The greatest," snapped Dino. "Not just as a rider but as a human being. If he walked out on the games, he must have a good reason, OK? I guess he wanted to protect Helen from her bastard of a husband."

On the way to Hardy's box Dino started kissing Fen again.

"Give him to me," said Sarah, grabbing Hardy. "You are in no fit condition. Take her away, Dino. She deserves the afternoon off. Make a change from taking Ivor around Disneyland."

Dino put his arm through Fen's "I'm staying at Carl Kennedy's place just up the road. Let's go there. At least we can be alone."

"I ought to have a bath," said Fen, suddenly aware of her sweaty hair and clothes.

"I'll give you one," said Dino. "It'll take hours."

Fen blushed scarlet.

"Dino," shouted a voice.

It was a middle-aged woman with the kind of lean muscular body that looks better in breeches than in the summer dress she was wearing.

"We thought you weren't coming," said her husband.

"Changed my mind."

"We were real sorry about Manny."

"Yeah, it was tough."

There was a pause. The couple looked inquiringly at Fen whose hand was still firmly held by Dino. Aware she must look hot and shiny from being kissed, she hung her head. Dropping her hand, Dino took hold of her hair at the back and very gently yanked her head upwards.

"You haven't met Fenella Maxwell," he said in his most drawling voice, "my future wife."

Fen jumped out of her skin, then looked up at him with such startled anxious eyes that he let go her hair and put a comforting arm around her shoulders.

"Truly?" she gasped.

"Very very truly," Dino said, laughing.

"Your future wife," said the woman in delighted surprise. "Is that a fact, Fenella—er—Maxwell?"

"Jake Lovell's sister-in-law, you were too polite to say," said Dino. "She's with the British team."

"Well congratulations," said the husband, pumping Fen by the hand.

"How long have you been engaged?"

Dino looked at his watch and laughed again. "About fifteen seconds," he said, "perhaps sixteen by now."

"Oh wow, this may not be the best way of relaxing before a mega-competition," said Dino, "but it's certainly the nicest."

He eased himself out of her and collapsed on to the flowered sheets. Carl Kennedy's house was near Suzy Erikson's. Out of the window they could see the mountains.

"I feel so relaxed I don't think I'll ever get up again," said Fen.

"It sure went through the top of the Richter scale," said Dino. "Were you scared?"

"Not as much as I thought I was going to be."

"Nor was I. It didn't matter if we bombed, we've got all our lives to get it right. Shall we have lots of kids? My Daddy's dying to be a grandfather."

Fen rolled over. "Are you sure you want to get married?"

"Don't you?" he said appalled.

"Oh yes, more than anything. I just don't want you to feel trapped."

"I want to be trapped. You gotta make an honest man of me."

He leaned on his elbow, running his hand down her body, stroking the hollow of her stomach.

"I'm going to feed you up."

"I'm sorry I was so vile in England."

"Well I came on pretty hostile too. You were bent out of shape over Billy. I over-reacted and backed off too hard not to crowd you."

"But all that stupid business with Enrico," protested Fen. "Ouch that's my boob you've dug your nails into."

"Anyone else I wouldn't have minded, but he's such a bastard. No that's not true. I'd have killed you if it had been anyone, I was so jealous."

"I haven't been out with a single man since you left."

"What about married guys?" said Dino. Fen giggled. "Nor them either. How about you?"

"Um—well I did try to screw my way out of it, but it didn't do any good. I knew I'd never love anyone else. I worked and worked. I had fantasies about getting the gold and dazzling you into loving me back."

Fen snuggled up to him. "You didn't need a gold. God, I feel guilty feeling so ridiculously happy, when everything else is so awful."

She knew she ought to put a call through to Tory, but couldn't bring herself to burst the bubble of bliss just yet. She looked at the lean brown length of him, revelling once again in the thick blonde hair, the Siamese cat eyes, the wide curling mouth. "I never dreamed I'd end up with anyone as stunningly attractive as you," she said humbly. "In fact your looks have definitely improved with age. D'you think I ought to call Malise just in case he thinks his entire team is doing a disappearing act?"

"He knows." Very gently Dino began to stroke the inside of her thighs. "I wanted to test the water so I made sure I bumped into him first this morning. He told me where to find you. He also reckoned," Dino smirked slightly, "you were going into a decline."

"I was not," said Fen indignantly. Then, as Dino moved his hand upwards and began to slide two fingers in and out of her, she gasped and said, "Well, perhaps I was."

"Come here," said Dino, bending over to kiss her. "I need a fix again."

In the end it was he who made her call Tory. She heard the operator saying the call came from L.A.

"Jake, is that you?" Tory's voice trembled with hope.

"No I'm afraid it's only me, Fen. You OK? No, I'm awfully sorry, there's really no news of him this end. How are the children taking it?"

"We're managing very well," said Tory in an unnaturally bright voice. "I just hope Jake isn't too shattered by the press furore to come out of hiding." She started to cry.

"Oh please don't," said Fen, feeling her eyes fill with tears. "Look, Dino Ferranti turned up today. Have a word with him." She handed the receiver to Dino.

Dino was immensely kind but very practical. Did she have enough food in the house? Was anyone helping her with the kids and the horses?

Who was fending off the press?

"Everyone's being marvelous," said Tory, "but they're so embarrassed. They were so proud of Jakey and were planning this huge welcome-home bonanza. Now they don't know what to do."

"Tell them to cheer for Fen. Angel, please don't cry." He raised a palm upwards in a particularly Latin gesture of despair, then said, "Listen, I'm going to get a night flight, right?"

"Oh no," whispered Fen in horror. "You can't do that. I need you."

"I'll be with you some time tomorrow," he went on. "Don't bother to meet me. I'll call from Heathrow. I'll sort everything out. We'll just cross our fingers."

Putting down the telephone he gathered Fen into his arms.

"I can't bear it, not so soon after I've found you. I need you just as much as she does," she sobbed. "I'm sorry to be so selfish."

Dino let her cry, stroking her hair, cradling her.

"It's the most awful thing I've ever had to do," he said, "but if I'm joining your family, right, I have a responsibility towards all of them. Things are simmering along at the moment but if Jake doesn't show on Sunday, the shit is going to really hit the fan. He's already blown the monetary advantages of his silver. The press is gonna assassinate him for letting down his country and you've no idea of Rupert's capacity for vengeance. Every door'll be shut to him. He'll probably be suspended for ten years."

"Oh poor Jake," said Fen in horror. "Why *did* he do it?"

Dino brushed her damp hair and kissed her forehead. "I guess he fell in love. We know how potent that is. Helen was suicidal, frantic to escape from Rupert. Jake momentarily wanted someone glamorous to complement his new star status, probably wanted to deal the coup de grace to Rupert. Nothing like cuckolding your enemy. All the same I figure Helen's to blame. However much Rupert hammers Jake for enticement, I guess it was Helen who pulled the plug out. She blew it to Rupert, knowing it would trigger Jake into leaving. But whatever happens, Jake's on a collision course. Rupert'll ruin them both."

He glanced at her watch. "I'd better book that flight."

As he came off the telephone Fen put her arms round him. "I didn't believe it was possible, but I love you about a million times more than I did an hour ago; all the same I wouldn't tell Tory about us yet. Other people's happiness tends to push you over the edge."

61

*I*t was like the House of Atreus as disaster after disaster hit the British team. Despite every effort, Desdemona was still not fit, which meant that, unless Jake came back, Fen would have to ride Hardy.

"He's a misogynist," grumbled Fen next morning, after he'd thrown her off for the second time. "I'll never get him out of the collecting ring in this mood."

"Well, we've got to have someone whose round we can drop," said Grisel, kicking Mr. Punch on and clearing the combination on a perfect stride.

"Bitch." thought Fen, "may you be struck down by toads and pestilence."

She spoke too soon. Coming back to the Olympic village that evening she found Grisel staggering out of the john, as green as the elephant who ate the mushroom in the Babar books.

"I've vomited fifteen times," she announced, collapsing onto her bed.

"Too many cyclists," muttered Fen under her berath. "Shall I get a doctor?"

"No," groaned Grisel. "I'll be OK."

By late evening poor Grisel's temperature had gone up to 104 and she was admitted to the hospital with suspected food poisoning.

"And then there were three," said Rupert next morning, as they had a final workout before the competition the following day. Despite his appearance of icy indifference, Rupert was in a terrible state. Rage against both Helen and Jake kept bubbling up inside him, corrosive as black bile. Despite the quantities of whisky he'd drunk each night in search of oblivion, he had hardly slept since they'd gone. Drink had never affected his eyes in the past, but watching Humphrey Bogart movies on television all night hadn't helped. In the relentless Los Angeles sunshine that morning, as he was cantering towards a huge upright, Jesus the Mexican decided to gallop across his path ten yards beyond the fence. Just for a second Rocky panicked, took off too early, clouting the heavy pole with his forelegs. Turning a somersault in the air, he crashed down with Rupert under him.

By the time Fen, Malise and Jesus the Mexican had reached them, Rocky had scrambled to his feet. Shaking himself gingerly, he decided he wasn't hurt and cantered off. Rupert tried to get up, groaned and fell back, clutching his shoulder.

"What is it?" said Malise, dropping to his knees.

"Shoulder," said Rupert through clenched teeth. "Dislocated. Get me to a fucking hospital at once and get it put back. Jesus!"

"*Si,*" said the Mexican, "I am here."

Just for a second a ghost of a smile flickered across Rupert's face.

"Not you," he said. "I was talking to an earlier model."

Malise went with Rupert to the Emergency Room. He lay stretched out in the ambulance, his face grey-green, sweat beads drenching his forehead and upper lip, cursing quietly to himself the whole way. Just to look at the horrible angle of his arm made Malise feel sick.

"At least it's not fractured," said the doctor after the X-Ray. "Pretty straightforward to put back. You'll just be out of action for a few days."

Malise and Rupert exchanged glances. Rupert turned to the doctor.

"I don't want an anesthetic."

"Don't be ridiculous," said Malise.

"I don't need one. How did they manage before they had chloroform? I don't want my reflexes fucked up for tomorrow."

"You're not jumping tomorrow," said Malise.

"What other alternative do we have?"

"Appealing to Jake to come back."

"If he shows his face within fifty miles of the show ring he'll end up in here as well," said Rupert. "In the morgue."

"Have you any idea how painful it will be without an anesthetic?" said the doctor.

"Yes," said Rupert. "Our doctor at home put it back for me once out hunting. I carried on for the rest of the day."

"You were younger then." said Malise.

"This is the second time," said the doctor.

"I know," said Rupert, throwing back his head and clenching his teeth. "Come here, sweetheart," he added to the beautiful nurse who was gazing at him with pity and admiration, "and hold my hand."

He was about to say he expected he'd do it a third time, but as the doctor got to work he fainted.

"At least the pain should take my mind off my erring wife," he said when he came round. But despite repeated shots of morphine, he had never known such agony.

At five o'clock Malise called a press conference: "The British team is down to three riders. One of them Rupert Campbell-Black, has been very seriously injured today but is determined to ride tomorrow. I want to make one more appeal to Jake Lovell to think seriously about coming back. Great Britain needs him. Rupert has agreed there will be no reprisals."

Fen's night was scarcely better than Rupert's. She had thought that now Dino had reappeared everything would be easier. But she found herself even twitchier than ever. Had he really been there at all?

Did he really love her and want to marry her? She felt bitterly ashamed of the resentment she felt that he'd gone to look after Tory. If he really loved you, mocked a voice as she got dressed at four o'clock in the morning, he wouldn't have been able to tear himself away. She'd been miserable for so long, she couldn't adjust to happiness. In a few hours she was going to face the worst ordeal of her life and she felt quite unprepared to cope with it. She must get herself into the right frame of mind.

"Tell me how stupid I am," she said to Lester the teddy bear as she tied her tie.

But Lester didn't answer.

"Have a nice day," she said to him as she left the room. "It's more than I shall have."

Malise was standing by the car. Ivor was already in the back, looking green. "I slept like a log," he said in a surprised voice.

"Lucky you," said Fen.

The press surged forward.

"Any news from Jake?"

"Nothing," said Malise bleakly. "We shall only be fielding three riders. It's too late for him to declare now."

Rupert was glad when the night was over. He'd always assumed he would be able to withstand torture; now he wasn't sure. He wondered if the doctor had trapped a nerve when he'd put the shoulder back.

At five-thirty he had a bath. The hot water helped to relax him, but after a quarter of an hour he found he couldn't get out of the tub. The slightest move to raise himself up produced absolute agony in his shoulder. Another half-hour passed, as he slumped between each thwarted attempt. He was terrified of slipping. With his left foot he pulled out the plug, waiting for the enamel surface to dry, so he might have more grip. It must be getting on for six-thirty. They'd be walking the course in an hour. He'd have to yell for Suzy, who probably had a hangover and wouldn't wake up. He was almost sobbing with pain and frustration. If only he could crawl to the bedroom, he could give himself another shot of morphine. Then he heard the doorbell go, then again. He made another attempt to get out. Then he heard Suzy's door open.

"Suzy," he croaked. Then he heard voices in the hall. Probably Malise wondering where the hell he was.

"He's not in his room, he must be in the bath," Suzy was saying sleepily.

Thank God he hadn't locked the door. Suzy banged on it.

"Someone to see you Rupe."

"Who the hell is it?" he said.

"It's me," said a blissfully familiar voice, and there in the doorway stood Billy.

For a second Rupert gazed at him dumbfounded.

"Christ, do I ever need you." he said in an unsteady voice.

"I know. I'm terribly sorry about Helen."

"Now, to get me out of this bloody bath," said Rupert. "But give me a shot of morphine first. It's on the chest of drawers in my bedroom."

The sting of the needle entering his shoulder was the most wonderful sensation he could imagine.

"How the hell did you manage to get out of Janey's clutches?" he asked.

Billy grinned. "I told her that sometimes water was thicker than blood."

"Draw's good," said Malise. "We're fourteenth out of sixteen. All the other riders were tremendously sympathetic and friendly."

"They can afford to be," said Rupert. "They think we've had it."

"Who are the favorites?" asked Fen.

"Americans, Germans, Swiss," said Rupert. "We're about a million to one. I've put a monkey on."

"Don't let Fen see any of the papers," hissed Malise. "They've all crucified Jake."

"Good," said Rupert. Then, shooting a sidelong glance at Malise, "It's not the winning that matters, it's the being taken apart."

It was a tremendous boost to the British team to see Billy.

"Can't you jump?" said Ivor.

"I'm going to sit in the commentary box with Dudley," said Billy, "and be wildly partisan."

"At least you'll get the names right," said Fen.

"I'm glad you think so, Fiona," said Billy. "How's Rupe bearing up?" he added in an undertone.

"He won't talk about either her or Jake except to make the odd flip crack. He probably will to you. I think he's going through hell, but I can't quite work out if it's violent possessiveness or murdered pride, or whether he's suddenly realized he loves her."

At seven-thirty they walked the course. Everyone agreed it was the biggest ever built in show-jumping. Fen could walk straight underneath the parallel without bumping her head. Close up, first time she realized how huge the fences were.

"Can't think why they don't stage the Olympic swimming contest in the water jump," she said.

Ivor's mouth was open wider than ever. "It's even worse than the individual."

In front sauntered the American team. In their white short-sleeved shirts and breeches, showing off their mahogany suntans, long bodies and thoroughbred legs, laughing and exuding quiet confidence, they looked as though they'd been fed on peaches and T-bones all their lives. The crowd gave them a colossal cheer of encouragement as they passed. The German team looked equally together as they goose-stepped out the distances. But for the first time Fen felt there was real solidarity within the British team.

The arena was like an oven already. By the time I go in, thought Fen, it'll be turned up to 110°.

"That's going to cause the most trouble," said Malise, looking at the fence constructed in the shape of a huge brown derby hat. "It's so unfamiliar, you'll have to ride them really hard at it, then there's that big gate immediately after."

"At least they've scrapped the hotdog," said Ivor in relief. "All these flowers are giving me hay fever."

Rupert broke off a frangipani and gave it to Fen.

"You'll be had up for demolishing the course even before you start," she said.

Malise was right. The derby upset everyone. Ludwig, the German pathfinder, expected to go clear, was nearly brought down by it, and knocked up sixteen faults.

"Roll on ze next Olympics," he said ruefully as he came out of the ring. "I am very bored of being ze good loser."

Canadian, Australian, Italian and French riders all came to grief. Jesus the Mexican had a punishing fall. The first American rider, Lizzie Dean, came in and cleared the derby, but ran slap into the gate and had eight faults at the combination.

"I can't watch any more. My self-confidence is in tatters," said Fen. "The only good thing about this competition is Billy doing the commentary. He keeps saying 'Hooray' every time a foreign rider kicks out a fence."

"You'll be jumping in three-quarters of an hour," said Malise. "Better go and warm Hardy up. By the way, some flowers arrived for you. They're in the tackroom."

He allowed himself a small smile as Fen bolted the 400 yards to the stables. The flowers were two dozen pale pink roses and the card inside said, "To darling Fen, Good Luck, I love you, Dino."

"How the hell did they get them delivered here?" she said.

"Carl Kennedy bought them," said Sarah. "He promised Dino he'd make sure you got them. Stop grinning like a Cheshire cat. This is no time to be worrying about the opposite sex."

"Having got these," said Fen, putting them in a bucket of water, "I can now stop worrying about it."

Because they were only fielding three riders, the British team
only started jumping with the second riders of the other teams.
Among these, Hans Schmidt only had a couple of poles down for eight
faults and Mary Jo came in and showed everyone how to do it with a
glorious clear.

"That should encourage Ivor," said Fen, who had jumped off
Hardy for a second to watch him.

Ivor rode in blinking. Not a seat was empty. After Mary Jo's gold
earlier in the week, and her clear now, the huge crowd was at fever
pitch.

"I always enjoy Ivor's intellectual approach to the sport," said
Rupert from the shade of riders' stand. "Now he has removed his hat
will he ever find his head again?"

After Tuesday's fiasco, Ivor started well and rode with colossal
determination. The sailboat, the derby, the high gate, the huge wall,
the massive blue water jump caused him no trouble at all. Then he
unaccountably stopped twice at the parallels.

"That's that then," said Rupert. "Let's go and have a screw, Dizz."

"For God's sake get your bat out Ivor," Billy was yelling in the
commentary box, to the startled delight of the viewers. "One more
stop and the whole team's eliminated."

Scarlet in the face, as if by telepathy, Ivor pulled his whip out of
his boot, in which it was tucked, and gave John half a dozen hefty
whacks.

"Good God," said Malise.

The picture of injured pride, John heaved himself over the parallel, and, swishing his tail in rage, proceeded to go clear, except for
bringing down the middle element of the combination.

"Absolutely marvelous. Well done Ivor," said Billy in excitement
from the commentary box. "Do you know, he only paid £1000 for that
horse?"

"Ten faults, plus one time fault. That's not at all bad," said
Malise.

Fen knew she should have some inner tap which could turn off all
outside excitement and leave her icily calm. On Desdemona she'd always jumped best when she was angry. But Hardy needed to be kept
serene. He seemed a little tired after his medal-winning adventures on
Monday, which would at least make him jump more carefully. Following Jake's lead, she had removed the cotton wool from his ears and let
him go to the entrance of the arena, so he could watch the preceding
round. It was both inspiring and daunting. Carl Kennedy went clear,
to colossal applause, which meant the Americans were on twelve faults
at the end of their third round, and could probably scrap Lizzie Dean's

round. The Tarzan howls and the waving American flags had Hardy hopping all over the place.

"The time is incredibly tight," said Malise. "Don't waste any of it in the corners. But remember, the important thing is to get round at all costs. If you're disqualified we're out."

"You do say the cheeriest things," said Fen.

"Good luck," said Rupert.

Fen felt the butterflies going berserk in her stomach, as the terror finally got to her.

"I can't face it," she said in panic. "I simply can't jump in front of all those people."

"Yes, you can," said Rupert, putting his good left hand up to squeeze her thigh. "Come on darling, you'll float over them. Hardy's done it all before. Leave it to him.

"Are you sure?" Suddenly she looked terribly young.

Rupert smiled. "Quite sure."

Out in the arena there was nothing like it. Nothing like the fear and the exposure in that blazing white hot heat, watched by 200,000 eyes and millions and millions of television viewers.

Billy, who by now was well into the whisky, admired the slender figure in the black coat, her blonde hair just curling under her hat, one of Dino's pink roses in her buttonhole.

"This is certainly the most beautiful girl rider in the world," he said. "Riding Hardy, with whom her brother-in-law, Jake Lovell, did so brilliantly on Monday to get the silver medal. Now come on, darling."

"I told you not to mention Jake," hissed Dudley, putting his hand over the microphone, "and don't call Fiona darling."

The relief of the bell stopped all thought process. Suddenly Fen's nerves vanished.

"It's you and me, babe," she whispered to Hardy as he cleared the first four fences without any trouble, kicking up the tan bank, following the hoof prints of earlier riders. She steadied him for the derby. He didn't like it, then decided he did and took a mighty leap, clearing it by a foot. The yell of the crowd distracted him, and the heat haze above the gate made judging the distance difficult. Fen asked him to take off too early, he kicked out the fence, and then toppled the wall after that, hurting himself, eyes flashing, ears flattened, tail whisking like an angry cat.

"Now she'll go to pieces," thought Malise in despair. But Fen held him together and drove him on, picking her way over the obstacles, not touching any of them.

"Look at him," said Sarah in ecstasy. "He's really, really trying."

Coming up to the last fence, Hardy started showing off and gave a huge kick back. The crowd laughed. He kicked back again. Lazily whisking over the last fence, he gave it an almighty clout. For a second the pole shuddered, trembled on the edge, then fell back into the cup.

"God is on our side after all," said Malise.

"Bloody good," said Rupert, as Fen slipped off the huge horse, flinging her arms round Hardy's neck, and taking back all the beastly things she'd ever said about him.

"Until the next time," said Sarah.

Now the last riders in each team had to jump. Peter Colgate, riding instead of Dino, knocked up a surprising fifteen faults, so his was the round the Americans dropped. Hans Schmidt went clear.

The round, however, the world was waiting for was Rupert's. Fen straightened his tie and did up one brass button of his red coat which was draped over his damaged right shoulder: "Are you OK? Does it hurt horribly?"

"Yes, but I've just had another shot, I'm so spaced out I'll probably carry Rocky over the fences with one finger."

Not by a flicker as he rode into the ring did Rupert betray his awareness that every camera in the world was trained on him to see what the effect had been of Helen leaving. If the press had gone to town on Jake that morning, it was without Rupert's help. He had refused to say a word to them.

He held the reins lightly in his left hand. He carried no whip. The crowd, seeing that he was coming in to jump the most punishing course in history with one arm in a sling, roared their approval and encouragement.

Dropping his reins, he removed his hat. His blonde hair glittered golder than any medal. The pain was terrible, even the gentlest pop in the collecting ring had jolted his shoulder unbearably, but none of this showed in his face.

Rocky was a gallant and kind horse. Something was different today, perhaps it was the sympathetic almost helpless way Rupert had jumped him earlier, perhaps it was because for once his master wasn't carrying a whip. Suddenly there was an expression of deep responsibility on Rocky's handsome golden face.

I will take care of you today, he seemed to be saying, just to make you feel a sod for all the times you've beaten me up in the past.

Over the first two fences Rupert had the greatest difficulty balancing himself, then he settled in. Rocky was jumping really carefully, only clearing each fence by an inch or so. Now he was thundering down to the water—and over. Now he was over the derby gate, now turning for the huge three-part combination.

"Undoubtedly Rupert is the best rider in the world," shouted

Billy in jubilation in the commentary box. "Look at the power of those leg muscles; he isn't even shifting in the saddle. Go on Rupe, go on."

For a miraculous moment it looked as if he was going to go clear; then Rocky trailed a leg at the last fence and, unlike Fen, brought it down. Out he rode to almost the biggest cheer of the day.

Billy bolted out of the commentary box to congratulate him. "Wait," wailed Dudley. "There are still the Japs and the Portuguese to jump."

"That was absolutely brilliant," said Billy, rushing up to Rupert. "God knows how you did it."

"Should have been a clear," said Rupert, kicking his right foot out of the stirrup and wincing and biting his lip as he lowered himself down.

"Tremendous performance, Rupert," said Malise, looking at his score sheet, "The Yanks are on twelve, the Germans on sixteen, the Swiss on eighteen, the French on twenty. We're fifth with twenty-two," he added with quiet satisfaction.

"You shouldn't be jumping, but I'm sure glad I saw you. Congratulations," said a voice. It was the doctor from the hospital.

Rupert smiled, but the doctor, noticing his pallor and how much he was sweating, waved his medical kit. "I thought you'd probably need something stronger to face this afternoon."

"I need an enormous whisky," said Rupert.

"Not too enormous," said Malise.

*F*en never knew afterwards if she ate any lunch. Ivor ate his way solemnly through two steaks without realizing it. Billy came too, cracking jokes with Rupert, keeping up everybody's spirits. They knew they wouldn't win, the margin was too big, but they were quietly elated. They had conducted themselves with honor.

Prince Philip, who was an old admirer of Rupert's, came up and congratulated them.

"Really tremendous! Well done of all of you! Don't know why you bother to ride with any hands at all, Rupert."

"I'd better go back and wind up Dudley," said Billy, getting to his feet. "He says I must be more enthusiastic about the other nations. Good luck everyone. Take care of yourself, Rupe."

Rupert raised his hand. He wished Billy could stay. He was beginning to feel desperately tired and the pain was really getting to him.

"Can you give me something?" he said to the doctor.

"It'd be better nearer your round or the effect might wear off. I daren't give you two shots or you'll pass out in the ring."

When the riders came out for the second round, it was soon apparent that the first round had overstretched the horses. Despite violent clouds on the horizon and the rumble of thunder, the sun was at its height, beating down into the stadium at a heat of over 100 degrees.

Only the top ten teams went through, but it still meant nearly forty rounds for the crowd to watch. The Americans, who had been led to believe that their team couldn't lose, came back in anticipation of slaughter. Bored now by foreign rounds, screaming and hysterically cheering on their own riders, their chauvinism was only equaled by Billy's in the commentary box.

"He's a nice guy, he deserves it," he said when Ludwig went clear, dashing British hopes, but he was unashamedly delighted when Mary Jo put in an unexpected twelve faults, and Lizzie Dean hit two fences and put in a stop, and the early French and Swiss riders knocked up cricket scores.

Ivor came in so elated by his first round success that he only knocked up eight faults.

"Marvelous," said Billy. "That's really marvelous. Now with all the second riders gone, Great Britain's edged up to third place, and the Germans are moving right up behind the Americans."

As it became apparent that a duel to the death was setting in, people ran in from the halls and the stands filled up to bursting.

"I must have another shot," said Rupert.

"You can't risk it, said the doctor.

Carl Kennedy went clear agian. Once again Fen had to follow him.

"The Americans are on thirty-one; we are on thirty," Malise told her. Fen's nerves were worse. Last time they'd had so little to lose; now they were in with a chance. If Hardy started kicking out fences all was lost.

"Kiss me Hardy, e'er I die of fright," she said.

In England they were only televising the second round of the competition. Dino checked the video for the hundredth time to see if there was enough tape for Fen's round.

"Tory darling," he called into the bedroom, "Fen's about to jump. I think you ought to come and watch."

He could hardly bear to watch her, she looked so small and defenseless as she rode into the ring. He had seen Rupert patting her hand and giving her encouragement. The bastard looked so impossibly handsome and, with his dislocated shoulder, a more romantic figure than ever. And even worse, Billy Lloyd-Foxe was doing the commentary. What the hell was he doing in America?

"And here comes Fenella Maxwell, riding her second round for Great Britain," said Billy. "Only nineteen and easily our most brilliant and beautiful girl rider, and voted Sports Personality of the Year. Come on now Fen, darling."

"Oh shut up Billy," howled Janey and Dino from different parts of England.

"Please don't cheer," Fen prayed to the crowd as Hardy plunged all over the place. "Please don't distract him. Let us get around. Concentrate, Hardy my darling."

Suddenly Hardy decided to behave, jumping over the fences as though they were fallen logs in the wood.

"I want to go clear, oh please let me go clear," prayed Fen, getting excited. But Hardy took such an unexpectedly huge jump over the wall that it didn't give him enough run into the water and he landed well in with a splash. Fen felt her face covered with tepid water. Hardy was drenched. He loathed getting wet. He lashed his tail, ears flattened.

"That's done it," groaned Rupert. "He'll never clear the upright; he's come in too close."

Determined to prove Rupert wrong, Hardy did an incredible cat jump, up and up he went as though he was climbing a ladder. Then with a merry flick of his back feet he was over.

Dino put his arm around Tory.

"Go on Fen," yelled Darklis.

"Don't look around," screamed Isa, "Daddy'll murder you." He stopped, remembering, and looked in embarrassed apology at his mother. "I mean, for goodness sake hurry."

Fen thundered down to the last triple—she was over.

"Hooray," yelled Billy, stamping his feet in the commentary box.

The applause was so colossal, Fen didn't realize she'd got a time fault.

Once again, everyone got out their calculators.

"That puts us on thirty-five, very much in contention," said Malise. "The Germans are on thiry-four, the Americans on thirty. But we can't afford any complacency. The Italians are on thirty-nine, with Piero Fratinelli to come."

Rupert was seriously worried. The morphine wasn't having the desired effect this time. He hardly warmed up Rocky at all; every stride was agony. There was no point risking a fall and finishing himself off altogether over a practice fence. He sat in the tackroom on an upturned bucket, with his head in his hands. He daren't go near the First Aid Post in case they stopped him riding.

"You going to be able to make it?" said the doctor.

"Sure." said Rupert, "but I hope they bloody hurry."

Hans Schmidt had eight faults.

"That's not at all good for us," sighed Billy. "Good round though."

He grinned across at Fen, who was biting her nails in the riders' stand, and mopped his brow.

In came Peter Colgate, who'd replaced Dino. The American crowd was in a state of hysteria. All across the stands American flags were being waved in encouragement, as the big striding bay thoroughbred, who'd won several races in his youth, ate up the course.

"I don't fancy anyone's chances against him if there's a jump off," said Billy.

The thoroughbred's racetrack origins were his undoing, however. Picking up the tension from his rider, hearing the hysterical yelling of the crowd, he was reminded of his youth and, thundering towards the final fences, he cleared the pink wall with ease, then accelerated and flattened both parts of the double and, hearing the howl and groan of the crowd, only just scraped over the last massive triple.

"Hooray," said Billy from the commentary box. "That's absolutely marvelous for us, but admittedly not great for the Americans."

Carl Kennedy turned to Fen, shaking his head. "Our mutual friend would have gone clear."

"What's the score?" Fen asked Malise.

"Italians forty, Americans thirty-eight, Germans forty-three."

They looked at each other for a minute.

"That means if Rupert goes clear we get the gold, four faults we get the silver, eight faults we'll have to jump off, which will be too much for Rupert."

Rupert rode into the ring.

"And here comes Rupert Campbell-Black on Popstar," said Dudley, "with a dislocated shoulder, which was put back yesterday. The suspense is absolutely terrible, but I think we are about to witness a great display of courage."

"Courage is a quality the Campbell-Blacks have never lacked," said Billy. "One of Rupert's ancestors was on the King's side during the Civil War, but, tortured by Roundheads, he never squealed."

All the vengeful heat of the sun seemed to be concentrated on Rupert's black velvet hat. The colored poles and the flower arrangements swam before his eyes. The officials in their coral blazers seemed to be dancing, the derby rising and falling by itself, the red and blue boat sailing away. The pain was excruciating now. If Rocky played up, he was doomed. Somehow he removed his hat, but, as Rocky sidled away, it took hours to get it back on again.

Where the hell was the first fence? For a panic-stricken moment he couldn't remember. He looked up at the sea of faces, curiously still for once, the peaks of their caps like a million beaks. He had a terrifying hallucination—they were going to swoop down and peck him to death. Everything went black, he swayed then forced himself to look down at Rocky's blond braids. His good hand was shaking violently—like a jerking off schoolboy—the thought made him laugh. Thank God, there was the first fence. He kicked Rocky into a canter.

"And there goes Rupert," said Billy in a voice that was not quite steady. "All our hopes go with him."

Rocky, aware that his master was wildly untogether, jumped the first fence wrong, rapping it really hard, jarring Rupert's shoulder appallingly. To a man, the crowd winced. The next jump was almost as unhappy. Rupert lost a stirrup, his balance all awry. Then he jabbed Rocky's mouth over the sailboat and the horse pecked on landing.

"God, that must hurt," moaned Billy.

Coming up to the derby, Rupert found his iron and managed to stay on somehow.

"Oughtn't he to retire?" said Fen in anguish. "It must be killing him."

Suddenly, with a relentless surge of courage, Rupert cleared the gate, and turned to the water, riding at it like a man possessed, clearing it by two feet. The crowd roared in ecstasy and then in apprehension. Rupert was beginning to do it well. Suddenly an American victory was in danger. Now he was turning towards the big combination: three vast brick-red fences with their clashing bright green pools of ferns. He left the first element to Rocky, who jumped it big, leaving him too close to the second element. With a brilliant shift in the saddle, Rupert swung Rocky to the right so he had more room and could get in an extra stride before clearing it, then swung him back again so he had the same extra diagonal. Rocky clouted the final pole, which was almost indistinguishable from the greenery filling the jump, but it stayed put.

The crowd burst into a spontaneous yell of applause.

"The Gods who live forever," muttered Malise to himself, "are on our side today."

"That was the most glorious piece of riding," said Billy. "Oh come on Rupe. I can't bear to look any more. You take over, Dudley."

There were only three fences between Britain and a medal and, because of this, they all seemed higher than the grandstand.

Rocky was jumping majestically, but Rupert realized he must

speed up. He couldn't afford time faults. Through a haze of pain the three fences receded and came towards him; he'd never judge the distances; he couldn't really gallop on with only one hand.

"He can either go carefully and risk time faults, or risk knocking them down," said Billy. "Knowing Rupe, I bet he chooses the latter."

Rupert did. He came thundering down to the first fence.

"Oh steady," said Malise in anguish.

"Too fast, gasped Fen. "Oh God help him."

Rupert was over the first fence, meeting it absolutely perfectly.

"We'll have to jump off for the bronze," shouted Billy in excitement.

Rupert was somehow over the two treacherous uprights of the double.

"We've got the silver," yelled Billy, Come on, Rupe, come on."

Rocky gathered himself together, took a mighty leap and sailed through the air, over the triple and into the history books. Pandemonium broke out in the commentary box. Billy was hugging Dudley, both yelling at once. Dizzy burst into tears.

"I'm awfully sorry, Ma'am," said Fen, realizing she was hugging Princess Anne. Suddenly she heard a hoarse strangulated sound behind her; it was Ivor, cheering like an old mule.

"We got the gold," screamed Fen, jumping up and down. "We got the gold."

As Rupert rode out of the arena at a walk, the whole stadium rose to their feet to applaud him. The cheers went on for a full five minutes.

Naturally disappointed the home team hadn't made it, the crowd was prepared to honor such a display of courage.

Rupert rode up to Malise. His face was expressionless.

"What price fairies now?" he said.

Malise grinned up at him. "On the day my pansies came good. Bloody marvelous," then, surprised at Rupert's lack of excitement, "You went clear you know. We've got the gold."

Rupert shook his head. A loudspeaker confirmed his victory. He stayed absolutely calm. He didn't smile or give Rocky great slaps of joy on the neck which was normal practice. His hand didn't even tremble. He slid off the horse, gave him a quick pat, leaned his head for a second against the red-gold satin neck. Everyone swarmed around him, cheering and yelling.

"Great Rupe, terrific, you showed them."

Rupe broke away from them and stumbled towards the tunnel. Everyone followed him, cheering. Malise fought his way back to Rupert's side.

"Leave him alone," he snarled at the pack, suddenly losing his temper. "Can't you understand the strain he's been under?"

"It's all right," he said gently to Rupert.

Rupert turned, his eyes streaming. "A moron, a schoolgirl and a cuckold," he said, "we took on the whole bloody world."

"And beat them," said Malise.

Halfway down the tunnel Rupert slumped against the wall, shutting his eyes, battling to stop the tears.

"I'm sorry," he mumbled. "Been a bit of a strain the last few days. Too much dope, not much sleep. Oh Christ."

"Look," said Malise, patting Rupert's good shoulder, "over the years I've seldom seen eye to eye with you. But I have to hand it to you today. Without doubt you produced the finest and bravest display of riding I've ever seen. You made the other riders look like gymkhana kids. No one in that stadium or watching it on television will ever forget it."

Rupert sniffed and wiped away the tears with the back of his hand.

"Think Jake would've beaten me?"

"My dear boy, today no one could have beaten you."

Rupert stretched out his good hand and grabbed Malise's arm.

"I've always given you a hard time," he said shakily, "but I guess you're the best too."

Odd, thought Malise, how the moments of greatest happiness come from people you least expect.

Suddenly Rupert brightened perceptibly. "I put money on our winning," he said. "I must have made a fortune."

Chestnut, dappled grey and dark bay, they walked proudly into the arena, ears pricked, eyes bright, knowing they were the best in the world. On their backs rode Rupert and Ivor in their red coats, with Fen in black in the center. And realizing once again they were riding one man short, the magnanimous crowd cheered them to the top of the stadium. Everywhere Union Jacks seemed to be waving.

"And straight against that great array/Forth went the dauntless three," thought Malise.

"Mummy," said Georgina Hamilton in Scotland, "you really must allow me to meet Rupert. I mean, he may be old and frightfully wicked, but he is phenomenally attractive. And they always say it's best to start with older men."

Tabitha, who'd been allowed to stay up, bounced on Amanda's knee.

"Daddy jump," she said. "Daddy jump well."

"He did indeed, darling," said Amanda. She turned to Rollo, trying to keep her elation within bounds. "If that doesn't get Rupert a safe seat, nothing will."

"He is stunning," said Georgina. "Oh promise you'll introduce me."

"It's a good thing," thought Amanda, "that Georgina is going back to boarding school next week."

"Want Mummy. When will I see Mummy?" said Marcus for the hundredth time that day.

"I'm so proud of her," said Tory. "She rode so wonderfully well. It's so awful that such a marvelous victory should be blighted by the other thing. Jakey must be heartbroken not to be part of it."

"He couldn't come back into that," said Dino. "I guess he didn't want to rock any more boats. If he's coming back, I figure it'll be later."

Malise followed them with his military walk, marching on air. The crowd once again gave an extra cheer in appreciation of Dizzy and Sarah in their Union Jack shorts.

As she stood on the highest middle step of the podium, Fen was still smaller than Carl Kennedy.

"Dino will be very proud of you," he said, kissing her.

"You'd have pulled it off if he hadn't dropped out," said Fen.

Carl shrugged: "You'd have pulled it off even more if you'd had Jake."

"We might not have," said Fen. "We were more of a team than ever before."

The President's wife came forward in a pale blue dress and Fen bowed her head as the pink, blue and green ribbon was hung around her neck. Almost like braille, she put her hand up to touch the gold, tracing the lady with her sheaf of corn on one side, the athlete borne aloft on the other.

"We got a gold," she said incredulously.

"Team gold's the best," said Rupert.

They watched the British flag slide up the white pole. A breath of wind stretched it out. Never had the national anthem sounded so beautiful.

"God save," began Fen, then found she couldn't go on. Tears splashed on to her high cheekbones. Rupert put his hand on her shoulder, squeezing it reassuringly.

When the music stopped she turned back to him, burying her face in his shoulder.

"What shall we do this evening?" he said.

"You ought to go to bed," said Fen.

"How about a really marvelous fuck?" said Rupert.

Fen burst out laughing.

"I've always wanted you," said Rupert, kissing her.

"Hey lay off," howled Dino, hurling a cushion at the television set.

—

"Lucky thing," said Georgina Hamilton. "She's seriously attractive. Mind you, I expect she'll console him now Helen's pushed off."

Amanda Hamilton was surprised how much she minded that embrace. She knew it was victory euphoria, but Fen really was very pretty. Amanda caught a glimpse of herself in the mirror, and pulled in her tummy. She'd been eating too much; she must go on a diet before Rupert got back.

I've seen a lot of things," Malise told Prince Philip, wiping away a tear, as the riders galloped around the arena, their ribbons streaming like colored meteors. "I went all through the war, but this is the greatest experience of my life. Makes you very proud to be British."

"That was a staggering piece of riding by Rupert Campbell-Black," said Prince Philip.

Jake Lovell, in a scruffy motel near Kennedy airport, and rapidly running out of money, decided not to have another cigarette yet, as he had only half a pack left. Holding Helen in his arms, he lay in bed watching television.

"Hardy was your horse," sobbed Helen. "You ought to have been up there getting a gold too."

"I'm on the winners' rostrum already. I've got you," said Jake. But his heart was like lead. Helen must never realize the colossal sacrifice he had made, or she'd never forgive herself.

Dino tucked Tory into bed, making sure that she took both her sleeping pills. Her apathy worried him; he felt it would be healthier if she raged against Helen and Jake. Then he put the children to bed. Darklis was so overexcited she wanted a story. Every time Dino tried to skip, or missed a word because he was tired, she corrected him. He found Isa in floods of tears. Why had his father gone off with Helen? Why was the paper calling him a traitor and a deserter? What did treachery mean? Who would look after his mother now? Was it something that he, Isa, had done?

Dino comforted him as best he could. He didn't really know the answer to any of those questions either, but he knew Jake going off had nothing to do with Isa, and he was sure that once the Games were over, Jake would want to see him and Darklis again. At last Isa fell asleep.

It was two o'clock in the morning. The Mill seemed bitterly cold after America. Dino supposed it was the changeover from summer to fall. Now jet lag was catching up with him and he felt absolutely shattered. For the millionth time he asked himself if he'd been insane to indulge in this quixotic geesture of rushing off to Europe to look after Tory.

He had avoided going into Fen's room because he was missing her so much. Now, desperate for reassurance, he pushed open the door, breathing in the faint trace of her perfume and the mustiness of damp and dust and lack of use. All the china horses on the shelves and the teddy bears that used to fill up the entire window seat had been put away. Perhaps that was his fault for telling her she ought to grow up during that terrible last row. He'd liked the room better as it was before—except for the photograph of Billy Lloyd-Foxe, which had been removed.

Feeling he should't be snooping, he opened the top drawer of the chest and found a small pile of newspaper clippings and photographs held together by a pink plastic paper clip. They were all of himself, making him feel slightly better. All the same, he'd been mad to leave her with Rupert and Billy. He went back into the living room and opened a bottle of red wine. He felt shattered but not really sleepy; his time clock was still up the creek.

Turning on the television, he stretched out on the sofa. They were now showing the press conference. Everyone cheered and whooped as Malise and the British team filed in. There was a tremendous popping of champagne corks.

Rupert, who sat next to Fen with his good arm along the back of her chair in a vaguely proprietorial way, did most of the talking. He looked great; the earlier tears might never have occurred. He must have lost another five pounds since Helen left him, but it merely made his arrogant, slightly depraved face more finely planed than ever.

"Now, none of us want to talk about my wife of Fen's brother-in-law, so please shut up about that," he said. "I think we proved that we can win medals without them. Ivor had the most difficult task as the pathfinder. He jumped quite brilliantly. Fen had to jump on a different horse, and he can be a sod, I promise you. He's much too strong for her, but she kept him sweet, and I'd like to remind you that she's only just nineteen and jumping in her first Olympic competition."

Fen blushed as a huge cheer went round the room.

"I'm incredibly proud of them," said Malise. "I think today they all moved up a gear and that people will talk about Rupert's legendary second round as long as show-jumping lasts."

"And it wasn't just us either," said Fen, holding out her glass for more champagne as the cheers subsided. "It was Malise who kept us all calm when we looked like going to pieces, and Dizzy and Sarah, our grooms, and poor Grisel who's in the hospital, and our families, who've had to put up with us being offish, and totally self-obsessed for the last month . . . Also," she added defiantly, "there's my brother-in-law, Jake Lovell."

Somebody booed, then everybody followed suit, stamping their feet, shouting "Out, out, out."

"No, shut up," said Fen furiously. "He taught me everything I know, and he made Hardy, who got a silver and a gold, so we ought to thank him and give him credit as well."

"Particularly," drawled Rupert, "for taking my wife off my hands."

For a second there was a very embarrassed pause, then everyone roared with laughter.

Rupert seized the champagne bottle, filling up his glass.

"In fact, the toast definitely isn't absent friends. We like the people who stuck by us, don't we angel?" He stroked the back of Fen's neck. There wasn't a reporter in the room who didn't respond to his magnetism.

"We noticed you had Fen in a clinch on the podium," said the man from the *Daily Mirror*.

"Who can blame me?" said Rupert insolently.

Fen looked wary. "Our horses are just good friends," she said.

"What about you two?" said the men from the *Daily Mirror*.

"This is quite unnecessary," snapped Malise. "They came here to discuss the gold."

The man from the *Mirror* ignored him. "Might be nice if you consoled Rupert," he said.

"No it would not," said Fen furiously. "I'm going to marry Dino Ferranti." Then she clapped her hands over her mouth in horror.

Dino knew that, where Rupert was concerned, Fen was unfinished business. He trusted Fen, but for the last three hours he had been through all the agonizing jealousy of a man deeply in love.

"Yippee," he shouted, "Yippee." Then, exactly on cue, he heard the bells pealing out in the village. He opened the window. It was a clear starlit night. Orion was climbing out of bed on the horizon, pulling on his boots. Not a breath of wind ruffled the curtains. The peal of the bells must be carrying miles down the valley. His darling, darling Fen had won the gold. The village hadn't known what to do; they had been shell-shocked by Jake walking out. Now they had another heroic exploit to celebrate. They could carry on with their Welcome Home celebrations. Not many villages in England could boast a silver *and* a gold.

Tory, woken by Dino's shout of joy, pulled the blankets and pillows over her head to blot out the sound of the bells, remembering in anguish how they had rung out for Jake only six nights ago. Oh God, please bring him back. As the telephone rang, she experienced a frantic surge of hope, then the black, black despair overwhelmed her again as she heard Dino say,

"Fen darling, you were fantastic, a bloody miracle. I never figured I'd want another country to beat America, but you were just great, great, great."

"Dino," said Fen in a small voice, "I've got something to tell you. I didn't mean to force your hand. But they goaded me about Rupert at the press conference and I told them I was going to marry you."

"I know," said Dino. "Best program I've ever seen."

"You saw it?" said Fen in amazement.

"I taped it, so you can't change your mind. Means we won't have to put an announcement in the *New York Times* either."

Fen giggled. "Oh you are lovely. I didn't want to trap you."

"Baby, how many times do I have to tell you? Look, are you coming home tomorrow? I've got the most god awful withdrawal symptoms."

"Oh yes," said Fen. "I can't bear another minute away from you."

"And when you get back, I'm going to march you into the nearest Registrar's office and marry you. What the hell's Billy doing out there?"

"Were you jealous?"

"Insanely—that's why I want you home. I don't trust either of those bastards."

For a few minutes they talked nonsense.

"Have you said anything to Tory about us?"

"No not really. I guess she knows. She's not in very good shape."

Tory, who had been listening at the top of the stairs, desperate for some crumb of comfort, some tiny piece of news about Jake, slunk back to bed. Only when Dino had checked that she was asleep did she give way to tears.

63

*A*utumn came, bringing huge red suns and frosty mornings and clogging the mill stream with yellow leaves. Tory carried on as though there was a key in her back. They were no money problems. Fen came back from L.A. to a heroine's welcome. She and Dino carried on taking the horses to shows and trying to keep their delirious happiness within bounds, at least when they were with Tory. The children, particularly Isa, were at first bewildered, even distraught, by Jake's disappearance, but soon got involved in a new term, where they were the object of increased sympathy and interest. Dino, whom they both adored, was back and he and Fen infected the children with their happiness and took them out a lot to give Tory a break. To Tory they seemed like four children, or very young parents with two kids. She was glad Dino and Fen had finally got it together, but it didn't ease her own despair.

Tory normally loved autumn best of all, chopping logs for huge fires, making chutney, jam and elderberry wine, loading up the deep freeze with vegetables and apple pies. But this year there seemed to be a glut of everything. Too many green tomatoes, too many apples thudding from the trees. She tried to pick them and gave up. She was always cold, always shivering. She covered herself up with three or four sweaters, so no one realized how much weight she had lost, or that she wasn't eating. Alone in the house, she spent her time crying, then creeping into bed at night to clutch an equally shivering Wolf, who missed Jake as much as she did. Malise came down to offer comfort, but was daunted by her grief. His own sadness that Helen had run off he kept to himself.

To buck Tory up, Dino and Fen tried to persuade her to come to Wembley. But she couldn't face the prying eyes or the memories. Billy Lloyd-Foxe had a brilliant week and won the Victor Ludorum. Every night Ivor Braine, Fen and Rupert, with his arm in a sling, appeared at the end of the Personality Parade, and brought the house down as they displayed their gold medals. Otherwise Rupert was off the circuit for two months. The doctor in L. A. had, in fact, trapped a nerve when he put Rupert's shoulder back. An operation was needed to sort it out. That Rupert had been brave enough to carry on jumping, despite such excruciating pain, only enhanced his almost magical prestige. The press reported his increased involvement in politics. He was tipped to take over a safe seat in Gloucestershire.

The press was also wildly interested in Jake, keeping a watch on all the airports, and continually ringing the Mill in case there was news of him. But there was none. He simply hadn't got in touch. Heaven knows what he and Helen were living on.

Then in the middle of October the press caught Jake and Helen arriving at Heathrow, huddled behind dark glasses. Neither would say a word to anyone, and somehow, as elusive as his gypsy forebears, Jake managed to shake off the pack of reporters and vanish. But not for long. The press's blood was up and within a few days they had hunted them down, staying near Gloucester with a horse-dealing friend of Jake's. Again he and Helen refused to talk, despite the astronomical sums of money which were offered for their story. And two days later, blazoned across every paper, were pictures of Jake, again huddled behind dark glasses, applying for the dole at Gloucester Labor Exchange.

The fact that Jake was so near, yet still hadn't contacted Tory, was for Dino the final straw. He saw how Tory was being crucified. He was all for driving over to Gloucester and beating the hell out of Jake, but Fen managed to restrain him.

"You can't make him come back if he doesn't want to. Tory would hate that more than anything."

—

Once back in England, when he wasn't dodging the press, Jake made heroic efforts to get work, but found every door shut. There was no point ringing Garfield Boyson, as he hadn't kept his nose clean, but he rang all the other sponsors who'd been pursuing him before the games. They all gave him an earful or hung up. He buried his pride and applied for jobs running riding schools or working as a stud groom. A few people saw him out of curiosity before rejecting him. No one wanted a fallen idol.

Horse and Hound had announced that the inquiry into his defection at the Olympic Games would be held at the B. S. J. A. headquarters in November. Jake was expected to turn up and defend himself. If he didn't, the general consensus was that he'd be suspended for at least ten years, if not for life.

Jake could have handled all this if he and Helen had been happy. But, as the days passed, he began to realize the full extent of her neurosis and egotism. Even if he did get a job, her insecurity was such that she couldn't bear him out of her sight for an instant.

Before the Games all they had really talked about was their love for one another and the situation. Like a prisoner of war, Helen had dreamed of escape, but, having escaped, she now found she was living in some bleak grey Eastern European zone. By running off she and Jake had deprived themselves of everything except each other. Claustrophobically thrown on their own resources, they found they had nothing in common.

Helen longed for her beautiful house and garden, her children, particularly Marcus, her checkbook and her status as Rupert's wife. Rupert blocked her application to see the children, so she would have to go to court and, as they had no money, that would mean applying for legal aid.

Horses had been Jake's life. Deprived of them, he was like a junkie without a fix. He missed the Mill, the children, Wolf, but most of all he found he missed Tory. And yet some strange pride stopped him getting in touch. He was convinced they were all managing perfectly without him. It would look as though he was only slinking back because he'd run out of money and couldn't cope. He also realized the enormity of his crime towards her and towards his country and was too ashamed to show his face. Above all, he'd given Helen the handkerchief; he must stick by the rules.

He never blamed her once for forcing his hand, but he retreated inside himself. Knowing he was miserable, she became obsessively jealous of Tory, the good wife, who never made a fuss. Why the hell couldn't Jake bitch about her occasionally? But Jake realized now that Tory had loved him for himself. Helen only loved the new infinitely desirable image of herself which his love had created, and which must be preserved at all costs.

Feeling that the horse dealer who'd put them up shouldn't be subjected to such a bombardment from the press, Helen and Jake moved into a studio apartment in Gloucester. But they were flat broke The Labor Exchange came up with one reason after another why they shouldn't give Jake any money. He sold his cufflinks and some of Helen's jewelry. Soon the only thing left would be his silver medal. And all the time Fleet Street was tempting him, offering more than a quarter of a million for their story.

Jake was accustomed to being poor. Helen was not. She tried to economize, but she was used to going to the hairdresser at least twice a week, and never having a run in her stockings and paying £15 for a jar of night cream. Having run away in Los Angeles with only summer clothes, she was desperate to buy winter ones, and thought wistfully of her furs in the closets at Penscombe.

The last Monday in October began badly for Tory. She got up and took the children to school, only realizing when she got there and found the doors locked that it was vacation. Later, making her bed, she retrieved her hot water bottle from the bottom and, unscrewing it, found herself solemnly emptying it into her sweater drawer. In the middle of the morning Dino found her in floods of tears, spilling out the contents of the vacuum cleaner in the sitting-room, because she'd vacuumed up a moth by mistake.

"The poor little thing was alive," she sobbed, scrabbling frantically through the dust. "I can't find it anywhere."

Dino cleared up the mess, then sat her down.

"Angel, you're very very tired. Fen and I have got to go up to London for this program." (They were doing Billy Lloyd-Foxe on *This is Your Life* that evening.) "We're going to take the kids to get them out of your hair for twenty-four hours. They'll enjoy seeing the inside of a studio. Hannah will be here to keep an eye on you. Sarah'll be back first thing tomorrow morning, so you don't have to worry about the horses. Tomorrow, when we get back, I am taking you to a doctor."

"I'm all right," protest Tory.

But the children's wild delight at the prospect of a jaunt only depressed her more. They're bored by me, she thought miserably, I'm no fun anymore.

"You do promise to look after her, don't you?" said Fen to Hannah as they left.

After they'd gone, Tory tried to pull herself together and get down to making green tomato chutney. But as she was chopping the onions, she remembered it had been Jake's favorite, and how he used to eat it out of the jar with a spoon, which made her cry again.

She started as the doorbell rang. Why did she still harbor some insane hope that it might be Jake? But it was her mother, in a new burgundy suit, looking very chic despite a burgundy face from the car heater.

"I'm not crying," lied Tory, wiping her hands on her skirt.

"No, I can smell you're not," said Molly, backing off slightly. "We're on our way to stay with some of Bernard's dreary relations. I left him in the car." As though he was a smelly old labrador behind a grill, thought Tory.

"Doesn't he want to come in?"

"No, we won't be able to gossip."

"Would you like a cup of coffee?"

Molly looked pointedly at her watch.

"I would have thought it was more like sherry time."

As Tory poured her a glass, Molly said how pleased she was about Fen and Dino. Tory returned to chopping onions.

"Seems a nice chap," Molly went on. "Very good-looking and very rich. You should have married someone like that in the first place. Now I want to have a serious talk with you."

Tory gritted her teeth.

"What are you going to do about your future?" said Molly. "Fen and Dino won't want to stay here forever with you and the children. They'll need a place of their own—probably go back to America."

Tory looked up in horror. "D'you think so?"

"I know so. Of course, they're too nice to say anything, but you can't hold them back for ever."

Tory said nothing, but chopped one piece of onion to a pulp.

"And when are you going to divorce Jake? I mean, he's deserted you, so you shouldn't have any difficulty. His father did the same thing to his mother. Like father like son, I suppose."

"Please Mummy, don't." Tory's voice broke. "I can't bear it."

"Can't think why you mind so much," said Molly. "You always knew he never loved you. Only married you for your money. What d'you expect?"

Tory looked down at the garbage pail. It was a disgusting mess of bacon rinds, spaghetti hoops, rusty Brillo pads and old tea bags. Like me, she thought I'm as useless as an old tea bag.

"Let's be positive," Molly was going on. "I'm pleased to see you've lost a lot of weight. You may be looking quite frightful, but at least you've got a waist, and even ankles now. But you really shouldn't have let yourself go like that. Can't blame Jake pushing off really. You never tried to hold him.

"However, Bernard and I have a plan. We're going to send you to a health farm for a week. There's a special offer for one in *Harpers* this month. No, I won't take no for an answer. We've filled in the form and sent if off. You can have it as an early Christmas present."

Tory was obviously not going to offer her another glass of sherry, so Molly helped herself. She wondered if the child was quite right in the head at the moment.

"Cheer up," she said. "You're only twenty-eight. If you smarten yourself up, you might easily get another man. One of your own class this time."

After her mother had gone, Tory sat down and cried and cried. Wolf sat at her feet, raking her knee with his paw, licking her face, desperately trying to comfort her.

Eventually she responded to his sympathy. She had to go up to the village to buy brown sugar for the chutney, and afterwards she'd take him for a walk. She couldn't be bothered with lunch. As she got her coat and purse, the telephone rang. But it was for Hannah, who took it in the tackroom.

Going out into the yard Tory met Hannah, standing on one leg. Her boyfriend, she explained, had got tickets for the Rolling Stones that night. Of course she must go, said Tory. If Hannah gave the horses their final feed Tory would check them last thing to see everything was all right.

"Are you sure you'll be O.K.?" said Hannah.

"I'll be fine," Tory reassured her. "It'll be rather peaceful to have the house to myself."

She didn't need a leash for Wolf any more. Since Jake had gone he never left her heels, waiting outside the village shop for her, with an anxious expression on his pointed brindle face. As she came out of the bakers, the low afternoon sun shone directly into her eyes. Suddenly she gave a gasp of excitement. Across the road a black-haired man was watching them. Then she felt a desperate thud of disappointment. It was very like him—but it was not Jake. Wolf, however, gave a bark of joyful recognition and shot across the road into the path of an oncoming truck. The passers-by, watching in horror, couldn't work out if the dog or the girl crouched frantically over him was screaming.

Everyone was very kind. They recognized poor Mrs. Lovell. A man offered her a lift to the vet, but Wolf died on the way. He licked Tory's hand and gave a last thump of his shepherd's crook tail, as if to apologize for deserting her too, and his head fall back.

The vet drove Tory home, dug a grave for Wolf beside Sailor and various of the children's guinea pigs and hamsters, and buried him in his blanket with his old shoe. He didn't like what he saw. Tory was shivering uncontrollably; there was no color in her cheeks; her clothes hung off her. She insisted on making him a cup of tea, but forgot to put any tea in the pot and didn't even notice that she'd handed him just hot water and milk.

"It was Jake's dog," she kept saying. "I should have had him on a leash."

"Now you're not going to be by yourself?" asked the vet.

"No, no, the others'll be back soon."

Hannah, going off at dusk, her thoughts full of her boyfriend and the Rolling Stones, wondered if she ought to call Dino and Fen in London. Tory was just sitting at the kitchen table, twisting a dish towel, gazing unseeingly at a mountain of chopped onions.

"Honestly, I'm perfectly OK." she said. "Sarah'll be back first thing and I've got an awful lot of chutney to make."

At nine o'clock Tory checked the horses. They were all dozing or lying down. She gave Macaulay an apple and a cuddle and then shut all the top doors. Then she took a flashlight and looked at Wolf's grave.

"You're lucky," she said. "You won't miss him anymore."

Life without Jake, she reflected, wasn't worth a farthing. A far thing. Nothing could be further away now than he was. She was useless as a mother, no good as a human being. If she wasn't there Jake could come home with Helen when Dino and Fen went to America and take over the stable.

The note took her hours, her mind was working so slowly. She tore up several drafts and chucked them in the wastebasket. In the top of Jake's chest of drawers in the bedroom, under the lining paper, she found the key to the poison cupboard. Back in the tackroom, she had to stand on a chair to open it. What a choice awaited her. Like Jake asking her what she wanted to drink the first time he'd taken her to a pub. There was henbane, used by Doctor Crippen, and hemlock water dropwort, which Jake often used as a poultice for horses with sore backs. Deadly poison it was, but it also paralyzed you, leaving your mind clear to the end. She couldn't cope with that. Then there was deadly nightshade, or belladonna as it was called. A more appropriate name for Helen than herself. Jake had once told her that there was enough poison in that bottle to kill off a dozen Campbell-Blacks, with all their phenomenal strength. It should be enough for her. She took down the bottle.

Next morning Jake walked towards Gloucester Labor Exchange to have another crack at getting some dole. It was totally against his nature, hustling or wheedling for money—but things were getting desperate.

"Hello Jake," said a voice.

Wary of rejection, he turned, frowning. But it was Tanya, his old groom, now married and wheeling a baby in a stroller. Jake knelt down to admire the child, picking up his little hands, tickling his ribs to make him laugh. He'd always been sweet with kids, thought Tanya, he must miss his own horribly. She was dying to ask how he was getting on with Helen. He looked terrible, his face grey, his eyes deeply shadowed. The cotton jacket and jeans were far too thin for a bitter cold morning.

"He's beautiful," he said, getting reluctantly to his feet.

"I'm sorry about Wolf," she said.

"What about him?" said Jake, suddenly tense.

"Oh God, perhaps I shouldn't have told you. Hannah called me, he was run over yesterday afternoon."

An hour later Jake got back to the studio to find Helen painting her nails and not in a good mood. She had just read in the *Daily Mail* that her husband had joined the Tory party and was expecting to be given a safe seat at any minute. Tory, Helen reflected bitterly, was not her favorite word at the moment. She thought so even less when she saw Jake's face.

"What's the matter?" she asked in alarm.

"I've got to go home." She winced at the word. "There's been an accident."

"Oh God, not one of the kids?"

"No, Wolf."

"Wolf? Is that a horse?"

"No, the dog. He was run over yesterday."

"A dog?" said Helen incredulously. "A dog! You're going back just for that? I could appreciate it if it was a child."

"Wolf was like a child to Tory." And to me, he wanted to add.

Helen looked at him in bewilderment. It was all part of this hideous conspiracy between the English and their animals.

"I simply don't get it," she said. "You refuse to go back when Malise appeals to you over and over again to jump for your country, then you scuttle home because some goddam dog's been run over. I just don't understand you."

There was a pause.

"How long will you be?" she asked. "I suppose you'll want the car."

Jake looked at his watch. "I'll be back in time for you to go the hairdresser. If I get delayed, take a taxi."

"We can't afford it, and I've got to pay the hairdresser."

Jake pulled a wad of tenners out of his pocket.

"Did you rob a bank?" asked Helen in amazement.

Jake shook his head. "I pawned my silver."

"Oh Jake," she wailed. "How could you? It was the one thing we had, your one link with immortality. We've scrimped and saved so much so that you could keep it."

He gave her a hundred and fifty pounds—"Now you can buy some winter clothes"—and kept a hundred for himself.

With it, he went to his friend Harry, who bred lurchers, and bought a puppy, a tiny replica of Wolf, with a brindle fluffy coat, a nose like an anteater and huge anxious eyes. By the time he drove over the bridge at Withrington the puppy had been sick five times. As he gently lifted the little creature out of the car, she was sick again all over Jake's coat. Jake hardly noticed. Unsure of his reception, his heart was thumping, his throat dry.

The yard seemed curiously deserted, except for the stable cat who arched his back at the puppy, and the horses, particularly Macaulay, who nearly broke down their half-doors in their delight at seeing their master again. The back door was open but there was no one in the house. As Jake washed the vomit off, he was tempted to go upstairs and get a sweater. But Helen would be frantic if he came back wearing something different. His heart was still thumping when the telephone rang and he automatically picked it up. He had great difficulty even saying "Hello."

"Dino," said a voice, "this is Malise. I'm desperately sorry. Just wondered if there was any more news of Tory."

"What about Tory?" snapped Jake.

"Who's that?"

"Jake"

"What the hell are you doing there?"

"What about Tory?" said Jake on a rising note of fear.

"She tried to commit suicide last night."

"Must have been a mistake."

"I'm afraid not," said Malise, losing his temper. "She took a massive overdose of one of your bloody posions. She wasn't expecting anyone back till this morning. Dino and Fen got worried, came back and found her last night."

"Oh my God," whispered Jake. "Is she, is she . . . ?"

Malise realized he'd been too harsh. "I'm afraid she's dying, Jake."

"Where is she?"

"The Great Warwickshire."

Jake took Fen's car because it was faster. It has never been driven so fast in its life. The poor puppy ratled back and forth in the back like a shuttle. The hospital steps were swarming with press.

"Hullo Gyppo, shown up at last have you?" shouted the *Daily Mail*.

"About bloody time. You come to pay for the funeral?" asked *The Sun*.

"Fuck off," snarled Jake.

Mrs. Lovell was in intensive care on the second floor, said the receptionist, giving Jake a strange look. "You can't bring that puppy in here."

But Jake was off, limping across the polished floor, pulling the heavy gates of the lift with one hand, holding the puppy with the other. On the way up, she licked Jake's face. Oh please, God, he prayed frantically, don't let her die.

As he walked down the passage, a voice said, "What the hell are you doing here?"

It was Dino towering over him, barring his way, like the Archangel Michael with the flaming sword. For a second Jake thought Dino was going to smash his face in, knocking him flying back into a trolley of instruments. Jake stood his ground.

"I want to see Tory."

"Well, you bloody can't. She's in a coma and fading fast, and it's all your bloody fault, you bastard, you and your lousy poisons. My God, you wouldn't treat a horse, or even a dog, the way you treated her, leaving her without a fucking word, never getting in touch, letting her just pine away."

For two minutes Dino carried on in the same vein, calling Jake every name under the sun. His eloquence was fueled by misery and guilt that he and Fen had left Tory on her own yesterday, not appreciating how desperate she was. Jake let him finish.

"Everything you say is right," he said.

Hearing the din, a nurse came out of Tory's room.

"If you'd like to come in, Mr. Ferranti."

Jake stepped forward. "I'm her husband, I've got to see her."

But at that moment Fen came out, fighting back the tears, and went straight into Dino's arms.

"Look who's just turned up," said Dino bitterly.

Fen spun round. "Jake, where the hell have you been?" She gave a sob. "You're too bloody late, that's all; she's dying. She was just conscious when we got to her, but she's got no will to live."

Not waiting to hear any more, Jake pushed past them into the room. At first he thought he was hallucinating. For there on the bed was Fen. Then he realized it was Tory—she'd lost so much weight since he'd seen her. Her face, still flushed from the belladonna, gave an illusion of health. Long lashes swept her hollowed cheeks. All Jake could think was how beautiful she looked. He sat down beside the bed, taking her hand. It felt so small and bony now, almost like Helen's. Oh Christ, how could he have done this to her? It was he who'd killed her, not the poison.

The doctor came in, deciding to overlook the sleeping puppy curled upon Jake's knee. This was really no time to worry about hygiene.

"Can't you do anything?" asked Jake in desperation.

The doctor shook his head. "We've done all we can. She took a massive overdose, enough to kill four people. Luckily we caught it very early, but I'm surprised she's lasted this long. We pumped her stomach of course, but she's got no resistance. There was nothing in her stomach. She can't have eaten for days. I'm afraid there's very little hope she'll ever regain consciousness. I'm so sorry."

Jake was frantically wracking his brain. When he was living with the gypsies one of the girls had taken an overdose of belladonna because her lover had walked out. The old gypsy grandmother had produced some antidote or emetic and saved her. What the hell had she used? But it was such a long time ago. He must concentrate and try and remember.

"Did she leave a note?" he asked Fen.

Fen got it out of her jeans pocket. "It was addressed to you. She's left you everything. She knew horses were the only thing that mattered to you, that you and Helen could only come back if she was out of the way."

But Jake was reading the note.

"She loved you," said Fen bitterly. "Isa, Darklis, me, the horses, Wolf, were only extensions of how much she loved you. She knew you didn't love her, but she felt you needed her. That she made life easier, that was enough."

"Oh Christ," Jake groaned, putting his head in his hands. "I only realized in L. A. how much I loved her. Then Helen spilled the beans to Rupert. I couldn't let her down. I was frightened what Rupert would do to her. I'd got myself into such a stupid fucking corner."

"You could have got in touch," said Fen bleakly. "Nothing, not a word to anyone since you walked out."

"I didn't know what to say. I'd treated her so horrendously. I felt so guilty, and beside I'd given Helen the handkerchief."

Fen lost her temper. "What about the handkerchief you once gave Tory?" she hissed. "You conveniently forgot about that when it suited you, didn't you? So much for your bloody gypsy integrity. Tory was clutching it when we found her."

Jake was stunned. "She always seemed so strong that she could cope with anything. I didn't realize I meant so much to her." He looked down at Tory, touching her cheek. With a lurch of fear, he realized her breathing was even fainter. Both he and Fen jumped as Dino came in.

"You've been here long enough," he said to Jake, making absolutely no attempt to conceal his contempt and loathing.

Suddenly Jake seemed roused out of his state of apathy.

"She's my wife," he snarled, "and I love her."

"Funny way of showing it," said Dino, holding the door open for him.

Tipping the puppy gently on to the floor, Jake stood up. "Well, they won't cure her in here."

"What the hell are you doing?"

"Taking her home."

"She's dying, Godammit."

"Then she might as well die at home, surrounded by people and animals she loves."

Pulling one of the thick grey blankets off the bed, Jake wrapped it around Tory and picked her up. She was so light now, he could carry her easily. The puppy, already recognizing Jake as her new master, wagged her tail and trotted after him out of the room. Deaf to the protestations of doctors and nurses, desperately trying to remember the name of that miracle cure of the old gypsy grandmother, Jake hardly seemed to recognize Malise coming out the lift.

"Where d'you think you're going?" said Malise icily.

"Back to the Mill."

"What about Helen?"

"Helen?" Jake wrinkled his brow. It was as if Malise were asking him whether he'd turned off the tap in his cabin as the *Titanic* sank under the waves.

"Yes, Helen," said Malise grimly, holding the lift door shut, blocking Jake's path.

Dragging his mind back, Jake gave Malise the address in Gloucester. "She doesn't know what's happened. Could you go to her, explain to her, look after her, say I'm sorry?"

Back at the Mill, Jake had tucked Tory up in the big double bed and lit a fire in the grate. Then he settled down in an armchair, as near her as possible, to pore over his ancient flower books and herbals, frantically searching for a clue to the missing ingredient that might cure her.

Late in the afternoon the children came home. Jake braced himself, longing to see them but prepared for sullen antagonism, even abuse. He nearly wept at their incredulous joy that he was home again, hurling themselves into his arms without a word of reproach.

Isa was clearly demented with worry about his mother. Darklis was young enough to be distracted. The puppy was a godsend and was soon taken over by both children. What frightened Jake was their touching faith that, now he was back, their mother would recover. Macaulay and Hardy had been close to death, numerous other horses, dogs and members of the family had been ill and Jake had cured them.

"Mummy definitely won't have to be put down now," Jake heard Darklis telling Dino.

But Tory showed absolutely no sign of regaining consciousness, gradually growing weaker and weaker. Jake hardly left her side, not eating or sleeping. His anguish was so obvious, Fen, and even Dino, came to respect it, leaving him on his own with Tory, fending off the press, keeping the children away if they became quarrelsome, although most of the time Jake seemed to gain strength from their presence.

Two more days crawled by. Doctors and specialists, wheeled in by Dino, came and shook their heads. They no longer suggested Tory should go back into the hospital, there was nothing anyone could do.

Jake refused to give up. If only it had been high summer, or even spring, some of the plants he suspected might cure her might have been flowering, or at least in leaf, and identifiable. Anyway, he was terrified to leave her too long in order to search, in case she died when he wasn't there. Hour after hour he turned the pages with his right hand, holding her hand with his left, hoping against hope that she might return the pressure and show some sign of life.

And now it was midnight on the third day. Outside the foxes were barking. The fire was dying in the grate. Tory's breathing had almost stopped. Her heartbeat was so faint he kept thinking he had lost her. She was deathly pale; the belladonna flush had long since gone. If only she could regain consciousness just for a second, so she could die knowing how much he loved her.

In one last desperate hope, he turned back to the most ancient flower book. He was so exhausted and he'd been reading small print so long now that the words blurred before his eyes.

The only possibility had been the lesser spearwort, but it was such a strong emetic it would finish Tory off completely in her hopelessly weakened state. It was no good; he was powerless to save her.

Frantic, he took her in his arms, trying to warm some life into the frail body. He remembered how she had held Africa for him when he'd rushed off to be sick that first hot afternoon at the Bilborough Show, never letting on she was scared stiff of horses. He remembered how she'd got tight and bought Africa for him, how she'd never complained at the long hours away, had always welcomed him home, delighting in every victory, yet boosting his morale, professing her faith in him whenever he lost. Believing she would always be there, he had taken her for granted. He knew she was going to be taken away from him. At the end he had failed her again, by not being able to remember that missing ingredient.

"Don't die," he pleaded for the thousandth time. "Please don't die."

Laying her very gently back on the pillow, he noticed the fire was nearly out and got up to put on another log. He hadn't even bothered to draw the curtains. Stiff from sitting so long, he went to the window. There were no stars. The sky was already in mourning. He couldn't bear it. Despairingly he lent his forehead against the cold windowpane. He had no idea how long he stood there.

"Jake," came the faintest, faintest whisper.

He swung round in terror, drenched in sweat, his heart pounding. It must be her ghost come back to mock him.

"Jake," she whispered again.

He was beside her in an instant, seizing her hands, willing her to speak.

"Is it really you?" she murmured.

"Really me."

"You came back." The words were so faint he had to bend close to catch them. "Or have I gone to Heaven?"

"Must be Hell," he said unsteadily, "if you found me there. Please don't die, I love you so so much."

"You need to shave," she said and drifted into unconsciousness.

Sick with terror, Jake had to wait, cradling her in his arms, frightened even to move. He'd only asked to be able to have time to tell her he loved her, but now it wasn't enough and didn't make him feel any better. He longed to call for Fen and Dino, but panic-stricken that she might die at any moment, he knew he could only face it alone.

After a couple of hours she gave a little sigh, shuddered and opened her eyes again.

"I'm sorry I took all your belladonna. I couldn't go on without you."

Jake kissed her forehead. "I was the same. I just didn't know how to come back. Please get better. I'll never survive unless you do."

"I'm sorry about Wolf. I should have had him on a lead, but he stuck so close since you, since you . . ." Her voice faltered.

"I know. I got you a puppy." He picked the sleeping lurcher out of her basket, laid her beside Tory on the bed, placing Tory's hand on the fluffy narrow head. The puppy gave a deep contented sigh, licked the inside of Tory's wrist and snuggled back to sleep again.

Tory smiled weakly. "She's lovely. I didn't mean to blackmail you into coming back."

"You didn't have to. I didn't even know you'd taken the belladonna until I turned up here with the puppy. Tanya told me about Wolf being run over. All I needed was an excuse to come back. I never stopped missing you the whole time I was away. Please don't talk, you rest."

"Can I see your silver?" she said drowsily.

"I pawned it to buy the puppy."

As he drew the blankets up around her, the door opened softly. It was Fen. Jake put his finger to his lips. Shaking with sudden hope, Fen tiptoed towards the bed.

"You were speaking to her?"

"Twice."

"Did she make sense?"

"Perfect."

"Oh, my God. Is she going to be all right?"

"I don't know, it's too early to say."

Together they gazed at the sleeping Tory. Then Fen put a hand on Jake's shoulder.

"You made her better," she said softly.

For a second, he glanced up, his face soaked with tears.

"I failed her," he mumbled. "I tried and tried, but I couldn't remember the missing ingredient."

"You blind stupid idiot," said Fen very gently. "Only you could have cured her. Don't you understand? The missing ingredient was love."

Epilogue

The following afternoon Rupert Campbell-Black passed his first interview with the Birdlip and Chalford constituency committee with flying colors. There was only one sticky moment, when deaf old Lady Oakridge, who never read the papers, asked Rupert if he and his wife would be living in the constituency.

Everyone held their breath in embarrassment.

"My wife will certainly be living in the constituency," said Rupert emphatically.

"Good, good, glad to hear it," said Lady Oakridge.

"But not actually with me," said Rupert.

Everyone, except Lady Oakridge, suppressed smiles.

"Better to have a wife," she said.

"I absolutely agree," said Rupert. "Unfortunately mine's only just pushed off, so I haven't had time to get another one."

"Fellow's certainly got charm," said Lord Oakridge after the meeting.

"Views are sound too," said the Brigadier. "Think we should seriously consider him."

"You did so well," said Amanda, patting Rupert's thigh as she drove him back to London. "It's a cinch."

"Glad you think so." Privately Rupert wondered how much he would enjoy listening to his constituents grumbling about one-way streets and their rows with their neighbors. Being off the circuit for two months had made him realize how desperately he missed show jumping. With any luck he should be back for Olympia.

"Oh damn," said Amanda, as they drew up at her house in

Rutland Gate. "Conceptione's left the drawing-room light on. She's getting awfully slack."

"Hope it isn't Rollo."

"Rollo's in Paris," said Amanda, opening the front door. "Anyway he knows I'm driving you around. Georgina!" she cried in outraged tones as she went into the drawing-room. "What on earth are you doing here?"

"The rest of the class has gone to the Old Vic. I couldn't face it. I thought it would be more fun to come and see you," said Georgina. "Hello," she turned to Rupert. "Mummy's never allowed us to meet."

"Oh Christ," thought Rupert helplessly.

For there, in school uniform, exuding lascivious innocence, was a replica of Amanda, just as beautiful, but twenty-five years younger. No, he told himself firmly, it simply wouldn't do. Now that he was almost a prospective Tory candidate, he had to behave himself—although, heaven knows, they all seemed to be at it.

"What was the play?" he heard himself saying in an abnormally avuncular voice.

"All's well that ends well," said Georgina smiling dreamily. "I hear you're going into politics."

"Not sure I'll be very good," said Rupert. "The only babies I like kissing are female and over fifteen."

"Oh great!" said Georgina. "I was sixteen last week."

Billy Lloyd-Foxe, just back from Amsterdam, watched his beautiful wife feeding his beautiful son with enormous pride and decided against pouring himself another glass of whisky yet. He was just getting over the glow of being on *This is Your Life*. So many people had emerged from his past and said such amazingly nice things.

"I heard the most riveting bit of gossip today," said Janey.

"What was it?"

"Well Tracey told me she heard it from Dizzy, who heard it from Sarah, who heard it from Bridie, who's just got this tremendously intellectual boyfriend, who actually takes her to the opera. Poor Bridie had to sit through *Parsifal* the other night. Said she nearly died of boredom."

"Oh get on with it," said Billy grinning.

Janey's eyes gleamed. "I'll give you three guesses who she saw in a box together, looking radiant and not at all bored."

"You know I can never guess anyone."

"Malise and Helen."

"Good God," said Billy astounded. "Isn't Helen rather too young for him?"

"I would have thought so," said Janey, "and Monica Carlton will certainly call Malise out."

—

Tory was getting better by the minute, but Jake, terrified that she might still elude him, hardly left her alone for a second.

"From the way he bullies her into resting and polices her every mouthful, you'd think she was Macaulay," grumbled Fen, but she was so happy for them both.

As the doctor said, it was little short of a miracle.

A few days later, however, when Tory was definitely out of danger, Jake was persuaded downstairs to see Garfield Boyson.

"Well, lad," said Boyson.

"Well," said Jake.

"You've made a right fuck-up of your career, haven't you?"

"I don't need anyone else to tell me."

"I gather you've been to see every other sponsor touting for business. Didn't come to me. Not much faith, have you? I said I'd keep my side of the bargain, if you kept yours, and you did. You got your medal. I'm still ready to back you."

"The B. S. J. A. are going to suspend me."

"Happen they won't. Under the circs, you may get off with a hefty fine."

"I'm not interested," said Jake. "I'm not going back on the circuit. I'm going to train instead. I don't want to leave Tory or the children any more, and Dino and Fen are going back to the States."

Looking out the kitchen window, he saw Fen ride into the yard and collapse off Macaulay into Dino's arms. He wouldn't have believed it was possible for anyone to go on kissing for so long. Boyson brought him back to earth.

"You'll be looking for riders then. My lad can be your first jockey."

Jake looked sceptical, so Boyson went on:

"I've just had a look at Africa's foal. Dino said she jumped six foot out of her field this morning."

Jake laughed for the first time since the night he won his silver.

"I suppose you're trying to tell me that she and your boy'll be ready for the next Olympics," he said.